TALES OF MYSTERY & THE SUPERNATURAL

General Editor: David Stuart Davies

THE HAUNTER
OF THE DARK

and other stories

COLLECTED SHORT STORIES, VOLUME THREE

THE HAUNTER
OF THE DARK
and other stories

H. P. Lovecraft

Selected and introduced
by M. J. Elliott

WORDSWORTH EDITIONS

Readers interested in other titles from
Wordsworth Editions are invited to visit our
website at www.wordsworth-editions.com

This edition published 2011 by
Wordsworth Editions Limited
8B East Street, Ware,
Hertfordshire SG12 9HJ

ISBN 978 1 84022 667 6

Typeset in Great Britain by Roperford Editorial
Printed by Clays Ltd, St Ives plc

CONTENTS

*To my uncle, Maurice Crumley, the Lovecraft
enthusiast who was probably right not to tell
me that I share my name with a character
from* The Shadow Over Innsmouth

INTRODUCTION

In the decades since his death, the works of Howard Phillips Love-craft (1890–1937) have become a global sensation. An examination of his tortuously complex catalogue of inter-related underwater or intergalactic horrors brings us no closer to an understanding of the man who created them. But one of Lovecraft's most remarkable and underestimated talents was his ability to place his unconscious on the page, and it is perhaps through his dreams and the dreams of his creations that we may know him better.

Throughout his life, Lovecraft experienced extraordinarily vivid dreams – 'the real scenes frequently merge into unknown and fantastic realms, and include landscapes and architectural vistas which could scarcely be on this planet.' Many of these landscapes and architectural vistas made their way into what is known as Lovecraft's Dream Quest Cycle. This sequence is not as highly regarded as the Cthulhu Mythos, largely because of the lack of any horrific elements and its (by necess-ity) meandering, fantastical stream-of-unconsciousness narrative.

The story 'Polaris' was inspired by one of his dreams. 'I had a strange dream, of a strange city. A city of many palaces and gilded domes, lying in a hollow betwixt ranges of grey and horrible hills. I was, as I said, aware of this city visually. I was in it and around it, but certainly I had no corporeal existence.' 'Polaris' concerns an unnamed narrator who is plagued by visions of a magnificent city on a vast plateau. The people of the city of Lomar are under siege from the Inutos, a race from which the Inuit evolved. The protagonist, a frail but learned fellow, well-versed in the *Pnakotic Manuscripts* (a forerunner of Lovecraft's more famous forbidden text *The Necro-nomicon*, about which a brief and unreliable history is included in this volume) is unable to fight because 'I was feeble and given to strange faintings when subjected to stress and hardships', and so is given the job of lookout, a post in which he fails utterly. Lovecraft, who was too sickly to participate in World War I, or even complete his formal education, would doubtless have been all too familiar with his creation's sense of impotence.

The people of Sarnath fare no better than those of Lomar, though in a reversal of the usual order of things in such stories, man is the enemy here, having settled in Sarnath because of the presence of precious metals and learning to loathe his green-skinned neighbours before eventually committing an act of genocide.

While it is not entirely clear whether Sarnath and Lomar are once to be found on our world, there can be little doubt that the timeless city of Celephaïs is a fantasy realm, again inspired by another of Lovecraft's dreams, although in the story of the same name, the dreams are experienced by a British millionaire brewer referred to as Kuranes, who returns in 'The Dream-Quest of Unknown Kadath', having achieved kinghood in the Dream Lands at the cost of his life in the physical world.

Another dream provided the inspiration for the author's 1919 story 'The Statement of Randolph Carter'. Carter reappears in four further stories, but to call him Lovecraft's recurring hero might be presumptous, given his unfortunate habit of freezing in terror at crucial moments – even his best friend Harley Warren describes him as 'a bundle of nerves' when they explore a graveyard late at night.

Though short and snappy, 'The Statement of Randolph Carter' features some of Lovecraft's worst literary affectations, relying heavily upon phrases in capitals and italics to emphasize moments where he wishes the reader to be terrified. Like many of his stories, 'Statement' contains what the author himself described as his 'adjectival heaviness', relying too much upon the frequent use of such terms as 'terrible', 'hideous', 'shocking' and 'repellent'. By the time he wrote 'The Shadow Out of Time' in 1936, he was trying to control his excesses, and was "pausing now and then to cut out involuntary bits of overcolouring which insist on creeping in – references to 'monstrous and maddening arcana of daemoniac palaeogean horror" &c. &c.' But despite its flaws, 'Statement' marks the first step towards his Dream-Quest cycle.

The fantasy tale 'The Cats of Ulthar' demonstrates a rather mischievous sense of humour in the famously grim author, who here adds his own grisly twist to the tale of the Pied Piper. The story of Ulthar is continued in 'The Other Gods', in which Atal, the innkeeper's son, reappears as an adult. The introduction also mentions 'the Pnakotic manuscripts of distant and frozen Lomar', tying both tales in with 'Polaris'. Such instances of continuity are more likely to have been for Lovecraft's amusement rather than for the reader's satisfaction, since the author is unlikely to have imagined that readers were following his work from one obscure amateur publication to another. Both Ulthar and the Other Gods are referenced in the perhaps *too* dream-like 'The Strange High House in the Mist'. Its climax – in which philosopher Thomas Olney rides inside a giant conch in the company of Neptune and other mythological characters – proves either fantastical or absurd, depending upon the reader's disposition.

'Herbert West – Reanimator', the first of many Lovecraft stories to feature the fictional town of Arkham and that venerable institution Miskatonic University, originally appeared in the humorous magazine *Home Brew* as a serial entitled 'Grewsome Tales'. The story is the closest to a penny-dreadful he ever wrote, and is easily the guiltiest pleasure in the Lovecraft canon, despite the repetitive manner in which West's increasingly Frankenstein-like attempts to bring the recently deceased back to life are quashed. Very likely, given the nature of the publication in which it first appeared, Lovecraft thought of 'Reanimator' more as comedy than as true horror.

For 'The Shunned House', Lovecraft combined a legend recorded in Charles M. Skinner's *Myths and Legends of Our Own Land* with a real location – 135 Benefit Street, Providence, home for a time to his Aunt Lillian. It proved to be the first of his stories rejected by *Weird Tales Magazine*'s editor Farnsworth Wright, who felt that it was too long. Lovecraft refused to amend it, though Wright's criticism is undoubtedly valid. The author's verbosity acts against his attempts to create atmosphere in what is, in essence, a simple scenario – a night in a haunted house. Lovecraft's fertile imaginings can be appreciated even more when he mentions the possibility of a vampire despatching the residents of the house – such supernatural beings seem mundane and puerile by comparison with Old Ones, Nightgaunts and Outer Gods.

Lovecraft drew upon his experience of living briefly in Red Hook, a district of Brooklyn, to create the vivid and colourful 'The Horror at

Red Hook'. This tale has a rather confusing climax – the hero, Irish cop Thomas Malone, is uncertain whether he has actually witnessed the events described or dreamt them as his creator might have done. Malone's profession sets him apart from the crowd, and this is perhaps explained by the fact that Lovecraft attempted to submit this story and 'The Shunned House' to a detective magazine, although they both inevitably appeared in *Weird Tales*. Of 'The Horror of Red Hook', he wrote: 'The tale is rather long and rambling, and I don't think it's very good. But it represents at least an attempt to extract horror from an atmosphere to which you deny any qualities, save vulgar commonplaceness.'

With 'Pickman's Model', Lovecraft employed a different and entirely successful narrative technique: the protagonist, Thurber, is not only relating the account of his visit to Richard Upton Pickman's studio to the unseen listener Elliot, but also responding to Elliot's unheard questions. His vivid descriptions of each of Pickman's paintings are presented as mini horror stories in themselves. There's also a sly dig at Margaret Brundage's famously eye-catching but sexually risqué artwork for *Weird Tales* when the narrator comments: 'Any magazine-cover hack can splash paint around wildly and call it a nightmare or a Witches' Sabbath or a portrait of the devil, but only a great painter can make such a thing really scare or ring true.' Brundage's pieces usually featured naked women in various states of distress; Lovecraft used to tear the covers from his copies of *Weird Tales* so that he might not be ashamed to be seen with them.

The opening of this story makes it clear that Pickman has disappeared, but we do not learn just where he has gone until 'The Dream-Quest of Unknown Kadath' where, in an otherworldly form, he assists Randolph Carter of the Dream Quest cycle. However, this Carter seems a vastly different man from the one we have already encountered. For example in 'The Silver Key', he is said to have served in the Foreign Legion during World War I. Carter's melancholy state at the beginning of 'The Silver Key' no doubt originates from his creator's own situation, for he had recently fled from New York and a disastrous marriage. During this time Lovecraft was at the lowest ebb of his life thus far; following his separation from his wife Sonia, he had taken to keeping a bottle of poison about his person. Carter also contemplates suicide, but chooses instead to recapture the fantasy lands of his dreams when a younger man, lands to which the way is now barred.

Carter's state of mind might well have its origins in Lovecraft's atheism – his belief that if all existence is ultimately futile, then why should our unconscious experiences be less worthy or relevant than the conscious ones? For a man whose dreams were so extraordinary, and for whom reality had been such a disappointment, denying him the success and happiness we each imagine we deserve, it is easy to see how Lovecraft might have desired to put himself in Randolph Carter's place.

In writing 'The Dream-Quest of Unknown Kadath', Lovecraft dipped into his own childhood nightmares: at the age of six or seven, he was tormented by a recurring dream in which a monstrous race of entities called Night-Gaunts would snatch him up and carry him off. In this story, the Night-Gaunts are the guards of Ngarek, who carry off trespassers in the manner recalled by their creator.

'The Colour Out of Space' does not have any obvious connections to either of Lovecraft's great sagas, but the title is repeated in the key Cthulhu Mythos story 'At the Mountains of Madness', published four years later. It is interesting to note that Lovecraft insisted upon the English spelling 'colour' – just one of his many deliberate affect- ations, along with the insistence upon peculiar and archaic turns of phrase. Lovecraft's wearisome habit of presenting the dialogue of rural folk phonetically is overused here and to an even greater extent in 'The Shadow Over Innsmouth'.

The hero of 'Innsmouth' – unnamed, but referred to as 'Robert Olmstead' in Lovecraft's notes – is travelling the country, just as the author himself had taken to doing at this stage of his life. Luckily, he never found himself in a town like Innsmouth, where the Dagon- worshipping inhabitants have taken to interbreeding with a race of fish-creatures – common local surnames, such as Gilman and Marsh, serve as an uneasy reminder of their antecedents. The latter half of the story, in which 'Olmstead' attempts to flee Innsmouth with virtually the entire population in pursuit, is both effectively suspenseful and unusually action-packed, although Lovecraft did not think so: 'Use of any other style was like working in a foreign language – hence I was left high and dry.'

A few criticisms from his correspondents, plus his own gloomy state of mind at the time, caused him to file the story away. 'I don't intend to offer 'The Shadow Over Innsmouth' for publication, for it would probably stand no chance of acceptance,' he explained, going on to describe it as 'my own verbose and doubtful swan-song'.

In 'Dreams in the Witch House', Miskatonic University undergraduate Walter Gilman (no apparent relation to the good folk of Innsmouth) rents a room of peculiar dimensions, and finds his dreams inhabited by a witch, her rat-like familiar and strange geometrical shapes. Lovecraft's own enthusiasm for the story was blunted, once again, by a harsh review by August Derleth. Disheartened, he wrote: 'The whole incident shows me that my fictional days are probably over'.

'The Thing on the Doorstep' is noteworthy because of the appearance of Miskatonic University's only female student, Asenath Waite, a former Innsmouth resident. Female characters of any sort are extremely rare in any Lovecraft tale, which perhaps invites more examination of her significance than is warranted. It is impossible for anyone with some knowledge of Lovecraft's personal life not to see in this story of a female controlling and eventually engulfing a young man's mind and nature, elements of his own experiences with his mother, his aunts and, most likely, his former wife Sonia Haft Greene.

If Asenath is indeed possessed by her own father Ephraim, it raises further questions about Edward's intimate relations with his wife. Or it might, if the sexual act were not practically non-existent in Lovecraft's universe (save for talk of cross-species mating in 'The Shadow Over Innsmouth'). Some have speculated that Lovecraft might have been gay, but speculations they must remain, since there is nothing in his known life, his letters, or the recollections of Sonia H. Greene to verify them. It has been noted that many of the creatures frequenting his work possess tentacles which may represent male genitalia, suggesting either a fascination or horror with the male member . . . or perhaps the tentacles simply represent tentacles.

A masterpiece of plot construction and sheer force of imagination, 'The Shadow Out of Time' concerns Nathaniel Wingate Peaslee, a professor at Miskatonic University, who undergoes a massive personality change and becomes unrecognisable to his family – Lovecraft's own father, Winfield Scott Lovecraft, suffered from paralytic dementia, very likely brought on by syphilis, and died in hospital. Unlike Winfield, Peaslee regains his senses, albeit after a gap of five years. Through his dreams, he discerns the truth – that his body was inhabited by a member of an ancient alien race known as the Yithians, while he existed in a Yithian body on Earth during the Triassic era. Though generally regarded as one of his finest works, Lovecraft was, as usual, far more critical: 'Its total loss would entail no great harm and I may junk it in the end.'

Published in the December 1936 issue of *Weird Tales*, 'The Haunter of the Dark' is dedicated to Lovecraft's fellow *Weird Tales* author, the prolific Robert Bloch. In 1935, Bloch wrote a story for *Weird Tales* entitled 'The Shambler from the Stars', which features not only the *Necronomicon* but also an unnamed 'mystic dreamer in New England', very obviously based upon Lovecraft himself. It was Bloch's intention that the New Englander suffer a gory fate, but he contacted his colleague first to ask his permission. Lovecraft replied:

This is to certify that Robert Bloch, Esq., of Milwaukee, Wisconsin, U.S.A. – reincarnation of Mijnheer Ludvig Prinn, author of *De Vermis Mysteriis* – is fully authorized to portray, murder, annihilate, disintegrate, transfigure, metamorphose, or otherwise manhandle the undersigned in the tale entitled *The Shambler from the Stars*.

The hero of Lovecraft's 'The Haunter in the Dark' is one Robert Blake, a name not a million miles removed from Robert Bloch. Blake too suffers a horrible fate after discovering a Trapezohedron constructed on Yuggoth, Lovecraft's name for the planet Pluto (the poem 'Fungi from Yuggoth' can also be found in this volume). Bloch concluded his story fourteen years later with 'The Shadow in the Steeple'.

If by a man's works you shall know him, then Howard Phillips Lovecraft was a unique individual. It may be, of course, that no more is gained from the experience of reading these works than an appreciation of the finest horror writer of the twentieth century, which is no small thing. And should you ever happen to dream that you are visiting unknown and fantastic realms that could not possibly exist in our world . . . don't be surprised at who you might bump into there.

M. J. ELLIOTT

M. J. Elliott is a writer and radio dramatist whose articles, fiction and reviews have appeared in the magazines *SHERLOCK*, *Total DVD* and *Scarlet Street*. For American radio, he has scripted episodes of *The Twilight Zone*, *The Further Adventures of Sherlock Holmes*, *The Classic Adventures of Sherlock Holmes*, *Raffles the Gentleman Thief*, *The Father Brown Mysteries*, *Kincaid the Strangeseeker*, *The Adventures of Harry Nile*, *The Perry Mason Radio Dramas*, *Vincent Price Presents* and the Audie Award-nominated *New Adventures of Mickey Spillane's Mike Hammer*. He is the creator of *The Hilary Caine Mysteries*, which first aired in 2005. For Wordsworth, he has contributed to *The Game's Afoot* and edited *The Whisperer in Darkness* and *The Horror in the Museum* by H. P. Lovecraft, *The Right Hand of Doom* and *The Haunter of the Ring* by Robert E. Howard, and *A Charlie Chan Omnibus* by Earl Derr Biggers.

THE HAUNTER OF THE DARK
AND OTHER STORIES

The Haunter of the Dark

[*dedicated to Robert Bloch*]

> I have seen the dark universe yawning
> Where the black planets roll without aim –
> Where they roll in their horror unheeded,
> Without knowledge or lustre or name.
>
> *Nemesis*

Cautious investigators will hesitate to challenge the common belief that Robert Blake was killed by lightning, or by some profound nervous shock derived from an electrical discharge. It is true that the window he faced was unbroken, but Nature has shewn herself capable of many freakish performances. The expression on his face may easily have arisen from some obscure muscular source unrelated to anything he saw, while the entries in his diary are clearly the result of a fantastic imagination aroused by certain local superstitions and by certain old matters he had uncovered. As for the anomalous conditions at the deserted church on Federal Hill – the shrewd analyst is not slow in attributing them to some charlatanry, conscious or unconscious, with at least some of which Blake was secretly connected.

For after all, the victim was a writer and painter wholly devoted to the field of myth, dream, terror, and superstition, and avid in his quest for scenes and effects of a bizarre, spectral sort. His earlier stay in the city – a visit to a strange old man as deeply given to occult and forbidden lore as he – had ended amidst death and flame, and it must have been some morbid instinct which drew him back from his home in Milwaukee. He may have known of the old stories despite his statements to the contrary in the diary, and his death may have nipped in the bud some stupendous hoax destined to have a literary reflection.

Among those, however, who have examined and correlated all this evidence, there remain several who cling to less rational and commonplace theories. They are inclined to take much of Blake's diary at its face value, and point significantly to certain facts such as the undoubted genuineness of the old church record, the verified existence of the disliked and unorthodox Starry Wisdom sect prior to 1877, the recorded disappearance of an inquisitive reporter named Edwin M. Lillibridge in 1893, and – above all – the look of monstrous, transfiguring fear on the face of the young writer when he died. It was one of these believers who, moved to fanatical extremes, threw into the bay the curiously angled stone and its strangely adorned metal box found in the old church steeple – the black windowless steeple, and not the tower where Blake's diary said those things originally were. Though widely censured both officially and unofficially, this man – a reputable physician with a taste for odd folklore – averred that he had rid the earth of something too dangerous to rest upon it.

Between these two schools of opinion the reader must judge for himself. The papers have given the tangible details from a sceptical angle, leaving for others the drawing of the picture as Robert Blake saw it – or thought he saw it – or pretended to see it. Now, studying the diary closely, dispassionately, and at leisure, let us summarise the dark chain of events from the expressed point of view of their chief actor.

Young Blake returned to Providence in the winter of 1934–5, taking the upper floor of a venerable dwelling in a grassy court off College Street – on the crest of the great eastward hill near the Brown University campus and behind the marble John Hay Library. It was a cosy and fascinating place, in a little garden oasis of village-like antiquity where huge, friendly cats sunned themselves atop a convenient shed. The square Georgian house had a monitor roof, classic doorway with fan carving, small-paned windows, and all the other earmarks of early nineteenth-century workmanship. Inside were six-panelled doors, wide floor-boards, a curving colonial staircase, white Adam-period mantels, and a rear set of rooms three steps below the general level.

Blake's study, a large southwest chamber, overlooked the front garden on one side, while its west windows – before one of which he had his desk – faced off from the brow of the hill and commanded a splendid view of the lower town's outspread roofs and of the mystical sunsets that flamed behind them. On the far horizon were the open countryside's purple slopes. Against these, some two miles away, rose the spectral hump of Federal Hill, bristling with huddled roofs and steeples whose remote outlines wavered mysteriously, taking fantastic forms as the smoke of the city swirled up and enmeshed them. Blake had a curious sense that he was looking upon some unknown, ethereal world which might or might not vanish in dream if ever he tried to seek it out and enter it in person.

Having sent home for most of his books, Blake bought some antique furniture suitable to his quarters and settled down to write and paint – living alone, and attending to the simple housework himself. His studio was in a north attic room, where the panes of the monitor roof furnished admirable lighting. During that first winter he produced five of his best-known short stories – 'The Burrower Beneath', 'The Stairs in the Crypt', 'Shaggai', 'In the Vale of Pnath', and 'The Feaster from the Stars' – and painted seven canvases; studies of nameless, unhuman monsters, and profoundly alien, non-terrestrial landscapes.

At sunset he would often sit at his desk and gaze dreamily off at the outspread west – the dark towers of Memorial Hall just below, the Georgian court-house belfry, the lofty pinnacles of the downtown section, and that shimmering, spire-crowned mound in the distance whose unknown streets and labyrinthine gables so potently provoked his fancy. From his few local acquaintances he learned that the far-off slope was a vast Italian quarter, though most of the houses were remnants of older Yankee and Irish days. Now and then he would train his field-glasses on that spectral, unreachable world beyond the curling smoke; picking out individual roofs and chimneys and steeples, and speculating upon the bizarre and curious mysteries they might house. Even with optical aid Federal Hill seemed somehow alien, half fabulous, and linked to the unreal, intangible marvels of Blake's own tales and pictures. The feeling would persist long after the hill had faded into the violet, lamp-starred twilight, and the court-house floodlights and the red Industrial Trust beacon had blazed up to make the night grotesque.

Of all the distant objects on Federal Hill, a certain huge, dark church most fascinated Blake. It stood out with especial distinctness at certain hours of the day, and at sunset the great tower and tapering steeple loomed blackly against the flaming sky. It seemed to rest on especially high ground; for the grimy façade, and the obliquely seen north side with sloping roof and the tops of great pointed windows, rose boldly above the tangle of surrounding ridgepoles and chimney-pots. Peculiarly grim and austere, it appeared to be built of stone, stained and weathered with the smoke and storms of a century and more. The style, so far as the glass could shew, was that earliest experimental form of Gothic revival which preceded the stately Upjohn period and held over some of the outlines and proportions of the Georgian age. Perhaps it was reared around 1810 or 1815.

As months passed, Blake watched the far-off, forbidding structure with an oddly mounting interest. Since the vast windows were never lighted, he knew that it must be vacant. The longer he watched, the more his imagination worked, till at length he began to fancy curious things. He believed that a vague, singular aura of desolation hovered over the place, so that even the pigeons and swallows shunned its smoky eaves. Around other towers and belfries his glass would reveal great flocks of birds, but here they never rested. At least, that is what he thought and set down in his diary. He pointed the place out to several friends, but none of them had even been on Federal Hill or possessed the faintest notion of what the church was or had been.

In the spring a deep restlessness gripped Blake. He had begun his long-planned novel – based on a supposed survival of the witch-cult in Maine – but was strangely unable to make progress with it. More and more he would sit at his westward window and gaze at the distant hill and the black, frowning steeple shunned by the birds. When the delicate leaves came out on the garden boughs the world was filled with a new beauty, but Blake's restlessness was merely increased. It was then that he first thought of crossing the city and climbing bodily up that fabulous slope into the smoke-wreathed world of dream.

Late in April, just before the aeon-shadowed Walpurgis time, Blake made his first trip into the unknown. Plodding through the endless downtown streets and the bleak, decayed squares beyond, he came finally upon the ascending avenue of century-worn steps, sagging Doric porches, and blear-paned cupolas which he felt must lead up to the long-known, unreachable world beyond the mists. There were dingy blue-and-white street signs which meant nothing to him, and presently he noted the strange, dark faces of the drifting crowds, and the foreign signs over curious shops in brown, decade-weathered buildings. Nowhere could he find any of the objects he had seen from afar; so that once more he half fancied that the Federal Hill of that distant view was a dream-world never to be trod by living human feet.

Now and then a battered church façade or crumbling spire came in sight, but never the blackened pile that he sought. When he asked a shopkeeper about a great stone church the man smiled and shook his head, though he spoke English freely. As Blake climbed higher, the region seemed stranger and stranger, with bewildering mazes of brooding brown alleys leading eternally off to the south. He crossed two or three broad avenues, and once thought he glimpsed a familiar tower. Again he asked a merchant about the massive church of stone, and this time he could have sworn that the plea of ignorance was feigned. The dark man's face had a look of fear which he tried to hide, and Blake saw him make a curious sign with his right hand.

Then suddenly a black spire stood out against the cloudy sky on his left, above the tiers of brown roofs lining the tangled southerly alleys. Blake knew at once what it was, and plunged toward it through the squalid, unpaved lanes that climbed from the avenue. Twice he lost his way, but he somehow dared not ask any of the patriarchs or housewives who sat on their doorsteps, or any of the children who shouted and played in the mud of the shadowy lanes.

At last he saw the tower plain against the southwest, and a huge stone bulk rose darkly at the end of an alley. Presently he stood in a windswept open square, quaintly cobble-stoned, with a high bank wall on the farther side. This was the end of his quest; for upon the wide, iron-railed, weed-grown plateau which the wall supported – a separate, lesser world raised fully six feet above the surrounding streets – there stood a grim, titan bulk whose identity, despite Blake's new perspective, was beyond dispute.

The vacant church was in a state of great decrepitude. Some of the high stone buttresses had fallen, and several delicate finials lay half lost among the brown, neglected weeds and grasses. The sooty Gothic windows were largely unbroken, though many of the stone mullions were missing. Blake wondered how the obscurely painted panes could have survived so well, in view of the known habits of small boys the world over. The massive doors were intact and tightly closed. Around the top of the bank wall, fully enclosing the grounds, was a rusty iron fence whose gate – at the head of a flight of steps from the square – was visibly padlocked. The path from the gate to the building was completely overgrown. Desolation and decay hung like a pall above the place, and in the birdless eaves and black, ivyless walls Blake felt a touch of the dimly sinister beyond his power to define.

There were very few people in the square, but Blake saw a policeman at the northerly end and approached him with questions about the church. He was a great wholesome Irishman, and it seemed odd that he would do little more than make the sign of the cross and mutter that people never spoke of that building. When Blake pressed him he said very hurriedly that the Italian priests warned everybody against it, vowing that a monstrous evil had once dwelt there and left its mark. He himself had heard dark whispers of it from his father, who recalled certain sounds and rumours from his boyhood.

There had been a bad sect there in the ould days – an outlaw sect that called up awful things from some unknown gulf of night. It had taken a good priest to exorcise what had come, though there did be those who said that merely the light could do it. If Father O'Malley were alive there would be many the thing he could tell. But now there was nothing to do but let it alone. It hurt nobody now, and those that owned it were dead or far away. They had run away like rats after the threatening talk in '77, when people began to mind the way folks vanished now and then in the neighbourhood. Some day the city would step in and take the property for lack of heirs, but little good would come of anybody's touching it. Better it be left alone for the years to topple, lest things be stirred that ought to rest forever in their black abyss.

After the policeman had gone Blake stood staring at the sullen steepled pile. It excited him to find that the structure seemed as sinister to others as to him, and he wondered what grain of truth might lie behind the old tales the bluecoat had repeated. Probably they were mere legends evoked by the evil look of the place, but even so, they were like a strange coming to life of one of his own stories.

The afternoon sun came out from behind dispersing clouds, but seemed unable to light up the stained, sooty walls of the old temple that towered on its high plateau. It was odd that the green of spring had not touched the brown, withered growths in the raised, iron-fenced yard. Blake found himself edging nearer the raised area and examining the bank wall and rusted fence for possible avenues of ingress. There was a terrible lure about the blackened fane which was not to be resisted. The fence had no opening near the steps, but around on the north side were some missing bars. He could go up the steps and walk around on the narrow coping outside the fence till he came to the gap. If the people feared the place so wildly, he would encounter no interference.

He was on the embankment and almost inside the fence before anyone noticed him. Then, looking down, he saw the few people in the square edging away and making the same sign with their right hands that the shopkeeper in the avenue had made. Several windows were slammed down, and a fat woman darted into the street and pulled some small children inside a rickety, unpainted house. The gap in the fence was very easy to pass through, and before long Blake found himself wading amidst the rotting, tangled growths of the deserted yard. Here and there the worn stump of a headstone told him that there had once been burials in this field; but that, he saw, must have been very long ago. The sheer bulk of the church was oppressive now that he was close to it, but he conquered his mood and approached to try the three great doors in the façade. All were securely locked, so he began a circuit of the Cyclopean building in quest of some minor and more penetrable opening. Even then he could not be sure that he wished to enter that haunt of desertion and shadow, yet the pull of its strangeness dragged him on automatically.

A yawning and unprotected cellar window in the rear furnished the needed aperture. Peering in, Blake saw a subterrene gulf of cobwebs and dust faintly litten by the western sun's filtered rays. Debris, old barrels, and ruined boxes and furniture of numerous sorts met his eye, though over everything lay a shroud of dust which softened all sharp outlines. The rusted remains of a hot-air furnace shewed that the building had been used and kept in shape as late as mid-Victorian times.

Acting almost without conscious initiative, Blake crawled through the window and let himself down to the dust-carpeted and debris-strown concrete floor. The vaulted cellar was a vast one, without partitions; and in a corner far to the right, amid dense shadows, he saw a black archway evidently leading upstairs. He felt a peculiar sense of oppression at being actually within the great spectral building, but kept it in check as he cautiously scouted about – finding a still-intact barrel amid the dust, and rolling it over to the open window to provide for his exit. Then, bracing himself, he crossed the wide, cobweb-festooned space toward the arch. Half choked with the omnipresent dust, and covered with ghostly gossamer fibres, he reached and began to climb the worn stone steps which rose into the darkness. He had no light, but groped carefully with his hands. After a sharp turn he felt a closed door ahead, and a little fumbling revealed its ancient latch. It opened inward, and beyond it he saw a dimly illumined corridor lined with worm-eaten panelling.

Once on the ground floor, Blake began exploring in a rapid fashion. All the inner doors were unlocked, so that he freely passed from room to room. The colossal nave was an almost eldritch place with its drifts and mountains of dust over box pews, altar, hourglass pulpit, and sounding-board, and its titanic ropes of cobweb stretching among the pointed arches of the gallery and entwining the clustered Gothic columns. Over all this hushed desolation played a hideous leaden light as the declining afternoon sun sent its rays through the strange, half-blackened panes of the great apsidal windows.

The paintings on those windows were so obscured by soot that Blake could scarcely decipher what they had represented, but from the little he could make out he did not like them. The designs were largely conventional, and his knowledge of obscure symbolism told him much concerning some of the ancient patterns. The few saints depicted bore expressions distinctly open to criticism, while one of the windows seemed to shew merely a dark space with spirals of curious luminosity scattered about in it. Turning away from the windows, Blake noticed that the cobwebbed cross above the altar was not of the ordinary kind, but resembled the primordial ankh or *crux ansata* of shadowy Egypt.

In a rear vestry room beside the apse Blake found a rotting desk and ceiling-high shelves of mildewed, disintegrating books. Here for the first time he received a positive shock of objective horror, for the titles of those books told him much. They were the black, forbidden things which most sane people have never even heard of, or have heard of only in furtive, timorous whispers; the banned and dreaded repositories of equivocal secrets and immemorial formulae which have trickled down the stream of time from the days of man's youth, and the dim, fabulous days before man was. He had himself read many of them – a Latin version of the abhorred *Necronomicon*, the sinister *Liber Ivonis*, the infamous *Cultes des Goules* of Comte d'Erlette, the *Unaussprechlichen Kulten* of von Junzt, and old Ludvig Prinn's hellish *De Vermis Mysteriis*. But there were others he had known merely by reputation or not at all – the *Pnakotic Manuscripts*, the *Book of Dzyan*, and a crumbling volume in wholly unidentifiable characters yet with certain symbols and diagrams shudderingly recognisable to the occult student. Clearly, the lingering local rumours had not lied. This place had once been the seat of an evil older than mankind and wider than the known universe.

In the ruined desk was a small leather-bound record-book filled with entries in some odd cryptographic medium. The manuscript writing consisted of the common traditional symbols used today in astronomy and anciently in alchemy, astrology, and other dubious arts – the devices of the sun, moon, planets, aspects, and zodiacal signs – here massed in solid pages of text, with divisions and paragraphings suggesting that each symbol answered to some alphabetical letter.

In the hope of later solving the cryptogram, Blake bore off this volume in his coat pocket. Many of the great tomes on the shelves fascinated him unutterably, and he felt tempted to borrow them at some later time. He wondered how they could have remained undisturbed so long. Was he the first to conquer the clutching, pervasive fear which had for nearly sixty years protected this deserted place from visitors?

Having now thoroughly explored the ground floor, Blake ploughed again through the dust of the spectral nave to the front vestibule, where he had seen a door and staircase presumably leading up to the blackened tower and steeple – objects so long familiar to him at a distance. The ascent was a choking experience, for dust lay thick, while the spiders had done their worst in this constricted place. The staircase was a spiral with high, narrow wooden treads, and now and then Blake passed a clouded window looking dizzily out over the city. Though he had seen no ropes below, he expected to find a bell or peal of bells in the tower whose narrow, louver-boarded lancet windows his field-glass had studied so often. Here he was doomed to disappointment; for when he attained the top of the stairs he found the tower chamber vacant of chimes, and clearly devoted to vastly different purposes.

The room, about fifteen feet square, was faintly lighted by four lancet windows, one on each side, which were glazed within their screening of decayed louver-boards. These had been further fitted with tight, opaque screens, but the latter were now largely rotted away. In the centre of the dust-laden floor rose a curiously angled stone pillar some four feet in height and two in average diameter, covered on each side with bizarre, crudely incised, and wholly unrecognisable hieroglyphs. On this pillar rested a metal box of peculiarly asymmetrical form; its hinged lid thrown back, and its interior holding what looked beneath the decade-deep dust to be an egg-shaped or irregularly spherical object some four inches through. Around the pillar in a rough circle were seven high-backed Gothic chairs still largely intact, while behind them, ranging along the dark-panelled walls, were seven colossal images of crumbling, black-painted plaster, resembling more than anything else the cryptic carven megaliths of mysterious Easter Island. In one corner of the cobwebbed chamber a ladder was built into the wall, leading up to the closed trap-door of the windowless steeple above.

As Blake grew accustomed to the feeble light he noticed odd bas-reliefs on the strange open box of yellowish metal. Approaching, he tried to clear the dust away with his hands and handkerchief, and saw that the figurings were of a monstrous and utterly alien kind; depicting entities which, though seemingly alive, resembled no known life-form ever evolved on this planet. The four-inch seeming sphere turned out to be a nearly black, red-striated polyhedron with many irregular flat surfaces; either a very remarkable crystal of some sort, or an artificial object of carved and highly polished mineral matter. It did not touch the bottom of the box, but was held suspended by means of a metal band around its centre, with seven queerly designed supports extending horizontally to angles of the box's inner wall near the top. This stone, once exposed, exerted upon Blake an almost alarming fascination. He could scarcely tear his eyes from it, and as he looked at its glistening surfaces he almost fancied it was transparent, with half-formed worlds of wonder within. Into his mind floated pictures of alien orbs with great stone towers, and other orbs with titan mountains and no mark of life, and still remoter spaces where only a stirring in vague blacknesses told of the presence of consciousness and will.

When he did look away, it was to notice a somewhat singular mound of dust in the far corner near the ladder to the steeple. Just why it took his attention he could not tell, but something in its contours carried a message to his unconscious mind. Ploughing toward it, and brushing aside the hanging cobwebs as he went, he began to discern something grim about it. Hand and handkerchief soon revealed the truth, and Blake gasped with a baffling mixture of emotions. It was a human skeleton, and it must have been there for a very long time. The clothing was in shreds, but some buttons and fragments of cloth bespoke a man's grey suit. There were other bits of evidence – shoes, metal clasps, huge buttons for round cuffs, a stickpin of bygone pattern, a reporter's badge with the name of the old *Providence Telegram*, and a crumbling leather pocketbook. Blake examined the latter with care, finding within it several bills of antiquated issue, a celluloid advertising calendar for 1893, some cards with the name 'Edwin M. Lillibridge', and a paper covered with pencilled memoranda.

This paper held much of a puzzling nature, and Blake read it carefully at the dim westward window. Its disjointed text included such phrases as the following.

Prof. Enoch Bowen home from Egypt May 1844 – buys old Free-Will Church in July – his archaeological work & studies in occult well known.

Dr Drowne of 4th Baptist warns against Starry Wisdom in sermon Dec. 29, 1844.

Congregation 97 by end of '45.

1846 – 3 disappearances – first mention of Shining Trapezo-hedron.

7 disappearances 1848 – stories of blood sacrifice begin.

Investigation 1853 comes to nothing – stories of sounds.

Fr. O'Malley tells of devil-worship with box found in great Egyptian ruins – says they call up something that can't exist in light. Flees a little light, and banished by strong light. Then has to be summoned again. Probably got this from deathbed confession of Francis X. Feeney, who had joined Starry Wisdom in '49. These people say the Shining Trapezohedron shews them heaven & other worlds, & that the Haunter of the Dark tells them secrets in some way.

Story of Orrin B. Eddy 1857. They call it up by gazing at the crystal, & have a secret language of their own.

200 or more in cong. 1863, exclusive of men at front.

Irish boys mob church in 1869 after Patrick Regan's disappearance.

Veiled article in J. March 14, '72, but people don't talk about it.

6 disappearances 1876 – secret committee calls on Mayor Doyle.

Action promised Feb. 1877 – church closes in April.

Gang – Federal Hill Boys – threaten Dr — and vestrymen in May.

181 persons leave city before end of '77 – mention no names.

Ghost stories begin around 1880 – try to ascertain truth of report that no human being has entered church since 1877.

Ask Lanigan for photograph of place taken 1851 . . .

Restoring the paper to the pocketbook and placing the latter in his coat, Blake turned to look down at the skeleton in the dust. The implications of the notes were clear, and there could be no doubt but that this man had come to the deserted edifice forty-two years before in quest of a newspaper sensation which no one else had been bold enough to attempt. Perhaps no one else had known of his plan – who could tell? But he had never returned to his paper. Had some bravely suppressed fear risen to overcome him and bring on sudden heart-failure? Blake stooped over the gleaming bones and noted their peculiar state. Some of them were badly scattered, and a few seemed oddly *dissolved* at the ends. Others were strangely yellowed, with vague suggestions of charring. This charring extended to some of the fragments of clothing. The skull was in a very peculiar state – stained yellow, and with a charred aperture in the top as if some powerful acid had eaten through the solid bone. What had happened to the skeleton during its four decades of silent entombment here Blake could not imagine.

Before he realised it, he was looking at the stone again, and letting its curious influence call up a nebulous pageantry in his mind. He saw processions of robed, hooded figures whose outlines were not human, and looked on endless leagues of desert lined with carved, sky-reaching monoliths. He saw towers and walls in nighted depths under the sea, and vortices of space where wisps of black mist floated before thin shimmerings of cold purple haze. And beyond all else he glimpsed an infinite gulf of darkness, where solid and semi-solid forms were known only by their windy stirrings, and cloudy patterns of force seemed to superimpose order on chaos and hold forth a key to all the paradoxes and arcana of the worlds we know.

Then all at once the spell was broken by an access of gnawing, indeterminate panic fear. Blake choked and turned away from the stone, conscious of some formless alien presence close to him and watching him with horrible intentness. He felt entangled with something – something which was not in the stone, but which had looked through it at him – something which would ceaselessly follow him with a cognition that was not physical sight. Plainly, the place was getting on his nerves – as well it might in view of his gruesome find. The light was waning, too, and since he had no illuminant with him he knew he would have to be leaving soon.

It was then, in the gathering twilight, that he thought he saw a faint trace of luminosity in the crazily angled stone. He had tried to look away from it, but some obscure compulsion drew his eyes back. Was there a subtle phosphorescence of radio-activity about the thing? What was it that the dead man's notes had said concerning a *Shining Trapezohedron?* What, anyway, was this abandoned lair of cosmic evil? What had been done here, and what might still be lurking in the bird-shunned shadows? It seemed now as if an elusive touch of foetor had arisen somewhere close by, though its source was not apparent. Blake seized the cover of the long-open box and snapped it down. It moved easily on its alien hinges, and closed completely over the unmistakably glowing stone.

At the sharp click of that closing a soft stirring sound seemed to come from the steeple's eternal blackness overhead, beyond the trap-door. Rats, without question – the only living things to reveal their presence in this accursed pile since he had entered it. And yet that stirring in the steeple frightened him horribly, so that he plunged almost wildly down the spiral stairs, across the ghoulish nave, into the vaulted basement, out amidst the gathering dusk of the deserted square, and down through the teeming, fear-haunted alleys and avenues of Federal Hill toward the sane central streets and the home-like brick sidewalks of the college district.

During the days which followed, Blake told no one of his expedition. Instead, he read much in certain books, examined long years of newspaper files downtown, and worked feverishly at the cryptogram in that leather volume from the cobwebbed vestry room. The cipher, he soon saw, was no simple one; and after a long period of endeavour he felt sure that its language could not be English, Latin, Greek, French, Spanish, Italian, or German. Evidently he would have to draw upon the deepest wells of his strange erudition.

Every evening the old impulse to gaze westward returned, and he saw the black steeple as of yore amongst the bristling roofs of a distant and half-fabulous world. But now it held a fresh note of terror for him. He knew the heritage of evil lore it masked, and with the knowledge his vision ran riot in queer new ways. The birds of spring were returning, and as he watched their sunset flights he fancied they avoided the gaunt, lone spire as never before. When a flock of them approached it, he thought, they would wheel and scatter in panic confusion – and he could guess at the wild twitterings which failed to reach him across the intervening miles.

It was in June that Blake's diary told of his victory over the cryptogram. The text was, he found, in the dark Aklo language used by certain cults of evil antiquity, and known to him in a halting way through previous researches. The diary is strangely reticent about what Blake deciphered, but he was patently awed and disconcerted by his results. There are references to a Haunter of the Dark awaked by gazing into the Shining Trapezohedron, and insane conjectures about the black gulfs of chaos from which it was called. The being is spoken of as holding all knowledge, and demanding monstrous sacrifices. Some of Blake's entries shew fear lest the thing, which he seemed to regard as summoned, stalk abroad; though he adds that the street-lights form a bulwark which cannot be crossed.

Of the Shining Trapezohedron he speaks often, calling it a window on all time and space, and tracing its history from the days it was fashioned on dark Yuggoth, before ever the Old Ones brought it to earth. It was treasured and placed in its curious box by the crinoid things of Antarctica, salvaged from their ruins by the serpent-men of Valusia, and peered at aeons later in Lemuria by the first human beings. It crossed strange lands and stranger seas, and sank with Atlantis before a Minoan fisher meshed it in his net and sold it to swarthy merchants from nighted Khem. The Pharaoh Nephren-Ka built around it a temple with a windowless crypt, and did that which caused his name to be stricken from all monuments and records. Then it slept in the ruins of that evil fane which the priests and the new Pharaoh destroyed, till the delver's spade once more brought it forth to curse mankind.

Early in July the newspapers oddly supplement Blake's entries, though in so brief and casual a way that only the diary has called general attention to their contribution. It appears that a new fear had been growing on Federal Hill since a stranger had entered the dreaded church. The Italians whispered of unaccustomed stirrings and bumpings and scrapings in the dark windowless steeple, and called on their priests to banish an entity which haunted their dreams. Something, they said, was constantly watching at a door to see if it were dark enough to venture forth. Press items mentioned the long-standing local superstitions, but failed to shed much light on the earlier background of the horror. It was obvious that the young reporters of today are no antiquarians. In writing of these things in his diary, Blake expresses a curious kind of remorse, and talks of the duty of burying the Shining Trapezohedron and of banishing what he had evoked by letting daylight into the hideous jutting spire. At the same time, however, he displays the dangerous extent of his fascination, and admits a morbid longing – pervading even his dreams – to visit the accursed tower and gaze again into the cosmic secrets of the glowing stone.

Then something in the *Journal* on the morning of July 17 threw the diarist into a veritable fever of horror. It was only a variant of the other half-humorous items about the Federal Hill restlessness, but to Blake it was somehow very terrible indeed. In the night a thunderstorm had put the city's lighting-system out of commission for a full hour, and in that black interval the Italians had nearly gone mad with fright. Those living near the dreaded church had sworn that the thing in the steeple had taken advantage of the street-lamps' absence and gone down into the body of the church, flopping and bumping around in a viscous, altogether dreadful way. Toward the last it had bumped up to the tower, where there were sounds of the shattering of glass. It could go wherever the darkness reached, but light would always send it fleeing.

When the current blazed on again there had been a shocking commotion in the tower, for even the feeble light trickling through the grime-blackened, louver-boarded windows was too much for the thing. It had bumped and slithered up into its tenebrous steeple just in time – for a long dose of light would have sent it back into the abyss whence the crazy stranger had called it. During the dark hour praying crowds had clustered round the church in the rain with lighted candles and lamps somehow shielded with folded paper and umbrellas – a guard of light to save the city from the nightmare that stalks in darkness. Once, those nearest the church declared, the outer door had rattled hideously.

But even this was not the worst. That evening in the *Bulletin* Blake read of what the reporters had found. Aroused at last to the whimsical news value of the scare, a pair of them had defied the frantic crowds of Italians and crawled into the church through the cellar window after trying the doors in vain. They found the dust of the vestibule and of the spectral nave ploughed up in a singular way, with bits of rotted cushions and satin pew-linings scattered curiously around. There was a bad odour everywhere, and here and there were bits of yellow stain and patches of what looked like charring. Opening the door to the tower, and pausing a moment at the suspicion of a scraping sound above, they found the narrow spiral stairs wiped roughly clean.

In the tower itself a similarly half-swept condition existed. They spoke of the heptagonal stone pillar, the overturned Gothic chairs, and the bizarre plaster images; though strangely enough the metal box and the old mutilated skeleton were not mentioned. What disturbed Blake the most – except for the hints of stains and charring and bad odours – was the final detail that explained the crashing glass. Every one of the tower's lancet windows was broken, and two of them had been darkened in a crude and hurried way by the stuffing of satin pew-linings and cushion-horsehair into the spaces between the slanting exterior louver-boards. More satin fragments and bunches of horsehair lay scattered around the newly swept floor, as if someone had been interrupted in the act of restoring the tower to the absolute blackness of its tightly curtained days.

Yellowish stains and charred patches were found on the ladder to the windowless spire, but when a reporter climbed up, opened the horizontally sliding trap-door, and shot a feeble flashlight beam into the black and strangely foetid space, he saw nothing but darkness, and an heterogeneous litter of shapeless fragments near the aperture. The verdict, of course, was charlatanry. Somebody had played a joke on the superstitious hill-dwellers, or else some fanatic had striven to bolster up their fears for their own supposed good. Or perhaps some of the younger and more sophisticated dwellers had staged an elaborate hoax on the outside world. There was an amusing aftermath when the police sent an officer to verify the reports. Three men in succession found ways of evading the assignment, and the fourth went very reluctantly and returned very soon without adding to the account given by the reporters.

From this point onward Blake's diary shews a mounting tide of insidious horror and nervous apprehension. He upbraids himself for not doing something, and speculates wildly on the consequences of another electrical breakdown. It has been verified that on three occasions – during thunderstorms – he telephoned the electric light company in a frantic vein and asked that desperate precautions against a lapse of power be taken. Now and then his entries shew concern over the failure of the reporters to find the metal box and stone, and the strangely marred old skeleton, when they explored the shadowy tower room. He assumed that these things had been removed – whither, and by whom or what, he could only guess. But his worst fears concerned himself, and the kind of unholy rapport he felt to exist between his mind and that lurking horror in the distant steeple – that monstrous thing of night which his rashness had called out of the ultimate black spaces. He seemed to feel a constant tugging at his will, and callers of that period remember how he would sit abstractedly at his desk and stare out of the west window at that far-off, spire-bristling mound beyond the swirling smoke of the city. His entries dwell monotonously on certain terrible dreams, and on a strengthening of the unholy rapport in his sleep. There is mention of a night when he awaked to find himself fully dressed, outdoors, and headed automatically down College Hill toward the west. Again and again he dwells on the fact that the thing in the steeple knows where to find him.

The week following July 30 is recalled as the time of Blake's partial breakdown. He did not dress, and ordered all his food by telephone. Visitors remarked the cords he kept near his bed, and he said that sleep-walking had forced him to bind his ankles every night with knots which would probably hold or else waken him with the labour of untying.

In his diary he told of the hideous experience which had brought the collapse. After retiring on the night of the 30th he had suddenly found himself groping about in an almost black space. All he could see were short, faint, horizontal streaks of bluish light, but he could smell an overpowering foetor and hear a curious jumble of soft, furtive sounds above him. Whenever he moved he stumbled over something, and at each noise there would come a sort of answering sound from above – a vague stirring, mixed with the cautious sliding of wood on wood.

Once his groping hands encountered a pillar of stone with a vacant top, whilst later he found himself clutching the rungs of a ladder built into the wall, and fumbling his uncertain way upward toward some region of intenser stench where a hot, searing blast beat down against him. Before his eyes a kaleidoscopic range of phantasmal images played, all of them dissolving at intervals into the picture of a vast, unplumbed abyss of night wherein whirled suns and worlds of an even profounder blackness. He thought of the ancient legends of Ultimate Chaos, at whose centre sprawls the blind idiot god Azathoth, Lord of All Things, encircled by his flopping horde of mindless and amorphous dancers, and lulled by the thin monotonous piping of a daemoniac flute held in nameless paws.

Then a sharp report from the outer world broke through his stupor and roused him to the unutterable horror of his position. What it was, he never knew – perhaps it was some belated peal from the fireworks heard all summer on Federal Hill as the dwellers hail their various patron saints, or the saints of their native villages in Italy. In any event he shrieked aloud, dropped frantically from the ladder, and stumbled blindly across the obstructed floor of the almost lightless chamber that encompassed him.

He knew instantly where he was, and plunged recklessly down the narrow spiral staircase, tripping and bruising himself at every turn. There was a nightmare flight through a vast cobwebbed nave whose ghostly arches reached up to realms of leering shadow, a sightless scramble through a littered basement, a climb to regions of air and street-lights outside, and a mad racing down a spectral hill of gibbering gables, across a grim, silent city of tall black towers, and up the steep eastward precipice to his own ancient door.

On regaining consciousness in the morning he found himself lying on his study floor fully dressed. Dirt and cobwebs covered him, and every inch of his body seemed sore and bruised. When he faced the mirror he saw that his hair was badly scorched, while a trace of strange, evil odour seemed to cling to his upper outer clothing. It was then that his nerves broke down. Thereafter, lounging exhaustedly about in a dressing-gown, he did little but stare from his west window, shiver at the threat of thunder, and make wild entries in his diary.

The great storm broke just before midnight on August 8th. Lightning struck repeatedly in all parts of the city, and two remarkable fireballs were reported. The rain was torrential, while a constant fusillade of thunder brought sleeplessness to thousands. Blake was utterly frantic in his fear for the lighting system, and tried to telephone the company around 1 a.m., though by that time service had been temporarily cut off in the interest of safety. He recorded everything in his diary – the large, nervous, and often undecipherable hieroglyphs telling their own story of growing frenzy and despair, and of entries scrawled blindly in the dark.

He had to keep the house dark in order to see out the window, and it appears that most of his time was spent at his desk, peering anxiously through the rain across the glistening miles of downtown roofs at the constellation of distant lights marking Federal Hill. Now and then he would fumblingly make an entry in his diary, so that detached phrases such as 'The lights must not go'; 'It knows where I am'; 'I must destroy it'; and 'It is calling to me, but perhaps it means no injury this time'; are found scattered down two of the pages.

Then the lights went out all over the city. It happened at 2:12 a.m. according to power-house records, but Blake's diary gives no indication of the time. The entry is merely, 'Lights out – God help me.' On Federal Hill there were watchers as anxious as he, and rain-soaked knots of men paraded the square and alleys around the evil church with umbrella-shaded candles, electric flashlights, oil lanterns, crucifixes, and obscure charms of the many sorts common to southern Italy. They blessed each flash of lightning, and made cryptical signs of fear with their right hands when a turn in the storm caused the flashes to lessen and finally to cease altogether. A rising wind blew out most of the candles, so that the scene grew threateningly dark. Someone roused Father Merluzzo of Spirito Santo Church, and he hastened to the dismal square to pronounce whatever helpful syllables he could. Of the restless and curious sounds in the blackened tower, there could be no doubt whatever.

For what happened at 2:35 we have the testimony of the priest, a young, intelligent, and well-educated person; of Patrolman William J. Monahan of the Central Station, an officer of the highest reliability who had paused at that part of his beat to inspect the crowd; and of most of the seventy-eight men who had gathered around the church's high bank wall – especially those in the square where the eastward façade was visible. Of course there was nothing which can be proved as being outside the order of Nature. The possible causes of such an event are many. No one can speak with certainty of the obscure chemical processes arising in a vast, ancient, ill-aired, and long-deserted building of heterogeneous contents. Mephitic vapours – spontaneous combustion – pressure of gases born of long decay – any one of numberless phenomena might be responsible. And then, of course, the factor of conscious charlatanry can by no means be excluded. The thing was really quite simple in itself, and covered less than three minutes of actual time. Father Merluzzo, always a precise man, looked at his watch repeatedly.

It started with a definite swelling of the dull fumbling sounds inside the black tower. There had for some time been a vague exhalation of strange, evil odours from the church, and this had now become emphatic and offensive. Then at last there was a sound of splintering wood, and a large, heavy object crashed down in the yard beneath the frowning easterly façade. The tower was invisible now that the candles would not burn, but as the object neared the ground the people knew that it was the smoke-grimed louver-boarding of that tower's east window.

Immediately afterward an utterly unbearable foetor welled forth from the unseen heights, choking and sickening the trembling watchers, and almost prostrating those in the square. At the same time the air trembled with a vibration as of flapping wings, and a sudden east-blowing wind more violent than any previous blast snatched off the hats and wrenched the dripping umbrellas of the crowd. Nothing definite could be seen in the candleless night, though some upward-looking spectators thought they glimpsed a great spreading blur of denser blackness against the inky sky – something like a formless cloud of smoke that shot with meteor-like speed toward the east.

That was all. The watchers were half numbed with fright, awe, and discomfort, and scarcely knew what to do, or whether to do anything at all. Not knowing what had happened, they did not relax their vigil; and a moment later they sent up a prayer as a sharp flash of belated lightning, followed by an earsplitting crash of sound, rent the flooded heavens. Half an hour later the rain stopped, and in fifteen minutes more the street-lights sprang on again, sending the weary, bedraggled watchers relievedly back to their homes.

The next day's papers gave these matters minor mention in connexion with the general storm reports. It seems that the great lightning flash and deafening explosion which followed the Federal Hill occurrence were even more tremendous farther east, where a burst of the singular foetor was likewise noticed. The phenomenon was most marked over College Hill, where the crash awaked all the sleeping inhabitants and led to a bewildered round of speculations. Of those who were already awake only a few saw the anomalous blaze of light near the top of the hill, or noticed the inexplicable upward rush of air which almost stripped the leaves from the trees and blasted the plants in the gardens. It was agreed that the lone, sudden lightning-bolt must have struck somewhere in this neighbourhood, though no trace of its striking could afterward be found. A youth in the Tau Omega fraternity house thought he saw a grotesque and hideous mass of smoke in the air just as the preliminary flash burst, but his observation has not been verified. All of the few observers, however, agree as to the violent gust from the west and the flood of intolerable stench which preceded the belated stroke; whilst evidence concerning the momentary burned odour after the stroke is equally general.

These points were discussed very carefully because of their probable connexion with the death of Robert Blake. Students in the Psi Delta house, whose upper rear windows looked into Blake's study, noticed the blurred white face at the westward window on the morning of the 9th, and wondered what was wrong with the expression. When they saw the same face in the same position that evening, they felt worried, and watched for the lights to come up in his apartment. Later they rang the bell of the darkened flat, and finally had a policeman force the door.

The rigid body sat bolt upright at the desk by the window, and when the intruders saw the glassy, bulging eyes, and the marks of stark, convulsive fright on the twisted features, they turned away in sickened dismay. Shortly afterward the coroner's physician made an examination, and despite the unbroken window reported electrical shock, or nervous tension induced by electrical discharge, as the cause of death. The hideous expression he ignored altogether, deeming it a not improbable result of the profound shock as experienced by a person of such abnormal imagination and unbalanced emotions. He deduced these latter qualities from the books, paintings, and manuscripts found in the apartment, and from the blindly scrawled entries in the diary on the desk. Blake had prolonged his frenzied jottings to the last, and the broken-pointed pencil was found clutched in his spasmodically contracted right hand.

The entries after the failure of the lights were highly disjointed, and legible only in part. From them certain investigators have drawn conclusions differing greatly from the materialistic official verdict, but such speculations have little chance for belief among the conservative. The case of these imaginative theorists has not been helped by the action of superstitious Dr Dexter, who threw the curious box and angled stone – an object certainly self-luminous as seen in the black windowless steeple where it was found – into the deepest channel of Narragansett Bay. Excessive imagination and neurotic unbalance on Blake's part, aggravated by knowledge of the evil bygone cult whose startling traces he had uncovered, form the dominant interpretation given those final frenzied jottings. These are the entries – or all that can be made of them.

'Lights still out – must be five minutes now. Everything depends on lightning. Yaddith grant it will keep up! . . . Some influence seems beating through it . . . Rain and thunder and wind deafen . . . The thing is taking hold of my mind . . .

'Trouble with memory. I see things I never knew before. Other worlds and other galaxies . . . Dark . . . The lightning seems dark and the darkness seems light . . .

'It cannot be the real hill and church that I see in the pitch-darkness. Must be retinal impression left by flashes. Heaven grant the Italians are out with their candles if the lightning stops!

'What am I afraid of? Is it not an avatar of Nyarlathotep, who in antique and shadowy Khem even took the form of man? I remember Yuggoth, and more distant Shaggai, and the ultimate void of the black planets . . .

'The long, winging flight through the void . . . cannot cross the universe of light . . . re-created by the thoughts caught in the Shining Trapezohedron . . . send it through the horrible abysses of radiance . . .

'My name is Blake – Robert Harrison Blake of 620 East Knapp Street, Milwaukee, Wisconsin . . . I am on this planet . . .

'Azathoth have mercy! – the lightning no longer flashes – horrible – I can see everything with a monstrous sense that is not sight – light is dark and dark is light . . . those people on the hill . . . guard . . . candles and charms . . . their priests . . .

'Sense of distance gone – far is near and near is far. No light – no glass – see that steeple – that tower – window – can hear – Roderick Usher – am mad or going mad – the thing is stirring and fumbling in the tower – I am it and it is I – I want to get out . . . must get out and unify the forces . . . It knows where I am . . .

'I am Robert Blake, but I see the tower in the dark. There is a monstrous odour . . . senses transfigured . . . boarding at that tower window cracking and giving way . . . Iä . . . ngai . . . ygg . . .

'I see it – coming here – hell-wind – titan blur – black wings – Yog-Sothoth save me – the three-lobed burning eye . . .'

Polaris

Into the north window of my chamber glows the Pole Star with uncanny light. All through the long hellish hours of blackness it shines there. And in the autumn of the year, when the winds from the north curse and whine, and the red-leaved trees of the swamp mutter things to one another in the small hours of the morning under the horned waning moon, I sit by the casement and watch that star. Down from the heights reels the glittering Cassiopeia as the hours wear on, while Charles' Wain lumbers up from behind the vapour-soaked swamp trees that sway in the night-wind. Just before dawn Arcturus winks ruddily from above the cemetery on the low hillock, and Coma Berenices shimmers weirdly afar off in the mysterious east; but still the Pole Star leers down from the same place in the black vault, winking hideously like an insane watching eye which strives to convey some strange message, yet recalls nothing save that it once had a message to convey. Sometimes, when it is cloudy, I can sleep.

Well do I remember the night of the great Aurora, when over the swamp played the shocking coruscations of the daemon-light. After the beams came clouds, and then I slept.

And it was under a horned waning moon that I saw the city for the first time. Still and somnolent did it lie, on a strange plateau in a hollow betwixt strange peaks. Of ghastly marble were its walls and its towers, its columns, domes, and pavements. In the marble streets were marble pillars, the upper parts of which were carven into the images of grave bearded men. The air was warm and stirred not. And overhead, scarce ten degrees from the zenith, glowed that watching Pole Star. Long did I gaze on the city, but the day came not. When the red Aldebaran, which blinked low in the sky but never set, had crawled a quarter of the way around the horizon, I saw light and motion in the houses and the streets.

Forms strangely robed, but at once noble and familiar, walked abroad, and under the horned waning moon men talked wisdom in a tongue which I understood, though it was unlike any language I had ever known. And when the red Aldebaran had crawled more than half way around the horizon, there were again darkness and silence.

When I awaked, I was not as I had been. Upon my memory was graven the vision of the city, and within my soul had arisen another and vaguer recollection, of whose nature I was not then certain. Thereafter, on the cloudy nights when I could sleep, I saw the city often; sometimes under that horned waning moon, and sometimes under the hot yellow rays of a sun which did not set, but which wheeled low around the horizon. And on the clear nights the Pole Star leered as never before.

Gradually I came to wonder what might be my place in that city on the strange plateau betwixt strange peaks. At first content to view the scene as an all-observant uncorporeal presence, I now desired to define my relation to it, and to speak my mind amongst the grave men who conversed each day in the public squares. I said to myself, 'This is no dream, for by what means can I prove the greater reality of that other life in the house of stone and brick south of the sinister swamp and the cemetery on the low hillock, where the Pole Star peers into my north window each night?'

One night as I listened to the discourse in the large square containing many statues, I felt a change; and perceived that I had at last a bodily form. Nor was I a stranger in the streets of Olathoë, which lies on the plateau of Sarkis, betwixt the peaks Noton and Kadiphonek. It was my friend Alos who spoke, and his speech was one that pleased my soul, for it was the speech of a true man and patriot. That night had the news come of Daikos' fall, and of the advance of the Inutos; squat, hellish, yellow fiends who five years ago had appeared out of the unknown west to ravage the confines of our kingdom, and finally to besiege our towns. Having taken the fortified places at the foot of the mountains, their way now lay open to the plateau, unless every citizen could resist with the strength of ten men. For the squat creatures were mighty in the arts of war, and knew not the scruples of honour which held back our tall, grey-eyed men of Lomar from ruthless conquest.

Alos, my friend, was commander of all the forces on the plateau, and in him lay the last hope of our country. On this occasion he spoke of the perils to be faced, and exhorted the men of Olathoë, bravest of the Lomarians, to sustain the traditions of their ancestors, who when forced to move southward from Zobna before the advance of the great ice-sheet (even as our descendants must some day flee from the land of Lomar), valiantly and victoriously swept aside the hairy, long-armed, cannibal Gnophkehs that stood in their way. To me Alos denied a warrior's part, for I was feeble and given to strange faintings when subjected to stress and hardships. But my eyes were the keenest in the city, despite the long hours I gave each day to the study of the *Pnakotic Manuscripts* and the wisdom of the Zobnarian Fathers; so my friend, desiring not to doom me to inaction, rewarded me with that duty which was second to nothing in importance. To the watch-tower of Thapnen he sent me, there to serve as the eyes of our army. Should the Inutos attempt to gain the citadel by the narrow pass behind the peak Noton, and thereby surprise the garrison, I was to give the signal of fire which would warn the waiting soldiers and save the town from immediate disaster.

Alone I mounted the tower, for every man of stout body was needed in the passes below. My brain was sore dazed with excitement and fatigue, for I had not slept in many days; yet was my purpose firm, for I loved my native land of Lomar, and the marble city of Olathoë that lies betwixt the peaks of Noton and Kadiphonek.

But as I stood in the tower's topmost chamber, I beheld the horned waning moon, red and sinister, quivering through the vapours that hovered over the distant valley of Banof. And through an opening in the roof glittered the pale Pole Star, fluttering as if alive, and leering like a fiend and tempter. Methought its spirit whispered evil counsel, soothing me to traitorous somnolence with a damnable rhythmical promise which it repeated over and over.

> Slumber, watcher, till the spheres
> Six and twenty thousand years
> Have revolv'd, and I return
> To the spot where now I burn.
> Other stars anon shall rise
> To the axis of the skies;

> Stars that soothe and stars that bless
> With a sweet forgetfulness:
> Only when my round is o'er
> Shall the past disturb thy door.

Vainly did I struggle with my drowsiness, seeking to connect these strange words with some lore of the skies which I had learnt from the *Pnakotic Manuscripts*. My head, heavy and reeling, drooped to my breast, and when next I looked up it was in a dream; with the Pole Star grinning at me through a window from over the horrible swaying trees of a dream-swamp. And I am still dreaming.

In my shame and despair I sometimes scream frantically, begging the dream-creatures around me to waken me ere the Inutos steal up the pass behind the peak Noton and take the citadel by surprise; but these creatures are daemons, for they laugh at me and tell me I am not dreaming. They mock me whilst I sleep, and whilst the squat yellow foe may be creeping silently upon us. I have failed in my duty and betrayed the marble city of Olathoë; I have proven false to Alos, my friend and commander. But still these shadows of my dream deride me. They say there is no land of Lomar, save in my nocturnal imaginings; that in those realms where the Pole Star shines high and red Aldebaran crawls low around the horizon, there has been naught save ice and snow for thousands of years, and never a man save squat yellow creatures, blighted by the cold, whom they call 'Esquimaux'.

And as I writhe in my guilty agony, frantic to save the city whose peril every moment grows, and vainly striving to shake off this unnatural dream of a house of stone and brick south of a sinister swamp and a cemetery on a low hillock; the Pole Star, evil and monstrous, leers down from the black vault, winking hideously like an insane watching eye which strives to convey some strange message, yet recalls nothing save that it once had a message to convey.

The Doom That Came to Sarnath

There is in the land of Mnar a vast still lake that is fed by no stream and out of which no stream flows. Ten thousand years ago there stood by its shore the mighty city of Sarnath, but Sarnath stands there no more.

It is told that in the immemorial years when the world was young, before ever the men of Sarnath came to the land of Mnar, another city stood beside the lake; the grey stone city of Ib, which was old as the lake itself, and peopled with beings not pleasing to behold. Very odd and ugly were these beings, as indeed are most beings of a world yet inchoate and rudely fashioned. It is written on the brick cylinders of Kadatheron that the beings of Ib were in hue as green as the lake and the mists that rise above it; that they had bulging eyes, pouting, flabby lips, and curious ears, and were without voice. It is also written that they descended one night from the moon in a mist; they and the vast still lake and grey stone city Ib. However this may be, it is certain that they worshipped a sea-green stone idol chiselled in the likeness of Bokrug, the great water-lizard; before which they danced horribly when the moon was gibbous. And it is written in the papyrus of Ilarnek, that they one day discovered fire, and thereafter kindled flames on many ceremonial occasions. But not much is written of these beings, because they lived in very ancient times, and man is young, and knows little of the very ancient living things.

After many aeons men came to the land of Mnar; dark shepherd folk with their fleecy flocks, who built Thraa, Ilarnek, and Kadatheron on the winding river Ai. And certain tribes, more hardy than the rest, pushed on to the border of the lake and built Sarnath at a spot where precious metals were found in the earth.

Not far from the grey city of Ib did the wandering tribes lay the first stones of Sarnath, and at the beings of Ib they marvelled greatly. But with their marvelling was mixed hate, for they thought it not meet that beings of such aspect should walk about the world of men at dusk. Nor did they like the strange sculptures upon the grey monoliths of Ib, for those sculptures were terrible with great antiquity. Why the beings and the sculptures lingered so late in the world, even until the coming of men, none can tell; unless it was because the land of Mnar is very still, and remote from most other lands both of waking and of dream.

As the men of Sarnath beheld more of the beings of Ib their hate grew, and it was not less because they found the beings weak, and soft as jelly to the touch of stones and spears and arrows. So one day the young warriors, the slingers and the spearmen and the bowmen, marched against Ib and slew all the inhabitants thereof, pushing the queer bodies into the lake with long spears, because they did not wish to touch them. And because they did not like the grey sculptured monoliths of Ib they cast these also into the lake; wondering from the greatness of the labour how ever the stones were brought from afar, as they must have been, since there is naught like them in all the land of Mnar or in the lands adjacent.

Thus of the very ancient city of Ib was nothing spared save the sea-green stone idol chiselled in the likeness of Bokrug, the water-lizard. This the young warriors took back with them to Sarnath as a symbol of conquest over the old gods and beings of Ib, and a sign of leadership in Mnar. But on the night after it was set up in the temple a terrible thing must have happened, for weird lights were seen over the lake, and in the morning the people found the idol gone, and the high-priest Taran-Ish lying dead, as from some fear unspeakable. And before he died, Taran-Ish had scrawled upon the altar of chrysolite with coarse shaky strokes the sign of **DOOM**.

After Taran-Ish there were many high-priests in Sarnath, but never was the sea-green stone idol found. And many centuries came and went, wherein Sarnath prospered exceedingly, so that only priests and old women remembered what Taran-Ish had scrawled upon the altar of chrysolite. Betwixt Sarnath and the city of Ilarnek arose a caravan route, and the precious metals from the earth were exchanged for other metals and rare cloths and jewels and books and tools for artificers and all things of luxury that are known to the people who dwell along the winding river Ai and beyond. So Sarnath waxed mighty and learned and beautiful, and sent forth conquering armies to subdue the neighbouring cities; and in time there sate upon a throne in Sarnath the kings of all the land of Mnar and of many lands adjacent.

The wonder of the world and the pride of all mankind was Sarnath the magnificent. Of polished desert-quarried marble were its walls, in height 300 cubits and in breadth 75, so that chariots might pass each other as men drave them along the top. For full 500 stadia did they run, being open only on the side toward the lake; where a green stone sea-wall kept back the waves that rose oddly once a year at the festival of the destroying of Ib. In Sarnath were fifty streets from the lake to the gates of the caravans, and fifty more intersecting them. With onyx were they paved, save those whereon the horses and camels and elephants trod, which were paved with granite. And the gates of Sarnath were as many as the landward ends of the streets, each of bronze, and flanked by the figures of lions and elephants carven from some stone no longer known among men. The houses of Sarnath were of glazed brick and chalcedony, each having its walled garden and crystal lakelet. With strange art were they builded, for no other city had houses like them; and travellers from Thraa and Ilarnek and Kadatheron marvelled at the shining domes wherewith they were surmounted.

But more marvellous still were the palaces and the temples, and the gardens made by Zokkar the olden king. There were many palaces, the least of which were mightier than any in Thraa or Ilarnek or Kadatheron. So high were they that one within might sometimes fancy himself beneath only the sky; yet when lighted with torches dipt in the oil of Dothur their walls shewed vast paintings of kings and armies, of a splendour at once inspiring and stupefying to the beholder. Many were the pillars of the palaces, all of tinted marble, and carven into designs of surpassing beauty. And in most of the palaces the floors were mosaics of beryl and lapis-lazuli and sardonyx and carbuncle and other choice materials, so disposed that the beholder might fancy himself walking over beds of the rarest flowers. And there were likewise fountains, which cast scented waters about in pleasing jets arranged with cunning art. Outshining all others was the palace of the kings of Mnar and of the lands adjacent. On a pair of golden crouching lions rested the throne, many steps above the gleaming floor. And it was wrought of one piece of ivory, though no man lives who knows whence so vast a piece could have come. In that palace there were also many galleries, and many amphitheatres where lions and men and elephants battled at the pleasure of the kings. Sometimes the amphitheatres were flooded with water conveyed from the lake in mighty aqueducts, and then were enacted stirring sea-fights, or combats betwixt swimmers and deadly marine things.

Lofty and amazing were the seventeen tower-like temples of Sarnath, fashioned of a bright multi-coloured stone not known elsewhere. A full thousand cubits high stood the greatest among them, wherein the high-priests dwelt with a magnificence scarce less than that of the kings. On the ground were halls as vast and splendid as those of the palaces; where gathered throngs in worship of Zo-Kalar and Tamash and Lobon, the chief gods of Sarnath, whose incense-enveloped shrines were as the thrones of monarchs. Not like the eikons of other gods were those of Zo-Kalar and Tamash and Lobon, for so close to life were they that one might swear the graceful bearded gods themselves sate on the ivory thrones. And up unending steps of shining zircon was the tower-chamber, wherefrom the high-priests looked out over the city and the plains and the lake by day; and at the cryptic moon and significant stars and planets, and their reflections in the lake, by night. Here was done the very secret and ancient rite in detestation of Bokrug, the water-lizard, and here rested the altar of chrysolite which bore the **DOOM**-scrawl of Taran-Ish.

Wonderful likewise were the gardens made by Zokkar the olden king. In the centre of Sarnath they lay, covering a great space and encircled by a high wall. And they were surmounted by a mighty dome of glass, through which shone the sun and moon and stars and planets when it was clear, and from which were hung fulgent images of the sun and moon and stars and planets when it was not clear. In summer the gardens were cooled with fresh odorous breezes skilfully wafted by fans, and in winter they were heated with concealed fires, so that in those gardens it was always spring. There ran little streams over bright pebbles, dividing meads of green and gardens of many hues, and spanned by a multitude of bridges. Many were the waterfalls in their courses, and many were the lilied lakelets into which they expanded. Over the streams and lakelets rode white swans, whilst the music of rare birds chimed in with the melody of the waters. In ordered terraces rose the green banks, adorned here and there with bowers of vines and sweet blossoms, and seats and benches of marble and porphyry. And there were many small shrines and temples where one might rest or pray to small gods.

Each year there was celebrated in Sarnath the feast of the destroying of Ib, at which time wine, song, dancing, and merriment of every kind abounded. Great honours were then paid to the shades of those who had annihilated the odd ancient beings, and the memory of those beings and of their elder gods was derided by dancers and lutanists crowned with roses from the gardens of Zokkar. And the kings would look out over the lake and curse the bones of the dead that lay beneath it. At first the high-priests liked not these festivals, for there had descended amongst them queer tales of how the sea-green eikon had vanished, and how Taran-Ish had died from fear and left a warning. And they said that from their high tower they sometimes saw lights beneath the waters of the lake. But as many years passed without calamity even the priests laughed and cursed and joined in the orgies of the feasters. Indeed, had they not themselves, in their high tower, often performed the very ancient and secret rite in detestation of Bokrug, the water-lizard? And a thousand years of riches and delight passed over Sarnath, wonder of the world and pride of all mankind.

Gorgeous beyond thought was the feast of the thousandth year of the destroying of Ib. For a decade had it been talked of in the land of Mnar, and as it drew nigh there came to Sarnath on horses and camels and elephants men from Thraa, Ilarnek, and Kadatheron, and all the cities of Mnar and the lands beyond. Before the marble walls on the appointed night were pitched the pavilions of princes and the tents of travellers, and all the shore resounded with the song of happy revellers. Within his banquet-hall reclined Nargis-Hei, the king, drunken with ancient wine from the vaults of conquered Pnath, and surrounded by feasting nobles and hurrying slaves. There were eaten many strange delicacies at that feast; peacocks from the isles of Nariel in the Middle Ocean, young goats from the distant hills of Implan, heels of camels from the Bnazic desert, nuts and spices from Cydathrian groves, and pearls from wave-washed Mtal dissolved in the vinegar of Thraa. Of sauces there were an untold number, prepared by the subtlest cooks in all Mnar, and suited to the palate of every feaster. But most prized of all the viands were the great fishes from the lake, each of vast size, and served up on golden platters set with rubies and diamonds.

Whilst the king and his nobles feasted within the palace, and viewed the crowning dish as it awaited them on golden platters, others feasted elsewhere. In the tower of the great temple the priests held revels, and in pavilions without the walls the princes of neighbouring lands made merry. And it was the high-priest Gnai-Kah who first saw the shadows that descended from the gibbous moon into the lake, and the damnable green mists that arose from the lake to meet the moon and to shroud in a sinister haze the towers and the domes of fated Sarnath. Thereafter those in the towers and without the walls beheld strange lights on the water, and saw that the grey rock Akurion, which was wont to rear high above it near the shore, was almost submerged. And fear grew vaguely yet swiftly, so that the princes of Ilarnek and of far Rokol took down and folded their tents and pavilions and departed for the river Ai, though they scarce knew the reason for their departing.

Then, close to the hour of midnight, all the bronze gates of Sarnath burst open and emptied forth a frenzied throng that blackened the plain, so that all the visiting princes and travellers fled away in fright. For on the faces of this throng was writ a madness born of horror unendurable, and on their tongues were words so terrible that no hearer paused for proof. Men whose eyes were wild with fear shrieked aloud of the sight within the king's banquet-hall, where through the windows were seen no longer the forms of Nargis-Hei and his nobles and slaves, but a horde of indescribable green voiceless things with bulging eyes, pouting, flabby lips, and curious ears; things which danced horribly, bearing in their paws golden platters set with rubies and diamonds containing uncouth flames. And the princes and travellers, as they fled from the doomed city of Sarnath on horses and camels and elephants, looked again upon the mist-begetting lake and saw the grey rock Akurion was quite submerged.

Through all the land of Mnar and the lands adjacent spread the tales of those who had fled from Sarnath, and caravans sought that accursed city and its precious metals no more. It was long ere any traveller went thither, and even then only the brave and adventurous young men of distant Falona dared make the journey; adventurous young men of yellow hair and blue eyes, who are no kin to the men of Mnar. These men indeed went to the lake to view Sarnath; but though they found the vast still lake itself, and the grey rock Akurion which rears high above it near the shore, they beheld not the wonder of the world and pride of all mankind. Where once had risen walls of 300 cubits and towers yet higher, now stretched only the marshy shore, and where once had dwelt fifty millions of men now crawled only the detestable green water-lizard. Not even the mines of precious metal remained, for **DOOM** had come to Sarnath.

But half buried in the rushes was spied a curious green idol of stone; an exceedingly ancient idol coated with seaweed and chiselled in the likeness of Bokrug, the great water-lizard. That idol, enshrined in the high temple at Ilarnek, was subsequently worshipped beneath the gibbous moon throughout the land of Mnar.

The Statement of Randolph Carter

I repeat to you, gentlemen, that your inquisition is fruitless. Detain me here forever if you will; confine or execute me if you must have a victim to propitiate the illusion you call justice; but I can say no more than I have said already. Everything that I can remember, I have told with perfect candour. Nothing has been distorted or concealed, and if anything remains vague, it is only because of the dark cloud which has come over my mind – that cloud and the nebulous nature of the horrors which brought it upon me.

Again I say, I do not know what has become of Harley Warren; though I think – almost hope – that he is in peaceful oblivion, if there be anywhere so blessed a thing. It is true that I have for five years been his closest friend, and a partial sharer of his terrible researches into the unknown. I will not deny, though my memory is uncertain and indistinct, that this witness of yours may have seen us together as he says, on the Gainesville pike, walking toward Big Cypress Swamp, at half past eleven on that awful night. That we bore electric lanterns, spades, and a curious coil of wire with attached instruments, I will even affirm; for these things all played a part in the single hideous scene which remains burned into my shaken recollection. But of what followed, and of the reason I was found alone and dazed on the edge of the swamp next morning, I must insist that I know nothing save what I have told you over and over again. You say to me that there is nothing in the swamp or near it which could form the setting of that frightful episode. I reply that I know nothing beyond what I saw. Vision or nightmare it may have been – vision or nightmare I fervently hope it was – yet it is all that my mind retains of what took place in those shocking hours after we left the sight of men. And why Harley Warren did not return, he or his shade – or some nameless *thing* I cannot describe – alone can tell.

As I have said before, the weird studies of Harley Warren were well known to me, and to some extent shared by me. Of his vast collection of strange, rare books on forbidden subjects I have read all that are written in the languages of which I am master; but these are few as compared with those in languages I cannot understand. Most, I believe, are in Arabic; and the fiend-inspired book which brought on the end – the book which he carried in his pocket out of the world – was written in characters whose like I never saw elsewhere. Warren would never tell me just what was in that book. As to the nature of our studies – must I say again that I no longer retain full comprehension? It seems to me rather merciful that I do not, for they were terrible studies, which I pursued more through reluctant fascination than through actual inclination. Warren always dominated me, and sometimes I feared him. I remember how I shuddered at his facial expression on the night before the awful happening, when he talked so incessantly of his theory, *why certain corpses never decay, but rest firm and fat in their tombs for a thousand years.* But I do not fear him now, for I suspect that he has known horrors beyond my ken. Now I fear *for* him.

Once more I say that I have no clear idea of our object on that night. Certainly, it had much to do with something in the book which Warren carried with him – that ancient book in undecipherable characters which had come to him from India a month before – but I swear I do not know what it was that we expected to find. Your witness says he saw us at half past eleven on the Gainesville pike, headed for Big Cypress Swamp. This is probably true, but I have no distinct memory of it. The picture seared into my soul is of one scene only, and the hour must have been long after midnight; for a waning crescent moon was high in the vaporous heavens.

The place was an ancient cemetery; so ancient that I trembled at the manifold signs of immemorial years. It was in a deep, damp hollow, overgrown with rank grass, moss, and curious creeping weeds, and filled with a vague stench which my idle fancy associated absurdly with rotting stone. On every hand were the signs of neglect and decrepitude, and I seemed haunted by the notion that Warren and I were the first living creatures to invade a lethal silence of centuries. Over the valley's rim a wan, waning crescent moon peered through the noisome vapours that seemed to emanate from unheard-of catacombs, and by its feeble, wavering beams I could distinguish a repellent array of antique slabs, urns, cenotaphs, and mausoleum façades; all crumbling, moss-grown, and moisture-stained, and partly concealed by the gross luxuriance of the unhealthy vegetation. My first vivid impression of my own presence in this terrible necropolis concerns the act of pausing with Warren before a certain half-obliterated sepulchre, and of throwing down some burdens which we seemed to have been carrying. I now observed that I had with me an electric lantern and two spades, whilst my companion was supplied with a similar lantern and a portable telephone outfit. No word was uttered, for the spot and the task seemed known to us; and without delay we seized our spades and commenced to clear away the grass, weeds, and drifted earth from the flat, archaic mortuary. After uncovering the entire surface, which consisted of three immense granite slabs, we stepped back some distance to survey the charnel scene; and Warren appeared to make some mental calculations. Then he returned to the sepulchre, and using his spade as a lever, sought to pry up the slab lying nearest to a stony ruin which may have been a monument in its day. He did not succeed, and motioned to me to come to his assistance. Finally our combined strength loosened the stone, which we raised and tipped to one side.

The removal of the slab revealed a black aperture, from which rushed an effluence of miasmal gases so nauseous that we started back in horror. After an interval, however, we approached the pit again, and found the exhalations less unbearable. Our lanterns disclosed the top of a flight of stone steps, dripping with some detestable ichor of the inner earth, and bordered by moist walls encrusted with nitre. And now for the first time my memory records verbal discourse, Warren addressing me at length in his mellow tenor voice; a voice singularly unperturbed by our awesome surroundings.

'I'm sorry to have to ask you to stay on the surface,' he said, 'but it would be a crime to let anyone with your frail nerves go down there. You can't imagine, even from what you have read and from what I've told you, the things I shall have to see and do. It's fiendish work, Carter, and I doubt if any man without ironclad sensibilities could ever see it through and come up alive and sane. I don't wish to offend you, and heaven knows I'd be glad enough to have you with me; but the responsibility is in a certain sense mine, and I couldn't drag a bundle of nerves like you down to probable death or madness. I tell you, you can't imagine what the thing is really like! But I promise to keep you informed over the telephone of every move – you see I've enough wire here to reach to the centre of the earth and back!'

I can still hear, in memory, those coolly spoken words; and I can still remember my remonstrances. I seemed desperately anxious to accompany my friend into those sepulchral depths, yet he proved inflexibly obdurate. At one time he threatened to abandon the expedition if I remained insistent; a threat which proved effective, since he alone held the key to the *thing*. All this I can still remember, though I no longer know what manner of *thing* we sought. After he had secured my reluctant acquiescence in his design, Warren picked up the reel of wire and adjusted the instruments. At his nod I took one of the latter and seated myself upon an aged, discoloured gravestone close by the newly uncovered aperture. Then he shook my hand, shouldered the coil of wire, and disappeared within that indescribable ossuary. For a moment I kept sight of the glow of his lantern, and heard the rustle of the wire as he laid it down after him; but the glow soon disappeared abruptly, as if a turn in the stone staircase had been encountered, and the sound died away almost as quickly. I was alone, yet bound to the unknown depths by those magic strands whose insulated surface lay green beneath the struggling beams of that waning crescent moon.

In the lone silence of that hoary and deserted city of the dead, my mind conceived the most ghastly phantasies and illusions; and the grotesque shrines and monoliths seemed to assume a hideous personality – a half-sentience. Amorphous shadows seemed to lurk in the darker recesses of the weed-choked hollow and to flit as in some blasphemous ceremonial procession past the portals of the mouldering tombs in the hillside; shadows which could not have been cast by that pallid, peering crescent moon. I constantly consulted my watch by the light of my electric lantern, and listened with feverish anxiety at the receiver of the telephone; but for more than a quarter of an hour heard nothing. Then a faint clicking came from the instrument, and I called down to my friend in a tense voice. Apprehensive as I was, I was nevertheless unprepared for the words which came up from that uncanny vault in accents more alarmed and quivering than any I had heard before from Harley Warren. He who had so calmly left me a little while previously, now called from below in a shaky whisper more portentous than the loudest shriek.

'*God! If you could see what I am seeing!*'

I could not answer. Speechless, I could only wait. Then came the frenzied tones again.

'*Carter, it's terrible – monstrous – unbelievable!*'

This time my voice did not fail me, and I poured into the transmitter a flood of excited questions. Terrified, I continued to repeat, 'Warren, what is it? What is it?'

Once more came the voice of my friend, still hoarse with fear, and now apparently tinged with despair.

'*I can't tell you, Carter! It's too utterly beyond thought – I dare not tell you – no man could know it and live – Great God! I never dreamed of* **THIS***!*'

Stillness again, save for my now incoherent torrent of shuddering inquiry. Then the voice of Warren in a pitch of wilder consternation.

'*Carter! for the love of God, put back the slab and get out of this if you can! Quick! – leave everything else and make for the outside – it's your only chance! Do as I say, and don't ask me to explain!*'

I heard, yet was able only to repeat my frantic questions. Around me were the tombs and the darkness and the shadows; below me, some peril beyond the radius of the human imagination. But my friend was in greater danger than I, and through my fear I felt a vague resentment that he should deem me capable of deserting him under such circumstances. More clicking, and after a pause a piteous cry from Warren.

'*Beat it! For God's sake, put back the slab and beat it, Carter!*'

Something in the boyish slang of my evidently stricken companion unleashed my faculties. I formed and shouted a resolution, 'Warren, brace up! I'm coming down!' But at this offer the tone of my auditor changed to a scream of utter despair.

'*Don't! You can't understand! It's too late – and my own fault. Put back the slab and run – there's nothing else you or anyone can do now!*'

The tone changed again, this time acquiring a softer quality, as of hopeless resignation. Yet it remained tense through anxiety for me.

'*Quick – before it's too late!*'

I tried not to heed him; tried to break through the paralysis which held me, and to fulfil my vow to rush down to his aid. But his next whisper found me still held inert in the chains of stark horror.

'*Carter – hurry! It's no use – you must go – better one than two – the slab –* ' A pause, more clicking, then the faint voice of Warren:

'*Nearly over now – don't make it harder – cover up those damned steps and run for your life – you're losing time – So long, Carter – won't see you again.*' Here Warren's whisper swelled into a cry; a cry that gradually rose to a shriek fraught with all the horror of the ages –

'*Curse these hellish things – legions – My God! Beat it! Beat it! Beat it!*'

After that was silence. I know not how many interminable aeons I sat stupefied; whispering, muttering, calling, screaming into that telephone. Over and over again through those aeons I whispered and muttered, called, shouted, and screamed, 'Warren! Warren! Answer me – are you there?'

And then there came to me the crowning horror of all – the unbelievable, unthinkable, almost unmentionable thing. I have said that aeons seemed to elapse after Warren shrieked forth his last despairing warning, and that only my own cries now broke the hideous silence. But after a while there was a further clicking in the receiver, and I strained my ears to listen. Again I called down, 'Warren, are you there?', and in answer heard the *thing* which has brought this cloud over my mind. I do not try, gentlemen, to account for that *thing* – that voice – nor can I venture to describe it in detail, since the first words took away my consciousness and created a mental blank which reaches to the time of my awakening in the hospital. Shall I say that the voice was deep; hollow; gelatinous; remote; unearthly; inhuman; disembodied? What shall I say? It was the end of my experience, and is the end of my story. I heard it, and knew no more. Heard it as I sat petrified in that unknown cemetery in the hollow, amidst the crumbling stones and the falling tombs, the rank vegetation and the miasmal vapours. Heard it well up from the innermost depths of that damnable open sepulchre as I watched amorphous, necrophagous shadows dance beneath an accursed waning moon. And this is what it said.

'*YOU FOOL, WARREN IS DEAD!*'

The Cats of Ulthar

It is said that in Ulthar, which lies beyond the river Skai, no man may kill a cat; and this I can verily believe as I gaze upon him who sitteth purring before the fire. For the cat is cryptic, and close to strange things which men cannot see. He is the soul of antique Aegyptus, and bearer of tales from forgotten cities in Meroë and Ophir. He is the kin of the jungle's lords, and heir to the secrets of hoary and sinister Africa. The Sphinx is his cousin, and he speaks her language; but he is more ancient than the Sphinx, and remembers that which she hath forgotten.

In Ulthar, before ever the burgesses forbade the killing of cats, there dwelt an old cotter and his wife who delighted to trap and slay the cats of their neighbours. Why they did this I know not; save that many hate the voice of the cat in the night, and take it ill that cats should run stealthily about yards and gardens at twilight. But whatever the reason, this old man and woman took pleasure in trapping and slaying every cat which came near to their hovel; and from some of the sounds heard after dark, many villagers fancied that the manner of slaying was exceedingly peculiar. But the villagers did not discuss such things with the old man and his wife; because of the habitual expression on the withered faces of the two, and because their cottage was so small and so darkly hidden under spreading oaks at the back of a neglected yard. In truth, much as the owners of cats hated these odd folk, they feared them more; and instead of berating them as brutal assassins, merely took care that no cherished pet or mouser should stray toward the remote hovel under the dark trees. When through some unavoidable oversight a cat was missed, and sounds heard after dark, the loser would lament impotently; or console himself by thanking Fate that it was not one of his children who had thus vanished. For the people of Ulthar were simple, and knew not whence it is all cats first came.

One day a caravan of strange wanderers from the South entered the narrow cobbled streets of Ulthar. Dark wanderers they were, and unlike the other roving folk who passed through the village twice every year. In the market-place they told fortunes for silver, and bought gay beads from the merchants. What was the land of these wanderers none could tell; but it was seen that they were given to strange prayers, and that they had painted on the sides of their wagons strange figures with human bodies and the heads of cats, hawks, rams, and lions. And the leader of the caravan wore a head-dress with two horns and a curious disc betwixt the horns.

There was in this singular caravan a little boy with no father or mother, but only a tiny black kitten to cherish. The plague had not been kind to him, yet had left him this small furry thing to mitigate his sorrow; and when one is very young, one can find great relief in the lively antics of a black kitten. So the boy whom the dark people called Menes smiled more often than he wept as he sate playing with his graceful kitten on the steps of an oddly painted wagon.

On the third morning of the wanderers' stay in Ulthar, Menes could not find his kitten; and as he sobbed aloud in the market-place certain villagers told him of the old man and his wife, and of sounds heard in the night. And when he heard these things his sobbing gave place to meditation, and finally to prayer. He stretched out his arms toward the sun and prayed in a tongue no villager could understand; though indeed the villagers did not try very hard to understand, since their attention was mostly taken up by the sky and the odd shapes the clouds were assuming. It was very peculiar, but as the little boy uttered his petition there seemed to form overhead the shadowy, nebulous figures of exotic things; of hybrid creatures crowned with horn-flanked discs. Nature is full of such illusions to impress the imaginative.

That night the wanderers left Ulthar, and were never seen again. And the householders were troubled when they noticed that in all the village there was not a cat to be found. From each hearth the familiar cat had vanished; cats large and small, black, grey, striped, yellow, and white. Old Kranon, the burgomaster, swore that the dark folk had taken the cats away in revenge for the killing of Menes' kitten; and cursed the caravan and the little boy. But Nith, the lean notary, declared that the old cotter and his wife were more likely persons to suspect; for their hatred of cats was notorious and increasingly bold. Still, no one durst complain to the sinister couple; even when little Atal, the innkeeper's son, vowed that he had at twilight seen all the cats of Ulthar in that accursed yard under the trees, pacing very slowly and solemnly in a circle around the cottage, two abreast, as if in performance of some unheard-of rite of beasts. The villagers did not know how much to believe from so small a boy; and though they feared that the evil pair had charmed the cats to their death, they preferred not to chide the old cotter till they met him outside his dark and repellent yard.

So Ulthar went to sleep in vain anger; and when the people awaked at dawn – behold! every cat was back at his accustomed hearth! Large and small, black, grey, striped, yellow, and white, none was missing. Very sleek and fat did the cats appear, and sonorous with purring content. The citizens talked with one another of the affair, and marvelled not a little. Old Kranon again insisted that it was the dark folk who had taken them, since cats did not return alive from the cottage of the ancient man and his wife. But all agreed on one thing: that the refusal of all the cats to eat their portions of meat or drink their saucers of milk was exceedingly curious. And for two whole days the sleek, lazy cats of Ulthar would touch no food, but only doze by the fire or in the sun.

It was fully a week before the villagers noticed that no lights were appearing at dusk in the windows of the cottage under the trees. Then the lean Nith remarked that no one had seen the old man or his wife since the night the cats were away. In another week the burgomaster decided to overcome his fears and call at the strangely silent dwelling as a matter of duty, though in so doing he was careful to take with him Shang the blacksmith and Thul the cutter of stone as witnesses. And when they had broken down the frail door they found only this: two cleanly picked human skeletons on the earthen floor, and a number of singular beetles crawling in the shadowy corners.

There was subsequently much talk among the burgesses of Ulthar. Zath, the coroner, disputed at length with Nith, the lean notary; and Kranon and Shang and Thul were overwhelmed with questions. Even little Atal, the innkeeper's son, was closely questioned and given a sweetmeat as reward. They talked of the old cotter and his wife, of the caravan of dark wanderers, of small Menes and his black kitten, of the prayer of Menes and of the sky during that prayer, of the doings of the cats on the night the caravan left, and of what was later found in the cottage under the dark trees in the repellent yard.

And in the end the burgesses passed that remarkable law which is told of by traders in Hatheg and discussed by travellers in Nir; namely, that in Ulthar no man may kill a cat.

Celephaïs

In a dream Kuranes saw the city in the valley, and the sea-coast beyond, and the snowy peak overlooking the sea, and the gaily painted galleys that sail out of the harbour toward the distant regions where the sea meets the sky. In a dream it was also that he came by his name of Kuranes, for when awake he was called by another name. Perhaps it was natural for him to dream a new name; for he was the last of his family, and alone among the indifferent millions of London, so there were not many to speak to him and remind him who he had been. His money and lands were gone, and he did not care for the ways of people about him, but preferred to dream and write of his dreams. What he wrote was laughed at by those to whom he shewed it, so that after a time he kept his writings to himself, and finally ceased to write. The more he withdrew from the world about him, the more wonderful became his dreams; and it would have been quite futile to try to describe them on paper. Kuranes was not modern, and did not think like others who wrote. Whilst they strove to strip from life its embroidered robes of myth, and to shew in naked ugliness the foul thing that is reality, Kuranes sought for beauty alone. When truth and experience failed to reveal it, he sought it in fancy and illusion, and found it on his very doorstep, amid the nebulous memories of childhood tales and dreams.

There are not many persons who know what wonders are opened to them in the stories and visions of their youth; for when as children we listen and dream, we think but half-formed thoughts, and when as men we try to remember, we are dulled and prosaic with the poison of life. But some of us awake in the night with strange phantasms of enchanted hills and gardens, of fountains that sing in the sun, of golden cliffs overhanging murmuring seas, of plains that stretch down to sleeping cities of bronze and stone, and of shadowy companies of heroes that ride caparisoned white horses along the edges of thick forests; and then we know that we have looked back through the ivory gates into that world of wonder which was ours before we were wise and unhappy.

Kuranes came very suddenly upon his old world of childhood. He had been dreaming of the house where he was born; the great stone house covered with ivy, where thirteen generations of his ancestors had lived, and where he had hoped to die. It was moonlight, and he had stolen out into the fragrant summer night, through the gardens, down the terraces, past the great oaks of the park, and along the long white road to the village. The village seemed very old, eaten away at the edge like the moon which had commenced to wane, and Kuranes wondered whether the peaked roofs of the small houses hid sleep or death. In the streets were spears of long grass, and the window-panes on either side were either broken or filmily staring. Kuranes had not lingered, but had plodded on as though summoned toward some goal. He dared not disobey the summons for fear it might prove an illusion like the urges and aspirations of waking life, which do not lead to any goal. Then he had been drawn down a lane that led off from the village street toward the channel cliffs, and had come to the end of things – to the precipice and the abyss where all the village and all the world fell abruptly into the unechoing emptiness of infinity, and where even the sky ahead was empty and unlit by the crumbling moon and the peering stars. Faith had urged him on, over the precipice and into the gulf, where he had floated down, down, down; past dark, shapeless, undreamed dreams, faintly glowing spheres that may have been partly dreamed dreams, and laughing winged things that seemed to mock the dreamers of all the worlds. Then a rift seemed to open in the darkness before him, and he saw the city of the valley, glistening radiantly far, far below, with a background of sea and sky, and a snow-capped mountain near the shore.

Kuranes had awaked the very moment he beheld the city, yet he knew from his brief glance that it was none other than Celephaïs, in the Valley of Ooth-Nargai beyond the Tanarian Hills, where his spirit had dwelt all the eternity of an hour one summer afternoon very long ago, when he had slipt away from his nurse and let the warm sea-breeze lull him to sleep as he watched the clouds from the cliff near the village. He had protested then, when they had found him, waked him, and carried him home, for just as he was aroused he had been about to sail in a golden galley for those alluring regions where the sea meets the sky. And now he was equally resentful of awaking, for he had found his fabulous city after forty weary years.

But three nights afterward Kuranes came again to Celephaïs. As before, he dreamed first of the village that was asleep or dead, and of the abyss down which one must float silently; then the rift appeared again, and he beheld the glittering minarets of the city, and saw the graceful galleys riding at anchor in the blue harbour, and watched the gingko trees of Mount Aran swaying in the sea-breeze. But this time he was not snatched away, and like a winged being settled gradually over a grassy hillside till finally his feet rested gently on the turf. He had indeed come back to the Valley of Ooth-Nargai and the splendid city of Celephaïs.

Down the hill amid scented grasses and brilliant flowers walked Kuranes, over the bubbling Naraxa on the small wooden bridge where he had carved his name so many years ago, and through the whispering grove to the great stone bridge by the city gate. All was as of old, nor were the marble walls discoloured, nor the polished bronze statues upon them tarnished. And Kuranes saw that he need not tremble lest the things he knew be vanished; for even the sentries on the ramparts were the same, and still as young as he remembered them. When he entered the city, past the bronze gates and over the onyx pavements, the merchants and camel-drivers greeted him as if he had never been away; and it was the same at the turquoise temple of Nath-Horthath, where the orchid-wreathed priests told him that there is no time in Ooth-Nargai, but only perpetual youth. Then Kuranes walked through the Street of Pillars to the seaward wall, where gathered the traders and sailors, and strange men from the regions where the sea meets the sky. There he stayed long, gazing out over the bright harbour where the ripples sparkled beneath an unknown sun, and where rode lightly the galleys from far places over the water. And he gazed also upon Mount Aran rising regally from the shore, its lower slopes green with swaying trees and its white summit touching the sky.

More than ever Kuranes wished to sail in a galley to the far places of which he had heard so many strange tales, and he sought again the captain who had agreed to carry him so long ago. He found the man,

Athib, sitting on the same chest of spices he had sat upon before, and Athib seemed not to realise that any time had passed. Then the two rowed to a galley in the harbour, and giving orders to the oarsmen, commenced to sail out into the billowy Cerenerian Sea that leads to the sky. For several days they glided undulatingly over the water, till finally they came to the horizon, where the sea meets the sky. Here the galley paused not at all, but floated easily in the blue of the sky among fleecy clouds tinted with rose. And far beneath the keel Kuranes could see strange lands and rivers and cities of surpassing beauty, spread indolently in the sunshine which seemed never to lessen or disappear. At length Athib told him that their journey was near its end, and that they would soon enter the harbour of Serannian, the pink marble city of the clouds, which is built on that ethereal coast where the west wind flows into the sky; but as the highest of the city's carven towers came into sight there was a sound somewhere in space, and Kuranes awaked in his London garret.

For many months after that Kuranes sought the marvellous city of Celephaïs and its sky-bound galleys in vain; and though his dreams carried him to many gorgeous and unheard-of places, no one whom he met could tell him how to find Ooth-Nargai, beyond the Tanarian Hills. One night he went flying over dark mountains where there were faint, lone campfires at great distances apart, and strange, shaggy herds with tinkling bells on the leaders; and in the wildest part of this hilly country, so remote that few men could ever have seen it, he found a hideously ancient wall or causeway of stone zigzagging along the ridges and valleys; too gigantic ever to have risen by human hands, and of such a length that neither end of it could be seen. Beyond that wall in the grey dawn he came to a land of quaint gardens and cherry trees, and when the sun rose he beheld such beauty of red and white flowers, green foliage and lawns, white paths, diamond brooks, blue lakelets, carven bridges, and red-roofed pagodas, that he for a moment forgot Celephaïs in sheer delight. But he remembered it again when he walked down a white path toward a red-roofed pagoda, and would have questioned the people of that land about it, had he not found that there were no people there, but only birds and bees and butterflies. On another night Kuranes walked up a damp stone spiral stairway endlessly, and came to a tower window overlooking a mighty plain and river lit by the full moon; and in the silent city that spread away from the river-bank he thought he beheld some feature or arrangement which he had known before. He would have descended and asked the way to Ooth-Nargai had not a fearsome aurora sputtered up from some remote place beyond the horizon, shewing the ruin and antiquity of the city, and the stagnation of the reedy river, and the death lying upon that land, as it had lain since King Kynaratholis came home from his conquests to find the vengeance of the gods.

So Kuranes sought fruitlessly for the marvellous city of Celephaïs and its galleys that sail to Serannian in the sky, meanwhile seeing many wonders and once barely escaping from the high-priest not to be described, which wears a yellow silken mask over its face and dwells all alone in a prehistoric stone monastery on the cold desert plateau of Leng. In time he grew so impatient of the bleak intervals of day that he began buying drugs in order to increase his periods of sleep. Hasheesh helped a great deal, and once sent him to a part of space where form does not exist, but where glowing gases study the secrets of existence. And a violet-coloured gas told him that this part of space was outside what he had called infinity. The gas had not heard of planets and organisms before, but identified Kuranes merely as one from the infinity where matter, energy, and gravitation exist. Kuranes was now very anxious to return to minaret-studded Celephaïs, and increased his doses of drugs; but eventually he had no more money left, and could buy no drugs. Then one summer day he was turned out of his garret, and wandered aimlessly through the streets, drifting over a bridge to a place where the houses grew thinner and thinner. And it was there that fulfilment came, and he met the cortège of knights come from Celephaïs to bear him thither forever.

Handsome knights they were, astride roan horses and clad in shining armour with tabards of cloth-of-gold curiously emblazoned. So numerous were they, that Kuranes almost mistook them for an army, but their leader told him they were sent in his honour; since it was he who had created Ooth-Nargai in his dreams, on which account he was now to be appointed its chief god for evermore. Then they gave Kuranes a horse and placed him at the head of the cavalcade, and all rode majestically through the downs of Surrey and onward toward the region where Kuranes and his ancestors were born. It was very strange, but as the riders went on they seemed to gallop back through Time; for whenever they passed through a village in the twilight they saw only such houses and villages as Chaucer or men before him might have seen, and sometimes they saw knights on horseback with small companies of retainers. When it grew dark they travelled more swiftly, till soon they were flying uncannily as if in the air. In the dim dawn they came upon the village which Kuranes had seen alive in his childhood, and asleep or dead in his dreams. It was alive now, and early villagers courtesied as the horsemen clattered down the street and turned off into the lane that ends in the abyss of dream. Kuranes had previously entered that abyss only at night, and wondered what it would look like by day; so he watched anxiously as the column approached its brink. Just as they galloped up the rising ground to the precipice a golden glare came somewhere out of the east and hid all the landscape in its effulgent draperies. The abyss was now a seething chaos of roseate and cerulean splendour, and invisible voices sang exultantly as the knightly entourage plunged over the edge and floated gracefully down past glittering clouds and silvery coruscations. Endlessly down the horsemen floated, their chargers pawing the aether as if galloping over golden sands; and then the luminous vapours spread apart to reveal a greater brightness, the brightness of the city Celephaïs, and the sea-coast beyond, and the snowy peak overlooking the sea, and the gaily painted galleys that sail out of the harbour toward distant regions where the sea meets the sky.

And Kuranes reigned thereafter over Ooth-Nargai and all the neighbouring regions of dream, and held his court alternately in Celephaïs and in the cloud-fashioned Serannian. He reigns there still, and will reign happily forever, though below the cliffs at Innsmouth the channel tides played mockingly with the body of a tramp who had stumbled through the half-deserted village at dawn; played mockingly, and cast it upon the rocks by ivy-covered Trevor Towers, where a notably fat and especially offensive millionaire brewer enjoys the purchased atmosphere of extinct nobility.

The Other Gods

Atop the tallest of earth's peaks dwell the gods of earth, and suffer no man to tell that he hath looked upon them. Lesser peaks they once inhabited; but ever the men from the plains would scale the slopes of rock and snow, driving the gods to higher and higher mountains till now only the last remains. When they left their older peaks they took with them all signs of themselves; save once, it is said, when they left a carven image on the face of the mountain which they called Ngranek.

But now they have betaken themselves to unknown Kadath in the cold waste where no man treads, and are grown stern, having no higher peak whereto to flee at the coming of men. They are grown stern, and where once they suffered men to displace them, they now forbid men to come, or coming, to depart. It is well for men that they know not of Kadath in the cold waste, else they would seek injudiciously to scale it.

Sometimes when earth's gods are homesick they visit in the still night the peaks where once they dwelt, and weep softly as they try to play in the olden way on remembered slopes. Men have felt the tears of the gods on white-capped Thurai, though they have thought it rain; and have heard the sighs of the gods in the plaintive dawn-winds of Lerion. In cloud-ships the gods are wont to travel, and wise cotters have legends that keep them from certain high peaks at night when it is cloudy, for the gods are not lenient as of old.

In Ulthar, which lies beyond the river Skai, once dwelt an old man avid to behold the gods of earth; a man deeply learned in the seven cryptical books of Hsan, and familiar with the *Pnakotic Manuscripts* of distant and frozen Lomar. His name was Barzai the Wise, and the villagers tell of how he went up a mountain on the night of the strange eclipse.

Barzai knew so much of the gods that he could tell of their comings and goings, and guessed so many of their secrets that he was deemed half a god himself. It was he who wisely advised the burgesses of Ulthar when they passed their remarkable law against the slaying of cats, and who first told the young priest Atal where it is that black cats go at midnight on St John's Eve. Barzai was learned in the lore of earth's gods, and had gained a desire to look upon their faces. He believed that his great secret knowledge of gods could shield him from their wrath, so resolved to go up to the summit of high and rocky Hatheg-Kla on a night when he knew the gods would be there.

Hatheg-Kla is far in the stony desert beyond Hatheg, for which it is named, and rises like a rock statue in a silent temple. Around its peak the mists play always mournfully, for mists are the memories of the gods, and the gods loved Hatheg-Kla when they dwelt upon it in the old days. Often the gods of earth visit Hatheg-Kla in their ships of cloud, casting pale vapours over the slopes as they dance reminiscently on the summit under a clear moon. The villagers of Hatheg say it is ill to climb Hatheg-Kla at any time, and deadly to climb it by night when pale vapours hide the summit and the moon; but Barzai heeded them not when he came from neighbouring Ulthar with the young priest Atal, who was his disciple. Atal was only the son of an innkeeper, and was sometimes afraid; but Barzai's father had been a landgrave who dwelt in an ancient castle, so he had no common superstition in his blood, and only laughed at the fearful cotters.

Barzai and Atal went out of Hatheg into the stony desert despite the prayers of peasants, and talked of earth's gods by their campfires at night. Many days they travelled, and from afar saw lofty Hatheg-Kla with his aureole of mournful mist. On the thirteenth day they reached the mountain's lonely base, and Atal spoke of his fears. But Barzai was old and learned and had no fears, so led the way boldly up the slope that no man had scaled since the time of Sansu, who is written of with fright in the mouldy *Pnakotic Manuscripts*.

The way was rocky, and made perilous by chasms, cliffs, and falling stones. Later it grew cold and snowy; and Barzai and Atal often slipped and fell as they hewed and plodded upward with staves and axes. Finally the air grew thin, and the sky changed colour, and the climbers found it hard to breathe; but still they toiled up and up, marvelling at the strangeness of the scene and thrilling at the thought of what would happen on the summit when the moon was out and the pale vapours spread around. For three days they climbed higher, higher, and higher toward the roof of the world; then they camped to wait for the clouding of the moon.

For four nights no clouds came, and the moon shone down cold through the thin mournful mists around the silent pinnacle. Then on the fifth night, which was the night of the full moon, Barzai saw some dense clouds far to the north, and stayed up with Atal to watch them draw near. Thick and majestic they sailed, slowly and deliberately onward; ranging themselves round the peak high above the watchers, and hiding the moon and the summit from view. For a long hour the watchers gazed, whilst the vapours swirled and the screen of clouds grew thicker and more restless. Barzai was wise in the lore of earth's gods, and listened hard for certain sounds, but Atal felt the chill of the vapours and the awe of the night, and feared much. And when Barzai began to climb higher and beckon eagerly, it was long before Atal would follow.

So thick were the vapours that the way was hard, and though Atal followed on at last, he could scarce see the grey shape of Barzai on the dim slope above in the clouded moonlight. Barzai forged very far ahead, and seemed despite his age to climb more easily than Atal; fearing not the steepness that began to grow too great for any save a strong and dauntless man, nor pausing at wide black chasms that Atal scarce could leap. And so they went up wildly over rocks and gulfs, slipping and stumbling, and sometimes awed at the vastness and horrible silence of bleak ice pinnacles and mute granite steeps.

Very suddenly Barzai went out of Atal's sight, scaling a hideous cliff that seemed to bulge outward and block the path for any climber not inspired of earth's gods. Atal was far below, and planning what he should do when he reached the place, when curiously he noticed that the light had grown strong, as if the cloudless peak and moonlit meeting-place of the gods were very near. And as he scrambled on toward the bulging cliff and litten sky he felt fears more shocking than any he had known before. Then through the high mists he heard the voice of unseen Barzai shouting wildly in delight.

'I have heard the gods! I have heard earth's gods singing in revelry on Hatheg-Kla! The voices of earth's gods are known to Barzai the Prophet! The mists are thin and the moon is bright, and I shall see the gods dancing wildly on Hatheg-Kla that they loved in youth! The wisdom of Barzai hath made him greater than earth's gods, and against his will their spells and barriers are as naught; Barzai will behold the gods, the proud gods, the secret gods, the gods of earth who spurn the sight of men!'

Atal could not hear the voices Barzai heard, but he was now close to the bulging cliff and scanning it for foot-holds. Then he heard Barzai's voice grow shriller and louder.

'The mists are very thin, and the moon casts shadows on the slope; the voices of earth's gods are high and wild, and they fear the coming of Barzai the Wise, who is greater than they . . . The moon's light flickers, as earth's gods dance against it; I shall see the dancing forms of the gods that leap and howl in the moonlight . . . The light is dimmer and the gods are afraid . . . '

Whilst Barzai was shouting these things Atal felt a spectral change in the air, as if the laws of earth were bowing to greater laws; for though the way was steeper than ever, the upward path was now grown fearsomely easy, and the bulging cliff proved scarce an obstacle when he reached it and slid perilously up its convex face. The light of the moon had strangely failed, and as Atal plunged upward through the mists he heard Barzai the Wise shrieking in the shadows.

'The moon is dark, and the gods dance in the night; there is terror in the sky, for upon the moon hath sunk an eclipse foretold in no books of men or of earth's gods . . . There is unknown magic on Hatheg-Kla, for the screams of the frightened gods have turned to laughter, and the slopes of ice shoot up endlessly into the black heavens whither I am plunging . . . Hei! Hei! At last! *In the dim light I behold the gods of earth*!'

And now Atal, slipping dizzily up over inconceivable steeps, heard in the dark a loathsome laughing, mixed with such a cry as no man else ever heard save in the Phlegethon of unrelatable nightmares; a cry wherein reverberated the horror and anguish of a haunted lifetime packed into one atrocious moment.

'The *other* gods! The *other* gods! The gods of the outer hells that guard the feeble gods of earth! . . . Look away! . . . Go back! . . . Do not see! . . . Do not see! . . . The vengeance of the infinite abysses . . . That cursed, that damnable pit . . . Merciful gods of earth, *I am falling into the sky*!'

And as Atal shut his eyes and stopped his ears and tried to jump downward against the frightful pull from unknown heights, there resounded on Hatheg-Kla that terrible peal of thunder which awaked the good cotters of the plains and the honest burgesses of Hatheg and Nir and Ulthar, and caused them to behold through the clouds that strange eclipse of the moon that no book ever predicted. And when the moon came out at last Atal was safe on the lower snows of the mountain without sight of earth's gods, or of the *other* gods.

Now it is told in the mouldy *Pnakotic Manuscripts* that Sansu found naught but wordless ice and rock when he climbed Hatheg-Kla in the youth of the world. Yet when the men of Ulthar and Nir and Hatheg crushed their fears and scaled that haunted steep by day in search of Barzai the Wise, they found graven in the naked stone of the summit a curious and Cyclopean symbol fifty cubits wide, as if the rock had been riven by some titanic chisel. And the symbol was like to one that learned men have discerned in those frightful parts of the *Pnakotic Manuscripts* which are too ancient to be read. This they found.

Barzai the Wise they never found, nor could the holy priest Atal ever be persuaded to pray for his soul's repose. Moreover, to this day the people of Ulthar and Nir and Hatheg fear eclipses, and pray by night when pale vapours hide the mountain-top and the moon. And above the mists on Hatheg-Kla earth's gods sometimes dance reminiscently; for they know they are safe, and love to come from unknown Kadath in ships of cloud and play in the olden way, as they did when earth was new and men not given to the climbing of inaccessible places.

Herbert West – Reanimator

1 From the Dark

Of Herbert West, who was my friend in college and in after life, I can speak only with extreme terror. This terror is not due altogether to the sinister manner of his recent disappearance, but was engendered by the whole nature of his life-work, and first gained its acute form more than seventeen years ago, when we were in the third year of our course at the Miskatonic University Medical School in Arkham. While he was with me, the wonder and diabolism of his experiments fascinated me utterly, and I was his closest companion. Now that he is gone and the spell is broken, the actual fear is greater. Memories and possibilities are ever more hideous than realities.

The first horrible incident of our acquaintance was the greatest shock I ever experienced, and it is only with reluctance that I repeat it. As I have said, it happened when we were in the medical school, where West had already made himself notorious through his wild theories on the nature of death and the possibility of overcoming it artificially. His views, which were widely ridiculed by the faculty and his fellow-students, hinged on the essentially mechanistic nature of life; and concerned means for operating the organic machinery of mankind by calculated chemical action after the failure of natural processes. In his experiments with various animating solutions he had killed and treated immense numbers of rabbits, guinea-pigs, cats, dogs, and monkeys, till he had become the prime nuisance of the college. Several times he had actually obtained signs of life in animals supposedly dead; in many cases violent signs; but he soon saw that the perfection of this process, if indeed possible, would necessarily involve a lifetime of research. It likewise became clear that, since the same solution never worked alike on different organic species, he would require human subjects for further and more specialised progress. It was here that he first came into conflict with the college authorities, and was debarred from future experiments by no less a dignitary than the dean of the medical school himself – the learned and benevolent Dr Allan Halsey, whose work in behalf of the stricken is recalled by every old resident of Arkham.

I had always been exceptionally tolerant of West's pursuits, and we frequently discussed his theories, whose ramifications and corollaries were almost infinite. Holding with Haeckel that all life is a chemical and physical process, and that the so-called 'soul' is a myth, my friend believed that artificial reanimation of the dead can depend only on the condition of the tissues; and that unless actual decomposition has set in, a corpse fully equipped with organs may with suitable measures be set going again in the peculiar fashion known as life. That the psychic or intellectual life might be impaired by the slight deterioration of sensitive brain-cells which even a short period of death would be apt to cause, West fully realised. It had at first been his hope to find a reagent which would restore vitality before the actual advent of death, and only repeated failures on animals had shewn him that the natural and artificial life-motions were incompatible. He then sought extreme freshness in his specimens, injecting his solutions into the blood immediately after the extinction of life. It was this circumstance which made the professors so carelessly sceptical, for they felt that true death had not occurred in any case. They did not stop to view the matter closely and reasoningly.

It was not long after the faculty had interdicted his work that West confided to me his resolution to get fresh human bodies in some manner, and continue in secret the experiments he could no longer perform openly. To hear him discussing ways and means was rather ghastly, for at the college we had never procured anatomical specimens ourselves. Whenever the morgue proved inadequate, two local negroes attended to this matter, and they were seldom questioned. West was then a small, slender, spectacled youth with delicate features, yellow hair, pale blue eyes, and a soft voice, and it was uncanny to hear him dwelling on the relative merits of Christchurch Cemetery and the potter's field. We finally decided on the potter's field, because practically every body in Christchurch was embalmed; a thing of course ruinous to West's researches.

I was by this time his active and enthralled assistant, and helped him make all his decisions, not only concerning the source of bodies but concerning a suitable place for our loathsome work. It was I who thought of the deserted Chapman farmhouse beyond Meadow Hill, where we fitted up on the ground floor an operating room and a laboratory, each with dark curtains to conceal our midnight doings. The place was far from any road, and in sight of no other house, yet precautions were none the less necessary; since rumours of strange lights, started by chance nocturnal roamers, would soon bring disaster on our enterprise. It was agreed to call the whole thing a chemical laboratory if discovery should occur. Gradually we equipped our sinister haunt of science with materials either purchased in Boston or quietly borrowed from the college – materials carefully made unrecognisable save to expert eyes – and provided spades and picks for the many burials we should have to make in the cellar. At the college we used an incinerator, but the apparatus was too costly for our unauthorised laboratory. Bodies were always a nuisance – even the small guinea-pig bodies from the slight clandestine experiments in West's room at the boarding-house.

We followed the local death-notices like ghouls, for our specimens demanded particular qualities. What we wanted were corpses interred soon after death and without artificial preservation; preferably free from malforming disease, and certainly with all organs present. Accident victims were our best hope. Not for many weeks did we hear of anything suitable; though we talked with morgue and hospital authorities, ostensibly in the college's interest, as often as we could without exciting suspicion. We found that the college had first choice in every case, so that it might be necessary to remain in Arkham during the summer, when only the limited summer-school classes were held. In the end, though, luck favoured us; for one day we heard of an almost ideal case in the potter's field; a brawny young workman drowned only the morning before in Sumner's Pond, and buried at the town's expense without delay or embalming. That afternoon we found the new grave, and determined to begin work soon after midnight.

It was a repulsive task that we undertook in the black small hours, even though we lacked at that time the special horror of graveyards which later experiences brought to us. We carried spades and oil dark lanterns, for although electric torches were then manufactured, they were not as satisfactory as the tungsten contrivances of today. The process of unearthing was slow and sordid – it might have been gruesomely poetical if we had been artists instead of scientists – and we were glad when our spades struck wood. When the pine box was fully uncovered West scrambled down and removed the lid, dragging out and propping up the contents. I reached down and hauled the contents out of the grave, and then both toiled hard to restore the spot to its former appearance. The affair made us rather nervous, especially the stiff form and vacant face of our first trophy, but we managed to remove all traces of our visit. When we had patted down the last shovelful of earth we put the specimen in a canvas sack and set out for the old Chapman place beyond Meadow Hill.

On an improvised dissecting-table in the old farmhouse, by the light of a powerful acetylene lamp, the specimen was not very spectral looking. It had been a sturdy and apparently unimaginative youth of wholesome plebeian type – large-framed, grey-eyed, and brown-haired – a sound animal without psychological subtleties, and probably having vital processes of the simplest and healthiest sort. Now, with the eyes closed, it looked more asleep than dead; though the expert test of my friend soon left no doubt on that score. We had at last what West had always longed for – a real dead man of the ideal kind, ready for the solution as prepared according to the most careful calculations and theories for human use. The tension on our part became very great. We knew that there was scarcely a chance for anything like complete success, and could not avoid hideous fears at possible grotesque results of partial animation. Especially were we apprehensive concerning the mind and impulses of the creature, since in the space following death some of the more delicate cerebral cells might well have suffered deterioration. I, myself, still held some curious notions about the traditional 'soul' of man, and felt an awe at the secrets that might be told by one returning from the dead. I wondered what sights this placid youth might have seen in inaccessible spheres, and what he could relate if fully restored to life. But my wonder was not overwhelming, since for the most part I shared the materialism of my friend. He was calmer than I as he forced a large quantity of his fluid into a vein of the body's arm, immediately binding the incision securely.

The waiting was gruesome, but West never faltered. Every now and then he applied his stethoscope to the specimen, and bore the negative results philosophically. After about three-quarters of an hour without the least sign of life he disappointedly pronounced the solution inadequate, but determined to make the most of his opportunity and try one change in the formula before disposing of his ghastly prize. We had that afternoon dug a grave in the cellar, and would have to fill it by dawn – for although we had fixed a lock on the house we wished to shun even the remotest risk of a ghoulish discovery. Besides, the body would not be even approximately fresh the next night. So taking the solitary acetylene lamp into the adjacent laboratory, we left our silent guest on the slab in the dark, and bent every energy to the mixing of a new solution; the weighing and measuring supervised by West with an almost fanatical care.

The awful event was very sudden, and wholly unexpected. I was pouring something from one test-tube to another, and West was busy over the alcohol blast-lamp which had to answer for a Bunsen burner in this gasless edifice, when from the pitch-black room we had left there burst the most appalling and daemoniac succession of cries that either of us had ever heard. Not more unutterable could have been the chaos of hellish sound if the pit itself had opened to release the agony of the damned, for in one inconceivable caco-phony was centred all the supernal terror and unnatural despair of animate nature. Human it could not have been – it is not in man to make such sounds – and without a thought of our late employment or its possible discovery both West and I leaped to the nearest window like stricken animals; overturning tubes, lamp, and retorts, and vaulting madly into the starred abyss of the rural night. I think we screamed ourselves as we stumbled frantically toward the town, though as we reached the outskirts we put on a semblance of restraint – just enough to seem like belated revellers staggering home from a debauch.

We did not separate, but managed to get to West's room, where we whispered with the gas up until dawn. By then we had calmed ourselves a little with rational theories and plans for investigation, so that we could sleep through the day – classes being disregarded. But that evening two items in the paper, wholly unrelated, made it again impossible for us to sleep. The old deserted Chapman house had inexplicably burned to an amorphous heap of ashes; that we could understand because of the upset lamp. Also, an attempt had been made to disturb a new grave in the potter's field, as if by futile and spadeless clawing at the earth. That we could not understand, for we had patted down the mould very carefully.

And for seventeen years after that West would look frequently over his shoulder, and complain of fancied footsteps behind him. Now he has disappeared.

2 The Plague-Daemon

I shall never forget that hideous summer sixteen years ago, when like a noxious afrite from the halls of Eblis typhoid stalked leeringly through Arkham. It is by that satanic scourge that most recall the year, for truly terror brooded with bat-wings over the piles of coffins in the tombs of Christchurch Cemetery; yet for me there is a greater horror in that time – a horror known to me alone now that Herbert West has disappeared.

West and I were doing post-graduate work in summer classes at the medical school of Miskatonic University, and my friend had attained a wide notoriety because of his experiments leading toward the revivification of the dead. After the scientific slaughter of uncounted small animals the freakish work had ostensibly stopped by order of our sceptical dean, Dr Allan Halsey; though West had continued to perform certain secret tests in his dingy boarding-house room, and had on one terrible and unforgettable occasion taken a human body from its grave in the potter's field to a deserted farmhouse beyond Meadow Hill.

I was with him on that odious occasion, and saw him inject into the still veins the elixir which he thought would to some extent restore life's chemical and physical processes. It had ended horribly – in a delirium of fear which we gradually came to attribute to our own overwrought nerves – and West had never afterward been able to shake off a maddening sensation of being haunted and hunted. The body had not been quite fresh enough; it is obvious that to restore normal mental attributes a body must be very fresh indeed; and a burning of the old house had prevented us from burying the thing. It would have been better if we could have known it was underground.

After that experience West had dropped his researches for some time; but as the zeal of the born scientist slowly returned, he again became importunate with the college faculty, pleading for the use of the dissecting-room and of fresh human specimens for the work he regarded as so overwhelmingly important. His pleas, however, were wholly in vain; for the decision of Dr Halsey was inflexible, and the other professors all endorsed the verdict of their leader. In the radical theory of reanimation they saw nothing but the immature vagaries of a youthful enthusiast whose slight form, yellow hair, spectacled blue eyes, and soft voice gave no hint of the supernormal – almost diabolical – power of the cold brain within. I can see him now as he was then – and I shiver. He grew sterner of face, but never elderly. And now Sefton Asylum has had the mishap and West has vanished.

West clashed disagreeably with Dr Halsey near the end of our last undergraduate term in a wordy dispute that did less credit to him than to the kindly dean in point of courtesy. He felt that he was needlessly and irrationally retarded in a supremely great work; a work which he could of course conduct to suit himself in later years, but which he wished to begin while still possessed of the exceptional facilities of the university. That the tradition-bound elders should ignore his singular results on animals, and persist in their denial of the possibility of reanimation, was inexpressibly disgusting and almost incomprehensible to a youth of West's logical temperament. Only greater maturity could help him understand the chronic mental limitations of the 'professor-doctor' type – the product of generations of pathetic Puritanism; kindly, conscientious, and sometimes gentle and amiable, yet always narrow, intolerant, custom-ridden, and lacking in perspective. Age has more charity for these incomplete yet high-souled characters, whose worst real vice is timidity, and who are ultimately punished by general ridicule for their intellectual sins – sins like Ptolemaism, Calvinism, anti-Darwinism, anti-Nietzscheism, and every sort of Sabbatarianism and sumptuary legislation. West, young despite his marvellous scientific acquirements, had scant patience with good Dr Halsey and his erudite colleagues; and nursed an increasing resentment, coupled with a desire to prove his theories to these obtuse worthies in some striking and dramatic fashion. Like most youths, he indulged in elaborate day-dreams of revenge, triumph, and final magnanimous forgiveness.

And then had come the scourge, grinning and lethal, from the nightmare caverns of Tartarus. West and I had graduated about the time of its beginning, but had remained for additional work at the summer school, so that we were in Arkham when it broke with full daemoniac fury upon the town. Though not as yet licenced physicians, we now had our degrees, and were pressed frantically into public service as the numbers of the stricken grew. The situation was almost past management, and deaths ensued too frequently for the local undertakers fully to handle. Burials without embalming were made in rapid succession, and even the Christchurch Cemetery receiving tomb was crammed with coffins of the unembalmed dead. This circumstance was not without effect on West, who thought often of the irony of the situation – so many fresh specimens, yet none for his persecuted researches! We were frightfully overworked, and the terrific mental and nervous strain made my friend brood morbidly.

But West's gentle enemies were no less harassed with prostrating duties. College had all but closed, and every doctor of the medical faculty was helping to fight the typhoid plague. Dr Halsey in particular had distinguished himself in sacrificing service, applying his extreme skill with whole-hearted energy to cases which many others shunned because of danger or apparent hopelessness. Before a month was over the fearless dean had become a popular hero, though he seemed unconscious of his fame as he struggled to keep from collapsing with physical fatigue and nervous exhaustion. West could not withhold admiration for the fortitude of his foe, but because of this was even more determined to prove to him the truth of his amazing doctrines. Taking advantage of the disorganisation of both college work and municipal health regulations, he managed to get a recently deceased body smuggled into the university dissecting-room one night, and in my presence injected a new modification of his solution. The thing actually opened its eyes, but only stared at the ceiling with a look of soul-petrifying horror before collapsing into an inertness from which nothing could rouse it. West said it was not fresh enough – the hot summer air does not favour corpses. That time we were almost

caught before we incinerated the thing, and West doubted the advis-
ability of repeating his daring misuse of the college laboratory.

The peak of the epidemic was reached in August. West and I were
almost dead, and Dr Halsey did die on the 14th. The students all
attended the hasty funeral on the 15th, and bought an impressive
wreath, though the latter was quite overshadowed by the tributes
sent by wealthy Arkham citizens and by the municipality itself. It was
almost a public affair, for the dean had surely been a public benefactor. After the entombment we were all somewhat depressed, and
spent the afternoon at the bar of the Commercial House; where
West, though shaken by the death of his chief opponent, chilled the
rest of us with references to his notorious theories. Most of the
students went home, or to various duties, as the evening advanced;
but West persuaded me to aid him in 'making a night of it'. West's
landlady saw us arrive at his room about two in the morning, with a
third man between us; and told her husband that we had all evidently
dined and wined rather well.

Apparently this acidulous matron was right; for about 3 a.m. the
whole house was aroused by cries coming from West's room, where
when they broke down the door they found the two of us unconscious on the blood-stained carpet, beaten, scratched, and mauled,
and with the broken remnants of West's bottles and instruments
around us. Only an open window told what had become of our
assailant, and many wondered how he himself had fared after
the terrific leap from the second story to the lawn which he must
have made. There were some strange garments in the room, but
West upon regaining consciousness said they did not belong to the
stranger, but were specimens collected for bacteriological analysis
in the course of investigations on the transmission of germ diseases.
He ordered them burnt as soon as possible in the capacious fireplace.
To the police we both declared ignorance of our late companion's
identity. He was, West nervously said, a congenial stranger whom
we had met at some downtown bar of uncertain location. We had
all been rather jovial, and West and I did not wish to have our
pugnacious companion hunted down.

That same night saw the beginning of the second Arkham horror –
the horror that to me eclipsed the plague itself. Christchurch Cemetery was the scene of a terrible killing; a watchman having been

clawed to death in a manner not only too hideous for description, but raising a doubt as to the human agency of the deed. The victim had been seen alive considerably after midnight – the dawn revealed the unutterable thing. The manager of a circus at the neighbouring town of Bolton was questioned, but he swore that no beast had at any time escaped from its cage. Those who found the body noted a trail of blood leading to the receiving tomb, where a small pool of red lay on the concrete just outside the gate. A fainter trail led away toward the woods, but it soon gave out.

The next night devils danced on the roofs of Arkham, and unnatural madness howled in the wind. Through the fevered town had crept a curse which some said was greater than the plague, and which some whispered was the embodied daemon-soul of the plague itself. Eight houses were entered by a nameless thing which strewed red death in its wake – in all, seventeen maimed and shapeless remnants of bodies were left behind by the voiceless, sadistic monster that crept abroad. A few persons had half seen it in the dark, and said it was white and like a malformed ape or anthropomorphic fiend. It had not left behind quite all that it had attacked, for sometimes it had been hungry. The number it had killed was fourteen; three of the bodies had been in stricken homes and had not been alive.

On the third night frantic bands of searchers, led by the police, captured it in a house on Crane Street near the Miskatonic campus. They had organised the quest with care, keeping in touch by means of volunteer telephone stations, and when someone in the college district had reported hearing a scratching at a shuttered window, the net was quickly spread. On account of the general alarm and precautions, there were only two more victims, and the capture was effected without major casualties. The thing was finally stopped by a bullet, though not a fatal one, and was rushed to the local hospital amidst universal excitement and loathing.

For it had been a man. This much was clear despite the nauseous eyes, the voiceless simianism, and the daemoniac savagery. They dressed its wound and carted it to the asylum at Sefton, where it beat its head against the walls of a padded cell for sixteen years – until the recent mishap, when it escaped under circumstances that few like to mention. What had most disgusted the searchers of Arkham was the thing they noticed when the monster's face was cleaned – the mocking, unbelievable resemblance to a learned and self-sacrificing martyr who had been entombed but three days before – the late Dr Allan Halsey, public benefactor and dean of the medical school of Miskatonic University.

To the vanished Herbert West and to me the disgust and horror were supreme. I shudder tonight as I think of it; shudder even more than I did that morning when West muttered through his bandages,

'Damn it, it wasn't *quite* fresh enough!'

3 Six Shots by Midnight

It is uncommon to fire all six shots of a revolver with great sudden-ness when one would probably be sufficient, but many things in the life of Herbert West were uncommon. It is, for instance, not often that a young physician leaving college is obliged to conceal the principles which guide his selection of a home and office, yet that was the case with Herbert West. When he and I obtained our degrees at the medical school of Miskatonic University, and sought to relieve our poverty by setting up as general practitioners, we took great care not to say that we chose our house because it was fairly well isolated, and as near as possible to the potter's field.

Reticence such as this is seldom without a cause, nor indeed was ours; for our requirements were those resulting from a life-work distinctly unpopular. Outwardly we were doctors only, but beneath the surface were aims of far greater and more terrible moment – for the essence of Herbert West's existence was a quest amid black and forbidden realms of the unknown, in which he hoped to uncover the secret of life and restore to perpetual animation the graveyard's cold clay. Such a quest demands strange materials, among them fresh human bodies; and in order to keep supplied with these indispensable things one must live quietly and not far from a place of informal interment.

West and I had met in college, and I had been the only one to sympathise with his hideous experiments. Gradually I had come to be his inseparable assistant, and now that we were out of college we had to keep together. It was not easy to find a good opening for two doctors in company, but finally the influence of the university secured us a practice in Bolton – a factory town near Arkham, the seat of the college. The Bolton Worsted Mills are the largest in the Miskatonic Valley, and their polyglot employees are never popular as patients with the local physicians. We chose our house with the greatest care, seizing at last on a rather run-down cottage near the end of Pond Street; five numbers from the closest neighbour, and separated from the local potter's field by only a stretch of meadow land, bisected by a narrow neck of the rather dense forest which lies to the north. The distance was greater than we wished, but we could get no nearer house without going on the other side of the field, wholly out of the factory district. We were not much displeased, however, since there were no people between us and our sinister source of supplies. The walk was a trifle long, but we could haul our silent specimens undisturbed.

Our practice was surprisingly large from the very first – large enough to please most young doctors, and large enough to prove a bore and a burden to students whose real interest lay elsewhere. The mill-hands were of somewhat turbulent inclinations; and besides their many natural needs, their frequent clashes and stabbing affrays gave us plenty to do. But what actually absorbed our minds was the secret laboratory we had fitted up in the cellar – the laboratory with the long table under the electric lights, where in the small hours of the morning we often injected West's various solutions into the veins of the things we dragged from the potter's field. West was experimenting madly to find something which would start man's vital motions anew after they had been stopped by the thing we call death, but had encountered the most ghastly obstacles. The solution had to be differently compounded for different types – what would serve for guinea-pigs would not serve for human beings, and different human specimens required large modifications.

The bodies had to be exceedingly fresh, or the slight decomposition of brain tissue would render perfect reanimation impossible. Indeed, the greatest problem was to get them fresh enough – West had had horrible experiences during his secret college researches with corpses of doubtful vintage. The results of partial or imperfect animation were much more hideous than were the total failures, and we both held fearsome recollections of such things. Ever since our first daemoniac session in the deserted farmhouse on Meadow Hill in Arkham, we had felt a brooding menace; and West, though a calm, blond, blue-eyed scientific automaton in most respects, often confessed to a shuddering sensation of stealthy pursuit. He half felt that he was followed – a psychological delusion of shaken nerves, enhanced by the undeniably disturbing fact that at least one of our reanimated specimens was still alive – a frightful carnivorous thing in a padded cell at Sefton. Then there was another – our first – whose exact fate we had never learned.

We had fair luck with specimens in Bolton – much better than in Arkham. We had not been settled a week before we got an accident victim on the very night of burial, and made it open its eyes with an amazingly rational expression before the solution failed. It had lost an arm – if it had been a perfect body we might have succeeded better. Between then and the next January we secured three more: one total failure, one case of marked muscular motion, and one rather shivery thing – it rose of itself and uttered a sound. Then came a period when luck was poor; interments fell off, and those that did occur were of specimens either too diseased or too maimed for use. We kept track of all the deaths and their circumstances with systematic care.

One March night, however, we unexpectedly obtained a specimen which did not come from the potter's field. In Bolton the prevailing spirit of Puritanism had outlawed the sport of boxing – with the usual result. Surreptitious and ill-conducted bouts among the mill-workers were common, and occasionally professional talent of low grade was imported. This late winter night there had been such a match; evidently with disastrous results, since two timorous Poles had come to us with incoherently whispered entreaties to attend to a very secret and desperate case. We followed them to an abandoned barn, where the remnants of a crowd of frightened foreigners were watching a silent black form on the floor.

The match had been between Kid O'Brien – a lubberly and now quaking youth with a most un-Hibernian hooked nose – and Buck Robinson, 'The Harlem Smoke'. The negro had been knocked out, and a moment's examination shewed us that he would permanently remain so. He was a loathsome thing, with abnormally long arms which I could not help calling fore legs. The body must have looked even worse in life – but the world holds many ugly things. Fear was upon the whole pitiful crowd, for they did not know what the law would exact of them if the affair were not hushed up; and they were grateful when West, in spite of my involuntary shudders, offered to get rid of the thing quietly – for a purpose I knew too well.

There was bright moonlight over the snowless landscape, but we dressed the thing and carried it home between us through the deserted streets and meadows, as we had carried a similar thing one horrible night in Arkham. We approached the house from the field in the rear, took the specimen in the back door and down the cellar stairs, and prepared it for the usual experiment. Our fear of the police was absurdly great, though we had timed our trip to avoid the solitary patrolman of that section.

The result was wearily anticlimactic. Ghastly as our prize appeared, it was wholly unresponsive to every solution we injected in its black arm; solutions prepared from experience with white specimens only. So as the hour grew dangerously near to dawn, we did as we had done with the others – dragged the thing across the meadows to the neck of the woods near the potter's field, and buried it there in the best sort of grave the frozen ground would furnish. The grave was not very deep, but fully as good as that of the previous specimen – the thing which had risen of itself and uttered a sound. In the light of our dark lanterns we carefully covered it with leaves and dead vines, fairly certain that the police would never find it in a forest so dim and dense.

The next day I was increasingly apprehensive about the police, for a patient brought rumours of a suspected fight and death. West had still another source of worry, for he had been called in the afternoon to a case which ended very threateningly. An Italian woman had become hysterical over her missing child – a lad of five who had strayed off early in the morning and failed to appear for dinner – and had developed symptoms highly alarming in view of an always weak heart. It was a very foolish hysteria, for the boy had often run away before; but Italian peasants are exceedingly superstitious, and this woman seemed as much harassed by omens as by facts. About seven o'clock in the evening she had died, and her frantic husband had made a frightful scene in his efforts to kill West, whom he wildly blamed for not saving her life. Friends had held him when he drew a stiletto, but West departed amidst his inhuman shrieks, curses, and oaths of vengeance. In his latest affliction the fellow seemed to have forgotten his child, who was still missing as the night advanced. There was some talk of searching the woods, but most of the family's friends were busy with the dead woman and the screaming man. Altogether, the nervous strain upon West must have been tremendous. Thoughts of the police and of the mad Italian both weighed heavily.

We retired about eleven, but I did not sleep well. Bolton had a surprisingly good police force for so small a town, and I could not help fearing the mess which would ensue if the affair of the night before were ever tracked down. It might mean the end of all our local work – and perhaps prison for both West and me. I did not like those rumours of a fight which were floating about. After the clock had struck three the moon shone in my eyes, but I turned over without rising to pull down the shade. Then came the steady rattling at the back door.

I lay still and somewhat dazed, but before long heard West's rap on my door. He was clad in dressing-gown and slippers, and had in his hands a revolver and an electric flashlight. From the revolver I knew that he was thinking more of the crazed Italian than of the police.

'We'd better both go,' he whispered. 'It wouldn't do not to answer it anyway, and it may be a patient – it would be like one of those fools to try the back door.'

So we both went down the stairs on tiptoe, with a fear partly justified and partly that which comes only from the soul of the weird small hours. The rattling continued, growing somewhat louder. When we reached the door I cautiously unbolted it and threw it open, and as the moon streamed revealingly down on the form silhouetted there, West did a peculiar thing. Despite the obvious danger of attracting notice and bringing down on our heads the dreaded police investigation – a thing which after all was mercifully averted by the relative isolation of our cottage – my friend suddenly, excitedly, and unnecessarily emptied all six chambers of his revolver into the nocturnal visitor.

For that visitor was neither Italian nor policeman. Looming hideously against the spectral moon was a gigantic misshapen thing not to be imagined save in nightmares – a glassy-eyed, ink-black apparition nearly on all fours, covered with bits of mould, leaves, and vines, foul with caked blood, and having between its glistening teeth a snow-white, terrible, cylindrical object terminating in a tiny hand.

4 The Scream of the Dead

The scream of a dead man gave to me that acute and added horror of
Dr Herbert West which harassed the latter years of our companionship. It is natural that such a thing as a dead man's scream should
give horror, for it is obviously not a pleasing or ordinary occurrence;
but I was used to similar experiences, hence suffered on this occasion
only because of a particular circumstance. And, as I have implied, it
was not of the dead man himself that I became afraid.

Herbert West, whose associate and assistant I was, possessed
scientific interests far beyond the usual routine of a village physician. That was why, when establishing his practice in Bolton, he
had chosen an isolated house near the potter's field. Briefly and
brutally stated, West's sole absorbing interest was a secret study
of the phenomena of life and its cessation, leading toward the
reanimation of the dead through injections of an excitant solution.
For this ghastly experimenting it was necessary to have a constant
supply of very fresh human bodies; very fresh because even the least
decay hopelessly damaged the brain structure, and human because
we found that the solution had to be compounded differently for
different types of organisms. Scores of rabbits and guinea-pigs had
been killed and treated, but their trail was a blind one. West had
never fully succeeded because he had never been able to secure
a corpse sufficiently fresh. What he wanted were bodies from
which vitality had only just departed; bodies with every cell intact
and capable of receiving again the impulse toward that mode of
motion called life. There was hope that this second and artificial
life might be made perpetual by repetitions of the injection, but
we had learned that an ordinary natural life would not respond to
the action. To establish the artificial motion, natural life must be
extinct – the specimens must be very fresh, but genuinely dead.

The awesome quest had begun when West and I were students at
the Miskatonic University Medical School in Arkham, vividly conscious for the first time of the thoroughly mechanical nature of life.
That was seven years before, but West looked scarcely a day older
now – he was small, blond, clean-shaven, soft-voiced, and spectacled,
with only an occasional flash of a cold blue eye to tell of the hard-
ening and growing fanaticism of his character under the pressure of

his terrible investigations. Our experiences had often been hideous in the extreme; the results of defective reanimation, when lumps of graveyard clay had been galvanised into morbid, unnatural, and brainless motion by various modifications of the vital solution.

One thing had uttered a nerve-shattering scream; another had risen violently, beaten us both to unconsciousness, and run amuck in a shocking way before it could be placed behind asylum bars; still another, a loathsome African monstrosity, had clawed out of its shallow grave and done a deed – West had had to shoot that object. We could not get bodies fresh enough to shew any trace of reason when reanimated, so had perforce created nameless horrors. It was disturbing to think that one, perhaps two, of our monsters still lived – that thought haunted us shadowingly, till finally West disappeared under frightful circumstances. But at the time of the scream in the cellar laboratory of the isolated Bolton cottage, our fears were subordinate to our anxiety for extremely fresh specimens. West was more avid than I, so that it almost seemed to me that he looked half-covetously at any very healthy living physique.

It was in July, 1910, that the bad luck regarding specimens began to turn. I had been on a long visit to my parents in Illinois, and upon my return found West in a state of singular elation. He had, he told me excitedly, in all likelihood solved the problem of freshness through an approach from an entirely new angle – that of artificial preservation. I had known that he was working on a new and highly unusual embalming compound, and was not surprised that it had turned out well; but until he explained the details I was rather puzzled as to how such a compound could help in our work, since the objectionable staleness of the specimens was largely due to delay occurring before we secured them. This, I now saw, West had clearly recognised; creating his embalming compound for future rather than immediate use, and trusting to fate to supply again some very recent and unburied corpse, as it had years before when we obtained the negro killed in the Bolton prize-fight. At last fate had been kind, so that on this occasion there lay in the secret cellar laboratory a corpse whose decay could not by any possibility have begun. What would happen on reanimation, and whether we could hope for a revival of mind and reason, West did not venture to predict. The experiment would be a landmark in our studies, and he had saved the new body for my return, so that both might share the spectacle in accustomed fashion.

West told me how he had obtained the specimen. It had been a vigorous man; a well-dressed stranger just off the train on his way to transact some business with the Bolton Worsted Mills. The walk through the town had been long, and by the time the traveller paused at our cottage to ask the way to the factories his heart had become greatly overtaxed. He had refused a stimulant, and had suddenly dropped dead only a moment later. The body, as might be expected, seemed to West a heaven-sent gift. In his brief conversation the stranger had made it clear that he was unknown in Bolton, and a search of his pockets subsequently revealed him to be one Robert Leavitt of St Louis, apparently without a family to make instant inquiries about his disappearance. If this man could not be restored to life, no one would know of our experiment. We buried our materials in a dense strip of woods between the house and the potter's field. If, on the other hand, he could be restored, our fame would be brilliantly and perpetually established. So without delay West had injected into the body's wrist the compound which would hold it fresh for use after my arrival. The matter of the presumably weak heart, which to my mind imperiled the success of our experiment, did not appear to trouble West extensively. He hoped at last to obtain what he had never obtained before − a rekindled spark of reason and perhaps a normal, living creature.

So on the night of July 18, 1910, Herbert West and I stood in the cellar laboratory and gazed at a white, silent figure beneath the dazzling arc-light. The embalming compound had worked uncannily well, for as I stared fascinatedly at the sturdy frame which had lain two weeks without stiffening I was moved to seek West's assurance that the thing was really dead. This assurance he gave readily enough; reminding me that the reanimating solution was never used without careful tests as to life; since it could have no effect if any of the original vitality were present. As West proceeded to take preliminary steps, I was impressed by the vast intricacy of the new experiment; an intricacy so vast that he could trust no hand less delicate than his own. Forbidding me to touch the body, he first injected a drug in the wrist just beside the place his needle had punctured when injecting the embalming compound. This, he said, was to neutralise the compound and release the system to a normal relaxation so that the reanimating solution might freely work when injected. Slightly later, when a change and a gentle tremor seemed to affect the dead limbs, West stuffed a pillow-like object violently over the twitching face, not withdrawing it until the corpse appeared quiet and ready for our attempt at reanimation. The pale enthusiast now applied some last perfunctory tests for absolute lifelessness, withdrew satisfied, and finally injected into the left arm an accurately measured amount of the vital elixir, prepared during the afternoon with a greater care than we had used since college days, when our feats were new and groping. I cannot express the wild, breathless suspense with which we waited for results on this first really fresh specimen – the first we could reasonably expect to open its lips in rational speech, perhaps to tell of what it had seen beyond the unfathomable abyss.

West was a materialist, believing in no soul and attributing all the working of consciousness to bodily phenomena; consequently he looked for no revelation of hideous secrets from gulfs and caverns beyond death's barrier. I did not wholly disagree with him theoretically, yet held vague instinctive remnants of the primitive faith of my forefathers; so that I could not help eyeing the corpse with a certain amount of awe and terrible expectation. Besides – I could not extract from my memory that hideous, inhuman shriek we heard on the night we tried our first experiment in the deserted farmhouse at Arkham.

Very little time had elapsed before I saw the attempt was not to be a total failure. A touch of colour came to cheeks hitherto chalk-white, and spread out under the curiously ample stubble of sandy beard. West, who had his hand on the pulse of the left wrist, suddenly nodded significantly; and almost simultaneously a mist appeared on the mirror inclined above the body's mouth. There followed a few spasmodic muscular motions, and then an audible breathing and visible motion of the chest. I looked at the closed eyelids, and thought I detected a quivering. Then the lids opened, shewing eyes which were grey, calm, and alive, but still unintelligent and not even curious.

In a moment of fantastic whim I whispered questions to the reddening ears; questions of other worlds of which the memory might still be present. Subsequent terror drove them from my mind, but I think the last one, which I repeated, was: 'Where have you been?' I do not yet know whether I was answered or not, for no sound came from the well-shaped mouth; but I do know that at that moment I firmly thought the thin lips moved silently, forming syllables I would have vocalised as 'only now' if that phrase had possessed any sense or relevancy. At that moment, as I say, I was elated with the conviction that the one great goal had been attained; and that for the first time a reanimated corpse had uttered distinct words impelled by actual reason. In the next moment there was no doubt about the triumph; no doubt that the solution had truly accomplished, at least temporarily, its full mission of restoring rational and articulate life to the dead. But in that triumph there came to me the greatest of all horrors – not horror of the thing that spoke, but of the deed that I had witnessed and of the man with whom my professional fortunes were joined.

For that very fresh body, at last writhing into full and terrifying consciousness with eyes dilated at the memory of its last scene on earth, threw out its frantic hands in a life and death struggle with the air; and suddenly collapsing into a second and final dissolution from which there could be no return, screamed out the cry that will ring eternally in my aching brain:

'Help! Keep off, you cursed little tow-head fiend – keep that damned needle away from me!'

5 The Horror from the Shadows

Many men have related hideous things, not mentioned in print, which happened on the battlefields of the Great War. Some of these things have made me faint, others have convulsed me with devastating nausea, while still others have made me tremble and look behind me in the dark; yet despite the worst of them I believe I can myself relate the most hideous thing of all – the shocking, the unnatural, the unbelievable horror from the shadows.

In 1915 I was a physician with the rank of First Lieutenant in a Canadian regiment in Flanders, one of many Americans to precede the government itself into the gigantic struggle. I had not entered the army on my own initiative, but rather as a natural result of the enlistment of the man whose indispensable assistant I was – the celebrated Boston surgical specialist, Dr Herbert West. Dr West had been avid for a chance to serve as surgeon in a great war, and when the chance had come he carried me with him almost against my will. There were reasons why I would have been glad to let the war separate us; reasons why I found the practice of medicine and the companionship of West more and more irritating; but when he had gone to Ottawa and through a colleague's influence secured a medical commission as Major, I could not resist the imperious persuasion of one determined that I should accompany him in my usual capacity.

When I say that Dr West was avid to serve in battle, I do not mean to imply that he was either naturally warlike or anxious for the safety of civilisation. Always an ice-cold intellectual machine, slight, blond, blue-eyed, and spectacled, I think he secretly sneered at my occasional martial enthusiasms and censures of supine neutrality. There was, however, something he wanted in embattled Flanders; and in order to secure it he had to assume a military exterior. What he wanted was not a thing which many persons want, but something connected with the peculiar branch of medical science which he had chosen quite clandestinely to follow, and in which he had achieved amazing and occasionally hideous results. It was, in fact, nothing more or less than an abundant supply of freshly killed men in every stage of dismemberment.

Herbert West needed fresh bodies because his life-work was the reanimation of the dead. This work was not known to the fashionable clientèle who had so swiftly built up his fame after his arrival in Boston; but was only too well known to me, who had been his closest friend and sole assistant since the old days in Miskatonic University Medical School at Arkham. It was in those college days that he had begun his terrible experiments, first on small animals and then on human bodies shockingly obtained. There was a solution which he injected into the veins of dead things, and if they were fresh enough they responded in strange ways. He had had much trouble in discovering the proper formula, for each type of organism was found to need a stimulus especially adapted to it. Terror stalked him when he reflected on his partial failures; nameless things resulting from imperfect solutions or from bodies insufficiently fresh. A certain number of these failures had remained alive – one was in an asylum while others had vanished – and as he thought of conceivable yet virtually impossible eventualities he often shivered beneath his usual stolidity.

West had soon learned that absolute freshness was the prime requisite for useful specimens, and had accordingly resorted to frightful and unnatural expedients in body-snatching. In college, and during our early practice together in the factory town of Bolton, my attitude toward him had been largely one of fascinated admiration; but as his boldness in methods grew, I began to develop a gnawing fear. I did not like the way he looked at healthy living bodies; and then there came a nightmarish session in the cellar laboratory when I learned that a certain specimen had been a living body when he secured it. That was the first time he had ever been able to revive the quality of rational thought in a corpse; and his success, obtained at such a loathsome cost, had completely hardened him.

Of his methods in the intervening five years I dare not speak. I was held to him by sheer force of fear, and witnessed sights that no human tongue could repeat. Gradually I came to find Herbert West himself more horrible than anything he did – that was when it dawned on me that his once normal scientific zeal for prolonging life had subtly degenerated into a mere morbid and ghoulish curiosity and secret sense of charnel picturesqueness. His interest became a hellish and perverse addiction to the repellently and fiendishly abnormal; he gloated calmly over artificial monstrosities which would make most healthy men drop dead from fright and disgust; he became, behind his pallid intellectuality, a fastidious Baudelaire of physical experiment – a languid Elagabalus of the tombs.

Dangers he met unflinchingly; crimes he committed unmoved. I think the climax came when he had proved his point that rational life can be restored, and had sought new worlds to conquer by experimenting on the reanimation of detached parts of bodies. He had wild and original ideas on the independent vital properties of organic cells and nerve-tissue separated from natural physiological systems; and achieved some hideous preliminary results in the form of never-dying, artificially nourished tissue obtained from the nearly hatched eggs of an indescribable tropical reptile. Two biological points he was exceedingly anxious to settle – first, whether any amount of consciousness and rational action be possible without the brain, proceeding from the spinal cord and various nerve-centres; and second, whether any kind of ethereal, intangible relation distinct from the material cells may exist to link the surgically separated parts of what has previously been a single living organism. All this research work required a prodigious supply of freshly slaughtered human flesh – and that was why Herbert West had entered the Great War.

The phantasmal, unmentionable thing occurred one midnight late in March, 1915, in a field hospital behind the lines at St Eloi. I wonder even now if it could have been other than a daemoniac dream of delirium. West had a private laboratory in an east room of the barn-like temporary edifice, assigned him on his plea that he was devising new and radical methods for the treatment of hitherto hopeless cases of maiming. There he worked like a butcher in the midst of his gory wares – I could never get used to the levity with which he handled and classified certain things. At times he actually did perform marvels of surgery for the soldiers; but his chief delights were of a less public and philanthropic kind, requiring many explanations of sounds which seemed peculiar even amidst that babel of the damned. Among these sounds were frequent revolver-shots – surely not uncommon on a battlefield, but distinctly uncommon in a hospital. Dr West's reanimated specimens were not meant for long existence or a large audience. Besides human tissue, West employed much of the reptile embryo tissue which he had cultivated with such singular results. It was better than human material for maintaining life in organless fragments, and that was now my friend's chief activity. In a dark corner of the laboratory, over a queer incubating burner, he kept a large covered vat full of this reptilian cell-matter; which multiplied and grew puffily and hideously.

On the night of which I speak we had a splendid new specimen – a man at once physically powerful and of such high mentality that a sensitive nervous system was assured. It was rather ironic, for he was the officer who had helped West to his commission, and who was now to have been our associate. Moreover, he had in the past secretly studied the theory of reanimation to some extent under West. Major Sir Eric Moreland Clapham-Lee, D.S.O., was the greatest surgeon in our division, and had been hastily assigned to the St Eloi sector when news of the heavy fighting reached headquarters. He had come in an aeroplane piloted by the intrepid Lieut. Ronald Hill, only to be shot down when directly over his destination. The fall had been spectacular and awful; Hill was unrecognisable afterward, but the wreck yielded up the great surgeon in a nearly decapitated but otherwise intact condition. West had greedily seized the lifeless thing which had once been his friend and fellow-scholar; and I shuddered when he finished severing the head, placed it in his hellish vat of pulpy reptile-tissue to preserve it for future experiments, and proceeded to treat the decapitated body on the operating table. He injected new blood, joined certain veins, arteries, and nerves at the headless neck, and closed the ghastly aperture with engrafted skin from an unidentified specimen which had borne an officer's uniform. I knew what he wanted – to see if this highly organised body could exhibit, without its head, any of the signs of mental life which had distinguished Sir Eric Moreland Clapham-Lee. Once a student of reanimation, this silent trunk was now gruesomely called upon to exemplify it.

I can still see Herbert West under the sinister electric light as he injected his reanimating solution into the arm of the headless body. The scene I cannot describe – I should faint if I tried it, for there is madness in a room full of classified charnel things, with blood and lesser human debris almost ankle-deep on the slimy floor, and with hideous reptilian abnormalities sprouting, bubbling, and baking over a winking bluish-green spectre of dim flame in a far corner of black shadows.

The specimen, as West repeatedly observed, had a splendid nervous system. Much was expected of it; and as a few twitching motions began to appear, I could see the feverish interest on West's face. He was ready, I think, to see proof of his increasingly strong opinion that consciousness, reason, and personality can exist independently of the brain – that man has no central connective spirit, but is merely a machine of nervous matter, each section more or less complete in itself. In one triumphant demonstration West was about to relegate the mystery of life to the category of myth. The body now twitched more vigorously, and beneath our avid eyes commenced to heave in a frightful way. The arms stirred disquietingly, the legs drew up, and various muscles contracted in a repulsive kind of writhing. Then the headless thing threw out its arms in a gesture which was unmistakably one of desperation – an intelligent desperation apparently sufficient to prove every theory of Herbert West. Certainly, the nerves were recalling the man's last act in life; the struggle to get free of the falling aeroplane.

What followed, I shall never positively know. It may have been wholly an hallucination from the shock caused at that instant by the sudden and complete destruction of the building in a cataclysm of German shell-fire – who can gainsay it, since West and I were the only proved survivors? West liked to think that before his recent disappearance, but there were times when he could not; for it was queer that we both had the same hallucination. The hideous occurrence itself was very simple, notable only for what it implied.

The body on the table had risen with a blind and terrible groping, and we had heard a sound. I should not call that sound a voice, for it was too awful. And yet its timbre was not the most awful thing about it. Neither was its message – it had merely screamed, 'Jump, Ronald, for God's sake, jump!' The awful thing was its source.

For it had come from the large covered vat in that ghoulish corner of crawling black shadows.

6 The Tomb-Legions

When Dr Herbert West disappeared a year ago, the Boston police questioned me closely. They suspected that I was holding something back, and perhaps suspected graver things; but I could not tell them the truth because they would not have believed it. They knew, indeed, that West had been connected with activities beyond the credence of ordinary men; for his hideous experiments in the reanimation of dead bodies had long been too extensive to admit of perfect secrecy; but the final soul-shattering catastrophe held elements of daemoniac phantasy which make even me doubt the reality of what I saw.

I was West's closest friend and only confidential assistant. We had met years before, in medical school, and from the first I had shared his terrible researches. He had slowly tried to perfect a solution which, injected into the veins of the newly deceased, would restore life; a labour demanding an abundance of fresh corpses and therefore involving the most unnatural actions. Still more shocking were the products of some of the experiments – grisly masses of flesh that had been dead, but that West waked to a blind, brainless, nauseous animation. These were the usual results, for in order to reawaken the mind it was necessary to have specimens so absolutely fresh that no decay could possibly affect the delicate brain-cells.

This need for very fresh corpses had been West's moral undoing. They were hard to get, and one awful day he had secured his specimen while it was still alive and vigorous. A struggle, a needle, and a powerful alkaloid had transformed it to a very fresh corpse, and the experiment had succeeded for a brief and memorable moment; but West had emerged with a soul calloused and seared, and a hardened eye which sometimes glanced with a kind of hideous and calculating appraisal at men of especially sensitive brain and especially vigorous physique. Toward the last I became acutely afraid of West, for he began to look at me that way. People did not seem to notice his glances, but they noticed my fear; and after his disappearance used that as a basis for some absurd suspicions.

West, in reality, was more afraid than I; for his abominable pursuits entailed a life of furtiveness and dread of every shadow. Partly it was the police he feared; but sometimes his nervousness was deeper and more nebulous, touching on certain indescribable things into which he had injected a morbid life, and from which he had not seen that life depart. He usually finished his experiments with a revolver, but a few times he had not been quick enough. There was that first specimen on whose rifled grave marks of clawing were later seen. There was also that Arkham professor's body which had done cannibal things before it had been captured and thrust unidentified into a madhouse cell at Sefton, where it beat the walls for sixteen years. Most of the other possibly surviving results were things less easy to speak of – for in later years West's scientific zeal had degenerated to an unhealthy and fantastic mania, and he had spent his chief skill in vitalising not entire human bodies but isolated parts of bodies, or parts joined to organic matter other than human. It had become fiendishly disgusting by the time he disappeared; many of the experiments could not even be hinted at in print. The Great War, through which both of us served as surgeons, had intensified this side of West.

In saying that West's fear of his specimens was nebulous, I have in mind particularly its complex nature. Part of it came merely from knowing of the existence of such nameless monsters, while another part arose from apprehension of the bodily harm they might under certain circumstances do him. Their disappearance added horror to the situation – of them all West knew the whereabouts of only one, the pitiful asylum thing. Then there was a more subtle fear – a very fantastic sensation resulting from a curious experiment in the Canadian army in 1915. West, in the midst of a severe battle, had reanimated Major Sir Eric Moreland Clapham-Lee, D.S.O., a fellow-physician who knew about his experiments and could have duplicated them. The head had been removed, so that the possibilities of quasi-intelligent life in the trunk might be investigated. Just as the building was wiped out by a German shell, there had been a success. The trunk had moved intelligently; and, unbelievable to relate, we were both sickeningly sure that articulate sounds had come from the detached head as it lay in a shadowy corner of the laboratory. The shell had been merciful, in a way – but West could never feel as certain as he wished, that we two were the only survivors. He used to make shuddering conjectures about the possible actions of a headless physician with the power of reanimating the dead.

West's last quarters were in a venerable house of much elegance, overlooking one of the oldest burying-grounds in Boston. He had chosen the place for purely symbolic and fantastically aesthetic reasons, since most of the interments were of the colonial period and therefore of little use to a scientist seeking very fresh bodies. The laboratory was in a sub-cellar secretly constructed by imported workmen, and contained a huge incinerator for the quiet and complete disposal of such bodies, or fragments and synthetic mockeries of bodies, as might remain from the morbid experiments and unhallowed amusements of the owner. During the excavation of this cellar the workmen had struck some exceedingly ancient masonry; undoubtedly connected with the old burying-ground, yet far too deep to correspond with any known sepulchre therein. After a number of calculations West decided that it represented some secret chamber beneath the tomb of the Averills, where the last interment had been made in 1768. I was with him when he studied the nitrous, dripping walls laid bare by the spades and mattocks of the men, and was prepared for the gruesome thrill which would attend the uncovering of centuried grave-secrets; but for the first time West's new timidity conquered his natural curiosity, and he betrayed his degenerating fibre by ordering the masonry left intact and plastered over. Thus it remained till that final hellish night; part of the walls of the secret laboratory. I speak of West's decadence, but must add that it was a purely mental and intangible thing. Outwardly he was the same to the last – calm, cold, slight, and yellow-haired, with spectacled blue eyes and a general aspect of youth which years and fears seemed never to change. He seemed calm even when he thought of that clawed grave and looked over his shoulder; even when he thought of the carnivorous thing that gnawed and pawed at Sefton bars.

The end of Herbert West began one evening in our joint study when he was dividing his curious glance between the newspaper and me. A strange headline item had struck at him from the crumpled pages, and a nameless titan claw had seemed to reach down through sixteen years. Something fearsome and incredible had happened at Sefton Asylum fifty miles away, stunning the neighbourhood and baffling the police. In the small hours of the morning a body of silent men had entered the grounds and their leader had aroused the attendants. He was a menacing military figure who talked without moving his lips and whose voice seemed almost ventriloquially connected with an immense black case he carried. His expressionless face was handsome to the point of radiant beauty, but had shocked the superintendent when the hall light fell on it – for it was a wax face with eyes of painted glass. Some nameless accident had befallen this man. A larger man guided his steps; a repellent hulk whose bluish face seemed half eaten away by some unknown malady. The speaker had asked for the custody of the cannibal monster committed from Arkham sixteen years before; and upon being refused, gave a signal which precipitated a shocking riot. The fiends had beaten, trampled, and bitten every attendant who did not flee; killing four and finally succeeding in the liberation of the monster. Those victims who could recall the event without hysteria swore that the creatures had acted less like men than like unthinkable automata guided by the wax-faced leader. By the time help could be summoned, every trace of the men and of their mad charge had vanished.

From the hour of reading this item until midnight, West sat almost paralysed. At midnight the doorbell rang, startling him fearfully. All the servants were asleep in the attic, so I answered the bell. As I have told the police, there was no wagon in the street; but only a group of strange-looking figures bearing a large square box which they deposited in the hallway after one of them had grunted in a highly unnatural voice, 'Express – prepaid.' They filed out of the house with a jerky tread, and as I watched them go I had an odd idea that they were turning toward the ancient cemetery on which the back of the house abutted. When I slammed the door after them West came downstairs and looked at the box. It was about two feet square, and bore West's correct name and present address. It also bore the inscription, 'From Eric Moreland Clapham-Lee, St Eloi, Flanders'. Six years before, in Flanders, a shelled hospital had fallen upon the headless reanimated trunk of Dr Clapham-Lee, and upon the detached head which – perhaps – had uttered articulate sounds.

West was not even excited now. His condition was more ghastly. Quickly he said, 'It's the finish – but let's incinerate – this.' We carried the thing down to the laboratory – listening. I do not remember many particulars – you can imagine my state of mind – but it is a vicious lie to say it was Herbert West's body which I put into the incinerator. We both inserted the whole unopened wooden box, closed the door, and started the electricity. Nor did any sound come from the box, after all.

It was West who first noticed the falling plaster on that part of the wall where the ancient tomb masonry had been covered up. I was going to run, but he stopped me. Then I saw a small black aperture, felt a ghoulish wind of ice, and smelled the charnel bowels of a putrescent earth. There was no sound, but just then the electric lights went out and I saw outlined against some phosphorescence of the nether world a horde of silent toiling things which only insanity – or worse – could create. Their outlines were human, semi-human, fractionally human, and not human at all – the horde was grotesquely heterogeneous. They were removing the stones quietly, one by one, from the centuried wall. And then, as the breach became large enough, they came out into the laboratory in single file; led by a stalking thing with a beautiful head made of wax. A sort of mad-eyed monstrosity behind the leader seized on Herbert West. West did not resist or utter a sound. Then they all sprang at him and tore him to pieces before my eyes, bearing the fragments away into that subterranean vault of fabulous abominations. West's head was carried off by the wax-headed leader, who wore a Canadian officer's uniform. As it disappeared I saw that the blue eyes behind the spectacles were hideously blazing with their first touch of frantic, visible emotion.

Servants found me unconscious in the morning. West was gone. The incinerator contained only unidentifiable ashes. Detectives have questioned me, but what can I say? The Sefton tragedy they will not connect with West; not that, nor the men with the box, whose existence they deny. I told them of the vault, and they pointed to the unbroken plaster wall and laughed. So I told them no more. They imply that I am a madman or a murderer – probably I am mad. But I might not be mad if those accursed tomb-legions had not been so silent.

The Unnamable

We were sitting on a dilapidated seventeenth-century tomb in the late afternoon of an autumn day at the old burying-ground in Arkham, and speculating about the unnamable. Looking toward the giant willow in the centre of the cemetery, whose trunk has nearly engulfed an ancient, illegible slab, I had made a fantastic remark about the spectral and unmentionable nourishment which the colossal roots must be sucking in from that hoary, charnel earth; when my friend chided me for such nonsense and told me that since no interments had occurred there for over a century, nothing could possibly exist to nourish the tree in other than an ordinary manner. Besides, he added, my constant talk about 'unnamable' and 'unmentionable' things was a very puerile device, quite in keeping with my lowly standing as an author. I was too fond of ending my stories with sights or sounds which paralysed my heroes' faculties and left them without courage, words, or associations to tell what they had experienced. We know things, he said, only through our five senses or our religious intuitions; wherefore it is quite impossible to refer to any object or spectacle which cannot be clearly depicted by the solid definitions of fact or the correct doctrines of theology – preferably those of the Congregationalists, with whatever modifications tradition and Sir Arthur Conan Doyle may supply.

With this friend, Joel Manton, I had often languidly disputed. He was principal of the East High School, born and bred in Boston and sharing New England's self-satisfied deafness to the delicate overtones of life. It was his view that only our normal, objective experiences possess any aesthetic significance, and that it is the province of the artist not so much to rouse strong emotion by action, ecstasy, and astonishment, as to maintain a placid interest and appreciation by accurate, detailed transcripts of every-day affairs.

Especially did he object to my preoccupation with the mystical and
the unexplained; for although believing in the supernatural much
more fully than I, he would not admit that it is sufficiently commonplace for literary treatment. That a mind can find its greatest pleasure in escapes from the daily treadmill, and in original and dramatic
recombinations of images usually thrown by habit and fatigue into
the hackneyed patterns of actual existence, was something virtually
incredible to his clear, practical, and logical intellect. With him all
things and feelings had fixed dimensions, properties, causes, and
effects; and although he vaguely knew that the mind sometimes
holds visions and sensations of far less geometrical, classifiable, and
workable nature, he believed himself justified in drawing an arbitrary
line and ruling out of court all that cannot be experienced and
understood by the average citizen. Besides, he was almost sure that
nothing can be really 'unnamable'. It didn't sound sensible to him.

Though I well realised the futility of imaginative and metaphysical
arguments against the complacency of an orthodox sun-dweller,
something in the scene of this afternoon colloquy moved me to
more than usual contentiousness. The crumbling slate slabs, the
patriarchal trees, and the centuried gambrel roofs of the witch-
haunted old town that stretched around, all combined to rouse my
spirit in defence of my work; and I was soon carrying my thrusts
into the enemy's own country. It was not, indeed, difficult to begin
a counter-attack, for I knew that Joel Manton actually half clung to
many old-wives' superstitions which sophisticated people had long
outgrown; beliefs in the appearance of dying persons at distant
places, and in the impressions left by old faces on the windows
through which they had gazed all their lives. To credit these whisperings of rural grandmothers, I now insisted, argued a faith in
the existence of spectral substances on the earth apart from and
subsequent to their material counterparts. It argued a capability of
believing in phenomena beyond all normal notions; for if a dead
man can transmit his visible or tangible image half across the world,
or down the stretch of the centuries, how can it be absurd to
suppose that deserted houses are full of queer sentient things, or
that old graveyards teem with the terrible, unbodied intelligence
of generations? And since spirit, in order to cause all the manifestations attributed to it, cannot be limited by any of the laws

of matter, why is it extravagant to imagine psychically living dead things in shapes – or absences of shapes – which must for human spectators be utterly and appallingly 'unnamable'? 'Common sense' in reflecting on these subjects, I assured my friend with some warmth, is merely a stupid absence of imagination and mental flexibility.

Twilight had now approached, but neither of us felt any wish to cease speaking. Manton seemed unimpressed by my arguments, and eager to refute them, having that confidence in his own opinions which had doubtless caused his success as a teacher; whilst I was too sure of my ground to fear defeat. The dusk fell, and lights faintly gleamed in some of the distant windows, but we did not move. Our seat on the tomb was very comfortable, and I knew that my prosaic friend would not mind the cavernous rift in the ancient, root-disturbed brickwork close behind us, or the utter blackness of the spot brought by the intervention of a tottering, deserted seventeenth-century house between us and the nearest lighted road. There in the dark, upon that riven tomb by the deserted house, we talked on about the 'unnamable', and after my friend had finished his scoffing I told him of the awful evidence behind the story at which he had scoffed the most.

My tale had been called 'The Attic Window', and appeared in the January 1922 issue of *Whispers*. In a good many places, especially the South and the Pacific coast, they took the magazines off the stands at the complaints of silly milksops; but New England didn't get the thrill and merely shrugged its shoulders at my extravagance. The thing, it was averred, was biologically impossible to start with; merely another of those crazy country mutterings which Cotton Mather had been gullible enough to dump into his chaotic *Magnalia Christi Americana*, and so poorly authenticated that even he had not ventured to name the locality where the horror occurred. And as to the way I amplified the bare jotting of the old mystic – that was quite impossible, and characteristic of a flighty and notional scribbler! Mather had indeed told of the thing as being born, but nobody but a cheap sensationalist would think of having it grow up, look into people's windows at night, and be hidden in the attic of a house, in flesh and in spirit, till someone saw it at the window centuries later and couldn't describe what it was that turned his hair grey. All this was flagrant trashiness, and my friend Manton was not slow to insist on that fact. Then I told him what I had found in an old diary kept between 1706 and 1723, unearthed among family papers not a mile from where we were sitting; that, and the certain reality of the scars on my ancestor's chest and back which the diary described. I told him, too, of the fears of others in that region, and how they were whispered down for generations; and how no mythical madness came to the boy who in 1793 entered an abandoned house to examine certain traces suspected to be there.

It had been an eldritch thing – no wonder sensitive students shudder at the Puritan age in Massachusetts. So little is known of what went on beneath the surface – so little, yet such a ghastly festering as it bubbles up putrescently in occasional ghoulish glimpses. The witchcraft terror is a horrible ray of light on what was stewing in men's crushed brains, but even that is a trifle. There was no beauty; no freedom – we can see that from the architectural and household remains, and the poisonous sermons of the cramped divines. And inside that rusted iron strait-jacket lurked gibbering hideousness, perversion, and diabolism. Here, truly, was the apotheosis of the unnamable.

Cotton Mather, in that daemoniac sixth book which no one should read after dark, minced no words as he flung forth his anathema. Stern as a Jewish prophet, and laconically unamazed as none since his day could be, he told of the beast that had brought forth what was more than beast but less than man – the thing with the blemished eye – and of the screaming drunken wretch that they hanged for having such an eye. This much he baldly told, yet without a hint of what came after. Perhaps he did not know, or perhaps he knew and did not dare to tell. Others knew, but did not dare to tell – there is no public hint of why they whispered about the lock on the door to the attic stairs in the house of a childless, broken, embittered old man who had put up a blank slate slab by an avoided grave, although one may trace enough evasive legends to curdle the thinnest blood.

It is all in that ancestral diary I found; all the hushed innuendoes and furtive tales of things with a blemished eye seen at windows in the night or in deserted meadows near the woods. Something had caught my ancestor on a dark valley road, leaving him with marks of horns on his chest and of ape-like claws on his back; and when they looked for prints in the trampled dust they found the mixed marks of split hooves and vaguely anthropoid paws. Once a post-rider said he saw an old man chasing and calling to a frightful loping, name-less thing on Meadow Hill in the thinly moonlit hours before dawn, and many believed him. Certainly, there was strange talk one night in 1710 when the childless, broken old man was buried in the crypt behind his own house in sight of the blank slate slab. They never unlocked that attic door, but left the whole house as it was, dreaded and deserted. When noises came from it, they whispered and shivered; and hoped that the lock on that attic door was strong. Then they stopped hoping when the horror occurred at the parson-age, leaving not a soul alive or in one piece. With the years the legends take on a spectral character – I suppose the thing, if it was a living thing, must have died. The memory had lingered hideously – all the more hideous because it was so secret.

During this narration my friend Manton had become very silent, and I saw that my words had impressed him. He did not laugh as I paused, but asked quite seriously about the boy who went mad in 1793, and who had presumably been the hero of my fiction. I told him why the boy had gone to that shunned, deserted house, and remarked that he ought to be interested, since he believed that windows retained latent images of those who had sat at them. The boy had gone to look at the windows of that horrible attic, because of tales of things seen behind them, and had come back screaming maniacally.

Manton remained thoughtful as I said this, but gradually reverted to his analytical mood. He granted for the sake of argument that some unnatural monster had really existed, but reminded me that even the most morbid perversion of Nature need not be *unnamable* or scientifically indescribable. I admired his clearness and persistence, and added some further revelations I had collected among the old people. Those later spectral legends, I made plain, related to monstrous apparitions more frightful than anything organic could be; apparitions of gigantic bestial forms sometimes visible and sometimes only tangible, which floated about on moonless nights and haunted the old house, the crypt behind it, and the grave where a sapling had sprouted beside an illegible slab. Whether or not such apparitions had ever gored or smothered people to death, as told in uncorroborated traditions, they had produced a strong and consistent impression;

and were yet darkly feared by very aged natives, though largely forgotten by the last two generations – perhaps dying for lack of being thought about. Moreover, so far as aesthetic theory was involved, if the psychic emanations of human creatures be grotesque distortions, what coherent representation could express or portray so gibbous and infamous a nebulosity as the spectre of a malign, chaotic perversion, itself a morbid blasphemy against Nature? Moulded by the dead brain of a hybrid nightmare, would not such a vaporous terror constitute in all loathsome truth the exquisitely, the shriekingly *unnamable*?

The hour must now have grown very late. A singularly noiseless bat brushed by me, and I believe it touched Manton also, for although I could not see him I felt him raise his arm. Presently he spoke.

'But is that house with the attic window still standing and deserted?'

'Yes,' I answered. 'I have seen it.'

'And did you find anything there – in the attic or anywhere else?'

'There were some bones up under the eaves. They may have been what that boy saw – if he was sensitive he wouldn't have needed anything in the window-glass to unhinge him. If they all came from the same object it must have been an hysterical, delirious monstrosity. It would have been blasphemous to leave such bones in the world, so I went back with a sack and took them to the tomb behind the house. There was an opening where I could dump them in. Don't think I was a fool – you ought to have seen that skull. It had four-inch horns, but a face and jaw something like yours and mine.'

At last I could feel a real shiver run through Manton, who had moved very near. But his curiosity was undeterred.

'And what about the window-panes?'

'They were all gone. One window had lost its entire frame, and in the other there was not a trace of glass in the little diamond apertures. They were that kind – the old lattice windows that went out of use before 1700. I don't believe they've had any glass for an hundred years or more – maybe the boy broke 'em if he got that far; the legend doesn't say.'

Manton was reflecting again.

'I'd like to see that house, Carter. Where is it? Glass or no glass, I must explore it a little. And the tomb where you put those bones, and the other grave without an inscription – the whole thing must be a bit terrible.'

'You did see it – until it got dark.'

My friend was more wrought upon than I had suspected, for at this touch of harmless theatricalism he started neurotically away from me and actually cried out with a sort of gulping gasp which released a strain of previous repression. It was an odd cry, and all the more terrible because it was answered. For as it was still echoing, I heard a creaking sound through the pitchy blackness, and knew that a lattice window was opening in that accursed old house beside us. And because all the other frames were long since fallen, I knew that it was the grisly glassless frame of that daemoniac attic window.

Then came a noxious rush of noisome, frigid air from that same dreaded direction, followed by a piercing shriek just beside me on that shocking rifted tomb of man and monster. In another instant I was knocked from my gruesome bench by the devilish threshing of some unseen entity of titanic size but undetermined nature; knocked sprawling on the root-clutched mould of that abhorrent graveyard, while from the tomb came such a stifled uproar of gasping and whirring that my fancy peopled the rayless gloom with Miltonic legions of the misshapen damned. There was a vortex of withering, ice-cold wind, and then the rattle of loose bricks and plaster; but I had mercifully fainted before I could learn what it meant.

Manton, though smaller than I, is more resilient; for we opened our eyes at almost the same instant, despite his greater injuries. Our couches were side by side, and we knew in a few seconds that we were in St Mary's Hospital. Attendants were grouped about in tense curiosity, eager to aid our memory by telling us how we came there, and we soon heard of the farmer who had found us at noon in a lonely field beyond Meadow Hill, a mile from the old burying-ground, on a spot where an ancient slaughterhouse is reputed to have stood. Manton had two malignant wounds in the chest, and some less severe cuts or gougings in the back. I was not so seriously hurt, but was covered with welts and contusions of the most bewildering character, including the print of a split hoof. It was plain that Manton knew more than I, but he told nothing to the puzzled and interested physicians till he had learned what our injuries were. Then he said we were the victims of a vicious bull – though the animal was a difficult thing to place and account for.

After the doctors and nurses had left, I whispered an awestruck question.

'Good God, Manton, but *what was it*? Those scars – *was it like that*?'

And I was too dazed to exult when he whispered back a thing I had half expected –

'*No – it wasn't that way at all.* It was everywhere – a gelatin – a slime – yet it had shapes, a thousand shapes of horror beyond all memory. There were eyes – and a blemish. It was the pit – the maelstrom – the ultimate abomination. Carter, *it was the unnamable!*'

The Shunned House

I

From even the greatest of horrors irony is seldom absent. Sometimes it enters directly into the composition of the events, while sometimes it relates only to their fortuitous position among persons and places. The latter sort is splendidly exemplified by a case in the ancient city of Providence, where in the late forties Edgar Allan Poe used to sojourn often during his unsuccessful wooing of the gifted poetess, Mrs Whitman. Poe generally stopped at the Mansion House in Benefit Street – the renamed Golden Ball Inn whose roof has sheltered Washington, Jefferson, and Lafayette – and his favourite walk led northward along the same street to Mrs Whitman's home and the neighbouring hillside churchyard of St John's, whose hidden expanse of eighteenth-century gravestones had for him a peculiar fascination.

Now the irony is this. In this walk, so many times repeated, the world's greatest master of the terrible and the bizarre was obliged to pass a particular house on the eastern side of the street; a dingy, antiquated structure perched on the abruptly rising side-hill, with a great unkempt yard dating from a time when the region was partly open country. It does not appear that he ever wrote or spoke of it, nor is there any evidence that he even noticed it. And yet that house, to the two persons in possession of certain information, equals or outranks in horror the wildest phantasy of the genius who so often passed it unknowingly, and stands starkly leering as a symbol of all that is unutterably hideous.

The house was – and for that matter still is – of a kind to attract the attention of the curious. Originally a farm or semi-farm building, it followed the average New England colonial lines of the middle eighteenth century – the prosperous peaked-roof sort, with two stories and dormerless attic, and with the Georgian doorway and interior panelling dictated by the progress of taste at that time. It faced south, with one gable end buried to the lower windows in the eastward rising hill, and the other exposed to the foundations toward the street. Its construction, over a century and a half ago, had followed the grading and straightening of the road in that especial vicinity; for Benefit Street – at first called Back Street – was laid out as a lane winding amongst the graveyards of the first settlers, and straightened only when the removal of the bodies to the North Burial Ground made it decently possible to cut through the old family plots.

At the start, the western wall had lain some twenty feet up a precipitous lawn from the roadway; but a widening of the street at about the time of the Revolution sheared off most of the intervening space, exposing the foundations so that a brick basement wall had to be made, giving the deep cellar a street frontage with door and two windows above ground, close to the new line of public travel. When the sidewalk was laid out a century ago the last of the intervening space was removed; and Poe in his walks must have seen only a sheer ascent of dull grey brick flush with the sidewalk and surmounted at a height of ten feet by the antique shingled bulk of the house proper.

The farm-like grounds extended back very deeply up the hill, almost to Wheaton Street. The space south of the house, abutting on Benefit Street, was of course greatly above the existing sidewalk level, forming a terrace bounded by a high bank wall of damp, mossy stone pierced by a steep flight of narrow steps which led inward between canyon-like surfaces to the upper region of mangy lawn, rheumy brick walls, and neglected gardens whose dismantled cement urns, rusted kettles fallen from tripods of knotty sticks, and similar paraphernalia set off the weather-beaten front door with its broken fanlight, rotting Ionic pilasters, and wormy triangular pediment.

What I heard in my youth about the shunned house was merely that people died there in alarmingly great numbers. That, I was told, was why the original owners had moved out some twenty years after building the place. It was plainly unhealthy, perhaps because of the dampness and fungous growth in the cellar, the general sickish smell, the draughts of the hallways, or the quality of the well and pump water. These things were bad enough, and these were all that gained belief among the persons whom I knew. Only the notebooks of my antiquarian uncle, Dr Elihu Whipple, revealed to me at length the darker, vaguer surmises which formed an undercurrent of folklore among old-time servants and humble folk; surmises which never travelled far, and which were largely forgotten when Providence grew to be a metropolis with a shifting modern population.

The general fact is, that the house was never regarded by the solid part of the community as in any real sense 'haunted'. There were no widespread tales of rattling chains, cold currents of air, extinguished lights, or faces at the window. Extremists sometimes said the house was 'unlucky', but that is as far as even they went. What was really beyond dispute is that a frightful proportion of persons died there; or more accurately, *had* died there, since after some peculiar happenings over sixty years ago the building had become deserted through the sheer impossibility of renting it. These persons were not all cut off suddenly by any one cause; rather did it seem that their vitality was insidiously sapped, so that each one died the sooner from whatever tendency to weakness he may have naturally had. And those who did not die displayed in varying degree a type of anaemia or consumption, and sometimes a decline of the mental faculties, which spoke ill for the salubriousness of the building. Neighbouring houses, it must be added, seemed entirely free from the noxious quality.

This much I knew before my insistent questioning led my uncle to shew me the notes which finally embarked us both on our hideous investigation. In my childhood the shunned house was vacant, with barren, gnarled, and terrible old trees, long, queerly pale grass, and nightmarishly misshapen weeds in the high terraced yard where birds never lingered. We boys used to overrun the place, and I can still recall my youthful terror not only at the morbid strangeness of this sinister vegetation, but at the eldritch atmosphere and odour of the dilapidated house, whose unlocked front door was often entered in quest of shudders. The small-paned windows were largely broken, and a nameless air of desolation hung round the precarious panelling, shaky interior shutters, peeling wall-paper, falling plaster, rickety staircases, and such fragments of battered furniture as still remained. The dust and cobwebs added their touch of the fearful; and brave indeed was the boy who would voluntarily ascend the ladder to the attic, a vast raftered length lighted only by small blinking windows in the gable ends, and filled with a massed wreckage of chests, chairs, and spinning-wheels which infinite years of deposit had shrouded and festooned into monstrous and hellish shapes.

But after all, the attic was not the most terrible part of the house. It was the dank, humid cellar which somehow exerted the strongest repulsion on us, even though it was wholly above ground on the street side, with only a thin door and window-pierced brick wall to separate it from the busy sidewalk. We scarcely knew whether to haunt it in spectral fascination, or to shun it for the sake of our souls and our sanity. For one thing, the bad odour of the house was strongest there; and for another thing, we did not like the white fungous growths which occasionally sprang up in rainy summer weather from the hard earth floor. Those fungi, grotesquely like the vegetation in the yard outside, were truly horrible in their outlines; detestable parodies of toadstools and Indian pipes, whose like we had never seen in any other situation. They rotted quickly, and at one stage became slightly phosphorescent; so that nocturnal passers-by sometimes spoke of witch-fires glowing behind the broken panes of the foetor-spreading windows.

We never – even in our wildest Hallowe'en moods – visited this cellar by night, but in some of our daytime visits could detect the phosphorescence, especially when the day was dark and wet. There was also a subtler thing we often thought we detected – a very strange thing which was, however, merely suggestive at most. I refer to a sort of cloudy whitish pattern on the dirt floor – a vague, shifting deposit of mould or nitre which we sometimes thought we could trace amidst the sparse fungous growths near the huge fireplace of the basement kitchen. Once in a while it struck us that this patch bore an uncanny resemblance to a doubled-up human figure, though generally no such kinship existed, and often there was no whitish deposit whatever. On a certain rainy afternoon when this illusion seemed phenomenally strong, and when, in addition, I had fancied I glimpsed a kind of thin, yellowish, shimmering exhalation rising from the nitrous pattern toward the yawning fireplace, I spoke to my uncle about the matter. He smiled at this odd conceit, but it seemed that his smile was tinged with reminiscence. Later I heard that a similar notion entered into some of the wild ancient tales of the common folk – a notion likewise alluding to ghoulish, wolfish shapes taken by smoke from the great chimney, and queer contours assumed by certain of the sinuous tree-roots that thrust their way into the cellar through the loose foundation-stones.

2

Not till my adult years did my uncle set before me the notes and data which he had collected concerning the shunned house. Dr Whipple was a sane, conservative physician of the old school, and for all his interest in the place was not eager to encourage young thoughts toward the abnormal. His own view, postulating simply a building and location of markedly unsanitary qualities, had nothing to do with abnormality; but he realised that the very picturesqueness which aroused his own interest would in a boy's fanciful mind take on all manner of gruesome imaginative associations.

The doctor was a bachelor; a white-haired, clean-shaven, old-fashioned gentleman, and a local historian of note, who had often broken a lance with such controversial guardians of tradition as Sidney S. Rider and Thomas W. Bicknell. He lived with one man-servant in a Georgian homestead with knocker and iron-railed steps, balanced eerily on a steep ascent of North Court Street beside the ancient brick court and colony house where his grandfather – a cousin of that celebrated privateersman, Capt. Whipple, who burnt His Majesty's armed schooner *Gaspee* in 1772 – had voted in the legislature on May 4, 1776, for the independence of the Rhode Island Colony. Around him in the damp, low-ceiled library with the musty white panelling, heavy carved overmantel, and small-paned, vine-shaded windows, were the relics and records of his ancient family, among which were many dubious allusions to the shunned house in Benefit Street. That pest spot lies not far distant – for Benefit runs ledgewise just above the court-house along the precipitous hill up which the first settlement climbed.

When, in the end, my insistent pestering and maturing years evoked from my uncle the hoarded lore I sought, there lay before me a strange enough chronicle. Long-winded, statistical, and drearily genealogical as some of the matter was, there ran through it a continuous thread of brooding, tenacious horror and preternatural malevolence which impressed me even more than it had impressed the good doctor. Separate events fitted together uncannily, and seemingly irrelevant details held mines of hideous possibilities. A new and burning curiosity grew in me, compared to which my boyish curiosity was feeble and inchoate. The first revelation led to an exhaustive research, and finally to that shuddering quest which proved so disastrous to myself and mine. For at last my uncle insisted on joining the search I had commenced, and after a certain night in that house he did not come away with me. I am lonely without that gentle soul whose long years were filled only with honour, virtue, good taste, benevolence, and learning. I have reared a marble urn to his memory in St John's churchyard – the place that Poe loved – the hidden grove of giant willows on the hill, where tombs and headstones huddle quietly between the hoary bulk of the church and the houses and bank walls of Benefit Street.

The history of the house, opening amidst a maze of dates, revealed no trace of the sinister either about its construction or about the prosperous and honourable family who built it. Yet from the first a taint of calamity, soon increased to boding significance, was apparent. My uncle's carefully compiled record began with the building of the structure in 1763, and followed the theme with an unusual amount of detail. The shunned house, it seems, was first inhabited by William Harris and his wife Rhoby Dexter, with their children, Elkanah, born in 1755, Abigail, born in 1757, William, Jr., born in 1759, and Ruth, born in 1761. Harris was a substantial merchant and seaman in the West India trade, connected with the firm of Obadiah Brown and his nephews. After Brown's death in 1761, the new firm of Nicholas Brown & Co. made him master of the brig *Prudence*, Providence-built, of 120 tons, thus enabling him to erect the new homestead he had desired ever since his marriage.

The site he had chosen – a recently straightened part of the new and fashionable Back Street, which ran along the side of the hill above crowded Cheapside – was all that could be wished, and the building did justice to the location. It was the best that moderate means could afford, and Harris hastened to move in before the birth of a fifth child which the family expected. That child, a boy, came in December; but was still-born. Nor was any child to be born alive in that house for a century and a half.

The next April sickness occurred among the children, and Abigail and Ruth died before the month was over. Dr Job Ives diagnosed the trouble as some infantile fever, though others declared it was more of a mere wasting-away or decline. It seemed, in any event, to be contagious; for Hannah Bowen, one of the two servants, died of it in the following June. Eli Liddeason, the other servant, constantly complained of weakness, and would have returned to his father's farm in Rehoboth but for a sudden attachment for Mehitabel Pierce, who was hired to succeed Hannah. He died the next year – a sad year indeed, since it marked the death of William Harris himself, enfeebled as he was by the climate of Martinique, where his occupation had kept him for considerable periods during the preceding decade.

The widowed Rhoby Harris never recovered from the shock of her husband's death, and the passing of her first-born Elkanah two years later was the final blow to her reason. In 1768 she fell victim to a mild form of insanity, and was thereafter confined to the upper part of the house; her elder maiden sister, Mercy Dexter, having moved in to take charge of the family. Mercy was a plain, raw-boned woman of great strength; but her health visibly declined from the time of her advent. She was greatly devoted to her unfortunate sister, and had an especial affection for her only surviving nephew William, who from a sturdy infant had become a sickly, spindling lad. In this year the servant Mehitabel died, and the other servant, Preserved Smith, left without coherent explanation – or at least, with only some wild tales and a complaint that he disliked the smell of the place. For a time Mercy could secure no more help, since the seven deaths and case of madness, all occurring within five years' space, had begun to set in motion the body of fireside rumour which later became so bizarre. Ultimately, however, she obtained new servants from out of town: Ann White, a morose woman from that part of North Kingstown now set off as the township of Exeter, and a capable Boston man named Zenas Low.

It was Ann White who first gave definite shape to the sinister idle talk. Mercy should have known better than to hire anyone from the Nooseneck Hill country, for that remote bit of backwoods was then, as now, a seat of the most uncomfortable superstitions. As lately as 1892 an Exeter community exhumed a dead body and ceremoniously burnt its heart in order to prevent certain alleged visitations injurious to the public health and peace, and one may imagine the point of view of the same section in 1768. Ann's tongue was perniciously active, and within a few months Mercy discharged her, filling her place with a faithful and amiable Amazon from Newport, Maria Robbins.

Meanwhile poor Rhoby Harris, in her madness, gave voice to dreams and imaginings of the most hideous sort. At times her screams became insupportable, and for long periods she would utter shrieking horrors which necessitated her son's temporary residence with his cousin, Peleg Harris, in Presbyterian-Lane near the new college building. The boy would seem to improve after these visits, and had Mercy been as wise as she was well-meaning, she would have let him live permanently with Peleg. Just what Mrs Harris cried out in her fits of violence, tradition hesitates to say; or rather, presents such extravagant accounts that they nullify themselves through sheer absurdity. Certainly it sounds absurd to hear that a woman educated only in the rudiments of French often shouted for hours in a coarse and idiomatic form of that language, or that the same person, alone and guarded, complained wildly of a staring thing which bit and chewed at her. In 1772 the servant Zenas died, and when Mrs Harris heard of it she laughed with a shocking delight utterly foreign to her. The next year she herself died, and was laid to rest in the North Burial Ground beside her husband.

Upon the outbreak of trouble with Great Britain in 1775, William Harris, despite his scant sixteen years and feeble constitution, managed to enlist in the Army of Observation under General Greene; and from that time on enjoyed a steady rise in health and prestige. In 1780, as a Captain in Rhode Island forces in New Jersey under Colonel Angell, he met and married Phebe Hetfield of Elizabethtown, whom he brought to Providence upon his honourable discharge in the following year.

The young soldier's return was not a thing of unmitigated happiness. The house, it is true, was still in good condition; and the street had been widened and changed in name from Back Street to Benefit Street. But Mercy Dexter's once robust frame had undergone a sad and curious decay, so that she was now a stooped and pathetic figure with hollow voice and disconcerting pallor – qualities shared to a singular degree by the one remaining servant Maria. In the autumn of 1782 Phebe Harris gave birth to a still-born daughter, and on the fifteenth of the next May Mercy Dexter took leave of a useful, austere, and virtuous life.

William Harris, at last thoroughly convinced of the radically unhealthful nature of his abode, now took steps toward quitting it and closing it forever. Securing temporary quarters for himself and his wife at the newly opened Golden Ball Inn, he arranged for the building of a new and finer house in Westminster Street, in the growing part of the town across the Great Bridge. There, in 1785, his son Dutee was born; and there the family dwelt till the encroachments of commerce drove them back across the river and over the hill to Angell Street, in the newer East Side residence district, where the late Archer Harris built his sumptuous but hideous French-roofed mansion in 1876. William and Phebe both succumbed to the yellow fever epidemic of 1797, but Dutee was brought up by his cousin Rathbone Harris, Peleg's son.

Rathbone was a practical man, and rented the Benefit Street house despite William's wish to keep it vacant. He considered it an obligation to his ward to make the most of all the boy's property, nor did he concern himself with the deaths and illnesses which caused so many changes of tenants, or the steadily growing aversion with which the house was generally regarded. It is likely that he felt only vexation when, in 1804, the town council ordered him to fumigate the place with sulphur, tar, and gum camphor on account of the much-discussed deaths of four persons, presumably caused by the then diminishing fever epidemic. They said the place had a febrile smell.

Dutee himself thought little of the house, for he grew up to be a privateersman, and served with distinction on the *Vigilant* under Capt. Cahoone in the War of 1812. He returned unharmed, married in 1814, and became a father on that memorable night of September 23, 1815, when a great gale drove the waters of the bay over half the town, and floated a tall sloop well up Westminster Street so that its masts almost tapped the Harris windows in symbolic affirmation that the new boy, Welcome, was a seaman's son.

Welcome did not survive his father, but lived to perish gloriously at Fredericksburg in 1862. Neither he nor his son Archer knew of the shunned house as other than a nuisance almost impossible to rent – perhaps on account of the mustiness and sickly odour of unkempt old age. Indeed, it never was rented after a series of deaths culminating in 1861, which the excitement of the war tended to throw into obscurity. Carrington Harris, last of the male line, knew it only as a deserted and somewhat picturesque centre of legend until I told him my experience. He had meant to tear it down and build an apartment house on the site, but after my account decided to let it stand, install plumbing, and rent it. Nor has he yet had any difficulty in obtaining tenants. The horror has gone.

3

It may well be imagined how powerfully I was affected by the annals of the Harrises. In this continuous record there seemed to me to brood a persistent evil beyond anything in Nature as I had known it; an evil clearly connected with the house and not with the family. This impression was confirmed by my uncle's less systematic array of miscellaneous data – legends transcribed from servant gossip, cuttings from the papers, copies of death-certificates by fellow-physicians, and the like. All of this material I cannot hope to give, for my uncle was a tireless antiquarian and very deeply interested in the shunned house; but I may refer to several dominant points which earn notice by their recurrence through many reports from diverse sources. For example, the servant gossip was practically unanimous in attributing to the fungous and malodorous *cellar* of the house a vast supremacy in evil influence. There had been servants – Ann White especially – who would not use the cellar kitchen, and at least three well-defined legends bore upon the queer quasi-human or diabolic outlines assumed by tree-roots and patches of mould in that region. These latter narratives interested me profoundly, on account of what I had seen in my boyhood, but I felt that most of the significance had in each case been largely obscured by additions from the common stock of local ghost lore.

Ann White, with her Exeter superstition, had promulgated the most extravagant and at the same time most consistent tale, alleging that there must lie buried beneath the house one of those vampires – the dead who retain their bodily form and live on the blood or breath of the living – whose hideous legions send their preying shapes or spirits abroad by night. To destroy a vampire one must, the grandmothers say, exhume it and burn its heart, or at least drive a stake through that organ; and Ann's dogged insistence on a search under the cellar had been prominent in bringing about her discharge.

Her tales, however, commanded a wide audience, and were the more readily accepted because the house indeed stood on land once used for burial purposes. To me their interest depended less on this circumstance than on the peculiarly appropriate way in which they dovetailed with certain other things – the complaint of the departing servant Preserved Smith, who had preceded Ann and never heard of her, that something 'sucked his breath' at night; the death-certificates of fever victims of 1804, issued by Dr Chad Hopkins, and shewing the four deceased persons all unaccountably lacking in blood; and the obscure passages of poor Rhoby Harris's ravings, where she complained of the sharp teeth of a glassy-eyed, half-visible presence.

Free from unwarranted superstition though I am, these things produced in me an odd sensation, which was intensified by a pair of widely separated newspaper cuttings relating to deaths in the shunned house – one from the *Providence Gazette and Country-Journal* of April 12, 1815, and the other from the *Daily Transcript and Chronicle* of October 27, 1845 – each of which detailed an appallingly grisly circumstance whose duplication was remarkable. It seems that in both instances the dying person, in 1815 a gentle old lady named Stafford and in 1845 a school-teacher of middle age named Eleazar Durfee, became transfigured in a horrible way, glaring glassily and attempting to bite the throat of the attending physician. Even more puzzling, though, was the final case which put an end to the renting of the house – a series of anaemia deaths preceded by progressive madnesses wherein the patient would craftily attempt the lives of his relatives by incisions in the neck or wrist.

This was in 1860 and 1861, when my uncle had just begun his medical practice; and before leaving for the front he heard much of it from his elder professional colleagues. The really inexplicable thing was the way in which the victims – ignorant people, for the ill-smelling and widely shunned house could now be rented to no others – would babble maledictions in French, a language they could not possibly have studied to any extent. It made one think of poor Rhoby Harris nearly a century before, and so moved my uncle that he commenced collecting historical data on the house after listening, some time subsequent to his return from the war, to the first-hand account of Drs Chase and Whitmarsh. Indeed, I could see that my uncle had thought deeply on the subject, and that he was glad of my own interest – an open-minded and sympathetic interest which enabled him to discuss with me matters at which others would merely have laughed. His fancy had not gone so far as mine, but he felt that the place was rare in its imaginative potentialities, and worthy of note as an inspiration in the field of the grotesque and macabre.

For my part, I was disposed to take the whole subject with profound seriousness, and began at once not only to review the evidence, but to accumulate as much more as I could. I talked with the elderly Archer Harris, then owner of the house, many times before his death in 1916; and obtained from him and his still surviving maiden sister Alice an authentic corroboration of all the family data my uncle had collected. When, however, I asked them what connexion with France or its language the house could have, they confessed themselves as frankly baffled and ignorant as I. Archer knew nothing, and all that Miss Harris could say was that an old allusion her grandfather, Dutee Harris, had heard of might have shed a little light. The old seaman, who had survived his son Welcome's death in battle by two years, had not himself known the legend; but recalled that his earliest nurse, the ancient Maria Robbins, seemed darkly aware of something that might have lent a weird significance to the French ravings of Rhoby Harris, which she had so often heard during the last days of that hapless woman. Maria had been at the shunned house from 1769 till the removal of the family in 1783, and had seen Mercy Dexter die. Once she hinted to the child Dutee of a somewhat peculiar circumstance in Mercy's last moments, but he had soon forgotten all about it save that it was something peculiar. The granddaughter, moreover, recalled even this much with difficulty. She and her brother were not so much interested in the house as was Archer's son Carrington, the present owner, with whom I talked after my experience.

Having exhausted the Harris family of all the information it could furnish, I turned my attention to early town records and deeds with a zeal more penetrating than that which my uncle had occasionally shewn in the same work. What I wished was a comprehensive history of the site from its very settlement in 1636 – or even before, if any

Narragansett Indian legend could be unearthed to supply the data. I found, at the start, that the land had been part of the long strip of home lot granted originally to John Throckmorton; one of many similar strips beginning at the Town Street beside the river and extending up over the hill to a line roughly corresponding with the modern Hope Street. The Throckmorton lot had later, of course, been much subdivided; and I became very assiduous in tracing that section through which Back or Benefit Street was later run. It had, a rumour indeed said, been the Throckmorton graveyard; but as I examined the records more carefully, I found that the graves had all been transferred at an early date to the North Burial Ground on the Pawtucket West Road.

Then suddenly I came – by a rare piece of chance, since it was not in the main body of records and might easily have been missed – upon something which aroused my keenest eagerness, fitting in as it did with several of the queerest phases of the affair. It was the record of a lease, in 1697, of a small tract of ground to an Etienne Roulet and wife. At last the French element had appeared – that, and another deeper element of horror which the name conjured up from the darkest recesses of my weird and heterogeneous reading – and I feverishly studied the platting of the locality as it had been before the cutting through and partial straightening of Back Street between 1747 and 1758. I found what I had half expected, that where the shunned house now stood the Roulets had laid out their graveyard behind a one-story and attic cottage, and that no record of any transfer of graves existed. The document, indeed, ended in much confusion; and I was forced to ransack both the Rhode Island Historical Society and Shepley Library before I could find a local door which the name Etienne Roulet would unlock. In the end I did find something; something of such vague but monstrous import that I set about at once to examine the cellar of the shunned house itself with a new and excited minuteness.

The Roulets, it seemed, had come in 1696 from East Greenwich, down the west shore of Narragansett Bay. They were Huguenots from Caude, and had encountered much opposition before the Providence selectmen allowed them to settle in the town. Unpopularity had dogged them in East Greenwich, whither they had come in 1686, after the revocation of the Edict of Nantes, and rumour said that the cause of dislike extended beyond mere racial and national prejudice, or the land disputes which involved other French settlers with the English in rivalries which not even Governor Andros could quell. But their ardent Protestantism – too ardent, some whispered – and their evident distress when virtually driven from the village down the bay, had moved the sympathy of the town fathers. Here the strangers had been granted a haven; and the swarthy Etienne Roulet, less apt at agriculture than at reading queer books and drawing queer diagrams, was given a clerical post in the warehouse at Pardon Tillinghast's wharf, far south in Town Street. There had, however, been a riot of some sort later on – perhaps forty years later, after old Roulet's death – and no one seemed to hear of the family after that.

For a century and more, it appeared, the Roulets had been well remembered and frequently discussed as vivid incidents in the quiet life of a New England seaport. Etienne's son Paul, a surly fellow whose erratic conduct had probably provoked the riot which wiped out the family, was particularly a source of speculation; and though Providence never shared the witchcraft panics of her Puritan neighbours, it was freely intimated by old wives that his prayers were neither uttered at the proper time nor directed toward the proper object. All this had undoubtedly formed the basis of the legend known by old Maria Robbins. What relation it had to the French ravings of Rhoby Harris and other inhabitants of the shunned house, imagination or future discovery alone could determine. I wondered how many of those who had known the legends realised that additional link with the terrible which my wide reading had given me; that ominous item in the annals of morbid horror which tells of the creature *Jacques Roulet, of Caude*, who in 1598 was condemned to death as a daemoniac but afterward saved from the stake by the Paris parliament and shut in a madhouse. He had been found covered with blood and shreds of flesh in a wood, shortly after the killing and rending of a boy by a pair of wolves. One wolf was seen to lope away unhurt. Surely a pretty hearthside tale, with a queer significance as to name and place; but I decided that the Providence gossips could not have generally known of it. Had they known, the coincidence of names would have brought some drastic and frightened action – indeed, might not its limited whispering have precipitated the final riot which erased the Roulets from the town?

I now visited the accursed place with increased frequency; studying the unwholesome vegetation of the garden, examining all the walls of the building, and poring over every inch of the earthen cellar floor. Finally, with Carrington Harris's permission, I fitted a key to the disused door opening from the cellar directly upon Benefit Street, preferring to have a more immediate access to the outside world than the dark stairs, ground floor hall, and front door could give. There, where morbidity lurked most thickly, I searched and poked during long afternoons when the sunlight filtered in through the cobwebbed above-ground windows, and a sense of security glowed from the unlocked door which placed me only a few feet from the placid sidewalk outside. Nothing new rewarded my efforts – only the same depressing mustiness and faint suggestions of noxious odours and nitrous outlines on the floor – and I fancy that many pedestrians must have watched me curiously through the broken panes.

At length, upon a suggestion of my uncle's, I decided to try the spot nocturnally; and one stormy midnight ran the beams of an electric torch over the mouldy floor with its uncanny shapes and distorted, half-phosphorescent fungi. The place had dispirited me curiously that evening, and I was almost prepared when I saw – or thought I saw – amidst the whitish deposits a particularly sharp definition of the 'huddled form' I had suspected from boyhood. Its clearness was astonishing and unprecedented – and as I watched I seemed to see again the thin, yellowish, shimmering exhalation which had startled me on that rainy afternoon so many years before.

Above the anthropomorphic patch of mould by the fireplace it rose; a subtle, sickish, almost luminous vapour which as it hung trembling in the dampness seemed to develop vague and shocking suggestions of form, gradually trailing off into nebulous decay and passing up into the blackness of the great chimney with a foetor in its wake. It was truly horrible, and the more so to me because of what I knew of the spot. Refusing to flee, I watched it fade – and as I watched I felt that it was in turn watching me greedily with eyes more imaginable than visible. When I told my uncle about it he was greatly aroused; and after a tense hour of reflection, arrived at a definite and drastic decision. Weighing in his mind the importance of the matter, and the significance of our relation to it, he insisted that we both test – and if possible destroy – the horror of the house by a joint night or nights of aggressive vigil in that musty and fungus-cursed cellar.

4

On Wednesday, June 25, 1919, after a proper notification of Carrington Harris which did not include surmises as to what we expected to find, my uncle and I conveyed to the shunned house two camp chairs and a folding camp cot, together with some scientific mechanism of greater weight and intricacy. These we placed in the cellar during the day, screening the windows with paper and planning to return in the evening for our first vigil. We had locked the door from the cellar to the ground floor; and having a key to the outside cellar door, we were prepared to leave our expensive and delicate apparatus – which we had obtained secretly and at great cost – as many days as our vigils might need to be protracted. It was our design to sit up together till very late, and then watch singly till dawn in two-hour stretches, myself first and then my companion; the inactive member resting on the cot.

The natural leadership with which my uncle procured the instruments from the laboratories of Brown University and the Cranston Street Armoury, and instinctively assumed direction of our venture, was a marvellous commentary on the potential vitality and resilience of a man of eighty-one. Elihu Whipple had lived according to the hygienic laws he had preached as a physician, and but for what happened later would be here in full vigour today. Only two persons suspect what did happen – Carrington Harris and myself. I had to tell Harris because he owned the house and deserved to know what had gone out of it. Then too, we had spoken to him in advance of our quest; and I felt after my uncle's going that he would understand and assist me in some vitally necessary public explanations. He turned very pale, but agreed to help me, and decided that it would now be safe to rent the house.

To declare that we were not nervous on that rainy night of watching would be an exaggeration both gross and ridiculous. We were not, as I have said, in any sense childishly superstitious, but scientific study and reflection had taught us that the known universe of three dimensions embraces the merest fraction of the whole cosmos of substance and energy. In this case an overwhelming preponderance of evidence from numerous authentic sources pointed to the tenacious existence of certain forces of great power and, so far as the human point of view is concerned, exceptional malignancy. To say that we actually believed in vampires or werewolves would be a carelessly inclusive statement. Rather must it be said that we were not prepared to deny the possibility of certain unfamiliar and unclassified modifications of vital force and attenuated matter; existing very infrequently in three-dimensional space because of its more intimate connexion with other spatial units, yet close enough to the boundary of our own to furnish us occasional manifestations which we, for lack of a proper vantage-point, may never hope to understand.

In short, it seemed to my uncle and me that an incontrovertible array of facts pointed to some lingering influence in the shunned house; traceable to one or another of the ill-favoured French settlers of two centuries before, and still operative through rare and unknown laws of atomic and electronic motion. That the family of Roulet had possessed an abnormal affinity for outer circles of entity – dark spheres which for normal folk hold only repulsion and terror – their recorded history seemed to prove. Had not, then, the riots of those bygone seventeen-thirties set moving certain kinetic patterns in the morbid brain of one or more of them – notably the sinister Paul Roulet – which obscurely survived the bodies murdered and buried by the mob, and continued to function in some multiple-dimensioned space along the original lines of force determined by a frantic hatred of the encroaching community?

Such a thing was surely not a physical or biochemical impossibility in the light of a newer science which includes the theories of relativity and intra-atomic action. One might easily imagine an alien nucleus of substance or energy, formless or otherwise, kept alive by imperceptible or immaterial subtractions from the life-force or bodily tissues and fluids of other and more palpably living things into which it penetrates and with whose fabric it sometimes completely merges itself. It might be actively hostile, or it might be dictated merely by blind motives of self-preservation. In any case such a monster must of necessity be in our scheme of things an anomaly and an intruder, whose extirpation forms a primary duty with every man not an enemy to the world's life, health, and sanity.

What baffled us was our utter ignorance of the aspect in which we might encounter the thing. No sane person had even seen it, and few had ever felt it definitely. It might be pure energy – a form ethereal and outside the realm of substance – or it might be partly material; some unknown and equivocal mass of plasticity, capable of changing at will to nebulous approximations of the solid, liquid, gaseous, or tenuously unparticled states. The anthropomorphic patch of mould on the floor, the form of the yellowish vapour, and the curvature of the tree-roots in some of the old tales, all argued at least a remote and reminiscent connexion with the human shape; but how representative or permanent that similarity might be, none could say with any kind of certainty.

We had devised two weapons to fight it; a large and specially fitted Crookes tube operated by powerful storage batteries and provided with peculiar screens and reflectors, in case it proved intangible and opposable only by vigorously destructive ether radiations, and a pair of military flame-throwers of the sort used in the world-war, in case it proved partly material and susceptible of mechanical destruction – for like the superstitious Exeter rustics, we were prepared to burn the thing's heart out if heart existed to burn. All this aggressive mechanism we set in the cellar in positions carefully arranged with reference to the cot and chairs, and to the spot before the fireplace where the mould had taken strange shapes. That suggestive patch, by the way, was only faintly visible when we placed our furniture and instruments, and when we returned that evening for the actual vigil. For a moment I half doubted that I had ever seen it in the more definitely limned form – but then I thought of the legends.

Our cellar vigil began at 10 p.m., daylight saving time, and as it continued we found no promise of pertinent developments. A weak, filtered glow from the rain-harassed street-lamps outside, and a feeble phosphorescence from the detestable fungi within, shewed the dripping stone of the walls, from which all traces of whitewash had vanished; the dank, foetid, and mildew-tainted hard earth floor with its obscene fungi; the rotting remains of what had been stools, chairs, and tables, and other more shapeless furniture; the heavy planks and massive beams of the ground floor overhead; the decrepit plank door leading to bins and chambers beneath other parts of the house; the crumbling stone staircase with ruined wooden hand-rail; and the crude and cavernous fireplace of blackened brick where rusted iron fragments revealed the past presence of hooks, andirons, spit, crane, and a door to the Dutch oven – these things, and our austere cot and camp chairs, and the heavy and intricate destructive machinery we had brought.

We had, as in my own former explorations, left the door to the street unlocked, so that a direct and practical path of escape might lie open in case of manifestations beyond our power to deal with. It was our idea that our continued nocturnal presence would call forth whatever malign entity lurked there; and that being prepared, we could dispose of the thing with one or the other of our provided means as soon as we had recognised and observed it sufficiently. How long it might require to evoke and extinguish the thing, we had no notion. It occurred to us, too, that our venture was far from safe; for in what strength the thing might appear no one could tell. But we deemed the game worth the hazard, and embarked on it alone and unhesitatingly, conscious that the seeking of outside aid would only expose us to ridicule and perhaps defeat our entire purpose. Such was our frame of mind as we talked – far into the night, till my uncle's growing drowsiness made me remind him to lie down for his two-hour sleep.

Something like fear chilled me as I sat there in the small hours alone – I say alone, for one who sits by a sleeper is indeed alone; perhaps more alone than he can realise. My uncle breathed heavily, his deep inhalations and exhalations accompanied by the rain outside, and punctuated by another nerve-racking sound of distant dripping water within – for the house was repulsively damp even in dry weather, and in this storm positively swamp-like. I studied the loose, antique masonry of the walls in the fungus-light and the feeble rays which stole in from the street through the screened windows; and once, when the noisome atmosphere of the place seemed about to sicken me, I opened the door and looked up and down the street, feasting my eyes on familiar sights and my nostrils on the wholesome air. Still nothing occurred to reward my watching; and I yawned repeatedly, fatigue getting the better of apprehension.

Then the stirring of my uncle in his sleep attracted my notice. He had turned restlessly on the cot several times during the latter half of the first hour, but now he was breathing with unusual irregularity, occasionally heaving a sigh which held more than a few of the qualities of a choking moan. I turned my electric flashlight on him and found his face averted, so rising and crossing to the other side of the cot, I again flashed the light to see if he seemed in any pain. What I saw unnerved me most surprisingly, considering its relative triviality. It must have been merely the association of any odd circumstance with the sinister nature of our location and mission, for surely the circumstance was not in itself frightful or unnatural. It was merely that my uncle's facial expression, disturbed no doubt by the strange dreams which our situation prompted, betrayed considerable agitation, and seemed not at all characteristic of him. His habitual expression was one of kindly and well-bred calm, whereas now a variety of emotions seemed struggling within him. I think, on the whole, that it was this *variety* which chiefly disturbed me. My uncle, as he gasped and tossed in increasing perturbation and with eyes that had now started open, seemed not one but many men, and suggested a curious quality of alienage from himself.

All at once he commenced to mutter, and I did not like the look of his mouth and teeth as he spoke. The words were at first indistinguishable, and then – with a tremendous start – I recognised something about them which filled me with icy fear till I recalled the breadth of my uncle's education and the interminable translations he had made from anthropological and antiquarian articles in the *Revue des Deux Mondes*. For the venerable Elihu Whipple was muttering *in French*, and the few phrases I could distinguish seemed connected with the darkest myths he had ever adapted from the famous Paris magazine.

Suddenly a perspiration broke out on the sleeper's forehead, and he leaped abruptly up, half awake. The jumble of French changed to a cry in English, and the hoarse voice shouted excitedly, 'My breath, my breath!' Then the awakening became complete, and with a subsidence of facial expression to the normal state my uncle seized my hand and began to relate a dream whose nucleus of significance I could only surmise with a kind of awe.

He had, he said, floated off from a very ordinary series of dream-pictures into a scene whose strangeness was related to nothing he had ever read. It was of this world, and yet not of it – a shadowy geometrical confusion in which could be seen elements of familiar things

in most unfamiliar and perturbing combinations. There was a suggestion of queerly disordered pictures superimposed one upon another;
an arrangement in which the essentials of time as well as of space
seemed dissolved and mixed in the most illogical fashion. In this
kaleidoscopic vortex of phantasmal images were occasional snapshots,
if one might use the term, of singular clearness but unaccountable
heterogeneity.

Once my uncle thought he lay in a carelessly dug open pit, with a
crowd of angry faces framed by straggling locks and three-cornered
hats frowning down on him. Again he seemed to be in the interior of a
house – an old house, apparently – but the details and inhabitants were
constantly changing, and he could never be certain of the faces or the
furniture, or even of the room itself, since doors and windows seemed
in just as great a state of flux as the more presumably mobile objects. It
was queer – damnably queer – and my uncle spoke almost sheepishly,
as if half expecting not to be believed, when he declared that of the
strange faces many had unmistakably borne the features of the Harris
family. And all the while there was a personal sensation of choking, as
if some pervasive presence had spread itself through his body and
sought to possess itself of his vital processes. I shuddered at the
thought of those vital processes, worn as they were by eighty-one
years of continuous functioning, in conflict with unknown forces of
which the youngest and strongest system might well be afraid; but in
another moment reflected that dreams are only dreams, and that these
uncomfortable visions could be, at most, no more than my uncle's
reaction to the investigations and expectations which had lately filled
our minds to the exclusion of all else.

Conversation, also, soon tended to dispel my sense of strangeness;
and in time I yielded to my yawns and took my turn at slumber.
My uncle seemed now very wakeful, and welcomed his period of
watching even though the nightmare had aroused him far ahead of
his allotted two hours. Sleep seized me quickly, and I was at once
haunted with dreams of the most disturbing kind. I felt, in my
visions, a cosmic and abysmal loneness, with hostility surging from
all sides upon some prison where I lay confined. I seemed bound and
gagged, and taunted by the echoing yells of distant multitudes who
thirsted for my blood. My uncle's face came to me with less pleasant
associations than in waking hours, and I recall many futile struggles

and attempts to scream. It was not a pleasant sleep, and for a second I was not sorry for the echoing shriek which clove through the barriers of dream and flung me to a sharp and startled awakeness in which every actual object before my eyes stood out with more than natural clearness and reality.

5

I had been lying with my face away from my uncle's chair, so that in this sudden flash of awakening I saw only the door to the street, the more northerly window, and the wall and floor and ceiling toward the north of the room, all photographed with morbid vividness on my brain in a light brighter than the glow of the fungi or the rays from the street outside. It was not a strong or even a fairly strong light; certainly not nearly strong enough to read an average book by. But it cast a shadow of myself and the cot on the floor, and had a yellowish, penetrating force that hinted at things more potent than luminosity. This I perceived with unhealthy sharpness despite the fact that two of my other senses were violently assailed. For on my ears rang the reverberations of that shocking scream, while my nostrils revolted at the stench which filled the place. My mind, as alert as my senses, recognised the gravely unusual; and almost automatically I leaped up and turned about to grasp the destructive instruments which we had left trained on the mouldy spot before the fireplace. As I turned, I dreaded what I was to see; for the scream had been in my uncle's voice, and I knew not against what menace I should have to defend him and myself.

Yet after all, the sight was worse than I had dreaded. There are horrors beyond horrors, and this was one of those nuclei of all dreamable hideousness which the cosmos saves to blast an accursed and unhappy few. Out of the fungus-ridden earth steamed up a vaporous corpse-light, yellow and diseased, which bubbled and lapped to a gigantic height in vague outlines half-human and half-monstrous, through which I could see the chimney and fireplace beyond. It was all eyes – wolfish and mocking – and the rugose insect-like head dissolved at the top to a thin stream of mist which curled putridly about and finally vanished up the chimney. I say that I saw this thing, but it is only in conscious retrospection that I ever definitely traced its damnable approach to form. At the time it was to me only a seething, dimly phosphorescent cloud of fungous loathsomeness, enveloping and dissolving to an abhorrent plasticity the one object to which all my attention was focussed. That object was my uncle – the venerable Elihu Whipple – who with blackening and decaying features leered and gibbered at me, and reached out dripping claws to rend me in the fury which this horror had brought.

It was a sense of routine which kept me from going mad. I had drilled myself in preparation for the crucial moment, and blind training saved me. Recognising the bubbling evil as no substance reachable by matter or material chemistry, and therefore ignoring the flame-thrower which loomed on my left, I threw on the current of the Crookes tube apparatus, and focussed toward that scene of immortal blasphemousness the strongest ether radiations which man's art can arouse from the spaces and fluids of Nature. There was a bluish haze and a frenzied sputtering, and the yellowish phosphorescence grew dimmer to my eyes. But I saw the dimness was only that of contrast, and that the waves from the machine had no effect whatever.

Then, in the midst of that daemoniac spectacle, I saw a fresh horror which brought cries to my lips and sent me fumbling and staggering toward that unlocked door to the quiet street, careless of what abnormal terrors I loosed upon the world, or what thoughts or judgments of men I brought down upon my head. In that dim blend of blue and yellow the form of my uncle had commenced a nauseous liquefaction whose essence eludes all description, and in which there played across his vanishing face such changes of identity as only madness can conceive. He was at once a devil and a multitude, a charnel-house and a pageant. Lit by the mixed and uncertain beams, that gelatinous face assumed a dozen – a score – a hundred – aspects; grinning, as it sank to the ground on a body that melted like tallow, in the caricatured likeness of legions strange and yet not strange.

I saw the features of the Harris line, masculine and feminine, adult and infantile, and other features old and young, coarse and refined, familiar and unfamiliar. For a second there flashed a degraded counterfeit of a miniature of poor mad Rhoby Harris that I had seen in the School of Design Museum, and another time I thought I caught the raw-boned image of Mercy Dexter as I recalled her from a painting in Carrington Harris's house. It was frightful beyond conception; toward the last, when a curious blend of servant and baby visages flickered close to the fungous floor where a pool of greenish grease was spreading, it seemed as though the shifting features fought against themselves, and strove to form contours like those of my uncle's kindly face. I like to think that he existed at that moment, and that he tried to bid me farewell. It seems to me I hiccoughed a farewell from my own parched throat as I lurched out into the street, a thin stream of grease following me through the door to the rain-drenched sidewalk.

The rest is shadowy and monstrous. There was no one in the soaking street, and in all the world there was no one I dared tell. I walked aimlessly south past College Hill and the Athenaeum, down Hopkins Street, and over the bridge to the business section where tall buildings seemed to guard me as modern material things guard the world from ancient and unwholesome wonder. Then grey dawn unfolded wetly from the east, silhouetting the archaic hill and its venerable steeples, and beckoning me to the place where my terrible work was still unfinished. And in the end I went, wet, hatless, and dazed in the morning light, and entered that awful door in Benefit Street which I had left ajar, and which still swung cryptically in full sight of the early householders to whom I dared not speak.

The grease was gone, for the mouldy floor was porous. And in front of the fireplace was no vestige of the giant doubled-up form in nitre. I looked at the cot, the chairs, the instruments, my neglected hat, and the yellowed straw hat of my uncle. Dazedness was uppermost, and I could scarcely recall what was dream and what was reality. Then thought trickled back, and I knew that I had witnessed things more horrible than I had dreamed. Sitting down, I tried to conjecture as nearly as sanity would let me just what had happened, and how I might end the horror, if indeed it had been real. Matter it seemed not to be, nor ether, nor anything else conceivable by mortal mind. What, then, but some exotic *emanation*; some vampirish vapour such as Exeter rustics tell of as lurking over certain churchyards? This I felt was the clue, and again I looked at the floor before the fireplace where the mould and nitre had taken strange forms. In ten minutes my mind was made up, and taking my hat I set out for home, where I bathed, ate, and gave by telephone an order for a pickaxe, a spade, a military gas-mask, and six carboys of sulphuric acid, all to be delivered the next morning at the cellar door of the shunned house in Benefit Street. After that I tried to sleep; and failing, passed the hours in reading and in the composition of inane verses to counteract my mood.

At 11 a.m. the next day I commenced digging. It was sunny weather, and I was glad of that. I was still alone, for as much as I feared the unknown horror I sought, there was more fear in the thought of telling anybody. Later I told Harris only through sheer necessity, and because he had heard odd tales from old people which disposed him ever so little toward belief. As I turned up the stinking black earth in front of the fireplace, my spade causing a viscous yellow ichor to ooze from the white fungi which it severed, I trembled at the dubious thoughts of what I might uncover. Some secrets of inner earth are not good for mankind, and this seemed to me one of them.

My hand shook perceptibly, but still I delved, after a while standing in the large hole I had made. With the deepening of the hole, which was about six feet square, the evil smell increased; and I lost all doubt of my imminent contact with the hellish thing whose emanations had cursed the house for over a century and a half. I wondered what it would look like – what its form and substance would be, and how big it might have waxed through long ages of life-sucking. At length I climbed out of the hole and dispersed the heaped-up dirt, then arranging the great carboys of acid around and near two sides, so that when necessary I might empty them all down the aperture in quick succession. After that I dumped earth only along the other two sides; working more slowly and donning my gas-mask as the smell grew. I was nearly unnerved at my proximity to a nameless thing at the bottom of a pit.

Suddenly my spade struck something softer than earth. I shuddered, and made a motion as if to climb out of the hole, which was now as deep as my neck. Then courage returned, and I scraped away more dirt in the light of the electric torch I had provided. The surface I uncovered was fishy and glassy – a kind of semi-putrid congealed jelly with suggestions of translucency. I scraped further, and saw that it had form. There was a rift where a part of the substance was folded over. The exposed area was huge and roughly cylindrical; like a mammoth soft blue-white stovepipe doubled in two, its largest part some two feet in diameter. Still more I scraped, and then abruptly I leaped out of the hole and away from the filthy thing, frantically unstopping and tilting the heavy carboys, and precipitating their corrosive contents one after another down that charnel gulf and upon the unthinkable abnormality whose titan *elbow* I had seen.

The blinding maelstrom of greenish-yellow vapour which surged tempestuously up from that hole as the floods of acid descended, will never leave my memory. All along the hill people tell of the yellow day, when virulent and horrible fumes arose from the factory waste dumped in the Providence River, but I know how mistaken they are as to the source. They tell, too, of the hideous roar which at the same time came from some disordered water-pipe or gas main underground – but again I could correct them if I dared. It was unspeakably shocking, and I do not see how I lived through it. I did faint after emptying the fourth carboy, which I had to handle after the fumes had begun to penetrate my mask; but when I recovered I saw that the hole was emitting no fresh vapours.

The two remaining carboys I emptied down without particular result, and after a time I felt it safe to shovel the earth back into the pit. It was twilight before I was done, but fear had gone out of the place. The dampness was less foetid, and all the strange fungi had withered to a kind of harmless greyish powder which blew ash-like along the floor. One of earth's nethermost terrors had perished forever; and if there be a hell, it had received at last the daemon soul of an unhallowed thing. And as I patted down the last spadeful of mould, I shed the first of the many tears with which I have paid unaffected tribute to my beloved uncle's memory.

The next spring no more pale grass and strange weeds came up in the shunned house's terraced garden, and shortly afterward Carrington Harris rented the place. It is still spectral, but its strangeness fascinates me, and I shall find mixed with my relief a queer regret when it is torn down to make way for a tawdry shop or vulgar apartment building. The barren old trees in the yard have begun to bear small, sweet apples, and last year the birds nested in their gnarled boughs.

The Horror at Red Hook

> There are sacraments of evil as well as of good about us, and we live
> and move to my belief in an unknown world, a place where there
> are caves and shadows and dwellers in twilight. It is possible that
> man may sometimes return on the track of evolution, and it is my
> belief that an awful lore is not yet dead.
>
> *Arthur Machen*

I

Not many weeks ago, on a street corner in the village of Pascoag,
Rhode Island, a tall, heavily built, and wholesome-looking pedes-
trian furnished much speculation by a singular lapse of behaviour.
He had, it appears, been descending the hill by the road from
Chepachet; and encountering the compact section, had turned to
his left into the main thoroughfare where several modest business blocks convey a touch of the urban. At this point, without
visible provocation, he committed his astonishing lapse; staring
queerly for a second at the tallest of the buildings before him,
and then, with a series of terrified, hysterical shrieks, breaking
into a frantic run which ended in a stumble and fall at the next
crossing. Picked up and dusted off by ready hands, he was found
to be conscious, organically unhurt, and evidently cured of his sudden nervous attack. He muttered some shamefaced explanations
involving a strain he had undergone, and with downcast glance
turned back up the Chepachet road, trudging out of sight without
once looking behind him. It was a strange incident to befall so
large, robust, normal-featured, and capable-looking a man, and the
strangeness was not lessened by the remarks of a bystander who had
recognised him as the boarder of a well-known dairyman on the
outskirts of Chepachet.

He was, it developed, a New York police detective named Thomas
F. Malone, now on a long leave of absence under medical treatment

after some disproportionately arduous work on a gruesome local case which accident had made dramatic. There had been a collapse of several old brick buildings during a raid in which he had shared, and something about the wholesale loss of life, both of prisoners and of his companions, had peculiarly appalled him. As a result, he had acquired an acute and anomalous horror of any buildings even remotely suggesting the ones which had fallen in, so that in the end mental specialists forbade him the sight of such things for an indefinite period. A police surgeon with relatives in Chepachet had put forward that quaint hamlet of wooden colonial houses as an ideal spot for the psychological convalescence; and thither the sufferer had gone, promising never to venture among the brick-lined streets of larger villages till duly advised by the Woonsocket specialist with whom he was put in touch. This walk to Pascoag for magazines had been a mistake, and the patient had paid in fright, bruises, and humiliation for his disobedience.

So much the gossips of Chepachet and Pascoag knew; and so much, also, the most learned specialists believed. But Malone had at first told the specialists much more, ceasing only when he saw that utter incredulity was his portion. Thereafter he held his peace, protesting not at all when it was generally agreed that the collapse of certain squalid brick houses in the Red Hook section of Brooklyn, and the consequent death of many brave officers, had unseated his nervous equilibrium. He had worked too hard, all said, in trying to clean up those nests of disorder and violence; certain features were shocking enough, in all conscience, and the unexpected tragedy was the last straw. This was a simple explanation which everyone could understand, and because Malone was not a simple person he perceived that he had better let it suffice. To hint to unimaginative people of a horror beyond all human conception – a horror of houses and blocks and cities leprous and cancerous with evil dragged from elder worlds – would be merely to invite a padded cell instead of restful rustication, and Malone was a man of sense despite his mysticism. He had the Celt's far vision of weird and hidden things, but the logician's quick eye for the outwardly unconvincing; an amalgam which had led him far afield in the forty-two years of his life, and set him in strange places for a Dublin University man born in a Georgian villa near Phoenix Park.

And now, as he reviewed the things he had seen and felt and apprehended, Malone was content to keep unshared the secret of what could reduce a dauntless fighter to a quivering neurotic; what could make old brick slums and seas of dark, subtle faces a thing of nightmare and eldritch portent. It would not be the first time his sensations had been forced to bide uninterpreted – for was not his very act of plunging into the polyglot abyss of New York's underworld a freak beyond sensible explanation? What could he tell the prosaic of the antique witcheries and grotesque marvels discernible to sensitive eyes amidst the poison cauldron where all the varied dregs of unwholesome ages mix their venom and perpetuate their obscene terrors? He had seen the hellish green flame of secret wonder in this blatant, evasive welter of outward greed and inward blasphemy, and had smiled gently when all the New-Yorkers he knew scoffed at his experiment in police work. They had been very witty and cynical, deriding his fantastic pursuit of unknowable mysteries and assuring him that in these days New York held nothing but cheapness and vulgarity. One of them had wagered him a heavy sum that he could not – despite many poignant things to his credit in the *Dublin Review* – even write a truly interesting story of New York low life; and now, looking back, he perceived that cosmic irony had justified the prophet's words while secretly confuting their flippant meaning. The horror, as glimpsed at last, could not make a story – for like the book cited by Poe's German authority, '*es lässt sich nicht lesen*' – 'it does not permit itself to be read.'

2

To Malone the sense of latent mystery in existence was always present. In youth he had felt the hidden beauty and ecstasy of things, and had been a poet; but poverty and sorrow and exile had turned his gaze in darker directions, and he had thrilled at the imputations of evil in the world around. Daily life had for him come to be a phantasmagoria of macabre shadow-studies; now glittering and leering with concealed rottenness as in Beardsley's best manner, now hinting terrors behind the commonest shapes and objects as in the subtler and less obvious work of Gustave Doré. He would often regard it as merciful that most persons of high intelligence jeer at the inmost mysteries; for, he argued, if superior minds were ever placed in fullest contact with the secrets preserved by ancient and lowly cults, the resultant abnormalities would soon not only wreck the world, but threaten the very integrity of the universe. All this reflection was no doubt morbid, but keen logic and a deep sense of humour ably offset it. Malone was satisfied to let his notions remain as half-spied and forbidden visions to be lightly played with; and hysteria came only when duty flung him into a hell of revelation too sudden and insidious to escape.

He had for some time been detailed to the Butler Street station in Brooklyn when the Red Hook matter came to his notice. Red Hook is a maze of hybrid squalor near the ancient waterfront opposite Governor's Island, with dirty highways climbing the hill from the wharves to that higher ground where the decayed lengths of Clinton and Court Streets lead off toward the Borough Hall. Its houses are mostly of brick, dating from the first quarter to the middle of the nineteenth century, and some of the obscurer alleys and byways have that alluring antique flavour which conventional reading leads us to call 'Dickensian'. The population is a hopeless tangle and enigma, Syrian, Spanish, Italian, and negro elements impinging upon one another, and fragments of Scandinavian and American belts lying not far distant. It is a babel of sound and filth, and sends out strange cries to answer the lapping of oily waves at its grimy piers and the monstrous organ litanies of the harbour whistles. Here long ago a brighter picture dwelt, with clear-eyed mariners on the lower streets and homes of taste and substance where the larger houses line the hill. One can trace the relics of this former happiness in the trim shapes of the buildings, the occasional graceful churches, and the evidences of original art and background in bits of detail here and there – a worn flight of steps, a battered doorway, a wormy pair of decorative columns or pilasters, or a fragment of once green space with bent and rusted iron railing. The houses are generally in solid blocks, and now and then a many-windowed cupola arises to tell of days when the households of captains and ship-owners watched the sea.

From this tangle of material and spiritual putrescence the blasphemies of an hundred dialects assail the sky. Hordes of prowlers reel shouting and singing along the lanes and thoroughfares, occasional furtive hands suddenly extinguish lights and pull down curtains, and swarthy, sin-pitted faces disappear from windows when visitors pick their way through. Policemen despair of order or reform, and seek rather to erect barriers protecting the outside world from the contagion. The clang of the patrol is answered by a kind of spectral silence, and such prisoners as are taken are never communicative. Visible offences are as varied as the local dialects, and run the gamut from the smuggling of rum and prohibited aliens through diverse stages of lawlessness and obscure vice to murder and mutilation in their most abhorrent guises. That these visible affairs are not more frequent is not to the neighbourhood's credit, unless the power of concealment be an art demanding credit. More people enter Red Hook than leave it – or at least, than leave it by the landward side – and those who are not loquacious are the likeliest to leave.

Malone found in this state of things a faint stench of secrets more terrible than any of the sins denounced by citizens and bemoaned by priests and philanthropists. He was conscious, as one who united imagination with scientific knowledge, that modern people under lawless conditions tend uncannily to repeat the darkest instinctive patterns of primitive half-ape savagery in their daily life and ritual observances; and he had often viewed with an anthropologist's shudder the chanting, cursing processions of blear-eyed and pockmarked young men which wound their way along in the dark small hours of morning. One saw groups of these youths incessantly; sometimes in leering vigils on street corners, sometimes in doorways playing eerily on cheap instruments of music, sometimes in stupefied dozes or indecent dialogues around cafeteria tables near Borough Hall, and sometimes in whispering converse around dingy taxicabs drawn up at the high stoops of crumbling and closely shuttered old houses. They chilled and fascinated him more than he dared confess to his associates on the force, for he seemed to see in them some monstrous thread of secret continuity; some fiendish, cryptical, and ancient pattern utterly beyond and below the sordid mass of facts and habits and haunts listed with such conscientious technical care by the police. They must be, he felt inwardly, the heirs of some shocking and primordial tradition; the sharers of debased and broken scraps from cults and ceremonies older than mankind. Their coherence and definiteness suggested it, and it shewed in the singular suspicion of order which lurked beneath their squalid disorder. He had not read in vain such treatises as Miss Murray's *Witch-Cult in Western Europe*; and knew that up to recent years there had certainly survived among peasants and furtive folk a frightful and clandestine system of assemblies and orgies descended from dark religions antedating the Aryan world, and appearing in popular legends as Black Masses and Witches' Sabbaths. That these hellish vestiges of old Turanian-Asiatic magic and fertility-cults were even now wholly dead he could not for a moment suppose, and he frequently wondered how much older and how much blacker than the very worst of the muttered tales some of them might really be.

3

It was the case of Robert Suydam which took Malone to the heart of things in Red Hook. Suydam was a lettered recluse of ancient Dutch family, possessed originally of barely independent means, and inhabiting the spacious but ill-preserved mansion which his grandfather had built in Flatbush when that village was little more than a pleasant group of colonial cottages surrounding the steepled and ivy-clad Reformed Church with its iron-railed yard of Netherlandish gravestones. In his lonely house, set back from Martense Street amidst a yard of venerable trees, Suydam had read and brooded for some six decades except for a period a generation before, when he had sailed for the old world and remained there out of sight for eight years. He could afford no servants, and would admit but few visitors to his absolute solitude, eschewing close friendships and receiving his rare acquaintances in one of the three ground-floor rooms which he kept in order – a vast, high-ceiled library whose walls were solidly packed with tattered books of ponderous, archaic, and vaguely repellent aspect. The growth of the town and its final absorption in the Brooklyn district had meant nothing to Suydam, and he had come to mean less and less to the town. Elderly people still pointed him out on the streets, but to most of the recent population he was merely a queer, corpulent old fellow whose unkempt white hair, stubbly beard, shiny black clothes, and gold-headed cane earned him an amused glance and nothing more. Malone did not know him by sight till duty called him to the case, but had heard of him indirectly as a really profound authority on mediaeval superstition, and had once idly meant to look up an out-of-print pamphlet of his on the Kabbalah and the Faustus legend, which a friend had quoted from memory.

Suydam became a 'case' when his distant and only relatives sought court pronouncements on his sanity. Their action seemed sudden to the outside world, but was really undertaken only after prolonged observation and sorrowful debate. It was based on certain odd changes in his speech and habits; wild references to impending wonders, and unaccountable hauntings of disreputable Brooklyn neighbourhoods. He had been growing shabbier and shabbier with the years, and now prowled about like a veritable mendicant, seen occasionally by humiliated friends in subway stations, or loitering on the benches around Borough Hall in conversation with groups of swarthy, evil-looking strangers. When he spoke it was to babble of unlimited powers almost within his grasp, and to repeat with knowing leers such mystical words or names as 'Sephiroth', 'Ashmodai', and 'Samaël'. The court action revealed that he was using up his income and wasting his principal in the purchase of curious tomes imported from London and Paris, and in the maintenance of a squalid basement flat in the Red Hook district where he spent nearly every night, receiving odd delegations of mixed rowdies and foreigners, and apparently conducting some kind of ceremonial service behind the green blinds of secretive windows. Detectives assigned to follow him reported strange cries and chants and prancing of feet filtering out from these nocturnal rites, and shuddered at their peculiar ecstasy and abandon despite the commonness of weird orgies in that sodden section. When, however, the matter came to a hearing, Suydam managed to preserve his liberty. Before the judge his manner grew urbane and reasonable, and he freely admitted the queerness of demeanour and extravagant cast of language into which he had fallen through excessive devotion to study and research. He was, he said, engaged in the investigation of certain details of European tradition which required the closest contact with foreign groups and their songs and folk dances. The notion that any low secret society was preying upon him, as hinted by his relatives, was obviously absurd; and shewed how sadly limited was their understanding of him and his work. Triumphing with his calm explanations, he was suffered to depart unhindered; and the paid detectives of the Suydams, Corlears, and Van Brunts were withdrawn in resigned disgust.

It was here that an alliance of Federal inspectors and police, Malone with them, entered the case. The law had watched the Suydam action with interest, and had in many instances been called upon to aid the private detectives. In this work it developed that Suydam's new associates were among the blackest and most vicious criminals of Red Hook's devious lanes, and that at least a third of them were known and repeated offenders in the matter of thievery, disorder, and the importation of illegal immigrants. Indeed, it would not have been too much to say that the old scholar's particular circle coincided almost perfectly with the worst of the organised cliques which smuggled ashore certain nameless and unclassified Asian dregs wisely turned back by Ellis Island. In the teeming rookeries of Parker Place – since renamed – where Suydam had his basement flat, there had grown up a very unusual colony of unclassified slant-eyed folk who used the Arabic alphabet but were eloquently repudiated by the great mass of Syrians in and around Atlantic Avenue. They could all have been deported for lack of credentials, but legalism is slow-moving, and one does not disturb Red Hook unless publicity forces one to.

These creatures attended a tumbledown stone church, used Wednesdays as a dance-hall, which reared its Gothic buttresses near the vilest part of the waterfront. It was nominally Catholic, but priests throughout Brooklyn denied the place all standing and authenticity, and policemen agreed with them when they listened to the noises it emitted at night. Malone used to fancy he heard terrible cracked bass notes from a hidden organ far underground when the church stood empty and unlighted, whilst all observers dreaded the shrieking and drumming which accompanied the visible services. Suydam, when questioned, said he thought the ritual was some remnant of Nestorian Christianity tinctured with the Shamanism of Thibet. Most of the people, he conjectured, were of Mongoloid stock, originating somewhere in or near Kurdistan – and Malone could not help recalling that Kurdistan is the land of the Yezidis, last survivors of the Persian devil-worshippers. However this may have been, the stir of the Suydam investigation made it certain that these unauthorised newcomers were flooding Red Hook in increasing numbers, entering through some marine conspiracy unreached by revenue officers and harbour police, overrunning Parker Place and rapidly spreading up the hill, and welcomed with curious fraternalism by the other assorted denizens of the region. Their squat figures and characteristic squinting physiognomies, grotesquely combined with flashy American clothing, appeared more and more numerously among the loafers and nomad gangsters of the Borough Hall section, till at length it was deemed necessary to compute their numbers, ascertain their sources and occupations, and find if possible a way to round them up and deliver them to the proper immigration authorities. To this task Malone was assigned by agreement of Federal and city forces, and as he commenced his canvass of Red Hook he felt poised upon the brink of nameless terrors, with the shabby, unkempt figure of Robert Suydam as arch-fiend and adversary.

4

Police methods are varied and ingenious. Malone, through unostentatious rambles, carefully casual conversations, well-timed offers of hip-pocket liquor, and judicious dialogues with frightened prisoners, learned many isolated facts about the movement whose aspect had become so menacing. The newcomers were indeed Kurds, but of a dialect obscure and puzzling to exact philology. Such of them as worked lived mostly as dock-hands and unlicenced pedlars, though frequently serving in Greek restaurants and tending corner news stands. Most of them, however, had no visible means of support, and were obviously connected with underworld pursuits, of which smuggling and 'bootlegging' were the least indescribable. They had come in steamships, apparently tramp freighters, and had been unloaded by stealth on moonless nights in rowboats which stole under a certain wharf and followed a hidden canal to a secret subterranean pool beneath a house. This wharf, canal, and house Malone could not locate, for the memories of his informants were exceedingly confused, while their speech was to a great extent beyond even the ablest interpreters; nor could he gain any real data on the reasons for their systematic importation. They were reticent about the exact spot from which they had come, and were never sufficiently off guard to reveal the agencies which had sought them out and directed their course. Indeed, they developed something like acute fright when asked the reasons for their presence. Gangsters of other breeds were equally taciturn, and the most that could be gathered was that some god or great priesthood had promised them unheard-of powers and supernatural glories and rulerships in a strange land.

The attendance of both newcomers and old gangsters at Suydam's closely guarded nocturnal meetings was very regular, and the police soon learned that the erstwhile recluse had leased additional flats to accommodate such guests as knew his password; at last occupying three entire houses and permanently harbouring many of his queer companions. He spent but little time now at his Flatbush home, apparently going and coming only to obtain and return books; and his face and manner had attained an appalling pitch of wildness. Malone twice interviewed him, but was each time brusquely repulsed. He knew nothing, he said, of any mysterious plots or movements, and had no idea how the Kurds could have entered or what they wanted. His business was to study undisturbed the folklore of all the immigrants of the district; a business with which policemen had no legitimate concern. Malone mentioned his admiration for Suydam's old brochure on the Kabbalah and other myths, but the old man's softening was only momentary. He sensed an intrusion, and rebuffed his visitor in no uncertain way; till Malone withdrew disgusted, and turned to other channels of information.

What Malone would have unearthed could he have worked continuously on the case, we shall never know. As it was, a stupid conflict between city and Federal authority suspended the investigations for several months, during which the detective was busy with other assignments. But at no time did he lose interest, or fail to stand amazed at what began to happen to Robert Suydam. Just at the time when a wave of kidnappings and disappearances spread its excitement over New York, the unkempt scholar embarked upon a metamorphosis as startling as it was absurd. One day he was seen near Borough Hall with clean-shaved face, well-trimmed hair, and tastefully immaculate attire, and on every day thereafter some obscure improvement was noticed in him. He maintained

his new fastidiousness without interruption, added to it an unwonted sparkle of eye and crispness of speech, and began little
by little to shed the corpulence which had so long deformed him.
Now frequently taken for less than his age, he acquired an elasticity
of step and buoyancy of demeanour to match the new tradition,
and shewed a curious darkening of the hair which somehow did
not suggest dye. As the months passed, he commenced to dress
less and less conservatively, and finally astonished his new friends
by renovating and redecorating his Flatbush mansion, which he
threw open in a series of receptions, summoning all the acquaintances he could remember, and extending a special welcome to
the fully forgiven relatives who had so lately sought his restraint.
Some attended through curiosity, others through duty; but all
were suddenly charmed by the dawning grace and urbanity of the
former hermit. He had, he asserted, accomplished most of his
allotted work; and having just inherited some property from a
half-forgotten European friend, was about to spend his remaining
years in a brighter second youth which ease, care, and diet had
made possible to him. Less and less was he seen at Red Hook,
and more and more did he move in the society to which he was
born. Policemen noted a tendency of the gangsters to congregate
at the old stone church and dance-hall instead of at the basement
flat in Parker Place, though the latter and its recent annexes still
overflowed with noxious life.

Then two incidents occurred – wide enough apart, but both of
intense interest in the case as Malone envisaged it. One was a quiet
announcement in the *Eagle* of Robert Suydam's engagement to Miss
Cornelia Gerritsen of Bayside, a young woman of excellent position,
and distantly related to the elderly bridegroom-elect; whilst the
other was a raid on the dance-hall church by city police, after a
report that the face of a kidnapped child had been seen for a second
at one of the basement windows. Malone had participated in this
raid, and studied the place with much care when inside. Nothing was
found – in fact, the building was entirely deserted when visited –
but the sensitive Celt was vaguely disturbed by many things about
the interior. There were crudely painted panels he did not like –
panels which depicted sacred faces with peculiarly worldly and
sardonic expressions, and which occasionally took liberties that

even a layman's sense of decorum could scarcely countenance. Then, too, he did not relish the Greek inscription on the wall above the pulpit; an ancient incantation which he had once stumbled upon in Dublin college days, and which read, literally translated,

O friend and companion of night, thou who rejoicest in the baying of dogs and spilt blood, who wanderest in the midst of shades among the tombs, who longest for blood and bringest terror to mortals, Gorgo, Mormo, thousand-faced moon, look favourably on our sacrifices!

When he read this he shuddered, and thought vaguely of the cracked bass organ notes he fancied he had heard beneath the church on certain nights. He shuddered again at the rust around the rim of a metal basin which stood on the altar, and paused nervously when his nostrils seemed to detect a curious and ghastly stench from somewhere in the neighbourhood. That organ memory haunted him, and he explored the basement with particular assiduity before he left. The place was very hateful to him; yet after all, were the blasphemous panels and inscriptions more than mere crudities perpetrated by the ignorant?

By the time of Suydam's wedding the kidnapping epidemic had become a popular newspaper scandal. Most of the victims were young children of the lowest classes, but the increasing number of disappearances had worked up a sentiment of the strongest fury. Journals clamoured for action from the police, and once more the Butler Street station sent its men over Red Hook for clues, discoveries, and criminals. Malone was glad to be on the trail again, and took pride in a raid on one of Suydam's Parker Place houses. There, indeed, no stolen child was found, despite the tales of screams and the red sash picked up in the areaway; but the paintings and rough inscriptions on the peeling walls of most of the rooms, and the primitive chemical laboratory in the attic, all helped to convince the detective that he was on the track of something tremendous. The paintings were appalling – hideous monsters of every shape and size, and parodies on human outlines which cannot be described. The writing was in red, and varied from Arabic to Greek, Roman, and Hebrew letters. Malone could not read much of it, but what he did decipher was portentous and cabbalistic enough. One frequently repeated motto was in a sort of Hebraised Hellenistic Greek, and suggested the most terrible daemon-evocations of the Alexandrian decadence:

HEL • HELOYM • SOTHER • EMMANUEL • SABAOTH •
AGLA • TETRAGRAMMATON • AGYROS • OTHEOS •
ISCHYROS • ATHANATOS • IEHOVA • VA • ADONAI •
SADAY • HOMOUSION • MESSIAS • ESCHEREHEYE

Circles and pentagrams loomed on every hand, and told indubitably of the strange beliefs and aspirations of those who dwelt so squalidly here. In the cellar, however, the strangest thing was found – a pile of genuine gold ingots covered carelessly with a piece of burlap, and bearing upon their shining surfaces the same weird hieroglyphics which also adorned the walls. During the raid the police encountered only a passive resistance from the squinting Orientals that swarmed from every door. Finding nothing relevant, they had to leave all as it was; but the precinct captain wrote Suydam a note advising him to look closely to the character of his tenants and protégés in view of the growing public clamour.

5

Then came the June wedding and the great sensation. Flatbush was gay for the hour about high noon, and pennanted motors thronged the streets near the old Dutch church where an awning stretched from door to highway. No local event ever surpassed the Suydam-Gerritsen nuptials in tone and scale, and the party which escorted bride and groom to the Cunard Pier was, if not exactly the smartest, at least a solid page from the Social Register. At five o'clock adieux were waved, and the ponderous liner edged away from the long pier, slowly turned its nose seaward, discarded its tug, and headed for the widening water spaces that led to old world wonders. By night the outer harbour was cleared, and late passengers watched the stars twinkling above an unpolluted ocean.

Whether the tramp steamer or the scream was first to gain attention, no one can say. Probably they were simultaneous, but it is of no use to calculate. The scream came from the Suydam stateroom, and the sailor who broke down the door could perhaps have told frightful things if he had not forthwith gone completely mad – as it is, he shrieked more loudly than the first victims, and thereafter ran simpering about the vessel till caught and put in irons. The ship's doctor who entered the stateroom and turned on the lights a moment later did not go mad, but told nobody what he saw till afterward, when he corresponded with Malone in Chepachet. It was murder – strangulation – but one need not say that the claw-mark on Mrs Suydam's throat could not have come from her husband's or any other human hand, or that upon the white wall there flickered for an instant in hateful red a legend which, later copied from memory, seems to have been nothing less than the fearsome Chaldee letters of the word 'LILITH'. One need not mention these things because they vanished so quickly – as for Suydam, one could at least bar others from the room until one knew what to think oneself. The doctor has distinctly assured Malone that he did not see *IT*. The open porthole, just before he turned on the lights, was clouded for a second with a certain phosphorescence, and for a moment there seemed to echo in the night outside the suggestion of a faint and hellish tittering; but no real outline met the eye. As proof, the doctor points to his continued sanity.

Then the tramp steamer claimed all attention. A boat put off, and a horde of swart, insolent ruffians in officers' dress swarmed aboard the temporarily halted Cunarder. They wanted Suydam or his body – they had known of his trip, and for certain reasons were sure he would die. The captain's deck was almost a pandemonium; for at the instant, between the doctor's report from the stateroom and the demands of the men from the tramp, not even the wisest and gravest seaman could think what to do. Suddenly the leader of the visiting mariners, an Arab with a hatefully negroid mouth, pulled forth a dirty, crumpled paper and handed it to the captain. It was signed by Robert Suydam, and bore the following odd message.

> In case of sudden or unexplained accident or death on my part, please deliver me or my body unquestioningly into the hands of the bearer and his associates. Everything, for me, and perhaps for you, depends on absolute compliance. Explanations can come later – do not fail me now.
>
> ROBERT SUYDAM

Captain and doctor looked at each other, and the latter whispered something to the former. Finally they nodded rather helplessly and led the way to the Suydam stateroom. The doctor directed the captain's glance away as he unlocked the door and admitted the strange seamen, nor did he breathe easily till they filed out with their burden after an unaccountably long period of preparation. It was wrapped in bedding from the berths, and the doctor was glad that the outlines were not very revealing. Somehow the men got the thing over the side and away to their tramp steamer without uncovering it. The Cunarder started again, and the doctor and a ship's undertaker sought out the Suydam stateroom to perform what last services they could. Once more the physician was forced to reticence and even to mendacity, for a hellish thing had happened. When the undertaker asked him why he had drained off all of Mrs Suydam's blood, he neglected to affirm that he had not done so; nor did he point to the vacant bottle-spaces on the rack, or to the odour in the sink which shewed the hasty disposition of the bottles' original contents. The pockets of those men – if men they were – had bulged damnably when they left the ship. Two hours later, and the world knew by radio all that it ought to know of the horrible affair.

6

That same June evening, without having heard a word from the sea, Malone was desperately busy among the alleys of Red Hook. A sudden stir seemed to permeate the place, and as if apprised by 'grapevine telegraph' of something singular, the denizens clustered expectantly around the dance-hall church and the houses in Parker Place. Three children had just disappeared – blue-eyed Norwegians from the streets toward Gowanus – and there were rumours of a mob forming among the sturdy Vikings of that section. Malone had for weeks been urging his colleagues to attempt a general cleanup; and at last, moved by conditions more obvious to their common sense than the conjectures of a Dublin dreamer, they had agreed upon a final stroke. The unrest and menace of this evening had been the deciding factor, and just about midnight a raiding party recruited from three stations descended upon Parker Place and its environs. Doors were battered in, stragglers arrested, and candlelighted rooms forced to disgorge unbelievable throngs of mixed foreigners in figured robes, mitres, and other inexplicable devices. Much was lost in the mêlée, for objects were thrown hastily down unexpected shafts, and betraying odours deadened by the sudden kindling of pungent incense. But spattered blood was everywhere, and Malone shuddered whenever he saw a brazier or altar from which the smoke was still rising.

He wanted to be in several places at once, and decided on Suydam's basement flat only after a messenger had reported the complete emptiness of the dilapidated dance-hall church. The flat, he thought, must hold some clue to a cult of which the occult scholar had so obviously become the centre and leader; and it was with real expectancy that he ransacked the musty rooms, noted their vaguely charnel odour, and examined the curious books, instruments, gold ingots, and glass-stoppered bottles scattered carelessly here and there. Once a lean, black-and-white cat edged between his feet and tripped him, over-turning at the same time a beaker half full of a red liquid. The shock was severe, and to this day Malone is not certain of what he saw; but in dreams he still pictures that cat as it scuttled away with certain monstrous alterations and peculiarities. Then came the locked cellar door, and the search for something to break it down. A heavy stool stood near, and its tough seat was more than enough for the antique panels. A crack formed and enlarged, and the whole door gave way – but from the *other* side; whence poured a howling tumult of ice-cold wind with all the stenches of the bottomless pit, and whence reached a sucking force not of earth or heaven, which, coiling sentiently about the paralysed detective, dragged him through the aperture and down unmeasured spaces filled with whispers and wails, and gusts of mocking laughter.

Of course it was a dream. All the specialists have told him so, and he has nothing to prove the contrary. Indeed, he would rather have it thus; for then the sight of old brick slums and dark foreign faces would not eat so deeply into his soul. But at the time it was all horribly real, and nothing can ever efface the memory of those nighted crypts, those titan arcades, and those half-formed shapes of hell that strode gigantically in silence holding half-eaten things whose still surviving portions screamed for mercy or laughed with madness. Odours of incense and corruption joined in sickening concert, and the black air was alive with the cloudy, semi-visible bulk of shapeless elemental things with eyes. Somewhere dark sticky water was lapping at onyx piers, and once the shivery tinkle of raucous little bells pealed out to greet the insane titter of a naked phosphorescent thing which swam into sight, scrambled ashore, and climbed up to squat leeringly on a carved golden pedestal in the background.

Avenues of limitless night seemed to radiate in every direction, till one might fancy that here lay the root of a contagion destined to sicken and swallow cities, and engulf nations in the foetor of hybrid pestilence. Here cosmic sin had entered, and festered by unhallowed rites had commenced the grinning march of death that was to rot us all to fungous abnormalities too hideous for the grave's holding. Satan here held his Babylonish court, and in the blood of stainless childhood the leprous limbs of phosphorescent Lilith were laved. Incubi and succubae howled praise to Hecate, and headless moon-calves bleated to the Magna Mater. Goats leaped to the sound of thin accursed flutes, and aegipans chased endlessly after misshapen fauns over rocks twisted like swollen toads. Moloch and Ashtaroth were not absent; for in this quintessence of all damnation the bounds of consciousness were let down, and man's fancy lay open to vistas of every realm of horror and every forbidden dimension that evil had power to mould. The world and Nature were helpless against such assaults from unsealed wells of night, nor could any sign or prayer check the Walpurgis-riot of horror which had come when a sage with the hateful key had stumbled on a horde with the locked and brimming coffer of transmitted daemon-lore.

Suddenly a ray of physical light shot through these phantasms, and Malone heard the sound of oars amidst the blasphemies of things that should be dead. A boat with a lantern in its prow darted into sight, made fast to an iron ring in the slimy stone pier, and vomited forth several dark men bearing a long burden swathed in bedding. They took it to the naked phosphorescent thing on the carved golden pedestal, and the thing tittered and pawed at the bedding. Then they unswathed it, and propped upright before the pedestal the gangrenous corpse of a corpulent old man with stubbly beard and unkempt white hair. The phosphorescent thing tittered again, and the men produced bottles from their pockets and anointed its feet with red, whilst they afterward gave the bottles to the thing to drink from.

All at once, from an arcaded avenue leading endlessly away, there came the daemoniac rattle and wheeze of a blasphemous organ, choking and rumbling out the mockeries of hell in a cracked, sardonic bass. In an instant every moving entity was electrified; and forming at once into a ceremonial procession, the nightmare horde slithered away in quest of the sound – goat, satyr, and aegipan, incubus, succuba, and lemur, twisted toad and shapeless elemental, dog-faced howler and silent strutter in darkness – all led by the abominable naked phosphorescent thing that had squatted on the carved golden throne, and that now strode insolently bearing in its arms the glassy-eyed corpse of the corpulent old man. The strange dark men danced in the rear, and the whole column skipped and leaped with Dionysiac fury. Malone staggered after them a few steps, delirious and hazy, and doubtful of his place in this or in any world. Then he turned, faltered, and sank down on the cold damp stone, gasping and shivering as the daemon organ croaked on, and the howling and drumming and tinkling of the mad procession grew fainter and fainter.

Vaguely he was conscious of chanted horrors and shocking croakings afar off. Now and then a wail or whine of ceremonial devotion would float to him through the black arcade, whilst eventually there rose the dreadful Greek incantation whose text he had read above the pulpit of that dance-hall church.

O friend and companion of night, thou who rejoicest in the baying of dogs [*here a hideous howl burst forth*] and spilt blood [*here nameless sounds vied with morbid shriekings*], who wanderest in the midst of shades among the tombs [*here a whistling sigh occurred*], who longest for blood and bringest terror to mortals [*short, sharp cries from myriad throats*], Gorgo [*repeated as response*], Mormo [*repeated with ecstasy*], thousand-faced moon [*sighs and flute notes*], look favourably on our sacrifices!

As the chant closed, a general shout went up, and hissing sounds nearly drowned the croaking of the cracked bass organ. Then a gasp as from many throats, and a babel of barked and bleated words – 'Lilith, Great Lilith, behold the Bridegroom!' More cries, a clamour of rioting, and the sharp, clicking footfalls of a running figure. The footfalls approached, and Malone raised himself to his elbow to look.

The luminosity of the crypt, lately diminished, had now slightly increased; and in that devil-light there appeared the fleeing form of that which should not flee or feel or breathe – the glassy-eyed, gangrenous corpse of the corpulent old man, now needing no support, but animated by some infernal sorcery of the rite just closed. After it raced the naked, tittering, phosphorescent thing that belonged on the carven pedestal, and still farther behind panted the dark men, and all the dread crew of sentient loathsomenesses. The corpse was gaining on its pursuers, and seemed bent on a definite object, straining with every rotting muscle toward the carved golden pedestal, whose necromantic importance was evidently so great. Another moment and it had reached its goal, whilst the trailing throng laboured on with more frantic speed. But they were too late, for in one final spurt of strength which ripped tendon from tendon and sent its noisome bulk floundering to the floor in a state of jellyish dissolution, the staring corpse which had been Robert Suydam achieved its object and its triumph. The push had been tremendous, but the force had held out; and as the pusher collapsed to a muddy blotch of corruption the pedestal he had pushed tottered, tipped, and finally careened from its onyx base into the thick waters below, sending up a parting gleam of carven gold as it sank heavily to undreamable gulfs of lower Tartarus. In that instant, too, the whole scene of horror faded to nothingness before Malone's eyes; and he fainted amidst a thunderous crash which seemed to blot out all the evil universe.

7

Malone's dream, experienced in full before he knew of Suydam's death and transfer at sea, was curiously supplemented by some odd realities of the case; though that is no reason why anyone should believe it. The three old houses in Parker Place, doubtless long rotten with decay in its most insidious form, collapsed without visible cause while half the raiders and most of the prisoners were inside; and of both the greater number were instantly killed. Only in the basements and cellars was there much saving of life, and Malone was lucky to have been deep below the house of Robert Suydam. For he really was there, as no one is disposed to deny. They found him unconscious by the edge of a night-black pool, with a grotesquely horrible jumble of decay and bone, identifiable through dental work as the body of Suydam, a few feet away. The case was plain, for it was hither that the smugglers' underground canal led; and the men who took Suydam from the ship had brought him home. They themselves were never found, or at least never identified; and the ship's doctor is not yet satisfied with the simple certitudes of the police.

Suydam was evidently a leader in extensive man-smuggling operations, for the canal to his house was but one of several subterranean channels and tunnels in the neighbourhood. There was a tunnel from this house to a crypt beneath the dance-hall church; a crypt accessible from the church only through a narrow secret passage in the north wall, and in whose chambers some singular and terrible things were discovered. The croaking organ was there, as well as a vast arched chapel with wooden benches and a strangely figured altar. The walls were lined with small cells, in seventeen of which – hideous to relate – solitary prisoners in a state of complete idiocy were found chained, including four mothers with infants of disturbingly strange appearance. These infants died soon after exposure to the light; a circumstance which the doctors thought rather merciful. Nobody but Malone, among those who inspected them, remembered the sombre question of old Delrio: *'An sint unquam daemones incubi et succubae, et an ex tali congressu proles nasci queat?'* *

Before the canals were filled up they were thoroughly dredged, and yielded forth a sensational array of sawed and split bones of all sizes. The kidnapping epidemic, very clearly, had been traced home, though only two of the surviving prisoners could by any legal thread be connected with it. These men are now in prison, since they failed of conviction as accessories in the actual murders. The carved golden pedestal or throne so often mentioned by Malone as of primary occult importance was never brought to light, though at one place under the Suydam house the canal was observed to sink into a well too deep for dredging. It was choked up at the mouth and cemented over when the cellars of the new houses were made, but Malone often speculates on what lies beneath. The police, satisfied that they had shattered a dangerous gang of maniacs and man-smugglers, turned over to the Federal authorities the unconvicted Kurds, who before

---

* Whether there can ever exist daemons who are incubi and succubae, and whether offspring can be born from such a union.

their deportation were conclusively found to belong to the Yezidi clan of devil-worshippers. The tramp ship and its crew remain an elusive mystery, though cynical detectives are once more ready to combat its smuggling and rum-running ventures. Malone thinks these detectives shew a sadly limited perspective in their lack of wonder at the myriad unexplainable details, and the suggestive obscurity of the whole case; though he is just as critical of the newspapers, which saw only a morbid sensation and gloated over a minor sadist cult which they might have proclaimed a horror from the universe's very heart. But he is content to rest silent in Chepachet, calming his nervous system and praying that time may gradually transfer his terrible experience from the realm of present reality to that of picturesque and semi-mythical remoteness.

Robert Suydam sleeps beside his bride in Greenwood Cemetery. No funeral was held over the strangely released bones, and relatives are grateful for the swift oblivion which overtook the case as a whole. The scholar's connexion with the Red Hook horrors, indeed, was never emblazoned by legal proof, since his death forestalled the inquiry he would otherwise have faced. His own end is not much mentioned, and the Suydams hope that posterity may recall him only as a gentle recluse who dabbled in harmless magic and folklore.

As for Red Hook – it is always the same. Suydam came and went; a terror gathered and faded; but the evil spirit of darkness and squalor broods on amongst the mongrels in the old brick houses, and prowling bands still parade on unknown errands past windows where lights and twisted faces unaccountably appear and disappear. Age-old horror is a hydra with a thousand heads, and the cults of darkness are rooted in blasphemies deeper than the well of Democritus. The soul of the beast is omnipresent and triumphant, and Red Hook's legions of blear-eyed, pockmarked youths still chant and curse and howl as they file from abyss to abyss, none knows whence or whither, pushed on by blind laws of biology which they may never understand. As of old, more people enter Red Hook than leave it on the landward side, and there are already rumours of new canals running underground to certain centres of traffic in liquor and less mentionable things.

The dance-hall church is now mostly a dance-hall, and queer faces have appeared at night at the windows. Lately a policeman expressed the belief that the filled-up crypt has been dug out again, and for no simply explainable purpose. Who are we to combat poisons older than history and mankind? Apes danced in Asia to those horrors, and the cancer lurks secure and spreading where furtiveness hides in rows of decaying brick.

Malone does not shudder without cause – for only the other day an officer overheard a swarthy squinting hag teaching a small child some whispered patois in the shadow of an areaway. He listened, and thought it very strange when he heard her repeat over and over again,

'O friend and companion of night, thou who rejoicest in the baying of dogs and spilt blood, who wanderest in the midst of shades among the tombs, who longest for blood and bringest terror to mortals, Gorgo, Mormo, thousand-faced moon, look favourably on our sacrifices!'

Pickman's Model

You needn't think I'm crazy, Eliot – plenty of others have queerer prejudices than this. Why don't you laugh at Oliver's grandfather, who won't ride in a motor? If I don't like that damned subway, it's my own business; and we got here more quickly anyhow in the taxi. We'd have had to walk up the hill from Park Street if we'd taken the car.

I know I'm more nervous than I was when you saw me last year, but you don't need to hold a clinic over it. There's plenty of reason, God knows, and I fancy I'm lucky to be sane at all. Why the third degree? You didn't use to be so inquisitive.

Well, if you must hear it, I don't know why you shouldn't. Maybe you ought to, anyhow, for you kept writing me like a grieved parent when you heard I'd begun to cut the Art Club and keep away from Pickman. Now that he's disappeared I go around to the club once in a while, but my nerves aren't what they were.

No, I don't know what's become of Pickman, and I don't like to guess. You might have surmised I had some inside information when I dropped him – and that's why I don't want to think where he's gone. Let the police find what they can – it won't be much, judging from the fact that they don't know yet of the old North End place he hired under the name of Peters. I'm not sure that I could find it again myself – not that I'd ever try, even in broad daylight! Yes, I do know, or am afraid I know, why he maintained it. I'm coming to that. And I think you'll understand before I'm through why I don't tell the police. They would ask me to guide them, but I couldn't go back there even if I knew the way. There was something there – and now I can't use the subway or (and you may as well have your laugh at this, too) go down into cellars any more.

I should think you'd have known I didn't drop Pickman for the same silly reasons that fussy old women like Dr Reid or Joe Minot or

Bosworth did. Morbid art doesn't shock me, and when a man has the genius Pickman had I feel it an honour to know him, no matter what direction his work takes. Boston never had a greater painter than Richard Upton Pickman. I said it at first and I say it still, and I never swerved an inch, either, when he shewed that 'Ghoul Feeding'. That, you remember, was when Minot cut him.

You know, it takes profound art and profound insight into Nature to turn out stuff like Pickman's. Any magazine-cover hack can splash paint around wildly and call it a nightmare or a Witches' Sabbath or a portrait of the devil, but only a great painter can make such a thing really scare or ring true. That's because only a real artist knows the actual anatomy of the terrible or the physiology of fear – the exact sort of lines and proportions that connect up with latent instincts or hereditary memories of fright, and the proper colour contrasts and lighting effects to stir the dormant sense of strangeness. I don't have to tell you why a Fuseli really brings a shiver while a cheap ghost-story frontispiece merely makes us laugh. There's something those fellows catch – beyond life – that they're able to make us catch for a second. Doré had it. Sime has it. Angarola of Chicago has it. And Pickman had it as no man ever had it before or – I hope to heaven – ever will again.

Don't ask me what it is they see. You know, in ordinary art, there's all the difference in the world between the vital, breathing things drawn from Nature or models and the artificial truck that commercial small fry reel off in a bare studio by rule. Well, I should say that the really weird artist has a kind of vision which makes models, or summons up what amounts to actual scenes from the spectral world he lives in. Anyhow, he manages to turn out results that differ from the pretender's mince-pie dreams in just about the same way that the life painter's results differ from the concoctions of a correspondence-school cartoonist. If I had ever seen what Pickman saw – but no! Here, let's have a drink before we get any deeper. Gad, I wouldn't be alive if I'd ever seen what that man – if he was a man – saw!

You recall that Pickman's forte was faces. I don't believe anybody since Goya could put so much of sheer hell into a set of features or a twist of expression. And before Goya you have to go back to the mediaeval chaps who did the gargoyles and chimaeras on Notre Dame and Mont Saint-Michel. They believed all sorts of things – and maybe they saw all sorts of things, too, for the Middle Ages had some curious phases. I remember your asking Pickman yourself once, the year before you went away, wherever in thunder he got such ideas and visions. Wasn't that a nasty laugh he gave you? It was partly because of that laugh that Reid dropped him. Reid, you know, had just taken up comparative pathology, and was full of pompous 'inside stuff' about the biological or evolutionary significance of this or that mental or physical symptom. He said Pickman repelled him more and more every day, and almost frightened him toward the last – that the fellow's features and expression were slowly developing in a way he didn't like; in a way that wasn't human. He had a lot of talk about diet, and said Pickman must be abnormal and eccentric to the last degree. I suppose you told Reid, if you and he had any correspondence over it, that he'd let Pickman's paintings get on his nerves or harrow up his imagination. I know I told him that myself – then.

But keep in mind that I didn't drop Pickman for anything like this. On the contrary, my admiration for him kept growing; for that 'Ghoul Feeding' was a tremendous achievement. As you know, the club wouldn't exhibit it, and the Museum of Fine Arts wouldn't accept it as a gift; and I can add that nobody would buy it, so Pickman had it right in his house till he went. Now his father has it in Salem – you know Pickman comes of old Salem stock, and had a witch ancestor hanged in 1692.

I got into the habit of calling on Pickman quite often, especially after I began making notes for a monograph on weird art. Probably it was his work which put the idea into my head, and anyhow, I found him a mine of data and suggestions when I came to develop it. He shewed me all the paintings and drawings he had about; including some pen-and-ink sketches that would, I verily believe, have got him kicked out of the club if many of the members had seen them. Before long I was pretty nearly a devotee, and would listen for hours like a schoolboy to art theories and philosophic speculations wild enough to qualify him for the Danvers asylum. My hero-worship, coupled with the fact that people generally were commencing to have less and less to do with him, made him get very confidential with me; and one evening he hinted that if I were fairly close-mouthed and none too squeamish, he might shew me something rather unusual – something a bit stronger than anything he had in the house.

'You know,' he said, 'there are things that won't do for Newbury Street – things that are out of place here, and that can't be conceived here, anyhow. It's my business to catch the overtones of the soul, and you won't find those in a parvenu set of artificial streets on made land. Back Bay isn't Boston – it isn't anything yet, because it's had no time to pick up memories and attract local spirits. If there are any ghosts here, they're the tame ghosts of a salt marsh and a shallow cove; and I want human ghosts – the ghosts of beings highly organised enough to have looked on hell and known the meaning of what they saw.

'The place for an artist to live is the North End. If any aesthete were sincere, he'd put up with the slums for the sake of the massed traditions. God, man! Don't you realise that places like that weren't merely *made*, but actually *grew*? Generation after generation lived and felt and died there, and in days when people weren't afraid to live and feel and die. Don't you know there was a mill on Copp's Hill in 1632, and that half the present streets were laid out by 1650? I can shew you houses that have stood two centuries and a half and more; houses that have witnessed what would make a modern house crumble into powder. What do moderns know of life and the forces behind it? You call the Salem witchcraft a delusion, but I'll wager my four-times-great-grandmother could have told you things. They hanged her on Gallows Hill, with Cotton Mather looking sanctimoniously on. Mather, damn him, was afraid somebody might succeed in kicking free of this accursed cage of monotony – I wish someone had laid a spell on him or sucked his blood in the night!

'I can shew you a house he lived in, and I can shew you another one he was afraid to enter in spite of all his fine bold talk. He knew things he didn't dare put into that stupid *Magnalia* or that puerile *Wonders of the Invisible World*. Look here, do you know the whole North End once had a set of tunnels that kept certain people in touch with each other's houses, and the burying-ground, and the sea? Let them prosecute and persecute above ground – things went on every day that they couldn't reach, and voices laughed at night that they couldn't place!

'Why, man, out of ten surviving houses built before 1700 and not moved since I'll wager that in eight I can shew you something queer in the cellar. There's hardly a month that you don't read of workmen finding bricked-up arches and wells leading nowhere in this or that old place as it comes down – you could see one near Henchman Street from the elevated last year. There were witches and what their spells summoned; pirates and what they brought in from the sea; smugglers; privateers – and I tell you, people knew how to live, and how to enlarge the bounds of life, in the old times! This wasn't the only world a bold and wise man could know – faugh! And to think of today in contrast, with such pale-pink brains that even a club of supposed artists gets shudders and convulsions if a picture goes beyond the feelings of a Beacon Street tea-table!

'The only saving grace of the present is that it's too damned stupid to question the past very closely. What do maps and records and guide-books really tell of the North End? Bah! At a guess I'll guarantee to lead you to thirty or forty alleys and networks of alleys north of Prince Street that aren't suspected by ten living beings outside of the foreigners that swarm them. And what do those Dagoes know of their meaning? No, Thurber, these ancient places are dreaming gorgeously and overflowing with wonder and terror and escapes from the commonplace, and yet there's not a living soul to understand or profit by them. Or rather, there's only one living soul – for I haven't been digging around in the past for nothing!

'See here, you're interested in this sort of thing. What if I told you that I've got another studio up there, where I can catch the night-spirit of antique horror and paint things that I couldn't even think of in Newbury Street? Naturally I don't tell those cursed old maids at the club – with Reid, damn him, whispering even as it is that I'm a sort of monster bound down the toboggan of reverse evolution. Yes, Thurber, I decided long ago that one must paint terror as well as beauty from life, so I did some exploring in places where I had reason to know terror lives.

'I've got a place that I don't believe three living Nordic men besides myself have ever seen. It isn't so very far from the elevated as distance goes, but it's centuries away as the soul goes. I took it because of the queer old brick well in the cellar – one of the sort I told you about. The shack's almost tumbling down, so that nobody else would live there, and I'd hate to tell you how little I pay for it. The windows are boarded up, but I like that all the better, since I don't want daylight for what I do. I paint in the cellar, where the inspiration is thickest, but I've other rooms furnished on the ground floor. A Sicilian owns it, and I've hired it under the name of Peters.

'Now if you're game, I'll take you there tonight. I think you'd enjoy the pictures, for as I said, I've let myself go a bit there. It's no vast tour – I sometimes do it on foot, for I don't want to attract attention with a taxi in such a place. We can take the shuttle at the South Station for Battery Street, and after that the walk isn't much.'

Well, Eliot, there wasn't much for me to do after that harangue but to keep myself from running instead of walking for the first vacant cab we could sight. We changed to the elevated at the South Station, and at about twelve o'clock had climbed down the steps at Battery Street and struck along the old waterfront past Constitution Wharf. I didn't keep track of the cross streets, and can't tell you yet which it was we turned up, but I know it wasn't Greenough Lane.

When we did turn, it was to climb through the deserted length of the oldest and dirtiest alley I ever saw in my life, with crumbling-looking gables, broken small-paned windows, and archaic chimneys that stood out half-disintegrated against the moonlit sky. I don't believe there were three houses in sight that hadn't been standing in Cotton Mather's time – certainly I glimpsed at least two with an overhang, and once I thought I saw a peaked roof-line of the almost forgotten pre-gambrel type, though antiquarians tell us there are none left in Boston.

From that alley, which had a dim light, we turned to the left into an equally silent and still narrower alley with no light at all; and in a minute made what I think was an obtuse-angled bend toward the right in the dark. Not long after this Pickman produced a flash-light and revealed an antediluvian ten-panelled door that looked damnably worm-eaten. Unlocking it, he ushered me into a barren hallway with what was once splendid dark-oak panelling – simple, of course, but thrillingly suggestive of the times of Andros and Phipps and the Witchcraft. Then he took me through a door on the left, lighted an oil lamp, and told me to make myself at home.

Now, Eliot, I'm what the man in the street would call fairly 'hard-boiled', but I'll confess that what I saw on the walls of that room gave me a bad turn. They were his pictures, you know – the ones he couldn't paint or even shew in Newbury Street – and he was right when he said he had 'let himself go'. Here – have another drink – I need one anyhow!

There's no use in my trying to tell you what they were like, because the awful, the blasphemous horror, and the unbelievable loathsomeness and moral foetor came from simple touches quite beyond the power of words to classify. There was none of the exotic technique you see in Sidney Sime, none of the trans-Saturnian landscapes and lunar fungi that Clark Ashton Smith uses to freeze the blood. The backgrounds were mostly old churchyards, deep woods, cliffs by the sea, brick tunnels, ancient panelled rooms, or simple vaults of masonry. Copp's Hill Burying Ground, which could not be many blocks away from this very house, was a favourite scene.

The madness and monstrosity lay in the figures in the foreground – for Pickman's morbid art was preeminently one of daemoniac portraiture. These figures were seldom completely human, but often approached humanity in varying degree. Most of the bodies, while roughly bipedal, had a forward slumping, and a vaguely canine cast. The texture of the majority was a kind of unpleasant rubberiness. Ugh! I can see them now! Their occupations – well, don't ask me to be too precise. They were usually feeding – I won't say on what. They were sometimes shewn in groups in cemeteries or underground passages, and often appeared to be in battle over their prey – or rather, their treasure-trove. And what damnable expressiveness Pickman sometimes gave the sightless faces of this charnel booty! Occasionally the things were shewn leaping through open windows at night, or squatting on the chests of sleepers, worrying at their throats. One canvas shewed a ring of them baying about a hanged witch on Gallows Hill, whose dead face held a close kinship to theirs.

But don't get the idea that it was all this hideous business of theme and setting which struck me faint. I'm not a three-year-old kid, and I'd seen much like this before. It was the *faces*, Eliot, those accursed *faces*, that leered and slavered out of the canvas with the very breath of life! By God, man, I verily believe they *were* alive! That nauseous wizard had waked the fires of hell in pigment, and his brush had been a nightmare-spawning wand. Give me that decanter, Eliot!

There was one thing called 'The Lesson' – heaven pity me, that I ever saw it! Listen – can you fancy a squatting circle of nameless dog-like things in a churchyard teaching a small child how to feed like themselves? The price of a changeling, I suppose – you know the old myth about how the weird people leave their spawn in cradles in exchange for the human babes they steal. Pickman was shewing what happens to those stolen babes – how they grow up – and then I began to see a hideous relationship in the faces of the human and non-human figures. He was, in all his gradations of morbidity between the frankly non-human and the degradedly human, establishing a sardonic linkage and evolution. The dog-things were developed from mortals!

And no sooner had I wondered what he made of their own young as left with mankind in the form of changelings, than my eye caught a picture embodying that very thought. It was that of an ancient Puritan interior – a heavily beamed room with lattice windows, a settle, and clumsy seventeenth-century furniture, with the family sitting about while the father read from the Scriptures. Every face but one shewed nobility and reverence, but that one reflected the mockery of the pit. It was that of a young man in years, and no doubt belonged to a supposed son of that pious father, but in essence it was the kin of the unclean things. It was their changeling – and in a spirit of supreme irony Pickman had given the features a very perceptible resemblance to his own.

By this time Pickman had lighted a lamp in an adjoining room and was politely holding open the door for me; asking me if I would care to see his 'modern studies'. I hadn't been able to give him much of my opinions – I was too speechless with fright and loathing – but I think he fully understood and felt highly complimented. And now I want to assure you again, Eliot, that I'm no mollycoddle to scream at anything which shews a bit of departure from the usual. I'm middle-aged and decently sophisticated, and I guess you saw enough of me in France to know I'm not easily knocked out. Remember, too, that I'd just about recovered my wind and gotten used to those frightful pictures which turned colonial New England into a kind of annex of hell. Well, in spite of all this, that next room forced a real scream out of me, and I had to clutch at the doorway to keep from keeling over. The other chamber had shewn a pack of ghouls and witches over-running the world of our forefathers, but this one brought the horror right into our own daily life!

Gad, how that man could paint! There was a study called 'Subway Accident', in which a flock of the vile things were clambering up from some unknown catacomb through a crack in the floor of the Boylston Street subway and attacking a crowd of people on the platform. Another shewed a dance on Copp's Hill among the tombs with the background of today. Then there were any number of cellar views, with monsters creeping in through holes and rifts in the masonry and grinning as they squatted behind barrels or furnaces and waited for their first victim to descend the stairs.

One disgusting canvas seemed to depict a vast cross-section of Beacon Hill, with ant-like armies of the mephitic monsters squeezing themselves through burrows that honeycombed the ground. Dances in the modern cemeteries were freely pictured, and another conception somehow shocked me more than all the rest – a scene in an unknown vault, where scores of the beasts crowded about one who held a well-known Boston guide-book and was evidently reading aloud. All were pointing to a certain passage, and every face seemed so distorted with epileptic and reverberant laughter that I almost thought I heard the fiendish echoes. The title of the picture was, 'Holmes, Lowell, and Longfellow Lie Buried in Mount Auburn'.

As I gradually steadied myself and got readjusted to this second room of deviltry and morbidity, I began to analyse some of the points in my sickening loathing. In the first place, I said to myself, these things repelled because of the utter inhumanity and callous cruelty they shewed in Pickman. The fellow must be a relentless enemy of all mankind to take such glee in the torture of brain and flesh and the degradation of the mortal tenement. In the second place, they terrified because of their very greatness. Their art was the art that convinced – when we saw the pictures we saw the daemons themselves and were afraid of them. And the queer part was, that Pickman got none of his power from the use of selectiveness or bizarrerie. Nothing was blurred, distorted, or conventionalised; outlines were sharp and life-like, and details were almost painfully defined. And the faces!

It was not any mere artist's interpretation that we saw; it was pandemonium itself, crystal clear in stark objectivity. That was it, by heaven! The man was not a *fantaisiste* or romanticist at all – he did not even try to give us the churning, prismatic ephemera of dreams, but coldly and sardonically reflected some stable, mechanistic, and well-established horror-world which he saw fully, brilliantly, squarely, and unfalteringly. God knows what that world can have been, or where he ever glimpsed the blasphemous shapes that loped and trotted and crawled through it; but whatever the baffling source of his images, one thing was plain. Pickman was in every sense – in conception and in execution – a thorough, painstaking, and almost scientific *realist*.

My host was now leading the way down cellar to his actual studio, and I braced myself for some hellish effects among the unfinished canvases. As we reached the bottom of the damp stairs he turned his flashlight to a corner of the large open space at hand, revealing the circular brick curb of what was evidently a great well in the earthen floor. We walked nearer, and I saw that it must be five feet across, with walls a good foot thick and some six inches above the ground level – solid work of the seventeenth century, or I was much mistaken. That, Pickman said, was the kind of thing he had been talking about – an aperture of the network of tunnels that used to undermine the hill. I noticed idly that it did not seem to be bricked up, and that a heavy disc of wood formed the apparent cover. Thinking of the things this well must have been connected with if Pickman's wild hints had not been mere rhetoric, I shivered slightly; then turned to follow him up a step and through a narrow door into a room of fair size, provided with a wooden floor and furnished as a studio. An acetylene gas outfit gave the light necessary for work.

The unfinished pictures on easels or propped against the walls were as ghastly as the finished ones upstairs, and shewed the painstaking methods of the artist. Scenes were blocked out with extreme care, and pencilled guide lines told of the minute exactitude which Pickman used in getting the right perspective and proportions. The man was great – I say it even now, knowing as much as I do. A large camera on a table excited my notice, and Pickman told me that he used it in taking scenes for backgrounds, so that he might paint them from photographs in the studio instead of carting his outfit around the town for this or that view. He thought a photograph quite as good as an actual scene or model for sustained work, and declared he employed them regularly.

There was something very disturbing about the nauseous sketches and half-finished monstrosities that leered around from every side of the room, and when Pickman suddenly unveiled a huge canvas on the side away from the light I could not for my life keep back a loud scream – the second I had emitted that night. It echoed and echoed through the dim vaultings of that ancient and nitrous cellar, and I had to choke back a flood of reaction that threatened to burst out as hysterical laughter. Merciful Creator! Eliot, but I don't know how much was real and how much was feverish fancy. It doesn't seem to me that earth can hold a dream like that!

It was a colossal and nameless blasphemy with glaring red eyes, and it held in bony claws a thing that had been a man, gnawing at the head as a child nibbles at a stick of candy. Its position was a kind of crouch, and as one looked one felt that at any moment it might drop its present prey and seek a juicier morsel. But damn it all, it wasn't even the fiendish subject that made it such an immortal fountain-head of all panic – not that, nor the dog face with its pointed ears, bloodshot eyes, flat nose, and drooling lips. It wasn't the scaly claws nor the mould-caked body nor the half-hooved feet – none of these, though any one of them might well have driven an excitable man to madness.

It was the technique, Eliot – the cursed, the impious, the unnatural technique! As I am a living being, I never elsewhere saw the actual breath of life so fused into a canvas. The monster was there – it glared and gnawed and gnawed and glared – and I knew that only a suspension of Nature's laws could ever let a man paint a thing like that without a model – without some glimpse of the nether world which no mortal unsold to the Fiend has ever had.

Pinned with a thumb-tack to a vacant part of the canvas was a piece of paper now badly curled up – probably, I thought, a photograph from which Pickman meant to paint a background as hideous as the nightmare it was to enhance. I reached out to uncurl and look at it, when suddenly I saw Pickman start as if shot. He had been listening with peculiar intensity ever since my shocked scream had waked unaccustomed echoes in the dark cellar, and now he seemed struck with a fright which, though not comparable to my own, had in it more of the physical than of the spiritual. He drew a revolver and motioned me to silence, then stepped out into the main cellar and closed the door behind him.

I think I was paralysed for an instant. Imitating Pickman's listening, I fancied I heard a faint scurrying sound somewhere, and a series of squeals or bleats in a direction I couldn't determine. I thought of huge rats and shuddered. Then there came a subdued sort of clatter which somehow set me all in gooseflesh – a furtive, groping kind of clatter, though I can't attempt to convey what I mean in words. It was like heavy wood falling on stone or brick – wood on brick – what did that make me think of?

It came again, and louder. There was a vibration as if the wood had fallen farther than it had fallen before. After that followed a sharp grating noise, a shouted gibberish from Pickman, and the deafening discharge of all six chambers of a revolver, fired spectacularly as a lion-tamer might fire in the air for effect. A muffled squeal or squawk, and a thud. Then more wood and brick grating, a pause, and the opening of the door – at which I'll confess I started violently. Pickman reappeared with his smoking weapon, cursing the bloated rats that infested the ancient well.

'The deuce knows what they eat, Thurber,' he grinned, 'for those archaic tunnels touched graveyard and witch-den and sea-coast. But whatever it is, they must have run short, for they were devilish anxious to get out. Your yelling stirred them up, I fancy. Better be cautious in these old places – our rodent friends are the one drawback, though I sometimes think they're a positive asset by way of atmosphere and colour.'

Well, Eliot, that was the end of the night's adventure. Pickman had promised to shew me the place, and heaven knows he had done it. He led me out of that tangle of alleys in another direction, it seems, for when we sighted a lamp post we were in a half-familiar street with monotonous rows of mingled tenement blocks and old houses. Charter Street, it turned out to be, but I was too flustered to notice just where we hit it. We were too late for the elevated, and walked back downtown through Hanover Street. I remember that walk. We switched from Tremont up Beacon, and Pickman left me at the corner of Joy, where I turned off. I never spoke to him again.

Why did I drop him? Don't be impatient. Wait till I ring for coffee. We've had enough of the other stuff, but I for one need something. No – it wasn't the paintings I saw in that place; though I'll swear they were enough to get him ostracised in nine-tenths of the homes and clubs of Boston, and I guess you won't wonder now why I have to steer clear of subways and cellars. It was – something I found in my coat the next morning. You know, the curled-up paper tacked to that frightful canvas in the cellar; the thing I thought was a photograph of some scene he meant to use as a background for that monster. That last scare had come while I was reaching to uncurl it, and it seems I had vacantly crumpled it into my pocket. But here's the coffee – take it black, Eliot, if you're wise.

Yes, that paper was the reason I dropped Pickman; Richard Upton Pickman, the greatest artist I have ever known – and the foulest being that ever leaped the bounds of life into the pits of myth and madness. Eliot – old Reid was right. He wasn't strictly human. Either he was born in strange shadow, or he'd found a way to unlock the forbidden gate. It's all the same now, for he's gone – back into the fabulous darkness he loved to haunt. Here, let's have the chandelier going.

Don't ask me to explain or even conjecture about what I burned. Don't ask me, either, what lay behind that mole-like scrambling Pickman was so keen to pass off as rats. There are secrets, you know, which might have come down from old Salem times, and Cotton Mather tells even stranger things. You know how damned life-like Pickman's paintings were – how we all wondered where he got those faces.

Well – that paper wasn't a photograph of any background, after all. What it shewed was simply the monstrous being he was painting on that awful canvas. It was the model he was using – and its background was merely the wall of the cellar studio in minute detail. But by God, Eliot, *it was a photograph from life*.

The Silver Key

When Randolph Carter was thirty he lost the key of the gate of dreams. Prior to that time he had made up for the prosiness of life by nightly excursions to strange and ancient cities beyond space, and lovely, unbelievable garden lands across ethereal seas; but as middle age hardened upon him he felt these liberties slipping away little by little, until at last he was cut off altogether. No more could his galleys sail up the river Oukranos past the gilded spires of Thran, or his elephant caravans tramp through perfumed jungles in Kled, where forgotten palaces with veined ivory columns sleep lovely and unbroken under the moon.

He had read much of things as they are, and talked with too many people. Well-meaning philosophers had taught him to look into the logical relations of things, and analyse the processes which shaped his thoughts and fancies. Wonder had gone away, and he had forgotten that all life is only a set of pictures in the brain, among which there is no difference betwixt those born of real things and those born of inward dreamings, and no cause to value the one above the other. Custom had dinned into his ears a superstitious reverence for that which tangibly and physically exists, and had made him secretly ashamed to dwell in visions. Wise men told him his simple fancies were inane and childish, and he believed it because he could see that they might easily be so. What he failed to recall was that the deeds of reality are just as inane and childish, and even more absurd because their actors persist in fancying them full of meaning and purpose as the blind cosmos grinds aimlessly on from nothing to something and from something back to nothing again, neither heeding nor knowing the wishes or existence of the minds that flicker for a second now and then in the darkness.

They had chained him down to things that are, and had then explained the workings of those things till mystery had gone out of the world. When he complained, and longed to escape into twilight realms where magic moulded all the little vivid fragments and prized associations of his mind into vistas of breathless expectancy and unquenchable delight, they turned him instead toward the new-found prodigies of science, bidding him find wonder in the atom's vortex and mystery in the sky's dimensions. And when he had failed to find these boons in things whose laws are known and measurable, they told him he lacked imagination, and was immature because he preferred dream-illusions to the illusions of our physical creation.

So Carter had tried to do as others did, and pretended that the common events and emotions of earthy minds were more important than the fantasies of rare and delicate souls. He did not dissent when they told him that the animal pain of a stuck pig or dyspeptic ploughman in real life is a greater thing than the peerless beauty of Narath with its hundred carven gates and domes of chalcedony, which he dimly remembered from his dreams; and under their guid-ance he cultivated a painstaking sense of pity and tragedy.

Once in a while, though, he could not help seeing how shallow, fickle, and meaningless all human aspirations are, and how emptily our real impulses contrast with those pompous ideals we profess to hold. Then he would have recourse to the polite laughter they had taught him to use against the extravagance and artificiality of dreams; for he saw that the daily life of our world is every inch as extravagant and artificial, and far less worthy of respect because of its poverty in beauty and its silly reluctance to admit its own lack of reason and purpose. In this way he became a kind of humorist, for he did not see that even humour is empty in a mindless universe devoid of any true standard of consistency or inconsistency.

In the first days of his bondage he had turned to the gentle churchly faith endeared to him by the naive trust of his fathers, for thence stretched mystic avenues which seemed to promise escape from life. Only on closer view did he mark the starved fancy and beauty, the stale and prosy triteness, and the owlish gravity and grotesque claims of solid truth which reigned boresomely and over-whelmingly among most of its professors; or feel to the full the awkwardness with which it sought to keep alive as literal fact the outgrown fears and guesses of a primal race confronting the un-known. It wearied Carter to see how solemnly people tried to make earthly reality out of old myths which every step of their boasted science confuted, and this misplaced seriousness killed the attachment he might have kept for the ancient creeds had they been content to offer the sonorous rites and emotional outlets in their true guise of ethereal fantasy.

But when he came to study those who had thrown off the old myths, he found them even more ugly than those who had not. They did not know that beauty lies in harmony, and that loveliness of life has no standard amidst an aimless cosmos save only its harmony with the dreams and the feelings which have gone before and blindly moulded our little spheres out of the rest of chaos. They did not see that good and evil and beauty and ugliness are only ornamental fruits of perspective, whose sole value lies in their linkage to what chance made our fathers think and feel, and whose finer details are different for every race and culture. Instead, they either denied these things altogether or transferred them to the crude, vague instincts which they shared with the beasts and peasants; so that their lives were dragged malodorously out in pain, ugliness, and disproportion, yet filled with a ludicrous pride at having escaped from something no more unsound than that which still held them. They had traded the false gods of fear and blind piety for those of licence and anarchy.

Carter did not taste deeply of these modern freedoms; for their cheapness and squalor sickened a spirit loving beauty alone, while his reason rebelled at the flimsy logic with which their champions tried to gild brute impulse with a sacredness stripped from the idols they had discarded. He saw that most of them, in common with their cast-off priestcraft, could not escape from the delusion that life has a meaning apart from that which men dream into it; and could not lay aside the crude notion of ethics and obligations beyond those of beauty, even when all Nature shrieked of its unconsciousness and impersonal unmorality in the light of their scientific discoveries. Warped and bigoted with preconceived illusions of justice, freedom, and consistency, they cast off the old lore and the old ways with the old beliefs; nor ever stopped to think that that lore and those ways were the sole makers of their present thoughts and judgments, and the sole guides and standards in a meaningless universe without fixed aims or stable points of reference. Having lost these artificial settings, their lives grew void of direction and dramatic interest; till at length they strove to drown their ennui in bustle and pretended usefulness, noise and excitement, barbaric display and animal sensation. When these things palled, disappointed, or grew nauseous through revulsion, they cultivated irony and bitterness, and found fault with the social order. Never could they realise that their brute foundations were as shifting and contradictory as the gods of their elders, and that the satisfaction of one moment is the bane of the next. Calm, lasting beauty comes only in dream, and this solace the world had thrown away when in its worship of the real it threw away the secrets of childhood and innocence.

Amidst this chaos of hollowness and unrest Carter tried to live as befitted a man of keen thought and good heritage. With his dreams fading under the ridicule of the age he could not believe in anything, but the love of harmony kept him close to the ways of his race and station. He walked impassive through the cities of men, and sighed because no vista seemed fully real; because every flash of yellow sunlight on tall roofs and every glimpse of balustraded plazas in the first lamps of evening served only to remind him of dreams he had once known, and to make him homesick for ethereal lands he no longer knew how to find. Travel was only a mockery; and even the Great War stirred him but little, though he served from the first in the Foreign Legion of France. For a while he sought friends, but soon grew weary of the crudeness of their emotions, and the sameness and earthiness of their visions. He felt vaguely glad that all his relatives were distant and out of touch with him, for they could not have understood his mental life. That is, none but his grandfather and great-uncle Christopher could, and they were long dead.

Then he began once more the writing of books, which he had left off when dreams first failed him. But here, too, was there no satisfaction or fulfilment; for the touch of earth was upon his mind, and he could not think of lovely things as he had done of yore. Ironic humour dragged down all the twilight minarets he reared, and the earthy fear of improbability blasted all the delicate and amazing flowers in his faery gardens. The convention of assumed pity spilt mawkishness on his characters, while the myth of an important reality and significant human events and emotions debased all his high fantasy into thin-veiled allegory and cheap social satire. His new novels were successful as his old ones had never been; and because he knew how empty they must be to please an empty herd, he burned them and ceased his writing. They were very graceful novels, in which he urbanely laughed at the dreams he lightly sketched; but he saw that their sophistication had sapped all their life away.

It was after this that he cultivated deliberate illusion, and dabbled in the notions of the bizarre and the eccentric as an antidote for the commonplace. Most of these, however, soon shewed their poverty and barrenness; and he saw that the popular doctrines of occultism are as dry and inflexible as those of science, yet without even the slender palliative of truth to redeem them. Gross stupidity, falsehood, and muddled thinking are not dream, and form no escape from life to a mind trained above their level. So Carter bought stranger books and sought out deeper and more terrible men of fantastic erudition, delving into arcana of consciousness that few have trod, and learning things about the secret pits of life, legend, and immemorial antiquity which disturbed him ever afterward. He decided to live on a rarer plane, and furnished his Boston home to suit his changing moods; one room for each, hung in appropriate colours, furnished with befitting books and objects, and provided with sources of the proper sensations of light, heat, sound, taste, and odour.

Once he heard of a man in the South who was shunned and feared for the blasphemous things he read in prehistoric books and clay tablets smuggled from India and Arabia. Him he visited, living with him and sharing his studies for seven years, till horror overtook them one midnight in an unknown and archaic graveyard, and only one emerged where two had entered. Then he went back to Arkham, the terrible witch-haunted old town of his forefathers in New England, and had experiences in the dark, amidst the hoary willows and tottering gambrel roofs, which made him seal forever certain pages in the diary of a wild-minded ancestor. But these horrors took him only to the edge of reality, and were not of the true dream country he had known in youth; so that at fifty he despaired of any rest or contentment in a world grown too busy for beauty and too shrewd for dream.

Having perceived at last the hollowness and futility of real things, Carter spent his days in retirement, and in wistful disjointed memories of his dream-filled youth. He thought it rather silly that he bothered to keep on living at all, and got from a South American acquaintance a very curious liquid to take him to oblivion without suffering. Inertia and force of habit, however, caused him to defer action; and he lingered indecisively among thoughts of old times, taking down the strange hangings from his walls and refitting the house as it was in his early boyhood – purple panes, Victorian furniture, and all.

With the passage of time he became almost glad he had lingered, for his relics of youth and his cleavage from the world made life and sophistication seem very distant and unreal; so much so that a touch of magic and expectancy stole back into his nightly slumbers. For years those slumbers had known only such twisted reflections of every-day things as the commonest slumbers know, but now there returned a flicker of something stranger and wilder; something of vaguely awe-some immanence which took the form of tensely clear pictures from his childhood days, and made him think of little inconsequential things he had long forgotten. He would often awake calling for his mother and grandfather, both in their graves a quarter of a century.

Then one night his grandfather reminded him of a key. The grey old scholar, as vivid as in life, spoke long and earnestly of their ancient line, and of the strange visions of the delicate and sensitive men who composed it. He spoke of the flame-eyed Crusader who learnt wild secrets of the Saracens that held him captive; and of the first Sir Randolph Carter who studied magic when Elizabeth was queen. He spoke, too, of that Edmund Carter who had just escaped hanging in the Salem witchcraft, and who had placed in an antique box a great silver key handed down from his ancestors. Before Carter awaked, the gentle visitant had told him where to find that box; that carved oak box of archaic wonder whose grotesque lid no hand had raised for two centuries.

In the dust and shadows of the great attic he found it, remote and forgotten at the back of a drawer in a tall chest. It was about a foot square, and its Gothic carvings were so fearful that he did not marvel no person since Edmund Carter had dared to open it. It gave forth no noise when shaken, but was mystic with the scent of unremem-bered spices. That it held a key was indeed only a dim legend, and Randolph Carter's father had never known such a box existed. It was bound in rusty iron, and no means was provided for working the formidable lock. Carter vaguely understood that he would find within it some key to the lost gate of dreams, but of where and how to use it his grandfather had told him nothing.

An old servant forced the carven lid, shaking as he did so at the hideous faces leering from the blackened wood, and at some unplaced familiarity. Inside, wrapped in a discoloured parchment, was a huge key of tarnished silver covered with cryptical arabesques; but of any legible explanation there was none. The parchment was voluminous, and held only the strange hieroglyphs of an unknown tongue written with an antique reed. Carter recognised the characters as those he had seen on a certain papyrus scroll belonging to that terrible scholar of the South who had vanished one midnight in a nameless cemetery. The man had always shivered when he read this scroll, and Carter shivered now.

But he cleaned the key, and kept it by him nightly in its aromatic box of ancient oak. His dreams were meanwhile increasing in vividness, and though shewing him none of the strange cities and incredible gardens of the old days, were assuming a definite cast whose purpose could not be mistaken. They were calling him back along the years, and with the mingled wills of all his fathers were pulling him toward some hidden and ancestral source. Then he knew he must go into the past and merge himself with old things, and day after day he thought of the hills to the north where haunted Arkham and the rushing Miskatonic and the lonely rustic homestead of his people lay.

In the brooding fire of autumn Carter took the old remembered way past graceful lines of rolling hill and stone-walled meadow, distant vale and hanging woodland, curving road and nestling farmstead, and the crystal windings of the Miskatonic, crossed here and there by rustic bridges of wood or stone. At one bend he saw the group of giant elms among which an ancestor had oddly vanished a century and a half before, and shuddered as the wind blew meaningly through them. Then there was the crumbling farmhouse of old Goody Fowler the witch, with its little evil windows and great roof sloping nearly to the ground on the north side. He speeded up his car as he passed it, and did not slacken till he had mounted the hill where his mother and her fathers before her were born, and where the old white house still looked proudly across the road at the breathlessly lovely panorama of rocky slope and verdant valley, with the distant spires of Kingsport on the horizon, and hints of the archaic, dreamladen sea in the farthest background.

Then came the steeper slope that held the old Carter place he had not seen in over forty years. Afternoon was far gone when he reached the foot, and at the bend half way up he paused to scan the outspread countryside golden and glorified in the slanting floods of magic poured out by a western sun. All the strangeness and expectancy of his recent dreams seemed present in this hushed and unearthly landscape, and he thought of the unknown solitudes of other planets as his eyes traced out the velvet and deserted lawns shining undulant between their tumbled walls, the clumps of faery forest setting off far lines of purple hills beyond hills, and the spectral wooded valley dipping down in shadow to dank hollows where trickling waters crooned and gurgled among swollen and distorted roots.

Something made him feel that motors did not belong in the realm he was seeking, so he left his car at the edge of the forest, and putting the great key in his coat pocket walked on up the hill. Woods now engulfed him utterly, though he knew the house was on a high knoll that cleared the trees except to the north. He wondered how it would look, for it had been left vacant and untended through his neglect since the death of his strange great-uncle Christopher thirty years before. In his boyhood he had revelled through long visits there, and had found weird marvels in the woods beyond the orchard.

Shadows thickened around him, for the night was near. Once a gap in the trees opened up to the right, so that he saw off across leagues of twilight meadow and spied the old Congregational steeple on Central Hill in Kingsport; pink with the last flush of day, the panes of the little round windows blazing with reflected fire. Then, when he was in deep shadow again, he recalled with a start that the glimpse must have come from childish memory alone, since the old white church had long been torn down to make room for the Congregational Hospital. He had read of it with interest, for the paper had told about some strange burrows or passages found in the rocky hill beneath.

Through his puzzlement a voice piped, and he started again at its familiarity after long years. Old Benijah Corey had been his Uncle Christopher's hired man, and was aged even in those far-off times of his boyhood visits. Now he must be well over a hundred, but that piping voice could come from no one else. He could distinguish no words, yet the tone was haunting and unmistakable. To think that 'Old Benijy' should still be alive!

'Mister Randy! Mister Randy! Whar be ye? D'ye want to skeer yer Aunt Marthy plumb to death? Hain't she tuld ye to keep nigh the place in the arternoon an' git back afur dark? Randy! Ran . . . dee! . . . He's the beatin'est boy fer runnin' off in the woods I ever see; haff the time a-settin' moonin' raound that snake-den in the upper timber-lot! . . . Hey, yew, Ran . . . dee!'

Randolph Carter stopped in the pitch darkness and rubbed his hand across his eyes. Something was queer. He had been somewhere he ought not to be; had strayed very far away to places where he had not belonged, and was now inexcusably late. He had not noticed the time on the Kingsport steeple, though he could easily have made it out with his pocket telescope; but he knew his lateness was something very strange and unprecedented. He was not sure he had his little telescope with him, and put his hand in his blouse pocket to see. No, it was not there, but there was the big silver key he had found in a box somewhere. Uncle Chris had told him something odd once about an old unopened box with a key in it, but Aunt Martha had stopped the story abruptly, saying it was no kind of thing to tell a child whose head was already too full of queer fancies. He tried to recall just where he had found the key, but something seemed very confused. He guessed it was in the attic at home in Boston, and dimly remembered bribing Parks with half his week's allowance to help him open the box and keep quiet about it; but when he remembered this, the face of Parks came up very strangely, as if the wrinkles of long years had fallen upon the brisk little Cockney.

'Ran . . . dee! Ran . . . dee! Hi! Hi! Randy!'

A swaying lantern came around the black bend, and old Benijah pounced on the silent and bewildered form of the pilgrim.

'Durn ye, boy, so thar ye be! Ain't ye got a tongue in yer head, that ye can't answer a body? I ben callin' this haff hour, an' ye must a heerd me long ago! Dun't ye know yer Aunt Marthy's all a-fidget over yer bein' off arter dark? Wait till I tell yer Uncle Chris when he gits hum! Ye'd orta know these here woods ain't no fitten place to be traipsin' this hour! They's things abroad what dun't do nobody no good, as my gran'sir' knowed afur me. Come, Mister Randy, or Hannah wun't keep supper no longer!'

So Randolph Carter was marched up the road where wondering stars glimmered through high autumn boughs. And dogs barked as the yellow light of small-paned windows shone out at the farther turn, and the Pleiades twinkled across the open knoll where a great gambrel roof stood black against the dim west. Aunt Martha was in the doorway, and did not scold too hard when Benijah shoved the truant in. She knew Uncle Chris well enough to expect such things of the Carter blood. Randolph did not shew his key, but ate his supper in silence and protested only when bedtime came. He sometimes dreamed better when awake, and he wanted to use that key.

In the morning Randolph was up early, and would have run off to the upper timber-lot if Uncle Chris had not caught him and forced him into his chair by the breakfast table. He looked impatiently around the low-pitched room with the rag carpet and exposed beams and corner-posts, and smiled only when the orchard boughs scratched at the leaded panes of the rear window. The trees and the hills were close to him, and formed the gates of that timeless realm which was his true country.

Then, when he was free, he felt in his blouse pocket for the key; and being reassured, skipped off across the orchard to the rise beyond, where the wooded hill climbed again to heights above even the treeless knoll. The floor of the forest was mossy and mysterious, and great lichened rocks rose vaguely here and there in the dim light like Druid monoliths among the swollen and twisted trunks of a sacred grove. Once in his ascent Randolph crossed a rushing stream whose falls a little way off sang runic incantations to the lurking fauns and aegipans and dryads.

Then he came to the strange cave in the forest slope, the dreaded 'snake-den' which country folk shunned, and away from which Benijah had warned him again and again. It was deep; far deeper than anyone but Randolph suspected, for the boy had found a fissure in the farthermost black corner that led to a loftier grotto beyond – a haunting sepulchral place whose granite walls held a curious illusion of conscious artifice. On this occasion he crawled in as usual, lighting his way with matches filched from the sitting-room match-safe, and edging through the final crevice with an eagerness hard to explain even to himself. He could not tell why he approached the farther wall so confidently, or why he instinctively drew forth the great silver key as he did so. But on he went, and when he danced back to the house that night he offered no excuses for his lateness, nor heeded in the least the reproofs he gained for ignoring the noontide dinner-horn altogether.

Now it is agreed by all the distant relatives of Randolph Carter that something occurred to heighten his imagination in his tenth year. His cousin, Ernest B. Aspinwall, Esq., of Chicago, is fully ten years his senior, and distinctly recalls a change in the boy after the autumn of 1883. Randolph had looked on scenes of fantasy that few others can ever have beheld, and stranger still were some of the qualities which he shewed in relation to very mundane things. He seemed, in fine, to have picked up an odd gift of prophecy, and reacted unusually to things which, though at the time without meaning, were later found to justify the singular impressions. In subsequent decades as new inventions, new names, and new events appeared one by one in the book of history, people would now and then recall wonderingly how Carter had years before let fall some careless word of undoubted connexion with what was then far in the future. He did not himself understand these words, or know why certain things made him feel certain emotions, but fancied that some un-remembered dream must be responsible. It was as early as 1897 that he turned pale when some traveller mentioned the French town of Belloy-en-Santerre, and friends remembered it when he was almost mortally wounded there in 1916, while serving with the Foreign Legion in the Great War.

Carter's relatives talk much of these things because he has lately disappeared. His little old servant Parks, who for years bore patiently with his vagaries, last saw him on the morning he drove off alone in his car with a key he had recently found. Parks had helped him get the key from the old box containing it, and had felt strangely affected by the grotesque carvings on the box, and by some other odd quality he could not name. When Carter left, he had said he was going to visit his old ancestral country around Arkham.

Half way up Elm Mountain, on the way to the ruins of the old Carter place, they found his motor set carefully by the roadside; and in it was a box of fragrant wood with carvings that frightened the countrymen who stumbled on it. The box held only a queer parchment whose characters no linguist or palaeographer has been able to decipher or identify. Rain had long effaced any possible footprints, though Boston investigators had something to say about evidences of disturbances among the fallen timbers of the Carter place. It was, they averred, as though someone had groped about the ruins at no distant period. A common white handkerchief found among forest rocks on the hillside beyond cannot be identified as belonging to the missing man.

There is talk of apportioning Randolph Carter's estate among his heirs, but I shall stand firmly against this course because I do not believe he is dead. There are twists of time and space, of vision and reality, which only a dreamer can divine; and from what I know of Carter I think he has merely found a way to traverse these mazes. Whether or not he will ever come back, I cannot say. He wanted the lands of dream he had lost, and yearned for the days of his childhood. Then he found a key, and I somehow believe he was able to use it to strange advantage.

I shall ask him when I see him, for I expect to meet him shortly in a certain dream-city we both used to haunt. It is rumoured in Ulthar, beyond the river Skai, that a new king reigns on the opal throne in Ilek-Vad, that fabulous town of turrets atop the hollow cliffs of glass overlooking the twilight sea wherein the bearded and finny Gnorri build their singular labyrinths, and I believe I know how to interpret this rumour. Certainly, I look forward impatiently to the sight of that great silver key, for in its cryptical arabesques there may stand symbolised all the aims and mysteries of a blindly impersonal cosmos.

The Strange High House in the Mist

In the morning mist comes up from the sea by the cliffs beyond Kingsport. White and feathery it comes from the deep to its brothers the clouds, full of dreams of dank pastures and caves of leviathan. And later, in still summer rains on the steep roofs of poets, the clouds scatter bits of those dreams, that men shall not live without rumour of old, strange secrets, and wonders that planets tell planets alone in the night. When tales fly thick in the grottoes of tritons, and conches in seaweed cities blow wild tunes learned from the Elder Ones, then great eager mists flock to heaven laden with lore, and oceanward eyes on the rocks see only a mystic whiteness, as if the cliff's rim were the rim of all earth, and the solemn bells of buoys tolled free in the aether of faery.

Now north of archaic Kingsport the crags climb lofty and curious, terrace on terrace, till the northernmost hangs in the sky like a grey frozen wind-cloud. Alone it is, a bleak point jutting in limitless space, for there the coast turns sharp where the great Miskatonic pours out of the plains past Arkham, bringing woodland legends and little quaint memories of New England's hills. The sea-folk in Kingsport look up at that cliff as other sea-folk look up at the pole-star, and time the night's watches by the way it hides or shews the Great Bear, Cassiopeia, and the Dragon. Among them it is one with the firmament, and truly, it is hidden from them when the mist hides the stars or the sun. Some of the cliffs they love, as that whose grotesque profile they call Father Neptune, or that whose pillared steps they term The Causeway; but this one they fear because it is so near the sky. The Portuguese sailors coming in from a voyage cross themselves when they first see it, and the old Yankees believe it would be much graver matter than death to climb it, if indeed that were possible. Nevertheless there is an ancient house on that cliff, and at evening men see lights in the small-paned windows.

The ancient house has always been there, and people say One dwells therein who talks with the morning mists that come up from the deep, and perhaps sees singular things oceanward at those times when the cliff's rim becomes the rim of all earth, and solemn buoys toll free in the white aether of faery. This they tell from hearsay, for that forbidding crag is always unvisited, and natives dislike to train telescopes on it. Summer boarders have indeed scanned it with jaunty binoculars, but have never seen more than the grey primeval roof, peaked and shingled, whose eaves come nearly to the grey foundations, and the dim yellow light of the little windows peeping out from under those eaves in the dusk. These summer people do not believe that the same One has lived in the ancient house for hundreds of years, but cannot prove their heresy to any real Kingsporter. Even the Terrible Old Man who talks to leaden pendulums in bottles, buys groceries with centuried Spanish gold, and keeps stone idols in the yard of his antediluvian cottage in Water Street can only say these things were the same when his grandfather was a boy, and that must have been inconceivable ages ago, when Belcher or Shirley or Pownall or Bernard was Governor of His Majesty's Province of the Massachusetts-Bay.

Then one summer there came a philosopher into Kingsport. His name was Thomas Olney, and he taught ponderous things in a college by Narragansett Bay. With stout wife and romping children he came, and his eyes were weary with seeing the same things for many years, and thinking the same well-disciplined thoughts. He looked at the mists from the diadem of Father Neptune, and tried to walk into their white world of mystery along the titan steps of The Causeway. Morning after morning he would lie on the cliffs and look over the world's rim at the cryptical aether beyond, listening to spectral bells and the wild cries of what might have been gulls. Then, when the mist would lift and the sea stand out prosy with the smoke of steamers, he would sigh and descend to the town, where he loved to thread the narrow olden lanes up and down hill, and study the crazy tottering gables and odd pillared doorways which had sheltered so many generations of sturdy sea-folk. And he even talked with the Terrible Old Man, who was not fond of strangers, and was invited into his fearsomely archaic cottage where low ceilings and wormy panelling hear the echoes of disquieting soliloquies in the dark small hours.

Of course it was inevitable that Olney should mark the grey un-visited cottage in the sky, on that sinister northward crag which is one with the mists and the firmament. Always over Kingsport it hung, and always its mystery sounded in whispers through Kings-port's crooked alleys. The Terrible Old Man wheezed a tale that his father had told him, of lightning that shot one night *up from* that peaked cottage to the clouds of higher heaven; and Granny Orne, whose tiny gambrel-roofed abode in Ship Street is all covered with moss and ivy, croaked over something her grandmother had heard at second-hand, about shapes that flapped out of the eastern mists straight into the narrow single door of that unreachable place – for the door is set close to the edge of the crag toward the ocean, and glimpsed only from ships at sea.

At length, being avid for new strange things and held back by neither the Kingsporter's fear nor the summer boarder's usual indol-ence, Olney made a very terrible resolve. Despite a conservative training – or because of it, for humdrum lives breed wistful longings of the unknown – he swore a great oath to scale that avoided north-ern cliff and visit the abnormally antique grey cottage in the sky. Very plausibly his saner self argued that the place must be tenanted by people who reached it from inland along the easier ridge beside the Miskatonic's estuary. Probably they traded in Arkham, knowing how little Kingsport liked their habitation, or perhaps being unable to climb down the cliff on the Kingsport side. Olney walked out along the lesser cliffs to where the great crag leaped insolently up to consort with celestial things, and became very sure that no human feet could mount it or descend it on that beetling southern slope. East and north it rose thousands of feet vertically from the water, so only the western side, inland and toward Arkham, remained.

One early morning in August Olney set out to find a path to the inaccessible pinnacle. He worked northwest along pleasant back roads, past Hooper's Pond and the old brick powder-house to where the pastures slope up to the ridge above the Miskatonic and give a lovely vista of Arkham's white Georgian steeples across leagues of river and meadow. Here he found a shady road to Arkham, but no trail at all in the seaward direction he wished. Woods and fields crowded up to the high bank of the river's mouth, and bore not a sign of man's presence; not even a stone wall or a straying cow, but only the tall grass and giant trees and tangles of briers that the first Indian might have seen. As he climbed slowly east, higher and higher above the estuary on his left and nearer and nearer the sea, he found the way growing in difficulty, till he wondered how ever the dwellers in that disliked place managed to reach the world outside, and whether they came often to market in Arkham.

Then the trees thinned, and far below him on his right he saw the hills and antique roofs and spires of Kingsport. Even Central Hill was a dwarf from this height, and he could just make out the ancient graveyard by the Congregational Hospital, beneath which rumour said some terrible caves or burrows lurked. Ahead lay sparse grass and scrub blueberry bushes, and beyond them the naked rock of the crag and the thin peak of the dreaded grey cottage. Now the ridge narrowed, and Olney grew dizzy at his loneness in the sky. South of him the frightful precipice above Kingsport, north of him the vertical drop of nearly a mile to the river's mouth. Suddenly a great chasm opened before him, ten feet deep, so that he had to let himself down by his hands and drop to a slanting floor, and then crawl perilously up a natural defile in the opposite wall. So this was the way the folk of the uncanny house journeyed betwixt earth and sky!

When he climbed out of the chasm a morning mist was gathering, but he clearly saw the lofty and unhallowed cottage ahead; walls as grey as the rock, and high peak standing bold against the milky white of the seaward vapours. And he perceived that there was no door on this landward end, but only a couple of small lattice windows with dingy bull's-eye panes leaded in seventeenth-century fashion. All around him was cloud and chaos, and he could see nothing below but the whiteness of illimitable space. He was alone in the sky with this queer and very disturbing house; and when he sidled around to the front and saw that the wall stood flush with the cliff's edge, so that the single narrow door was not to be reached save from the empty aether, he felt a distinct terror that altitude could not wholly explain. And it was very odd that shingles so worm-eaten could survive, or bricks so crumbled still form a standing chimney.

As the mist thickened, Olney crept around to the windows on the north and west and south sides, trying them but finding them all locked. He was vaguely glad they were locked, because the more he saw of that house the less he wished to get in. Then a sound halted him. He heard a lock rattle and bolt shoot, and a long creaking follow as if a heavy door were slowly and cautiously opened. This was on the oceanward side that he could not see, where the narrow portal opened on blank space thousands of feet in the misty sky above the waves.

Then there was heavy, deliberate tramping in the cottage, and Olney heard the windows opening, first on the north side opposite him, and then on the west just around the corner. Next would come the south windows, under the great low eaves on the side where he stood; and it must be said that he was more than uncomfortable as he thought of the detestable house on one side and the vacancy of upper air on the other. When a fumbling came in the nearer casements he crept around to the west again, flattening himself against the wall beside the now opened windows. It was plain that the owner had come home; but he had not come from the land, nor from any balloon or airship that could be imagined. Steps sounded again, and Olney edged round to the north; but before he could find a haven a voice called softly, and he knew he must confront his host.

Stuck out of a west window was a great black-bearded face whose eyes shone phosphorescently with the imprint of unheard-of sights. But the voice was gentle, and of a quaint olden kind, so that Olney did not shudder when a brown hand reached out to help him over the sill and into that low room of black oak wainscots and carved Tudor furnishings. The man was clad in very ancient garments, and had about him an unplaceable nimbus of sea-lore and dreams of tall galleons. Olney does not recall many of the wonders he told, or even who he was; but says that he was strange and kindly, and filled with the magic of unfathomed voids of time and space. The small room seemed green with a dim aqueous light, and Olney saw that the far windows to the east were not open, but shut against the misty aether with dull thick panes like the bottoms of old bottles.

That bearded host seemed young, yet looked out of eyes steeped in the elder mysteries; and from the tales of marvellous ancient things he related, it must be guessed that the village folk were right in saying he had communed with the mists of the sea and the clouds of the sky ever since there was any village to watch his taciturn dwelling from the plain below. And the day wore on, and still Olney listened to rumours of old times and far places, and heard how the Kings of

Atlantis fought with the slippery blasphemies that wriggled out of rifts in ocean's floor, and how the pillared and weedy temple of Poseidonis is still glimpsed at midnight by lost ships, who know by its sight that they are lost. Years of the Titans were recalled, but the host grew timid when he spoke of the dim first age of chaos before the gods or even the Elder Ones were born, and when only *the other gods* came to dance on the peak of Hatheg-Kla in the stony desert near Ulthar, beyond the river Skai.

It was at this point that there came a knocking on the door; that ancient door of nail-studded oak beyond which lay only the abyss of white cloud. Olney started in fright, but the bearded man motioned him to be still, and tiptoed to the door to look out through a very small peep-hole. What he saw he did not like, so pressed his fingers to his lips and tiptoed around to shut and lock all the windows before returning to the ancient settle beside his guest. Then Olney saw lingering against the translucent squares of each of the little dim windows in succession a queer black outline as the caller moved inquisitively about before leaving; and he was glad his host had not answered the knocking. For there are strange objects in the great abyss, and the seeker of dreams must take care not to stir up or meet the wrong ones.

Then the shadows began to gather; first little furtive ones under the table, and then bolder ones in the dark panelled corners. And the bearded man made enigmatical gestures of prayer, and lit tall candles in curiously wrought brass candlesticks. Frequently he would glance at the door as if he expected someone, and at length his glance seemed answered by a singular rapping which must have followed some very ancient and secret code. This time he did not even glance through the peep-hole, but swung the great oak bar and shot the bolt, unlatching the heavy door and flinging it wide to the stars and the mist.

And then to the sound of obscure harmonies there floated into that room from the deep all the dreams and memories of earth's sunken Mighty Ones. And golden flames played about weedy locks, so that Olney was dazzled as he did them homage. Trident-bearing Neptune was there, and sportive tritons and fantastic nereids, and upon dolphins' backs was balanced a vast crenulate shell wherein rode the grey and awful form of primal Nodens, Lord of the Great

Abyss. And the conches of the tritons gave weird blasts, and the nereids made strange sounds by striking on the grotesque resonant shells of unknown lurkers in black sea-caves. Then hoary Nodens reached forth a wizened hand and helped Olney and his host into the vast shell, whereat the conches and the gongs set up a wild and awesome clamour. And out into the limitless aether reeled that fabulous train, the noise of whose shouting was lost in the echoes of thunder.

All night in Kingsport they watched that lofty cliff when the storm and the mists gave them glimpses of it, and when toward the small hours the little dim windows went dark they whispered of dread and disaster. And Olney's children and stout wife prayed to the bland proper god of Baptists, and hoped that the traveller would borrow an umbrella and rubbers unless the rain stopped by morning. Then dawn swam dripping and mist-wreathed out of the sea, and the buoys tolled solemn in vortices of white aether. And at noon elfin horns rang over the ocean as Olney, dry and light-footed, climbed down from the cliffs to antique Kingsport with the look of far places in his eyes. He could not recall what he had dreamed in the sky-perched hut of that still nameless hermit, or say how he had crept down that crag untraversed by other feet. Nor could he talk of these matters at all save with the Terrible Old Man, who afterward mumbled queer things in his long white beard, vowing that the man who came down from that crag was not wholly the man who went up, and that somewhere under that grey peaked roof, or amidst inconceivable reaches of that sinister white mist, there lingered still the lost spirit of him who was Thomas Olney.

And ever since that hour, through dull dragging years of greyness and weariness, the philosopher has laboured and eaten and slept and done uncomplaining the suitable deeds of a citizen. Not any more does he long for the magic of farther hills, or sigh for secrets that peer like green reefs from a bottomless sea. The sameness of his days no longer gives him sorrow, and well-disciplined thoughts have grown enough for his imagination. His good wife waxes stouter and his children older and prosier and more useful, and he never fails to smile correctly with pride when the occasion calls for it. In his glance there is not any restless light, and if he ever listens for solemn bells or far elfin horns it is only at night when old dreams are wandering. He has never seen Kingsport again, for his family disliked the funny old houses, and complained that the drains were impossibly bad. They have a trim bungalow now at Bristol Highlands, where no tall crags tower, and the neighbours are urban and modern.

But in Kingsport strange tales are abroad, and even the Terrible Old Man admits a thing untold by his grandfather. For now, when the wind sweeps boisterous out of the north past the high ancient house that is one with the firmament, there is broken at last that ominous brooding silence ever before the bane of Kingsport's maritime cotters. And old folk tell of pleasing voices heard singing there, and of laughter that swells with joys beyond earth's joys; and say that at evening the little low windows are brighter than formerly. They say, too, that the fierce aurora comes oftener to that spot, shining blue in the north with visions of frozen worlds while the crag and the cottage hang black and fantastic against wild coruscations. And the mists of the dawn are thicker, and sailors are not quite so sure that all the muffled seaward ringing is that of the solemn buoys.

Worst of all, though, is the shrivelling of old fears in the hearts of Kingsport's young men, who grow prone to listen at night to the north wind's faint distant sounds. They swear no harm or pain can inhabit that high peaked cottage, for in the new voices gladness beats, and with them the tinkle of laughter and music. What tales the seamists may bring to that haunted and northernmost pinnacle they do not know, but they long to extract some hint of the wonders that knock at the cliff-yawning door when clouds are thickest. And patriarchs dread lest some day one by one they seek out that inaccessible peak in the sky, and learn what centuried secrets hide beneath the steep shingled roof which is part of the rocks and the stars and the ancient fears of Kingsport. That those venturesome youths will come back they do not doubt, but they think a light may be gone from their eyes, and a will from their hearts. And they do not wish quaint Kingsport with its climbing lanes and archaic gables to drag listless down the years while voice by voice the laughing chorus grows stronger and wilder in that unknown and terrible eyrie where mists and the dreams of mists stop to rest on their way from the sea to the skies.

They do not wish the souls of their young men to leave the pleasant hearths and gambrel-roofed taverns of old Kingsport, nor do they wish the laughter and song in that high rocky place to grow louder. For as the voice which has come has brought fresh mists from the sea and from the north fresh lights, so do they say that still other voices will bring more mists and more lights, till perhaps the olden gods (whose existence they hint only in whispers for fear the Congregational parson shall hear) may come out of the deep and from unknown Kadath in the cold waste and make their dwelling on that evilly appropriate crag so close to the gentle hills and valleys of quiet simple fisherfolk. This they do not wish, for to plain people things not of earth are unwelcome; and besides, the Terrible Old Man often recalls what Olney said about a knock that the lone dweller feared, and a shape seen black and inquisitive against the mist through those queer translucent windows of leaded bull's-eyes.

All these things, however, the Elder Ones only may decide; and meanwhile the morning mist still comes up by that lonely vertiginous peak with the steep ancient house, that grey low-eaved house where none is seen but where evening brings furtive lights while the north wind tells of strange revels. White and feathery it comes from the deep to its brothers the clouds, full of dreams of dank pastures and caves of leviathan. And when tales fly thick in the grottoes of tritons, and conches in seaweed cities blow wild tunes learned from the Elder Ones, then great eager vapours flock to heaven laden with lore; and Kingsport, nestling uneasy on its lesser cliffs below that awesome hanging sentinel of rock, sees oceanward only a mystic whiteness, as if the cliff's rim were the rim of all earth, and the solemn bells of the buoys tolled free in the aether of faery.

The Dream-Quest of Unknown Kadath

Three times Randolph Carter dreamed of the marvelous city, and three times was he snatched away while still he paused on the high terrace above it. All golden and lovely it blazed in the sunset, with walls, temples, colonnades and arched bridges of veined marble, silver-basined fountains of prismatic spray in broad squares and perfumed gardens, and wide streets marching between delicate trees and blossom-laden urns and ivory statues in gleaming rows; while on steep northward slopes climbed tiers of red roofs and old peaked gables harbouring little lanes of grassy cobbles. It was a fever of the gods, a fanfare of supernal trumpets and a clash of immortal cymbals. Mystery hung about it as clouds about a fabulous unvisited mountain; and as Carter stood breathless and expectant on that balustraded parapet there swept up to him the poignancy and suspense of almost-vanished memory, the pain of lost things and the maddening need to place again what once had been an awesome and momentous place.

He knew that for him its meaning must once have been supreme; though in what cycle or incarnation he had known it, or whether in dream or in waking, he could not tell. Vaguely it called up glimpses of a far forgotten first youth, when wonder and pleasure lay in all the mystery of days, and dawn and dusk alike strode forth prophetic to the eager sound of lutes and song, unclosing fiery gates toward further and surprising marvels. But each night as he stood on that high marble terrace with the curious urns and carven rail and looked off over that hushed sunset city of beauty and unearthly immanence, he felt the bondage of dream's tyrannous gods; for in no wise could he leave that lofty spot, or descend the wide marmoreal fights flung endlessly down to where those streets of elder witchery lay outspread and beckoning.

When for the third time he awakened with those flights still undescended and those hushed sunset streets still untraversed, he prayed long and earnestly to the hidden gods of dream that brood capricious above the clouds on unknown Kadath, in the cold waste where no man treads. But the gods made no answer and shewed no relenting, nor did they give any favouring sign when he prayed to them in dream, and invoked them sacrificially through the bearded priests of Nasht and Kaman-Thah, whose cavern-temple with its pillar of flame lies not far from the gates of the waking world. It seemed, however, that his prayers must have been adversely heard, for after even the first of them he ceased wholly to behold the marvellous city, as if his three glimpses from afar had been mere accidents or oversights, and against some hidden plan or wish of the gods.

At length, sick with longing for those glittering sunset streets and cryptical hill lanes among ancient tiled roofs, nor able sleeping or waking to drive them from his mind, Carter resolved to go with bold entreaty whither no man had gone before, and dare the icy deserts through the dark to where unknown Kadath, veiled in cloud and crowned with unimagined stars, holds secret and nocturnal the onyx castle of the Great Ones.

In light slumber he descended the seventy steps to the cavern of flame and talked of this design to the bearded priests Nasht and Kaman-Thah. And the priests shook their pshent-bearing heads and vowed it would be the death of his soul. They pointed out that the Great Ones had shown already their wish, and that it is not agreeable to them to be harassed by insistent pleas. They reminded him, too, that not only had no man ever been to Kadath, but no man had ever suspected in what part of space it may lie; whether it be in the dreamlands around our own world, or in those surrounding some unguessed companion of Fomalhaut or Aldebaran. If in our dream-land, it might conceivably be reached, but only three human souls since time began had ever crossed and recrossed the black impious gulfs to other dreamlands, and of that three, two had come back quite mad. There were, in such voyages, incalculable local dangers, as well as that shocking final peril which gibbers unmentionably outside the ordered universe, where no dreams reach; that last amorphous blight of nethermost confusion which blasphemes and bubbles at the centre of all infinity – the boundless daemon sultan Azathoth, whose name no lips dare speak aloud, and who gnaws hungrily in inconceivable, unlighted chambers beyond time amidst the muffled, maddening beating of vile drums and the thin, monotonous whine of accursed flutes; to which detestable pounding and piping dance slowly, awkwardly, and absurdly the gigantic ultimate gods, the blind, voiceless, tenebrous, mindless Other Gods whose soul and messenger is the crawling chaos Nyarlathotep.

Of these things was Carter warned by the priests Nasht and Kaman-Thah in the cavern of flame, but still he resolved to find the gods on unknown Kadath in the cold waste, wherever that might be, and to win from them the sight and remembrance and shelter of the marvellous sunset city. He knew that his journey would be strange and long, and that the Great Ones would be against it; but being old in the land of dream he counted on many useful memories and devices to aid him. So asking a formal blessing of the priests and thinking shrewdly on his course, he boldly descended the seven hundred steps to the Gate of Deeper Slumber and set out through the Enchanted Wood.

In the tunnels of that twisted wood, whose low prodigious oaks twine groping boughs and shine dim with the phosphorescence of strange fungi, dwell the furtive and secretive Zoogs; who know many obscure secrets of the dream world and a few of the waking world, since the wood at two places touches the lands of men, though it would be disastrous to say where. Certain unexplained rumours, events, and vanishings occur among men where the Zoogs have access, and it is well that they cannot travel far outside the world of dreams. But over the nearer parts of the dream world they pass freely, flitting small and brown and unseen and bearing back piquant tales to beguile the hours around their hearths in the forest they love. Most of them live in burrows, but some inhabit the trunks of the great trees; and although they live mostly on fungi it is muttered that they have also a slight taste for meat, either physical or spiritual, for certainly many dreamers have entered that wood who have not come out. Carter, however, had no fear; for he was an old dreamer and had learnt their fluttering language and made many a treaty with them, having found through their help the splendid city of Celephaïs in Ooth-Nargai beyond the Tanarian Hills, where reigns half the year the great King Kuranes, a man he had known by another name in life. Kuranes was the one soul who had been to the star-gulls and returned free from madness.

Threading now the low phosphorescent aisles between those gigantic trunks, Carter made fluttering sounds in the manner of the Zoogs, and listened now and then for responses. He remembered one particular village of the creatures was in the centre of the wood, where a circle of great mossy stones in what was once a clearing tells of older and more terrible dwellers long forgotten, and toward this spot he hastened. He traced his way by the grotesque fungi, which always seem better nourished as one approaches the dread circle where elder beings danced and sacrificed. Finally the great light of those thicker fungi revealed a sinister green and grey vastness pushing up through the roof of the forest and out of sight. This was the nearest of the great ring of stones, and Carter knew he was close to the Zoog village. Renewing his fluttering sound, he waited patiently; and was at last rewarded by an impression of many eyes watching him. It was the Zoogs, for one sees their weird eyes long before one can discern their small, slippery brown outlines.

Out they swarmed, from hidden burrow and honeycombed tree, till the whole dim-litten region was alive with them. Some of the wilder ones brushed Carter unpleasantly, and one even nipped loathsomely at his ear; but these lawless spirits were soon restrained by their elders. The Council of Sages, recognizing the visitor, offered a gourd of fermented sap from a haunted tree unlike the others, which had grown from a seed dropt down by someone on the moon; and as Carter drank it ceremoniously a very strange colloquy began. The Zoogs did not, unfortunately, know where the peak of Kadath lies, nor could they even say whether the cold waste is in our dream world or in another. Rumours of the Great Ones came equally from all points; and one might only say that they were likelier to be seen on high mountain peaks than in valleys, since on such peaks they dance reminiscently when the moon is above and the clouds beneath.

Then one very ancient Zoog recalled a thing unheard-of by the others; and said that in Ulthar, beyond the River Skai, there still lingered the last copy of those inconceivably old *Pnakotic Manuscripts* made by waking men in forgotten boreal kingdoms and borne into the land of dreams when the hairy cannibal Gnophkehs overcame many-templed Olathoe and slew all the heroes of the land of Lomar. Those manuscripts, he said, told much of the gods, and besides, in Ulthar there were men who had seen the signs of the gods, and even one old priest who had scaled a great mountain to behold them dancing by moonlight. He had failed, though his companion had succeeded and perished namelessly.

So Randolph Carter thanked the Zoogs, who fluttered amicably and gave him another gourd of moon-tree wine to take with him, and set out through the phosphorescent wood for the other side, where the rushing Skai flows down from the slopes of Lerion, and Hatheg and Nir and Ulthar dot the plain. Behind him, furtive and unseen, crept several of the curious Zoogs; for they wished to learn what might befall him, and bear back the legend to their people. The vast oaks grew thicker as he pushed on beyond the village, and he looked sharply for a certain spot where they would thin somewhat, standing quite dead or dying among the unnaturally dense fungi and the rotting mould and mushy logs of their fallen brothers. There he would turn sharply aside, for at that spot a mighty slab of stone rests on the forest floor; and those who have dared approach it say that it bears an iron ring three feet wide. Remembering the archaic circle of great mossy rocks, and what it was possibly set up for, the Zoogs do not pause near that expansive slab with its huge ring; for they realise that all which is forgotten need not necessarily be dead, and they would not like to see the slab rise slowly and deliberately.

Carter detoured at the proper place, and heard behind him the frightened fluttering of some of the more timid Zoogs. He had known they would follow him, so he was not disturbed; for one grows accustomed to the anomalies of these prying creatures. It was twilight when he came to the edge of the wood, and the strengthening glow told him it was the twilight of morning. Over fertile plains rolling down to the Skai he saw the smoke of cottage chimneys, and on every hand were the hedges and ploughed fields and thatched roofs of a peaceful land. Once he stopped at a farmhouse well for a cup of water, and all the dogs barked affrightedly at the inconspicuous Zoogs that crept through the grass behind. At another house, where people were stirring, he asked questions about the gods, and whether they danced often upon Lerion; but the farmer and his wife would only make the Elder Sign and tell him the way to Nir and Ulthar.

At noon he walked through the one broad high street of Nir, which he had once visited and which marked his farthest former travels in this direction; and soon afterward he came to the great stone bridge across the Skai, into whose central piece the masons had sealed a living human sacrifice when they built it thirteen-hundred years before. Once on the other side, the frequent presence of cats (who all arched their backs at the trailing Zoogs) revealed the near neighborhood of Ulthar; for in Ulthar, according to an ancient and significant law, no man may kill a cat. Very pleasant were the suburbs of Ulthar, with their little green cottages and neatly fenced farms; and still pleasanter was the quaint town itself, with its old peaked roofs and overhanging upper stories and numberless chimney-pots and narrow hill streets where one can see old cobbles whenever the graceful cats afford space enough. Carter, the cats being somewhat dispersed by the half-seen Zoogs, picked his way directly to the modest Temple of the Elder Ones where the priests and old records were said to be; and once within that venerable circular tower of ivied stone – which crowns Ulthar's highest hill – he sought out the patriarch Atal, who had been up the forbidden peak Hatheg-Kia in the stony desert and had come down again alive.

Atal, seated on an ivory dais in a festooned shrine at the top of the temple, was fully three centuries old, but still very keen of mind and memory. From him Carter learned many things about the gods, but mainly that they are indeed only Earth's gods, ruling feebly our own dreamland and having no power or habitation elsewhere. They might, Atal said, heed a man's prayer if in good humour; but one must not think of climbing to their onyx stronghold atop Kadath in the cold waste. It was lucky that no man knew where Kadath towers, for the fruits of ascending it would be very grave. Atal's companion Banni the Wise had been drawn screaming into the sky for climbing merely the known peak of Hatheg-Kia. With unknown Kadath, if ever found, matters would be much worse; for although Earth's gods may sometimes be surpassed by a wise mortal, they are protected by the Other Gods from Outside, whom it is better not to discuss. At least twice in the world's history the Other Gods set their seal upon Earth's primal granite; once in antediluvian times, as guessed from a drawing in those parts of the *Pnakotic Manuscripts* too ancient to be read, and once on Hatheg-Kia when Barzai the Wise tried to see Earth's gods dancing by moonlight. So, Atal said, it would be much better to let all gods alone except in tactful prayers.

Carter, though disappointed by Atal's discouraging advice and by the meagre help to be found in the *Pnakotic Manuscripts* and the Seven Cryptical Books of Hsan, did not wholly despair. First he questioned the old priest about that marvellous sunset city seen from the railed terrace, thinking that perhaps he might find it without the gods' aid; but Atal could tell him nothing. Probably, Atal said, the place belonged to his especial dream world and not to the general land of vision that many know; and conceivably it might be on another planet. In that case Earth's gods could not guide him if they would. But this was not likely, since the stopping of the dreams shewed pretty clearly that it was something the Great Ones wished to hide from him.

Then Carter did a wicked thing, offering his guileless host so many draughts of the moon-wine which the Zoogs had given him that the old man became irresponsibly talkative. Robbed of his reserve, poor Atal babbled freely of forbidden things, telling of a great image reported by travellers as carved on the solid rock of the mountain Ngranek, on the isle of Oriab in the Southern Sea, and hinting that it may be a likeness which Earth's gods once wrought of their own features in the days when they danced by moonlight on that mountain. And he hiccoughed likewise that the features of that image are very strange, so that one might easily recognize them, and that they are sure signs of the authentic race of the gods.

Now the use of all this in finding the gods became at once apparent to Carter. It is known that in disguise the younger among the Great Ones often espouse the daughters of men, so that around the borders of the cold waste wherein stands Kadath the peasants must all bear their blood. This being so, the way to find that waste must be to see the stone face on Ngranek and mark the features; then, having noted them with care, to search for such features among living men. Where they are plainest and thickest, there must the gods dwell nearest; and whatever stony waste lies back of the villages in that place must be that wherein stands Kadath.

Much of the Great Ones might be learnt in such regions, and those with their blood might inherit little memories very useful to a seeker. They might not know their parentage, for the gods so dislike to be known among men that none can be found who has seen their faces wittingly; a thing which Carter realized even as he sought to scale Kadath. But they would have queer lofty thoughts misunderstood by their fellows, and would sing of far places and gardens so unlike any known even in the dreamland that common folk would call them fools; and from all this one could perhaps learn old secrets of Kadath, or gain hints of the marvellous sunset city which the gods held secret. And more, one might in certain cases seize some well-loved child of a god as hostage; or even capture some young god himself, disguised and dwelling amongst men with a comely peasant maiden as his bride.

Atal, however, did not know how to find Ngranek on its isle of Oriab; and recommended that Carter follow the singing Skai under its bridges down to the Southern Sea, where no burgess of Ulthar has ever been, but whence the merchants come in boats or with long caravans of mules and two-wheeled carts. There is a great city there, Dylath-Leen, but in Ulthar its reputation is bad because of the black three-banked galleys that sail to it with rubies from no clearly named shore. The traders that come from those galleys to deal with the jewellers are human, or nearly so, but the rowers are never beheld; and it is not thought wholesome in Ulthar that merchants should trade with black ships from unknown places whose rowers cannot be exhibited.

By the time he had given this information Atal was very drowsy, and Carter laid him gently on a couch of inlaid ebony and gathered his long beard decorously on his chest. As he turned to go, he observed that no suppressed fluttering followed him, and wondered why the Zoogs had become so lax in their curious pursuit. Then he noticed all the sleek complacent cats of Ulthar licking their chops with unusual gusto, and recalled the spitting and caterwauling he had faintly heard, in lower parts of the temple, while absorbed in the old priest's conversation. He recalled, too, the evilly hungry way in which an especially impudent young Zoog had regarded a small black kitten in the cobbled street outside. And because he loved nothing on earth more than small black kittens, he stooped and petted the sleek cats of Ulthar as they licked their chops, and did not mourn because those inquisitive Zoogs would escort him no farther.

It was sunset now, so Carter stopped at an ancient inn on a steep little street overlooking the lower town. And as he went out on the balcony of his room and gazed down at the sea of red tiled roofs and cobbled ways and the pleasant fields beyond, all mellow and magical in the slanted light, he swore that Ulthar would be a very likely place to dwell in always, were not the memory of a greater sunset city ever goading one onward toward unknown perils. Then twilight fell, and the pink walls of the plastered gables turned violet and mystic, and little yellow lights floated up one by one from old lattice windows. And sweet bells pealed in the temple tower above, and the first star winked softly above the meadows across the Skai. With the night came song, and Carter nodded as the lutanists praised ancient days from beyond the filigreed balconies and tesselated courts of simple Ulthar. And there might have been sweetness even in the voices of Ulthar's many cats, but that they were mostly heavy and silent from strange feasting. Some of them stole off to those cryptical realms which are known only to cats and which villagers say are on the moon's dark side, whither the cats leap from tall housetops, but one small black kitten crept upstairs and sprang in Carter's lap to purr and play, and curled up near his feet when he lay down at last on the little couch whose pillows were stuffed with fragrant, drowsy herbs.

In the morning Carter joined a caravan of merchants bound for Dylath-Leen with the spun wool of Ulthar and the cabbages of Ulthar's busy farms. And for six days they rode with tinkling bells on the smooth road beside the Skai, stopping some nights at the inns of little quaint fishing towns, and on other nights camping under the stars while snatches of boatmen's songs came from the placid river. The country was very beautiful, with green hedges and groves and picturesque peaked cottages and octagonal windmills.

On the seventh day a blur of smoke rose on the horizon ahead, and then the tall black towers of Dylath-Leen, which is built mostly of basalt. Dylath-Leen with its thin angular towers looks in the distance like a bit of the Giant's Causeway, and its streets are dark and uninviting. There are many dismal sea-taverns near the myriad wharves, and all the town is thronged with the strange seamen of every land on earth and of a few which are said to be not on earth. Carter questioned the oddly robed men of that city about the peak of Ngranek on the isle of Oriab, and found that they knew of it well.

Ships came from Baharna on that island, one being due to return thither in only a month, and Ngranek is but two days' zebra-ride from that port. But few had seen the stone face of the god, because it is on a very difficult side of Ngranek, which overlooks only sheer crags and a valley of sinister lava. Once the gods were angered with men on that side, and spoke of the matter to the Other Gods.

It was hard to get this information from the traders and sailors in Dylath-Leen's sea taverns, because they mostly preferred to whisper of the black galleys. One of them was due in a week with rubies from its unknown shore, and the townsfolk dreaded to see it dock. The mouths of the men who came from it to trade were too wide, and the way their turbans were humped up in two points above their foreheads was in especially bad taste. And their shoes were the shortest and queerest ever seen in the Six Kingdoms. But worst of all was the matter of the unseen rowers. Those three banks of oars moved too briskly and accurately and vigorously to be comfortable, and it was not right for a ship to stay in port for weeks while the merchants traded, yet to give no glimpse of its crew. It was not fair to the tavern-keepers of Dylath-Leen, or to the grocers and butchers, either; for not a scrap of provisions was ever sent aboard. The merchants took only gold and stout black slaves from Parg across the river. That was all they ever took, those unpleasantly featured merchants and their unseen rowers; never anything from the butchers and grocers, but only gold and the fat black men of Parg whom they bought by the pound. And the odours from those galleys which the south wind blew in from the wharves are not to be described. Only by constantly smoking strong thagweed could even the hardiest denizen of the old sea-taverns bear them. Dylath-Leen would never have tolerated the black galleys had such rubies been obtainable elsewhere, but no mine in all Barth's dreamland was known to produce their like.

Of these things Dylath-Leen's cosmopolitan folk chiefly gossiped whilst Carter waited patiently for the ship from Baharna, which might bear him to the isle whereon carven Ngranek towers lofty and barren. Meanwhile he did not fail to seek through the haunts of far travellers for any tales they might have concerning Kadath in the cold waste or a marvellous city of marble walls and silver fountains seen below terraces in the sunset. Of these things, however, he learned nothing, though he once thought that a certain old slant-eyed merchant looked queerly intelligent when the cold waste was spoken of. This man was reputed to trade with the horrible stone villages on the icy desert plateau of Leng, which no healthy folk visit and whose evil fires are seen at night from afar. He was even rumoured to have dealt with that High-Priest Not To Be Described, which wears a yellow silken mask over its face and dwells all alone in a prehistoric stone monastery. That such a person might well have had nibbling traffick with such beings as may conceivably dwell in the cold waste was not to be doubted, but Carter soon found that it was no use questioning him.

Then the black galley slipped into the harbour past the basalt wale and the tall lighthouse, silent and alien, and with a strange stench that the south wind drove into the town. Uneasiness rustled through the taverns along that waterfront, and after a while the dark wide-mouthed merchants with humped turbans and short feet clumped steathily ashore to seek the bazaars of the jewellers. Carter observed them closely, and disliked them more the longer he looked at them. Then he saw them drive the stout black men of Parg up the gang-plank grunting and sweating into that singular galley, and wondered in what lands – or if in any lands at all – those fat pathetic creatures might be destined to serve.

And on the third evening of that galley's stay one of the uncomfortable merchants spoke to him, smirking sinfully and hinting of what he had heard in the taverns of Carter's quest. He appeared to have knowledge too secret for public telling; and although the sound of his voice was unbearably hateful, Carter felt that the lore of so far a traveller must not be overlooked. He bade him therefore be his guest in locked chambers above, and drew out the last of the Zoogs' moon-wine to loosen his tongue. The strange merchant drank heavily, but smirked unchanged by the draught. Then he drew forth a curious bottle with wine of his own, and Carter saw that the bottle was a single hollowed ruby, grotesquely carved in patterns too fabulous to be comprehended. He offered his wine to his host, and though Carter took only the least sip, he felt the dizziness of space and the fever of unimagined jungles. All the while the guest had been smiling more and more broadly, and as Carter slipped into blankness the last thing he saw was that dark odious face convulsed with evil laughter and something quite unspeakable where one of the two frontal puffs of that orange turban had become disarranged with the shakings of that epileptic mirth.

Carter next had consciousness amidst horrible odours beneath a tent-like awning on the deck of a ship, with the marvellous coasts of the Southern Sea flying by in unnatural swiftness. He was not chained, but three of the dark sardonic merchants stood grinning nearby, and the sight of those humps in their turbans made him almost as faint as did the stench that filtered up through the sinister hatches. He saw slip past him the glorious lands and cities of which a fellow-dreamer of earth – a lighthouse-keeper in ancient Kingsport – had often discoursed in the old days, and recognized the templed terraces of Zak, abode of forgotten dreams; the spires of infamous Thalarion, that daemon-city of a thousand wonders where the eidolon Lathi reigns; the charnel gardens of Zura, land of pleasures unattained, and the twin headlands of crystal, meeting above in a resplendent arch, which guard the harbour of Sona-Nyl, blessed land of fancy.

Past all these gorgeous lands the malodorous ship flew unwholesomely, urged by the abnormal strokes of those unseen rowers below. And before the day was done Carter saw that the steersman could have no other goal than the Basalt Pillars of the West, beyond which simple folk say splendid Cathuria lies, but which wise dreamers well know are the gates of a monstrous cataract wherein the oceans of earth's dreamland drop wholly to abysmal nothingness and shoot through the empty spaces toward other worlds and other stars and the awful voids outside the ordered universe where the daemon sultan Azathoth gnaws hungrily in chaos amid pounding and piping and the hellish dancing of the Other Gods, blind, voiceless, tenebrous, and mindless, with their soul and messenger Nyarlathotep.

Meanwhile the three sardonic merchants would give no word of their intent, though Carter well knew that they must be leagued with those who wished to hold him from his quest. It is understood in the land of dream that the Other Gods have many agents moving among men; and all these agents, whether wholly human or slightly less than human, are eager to work the will of those blind and mindless things in return for the favour of their hideous soul and messenger, the crawling chaos Nyarlathotep. So Carter inferred that the merchants of the humped turbans, hearing of his daring search for the Great Ones in their castle of Kadath, had decided to take him away and deliver him to Nyarlathotep for whatever nameless bounty might be offered for such a prize. What might be the land of those merchants in our known universe or in the eldritch spaces outside, Carter could not guess; nor could he imagine at what hellish trysting-place they would meet the crawling chaos to give him up and claim their reward. He knew, however, that no beings as nearly human as these would dare approach the ultimate nighted throne of the daemon Azathoth in the formless central void.

At the set of sun the merchants licked their excessively wide lips and glared hungrily and one of them went below and returned from some hidden and offensive cabin with a pot and basket of plates. Then they squatted close together beneath the awning and ate the smoking meat that was passed around. But when they gave Carter a portion, he found something very terrible in the size and shape of it, so that he turned even paler than before and cast that portion into the sea when no eye was on him. And again he thought of those unseen rowers beneath, and of the suspicious nourishment from which their far too mechanical strength was derived.

It was dark when the galley passed betwixt the Basalt Pillars of the West and the sound of the ultimate cataract swelled portentous from ahead. And the spray of that cataract rose to obscure the stars, and the deck grew damp, and the vessel reeled in the surging current of the brink. Then with a queer whistle and plunge the leap was taken, and Carter felt the terrors of nightmare as earth fell away and the great boat shot silent and comet-like into planetary space. Never before had he known what shapeless black things lurk and caper and flounder all through the aether, leering and grinning at such voyagers as may pass, and sometimes feeling about with slimy paws when some moving object excites their curiosity. These are the nameless larvae of the Other Gods, and like them are blind and without mind, and possessed of singular hungers and thirsts.

But that offensive galley did not aim as far as Carter had feared, for he soon saw that the helmsman was steering a course directly for the moon. The moon was a crescent shining larger and larger as they approached it, and shewing its singular craters and peaks uncomfortably. The ship made for the edge, and it soon became clear that its destination was that secret and mysterious side which is always turned away from earth, and which no fully human person, save perhaps the dreamer Snireth-Ko, has ever beheld. The close aspect of the moon as the galley drew near proved very disturbing to Carter, and he did not like the size and shape of the ruins which crumbled here and there. The dead temples on the mountains were so placed that they could have glorified no suitable or wholesome gods, and in the symmetries of the broken columns there seemed to be some dark and inner meaning which did not invite solution. And what the structure and proportions of the olden worshippers could have been, Carter steadily refused to conjecture.

When the ship rounded the edge, and sailed over those lands unseen by man, there appeared in the queer landscape certain signs of life, and Carter saw many low, broad, round cottages in fields of grotesque whitish fungi. He noticed that these cottages had no windows, and thought that their shape suggested the huts of Esquimaux. Then he glimpsed the oily waves of a sluggish sea, and knew that the voyage was once more to be by water – or at least through some liquid. The galley struck the surface with a peculiar sound, and the odd elastic way the waves received it was very perplexing to Carter.

They now slid along at great speed, once passing and hailing another galley of kindred form, but generally seeing nothing but that curious sea and a sky that was black and star-strewn even though the sun shone scorchingly in it.

There presently rose ahead the jagged hills of a leprous-looking coast, and Carter saw the thick unpleasant grey towers of a city. The way they leaned and bent, the manner in which they were clustered, and the fact that they had no windows at all, was very disturbing to the prisoner; and he bitterly mourned the folly which had made him sip the curious wine of that merchant with the humped turban. As the coast drew nearer, and the hideous stench of that city grew stronger, he saw upon the jagged hills many forests, some of whose trees he recognized as akin to that solitary moon-tree in the enchanted wood of earth, from whose sap the small brown Zoogs ferment their curious wine.

Carter could now distinguish moving figures on the noisome wharves ahead, and the better he saw them the worse he began to fear and detest them. For they were not men at all, or even approximately men, but great greyish-white slippery things which could expand and contract at will, and whose principal shape – though it often changed – was that of a sort of toad without any eyes, but with a curious vibrating mass of short pink tentacles on the end of its blunt, vague snout. These objects were waddling busily about the wharves, moving bales and crates and boxes with preternatural strength, and now and then hopping on or off some anchored galley with long oars in their forepaws. And now and then one would appear driving a herd of clumping slaves, which indeed were approximate human beings with wide mouths like those merchants who traded in Dylath-Leen; only these herds, being without turbans or shoes or clothing, did not seem so very human after all. Some of the slaves – the fatter ones, whom a sort of overseer would pinch experimentally – were unloaded from ships and nailed in crates which workers pushed into the low warehouses or loaded on great lumbering vans.

Once a van was hitched and driven off, and the fabulous thing which drew it was such that Carter gasped, even after having seen the other monstrosities of that hateful place. Now and then a small herd of slaves dressed and turbaned like the dark merchants would be driven aboard a galley, followed by a great crew of the slippery toad-things as officers, navigators, and rowers. And Carter saw that the almost-human creatures were reserved for the more ignominious kinds of servitude which required no strength, such as steering and cooking, fetching and carrying, and bargaining with men on the earth or other planets where they traded. These creatures must have been convenient on earth, for they were truly not unlike men when dressed and carefully shod and turbaned, and could haggle in the shops of men without embarrassment or curious explanations. But most of them, unless lean or ill-favoured, were unclothed and packed in crates and drawn off in lumbering lorries by fabulous things. Occasionally other beings were unloaded and crated; some very like these semi-humans, some not so similar, and some not similar at all. And he wondered if any of the poor stout black men of Parg were left to be unloaded and crated and shipped inland in those obnoxious drays.

When the galley landed at a greasy-looking quay of spongy rock a nightmare horde of toad-things wiggled out of the hatches, and two of them seized Carter and dragged him ashore. The smell and aspect of that city are beyond telling, and Carter held only scattered images of the tiled streets and black doorways and endless precipices of grey vertical walls without windows. At length he was dragged within a low doorway and made to climb infinite steps in pitch blackness. It was, apparently, all one to the toad-things whether it were light or dark. The odour of the place was intolerable, and when Carter was locked into a chamber and left alone he scarcely had strength to crawl around and ascertain its form and dimensions. It was circular, and about twenty feet across.

From then on time ceased to exist. At intervals food was pushed in, but Carter would not touch it. What his fate would be, he did not know; but he felt that he was held for the coming of that frightful soul and messenger of infinity's Other Gods, the crawling chaos Nyarlathotep. Finally, after an unguessed span of hours or days, the great stone door swung wide again, and Carter was shoved down the stairs and out into the red-litten streets of that fearsome city. It was night on the moon, and all through the town were stationed slaves bearing torches.

In a detestable square a sort of procession was formed; ten of the toad-things and twenty-four almost human torch-bearers, eleven on either side, and one each before and behind. Carter was placed in the middle of the line, five toad-things ahead and five behind, and one almost-human torch-bearer on either side of him. Certain of the toad-things produced disgustingly carven flutes of ivory and made loathsome sounds. To that hellish piping the column advanced out of the tiled streets and into nighted plains of obscene fungi, soon commencing to climb one of the lower and more gradual hills that lay behind the city. That on some frightful slope or blasphemous plateau the crawling chaos waited, Carter could not doubt; and he wished that the suspense might soon be over. The whining of those impious flutes was shocking, and he would have given worlds for some even half-normal sound; but these toad-things had no voices, and the slaves did not talk.

Then through that star-specked darkness there did come a normal sound. It rolled from the higher hills, and from all the jagged peaks around it was caught up and echoed in a swelling pandaemoniac chorus. It was the midnight yell of the cat, and Carter knew at last that the old village folk were right when they made low guesses about the cryptical realms which are known only to cats, and to which the elders among cats repair by stealth nocturnally, springing from high housetops. Verily, it is to the moon's dark side that they go to leap and gambol on the hills and converse with ancient shadows, and here amidst that column of foetid things Carter heard their homely, friendly cry, and thought of the steep roofs and warm hearths and little lighted windows of home.

Now much of the speech of cats was known to Randolph Carter, and in this far terrible place he uttered the cry that was suitable. But that he need not have done, for even as his lips opened he heard the chorus wax and draw nearer, and saw swift shadows against the stars as small graceful shapes leaped from hill to hill in gathering legions. The call of the clan had been given, and before the foul procession had time even to be frightened a cloud of smothering fur and a phalanx of murderous claws were tidally and tempestuously upon it. The flutes stopped, and there were shrieks in the night. Dying almost-humans screamed, and cats spit and yowled and roared, but the toad-things made never a sound as their stinking green ichor oozed fatally upon that porous earth with the obscene fungi.

It was a stupendous sight while the torches lasted, and Carter had never before seen so many cats. Black, grey, and white; yellow, tiger, and mixed; common, Persian, and Marix; Thibetan, Angora, and Egyptian; all were there in the fury of battle, and there hovered over them some trace of that profound and inviolate sanctity which made their goddess great in the temples of Bubastis. They would leap seven strong at the throat of an almost-human or the pink tentacled snout of a toad-thing and drag it down savagely to the fungous plain, where myriads of their fellows would surge over it and into it with the frenzied claws and teeth of a divine battle-fury. Carter had seized a torch from a stricken slave, but was soon overborne by the surging waves of his loyal defenders. Then he lay in the utter blackness hearing the clangour of war and the shouts of the victors, and feeling the soft paws of his friends as they rushed to and fro over him in the fray.

At last awe and exhaustion closed his eyes, and when he opened them again it was upon a strange scene. The great shining disc of the earth, thirteen times greater than that of the moon as we see it, had risen with floods of weird light over the lunar landscape; and across all those leagues of wild plateau and ragged crest there squatted one endless sea of cats in orderly array. Circle on circle they reached, and two or three leaders out of the ranks were licking his face and purring to him consolingly. Of the dead slaves and toad-things there were not many signs, but Carter thought he saw one bone a little way off in the open space between him and the warriors.

Carter now spoke with the leaders in the soft language of cats, and learned that his ancient friendship with the species was well known and often spoken of in the places where cats congregate. He had not been unmarked in Ulthar when he passed through, and the sleek old cats had remembered how he patted them after they had attended to the hungry Zoogs who looked evilly at a small black kitten. And they recalled, too, how he had welcomed the very little kitten who came to see him at the inn, and how he had given it a saucer of rich cream in the morning before he left. The grandfather of that very little kitten was the leader of the army now assembled, for he had seen the evil procession from a far hill and recognized the prisoner as a sworn friend of his kind on earth and in the land of dream.

A yowl now came from the farther peak, and the old leader paused abruptly in his conversation. It was one of the army's outposts, stationed on the highest of the mountains to watch the one foe which Earth's cats fear; the very large and peculiar cats from Saturn, who for some reason have not been oblivious of the charm of our moon's dark side. They are leagued by treaty with the evil toad-things, and are notoriously hostile to our earthly cats; so that at this juncture a meeting would have been a somewhat grave matter.

After a brief consultation of generals, the cats rose and assumed a closer formation, crowding protectingly around Carter and preparing to take the great leap through space back to the housetops of our earth and its dreamland. The old field-marshal advised Carter to let himself be borne along smoothly and passively in the massed ranks of furry leapers, and told him how to spring when the rest sprang and land gracefully when the rest landed. He also offered to deposit him in any spot he desired, and Carter decided on the city of

Dylath-Leen whence the black galley had set out; for he wished to sail thence for Oriab and the carven crest Ngranek, and also to warn the people of the city to have no more traffick with black galleys, if indeed that traffick could be tactfully and judiciously broken off. Then, upon a signal, the cats all leaped gracefully with their friend packed securely in their midst, while in a black cave on an unhallowed summit of the moon-mountains still vainly waited the crawling chaos Nyarlathotep.

The leap of the cats through space was very swift; and being surrounded by his companions Carter did not see this time the great black shapelessnesses that lurk and caper and flounder in the abyss. Before he fully realised what had happened he was back in his familiar room at the inn at Dylath-Leen, and the stealthy, friendly cats were pouring out of the window in streams. The old leader from Ulthar was the last to leave, and as Carter shook his paw he said he would be able to get home by cockcrow. When dawn came, Carter went downstairs and learned that a week had elapsed since his capture and leaving. There was still nearly a fortnight to wait for the ship bound toward Oriab, and during that time he said what he could against the black galleys and their infamous ways. Most of the townsfolk believed him; yet so fond were the jewellers of great rubies that none would wholly promise to cease trafficking with the wide-mouthed merchants. If aught of evil ever befalls Dylath-Leen through such traffick, it will not be his fault.

In about a week the desiderate ship put in by the black wale and tall lighthouse, and Carter was glad to see that she was a barque of wholesome men, with painted sides and yellow lateen sails and a grey captain in silken robes. Her cargo was the fragrant resin of Oriab's inner groves, and the delicate pottery baked by the artists of Baharna, and the strange little figures carved from Ngranek's ancient lava. For this they were paid in the wool of Ulthar and the iridescent textiles of Hatheg and the ivory that the black men carve across the river in Parg. Carter made arrangements with the captain to go to Baharna and was told that the voyage would take ten days. And during his week of waiting he talked much with that captain of Ngranek, and was told that very few had seen the carven face thereon; but that most travellers are content to learn its legends from old people and lava-gatherers and image-makers in Baharna and afterward say in their far homes that they have indeed beheld it. The captain was not even sure that any person now living had beheld that carven face, for the wrong side of Ngranek is very difficult and barren and sinister, and there are rumours of caves near the peak wherein dwell the night-gaunts. But the captain did not wish to say just what a night-gaunt might be like, since such cattle are known to haunt most persistently the dreams of those who think too often of them. Then Carter asked that captain about unknown Kadath in the cold waste, and the marvellous sunset city, but of these the good man could truly tell nothing.

Carter sailed out of Dylath-Leen one early morning when the tide turned, and saw the first rays of sunrise on the thin angular towers of that dismal basalt town. And for two days they sailed eastward in sight of green coasts, and saw often the pleasant fishing towns that climbed up steeply with their red roofs and chimney-pots from old dreaming wharves and beaches where nets lay drying. But on the third day they turned sharply south where the roll of water was stronger, and soon passed from sight of any land. On the fifth day the sailors were nervous, but the captain apologized for their fears, saying that the ship was about to pass over the weedy walls and broken columns of a sunken city too old for memory, and that when the water was clear one could see so many moving shadows in that deep place that simple folk disliked it. He admitted, moreover, that many ships had been lost in that part of the sea, having been hailed when quite close to it, but never seen again.

That night the moon was very bright, and one could see a great way down in the water. There was so little wind that the ship could not move much, and the ocean was very calm. Looking over the rail Carter saw many fathoms deep the dome of the great temple, and in front of it an avenue of unnatural sphinxes leading to what was once a public square. Dolphins sported merrily in and out of the ruins, and porpoises revelled clumsily here and there, sometimes coming to the surface and leaping clear out of the sea. As the ship drifted on a little the floor of the ocean rose in hills, and one could clearly mark the lines of ancient climbing streets and the washed-down walls of myriad little houses.

Then the suburbs appeared, and finally a great lone building on a hill, of simpler architecture than the other structures, and in much better repair. It was dark and low and covered four sides of a square, with a tower at each corner, a paved court in the centre, and small curious round windows all over it. Probably it was of basalt, though weeds draped the greater part; and such was its lonely and impressive place on that far hill that it may have been a temple or a monastery. Some phosphorescent fish inside it gave the small round windows an aspect of shining, and Carter did not blame the sailors much for their fears. Then by the watery moonlight he noticed an odd high mono-lith in the middle of that central court, and saw that something was tied to it. And when after getting a telescope from the captain's cabin he saw that that bound thing was a sailor in the silk robes of Oriab, head downward and without any eyes, he was glad that a rising breeze soon took the ship ahead to more healthy parts of the sea.

The next day they spoke with a ship with violet sails bound for Zar, in the land of forgotten dreams, with bulbs of strange coloured lilies for cargo. And on the evening of the eleventh day they came in sight of the isle of Oriab with Ngranek rising jagged and snow-crowned in the distance. Oriab is a very great isle, and its port of Baharna a mighty city. The wharves of Baharna are of porphyry, and the city rises in great stone terraces behind them, having streets of steps that are frequently arched over by buildings and the bridges between buildings. There is a great canal which goes under the whole city in a tunnel with granite gates and leads to the inland lake of Yath, on whose farther shore are the vast clay-brick ruins of a primal city whose name is not remembered. As the ship drew into the harbour at evening the twin beacons Thon and Thal gleamed a welcome, and in all the million windows of Baharna's terraces mellow lights peeped out quietly and gradually as the stars peep out overhead in the dusk, till that steep and climbing seaport became a glittering constellation hung between the stars of heaven and the reflections of those stars in the still harbour.

The captain, after landing, made Carter a guest in his own small house on the shores of Yath where the rear of the town slopes down to it; and his wife and servants brought strange toothsome foods for the traveller's delight. And in the days after that Carter asked for rumours and legends of Ngranek in all the taverns and public places where lava-gatherers and image-makers meet, but could find no one who had been up the higher slopes or seen the carven face. Ngranek was a hard mountain with only an accursed valley behind it, and besides, one could never depend on the certainty that night-gaunts are altogether fabulous.

When the captain sailed hack to Dylath-Leen Carter took quarters in an ancient tavern opening on an alley of steps in the original part of the town, which is built of brick and resembles the ruins of Yath's farther shore. Here he laid his plans for the ascent of Ngranek, and correlated all that he had learned from the lava-gatherers about the roads thither. The keeper of the tavern was a very old man, and had heard so many legends that he was a great help. He even took Carter to an upper room in that ancient house and shewed him a crude picture which a traveller had scratched on the clay wall in the old days when men were bolder and less reluctant to visit Ngranek's higher slopes. The old tavern-keeper's great-grandfather had heard from his great-grandfather that the traveller who scratched that picture had climbed Ngranek and seen the carven face, here drawing it for others to behold, but Carter had very great doubts, since the large rough features on the wall were hasty and careless, and wholly overshadowed by a crowd of little companion shapes in the worst possible taste, with horns and wings and claws and curling tails.

At last, having gained all the information he was likely to gain in the taverns and public places of Baharna, Carter hired a zebra and set out one morning on the road by Yath's shore for those inland parts wherein towers stony Ngranek. On his right were rolling hills and pleasant orchards and neat little stone farmhouses, and he was much reminded of those fertile fields that flank the Skai. By evening he was near the nameless ancient ruins on Yath's farther shore, and though old lava-gatherers had warned him not to camp there at night, he tethered his zebra to a curious pillar before a crumbling wall and laid his blanket in a sheltered corner beneath some carvings whose meaning none could decipher. Around him he wrapped another blanket, for the nights are cold in Oriab; and when upon awaking once he thought he felt the wings of some insect brushing his face he covered his head altogether and slept in peace till roused by the magah birds in distant resin groves.

The sun had just come up over the great slope whereon leagues of primal brick foundations and worn walls and occasional cracked pillars and pedestals stretched down desolate to the shore of Yath, and Carter looked about for his tethered zebra. Great was his dismay to see that docile beast stretched prostrate beside the curious pillar to which it had been tied, and still greater was he vexed on finding that the steed was quite dead, with its blood all sucked away through a singular wound in its throat. His pack had been disturbed, and several shiny knickknacks taken away, and all round on the dusty soil were great webbed footprints for which he could not in any way account. The legends and warnings of lava-gatherers occurred to him, and he thought of what had brushed his face in the night. Then he shouldered his pack and strode on toward Ngranek, though not without a shiver when he saw close to him as the highway passed through the ruins a great gaping arch low in the wall of an old temple, with steps leading down into darkness farther than he could peer.

His course now lay uphill through wilder and partly wooded country, and he saw only the huts of charcoal-burners and the camp of those who gathered resin from the groves. The whole air was fragrant with balsam, and all the magah birds sang blithely as they flashed their seven colours in the sun. Near sunset he came on a new camp of lava-gatherers returning with laden sacks from Ngranek's lower slopes; and here he also camped, listening to the songs and tales of the men, and overhearing what they whispered about a companion they had lost. He had climbed high to reach a mass of fine lava above him, and at nightfall did not return to his fellows. When they looked for him the next day they found only his turban, nor was there any sign on the crags below that he had fallen. They did not search any more, because the old men among them said it would be of no use.

No one ever found what the night-gaunts took, though those beasts themselves were so uncertain as to be almost fabulous. Carter asked them if night-gaunts sucked blood and liked shiny things and left webbed footprints, but they all shook their heads negatively and seemed frightened at his making such an inquiry. When he saw how taciturn they had become he asked them no more, but went to sleep in his blanket.

The next day he rose with the lava-gatherers and exchanged fare-wells as they rode west and he rode east on a zebra he bought of them. Their older men gave him blessings and warnings, and told him he had better not climb too high on Ngranek, but while he thanked them heartily he was in no wise dissuaded. For still did he feel that he must find the gods on unknown Kadath; and win from them a way to that haunting and marvellous city in the sunset. By noon, after a long uphill ride, he came upon some abandoned brick villages of the hill-people who had once dwelt thus close to Ngranek and carved images from its smooth lava. Here they had dwelt till the days of the old tavern-keeper's grandfather, but about that time they felt that their presence was disliked. Their homes had crept even up the mountain's slope, and the higher they built the more people they would miss when the sun rose. At last they decided it would be better to leave altogether, since things were sometimes glimpsed in the darkness which no one could interpret favourably; so in the end all of them went down to the sea and dwelt in Baharna, inhabiting a very old quarter and teaching their sons the old art of image-making which to this day they carry on. It was from these children of the exiled hill-people that Carter had heard the best tales about Ngranek when searching through Bahama's ancient taverns.

All this time the great gaunt side of Ngranek was looming up higher and higher as Carter approached it. There were sparse trees on the lower slopes and feeble shrubs above them, and then the bare hideous rock rose spectral into the sky, to mix with frost and ice and eternal snow. Carter could see the rifts and ruggedness of that sombre stone, and did not welcome the prospect of climbing it. In places there were solid streams of lava, and scoriac heaps that littered slopes and ledges. Ninety aeons ago, before even the gods had danced upon its pointed peak, that mountain had spoken with fire and roared with the voices of the inner thunders. Now it towered all silent and sinister, bearing on the hidden side that secret titan image whereof rumour told. And there were caves in that mountain, which might be empty and alone with elder darkness, or might – if legend spoke truly – hold horrors of a form not to be surmised.

The ground sloped upward to the foot of Ngranek, thinly covered with scrub oaks and ash trees, and strewn with bits of rock, lava, and ancient cinder. There were the charred embers of many camps, where the lava-gatherers were wont to stop, and several rude altars which they had built either to propitiate the Great Ones or to ward off what they dreamed of in Ngranek's high passes and labyrinthine caves. At evening Carter reached the farthermost pile of embers and camped for the night, tethering his zebra to a sapling and wrapping himself well in his blankets before going to sleep. And all through the night a voonith howled distantly from the shore of some hidden pool, but Carter felt no fear of that amphibious terror, since he had been told with certainty that not one of them dares even approach the slope of Ngranek.

In the clear sunshine of morning Carter began the long ascent, taking his zebra as far as that useful beast could go, but tying it to a stunted ash tree when the floor of the thin wood became too steep. Thereafter he scrambled up alone; first through the forest with its ruins of old villages in overgrown clearings, and then over the tough grass where anaemic shrubs grew here and there. He regretted coming clear of the trees, since the slope was very precipitous and the whole thing rather dizzying. At length he began to discern all the countryside spread out beneath him whenever he looked about; the deserted huts of the image-makers, the groves of resin trees and the camps of those who gathered from them, the woods where prismatic magahs nest and sing, and even a hint very far away of the shores of Yath and of those forbidding ancient ruins whose name is forgotten. He found it best not to look around, and kept on climbing and climbing till the shrubs became very sparse and there was often nothing but the tough grass to cling to.

Then the soil became meagre, with great patches of bare rock cropping out, and now and then the nest of a condor in a crevice. Finally there was nothing at all but the bare rock, and had it not been very rough and weathered, he could scarcely have ascended farther. Knobs, ledges, and pinnacles, however, helped greatly; and it was cheering to see occasionally the sign of some lava-gatherer scratched clumsily in the friable stone, and know that wholesome human creatures had been there before him. After a certain height the presence of man was further shewn by handholds and footholds hewn where they were needed, and by little quarries and excavations where some choice vein or stream of lava had been found. In one place a narrow ledge had been chopped artificially to an especially rich deposit far to the right of the main line of ascent. Once or twice Carter dared to look around, and was almost stunned by the spread of landscape below. All the island betwixt him and the coast lay open to his sight, with Baharna's stone terraces and the smoke of its chimneys mystical in the distance. And beyond that the illimitable Southern Sea with all its curious secrets.

Thus far there had been much winding around the mountain, so that the farther and carven side was still hidden. Carter now saw a ledge running upward and to the left which seemed to head the way he wished, and this course he took in the hope that it might prove continuous. After ten minutes he saw it was indeed no cul-de-sac, but that it led steeply on in an arc which would, unless suddenly interrupted or deflected, bring him after a few hours' climbing to that unknown southern slope overlooking the desolate crags and the accursed valley of lava. As new country came into view below him he saw that it was bleaker and wilder than those seaward lands he had traversed. The mountain's side, too, was somewhat different, being here pierced by curious cracks and caves not found on the straighter route he had left. Some of these were above him and some beneath him, all opening on sheerly perpendicular cliffs and wholly unreachable by the feet of man. The air was very cold now, but so hard was the climbing that he did not mind it. Only the increasing rarity bothered him, and he thought that perhaps it was this which had turned the heads of other travellers and excited those absurd tales of night-gaunts whereby they explained the loss of such climbers as fell from these perilous paths. He was not much impressed by travellers' tales, but had a good curved scimitar in case of any trouble. All lesser thoughts were lost in the wish to see that carven face which might set him on the track of the gods atop unknown Kadath.

At last, in the fearsome iciness of upper space, he came round fully to the hidden side of Ngranek and saw in infinite gulfs below him the lesser crags and sterile abysses of lava which marked olden wrath of the Great Ones. There was unfolded, too, a vast expanse of country to the south; but it was a desert land without fair fields or cottage chimneys, and seemed to have no ending. No trace of the sea was visible on this side, for Oriab is a great island. Black caverns and odd crevices were still numerous on the sheer vertical cliffs, but none of them was accessible to a climber. There now loomed aloft a great beetling mass which hampered the upward view, and Carter was for a moment shaken with doubt lest it prove impassable. Poised in windy insecurity miles above earth, with only space and death on one side and only slippery walls of rock on the other, he knew for a moment the fear that makes men shun Ngranek's hidden side. He could not turn round, yet the sun was already low. If there were no way aloft, the night would find him crouching there still, and the dawn would not find him at all.

But there was a way, and he saw it in due season. Only a very expert dreamer could have used those imperceptible footholds, yet to Carter they were sufficient. Surmounting now the outward-hanging rock, he found the slope above much easier than that below, since a great glacier's melting had left a generous space with loam and ledges. To the left a precipice dropped straight from unknown heights to unknown depths, with a cave's dark mouth just out of reach above him. Elsewhere, however, the mountain slanted back strongly, and even gave him space to lean and rest.

He felt from the chill that he must be near the snow line, and looked up to see what glittering pinnacles might be shining in that late ruddy sunlight. Surely enough, there was the snow uncounted thousands of feet above, and below it a great beetling crag like that he had just climbed, hanging there forever in bold outline. And when he saw that crag he gasped and cried out aloud, and clutched at the jagged rock in awe; for the titan bulge had not stayed as earth's dawn had shaped it, but gleamed red and stupendous in the sunset with the carved and polished features of a god.

Stern and terrible shone that face that the sunset lit with fire. How vast it was no mind can ever measure, but Carter knew at once that man could never have fashioned it. It was a god chiselled by the hands of the gods, and it looked down haughty and majestic upon the seeker. Rumour had said it was strange and not to be mistaken, and Carter saw that it was indeed so; for those long narrow eyes and long-lobed ears, and that thin nose and pointed chin, all spoke of a race that is not of men but of gods.

He clung overawed in that lofty and perilous eyrie, even though it was this which he had expected and come to find; for there is in a god's face more of marvel than prediction can tell, and when that face is vaster than a great temple and seen looking downward at sunset in the scyptic silences of that upper world from whose dark lava it was divinely hewn of old, the marvel is so strong that none may escape it.

Here, too, was the added marvel of recognition; for although he had planned to search all dreamland over for those whose likeness to this face might mark them as the god's children, he now knew that he need not do so. Certainly, the great face carven on that mountain was of no strange sort, but the kin of such as he had seen often in the taverns of the seaport Celephaïs which lies in Ooth-Nargai beyond the Tanarian Hills and is ruled over by that King Kuranes whom Carter once knew in waking life. Every year sailors with such a face came in dark ships from the north to trade their onyx for the carved jade and spun gold and little red singing birds of Celephaïs, and it was clear that these could be no others than the hall-gods he sought. Where they dwelt, there must the cold waste lie close, and within it unknown Kadath and its onyx castle for the Great Ones. So to Celephaïs he must go, far distant from the isle of Oriab, and in such parts as would take him back to Dylath-Teen and up the Skai to the bridge by Nir, and again into the enchanted wood of the Zoogs, whence the way would bend northward through the garden lands by Oukranos to the gilded spires of Thran, where he might find a galleon bound over the Cerenarian Sea.

But dusk was now thick, and the great carven face looked down even sterner in shadow. Perched on that ledge night found the seeker; and in the blackness he might neither go down nor go up, but only stand and cling and shiver in that narrow place till the day came, praying to keep awake lest sleep loose his hold and send him down the dizzy miles of air to the crags and sharp rocks of the accursed valley. The stars came out, but save for them there was only black nothingness in his eyes; nothingness leagued with death, against whose beckoning he might do no more than cling to the rocks and lean back away from an unseen brink. The last thing of earth that he saw in the gloaming was a condor soaring close to the westward precipice beside him, and darting screaming away when it came near the cave whose mouth yawned just out of reach.

Suddenly, without a warning sound in the dark, Carter felt his curved scimitar drawn stealthily out of his belt by some unseen hand. Then he heard it clatter down over the rocks below. And between him and the Milky Way he thought he saw a very terrible outline of something noxiously thin and horned and tailed and bat-winged.

Other things, too, had begun to blot out patches of stars west of him, as if a flock of vague entities were flapping thickly and silently out of that inaccessible cave in the face of the precipice. Then a sort of cold rubbery arm seized his neck and something else seized his feet, and he was lifted inconsiderately up and swung about in space. Another minute and the stars were gone, and Carter knew that the night-gaunts had got him.

They bore him breathless into that cliffside cavern and through monstrous labyrinths beyond. When he struggled, as at first he did by instinct, they tickled him with deliberation. They made no sound at all themselves, and even their membranous wings were silent. They were frightfully cold and damp and slippery, and their paws kneaded one detestably. Soon they were plunging hideously downward through inconceivable abysses in a whirling, giddying, sickening rush of dank, tomb-like air; and Carter felt they were shooting into the ultimate vortex of shrieking and daemonic mad-ness. He screamed again and again, but whenever he did so the black paws tickled him with greater subtlety. Then he saw a sort of grey phosphorescence about, and guessed they were coming even to that inner world of subterrene horror of which dim legends tell, and which is litten only by the pale death-fire wherewith reeks the ghoulish air and the primal mists of the pits at earth's core.

At last far below him he saw faint lines of grey and ominous pinnacles which he knew must be the fabled Peaks of Throk. Awful and sinister they stand in the haunted disc of sunless and eternal depths; higher than man may reckon, and guarding terrible valleys where the Dholes crawl and burrow nastily. But Carter preferred to look at them than at his captors, which were indeed shocking and uncouth black things with smooth, oily, whale-like surfaces, unpleasant horns that curved inward toward each other, bat wings whose beating made no sound, ugly prehensile paws, and barbed tails that lashed needlessly and disquietingly. And worst of all, they never spoke or laughed, and never smiled because they had no faces at all to smile with, but only a suggestive blankness where a face ought to be. All they ever did was clutch and fly and tickle; that was the way of night-gaunts.

As the band flew lower the Peaks of Throk rose grey and towering on all sides, and one saw clearly that nothing lived on that austere and impressive granite of the endless twilight. At still lower levels the death-fires in the air gave out, and one met only the primal blackness of the void, save aloft where the thin peaks stood out goblin-like. Soon the peaks were very far away, and nothing about but great rushing winds with the dankness of nethermost grottoes in them. Then in the end the night-gaunts landed on a floor of unseen things which felt like layers of bones, and left Carter all alone in that black valley. To bring him thither was the duty of the night-gaunts that guard Ngranek; and this done, they flapped away silently. When Carter tried to trace their flight he found he could not, since even the Peaks of Throk had faded out of sight. There was nothing anywhere but blackness and horror and silence and bones.

Now Carter knew from a certain source that he was in the vale of Pnoth, where crawl and burrow the enormous Dholes; but he did not know what to expect, because no one has ever seen a Dhole or even guessed what such a thing may be like. Dholes are known only by dim rumour, from the rustling they make amongst mountains of bones and the slimy touch they have when they wriggle past one. They cannot be seen because they creep only in the dark. Carter did not wish to meet a Dhole, so listened intently for any sound in the unknown depths of bones about him. Even in this fearsome place he had a plan and an objective, for whispers of Pnoth were not unknown to one with whom he had talked much in the old days. In brief, it seemed fairly likely that this was the spot into which all the ghouls of the waking world cast the refuse of their feastings; and that if he but had good luck he might stumble upon that mighty crag taller even than Throk's peaks which marks the edge of their domain. Showers of bones would tell him where to look, and once found he could call to a ghoul to let down a ladder; for strange to say, he had a very singular link with these terrible creatures.

A man he had known in Boston – a painter of strange pictures with a secret studio in an ancient and unhallowed alley near a grave-yard – had actually made friends with the ghouls and had taught him to understand the simpler part of their disgusting meeping and glibbering. This man had vanished at last, and Carter was not sure but that he might find him now, and use for the first time in dream-land that far-away English of his dim waking life. In any case, he felt he could persuade a ghoul to guide him out of Pnoth; and it would be better to meet a ghoul, which one can see, than a Dhole, which one cannot see.

So Carter walked in the dark, and ran when he thought he heard something among the bones underfoot. Once he bumped into a stony slope, and knew it must be the base of one of Throk's peaks. Then at last he heard a monstrous rattling and clatter which reached far up in the air, and became sure he had come nigh the crag of the ghouls. He was not sure he could be heard from this valley miles below, but realised that the inner world has strange laws. As he pondered he was struck by a flying bone so heavy that it must have been a skull, and therefore realising his nearness to the fateful crag he sent up as best he might that meeping cry which is the call of the ghoul.

Sound travels slowly, so it was some time before he heard an answering glibber. But it came at last, and before long he was told that a rope ladder would be lowered. The wait for this was very tense, since there was no telling what might not have been stirred up among those bones by his shouting. Indeed, it was not long before he actually did hear a vague rustling afar off. As this thoughtfully approached, he became more and more uncomfortable; for he did not wish to move away from the spot where the ladder would come. Finally the tension grew almost unbearable, and he was about to flee in panic when the thud of something on the newly heaped bones nearby drew his notice from the other sound. It was the ladder, and after a minute of groping he had it taut in his hands. But the other sound did not cease, and followed him even as he climbed. He had gone fully five feet from the ground when the rattling beneath waxed emphatic, and was a good ten feet up when something swayed the ladder from below. At a height which must have been fifteen or twenty feet he felt his whole side brushed by a great slippery length which grew alternately convex and concave with wriggling; and hereafter he climbed desperately to escape the unendurable nuzzling of that loathsome and overfed Dhole whose form no man might see.

For hours he climbed with aching and blistered hands, seeing again the grey death-fire and Throk's uncomfortable pinnacles. At last he discerned above him the projecting edge of the great crag of the ghouls, whose vertical side he could not glimpse; and hours later he saw a curious face peering over it as a gargoyle peers over a parapet of Notre Dame. This almost made him lose his hold through faintness, but a moment later he was himself again; for his vanished friend Richard Pickman had once introduced him to a ghoul, and he knew well their canine faces and slumping forms and unmentionable idiosyncrasies. So he had himself well under control when that hideous thing pulled him out of the dizzy emptiness over the edge of the crag, and did not scream at the partly consumed refuse heaped at one side or at the squatting circles of ghouls who gnawed and watched curiously.

He was now on a dim-litten plain whose sole topographical features were great boulders and the entrances of burrows. The ghouls were in general respectful, even if one did attempt to pinch him while several others eyed his leanness speculatively. Through patient glibbering he made inquiries regarding his vanished friend, and found he had become a ghoul of some prominence in abysses nearer the waking world. A greenish elderly ghoul offered to conduct him to Pickman's present habitation, so despite a natural loathing he followed the creature into a capacious burrow and crawled after him for hours in the blackness of rank mould. They emerged on a dim plain strewn with singular relics of earth – old gravestones, broken urns, and grotesque fragments of monuments – and Carter realised with some emotion that he was probably nearer the waking world than at any other time since he had gone down the seven hundred steps from the cavern of flame to the Gate of Deeper Slumber.

There, on a tombstone of 1768 stolen from the Granary Burying Ground in Boston, sat a ghoul which was once the artist Richard Upton Pickman. It was naked and rubbery, and had acquired so much of the ghoulish physiognomy that its human origin was already obscure. But it still remembered a little English, and was able to converse with Carter in grunts and monosyllables, helped out now and then by the glibbering of ghouls. When it learned that Carter wished to get to the enchanted wood and from there to the city Celephaïs in Ooth-Nargai beyond the Tanarian Hills, it seemed rather doubtful; for these ghouls of the waking world do no business in the graveyards of upper dreamland (leaving that to the red-footed wamps that are spawned in dead cities), and many things intervene betwixt their gulf and the enchanted wood, including the terrible kingdom of the Gugs.

The Gugs, hairy and gigantic, once reared stone circles in that wood and made strange sacrifices to the Other Gods and the crawling chaos Nyarlathotep, until one night an abomination of theirs reached the ears of earth's gods and they were banished to caverns below. Only a great trap door of stone with an iron ring connects the abyss of the earth-ghouls with the enchanted wood, and this the Gugs are afraid to open because of a curse. That a mortal dreamer could traverse their cavern realm and leave by that door is inconceivable; for mortal dreamers were their former food, and they have legends of the toothsomeness of such dreamers even though banishment has restricted their diet to the ghasts, those repulsive beings which die in the light, and which live in the vaults of Zin and leap on long hind legs like kangaroos.

So the ghoul that was Pickman advised Carter either to leave the abyss at Sarkomand, that deserted city in the valley below Leng where black nitrous stairways guarded by winged diarite lions lead down from dreamland to the lower gulfs, or to return through a churchyard to the waking world and begin the quest anew down the seventy steps of light slumber to the cavern of flame and the seven hundred steps to the Gate of Deeper Slumber and the enchanted wood. This, however, did not suit the seeker; for he knew nothing of the way from Leng to Ooth-Nargai, and was likewise reluctant to awake lest he forget all he had so far gained in this dream. It was disastrous to his quest to forget the august and celestial faces of those seamen from the north who traded onyx in Celephaïs, and who, being the sons of gods, must point the way to the cold waste and Kadath where the Great Ones dwell.

After much persuasion the ghoul consented to guide his guest inside the great wall of the Gugs' kingdom. There was one chance that Carter might be able to steal through that twilight realm of circular stone towers at an hour when the giants would be all gorged and snoring indoors, and reach the central tower with the sign of Koth upon it, which has the stairs leading up to that stone trap door in the enchanted wood. Pickman even consented to lend three ghouls to help with a tombstone lever in raising the stone door; for of ghouls the Gugs are somewhat afraid, and they often flee from their own colossal graveyards when they see them feasting there.

He also advised Carter to disguise as a ghoul himself; shaving the beard he had allowed to grow (for ghouls have none), wallowing naked in the mould to get the correct surface, and loping in the usual slumping way, with his clothing carried in a bundle as if it were a choice morsel from a tomb. They would reach the city of Gugs – which is coterminous with the whole kingdom – through the proper burrows, emerging in a cemetery not far from the stair-containing Tower of Koth. They must beware, however, of a large cave near the cemetery; for this is the mouth of the vaults of Zin, and the vindictive ghasts are always on watch there murderously for those denizens of the upper abyss who hunt and prey on them. The ghasts try to come out when the Gugs sleep and they attack ghouls as readily as Gugs, for they cannot discriminate. They are very primitive, and eat one another. The Gugs have a sentry at a narrow in the vaults of Zin, but he is often drowsy and is sometimes surprised by a party of ghasts. Though ghasts cannot live in real light, they can endure the grey twilight of the abyss for hours.

So at length Carter crawled through endless burrows with three helpful ghouls bearing the slate gravestone of Col. Nepemiah Derby, *obiit* 1719, from the Charter Street Burying Ground in Salem. When they came again into open twilight they were in a forest of vast lichened monoliths reaching nearly as high as the eye could see and forming the modest gravestones of the Gugs. On the right of the hole out of which they wriggled, and seen through aisles of monoliths, was a stupendous vista of cyclopean round towers mounting up illimitable into the grey air of inner earth. This was the great city of the Gugs, whose doorways are thirty feet high. Ghouls come here often, for a buried Gug will feed a community for almost a year, and even with the added peril it is better to burrow for Gugs than to bother with the graves of men. Carter now understood the occasional titan bones he had felt beneath him in the vale of Pnoth.

Straight ahead, and just outside the cemetery, rose a sheer perpendicular cliff at whose base an immense and forbidding cavern yawned. This the ghouls told Carter to avoid as much as possible, since it was the entrance to the unhallowed vaults of Zin where Gugs hunt ghasts in the darkness. And truly, that warning was soon well justified; for the moment a ghoul began to creep toward the towers to see if the hour of the Gugs' resting had been rightly timed, there glowed in the gloom of that great cavern's mouth first one pair of yellowish-red eyes and then another, implying that the Gugs were one sentry less, and that ghasts have indeed an excellent sharpness of smell. So the ghoul returned to the burrow and motioned his companions to be silent. It was best to leave the ghasts to their own devices, and there was a possibility that they might soon withdraw, since they must naturally be rather tired after coping with a Gug sentry in the black vaults. After a moment something about the size of a small horse hopped out into the grey twilight, and Carter turned sick at the aspect of that scabrous and unwholesome beast, whose face is so curiously human despite the absence of a nose, a forehead, and other important particulars.

Presently three other ghasts hopped out to join their fellow, and a ghoul glibbered softly at Carter that their absence of battle-scars was a bad sign. It proved that they had not fought the Gug sentry at all, but had merely slipped past him as he slept, so that their strength and savagery were still unimpaired and would remain so till they had found and disposed of a victim. It was very unpleasant to see those filthy and disproportioned animals which soon numbered about fifteen, grubbing about and making their kangaroo leaps in the grey twilight where titan towers and monoliths arose, but it was still more unpleasant when they spoke among themselves in the coughing gutturals of ghasts. And yet, horrible as they were, they were not so horrible as what presently came out of the cave after them with disconcerting suddenness.

It was a paw, fully two feet and a half across, and equipped with formidable talons. Alter it came another paw, and after that a great black-furred arm to which both of the paws were attached by short forearms. Then two pink eyes shone, and the head of the awakened Gug sentry, large as a barrel, wobbled into view. The eyes jutted two inches from each side, shaded by bony protuberances overgrown with coarse hairs. But the head was chiefly terrible because of the mouth. That mouth had great yellow fangs and ran from the top to the bottom of the head, opening vertically instead of horizontally.

But before that unfortunate Gug could emerge from the cave and rise to his full twenty feet, the vindictive ghasts were upon him. Carter feared for a moment that he would give an alarm and arouse all his kin, till a ghoul softly glibbered that Gugs have no voice but talk by means of facial expression. The battle which then ensued was truly a frightful one. From all sides the venomous ghasts rushed feverishly at the creeping Gug, nipping and tearing with their muzzles, and mauling murderously with their hard pointed hooves. All the time they coughed excitedly, screaming when the great vertical mouth of the Gug would occasionally bite into one of their number, so that the noise of the combat would surely have aroused the sleeping city had not the weakening of the sentry begun to transfer the action farther and farther within the cavern. As it was, the tumult soon receded altogether from sight in the blackness, with only occasional evil echoes to mark its continuance.

Then the most alert of the ghouls gave the signal for all to advance, and Carter followed the loping three out of the forest of monoliths and into the dark noisome streets of that awful city whose rounded towers of cyclopean stone soared up beyond the sight. Silently they shambled over that rough rock pavement, hearing with disgust the abominable muffled snortings from great black doorways which marked the slumber of the Gugs. Apprehensive of the ending of the rest hour, the ghouls set a somewhat rapid pace; but even so the journey was no brief one, for distances in that town of giants are on a great scale. At last, however, they came to a somewhat open space before a tower even vaster than the rest; above whose colossal doorway was fixed a monstrous symbol in bas-relief which made one shudder without knowing its meaning. This was the central tower with the sign of Koth, and those huge stone steps just visible through the dusk within were the beginning of the great flight leading to upper dreamland and the enchanted wood.

There now began a climb of interminable length in utter blackness: made almost impossible by the monstrous size of the steps, which were fashioned for Gugs, and were therefore nearly a yard high. Of their number Carter could form no just estimate, for he soon became so worn out that the tireless and elastic ghouls were forced to aid him. All through the endless climb there lurked the peril of detection and pursuit; for though no Gug dares lift the stone door to the forest because of the Great One's curse, there are no such restraints concerning the tower and the steps, and escaped ghasts are often chased, even to the very top. So sharp are the ears of Gugs, that the bare feet and hands of the climbers might readily be heard when the city awoke; and it would of course take but little time for the striding giants, accustomed from their ghast-hunts in the vaults of Zin to seeing without light, to overtake their smaller and slower quarry on those cyclopean steps. It was very depressing to reflect that the silent pursuing Gugs would not be heard at all, but would come very suddenly and shockingly in the dark upon the climbers. Nor could the traditional fear of Gugs for ghouls be depended upon in that peculiar place where the advantages lay so heavily with the Gugs. There was also some peril from the furtive and venomous ghasts, which frequently hopped up onto the tower during the sleep hour of the Gugs. If the Gugs slept long, and the ghasts returned soon from their deed in the cavern, the scent of the climbers might easily be picked up by those loathsome and ill-disposed things; in which case it would almost be better to be eaten by a Gug.

Then, after aeons of climbing, there came a cough from the darkness above; and matters assumed a very grave and unexpected turn.

It was clear that a ghast, or perhaps even more, had strayed into that tower before the coming of Carter and his guides; and it was equally clear that this peril was very close. Alter a breathless second the leading ghoul pushed Carter to the wall and arranged his kinfolk in the best possible way, with the old slate tombstone raised for a crushing blow whenever the enemy might come in sight. Ghouls can see in the dark, so the party was not as badly off as Carter would have been alone. In another moment the clatter of hooves revealed the downward hopping of at least one beast, and the slab-bearing ghouls poised their weapon for a desperate blow. Presently two yellowish-red eyes flashed into view, and the panting of the ghast became audible above its clattering. As it hopped down to the step above the ghouls, they wielded the ancient gravestone with prodigious force, so that there was only a wheeze and a choking before the victim collapsed in a noxious heap. There seemed to be only this one animal, and after a moment of listening the ghouls tapped Carter as a signal to proceed again. As before, they were obliged to aid him; and he was glad to leave that place of carnage where the ghast's uncouth remains sprawled invisible in the blackness.

At last the ghouls brought their companion to a halt; and feeling above him, Carter realised that the great stone trap door was reached at last. To open so vast a thing completely was not to be thought of, but the ghouls hoped to get it up just enough to slip the gravestone under as a prop, and permit Carter to escape through the crack. They themselves planned to descend again and return through the city of the Gugs, since their elusiveness was great, and they did not know the way overland to spectral Sarkomand with its lion-guarded gate to the abyss.

Mighty was the straining of those three ghouls at the stone of the door above them, and Carter helped push with as much strength as he had. They judged the edge next the top of the staircase to be the right one, and to this they bent all the force of their disreputably nourished muscles. Alter a few moments a crack of light appeared; and Carter, to whom that task had been entrusted, slipped the end of the old gravestone in the aperture. There now ensued a mighty heaving; but progress was very slow, and they had of course to return to their first position every time they failed to turn the slab and prop the portal open.

Suddenly their desperation was magnified a thousand fold by a sound on the steps below them. It was only the thumping and rattling of the slain ghast's hooved body as it rolled down to lower levels; but of all the possible causes of that body's dislodgement and rolling, none was in the least reassuring. Therefore, knowing the ways of Gugs, the ghouls set to with something of a frenzy; and in a surprisingly short time had the door so high that they were able to hold it still whilst Carter turned the slab and left a generous opening. They now helped Carter through, letting him climb up to their rubbery shoulders and later guiding his feet as he clutched at the blessed soil of the upper dreamland outside. Another second and they were through themselves, knocking away the gravestone and closing the great trap door while a panting became audible beneath. Because of the Great One's curse no Gug might ever emerge from that portal, so with a deep relief and sense of repose Carter lay quietly on the thick grotesque fungi of the enchanted wood while his guides squatted near in the manner that ghouls rest.

Weird as was that enchanted wood through which he had fared so long ago, it was verily a haven and a delight after those gulfs he had now left behind. There was no living denizen about, for Zoogs shun the mysterious door in fear and Carter at once consulted with his ghouls about their future course. To return through the tower they no longer dared, and the waking world did not appeal to them when they learned that they must pass the priests Nasht and Kaman-Thah in the cavern of flame. So at length they decided to return through Sarkomand and its gate of the abyss, though of how to get there they knew nothing. Carter recalled that it lies in the valley below Leng, and recalled likewise that he had seen in Dylath-Leen a sinister, slant-eyed old merchant reputed to trade on Leng, therefore he advised the ghouls to seek out Dylath-Leen, crossing the fields to Nir and the Skai and following the river to its mouth. This they at once resolved to do, and lost no time in loping off, since the thickening of the dusk promised a full night ahead for travel. And Carter shook the paws of those repulsive beasts, thanking them for their help and sending his gratitude to the beast which once was Pickman; but could not help sighing with pleasure when they left. For a ghoul is a ghoul, and at best an unpleasant companion for man. After that Carter sought a forest pool and cleansed himself of the mud of nether earth, thereupon reassuming the clothes he had so carefully carried.

It was now night in that redoubtable wood of monstrous trees, but because of the phosphorescence one might travel as well as by day; wherefore Carter set out upon the well-known route toward Celephaïs, in Ooth-Nargai beyond the Tanarian Hills. And as he went he thought of the zebra he had left tethered to an ash-tree on Ngranek in far-away Oriab so many aeons ago, and wondered if any lava-gatherers had fed and released it. And he wondered, too, if he would ever return to Baharna and pay for the zebra that was slain by night in those ancient ruins by Yath's shore, and if the old tavern-keeper would remember him. Such were the thoughts that came to him in the air of the regained upper dreamland.

But presently his progress was halted by a sound from a very large hollow tree. He had avoided the great circle of stones, since he did not care to speak with Zoogs just now; but it appeared from the singular fluttering in that huge tree that important councils were in session elsewhere. Upon drawing nearer he made out the accents of a tense and heated discussion; and before long became conscious of matters which he viewed with the greatest concern. For a war on the cats was under debate in that sovereign assembly of Zoogs. It all came from the loss of the party which had sneaked after Carter to Ulthar, and which the cats had justly punished for unsuitable intentions. The matter had long rankled; and now, or at least within a month, the marshalled Zoogs were about to strike the whole feline tribe in a series of surprise attacks, taking individual cats or groups of cats unawares, and giving not even the myriad cats of Ulthar a proper chance to drill and mobilise. This was the plan of the Zoogs, and Carter saw that he must foil it before leaving upon his mighty quest.

Very quietly therefore did Randolph Carter steal to the edge of the wood and send the cry of the cat over the starlit fields. And a great grimalkin in a nearby cottage took up the burden and relayed it across leagues of rolling meadow to warriors large and small, black, grey, tiger, white, yellow, and mixed, and it echoed through Nir and beyond the Skai even into Ulthar, and Ulthar's numerous cats called in chorus and fell into a line of march. It was fortunate that the moon was not up, so that all the cats were on earth. Swiftly and silently leaping, they sprang from every hearth and housetop and poured in a great furry sea across the plains to the edge of the wood. Carter was there to greet them, and the sight of shapely, wholesome cats was indeed good for his eyes after the things he had seen and walked with in the abyss. He was glad to see his venerable friend and one-time rescuer at the head of Ulthar's detachment, a collar of rank around his sleek neck, and whiskers bristling at a martial angle. Better still, as a sub-lieutenant in that army was a brisk young fellow who proved to be none other than the very little kitten at the inn to whom Carter had given a saucer of rich cream on that long-vanished morning in Ulthar. He was a strapping and promising cat now, and purred as he shook hands with his friend. His grandfather said he was doing very well in the army, and that he might well expect a captaincy after one more campaign.

Carter now outlined the peril of the cat tribe, and was rewarded by deep-throated purrs of gratitude from all sides. Consulting with the generals, he prepared a plan of instant action which involved marching at once upon the Zoog council and other known strongholds of Zoogs; forestalling their surprise attacks and forcing them to terms before the mobilization of their army of invasion. Thereupon without a moment's loss that great ocean of cats flooded the enchanted wood and surged around the council tree and the great stone circle. Flutterings rose to panic pitch as the enemy saw the newcomers and there was very little resistance among the furtive and curious brown Zoogs. They saw that they were beaten in advance, and turned from thoughts of vengeance to thoughts of present self-preservation.

Half the cats now seated themselves in a circular formation with the captured Zoogs in the centre, leaving open a lane down which were marched the additional captives rounded up by the other cats in other parts of the wood. Terms were discussed at length, Carter acting as interpreter, and it was decided that the Zoogs might remain a free tribe on condition of rendering to the cats a large tribute of grouse, quail, and pheasants from the less fabulous parts of the forest. Twelve young Zoogs of noble families were taken as hostages to be kept in the Temple of Cats at Ulthar, and the victors made it plain that any disappearances of cats on the borders of the Zoog domain would be followed by consequences highly disastrous to Zoogs. These matters disposed of, the assembled cats broke ranks and permitted the Zoogs to slink off one by one to their respective homes, which they hastened to do with many a sullen backward glance.

The old cat general now offered Carter an escort through the forest to whatever border he wished to reach, deeming it likely that the Zoogs would harbour dire resentment against him for the frustration of their warlike enterprise. This offer he welcomed with gratitude; not only for the safety it afforded, but because he liked the graceful companionship of cats. So in the midst of a pleasant and playful regiment, relaxed after the successful performance of its duty, Randolph Carter walked with dignity through that enchanted and phosphorescent wood of titan trees, talking of his quest with the old general and his grandson whilst others of the band indulged in fantastic gambols or chased fallen leaves that the wind drove among the fungi of that primeval floor. And the old cat said that he had heard much of unknown Kadath in the cold waste, but did not know where it was. As for the marvellous sunset city, he had not even heard of that, but would gladly relay to Carter anything he might later learn.

He gave the seeker some passwords of great value among the cats of dreamland, and commended him especially to the old chief of the cats in Celephaïs, whither he was bound. That old cat, already slightly known to Carter, was a dignified maltese; and would prove highly influential in any transaction. It was dawn when they came to the proper edge of the wood, and Carter bade his friends a reluctant farewell. The young sub-lieutenant he had met as a small kitten would have followed him had not the old general forbidden it, but that austere patriarch insisted that the path of duty lay with the tribe and the army. So Carter set out alone over the golden fields that stretched mysterious beside a willow-fringed river, and the cats went back into the wood.

Well did the traveller know those garden lands that lie betwixt the wood of the Cerenerian Sea, and blithely did he follow the singing river Oukianos that marked his course. The sun rose higher over gentle slopes of grove and lawn, and heightened the colours of the thousand flowers that starred each knoll and dangle. A blessed haze lies upon all this region, wherein is held a little more of the sunlight than other places hold, and a little more of the summer's humming music of birds and bees; so that men walk through it as through a faery place, and feel greater joy and wonder than they ever afterward remember.

By noon Carter reached the jasper terraces of Kiran which slope down to the river's edge and bear that temple of loveliness wherein the King of Ilek-Vad comes from his far realm on the twilight sea once a year in a golden palanqnin to pray to the god of Oukianos, who sang to him in youth when he dwelt in a cottage by its banks. All of jasper is that temple, and covering an acre of ground with its walls and courts, its seven pinnacled towers, and its inner shrine where the river enters through hidden channels and the god sings softly in the night. Many times the moon hears strange music as it shines on those courts and terraces and pinnacles, but whether that music be the song of the god or the chant of the cryptical priests, none but the King of Ilek-Vad may say; for only he had entered the temple or seen the priests. Now, in the drowsiness of day, that carven and delicate fane was silent, and Carter heard only the murmur of the great stream and the hum of the birds and bees as he walked onward under the enchanted sun.

All that afternoon the pilgrim wandered on through perfumed meadows and in the lee of gentle riverward hills bearing peaceful thatched cottages and the shrines of amiable gods carven from jasper or chrysoberyl. Sometimes he walked close to the bank of Oukianos and whistled to the sprightly and iridescent fish of that crystal stream, and at other times he paused amidst the whispering rushes and gazed at the great dark wood on the farther side, whose trees came down clear to the water's edge. In former dreams he had seen quaint lumbering buopoths come shyly out of that wood to drink, but now he could not glimpse any. Once in a while he paused to watch a carnivorous fish catch a fishing bird, which it lured to the water by showing its tempting scales in the sun, and grasped by the beak with its enormous mouth as the winged hunter sought to dart down upon it.

Toward evening he mounted a low grassy rise and saw before him flaming in the sunset the thousand gilded spires of Thran. Lofty beyond belief are the alabaster walls of that incredible city, sloping inward toward the top and wrought in one solid piece by what means no man knows, for they are more ancient than memory. Yet lofty as they are with their hundred gates and two hundred turrets, the clustered towers within, all white beneath their golden spires, are loftier still; so that men on the plain around see them soaring into the sky, sometimes shining clear, sometimes caught at the top in tangles of cloud and mist, and sometimes clouded lower down with their utmost pinnacles blazing free above the vapours. And where Thran's gates open on the river are great wharves of marble, with ornate galleons of fragrant cedar and calamander riding gently at anchor, and strange bearded sailors sitting on casks and bales with the hieroglyphs of far places. Landward beyond the walls lies the farm country, where small white cottages dream between little hills, and narrow roads with many stone bridges wind gracefully among streams and gardens.

Down through this verdant land Carter walked at evening, and saw twilight float up from the river to the marvellous golden spires of Thran. And just at the hour of dusk he came to the southern gate, and was stopped by a red-robed sentry till he had told three dreams beyond belief, and proved himself a dreamer worthy to walk up Thran's steep mysterious streets and linger in the bazaars where the wares of the ornate galleons were sold. Then into that incredible city he walked; through a wall so thick that the gate was a tunnel, and thereafter amidst curved and undulant ways winding deep and narrow between the heavenward towers. Lights shone through grated and balconied windows, and the sound of lutes and pipes stole timid from inner courts where marble fountains bubbled. Carter knew his way, and edged down through darker streets to the river, where at an old sea tavern he found the captains and seamen he had known in myriad other dreams. There he bought his passage to Celephaïs on a great green galleon, and there he stopped for the night after speaking gravely to the venerable cat of that inn, who blinked dozing before an enormous hearth and dreamed of old wars and forgotten gods.

In the morning Carter boarded the galleon bound for Celephaïs, and sat in the prow as the ropes were cast off and the long sail down to the Cerenerian Sea begun. For many leagues the banks were much as they were above Thran, with now and then a curious temple rising on the farther hills toward the right, and a drowsy village on the shore, with steep red roofs and nets spread in the sun. Mindful of his search, Carter questioned all the mariners closely about those whom they had met in the taverns of Celephaïs, asking the names and ways of the strange men with long, narrow eyes, long-lobed ears, thin noses, and pointed chins who came in dark ships from the north and traded onyx for the carved jade and spun gold and little red singing birds of Celephaïs. Of these men the sailors knew not much, save that they talked but seldom and spread a kind of awe about them.

Their land, very far away, was called Inquanok, and not many people cared to go thither because it was a cold twilight land, and said to be close to unpleasant Leng; although high impassable mountains towered on the side where Leng was thought to lie, so that none might say whether this evil plateau with its horrible stone villages and unmentionable monastery were really there, or whether the rumour were only a fear that timid people felt in the night when those formidable barrier peaks loomed black against a rising moon. Certainly, men reached Leng from very different oceans. Of other boundaries of Inquanok those sailors had no notion, nor had they heard of the cold waste and unknown Kadath save from vague un-placed report. And of the marvellous sunset city which Carter sought they knew nothing at all. So the traveller asked no more of far things, but bided his time till he might talk with those strange men from cold and twilight Inquanok who are the seed of such gods as carved their features on Ngranek.

Late in the day the galleon reached those bends of the river which traverse the perfumed jungles of Kied. Here Carter wished he might disembark, for in those tropic tangles sleep wondrous palaces of ivory, lone and unbroken, where once dwelt fabulous monarchs of a land whose name is forgotten. Spells of the Elder Ones keep those places unharmed and undecayed, for it is written that there may one day be need of them again; and elephant caravans have glimpsed them from afar by moonlight, though none dares approach them closely because of the guardians to which their wholeness is due. But the ship swept on, and dusk hushed the hum of the day, and the first stars above blinked answers to the early fireflies on the banks as that jungle fell far behind, leaving only its fragrance as a memory that it had been. And all through the night that galleon floated on past mysteries unseen and unsuspected. Once a lookout reported fires on the hills to the east, but the sleepy captain said they had better not be looked at too much, since it was highly uncertain just who or what had lit them.

In the morning the river had broadened out greatly, and Carter saw by the houses along the banks that they were close to the vast trading city of Hlanith on the Cerenerian Sea. Here the walls are of rugged granite, and the houses peakedly fantastic with beamed and plastered gables. The men of Hlanith are more like those of the waking world than any others in dreamland; so that the city is not sought except for barter, but is prized for the solid work of its artisans. The wharves of Hlanith are of oak, and there the galleon made fast while the captain traded in the taverns. Carter also went ashore, and looked curiously upon the rutted streets where wooden ox carts lumbered and feverish merchants cried their wares vacuously in the bazaars. The sea taverns were all close to the wharves on cobbled lanes salted with the spray of high tides, and seemed exceedingly ancient with their low black-beamed ceilings and casements of greenish bull's-eye panes. Ancient sailors in those taverns talked much of distant ports, and told many stories of the curious men from twilight Inquanok, but had little to add to what the seamen of the galleon had told. Then at last, after much unloading and loading, the ship set sail once more over the sunset sea, and the high walls and gables of Hlanith grew less as the last golden light of day lent them a wonder and beauty beyond any that men had given them.

Two nights and two days the galleon sailed over the Cerenerian Sea, sighting no land and speaking to but one other vessel. Then near sunset of the second day there loomed up ahead the snowy peak of Aran with its gingko-trees swaying on the lower slope, and Carter knew that they were come to the land of Ooth-Nargai and the marvellous city of Celephaïs. Swiftly there came into sight the glittering minarets of that fabulous town, and the untarnished marble walls with their bronze statues, and the great stone bridge where Naraxa joins the sea. Then rose the gentle hills behind the town, with their groves and gardens of asphodels and the small shrines and cottages upon them; and far in the background the purple ridge of the Tanarians, potent and mystical, behind which lay forbidden ways into the waking world and toward other regions of dream.

The harbour was full of painted galleys, some of which were from the marble cloud-city of Serannian, that lies in ethereal space beyond where the sea meets the sky, and some of which were from more substantial parts of dreamland. Among these the steersman threaded his way up to the spice-fragrant wharves, where the galleon made fast in the dusk as the city's million lights began to twinkle out over the water. Ever new seemed this deathless city of vision, for here time has no power to tarnish or destroy. As it has always been is still the turquoise of Nath-Horthath, and the eighty orchid-wreathed priests are the same who builded it ten thousand years ago. Shining still is the bronze of the great gates, nor are the onyx pavements ever worn or broken. And the great bronze statues on the walls look down on merchants and camel drivers older than fable, yet without one grey hair in their forked beards.

Carter did not once seek out the temple or the palace or the citadel, but stayed by the seaward wall among traders and sailors. And when it was too late for rumours and legends he sought out an ancient tavern he knew well, and rested with dreams of the gods on unknown Kadath whom he sought. The next day he searched all along the quays for some of the strange mariners of Inquanok, but was told that none were now in port, their galley not being due from the north for full two weeks. He found, however, one Thorabonian sailor who had been to Inquanok and had worked in the onyx quarries of that twilight place; and this sailor said there was certainly a descent to the north of the peopled region, which everybody seemed to fear and shun. The

Thorabonian opined that this desert led around the utmost rim of impassable peaks into Leng's horrible plateau, and that this was why men feared it; though he admitted there were other vague tales of evil presences and nameless sentinels. Whether or not this could be the fabled waste wherein unknown Kadath stands he did not know; but it seemed unlikely that those presences and sentinels, if indeed they existed, were stationed for nought.

On the following day Carter walked up the Street of the Pillars to the turquoise temple and talked with the High-Priest. Though Nath-Horthath is chiefly worshipped in Celephaïs, all the Great Ones are mentioned in diurnal prayers; and the priest was reasonably versed in their moods. Like Atal in distant Ulthar, he strongly advised against any attempts to see them, declaring that they are testy and capricious, and subject to strange protection from the mindless Other Gods from Outside, whose soul and messenger is the crawling chaos Nyarlathotep. Their jealous hiding of the marvellous sunset city shewed clearly that they did not wish Carter to reach it, and it was doubtful how they would regard a guest whose object was to see them and plead before them. No man had ever found Kadath in the past, and it might be just as well if none ever found it in the future. Such rumours as were told about that onyx castle of the Great Ones were not by any means reassuring.

Having thanked the orchid-crowned High-Priest, Carter left the temple and sought out the bazaar of the sheep-butchers, where the old chief of Celephaïs' cats dwelt sleek and contented. That grey and dignified being was sunning himself on the onyx pavement, and extended a languid paw as his caller approached. But when Carter repeated the passwords and introductions furnished him by the old cat general of Ulthar, the furry patriarch became very cordial and communicative; and told much of the secret lore known to cats on the seaward slopes of Ooth-Nargai. Best of all, he repeated several things told him furtively by the timid waterfront cats of Celephaïs about the men of Inquanok, on whose dark ships no cat will go.

It seems that these men have an aura not of earth about them, though that is not the reason why no cat will sail on their ships. The reason for this is that Inquanok holds shadows which no cat can endure, so that in all that cold twilight realm there is never a cheering purr or a homely mew. Whether it be because of things wafted over the impassable peaks from hypothetical Leng, or because of things filtering down from the chilly desert to the north, none may say; but it remains a fact that in that far land there broods a hint of outer space which cats do not like, and to which they are more sensitive than men. Therefore they will not go on the dark ships that seek the basalt quays of Inquanok.

The old chief of the cats also told him where to find his friend King Kuranes, who in Carter's latter dreams had reigned alternately in the rose-crystal Palace of the Seventy Delights at Celephaïs and in the turreted cloud-castle of sky-floating Serannian. It seemed that he could no more find content in those places, but had formed a mighty longing for the English cliffs and downlands of his boyhood; where in little dreaming villages England's old songs hover at evening behind lattice windows, and where grey church towers peep lovely through the verdure of distant valleys. He could not go back to these things in the waking world because his body was dead; but he had done the next best thing and dreamed a small tract of such country-side in the region east of the city where meadows roll gracefully up from the sea-cliffs to the foot of the Tanarian Hills. There he dwelt in a grey Gothic manor-house of stone looking on the sea, and tried to think it was ancient Trevor Towers, where he was born and where thirteen generations of his forefathers had first seen the light. And on the coast nearby he had built a little Cornish fishing village with steep cobbled ways, settling therein such people as had the most English faces, and seeking ever to teach them the dear remembered accents of old Cornwall fishers. And in a valley not far off he had reared a great Norman Abbey whose tower he could see from his window, placing around it in the churchyard grey stones with the names of his ancestors carved thereon, and with a moss somewhat like Old England's moss. For though Kuranes was a monarch in the land of dream, with all imagined pomps and marvels, splendours and beauties, ecstasies and delights, novelties and excitements at his command, he would gladly have resigned forever the whole of his power and luxury and freedom for one blessed day as a simple boy in that pure and quiet England, that ancient, beloved England which had moulded his being and of which he must always be immutably a part.

So when Carter bade that old grey chief of the cats adieu, he did not seek the terraced palace of rose crystal but walked out the eastern gate and across the daisied fields toward a peaked gable which he glimpsed through the oaks of a park sloping up to the sea-cliffs. And in time he came to a great hedge and a gate with a little brick lodge, and when he rang the bell there hobbled to admit him no robed and anointed lackey of the palace, but a small stubby old man in a smock who spoke as best he could in the quaint tones of far Cornwall. And Carter walked up the shady path between trees as near as possible to England's trees, and climbed the terraces among gardens set out as in Queen Anne's time. At the door, flanked by stone cats in the old way, he was met by a whiskered butler in suitable livery; and was presently taken to the library where Kuranes, Lord of Ooth-Nargai and the Sky around Serannian, sat pensive in a chair by the window looking on his little seacoast village and wishing that his old nurse would come in and scold him because he was not ready for that hateful lawn-party at the vicar's, with the carriage waiting and his mother nearly out of patience.

Kuranes, clad in a dressing gown of the sort favoured by London tailors in his youth, rose eagerly to meet his guest; for the sight of an Anglo-Saxon from the waking world was very dear to him, even if it was a Saxon from Boston, Massachusetts, instead of from Cornwall. And for long they talked of old times, having much to say because both were old dreamers and well versed in the wonders of incredible places. Kuranes, indeed, had been out beyond the stars in the ultimate void, and was said to be the only one who had ever returned sane from such a voyage.

At length Carter brought up the subject of his quest, and asked of his host those questions he had asked of so many others. Kuranes did not know where Kadath was, or the marvellous sunset city; but he did know that the Great Ones were very dangerous creatures to seek out, and that the Other Gods had strange ways of protecting them from impertinent curiosity. He had learned much of the Other Gods in distant parts of space, especially in that region where form does not exist, and coloured gases study the innermost secrets. The violet gas S'ngac had told him terrible things of the crawling chaos Nyarlath-otep, and had warned him never to approach the central void where the daemon sultan Azathoth gnaws hungrily in the dark.

Altogether, it was not well to meddle with the Elder Ones; and if they persistently denied all access to the marvellous sunset city, it were better not to seek that city.

Kuranes furthermore doubted whether his guest would profit aught by coming to the city even were he to gain it. He himself had dreamed and yearned long years for lovely Celephaïs and the land of Ooth-Nargai, and for the freedom and colour and high experience of life devoid of its chains, and conventions, and stupidities. But now that he was come into that city and that land, and was the king thereof, he found the freedom and the vividness all too soon worn out, and monotonous for want of linkage with anything firm in his feelings and memories. He was a king in Ooth-Nargai, but found no meaning therein, and drooped always for the old familiar things of England that had shaped his youth. All his kingdom would he give for the sound of Cornish church bells over the downs, and all the thousand minarets of Celephaïs for the steep homely roofs of the village near his home. So he told his guest that the unknown sunset city might not hold quite that content he sought, and that perhaps it had better remain a glorious and half-remembered dream. For he had visited Carter often in the old waking days, and knew well the lovely New England slopes that had given him birth.

At the last, he was very certain, the seeker would long only for the early remembered scenes; the glow of Beacon Hill at evening, the tall steeples and winding hill streets of quaint Kingsport, the hoary gambrel roofs of ancient and witch-haunted Arkham, and the blessed meads and valleys where stone walls rambled and white farmhouse gables peeped out from bowers of verdure. These things he told Randolph Carter, but still the seeker held to his purpose. And in the end they parted each with his own conviction, and Carter went back through the bronze gate into Celephaïs and down the Street of Pillars to the old sea wall, where he talked more with the mariners of far ports and waited for the dark ship from cold and twilight Inquanok, whose strange-faced sailors and onyx-traders had in them the blood of the Great Ones.

One starlit evening when the Pharos shone splendid over the harbour the longed-for ship put in, and strange-faced sailors and traders appeared one by one and group by group in the ancient taverns along the sea wall. It was very exciting to see again those living faces so like the godlike features of Ngranek, but Carter did not hasten to speak with the silent seamen. He did not know how much of pride and secrecy and dim supernal memory might fill those children of the Great Ones, and was sure it would not be wise to tell them of his quest or ask too closely of that cold desert stretching north of their twilight land. They talked little with the other folk in those ancient sea taverns; but would gather in groups in remote corners and sing among themselves the haunting airs of unknown places, or chant long tales to one another in accents alien to the rest of dreamland. And so rare and moving were those airs and tales that one might guess their wonders from the faces of those who listened, even though the words came to common ears only as strange cadence and obscure melody.

For a week the strange seamen lingered in the taverns and traded in the bazaars of Celephaïs, and before they sailed Carter had taken passage on their dark ship, telling them that he was an old onyx miner and wishful to work in their quarries. That ship was very lovely and cunningly wrought, being of teakwood with ebony fittings and traceries of gold, and the cabin in which the traveller lodged had hangings of silk and velvet. One morning at the turn of the tide the sails were raised and the anchor lifted, and as Carter stood on the high stern he saw the sunrise-blazing walls and bronze statues and golden minarets of ageless Celephaïs sink into the distance, and the snowy peak of Mount Man grow smaller and smaller. By noon there was nothing in sight save the gentle blue of the Cerenerian Sea, with one painted galley afar off bound for that realm of Serannian where the sea meets the sky.

And the night came with gorgeous stars, and the dark ship steered for Charles' Wain and the Little Bear as they swung slowly round the pole. And the sailors sang strange songs of unknown places, and they stole off one by one to the forecastle while the wistful watchers murmured old chants and leaned over the rail to glimpse the luminous fish playing in bowers beneath the sea. Carter went to sleep at midnight, and rose in the glow of a young morning, marking that the sun seemed farther south than was its wont. And all through that second day he made progress in knowing the men of the ship, getting them little by little to talk of their cold twilight land, of their exquisite onyx city, and of their fear of the high and impassable peaks

beyond which Leng was said to be. They told him how sorry they
were that no cats would stay in the land of Inquanok, and how they
thought the hidden nearness of Leng was to blame for it. Only of the
stony desert to the north they would not talk. There was something
disquieting about that desert, and it was thought expedient not to
admit its existence.

On later days they talked of the quarries in which Carter said he
was going to work. There were many of them, for all the city of
Inquanok was builded of onyx, whilst great polished blocks of it
were traded in Rinar, Ogrothan, and Celephaïs and at home with
the merchants of Thraa, Flarnek, and Kadatheron, for the beautiful
wares of those fabulous ports. And far to the north, almost in the
cold desert whose existence the men of Inquanok did not care to
admit, there was an unused quarry greater than all the rest; from
which had been hewn in forgotten times such prodigious lumps and
blocks that the sight of their chiselled vacancies struck terror to all
who beheld. Who had mined those incredible blocks, and whither
they had been transported, no man might say; but it was thought
best not to trouble that quarry, around which such inhuman memories might conceivably cling. So it was left all alone in the twilight,
with only the raven and the rumoured Shantak-bird to brood on
its immensities. When Carter heard of this quarry he was moved
to deep thought, for he knew from old tales that the Great Ones'
castle atop unknown Kadath is of onyx.

Each day the sun wheeled lower and lower in the sky, and the mists
overhead grew thicker and thicker. And in two weeks there was not
any sunlight at all, but only a weird grey twilight shining through a
dome of eternal cloud by day, and a cold starless phosphorescence
from the under side of that cloud by night. On the twentieth day a
great jagged rock in the sea was sighted from afar, the first land
glimpsed since Man's snowy peak had dwindled behind the ship.
Carter asked the captain the name of that rock, but was told that it
had no name and had never been sought by any vessel because of the
sounds that came from it at night. And when, after dark, a dull and
ceaseless howling arose from that jagged granite place, the traveller
was glad that no stop had been made, and that the rock had no name.
The seamen prayed and chanted till the noise was out of earshot, and
Carter dreamed terrible dreams within dreams in the small hours.

Two mornings after that there loomed far ahead and to the east a line of great grey peaks whose tops were lost in the changeless clouds of that twilight world. And at the sight of them the sailors sang glad songs, and some knelt down on the deck to pray, so that Carter knew they were come to the land of Inquanok and would soon be moored to the basalt quays of the great town bearing that land's name. Toward noon a dark coastline appeared, and before three o'clock there stood out against the north the bulbous domes and fantastic spires of the onyx city. Rare and curious did that archaic city rise above its walls and quays, all of delicate black with scrolls, flutings, and arabesques of inlaid gold. Tall and many-windowed were the houses, and carved on every side with flowers and patterns whose dark symmetries dazzled the eye with a beauty more poignant than light. Some ended in swelling domes that tapered to a point, others in terraced pyramids whereon rose clustered minarets displaying every phase of strangeness and imagination. The walls were low, and pierced by frequent gates, each under a great arch rising high above the general level and capped by the head of a god chiselled with that same skill displayed in the monstrous face on distant Ngranek. On a hill in the centre rose a sixteen-angled tower greater than all the rest and bearing a high pinnacled belfry resting on a flattened dome. This, the seamen said, was the Temple of the Elder Ones, and was ruled by an old High-Priest sad with inner secrets.

At intervals the clang of a strange bell shivered over the onyx city, answered each time by a peal of mystic music made up of horns, viols, and chanting voices. And from a row of tripods on a galley round the high dome of the temple there burst flares of flame at certain moments; for the priests and people of that city were wise in the primal mysteries, and faithful in keeping the rhythms of the Great Ones as set forth in scrolls older than the *Pnakotic Manuscripts*. As the ship rode past the great basalt breakwater into the harbour the lesser noises of the city grew manifest, and Carter saw the slaves, sailors, and merchants on the docks. The sailors and merchants were of the strange-faced race of the gods, but the slaves were squat, slant-eyed folk said by rumour to have drifted somehow across or around the impassable peaks from the valleys beyond Leng. The wharves reached wide outside the city wall and bore upon them all manner of merchandise from the galleys anchored there, while at one end were great piles of onyx both carved and uncarved awaiting shipment to the far markets of Rinar, Ograthan and Celephaïs.

It was not yet evening when the dark ship anchored beside a jutting quay of stone, and all the sailors and traders filed ashore and through the arched gate into the city. The streets of that city were paved with onyx and some of them were wide and straight whilst others were crooked and narrow. The houses near the water were lower than the rest, and bore above their curiously arched doorways certain signs of gold said to be in honour of the respective small gods that favoured each. The captain of the ship took Carter to an old sea tavern where flocked the mariners of quaint countries, and promised that he would next day shew him the wonders of the twilight city, and lead him to the taverns of the onyx-miners by the northern wall. And evening fell, and little bronze lamps were lighted, and the sailors in that tavern sang songs of remote places. But when from its high tower the great bell shivered over the city, and the peal of the horns and viols and voices rose cryptical in answer thereto, all ceased their songs or tales and bowed silent till the last echo died away. For there is a wonder and a strangeness on the twilight city of Inquanok, and men fear to be lax in its rites lest a doom and a vengeance lurk unsuspectedly close.

Far in the shadows of that tavern Carter saw a squat form he did not like, for it was unmistakably that of the old slant-eyed merchant he had seen so long before in the taverns of Dylath-Leen, who was reputed to trade with the horrible stone villages of Leng which no healthy folk visit and whose evil fires are seen at night from afar, and even to have dealt with that High-Priest Not To Be Described, which wears a yellow silken mask over its face and dwells all alone in a prehistoric stone monastery. This man had seemed to shew a queer gleam of knowing when Carter asked the traders of Dylath-Leen about the cold waste and Kadath; and somehow his presence in dark and haunted Inquanok, so close to the wonders of the north, was not a reassuring thing. He slipped wholly out of sight before Carter could speak to him, and sailors later said that he had come with a yak caravan from some point not well determined, bearing the colossal and rich-flavoured eggs of the rumoured Shantak-bird to trade for the dextrous jade goblets that merchants brought from Ilarnek.

On the following morning the ship-captain led Carter through the onyx streets of Inquanok, dark under their twilight sky. The inlaid doors and figured house-fronts, carven balconies and crystal-paned oriels all gleamed with a sombre and polished loveliness; and now and then a plaza would open out with black pillars, colonnades, and the statues of curious beings both human and fabulous. Some of the vistas down long and unbending streets, or through side alleys and over bulbous domes, spires, and arabesqued roofs, were weird and beautiful beyond words; and nothing was more splendid than the massive heights of the great central Temple of the Elder Ones with its sixteen carven sides, its flattened dome, and its lofty pinnacled belfry, overtopping all else, and majestic whatever its foreground. And always to the east, far beyond the city walls and the leagues of pasture land, rose the gaunt grey sides of those topless and impassable peaks across which hideous Leng was said to lie.

The captain took Carter to the mighty temple, which is set with its walled garden in a great round plaza whence the streets go as spokes from a wheel's hub. The seven arched gates of that garden, each having over it a carven face like those on the city's gates, are always open, and the people roam reverently at will down the tiled paths and through the little lanes lined with grotesque termini and the shrines of modest gods. And there are fountains, pools, and basins there to reflect the frequent blaze of the tripods on the high balcony, all of onyx and having in them small luminous fish taken by divers from the lower bowers of ocean. When the deep clang from the temple belfry shivers over the garden and the city, and the answer of the horns and viols and voices peals out from the seven lodges by the garden gates, there issue from the seven doors of the temple long columns of masked and hooded priests in black, bearing at arm's length before them great golden bowls from which a curious steam rises. And all the seven columns strut peculiarly in single file, legs thrown far forward without bending the knees, down the walks that lead to the seven lodges, wherein they disappear and do not appear again. It is said that subterrene paths connect the lodges with the temple, and that the long files of priests return through them; nor is it unwhispered that deep flights of onyx steps go down to mysteries that are never told. But only a few are those who hint that the priests in the masked and hooded columns are not human beings.

Carter did not enter the temple, because none but the Veiled King is permitted to do that. But before he left the garden the hour of the bell came, and he heard the shivering clang deafening above him, and the wailing of the horns and viols and voices loud from the lodges by the gates. And down the seven great walks stalked the long files of bowl-bearing priests in their singular way, giving to the traveller a fear which human priests do not often give. When the last of them had vanished he left that garden, noting as he did so a spot on the pavement over which the bowls had passed. Even the ship-captain did not like that spot, and hurried him on toward the hill whereon the Veiled King's palace rises many-domed and marvellous.

The ways to the onyx palace are steep and narrow, all but the broad curving one where the king and his companions ride on yaks or in yak-drawn chariots. Carter and his guide climbed up an alley that was all steps, between inlaid walls bearing strange signs in gold, and under balconies and oriels whence sometimes floated soft strains of music or breaths of exotic fragrance. Always ahead loomed those titan walls, mighty buttresses, and clustered and bulbous domes for which the Veiled King's palace is famous; and at length they passed under a great black arch and emerged in the gardens of the monarch's pleasure. There Carter paused in faintness at so much beauty, for the onyx terraces and colonnaded walks, the gay parterres and delicate flower-ing trees espaliered to golden lattices, the brazen urns and tripods with cunning bas-reliefs, the pedestalled and almost breathing statues of veined black marble, the basalt-bottomed lagoon's tiled fountains with luminous fish, the tiny temples of iridescent singing birds atop carven columns, the marvellous scrollwork of the great bronze gates, and the blossoming vines trained along every inch of the polished walls all joined to form a sight whose loveliness was beyond reality, and half-fabulous even in the land of dreams. There it shimmered like a vision under that grey twilight sky, with the domed and fretted magnificence of the palace ahead, and the fantastic silhouette of the distant impassable peaks on the right. And ever the small birds and the fountains sang, while the perfume of rare blossoms spread like a veil over that incredible garden. No other human presence was there, and Carter was glad it was so. Then they turned and descended again the onyx alley of steps, for the palace itself no visitor may enter; and it is not well to look too long and steadily at the great central dome, since it is said to house the archaic father of all the rumoured Shantak-birds, and to send out queer dreams to the curious.

After that the captain took Carter to the north quarter of the town, near the Gate of the Caravans, where are the taverns of the yak-merchants and the onyx-miners. And there, in a low-ceiled inn of quarrymen, they said farewell; for business called the captain, whilst Carter was eager to talk with miners about the north. There were many men in that inn, and the traveller was not long in speaking to some of them, saying that he was an old miner of onyx, and anxious to know somewhat of Inquanok's quarries. But all that he learned was not much more than he knew before, for the miners were timid and evasive about the cold desert to the north and the quarry that no man visits. They had fears of fabled emissaries from around the mountains where Leng is said to lie, and of evil presences and nameless sentinels far north among the scattered rocks. And they whispered also that the rumoured Shantak-birds are no wholesome things, it being indeed for the best that no man has ever truly seen one (for that fabled father of Shantaks in the king's dome is fed in the dark).

The next day, saying that he wished to look over all the various mines for himself and to visit the scattered farms and quaint onyx villages of Inquanok, Carter hired a yak and stuffed great leathern saddle-bags for a journey. Beyond the Gate of the Caravans the road lay straight betwixt tilled fields, with many odd farmhouses crowned by low domes. At some of these houses the seeker stopped to ask questions, once finding a host so austere and reticent, and so full of an unplaced majesty like to that in the huge features on Ngranek, that he felt certain he had come at last upon one of the Great Ones themselves, or upon one with full nine-tenths of their blood, dwelling amongst men. And to that austere and reticent cotter he was careful to speak very well of the gods, and to praise all the blessings they had ever accorded him.

That night Carter camped in a roadside meadow beneath a great lygath-tree to which he tied his yak, and in the morning resumed his northward pilgrimage. At about ten o'clock he reached the small-domed village of Urg, where traders rest and miners tell their tales, and paused in its taverns till noon. It is here that the great caravan road turns west toward Selarn, but Carter kept on north by the quarry road. All the afternoon he followed that rising road, which was somewhat narrower than the great highway, and which now led through a region with more rocks than tilled fields. And by evening the low hills on his left had risen into sizable black cliffs, so that he knew he was close to the mining country. All the while the great gaunt sides of the impassable mountains towered afar off at his right, and the farther he went, the worse tales he heard of them from the scattered farmers and traders and drivers of lumbering onyx-carts along the way.

On the second night he camped in the shadow of a large black crag, tethering his yak to a stake driven in the ground. He observed the greater phosphorescence of the clouds at his northerly point, and more than once thought he saw dark shapes outlined against them. And on the third morning he came in sight of the first onyx quarry, and greeted the men who there laboured with picks and chisels. Before evening he had passed eleven quarries, the land being here given over altogether to onyx cliffs and boulders, with no vegetation at all, but only great rocky fragments scattered about a floor of black earth, with the grey impassable peaks always rising gaunt and sinister on his right. The third night he spent in a camp of quarrymen whose flickering fires cast weird reflections on the polished cliffs to the west. And they sang many songs and told many tales, shewing such strange knowledge of the olden days and the habits of gods that Carter could see they held many latent memories of their sires the Great Ones. They asked him whither he went, and cautioned him not to go too far to the north; but he replied that he was seeking new cliffs of onyx, and would take no more risks than were common among prospectors. In the morning he bade them adieu and rode on into the darkening north, where they had warned him he would find the feared and unvisited quarry whence hands older than men's hands had wrenched prodigious blocks. But he did not like it when, turning back to wave a last farewell, he thought he saw approaching the camp that squat and evasive old merchant with slanting eyes, whose conjectured traffick with Leng was the gossip of distant Dylath-Leen.

After two more quarries the inhabited part of Inquanok seemed to end, and the road narrowed to a steeply rising yak-path among forbidding black cliffs. Always on the right towered the gaunt and distant peaks, and as Carter climbed farther and farther into this untraversed realm he found it grew darker and colder. Soon he perceived that there were no prints of feet or hooves on the black path beneath, and realised that he was indeed come into strange and deserted ways of elder time. Once in a while a raven would croak far overhead, and now and then a flapping behind some vast rock would make him think uncomfortably of the rumoured Shantak-bird. But in the main he was alone with his shaggy steed, and it troubled him to observe that this excellent yak became more and more reluctant to advance, and more and more disposed to snort affrightedly at any small noise along the route.

The path now contracted between sable and glistening walls, and began to display an even greater steepness than before. It was a bad footing, and the yak often slipped on the stony fragments strewn thickly about. In two hours Carter saw ahead a definite crest, beyond which was nothing but dull grey sky, and blessed the prospect of a level or downward course. To reach this crest, however, was no easy task; for the way had grown nearly perpendicular, and was perilous with loose black gravel and small stones. Eventually Carter dismounted and led his dubious yak, pulling very hard when the animal balked or stumbled, and keeping his own footing as best he might. Then suddenly he came to the top and saw beyond, and gasped at what he saw.

The path indeed led straight ahead and slightly down, with the same lines of high natural walls as before; but on the left hand there opened out a monstrous space, vast acres in extent, where some archaic power had riven and rent the native cliffs of onyx in the form of a giant's quarry. Far back into the solid precipice ran that cyclopean gouge, and deep down within earth's bowels its lower delvings yawned. It was no quarry of man, and the concave sides were scarred with great squares, yards wide, which told of the size of the blocks once hewn by nameless hands and chisels. High over its jagged rim huge ravens flapped and croaked, and vague whirrings in the unseen depths told of bats or urhags or less mentionable presences haunting the endless blackness. There Carter stood in the narrow way amidst the twilight with the rocky path sloping down before him; tall onyx cliffs on his right that led on as far as he could see and tall cliffs on the left chopped off just ahead to make that terrible and unearthly quarry.

All at once the yak uttered a cry and burst from his control, leaping past him and darting on in a panic till it vanished down the narrow slope toward the north. Stones kicked by its flying hooves fell over the brink of the quarry and lost themselves in the dark without any sound of striking bottom; but Carter ignored the perils of that scanty path as he raced breathlessly after the flying steed. Soon the left-behind cliffs resumed their course, making the way once more a narrow lane; and still the traveller leaped on after the yak whose great wide prints told of its desperate flight.

Once he thought he heard the hoofbeats of the frightened beast, and doubled his speed from this encouragement. He was covering miles, and little by little the way was broadening in front till he knew he must soon emerge on the cold and dreaded desert to the north. The gaunt grey flanks of the distant impassable peaks were again visible above the right-hand crags, and ahead were the rocks and boulders of an open space which was clearly a foretaste of the dark and limitless plain. And once more those hoofbeats sounded in his ears, plainer than before, but this time giving terror instead of encouragement because he realised that they were not the frightened hoofbeats of his fleeing yak. The beats were ruthless and purposeful, and they were behind him.

Carter's pursuit of the yak became now a flight from an unseen thing, for though he dared not glance over his shoulder he felt that the presence behind him could be nothing wholesome or mentionable. His yak must have heard or felt it first, and he did not like to ask himself whether it had followed him from the haunts of men or had floundered up out of that black quarry pit. Meanwhile the cliffs had been left behind, so that the oncoming night fell over a great waste of sand and spectral rocks wherein all paths were lost. He could not see the hoofprints of his yak, but always from behind him there came that detestable clopping, mingled now and then with what he fancied were titanic flappings and whirrings. That he was losing ground seemed unhappily clear to him, and he knew he was hopelessly lost in this broken and blasted desert of meaningless rocks and untravelled sands. Only those remote and impassable peaks on the right gave him any sense of direction, and even they were less clear as the grey twilight waned and the sickly phosphorescence of the clouds took its place.

Then dim and misty in the darkling north before him he glimpsed a terrible thing. He had thought it for some moments a range of black mountains, but now he saw it was something more. The phosphorescence of the brooding clouds shewed it plainly, and even silhouetted parts of it as vapours glowed behind. How distant it was he could not tell, but it must have been very far. It was thousands of feet high, stretching in a great concave arc from the grey impassable peaks to the unimagined westward spaces, and had once indeed been a ridge of mighty onyx hills. But now these hills were hills no more, for some hand greater than man's had touched them. Silent they squatted there atop the world like wolves or ghouls, crowned with clouds and mists and guarding the secrets of the north forever. All in a great half circle they squatted, those dog-like mountains carven into monstrous watching statues, and their right hands were raised in menace against mankind.

It was only the flickering light of the clouds that made their mitred double heads seem to move, but as Carter stumbled on he saw arise from their shadowy caps great forms whose motions were no delusion. Winged and whirring, those forms grew larger each moment, and the traveller knew his stumbling was at an end. They were not any birds or bats known elsewhere on earth or in dreamland, for they were larger than elephants and had heads like a horse's. Carter knew that they must be the Shantak-birds of ill rumour, and wondered no more what evil guardians and nameless sentinels made men avoid the boreal rock desert. And as he stopped in final resignation he dared at last to look behind him, where indeed was trotting the squat slant-eyed trader of evil legend, grinning astride a lean yak and leading on a noxious horde of leering Shantaks to whose wings still clung the rime and nitre of the nether pits.

Trapped though he was by fabulous and hippocephalic winged nightmares that pressed around in great unholy circles, Randolph Carter did not lose consciousness. Lofty and horrible those titan gargoyles towered above him, while the slant-eyed merchant leaped down from his yak and stood grinning before the captive. Then the man motioned Carter to mount one of the repugnant Shantaks, helping him up as his judgement struggled with his loathing. It was hard work ascending, for the Shantak-bird has scales instead of feathers, and those scales are very slippery. Once he was seated, the slant-eyed man hopped up behind him, leaving the lean yak to be led away northward toward the ring of carven mountains by one of the incredible bird colossi.

There now followed a hideous whirl through frigid space, endlessly up and eastward toward the gaunt grey flanks of those impassable mountains beyond which Leng was said to be. Far above the clouds they flew, till at last there lay beneath them those fabled summits which the folk of Inquanok have never seen, and which lie always in high vortices of gleaming mist. Carter beheld them very plainly as they passed below, and saw upon their topmost peaks strange caves which made him think of those on Ngranek; but he did not question his captor about these things when he noticed that both the man and the horse-headed Shantak appeared oddly fearful of them, hurrying past nervously and shewing great tension until they were left far in the rear.

The Shantak now flew lower, revealing beneath the canopy of cloud a grey barren plain whereon at great distances shone little feeble fires. As they descended there appeared at intervals lone huts of granite and bleak stone villages whose tiny windows glowed with pallid light. And there came from those huts and villages a shrill droning of pipes and a nauseous rattle of crotala which proved at once that Inquanok's people are right in their geographic rumours. For travellers have heard such sounds before, and know that they float only from the cold desert plateau which healthy folk never visit, that haunted place of evil and mystery which is Leng.

Around the feeble fires dark forms were dancing, and Carter was curious as to what manner of beings they might be; for no healthy folk have ever been to Leng, and the place is known only by its fires and stone huts as seen from afar. Very slowly and awkwardly did those forms leap, and with an insane twisting and bending not good to behold; so that Carter did not wonder at the monstrous evil imputed to them by vague legend, or the fear in which all dreamland holds their abhorrent frozen plateau. As the Shantak flew lower, the repulsiveness of the dancers became tinged with a certain hellish familiarity; and the prisoner kept straining his eyes and racking his memory for clues to where he had seen such creatures before.

They leaped as though they had hooves instead of feet, and seemed to wear a sort of wig or headpiece with small horns. Of other clothing they had none, but most of them were quite furry. Behind they had dwarfish tails, and when they glanced upward he saw the excessive width of their mouths. Then he knew what they were, and that they did not wear any wigs or headpieces after all. For the cryptic folk of Leng were of one race with the uncomfortable merchants of the black galleys that traded rubies at Dylath-Leen, those not quite human merchants who are the slaves of the monstrous moon-things! They were indeed the same dark folk who had shanghaied Carter on their noisome galley so long ago, and whose kith he had seen driven in herds about the unclean wharves of that accursed lunar city, with the leaner ones toiling and the fatter ones taken away in crates for other needs of their polypous and amorphous masters. Now he saw where such ambiguous creatures came from, and shuddered at the thought that Leng must be known to these formless abominations from the moon.

But the Shantak flew on past the fires and the stone huts and the less than human dancers, and soared over sterile hills of grey granite and dim wastes of rock and ice and snow. Day came, and the phosphorescence of low clouds gave place to the misty twilight of that northern world, and still the vile bird winged meaningly through the cold and silence. At times the slant-eyed man talked with his steed in a hateful and guttural language, and the Shantak would answer with tittering tones that rasped like the scratching of ground glass. All this while the land was getting higher, and finally they came to a windswept table-land which seemed the very roof of a blasted and tenantless world. There, all alone in the hush and the dusk and the cold, rose the uncouth stones of a squat windowless building, around which a circle of crude monoliths stood. In all this arrangement there was nothing human, and Carter surmised from old tales that he was indeed come to that most dreadful and legendary of all places, the remote and prehistoric monastery wherein dwells uncompanioned the High-Priest Not To Be Described, which wears a yellow silken mask over its face and prays to the Other Gods and their crawling chaos Nyarlathotep.

The loathsome bird now settled to the ground, and the slant-eyed man hopped down and helped his captive alight. Of the purpose of his seizure Carter now felt very sure; for clearly the slant-eyed merchant was an agent of the darker powers, eager to drag before his masters a mortal whose presumption had aimed at the finding of unknown Kadath and the saying of a prayer before the faces of the Great Ones in their onyx castle. It seemed likely that this merchant had caused his former capture by the slaves of the moon-things in Dylath-Leen, and that he now meant to do what the rescuing cats had baffled; taking the victim to some dread rendezvous with monstrous Nyarlathotep and telling with what boldness the seeking of unknown Kadath had been tried. Leng and the cold waste north of Inquanok must be close to the Other Gods, and there the passes to Kadath are well guarded.

The slant-eyed man was small, but the great hippocephalic bird was there to see he was obeyed; so Carter followed where he led, and passed within the circle of standing rocks and into the low arched doorway of that windowless stone monastery. There were no lights inside, but the evil merchant lit a small clay lamp bearing morbid bas-reliefs and prodded his prisoner on through mazes of narrow winding corridors. On the walls of the corridors were printed frightful scenes older than history, and in a style unknown to the archaeologists of earth. After countless aeons their pigments were brilliant still, for the cold and dryness of hideous Leng keep alive many primal things. Carter saw them fleetingly in the rays of that dim and moving lamp, and shuddered at the tale they told.

Through those archaic frescoes Leng's annals stalked; and the horned, hooved, and wide-mouthed almost-humans danced evilly amidst forgotten cities. There were scenes of old wars, wherein Leng's almost-humans fought with the bloated purple spiders of the neighbouring vales; and there were scenes also of the coming of the black galleys from the moon, and of the submission of Leng's people to the polypous and amorphous blasphemies that hopped and floundered and wriggled out of them. Those slippery greyish-white blasphemies they worshipped as gods, nor ever complained when scores of their best and fatted males were taken away in the black galleys. The monstrous moon-beasts made their camp on a jagged isle in the sea, and Carter could tell from the frescoes that this was none other than the lone nameless rock he had seen when sailing to Inquanok; that grey accursed rock which Inquanok's seamen shun, and from which vile howlings reverberate all through the night.

And in those frescoes was shewn the great seaport and capital of the almost-humans; proud and pillared betwixt the cliffs and the basalt wharves, and wondrous with high fanes and carven places. Great gardens and columned streets led from the cliffs and from each of the six sphinx-crowned gates to a vast central plaza, and in that plaza was a pair of winged colossal lions guarding the top of a subterrene staircase. Again and again were those huge winged lions shewn, their mighty flanks of diarite glistening in the grey twilight of the day and the cloudy phosphorescence of the night. And as Carter stumbled past their frequent and repeated pictures it came to him at last what indeed they were, and what city it was that the almost-humans had ruled so anciently before the coming of the black galleys. There could be no mistake, for the legends of dreamland are generous and profuse. Indubitably that primal city was no less a place than storied Sarkomand, whose ruins had bleached for a million years before the first true human saw the light, and whose twin titan lions guard eternally the steps that lead down from dreamland to the Great Abyss.

Other views shewed the gaunt grey peaks dividing Leng from Inquanok, and the monstrous Shantak-birds that build nests on the ledges half way up. And they shewed likewise the curious caves near the very topmost pinnacles, and how even the boldest of the Shantaks fly screaming away from them. Carter had seen those caves when he passed over them, and had noticed their likeness to the caves on Ngranek. Now he knew that the likeness was more than a chance one, for in these pictures were shewn their fearsome denizens; and those bat-wings, curving horns, barbed tails, prehensile paws and rubbery bodies were not strange to him. He had met those silent, flitting and clutching creatures before; those mindless guardians of the Great Abyss whom even the Great Ones fear, and who own not Nyarlathotep but hoary Nodens as their lord. For they were the dreaded night-gaunts, who never laugh or smile because they have no faces, and who flop unendingly in the dark betwixt the Vale of Pnath and the passes to the outer world.

The slant-eyed merchant had now prodded Carter into a great domed space whose walls were carved in shocking bas-reliefs, and whose centre held a gaping circular pit surrounded by six malignly stained stone altars in a ring. There was no light in this vast evil-smelling crypt, and the small lamp of the sinister merchant shone so feebly that one could grasp details only little by little. At the farther end was a high stone dais reached by five steps; and there on a golden throne sat a lumpish figure robed in yellow silk figured with red and having a yellow silken mask over its face. To this being the slant-eyed man made certain signs with his hands, and the lurker in the dark replied by raising a disgustingly carven flute of ivory in silk-covered paws and blowing certain loathsome sounds from beneath its flowing yellow mask. This colloquy went on for some time, and to Carter there was something sickeningly familiar in the sound of that flute and the stench of the malodorous place. It made him think of a frightful red-litten city and of the revolting procession that once filed through it; of that, and of an awful climb through lunar countryside beyond, before the rescuing rush of earth's friendly cats. He knew that the creature on the dais was without doubt the High-Priest Not To Be Described, of which legend whispers such fiendish and abnormal possibilities, but he feared to think just what that abhorred High-Priest might be.

Then the figured silk slipped a trifle from one of the greyish-white paws, and Carter knew what the noisome High-Priest was. And in that hideous second, stark fear drove him to something his reason would never have dared to attempt, for in all his shaken consciousness there was room only for one frantic will to escape from what squatted on that golden throne. He knew that hopeless labyrinths of stone lay betwixt him and the cold table-land outside, and that even on that table-land the noxious Shantek still waited; yet in spite of all this there was in his mind only the instant need to get away from that wriggling, silk-robed monstrosity.

The slant-eyed man had set the curious lamp upon one of the high and wickedly stained altar-stones by the pit, and had moved forward somewhat to talk to the High-Priest with his hands. Carter, hitherto wholly passive, now gave that man a terrific push with all the wild strength of fear, so that the victim toppled at once into that gaping well which rumour holds to reach down to the hellish Vaults of Zin where Gugs hunt ghasts in the dark. In almost the same second he seized the lamp from the altar and darted out into the frescoed labyrinths, racing this way and that as chance determined and trying not to think of the stealthy padding of shapeless paws on the stones behind him, or of the silent wrigglings and crawlings which must be going on back there in lightless corridors.

After a few moments he regretted his thoughtless haste, and wished he had tried to follow backward the frescoes he had passed on the way in. True, they were so confused and duplicated that they could not have done him much good, but he wished none the less he had made the attempt. Those he now saw were even more horrible than those he had seen then, and he knew he was not in the corridors leading outside. In time he became quite sure he was not followed, and slackened his pace somewhat; but scarce had he breathed in half relief when a new peril beset him. His lamp was waning, and he would soon be in pitch blackness with no means of sight or guidance.

When the light was all gone he groped slowly in the dark, and prayed to the Great Ones for such help as they might afford. At times he felt the stone floor sloping up or down, and once he stumbled over a step for which no reason seemed to exist. The farther he went the damper it seemed to be, and when he was able to feel a junction or the mouth of a side passage he always chose the way which sloped downward the least. He believed, though, that his general course was down; and the vault-like smell and incrustations on the greasy walls and floor alike warned him he was burrowing deep in Leng's unwholesome table-land. But there was not any warning of the thing which came at last; only the thing itself with its terror and shock and breath-taking chaos. One moment he was groping slowly over the slippery floor of an almost level place, and the next he was shooting dizzily downward in the dark through a burrow which must have been well-nigh vertical.

Of the length of that hideous sliding he could never be sure, but it seemed to take hours of delirious nausea and ecstatic frenzy. Then he realized he was still, with the phosphorescent clouds of a northern night shining sickly above him. All around were crumbling walls and broken columns, and the pavement on which he lay was pierced by straggling grass and wrenched asunder by frequent shrubs and roots. Behind him a basalt cliff rose topless and perpendicular, its dark side sculptured into repellent scenes, and pierced by an arched and carven entrance to the inner blacknesses out of which he had come. Ahead stretched double rows of pillars, and the fragments and pedestals of pillars, that spoke of a broad and bygone street; and from the urns and basins along the way he knew it had been a great street of gardens. Far off at its end the pillars spread to mark a vast round plaza, and in that open circle there loomed gigantic under the lurid night clouds a pair of monstrous things. Huge winged lions of diarite they were, with blackness and shadow between them. Full twenty feet they reared their grotesque and unbroken heads, and snarled derisive on the ruins around them. And Carter knew right well what they must be, for legend tells of only one such twain. They were the changeless guardians of the Great Abyss, and these dark ruins were in truth primordial Sarkomand.

Carter's first act was to close and barricade the archway in the cliff with fallen blocks and odd debris that lay around. He wished no follower from Leng's hateful monastery, for along the way ahead would lurk enough of other dangers. Of how to get from Sarkomand to the peopled parts of dreamland he knew nothing at all; nor could he gain much by descending to the grottoes of the ghouls, since he knew they were no better informed than he. The three ghouls which had helped him through the city of Gugs to the outer world had not known how to reach Sarkomand in their journey back, but had planned to ask old traders in Dylath-Leen. He did not like to think of going again to the subterrene world of Gugs and risking once more that hellish tower of Koth with its Cyclopean steps leading to the enchanted wood, yet he felt he might have to try this course if all else failed. Over Leng's plateau past the lone monastery he dared not go unaided; for the High-Priest's emissaries must be many, while at the journey's end there would no doubt be the Shantaks and perhaps other things to deal with. If he could get a boat he might sail back to Inquanok past the jagged and hideous rock in the sea, for the primal frescoes in the monastery labyrinth had shewn that this frightful place lies not far from Sarkomand's basalt quays. But to find a boat in this aeon-deserted city was no probable thing, and it did not appear likely that he could ever make one.

Such were the thoughts of Randolph Carter when a new impression began beating upon his mind. All this while there had stretched before him the great corpse-like width of fabled Sarkomand with its black broken pillars and crumbling sphinx-crowned gates and titan stones and monstrous winged lions against the sickly glow of those luminous night clouds. Now he saw far ahead and on the right a glow that no clouds could account for, and knew he was not alone in the silence of that dead city. The glow rose and fell fitfully, flickering with a greenish tinge which did not reassure the watcher. And when he crept closer, down the littered street and through some narrow gaps between tumbled walls, he perceived that it was a campfire near the wharves with many vague forms clustered darkly around it, and a lethal odour hanging heavily over all. Beyond was the oily lapping of the harbour water with a great ship riding at anchor, and Carter paused in stark terror when he saw that the ship was indeed one of the dreaded black galleys from the moon.

Then, just as he was about to creep back from that detestable flame, he saw a stirring among the vague dark forms and heard a peculiar and unmistakable sound. It was the frightened meeping of a ghoul, and in a moment it had swelled to a veritable chorus of anguish. Secure as he was in the shadow of monstrous ruins, Carter allowed his curiosity to conquer his fear, and crept forward again instead of retreating. Once in crossing an open street he wriggled worm-like on his stomach, and in another place he had to rise to his feet to avoid making a noise among heaps of fallen marble. But always he succeeded in avoiding discovery, so that in a short time he had found a spot behind a titan pillar where he could watch the whole green-litten scene of action. There around a hideous fire fed by the obnoxious stems of lunar fungi, there squatted a stinking circle of the toad-like moonbeasts and their almost-human slaves. Some of these slaves were heating curious iron spears in the leaping flames, and at intervals applying their white-hot points to three tightly trussed prisoners that lay writhing before the leaders of the party. From the motions of their tentacles Carter could see that the blunt-snouted moonbeasts were enjoying the spectacle hugely, and vast was his horror when he suddenly recognised the frantic meeping and knew that the tortured ghouls were none other than the faithful trio which had guided him safely from the abyss, and had thereafter set out from the enchanted wood to find Sarkomand and the gate to their native deeps.

The number of malodorous moonbeasts about that greenish fire was very great, and Carter saw that he could do nothing now to save his former allies. Of how the ghouls had been captured he could not guess, but fancied that the grey toad-like blasphemies had heard them inquire in Dylath-Leen concerning the way to Sarkomand and had not wished them to approach so closely the hateful plateau of Leng and the High-Priest Not To Be Described. For a moment he pondered on what he ought to do, and recalled how near he was to the gate of the ghouls' black kingdom. Clearly it was wisest to creep east to the plaza of twin lions and descend at once to the gulf, where assuredly he would meet no horrors worse than those above, and where he might soon find ghouls eager to rescue their brethren and perhaps to wipe out the moonbeasts from the black galley. It occurred to him that the portal, like other gates to the abyss, might be guarded by flocks of night-gaunts; but he did not fear these faceless creatures now. He had learned that they are bound by solemn treaties with the ghouls, and the ghoul which was Pickman had taught him how to glibber a password they understood.

So Carter began another silent crawl through the ruins, edging slowly toward the great central plaza and the winged lions. It was ticklish work, but the moonbeasts were pleasantly busy and did not hear the slight noises which he twice made by accident among the scattered stones. At last he reached the open space and picked his way among the stunned trees and vines that had grown up therein. The gigantic lions loomed terrible above him in the sickly glow of the phosphorescent night clouds, but he manfully persisted toward them and presently crept round to their faces, knowing it was on that side he would find the mighty darkness which they guard. Ten feet apart crouched the mocking-faced beasts of diarite, brooding on cyclopean pedestals whose sides were chiselled in fearsome bas-reliefs. Betwixt them was a tiled court with a central space which had once been railed with balusters of onyx. Midway in this space a black well opened, and Carter soon saw that he had indeed reached the yawning gulf whose crusted and mouldy stone steps lead down to the crypts of nightmare.

Terrible is the memory of that dark descent in which hours wore themselves away whilst Carter wound sightlessly round and round down a fathomless spiral of steep and slippery stairs. So worn and narrow were the steps, and so greasy with the ooze of inner earth, that the climber never quite knew when to expect a breathless fall and hurtling down to the ultimate pits; and he was likewise uncertain just when or how the guardian night-gaunts would suddenly pounce upon him, if indeed there were any stationed in this primeval passage. All about him was a stifling odour of nether gulfs, and he felt that the air of these choking depths was not made for mankind. In time he became very numb and somnolent, moving more from automatic impulse than from reasoned will; nor did he realize any change when he stopped moving altogether as something quietly seized him from behind. He was flying very rapidly through the air before a malevolent tickling told him that the rubbery night-gaunts had performed their duty.

Awaked to the fact that he was in the cold, damp clutch of the faceless flutterers, Carter remembered the password of the ghouls and glibbered it as loudly as he could amidst the wind and chaos of flight. Mindless though night-gaunts are said to be, the effect was instantaneous; for all tickling stopped at once, and the creatures hastened to shift their captive to a more comfortable position. Thus encouraged Carter ventured some explanations, telling of the seizure and torture of three ghouls by the moonbeasts, and of the need of assembling a party to rescue them. The night-gaunts, though inarticulate, seemed to understand what was said, and shewed greater haste and purpose in their flight. Suddenly the dense blackness gave place to the grey twilight of inner earth, and there opened up ahead one of those flat sterile plains on which ghouls love to squat and gnaw. Scattered tombstones and osseous fragments told of the denizens of that place; and as Carter gave a loud meep of urgent summons, a score of burrows emptied forth their leathery, dog-like tenants. The night-gaunts now flew low and set their passenger upon his feet, afterward withdrawing a little and forming a hunched semicircle on the ground while the ghouls greeted the newcomer.

Carter glibbered his message rapidly and explicitly to the grotesque company, and four of them at once departed through different burrows to spread the news to others and gather such troops as might be available for a rescue. After a long wait a ghoul of some importance appeared, and made significant signs to the night-gaunts, causing two of the latter to fly off into the dark. Thereafter there were constant accessions to the hunched flock of night-gaunts on the plain, till at length the slimy soil was fairly black with them. Meanwhile fresh ghouls crawled out of the burrows one by one, all glibbering excitedly and forming in crude battle array not far from the huddled night-gaunts. In time there appeared that proud and influential ghoul which was once the artist Richard Pickman of Boston, and to him Carter glibbered a very full account of what had occurred. The erstwhile Pickman, pleased to greet his ancient friend again, seemed very much impressed, and held a conference with other chiefs a little apart from the growing throng.

Finally, after scanning the ranks with care, the assembled chiefs all meeped in unison and began glibbering orders to the crowds of ghouls and night-gaunts. A large detachment of the horned flyers vanished at once, while the rest grouped themselves two by two on their knees with extended forelegs, awaiting the approach of the ghouls one by one. As each ghoul reached the pair of night-gaunts to which he was assigned, he was taken up and borne away into the blackness; till at last the whole throng had vanished save for Carter, Pickman, and the other chiefs, and a few pairs of night-gaunts. Pickman explained that night-gaunts are the advance guard and battle steeds of the ghouls, and that the army was issuing forth to Sarkomand to deal with the moonbeasts. Then Carter and the ghoulish chiefs approached the waiting bearers and were taken up by the damp, slippery paws. Another moment and all were whirling in wind and darkness; endlessly up, up, up to the gate of the winged and the special ruins of primal Sarkomand.

When, after a great interval, Carter saw again the sickly light of Sarkomand's nocturnal sky, it was to behold the great central plaza swarming with militant ghouls and night-gaunts. Day, he felt sure, must be almost due; but so strong was the army that no surprise of the enemy would be needed. The greenish flare near the wharves still glimmered faintly, though the absence of ghoulish meeping shewed that the torture of the prisoners was over for the nonce. Softly glibbering directions to their steeds and to the flock of riderless night-gaunts ahead, the ghouls presently rose in wide whirring columns and swept on over the bleak ruins toward the evil flame. Carter was now beside Pickman in the front rank of ghouls, and saw as they approached the noisome camp that the moonbeasts were totally unprepared. The three prisoners lay bound and inert beside the fire, while their toad-like captors slumped drowsily about in no certain order. The almost-human slaves were asleep, even the sentinels shirking a duty which in this realm must have seemed to them merely perfunctory.

The final swoop of the night-gaunts and mounted ghouls was very sudden, each of the greyish toad-like blasphemies and their almost-human slaves being seized by a group of night-gaunts before a sound was made. The moonbeasts, of course, were voiceless; and even the slaves had little chance to scream before rubbery paws choked them into silence. Horrible were the writhings of those great jelly-fish abnormalities as the sardonic night-gaunts clutched them, but nothing availed against the strength of those black prehensile talons. When a moonbeast writhed too violently, a night-gaunt would seize and pull its quivering pink tentacles; which seemed to hurt so much that the victim would cease its struggles. Carter expected to see much slaughter, but found that the ghouls were far subtler in their plans. They glibbered certain simple orders to the night-gaunts which held the captives, trusting the rest to instinct; and soon the hapless creatures were borne silently away into the Great Abyss, to be distributed impartially amongst the Dholes, Gugs, ghasts and other dwellers in darkness whose modes of nourishment are not painless to their chosen victims. Meanwhile the three bound ghouls had been released and consoled by their conquering kinsfolk, whilst various parties searched the neighborhood for possible remaining moonbeasts, and boarded the evil-smelling black galley at the wharf to make sure that nothing had escaped the general defeat. Surely enough, the capture had been thorough, for not a sign of further life could the victors detect. Carter, anxious to preserve a means of access to the rest of dreamland, urged them not to sink the anchored galley; and this request was freely granted out of gratitude for his act in reporting the plight of the captured trio. On the ship were found some very curious objects and decorations, some of which Carter cast at once into the sea.

Ghouls and night-gaunts now formed themselves in separate groups, the former questioning their rescued fellows anent past happenings. It appeared that the three had followed Carter's directions and proceeded from the enchanted wood to Dylath-Leen by way of Nir and the Skin, stealing human clothes at a lonely farmhouse and loping as closely as possible in the fashion of a man's walk. In Dylath-Leen's taverns their grotesque ways and faces had aroused much comment; but they had persisted in asking the way to Sarko-mand until at last an old traveller was able to tell them. Then they knew that only a ship for Lelag-Leng would serve their purpose, and prepared to wait patiently for such a vessel.

But evil spies had doubtless reported much; for shortly a black galley put into port, and the wide-mouthed ruby merchants invited the ghouls to drink with them in a tavern. Wine was produced from one of those sinister bottles grotesquely carven from a single ruby, and after that the ghouls found themselves prisoners on the black galley as Carter had found himself. This time, however, the unseen rowers steered not for the moon but for antique Sarkomand, bent evidently on taking their captives before the High-Priest Not To Be Described. They had touched at the jagged rock in the northern sea which Inquanok's mariners shun, and the ghouls had there seen for the first time the red masters of the ship, being sickened despite their own callousness by such extremes of malign shapelessness and fearsome odour. There, too, were witnessed the nameless pastimes of the toad-like resident garrison – such pastimes as give rise to the night-howlings which men fear. After that had come the landing at ruined Sarkomand and the beginning of the tortures, whose continuance the present rescue had prevented.

Future plans were next discussed, the three rescued ghouls suggesting a raid on the jagged rock and the extermination of the toad-like garrison there. To this, however, the night-gaunts objected, since the prospect of flying over water did not please them. Most of the ghouls favoured the design, but were at a loss how to follow it without the help of the winged night-gaunts. Thereupon Carter, seeing that they could not navigate the anchored galley, offered to teach them the use of the great banks of oars; to which proposal they eagerly assented. Grey day had now come, and under that leaden northern sky a picked detachment of ghouls filed into the noisome ship and took their seats on the rowers' benches. Carter found them fairly apt at learning, and before night had risked several experimental trips around the harbour. Not till three days later, however, did he deem it safe to attempt the voyage of conquest. Then, the rowers trained and the night-gaunts safely stowed in the forecastle, the party set sail at last; Pickman and the other chiefs gathering on deck and discussing models of approach and procedure.

On the very first night the howlings from the rock were heard. Such was their timbre that all the galley's crew shook visibly; but most of all trembled the three rescued ghouls who knew precisely what those howlings meant. It was not thought best to attempt an attack by night, so the ship lay to under the phosphorescent clouds to wait for the dawn of a greyish day. When the light was ample and the howlings still the rowers resumed their strokes, and the galley drew closer and closer to that jagged rock whose granite pinnacles clawed fantastically at the dull sky. The sides of the rock were very steep, but on ledges here and there could be seen the bulging walls of queer windowless dwellings, and the low railings guarding travelled high-roads. No ship of men had ever come so near the place, or at least, had never come so near and departed again; but Carter and the ghouls were void of fear and kept inflexibly on, rounding the eastern face of the rock and seeking the wharves which the rescued trio described as being on the southern side within a harbour formed of steep headlands.

The headlands were prolongations of the island proper, and came so closely together that only one ship at a time might pass between them. There seemed to be no watchers on the outside, so the galley was steered boldly through the flume-like strait and into the stagnant putrid harbour beyond. Here, however, all was bustle and activity, with several ships lying at anchor along a forbidding stone quay, and scores of almost-human slaves and moonbeasts by the waterfront handling crates and boxes or driving nameless and fabulous horrors hitched to lumbering lorries. There was a small stone town hewn out of the vertical cliff above the wharves, with the start of a winding road that spiralled out of sight toward higher ledges of the rock. Of what lay inside that prodigious peak of granite none might say, but the things one saw on the outside were far from encouraging.

At sight of the incoming galley the crowds on the wharves displayed much eagerness; those with eyes staring intently, and those without eyes wriggling their pink tentacles expectantly. They did not, of course, realize that the black ship had changed hands; for ghouls look much like the horned and hooved almost-humans, and the night-gaunts were all out of sight below. By this time the leaders had fully formed a plan, which was to loose the night-gaunts as soon as the wharf was touched, and then to sail directly away, leaving matters wholly to the instincts of those almost-mindless creatures. Marooned on the rock, the horned flyers would first of all seize whatever living things they found there, and afterward, quite help-less to think except in terms of the homing instinct, would forget their fears of water and fly swiftly back to the abyss; bearing their noisome prey to appropriate destinations in the dark, from which not much would emerge alive.

The ghoul that was Pickman now went below and gave the night-gaunts their simple instructions, while the ship drew very near to the ominous and malodorous wharves. Presently a fresh stir rose along the waterfront, and Carter saw that the motions of the galley had begun to excite suspicion. Evidently the steersman was not making for the right dock, and probably the watchers had noticed the diff-erence between the hideous ghouls and the almost-human slaves whose places they were taking. Some silent alarm must have been given, for almost at once a horde of the mephitic moonbeasts began to pour from the little black doorways of the windowless houses and down the winding road at the right. A rain of curious javelins struck the galley as the prow hit the wharf felling two ghouls and slightly wounding another; but at this point all the hatches were thrown open to emit a black cloud of whirring night-gaunts which swarmed over the town like a flock of horned and cyclopean bats.

The jellyish moonbeasts had procured a great pole and were trying to push off the invading ship, but when the night-gaunts struck them they thought of such things no more. It was a very terrible spectacle to see those faceless and rubbery ticklers at their pastime, and trem-endously impressive to watch the dense cloud of them spreading through the town and up the winding roadway to the reaches above. Sometimes a group of the black flutterers would drop a toad-like prisoner from aloft by mistake, and the manner in which the victim would burst was highly offensive to the sight and smell. When the last of the night-gaunts had left the galley the ghoulish leaders glibbered an order of withdrawal, and the rowers pulled quietly out of the harbour between the grey headlands while still the town was a chaos of battle and conquest.

The Pickman ghoul allowed several hours for the night-gaunts to make up their rudimentary minds and overcome their fear of flying over the sea, and kept the galley standing about a mile off the jagged rock while he waited, and dressed the wounds of the injured men. Night fell, and the grey twilight gave place to the sickly phosphorescence of low clouds, and all the while the leaders watched the high peaks of that accursed rock for signs of the night-gaunts' flight. Toward morning a black speck was seen hovering timidly over the top-most pinnacle, and shortly afterward the speck had become a swarm. Just before daybreak the swarm seemed to scatter, and within a quarter of an hour it had vanished wholly in the distance toward the northeast. Once or twice something seemed to fall from the thing swarm into the sea; but Carter did not worry, since he knew from observation that the toad-like moonbeasts cannot swim. At length, when the ghouls were satisfied that all the night-gaunts had left for Sarkomand and the Great Abyss with their doomed burdens, the galley put back into the harbour betwixt the grey headlands; and all the hideous company landed and roamed curiously over the denuded rock with its towers and eyries and fortresses chiselled from the solid stone.

Frightful were the secrets uncovered in those evil and windowless crypts; for the remnants of unfinished pastimes were many, and in various stages of departure from their primal state. Carter put out of the way certain things which were after a fashion alive, and fled precipitately from a few other things about which he could not be very positive. The stench-filled houses were furnished mostly with grotesque stools and benches carven from moon-trees, and were painted inside with nameless and frantic designs. Countless weapons, implements, and ornaments lay about, including some large idols of solid ruby depicting singular beings not found on the earth. These latter did not, despite their material, invite either appropriation or long inspection; and Carter took the trouble to hammer five of them into very small pieces. The scattered spears and javelins he collected, and with Pickman's approval distributed among the ghouls. Such devices were new to the dog-like lopers, but their relative simplicity made them easy to master after a few concise hints.

The upper parts of the rock held more temples than private homes, and in numerous hewn chambers were found terrible carven altars and doubtfully stained fonts and shrines for the worship of things more monstrous than the wild gods atop Kadath. From the rear of one great temple stretched a low black passage which Carter followed far into the rock with a torch till he came to a lightless domed hall of vast proportions, whose vaultings were covered with demoniac carvings and in whose centre yawned a foul and bottomless well like that in the hideous monastery of Leng where broods alone the High-Priest Not To Be Described. On the distant shadowy side, beyond the noisome well, he thought he discerned a small door of strangely wrought bronze; but for some reason he felt an unaccountable dread of opening it or even approaching it, and hastened back through the cavern to his unlovely allies as they shambled about with an ease and abandon he could scarcely feel. The ghouls had observed the unfinished pastimes of the moonbeasts, and had profited in their fashion. They had also found a hogshead of potent moon-wine, and were rolling it down to the wharves for removal and later use in diplomatic dealings, though the rescued trio, remembering its effect on them in Dylath-Leen, had warned their company to taste none of it. Of rubies from lunar mines there was a great store, both rough and polished, in one of the vaults near the water; but when the ghouls found they were not good to eat they lost all interest in them. Carter did not try to carry any away, since he knew too much about those which had mined them.

Suddenly there came an excited meeping from the sentries on the wharves, and all the loathsome foragers turned from their tasks to stare seaward and cluster round the waterfront. Betwixt the grey headlands a fresh black galley was rapidly advancing, and it would be but a moment before the almost-humans on deck would perceive the invasion of the town and give the alarm to the monstrous things below. Fortunately the ghouls still bore the spears and javelins which Carter had distributed amongst them; and at his command, sustained by the being that was Pickman, they now formed a line of battle and prepared to prevent the landing of the ship. Presently a burst of excitement on the galley told of the crew's discovery of the changed state of things, and the instant stoppage of the vessel proved that the superior numbers of the ghouls had been noted and taken into account. After a moment of hesitation the newcomers silently turned and passed out between the headlands again, but not for an instant did the ghouls imagine that the conflict was averted. Either the dark ship would seek reinforcements or the crew would try to land elsewhere on the island; hence a party of scouts was at once sent up toward the pinnacle to see what the enemy's course would be.

In a very few minutes the ghoul returned breathless to say that the moonbeasts and almost-humans were landing on the outside of the more easterly of the rugged grey headlands, and ascending by hidden paths and ledges which a goat could scarcely tread in safety. Almost immediately afterward the galley was sighted again through the flume-like strait, but only for a second. Then a few moments later, a second messenger panted down from aloft to say that another party was landing on the other headland; both being much more numerous than the size of the galley would seem to allow for. The ship itself, moving slowly with only one sparsely manned tier of oars, soon hove in sight betwixt the cliffs, and lay to in the foetid harbour as if to watch the coming fray and stand by for any possible use.

By this time Carter and Pickman had divided the ghouls into three parties, one to meet each of the two invading columns and one to remain in the town. The first two at once scrambled up the rocks in their respective directions, while the third was subdivided into a land party and a sea party. The sea party, commanded by Carter, boarded the anchored galley and rowed out to meet the under-manned galley of the newcomers; whereat the latter retreated through the strait to the open sea. Carter did not at once pursue it, for he knew he might be needed more acutely near the town. Meanwhile the frightful detachments of the moonbeasts and almost-humans had lumbered up to the top of the headlands and were shockingly silhouetted on either side against the grey twilight sky. The thin hellish flutes of the invaders had now begun to whine, and the general effect of those hybrid, half-amorphous processions was as nauseating as the actual odour given off by the toad-like lunar blasphemies. Then the two parties of the ghouls swarmed into sight and joined the silhouetted panorama. Javelins began to fly from both sides, and the swelling meeps of the ghouls and the bestial howls of the almost-humans gradually joined the hellish whine of the flutes to form a frantick and indescribable chaos of daemon cacophony. Now and then bodies fell from the narrow ridges of the headlands into the sea outside or the harbour inside, in the latter case being sucked quickly under by certain submarine lurkers whose presence was indicated only by prodigious bubbles.

For half an hour this dual battle raged in the sky, till upon the west cliff the invaders were completely annihilated. On the east cliff, however, where the leader of the moonbeast party appeared to be present, the ghouls had not fared so well, and were slowly retreating to the slopes of the pinnacle proper. Pickman had quickly ordered reinforcements for this front from the party in the town, and these had helped greatly in the earlier stages of the combat. Then, when the western battle was over, the victorious survivors hastened across to the aid of their hard-pressed fellows, turning the tide and forcing the invaders back again along the narrow ridge of the headland. The almost-humans were by this time all slain, but the last of the toad-like horrors fought desperately with the great spears clutched in their powerful and disgusting paws. The time for javelins was now nearly past, and the fight became a hand-to-hand contest of what few spearmen could meet upon that narrow ridge.

As fury and recklessness increased, the number falling into the sea became very great. Those striking the harbour met nameless extinction from the unseen bubblers, but of those striking the open sea some were able to swim to the foot of the cliffs and land on tidal rocks, while the hovering galley of the enemy rescued several moon-beasts. The cliffs were unscalable except where the monsters had debarked, so that none of the ghouls on the rocks could rejoin their battle-line. Some were killed by javelins from the hostile galley or from the moonbeasts above, but a few survived to be rescued. When the security of the land parties seemed assured, Carter's galley sallied forth between the headlands and drove the hostile ship far out to sea, pausing to rescue such ghouls as were on the rocks or still swimming in the ocean. Several moonbeasts washed on rocks or reefs were speedily put out of the way.

Finally, the moonbeast galley being safely in the distance and the invading land army concentrated in one place, Carter landed a considerable force on the eastern headland in the enemy's rear; after which the fight was short-lived indeed. Attacked from both sides, the noisome flounderers were rapidly cut to pieces or pushed into the sea, till by evening the ghoulish chiefs agreed that the island was again clear of them. The hostile galley, meanwhile, had disappeared, and it was decided that the evil jagged rock had better be evacuated before any overwhelming horde of lunar horrors might be assembled and brought against the victors.

So by night Pickman and Carter assembled all the ghouls and counted them with care, finding that over a fourth had been lost in the day's battles. The wounded were placed on bunks in the galley, for Pickman always discouraged the old ghoulish custom of killing and eating one's own wounded, and the able-bodied troops were assigned to the oars or to such other places as they might most usefully fill. Under the low phosphorescent clouds of night the galley sailed, and Carter was not sorry to be departing from the island of unwholesome secrets, whose lightless domed hall with its bottomless well and repellent bronze door lingered restlessly in his fancy. Dawn found the ship in sight of Sarkomand's ruined quays of basalt, where a few night-gaunt sentries still waited, squatting like black horned gargoyles on the broken columns and crumbling sphinxes of that fearful city which lived and died before the years of man.

The ghouls made camp amongst the fallen stones of Sarkomand, despatching a messenger for enough night-gaunts to serve them as steeds. Pickman and the other chiefs were effusive in their gratitude for the aid Carter had lent them. Carter now began to feel that his plans were indeed maturing well, and that he would be able to command the help of these fearsome allies not only in quitting this part of dreamland, but in pursuing his ultimate quest for the gods atop unknown Kadath, and the marvellous sunset city they so strangely withheld from his slumbers. Accordingly he spoke of these things to the ghoulish leaders, telling what he knew of the cold waste wherein Kadath stands and of the monstrous Shantaks and the mountains carven into double-headed images which guard it. He spoke of the fear of Shantaks for night-gaunts, and of how the vast hippocephalic birds fly screaming from the black burrows high up on the gaunt grey peaks that divide Inquanok from hateful Leng. He spoke, too, of the things he had learned concerning night-gaunts from the frescoes in the windowless monastery of the High-Priest Not To Be Described; how even the Great Ones fear them, and how their ruler is not the crawling chaos Nyarlathotep at all, but hoary and immemorial Nodens, Lord of the Great Abyss.

All these things Carter glibbered to the assembled ghouls, and presently outlined that request which he had in mind and which he did not think extravagant considering the services he had so lately rendered the rubbery dog-like lopers. He wished very much, he said, for the services of enough night-gaunts to bear him safely through the air past the realm of Shantaks and carven mountains, and up into the old waste beyond the returning tracks of any other mortal. He desired to fly to the onyx castle atop unknown Kadath in the cold waste to plead with the Great Ones for the sunset city they denied him, and felt sure that the night-gaunts could take him thither without trouble; high above the perils of the plain, and over the hideous double heads of those carven sentinel mountains that squat eternally in the grey dusk. For the horned and faceless creatures there could be no danger from aught of earth since the Great Ones themselves dread them. And even were unexpected things to come from the Other Gods, who are prone to oversee the affairs of earth's milder gods, the night-gaunts need not fear; for the outer hells are indifferent matters to such silent and slippery flyers as own not Nyarlathotep for their master, but bow only to potent and archaic Nodens.

A flock of ten or fifteen night-gaunts, Carter glibbered, would surely be enough to keep any combination of Shantaks at a distance, though perhaps it might be well to have some ghouls in the party to manage the creatures, their ways being better known to their ghoulish allies than to men. The party could land him at some convenient point within whatever walls that fabulous onyx citadel might have, waiting in the shadows for his return or his signal whilst he ventured inside the castle to give prayer to the gods of earth. If any ghouls chose to escort him into the throne-room of the Great Ones, he would be thankful, for their presence would add weight and importance to his plea. He would not, however, insist upon this but merely wished transportation to and from the castle atop unknown Kadath; the final journey being either to the marvellous sunset city itself, in case of gods proving favourable, or back to the earthward Gate of Deeper Slumber in the Enchanted Wood in case his prayers were fruitless.

Whilst Carter was speaking all the ghouls listened with great attention, and as the moments advanced the sky became black with clouds of those night-gaunts for which messengers had been sent. The winged steeds settled in a semicircle around the ghoulish army, waiting respectfully as the dog-like chieftains considered the wish of the earthly traveller. The ghoul that was Pickman glibbered gravely with his fellows and in the end Carter was offered far more than he had at most expected. As he had aided the ghouls in their conquest of the moonbeasts, so would they aid him in his daring voyage to realms whence none had ever returned, lending him not merely a few of their allied night-gaunts, but their entire army as then encamped, veteran fighting ghouls and newly assembled night-gaunts alike, save only a small garrison for the captured black galley and such spoils as had come from the jagged rock in the sea. They would set out through the aft whenever he might wish, and once arrived on Kadath a suitable train of ghouls would attend him in state as he placed his petition before earth's gods in their onyx castle.

Moved by a gratitude and satisfaction beyond words, Carter made plans with the ghoulish leaders for his audacious voyage. The army would fly high, they decided, over hideous Leng with its nameless monastery and wicked stone villages, stopping only at the vast grey peaks to confer with the Shantak-frightening night-gaunts whose burrows honeycombed their summits. They would then, according to what advice they might receive from those denizens, choose their final course, approaching unknown Kadath either through the desert of carven mountains north of Inquanok, or through the more northerly reaches of repulsive Leng itself. Dog-like and soulless as they are, the ghouls and night-gaunts had no dread of what those untrodden deserts might reveal; nor did they feel any deterring awe at the thought of Kadath towering lone with its onyx castle of mystery.

About midday the ghouls and night-gaunts prepared for flight, each ghoul selecting a suitable pair of horned steeds to bear him. Carter was placed well up toward the head of the column beside Pickman, and in front of the whole a double line of riderless night-gaunts was provided as a vanguard. At a brisk meep from Pickman the whole shocking army rose in a nightmare cloud above the broken columns and crumbling sphinxes of primordial Sarkomand; higher and higher, till even the great basalt cliff behind the town was cleared, and the cold, sterile table-land of Leng's outskirts laid open to sight. Still higher flew the black host, till even this table-land grew small beneath them; and as they worked northward over the wind-swept plateau of horror Carter saw once again with a shudder the circle of crude monoliths and the squat windowless building which he knew held that frightful silken-masked blasphemy from whose clutches he had so narrowly escaped. This time no descent was made as the army swept bat-like over the sterile landscape, passing the feeble fires of the unwholesome stone villages at a great altitude, and pausing not at all to mark the morbid twistings of the hooved, horned almost-humans that dance and pipe eternally therein. Once they saw a Shantak-bird flying low over the plain, but when it saw them it screamed noxiously and flapped off to the north in grotesque panic.

At dusk they reached the jagged grey peaks that form the barrier of Inquanok, and hovered about these strange caves near the summits which Carter recalled as so frightful to the Shantaks. At the insistent meeping of the ghoulish leaders there issued forth from each lofty burrow a stream of horned black flyers with which the ghouls and night-gaunts of the party conferred at length by means of ugly gestures. It soon became clear that the best course would be that over the cold waste north of Inquanok, for Leng's northward reaches are full of unseen pitfalls that even the night-gaunts dislike; abysmal influences centering in certain white hemispherical buildings on curious knolls, which common folklore associates unpleasantly with the Other Gods and their crawling chaos Nyarlathotep.

Of Kadath the flutterers of the peaks knew almost nothing, save that there must be some mighty marvel toward the north, over which the Shantaks and the carven mountains stand guard. They hinted at rumoured abnormalities of proportion in those trackless leagues beyond, and recalled vague whispers of a realm where night broods eternally; but of definite data they had nothing to give. So Carter and his party thanked them kindly; and, crossing the top-most granite pinnacles to the skies of Inquanok, dropped below the level of the phosphorescent night clouds and beheld in the distance those terrible squatting gargoyles that were mountains till some titan hand carved fright into their virgin rock.

There they squatted in a hellish half-circle, their legs on the desert sand and their mitres piercing the luminous clouds; sinister, wolf-like, and double-headed, with faces of fury and right hands raised, dully and malignly watching the rim of man's world and guarding with horror the reaches of a cold northern world that is not man's. From their hideous laps rose evil Shantaks of elephantine bulk, but these all fled with insane titters as the vanguard of night-gaunts was sighted in the misty sky. Northward above those gargoyle mountains the army flew, and over leagues of dim desert where never a land-mark rose. Less and less luminous grew the clouds, till at length

Carter could see only blackness around him; but never did the winged steeds falter, bred as they were in earth's blackest crypts, and seeing not with any eyes, but with the whole dank surface of their slippery forms. On and on they flew, past winds of dubious scent and sounds of dubious import; ever in thickest darkness, and covering such prodigious spaces that Carter wondered whether or not they could still be within earth's dreamland.

Then suddenly the clouds thinned and the stars shone spectrally above. All below was still black, but those pallid beacons in the sky seemed alive with a meaning and directiveness they had never possessed elsewhere. It was not that the figures of the constellations were different, but that the same familiar shapes now revealed a significance they had formerly failed to make plain. Everything focussed toward the north; every curve and asterism of the glittering sky became part of a vast design whose function was to hurry first the eye and then the whole observer onward to some secret and terrible goal of convergence beyond the frozen waste that stretched endlessly ahead. Carter looked toward the east where the great ridge of barrier peaks had towered along all the length of Inquanok and saw against the stars a jagged silhouette which told of its continued presence. It was more broken now, with yawning clefts and fantastically erratic pinnacles; and Carter studied closely the suggestive turnings and inclinations of that grotesque outline, which seemed to share with the stars some subtle northward urge.

They were flying past at a tremendous speed, so that the watcher had to strain hard to catch details; when all at once he beheld just above the line of the topmost peaks a dark and moving object against the stars, whose course exactly paralleled that of his own bizarre party. The ghouls had likewise glimpsed it, for he heard their low glibbering all about him, and for a moment he fancied the object was a gigantic Shantak, of a size vastly greater than that of the average specimen. Soon, however, he saw that this theory would not hold; for the shape of the thing above the mountains was not that of any hippocephalic bird. Its outline against the stars, necessarily vague as it was, resembled rather some huge mitred head, or pair of heads infinitely magnified; and its rapid bobbing flight through the sky seemed most peculiarly a wingless one. Carter could not tell which side of the mountains it was on, but soon perceived that it had parts below the parts he had first seen, since it blotted out all the stars in places where the ridge was deeply cleft.

Then came a wide gap in the range, where the hideous reaches of transmontane Leng were joined to the cold waste on this side by a low pass trough which the stars shone wanly. Carter watched this gap with intense care, knowing that he might see outlined against the sky beyond it the lower parts of the vast thing that flew undulantly above the pinnacles. The object had now floated ahead a trifle, and every eye of the party was fixed on the rift where it would presently appear in full-length silhouette. Gradually the huge thing above the peaks neared the gap, slightly slackening its speed as if conscious of having outdistanced the ghoulish army. For another minute suspense was keen, and then the brief instant of full silhouette and revelation came, bringing to the lips of the ghouls an awed and half-choked meep of cosmic fear, and to the soul of the traveller a chill that never wholly left it. For the mammoth bobbing shape that overtopped the ridge was only a head – a mitred double head – and below it in terrible vastness loped the frightful swollen body that bore it; the mountain-high monstrosity that walked in stealth and silence; the hyaena-like distortion of a giant anthropoid shape that trotted blackly against the sky, its repulsive pair of cone-capped heads reaching half way to the zenith.

Carter did not lose consciousness or even scream aloud, for he was an old dreamer; but he looked behind him in horror and shuddered when he saw that there were other monstrous heads silhouetted above the level of the peaks, bobbing along stealthily after the first one. And straight in the rear were three of the mighty mountain shapes seen full against the southern stars, tiptoeing wolf-like and lumberingly, their tall mitres nodding thousands of feet in the aft. The carven mountains, then, had not stayed squatting in that rigid semicircle north of Inquanok, with right hands uplifted. They had duties to perform, and were not remiss. But it was horrible that they never spoke, and never even made a sound in walking.

Meanwhile the ghoul that was Pickman had glibbered an order to the night-gaunts, and the whole army soared higher into the air. Up toward the stars the grotesque column shot, till nothing stood out any longer against the sky; neither the grey granite ridge that was still nor the carven mitred mountains that walked. All was blackness beneath as the fluttering legion surged northward amidst rushing winds and invisible laughter in the aether, and never a Shantak or less mentionable entity rose from the haunted wastes to pursue them. The farther they went, the faster they flew, till soon their dizzying speed seemed to pass that of a rifle ball and approach that of a planet in its orbit. Carter wondered how with such speed the earth could still stretch beneath them, but knew that in the land of dream dimensions have strange properties. That they were in a realm of eternal night he felt certain, and he fancied that the constellations overhead had subtly emphasized their northward focus, gathering themselves up as it were to cast the flying army into the void of the boreal pole, as the folds of a bag are gathered up to cast out the last bits of substance therein.

Then he noticed with terror that the wings of the night-gaunts were not flapping any more. The horned and faceless steeds had folded their membranous appendages, and were resting quite passive in the chaos of wind that whirled and chuckled as it bore them on. A force not of earth had seized on the army, and ghouls and night-gaunts alike were powerless before a current which pulled madly and relentlessly into the north whence no mortal had ever returned. At length a lone pallid light was seen on the skyline ahead, thereafter rising steadily as they approached, and having beneath it a black mass that blotted out the stars. Carter saw that it must be some beacon on a mountain, for only a mountain could rise so vast as seen from so prodigious a height in the air.

Higher and higher rose the light and the blackness beneath it, till all the northern sky was obscured by the rugged conical mass. Lofty as the army was, that pale and sinister beacon rose above it, towering monstrous over all peaks and concernments of earth, and tasting the atomless aether where the cryptical moon and the mad planets reel. No mountain known of man was that which loomed before them. The high clouds far below were but a fringe for its foothills. The groping dizziness of topmost air was but a girdle for its loins. Scornful and spectral climbed that bridge betwixt earth and heaven, black in eternal night, and crowned with a pshent of unknown stars whose awful and significant outline grew every moment clearer. Ghouls meeped in wonder as they saw it, and Carter shivered in fear lest all the hurtling army be dashed to pieces on the unyielding onyx of that cyclopean cliff.

Higher and higher rose the light, till it mingled with the loftiest orbs of the zenith and winked down at the flyers with lurid mockery. All the north beneath it was blackness now; dread, stony blackness from infinite depths to infinite heights, with only that pale winking beacon perched unreachably at the top of all vision. Carter studied the light more closely, and saw at last what lines its inky background made against the stars. There were towers on that titan mountain-top; horrible domed towers in noxious and incalculable tiers and clusters beyond any dreamable workmanship of man; battlements and terraces of wonder and menace, all limned tiny and black and distant against the starry pshent that glowed malevolently at the uppermost rim of sight. Capping that most measureless of mountains was a castle beyond all mortal thought, and in it glowed the daemon-light. Then Randolph Carter knew that his quest was done, and that he saw above him the goal of all forbidden steps and audacious visions; the fabulous, the incredible home of the Great Ones atop unknown Kadath.

Even as he realised this thing, Carter noticed a change in the course of the helplessly wind-sucked party. They were rising abruptly now, and it was plain that the focus of their flight was the onyx castle where the pale light shone. So close was the great black mountain that its sides sped by them dizzily as they shot upward, and in the darkness they could discern nothing upon it. Vaster and vaster loomed the tenebrous towers of the nighted castle above, and Carter could see that it was well-nigh blasphemous in its immensity. Well might its stones have been quarried by nameless workmen in that horrible gulf rent out of the rock in the hill pass north of Inquanok, for such was its size that a man on its threshold stood even as air out on the steps of earth's loftiest fortress. The pshent of unknown stars above the myriad domed turrets glowed with a sallow, sickly flare, so that a kind of twilight hung about the murky walls of slippery onyx. The pallid beacon was now seen to be a single shining window high up in one of the loftiest towers, and as the helpless army neared the top of the mountain Carter thought he detected unpleasant shadows flitting across the feebly luminous expanse. It was a strangely arched window, of a design wholly alien to earth.

The solid rock now gave place to the giant foundations of the monstrous castle, and it seemed that the speed of the party was somewhat abated. Vast walls shot up, and there was a glimpse of a great gate through which the voyagers were swept. All was night in the titan courtyard, and then came the deeper blackness of inmost things as a huge arched portal engulfed the column. Vortices of cold wind surged dankly through sightless labyrinths of onyx, and Carter could never tell what Cyclopean stairs and corridors lay silent along the route of his endless aerial twisting. Always upward led the terrible plunge in darkness, and never a sound, touch or glimpse broke the dense pall of mystery. Large as the army of ghouls and night-gaunts was, it was lost in the prodigious voids of that more than earthly castle. And when at last there suddenly dawned around him the lurid light of that single tower room whose lofty window had served as a beacon, it took Carter long to discern the far walls and high, distant ceiling, and to realize that he was indeed not again in the boundless air outside.

Randolph Carter had hoped to come into the throne-room of the Great Ones with poise and dignity, flanked and followed by impressive lines of ghouls in ceremonial order, and offering his prayer as a free and potent master among dreamers. He had known that the Great Ones themselves are not beyond a mortal's power to cope with, and had trusted to luck that the Other Gods and their crawling chaos Nyarlathotep would not happen to come to their aid at the crucial moment, as they had so often done before when men sought out earth's gods in their home or on their mountains. And with his hideous escort he had half hoped to defy even the Other Gods if need were, knowing as he did that ghouls have no masters, and that night-gaunts own not Nyarlathotep but only archaic Nodens for their lord. But now he saw that supernal Kadath in its cold waste is indeed girt with dark wonders and nameless sentinels, and that the Other Gods are of a surety vigilant in guarding the mild, feeble gods of earth. Void as they are of lordship over ghouls and night-gaunts, the mindless, shapeless blasphemies of outer space can yet control them when they must; so that it was not in state as a free and potent master of dreamers that Randolph Carter came into the Great Ones' throne-room with his ghouls. Swept and herded by nightmare tempests from the stars, and dogged by unseen horrors of the northern waste, all that army floated captive and helpless in the lurid light, dropping numbly to the onyx floor when by some voiceless order the winds of fright dissolved.

Before no golden dais had Randolph Carter come, nor was there any august circle of crowned and haloed beings with narrow eyes, long-lobed ears, thin nose, and pointed chin whose kinship to the carven face on Ngranek might stamp them as those to whom a dreamer might pray. Save for the one tower room the onyx castle atop Kadath was dark, and the masters were not there. Carter had come to unknown Kadath in the cold waste, but he had not found the gods. Yet still the lurid light glowed in that one tower room whose size was so little less than that of all outdoors, and whose distant walls and roof were so nearly lost to sight in thin, curling mists. Earth's gods were not there, it was true, but of subtler and less visible presences there could be no lack. Where the mild gods are absent, the Other Gods are not unrepresented; and certainly, the onyx castle of castles was far from tenantless. In what outrageous form or forms terror would next reveal itself Carter could by no means imagine. He felt that his visit had been expected, and wondered how close a watch had all along been kept upon him by the crawling chaos Nyar-lathotep. It is Nyarlathotep, horror of infinite shapes and dread soul and messenger of the Other Gods, that the fungous moonbeasts serve; and Carter thought of the black galley that had vanished when the tide of battle turned against the toad-like abnormalities on the jagged rock in the sea.

Reflecting upon these things, he was staggering to his feet in the midst of his nightmare company when there rang without warning through that pale-litten and limitless chamber the hideous blast of a daemon trumpet. Three times pealed that frightful brazen scream, and when the echoes of the third blast had died chucklingly away Randolph Carter saw that he was alone. Whither, why and how the ghouls and night-gaunts had been snatched from sight was not for him to divine. He knew only that he was suddenly alone, and that whatever unseen powers lurked mockingly around him were no powers of earth's friendly dreamland. Presently from the chamber's uttermost reaches a new sound came. This, too, was a rhythmic trumpeting; but of a kind far removed from the three raucous blasts which had dissolved his goodly cohorts. In this low fanfare echoed all the wonder and melody of ethereal dream, exotic vistas of unimagined loveliness floating from each strange chord and subtly alien cadence. Odours of incense came to match the golden notes; and overhead a great light dawned, its colours changing in cycles unknown to earth's spectrum, and following the song of the trumpets in weird symphonic harmonies. Torches flared in the distance, and the beat of drums throbbed nearer amidst waves of tense expectancy.

Out of the thinning mists and the cloud of strange incenses filed twin columns of giant black slaves with loin-cloths of iridescent silk. Upon their heads were strapped vast helmet-like torches of glittering metal, from which the fragrance of obscure balsams spread in fumous spirals. In their right hands were crystal wands whose tips were carven into leering chimaeras, while their left hands grasped long thin silver trumpets which they blew in turn. Armlets and anklets of gold they had, and between each pair of anklets stretched a golden chain that held its wearer to a sober gait. That they were true black men of earth's dreamland was at once apparent, but it seemed less likely that their rites and costumes were wholly things of our earth. Ten feet from Carter the columns stopped, and as they did so each trumpet flew abruptly to its bearer's thick lips. Wild and ecstatic was the blast that followed, and wilder still the cry that chorused just after from dark throats somehow made shrill by strange artifice.

Then down the wide lane betwixt the two columns a lone figure strode; a tall, slim figure with the young face of an antique Pharaoh, gay with prismatic robes and crowned with a golden pshent that glowed with inherent light. Close up to Carter strode that regal figure, whose proud carriage and smart features had in them the fascination of a dark god or fallen archangel, and around whose eyes there lurked the languid sparkle of capricious humour. It spoke, and in its mellow tones there rippled the wild music of Lethean streams.

'Randolph Carter,' said the voice, 'you have come to see the Great Ones whom it is unlawful for men to see. Watchers have spoken of this thing, and the Other Gods have grunted as they rolled and tumbled mindlessly to the sound of thin flutes in the black ultimate void where broods the daemon-sultan whose name no lips dare speak aloud.

'When Barzai the Wise climbed Hatheg-Kia to see the Greater Ones dance and howl above the clouds in the moonlight he never returned. The Other Gods were there, and they did what was expected. Zenig of Aphorat sought to reach unknown Kadath in the cold waste, and his skull is now set in a ring on the little finger of one whom I need not name.

'But you, Randolph Carter, have braved all things of earth's dreamland, and burn still with the flame of quest. You came not as one curious, but as one seeking his due, nor have you failed ever in reverence toward the mild gods of earth. Yet have these gods kept you from the marvellous sunset city of your dreams, and wholly through their own small covetousness; for verily, they craved the weird loveliness of that which your fancy had fashioned, and vowed that henceforward no other spot should be their abode.

'They are gone from their castle on unknown Kadath to dwell in your marvellous city. All through its palaces of veined marble they revel by day, and when the sun sets they go out in the perfumed gardens and watch the golden glory on temples and colonnades, arched bridges and silver-basined fountains, and wide streets with blossom-laden urns and ivory statues in gleaming rows. And when night comes they climb tall terraces in the dew, and sit on carved benches of porphyry scanning the stars, or lean over pale balustrades to gaze at the town's steep northward slopes, where one by one the little windows in old peaked gables shine softly out with the calm yellow light of homely candles.

'The gods love your marvellous city, and walk no more in the ways of the gods. They have forgotten the high places of earth, and the mountains that knew their youth. The earth has no longer any gods that are gods, and only the Other Ones from outer space hold sway on unremembered Kadath. Far away in a valley of your own child-hood, Randolph Carter, play the heedless Great Ones. You have dreamed too well, O wise arch-dreamer, for you have drawn dream's gods away from the world of all men's visions to that which is wholly yours, having builded out of your boyhood's small fancies a city more lovely than all the phantoms that have gone before.

'It is not well that earth's gods leave their thrones for the spider to spin on, and their realm for the Others to sway in the dark manner of Others. Fain would the powers from outside bring chaos and horror to you, Randolph Carter, who are the cause of their upsetting, but that they know it is by you alone that the gods may be sent back to their world. In that half-waking dreamland which is yours, no power of uttermost night may pursue; and only you can send the selfish Great Ones gently out of your marvellous sunset city, back through the northern twilight to their wonted place atop unknown Kadath in the cold waste.

'So, Randolph Carter, in the name of the Other Gods I spare you and charge you to seek that sunset city which is yours, and to send thence the drowsy truant gods for whom the dream world waits. Not hard to find is that roseal fever of the gods, that fanfare of supernal trumpets and clash of immortal cymbals, that mystery whose place and meaning have haunted you through the halls of waking and the gulfs of dreaming, and tormented you with hints of vanished memory and the pain of lost things awesome and momentous. Not hard to find is that symbol and relic of your days of wonder, for truly, it is but the stable and eternal gem wherein all that wonder sparkles crystallised to light your evening path. Behold! it is not over unknown seas but back over well-known years that your quest must go; back to the bright strange things of infancy and the quick sun-drenched glimpses of magic that old scenes brought to wide young eyes.

'For know you, that your gold and marble city of wonder is only the sum of what you have seen and loved in youth. It is the glory of Boston's hillside roofs and western windows aflame with sunset, of the flower-fragrant Common and the great dome on the hill and the tangle of gables and chimneys in the violet valley where the many-bridged Charles flows drowsily. These things you saw, Randolph Carter, when your nurse first wheeled you out in the springtime, and they will be the last things you will ever see with eyes of memory and of love. And there is antique Salem with its brooding years, and spectral Marblehead scaling its rocky precipices into past centuries! And the glory of Salem's towers and spires seen afar from Marble-head's pastures across the harbour against the setting sun.

'There is Providence quaint and lordly on its seven hills over the blue harbour, with terraces of green leading up to steeples and citadels of living antiquity, and Newport climbing wraith-like from its dreaming breakwater. Arkham is there, with its moss-grown gambrel roofs and the rocky rolling meadows behind it; and antediluvian Kingsport hoary with stacked chimneys and deserted quays and overhanging gables, and the marvel of high cliffs and the milky-misted ocean with tolling buoys beyond.

'Cool vales in Concord, cobbled lands in Portsmouth, twilight bends of rustic New Hampshire roads where giant elms half hide white farmhouse walls and creaking well-sweeps. Gloucester's salt wharves and Truro's windy willows. Vistas of distant steepled towns and hills beyond hills along the North Shore, hushed stony slopes and low ivied cottages in the lee of huge boulders in Rhode Island's back country. Scent of the sea and fragrance of the fields; spell of the dark woods and joy of the orchards and gardens at dawn. These, Randolph Carter, are your city; for they are yourself. New England bore you, and into your soul she poured a liquid loveliness which cannot die. This loveliness, moulded, crystallised, and polished by years of memory and dreaming, is your terraced wonder of elusive sunsets; and to find that marble parapet with curious urns and carven rail, and descend at last these endless balustraded steps to the city of broad squares and prismatic fountains, you need only to turn back to the thoughts and visions of your wistful boyhood.

'Look! through that window shine the stars of eternal night. Even now they are shining above the scenes you have known and cherished, drinking of their charm that they may shine more lovely over the gardens of dream. There is Antares – he is winking at this moment over the roofs of Tremont Street, and you could see him from your window on Beacon Hill. Out beyond those stars yawn the gulfs from whence my mindless masters have sent me. Some day you too may traverse them, but if you are wise you will beware such folly; for of those mortals who have been and returned, only one preserves a mind unshattered by the pounding, clawing horrors of the void. Terrors and blasphemies gnaw at one another for space, and there is more evil in the lesser ones than in the greater; even as you know from the deeds of those who sought to deliver you into my hands, whilst I myself harboured no wish to shatter you, and would indeed have helped you hither long ago had I not been elsewhere busy, and certain that you would yourself find the way. Shun then, the outer hells, and stick to the calm, lovely things of your youth. Seek out your marvellous city and drive thence the recreant Great Ones, sending them back gently to those scenes which are of their own youth, and which wait uneasy for their return.

'Easier even then the way of dim memory is the way I will prepare for you. See! there comes hither a monstrous Shantak, led by a slave who for your peace of mind had best keep invisible. Mount and be ready – there! Yogash the Black will help you on the scaly horror. Steer for that brightest star just south of the zenith – it is Vega, and in two hours will be just above the terrace of your sunset city. Steer for it only till you hear a far-off singing in the high aether. Higher than that lurks madness, so rein your Shantak when the first note lures. Look then back to earth, and you will see shining the deathless altar-flame of Ired-Naa from the sacred roof of a temple. That temple is in your desiderate sunset city, so steer for it before you heed the singing and are lost.

'When you draw nigh the city steer for the same high parapet whence of old you scanned the outspread glory, prodding the Shan-tak till he cry aloud. That cry the Great Ones will hear and know as they sit on their perfumed terraces, and there will come upon them such a homesickness that all of your city's wonders will not console them for the absence of Kadath's grim castle and the pshent of eternal stars that crowns it.

'Then must you land amongst them with the Shantak, and let them see and touch that noisome and hippocephalic bird; meanwhile dis-coursing to them of unknown Kadath, which you will so lately have left, and telling them how its boundless halls are lovely and unlighted, where of old they used to leap and revel in supernal radiance. And the Shantak will talk to them in the manner of Shantaks, but it will have no powers of persuasion beyond the recalling of elder days.

'Over and over must you speak to the wandering Great Ones of their home and youth, till at last they will weep and ask to be shewn the returning path they have forgotten. Thereat can you loose the waiting Shantak, sending him skyward with the homing cry of his kind; hearing which the Great Ones will prance and jump with antique mirth, and forthwith stride after the loathly bird in the fashion of gods, through the deep gulfs of heaven to Kadath's familiar towers and domes.

'Then will the marvellous sunset city be yours to cherish and inhabit for ever, and once more will earth's gods rule the dreams of men from their accustomed seat. Go now – the casement is open and the stars await outside. Already your Shantak wheezes and titters with impatience. Steer for Vega through the night, but turn when the singing sounds. Forget not this warning, lest horrors unthinkable suck you into the gulf of shrieking and ululant madness. Remember the Other Gods; they are great and mindless and terrible, and lurk in the outer voids. They are good gods to shun.

'Hei! Aa-shanta 'nygh! You are off! Send back earth's gods to their haunts on unknown Kadath, and pray to all space that you may never meet me in my thousand other forms. Farewell, Randolph Carter, and beware; for I am Nyarlathotep, the Crawling Chaos.'

And Randolph Carter, gasping and dizzy on his hideous Shantak, shot screamingly into space toward the cold blue glare of boreal Vega, looking but once behind him at the clustered and chaotic turrets of the onyx nightmare wherein still glowed the lone lurid light of that window above the air and the clouds of earth's dreamland. Great polypous horrors slid darkly past, and unseen bat wings beat multitudinous around him, but still he clung to the unwholesome mane of that loathly and hippocephalic scaled bird. The stars danced mockingly, almost shifting now and then to form pale signs of doom that one might wonder one had not seen and feared before; and ever the winds of nether howled of vague blackness and loneliness beyond the cosmos.

Then through the glittering vault ahead there fell a hush of portent, and all the winds and horrors slunk away as night things slink away before the dawn. Trembling in waves that golden wisps of nebula made weirdly visible, there rose a timid hint of far-off melody, droning in faint chords that our own universe of stars knows not. And as that music grew, the Shantak raised its ears and plunged ahead, and Carter likewise bent to catch each lovely strain. It was a song, but not the song of any voice. Night and the spheres sang it, and it was old when space and Nyarlathotep and the Other Gods were born.

Faster flew the Shantak, and lower bent the rider, drunk with the marvel of strange gulfs, and whirling in the crystal coils of outer magic. Then came too late the warning of the evil one, the sardonic caution of the daemon legate who had bidden the seeker beware the madness of that song. Only to taunt had Nyarlathotep marked out the way to safety and the marvellous sunset city; only to mock had that black messenger revealed the secret of these truant gods whose steps he could so easily lead back at will. For madness and the void's wild vengeance are Nyarlathotep's only gifts to the presumptuous; and frantick though the rider strove to turn his disgusting steed, that leering, tittering Shantak coursed on impetuous and relentless, flapping its great slippery wings in malignant joy and headed for those unhallowed pits whither no dreams reach; that last amorphous blight of nethermost confusion where bubbles and blasphemes at infinity's centre the mindless daemon-sultan Azathoth, whose name no lips dare speak aloud.

Unswerving and obedient to the foul legate's orders, that hellish bird plunged onward through shoals of shapeless lurkers and caperers in darkness, and vacuous herds of drifting entities that pawed and groped and groped and pawed; the nameless larvae of the Other Gods, that are like them blind and without mind, and possessed of singular hungers and thirsts

Onward unswerving and relentless, and tittering hilariously to watch the chuckling and hysterics into which the risen song of night and the spheres had turned, that eldritch scaly monster bore its helpless rider; hurtling and shooting, cleaving the uttermost rim and spanning the outermost abysses; leaving behind the stars and the realms of matter, and darting meteor-like through stark formlessness toward those inconceivable, unlighted chambers beyond time wherein Azathoth gnaws shapeless and ravenous amidst the muffled, maddening beat of vile drums and the thin, monotonous whine of accursed flutes.

Onward – onward – through the screaming, cackling, and blackly populous gulfs – and then from some dim blessed distance there came an image and a thought to Randolph Carter the doomed. Too well had Nyarlathotep planned his mocking and his tantalising, for he had brought up that which no gusts of icy terror could quite efface. Home – New England – Beacon Hill – the waking world.

'For know you, that your gold and marble city of wonder is only the sum of what you have seen and loved in youth . . . the glory of Boston's hillside roofs and western windows aflame with sunset; of the flower-fragrant Common and the great dome on the hill and the tangle of gables and chimneys in the violet valley where the many-bridged Charles flows drowsily . . . this loveliness, moulded, crystallised, and polished by years of memory and dreaming, is your terraced wonder of elusive sunsets; and to find that marble parapet with curious urns and carven rail, and descend at last those endless balustraded steps to the city of broad squares and prismatic fountains, you need only to turn back to the thoughts and visions of your wistful boyhood.'

Onward – onward – dizzily onward to ultimate doom through the blackness where sightless feelers pawed and slimy snouts jostled and nameless things tittered and tittered and tittered. But the image and the thought had come, and Randolph Carter knew clearly that he was dreaming and only dreaming, and that somewhere in the background the world of waking and the city of his infancy still lay. Words came again – 'You need only turn back to the thoughts and visions of your wistful boyhood.' Turn – turn – blackness on every side, but Randolph Carter could turn.

Thick though the rushing nightmare that clutched his senses, Randolph Carter could turn and move. He could move, and if he chose he could leap off the evil Shantak that bore him hurtlingly doomward at the orders of Nyarlathotep. He could leap off and dare those depths of night that yawned interminably down, those depths of fear whose terrors yet could not exceed the nameless doom that lurked waiting at chaos' core. He could turn and move and leap – he could – he would – he would – he would.

Off that vast hippocephalic abomination leaped the doomed and desperate dreamer, and down through endless voids of sentient blackness he fell. Aeons reeled, universes died and were born again, stars became nebulae and nebulae became stars, and still Randolph Carter fell through those endless voids of sentient blackness.

Then in the slow creeping course of eternity the utmost cycle of the cosmos churned itself into another futile completion, and all things became again as they were unreckoned kalpas before. Matter and light were born anew as space once had known them; and comets, suns and worlds sprang flaming into life, though nothing survived to tell that they had been and gone, been and gone, always and always, back to no first beginning.

And there was a firmament again, and a wind, and a glare of purple light in the eyes of the falling dreamer. There were gods and presences and wills; beauty and evil, and the shrieking of noxious night robbed of its prey. For through the unknown ultimate cycle had lived a thought and a vision of a dreamer's boyhood, and now there were remade a waking world and an old cherished city to body and to justify these things. Out of the void S'ngac the violet gas had pointed the way, and archaic Nodens was bellowing his guidance from unhinted deeps.

Stars swelled to dawns, and dawns burst into fountains of gold, carmine, and purple, and still the dreamer fell. Cries rent the aether as ribbons of light beat back the fiends from outside. And hoary Nodens raised a howl of triumph when Nyarlathotep, close on his quarry, stopped baffled by a glare that seared his formless hunting-horrors to grey dust. Randolph Carter had indeed descended at last the wide marmoreal flights to his marvellous city, for he was come again to the fair New England world that had wrought him.

So to the organ chords of morning's myriad whistles, and dawn's blaze thrown dazzling through purple panes by the great gold dome of the State House on the hill, Randolph Carter leaped shoutingly awake within his Boston room. Birds sang in hidden gardens and the perfume of trellised vines came wistful from arbours his grandfather had reared. Beauty and light glowed from classic mantel and carven cornice and walls grotesquely figured, while a sleek black cat rose yawning from hearthside sleep that his master's start and shriek had disturbed. And vast infinities away, past the Gate of Deeper Slumber and the enchanted wood and the garden lands and the Cerenarian Sea and the twilight reaches of Inquanok, the crawling chaos Nyarlathotep strode brooding into the onyx castle atop unknown Kadath in the cold waste, and taunted insolently the mild gods of earth whom he had snatched abruptly from their scented revels in the marvellous sunset city.

The Colour Out of Space

West of Arkham the hills rise wild, and there are valleys with deep woods that no axe has ever cut. There are dark narrow glens where the trees slope fantastically, and where thin brooklets trickle without ever having caught the glint of sunlight. On the gentler slopes there are farms, ancient and rocky, with squat, moss-coated cottages brooding eternally over old New England secrets in the lee of great ledges; but these are all vacant now, the wide chimneys crumbling and the shingled sides bulging perilously beneath low gambrel roofs. The old folk have gone away, and foreigners do not like to live there. French-Canadians have tried it, Italians have tried it, and the Poles have come and departed. It is not because of anything that can be seen or heard or handled, but because of something that is imagined. The place is not good for the imagination, and does not bring restful dreams at night. It must be this which keeps the foreigners away, for old Ammi Pierce has never told them of anything he recalls from the strange days. Ammi, whose head has been a little queer for years, is the only one who still remains, or who ever talks of the strange days; and he dares to do this because his house is so near the open fields and the travelled roads around Arkham.

There was once a road over the hills and through the valleys, that ran straight where the blasted heath is now; but people ceased to use it and a new road was laid curving far toward the south. Traces of the old one can still be found amidst the weeds of a returning wilderness, and some of them will doubtless linger even when half the hollows are flooded for the new reservoir. Then the dark woods will be cut down and the blasted heath will slumber far below blue waters whose surface will mirror the sky and ripple in the sun. And the secrets of the strange days will be one with the deep's secrets; one with the hidden lore of old ocean, and all the mystery of primal earth.

When I went into the hills and vales to survey for the new reservoir they told me the place was evil. They told me this in Arkham, and because that is a very old town full of witch legends I thought the evil must be something which grandams had whispered to children through centuries. The name 'blasted heath' seemed to me very odd and theatrical, and I wondered how it had come into the folklore of a Puritan people. Then I saw that dark westward tangle of glens and slopes for myself, and ceased to wonder at anything besides its own elder mystery. It was morning when I saw it, but shadow lurked always there. The trees grew too thickly, and their trunks were too big for any healthy New England wood. There was too much silence in the dim alleys between them, and the floor was too soft with the dank moss and mattings of infinite years of decay.

In the open spaces, mostly along the line of the old road, there were little hillside farms, sometimes with all the buildings standing, some-times with only one or two, and sometimes with only a lone chimney or fast-filling cellar. Weeds and briers reigned, and furtive wild things rustled in the undergrowth. Upon everything was a haze of restless-ness and oppression; a touch of the unreal and the grotesque, as if some vital element of perspective or chiaroscuro were awry. I did not wonder that the foreigners would not stay, for this was no region to sleep in. It was too much like a landscape of Salvator Rosa; too much like some forbidden woodcut in a tale of terror.

But even all this was not so bad as the blasted heath. I knew it the moment I came upon it at the bottom of a spacious valley; for no other name could fit such a thing, or any other thing fit such a name. It was as if the poet had coined the phrase from having seen this one particular region. It must, I thought as I viewed it, be the outcome of a fire; but why had nothing new ever grown over those five acres of grey desolation that sprawled open to the sky like a great spot eaten by acid in the woods and fields? It lay largely to the north of the ancient road line, but encroached a little on the other side. I felt an odd reluctance about approaching, and did so at last only because my business took me through and past it. There was no vegetation of any kind on that broad expanse, but only a fine grey dust or ash which no wind seemed ever to blow about. The trees near it were sickly and stunted, and many dead trunks stood or lay rotting at the rim. As I walked hurriedly by I saw the tumbled bricks and stones of an old chimney and cellar on my right, and the yawning black maw of an abandoned well whose stagnant vapours played strange tricks with the hues of the sunlight. Even the long, dark woodland climb beyond seemed welcome in contrast, and I marvelled no more at the frightened whispers of Arkham people. There had been no house or ruin near; even in the old days the place must have been lonely and remote. And at twilight, dreading to repass that ominous spot, I walked circuitously back to the town by the curving road on the south. I vaguely wished some clouds would gather, for an odd timidity about the deep skyey voids above had crept into my soul.

In the evening I asked old people in Arkham about the blasted heath, and what was meant by that phrase 'strange days' which so many evasively muttered. I could not, however, get any good answers, except that all the mystery was much more recent than I had dreamed. It was not a matter of old legendry at all, but something within the lifetime of those who spoke. It had happened in the 'eighties, and a family had disappeared or was killed. Speakers would not be exact; and because they all told me to pay no attention to old Ammi Pierce's crazy tales, I sought him out the next morning, having heard that he lived alone in the ancient tottering cottage where the trees first begin to get very thick. It was a fearsomely archaic place, and had begun to exude the faint miasmal odour which clings about houses that have stood too long. Only with persistent knocking could I rouse the aged man, and when he shuffled timidly to the door I could tell he was not glad to see me. He was not so feeble as I had expected; but his eyes drooped in a curious way, and his unkempt clothing and white beard made him seem very worn and dismal. Not knowing just how he could best be launched on his tales, I feigned a matter of business; told him of my surveying, and asked vague questions about the district. He was far brighter and more educated than I had been led to think, and before I knew it had grasped quite as much of the subject as any man I had talked with in Arkham. He was not like other rustics I had known in the sections where reservoirs were to be. From him there were no protests at the miles of old wood and farmland to be blotted out, though perhaps there would have been had not his home lain outside the bounds of the future lake. Relief was all that he shewed; relief at the doom of the dark ancient valleys through which he had roamed all his life. They were better under water now – better under water since the strange days. And with this opening his husky voice sank low, while his body leaned forward and his right forefinger began to point shakily and impressively.

It was then that I heard the story, and as the rambling voice scraped and whispered on I shivered again and again despite the summer day. Often I had to recall the speaker from ramblings, piece out scientific points which he knew only by a fading parrot memory of professors' talk, or bridge over gaps where his sense of logic and continuity broke down. When he was done I did not wonder that his mind had snapped a trifle, or that the folk of Arkham would not speak much of the blasted heath. I hurried back before sunset to my hotel, unwilling to have the stars come out above me in the open; and the next day returned to Boston to give up my position. I could not go into that dim chaos of old forest and slope again, or face another time that grey blasted heath where the black well yawned deep beside the tumbled bricks and stones. The reservoir will soon be built now, and all those elder secrets will be safe forever under watery fathoms. But even then I do not believe I would like to visit that country by night – at least, not when the sinister stars are out; and nothing could bribe me to drink the new city water of Arkham.

It all began, old Ammi said, with the meteorite. Before that time there had been no wild legends at all since the witch trials, and even then these western woods were not feared half so much as the small island in the Miskatonic where the devil held court beside a curious stone altar older than the Indians. These were not haunted woods, and their fantastic dusk was never terrible till the strange days. Then there had come that white noontide cloud, that string of explosions in the air, and that pillar of smoke from the valley far in the wood. And by night all Arkham had heard of the great rock that fell out of the sky and bedded itself in the ground beside the well at the Nahum Gardner place. That was the house which had stood where the blasted heath was to come – the trim white Nahum Gardner house amidst its fertile gardens and orchards.

Nahum had come to town to tell people about the stone, and had dropped in at Ammi Pierce's on the way. Ammi was forty then, and all the queer things were fixed very strongly in his mind. He and his wife had gone with the three professors from Miskatonic University who hastened out the next morning to see the weird visitor from unknown stellar space, and had wondered why Nahum had called it so large the day before. It had shrunk, Nahum said as he pointed out the big brownish mound above the ripped earth and charred grass near the archaic well-sweep in his front yard; but the wise men answered that stones do not shrink. Its heat lingered persistently, and Nahum declared it had glowed faintly in the night. The professors tried it with a geologist's hammer and found it was oddly soft. It was, in truth, so soft as to be almost plastic; and they gouged rather than chipped a specimen to take back to the college for testing. They took it in an old pail borrowed from Nahum's kitchen, for even the small piece refused to grow cool. On the trip back they stopped at Ammi's to rest, and seemed thoughtful when Mrs Pierce remarked that the fragment was growing smaller and burning the bottom of the pail. Truly, it was not large, but perhaps they had taken less than they thought.

The day after that – all this was in June of '82 – the professors had trooped out again in a great excitement. As they passed Ammi's they told him what queer things the specimen had done, and how it had faded wholly away when they put it in a glass beaker. The beaker had gone, too, and the wise men talked of the strange stone's affinity for silicon. It had acted quite unbelievably in that well-ordered laboratory; doing nothing at all and shewing no occluded gases when heated on charcoal, being wholly negative in the borax bead, and soon proving itself absolutely non-volatile at any producible temperature, including that of the oxy-hydrogen blowpipe. On an anvil it appeared highly malleable, and in the dark its luminosity was very marked. Stubbornly refusing to grow cool, it soon had the college in a state of real excitement; and when upon heating before the spectroscope it displayed shining bands unlike any known colours of the normal spectrum there was much breathless talk of new elements, bizarre optical properties, and other things which puzzled men of science are wont to say when faced by the unknown.

Hot as it was, they tested it in a crucible with all the proper reagents. Water did nothing. Hydrochloric acid was the same. Nitric acid and even aqua regia merely hissed and spattered against its torrid invulnerability. Ammi had difficulty in recalling all these things, but recognised some solvents as I mentioned them in the usual order of use. There were ammonia and caustic soda, alcohol and ether, nauseous carbon disulphide and a dozen others; but although the weight grew steadily less as time passed, and the fragment seemed to be slightly cooling, there was no change in the solvents to shew that they had attacked the substance at all. It was a metal, though, beyond a doubt. It was magnetic, for one thing; and after its immersion in the acid solvents there seemed to be faint traces of the Widmannstätten figures found on meteoric iron. When the cooling had grown very considerable, the testing was carried on in glass; and it was in a glass beaker that they left all the chips made of the original fragment during the work. The next morning both chips and beaker were gone without trace, and only a charred spot marked the place on the wooden shelf where they had been.

All this the professors told Ammi as they paused at his door, and once more he went with them to see the stony messenger from the stars, though this time his wife did not accompany him. It had now most certainly shrunk, and even the sober professors could not doubt the truth of what they saw. All around the dwindling brown lump near the well was a vacant space, except where the earth had caved in; and whereas it had been a good seven feet across the day before, it was now scarcely five. It was still hot, and the sages studied its surface curiously as they detached another and larger piece with hammer and chisel. They gouged deeply this time, and as they pried away the smaller mass they saw that the core of the thing was not quite homogeneous.

They had uncovered what seemed to be the side of a large coloured globule imbedded in the substance. The colour, which resembled some of the bands in the meteor's strange spectrum, was almost impossible to describe; and it was only by analogy that they called it colour at all. Its texture was glossy, and upon tapping it appeared to promise both brittleness and hollowness. One of the professors gave it a smart blow with a hammer, and it burst with a nervous little pop. Nothing was emitted, and all trace of the thing vanished with the puncturing. It left behind a hollow spherical space about three inches across, and all thought it probable that others would be discovered as the enclosing substance wasted away.

Conjecture was vain; so after a futile attempt to find additional globules by drilling, the seekers left again with their new specimen – which proved, however, as baffling in the laboratory as its predecessor had been. Aside from being almost plastic, having heat, magnetism, and slight luminosity, cooling slightly in powerful acids, possessing an unknown spectrum, wasting away in air, and attacking silicon compounds with mutual destruction as a result, it presented no identifying features whatsoever; and at the end of the tests the college scientists were forced to own that they could not place it. It was nothing of this earth, but a piece of the great outside; and as such dowered with outside properties and obedient to outside laws.

That night there was a thunderstorm, and when the professors went out to Nahum's the next day they met with a bitter disappointment. The stone, magnetic as it had been, must have had some peculiar electrical property; for it had 'drawn the lightning', as Nahum said, with a singular persistence. Six times within an hour the farmer saw the lightning strike the furrow in the front yard, and when the storm was over nothing remained but a ragged pit by the ancient well-sweep, half-choked with caved-in earth. Digging had borne no fruit, and the scientists verified the fact of the utter vanishment. The failure was total; so that nothing was left to do but go back to the laboratory and test again the disappearing fragment left carefully cased in lead. That fragment lasted a week, at the end of which nothing of value had been learned of it. When it had gone, no residue was left behind, and in time the professors felt scarcely sure they had indeed seen with waking eyes that cryptic vestige of the fathomless gulfs outside; that lone, weird message from other universes and other realms of matter, force, and entity.

As was natural, the Arkham papers made much of the incident with its collegiate sponsoring, and sent reporters to talk with Nahum Gardner and his family. At least one Boston daily also sent a scribe, and Nahum quickly became a kind of local celebrity. He was a lean, genial person of about fifty, living with his wife and three sons on the pleasant farmstead in the valley. He and Ammi exchanged visits frequently, as did their wives; and Ammi had nothing but praise for him after all these years. He seemed slightly proud of the notice his place had attracted, and talked often of the meteorite in the succeeding weeks. That July and August were hot, and Nahum worked hard at his haying in the ten-acre pasture across Chapman's Brook; his rattling wain wearing deep ruts in the shadowy lanes between. The labour tired him more than it had in other years, and he felt that age was beginning to tell on him.

Then fell the time of fruit and harvest. The pears and apples slowly ripened, and Nahum vowed that his orchards were prospering as never before. The fruit was growing to phenomenal size and unwonted gloss, and in such abundance that extra barrels were ordered to handle the future crop. But with the ripening came sore disappointment; for of all that gorgeous array of specious lusciousness not one single jot was fit to eat. Into the fine flavour of the pears and apples had crept a stealthy bitterness and sickishness, so that even the smallest of bites induced a lasting disgust. It was the same with the melons and tomatoes, and Nahum sadly saw that his entire crop was lost. Quick to connect events, he declared that the meteorite had poisoned the soil, and thanked heaven that most of the other crops were in the upland lot along the road.

Winter came early, and was very cold. Ammi saw Nahum less often than usual, and observed that he had begun to look worried. The rest of his family, too, seemed to have grown taciturn, and were far from steady in their churchgoing or their attendance at the various social events of the countryside. For this reserve or melancholy no cause could be found, though all the household confessed now and then to poorer health and a feeling of vague disquiet. Nahum himself gave the most definite statement of anyone when he said he was disturbed about certain footprints in the snow. They were the usual winter prints of red squirrels, white rabbits, and foxes, but the brooding farmer professed to see something not quite right about their nature and arrangement. He was never specific, but appeared to think that they were not as characteristic of the anatomy and habits of squirrels and rabbits and foxes as they ought to be. Ammi listened without interest to this talk until one night when he drove past Nahum's house in his sleigh on the way back from Clark's Corners. There had been a moon, and a rabbit had run across the road, and the leaps of that rabbit were longer than either Ammi or his horse liked. The latter, indeed, had almost run away when brought up by a firm rein. Thereafter Ammi gave Nahum's tales more respect, and wondered why the Gardner dogs seemed so cowed and quivering every morning. They had, it developed, nearly lost the spirit to bark.

In February the McGregor boys from Meadow Hill were out shooting woodchucks, and not far from the Gardner place bagged a very peculiar specimen. The proportions of its body seemed slightly altered in a queer way impossible to describe, while its face had taken on an expression which no one ever saw in a woodchuck before. The boys were genuinely frightened, and threw the thing away at once, so that only their grotesque tales of it ever reached the people of the countryside. But the shying of the horses near Nahum's house had now become an acknowledged thing, and all the basis for a cycle of whispered legend was fast taking form.

People vowed that the snow melted faster around Nahum's than it did anywhere else, and early in March there was an awed discussion in Potter's general store at Clark's Corners. Stephen Rice had driven past Gardner's in the morning, and had noticed the skunk-cabbages coming up through the mud by the woods across the road. Never were things of such size seen before, and they held strange colours that could not be put into any words. Their shapes were monstrous, and the horse had snorted at an odour which struck Stephen as wholly unprecedented. That afternoon several persons drove past to see the abnormal growth, and all agreed that plants of that kind ought never to sprout in a healthy world. The bad fruit of the fall before was freely mentioned, and it went from mouth to mouth that there was poison in Nahum's ground. Of course it was the meteorite; and remembering how strange the men from the college had found that stone to be, several farmers spoke about the matter to them.

One day they paid Nahum a visit; but having no love of wild tales and folklore were very conservative in what they inferred. The plants were certainly odd, but all skunk-cabbages are more or less odd in shape and odour and hue. Perhaps some mineral element from the stone had entered the soil, but it would soon be washed away. And as for the footprints and frightened horses – of course this was mere country talk which such a phenomenon as the aëro-lite would be certain to start. There was really nothing for serious men to do in cases of wild gossip, for superstitious rustics will say and believe anything. And so all through the strange days the professors stayed away in contempt. Only one of them, when given two phials of dust for analysis in a police job over a year and a half later, recalled that the queer colour of that skunk-cabbage had been very like one of the anomalous bands of light shewn by the meteor fragment in the college spectroscope, and like the brittle globule found imbedded in the stone from the abyss. The samples in this analysis case gave the same odd bands at first, though later they lost the property.

The trees budded prematurely around Nahum's, and at night they swayed ominously in the wind. Nahum's second son Thaddeus, a lad of fifteen, swore that they swayed also when there was no wind; but even the gossips would not credit this. Certainly, however, restlessness was in the air. The entire Gardner family developed the habit of stealthy listening, though not for any sound which they could consciously name. The listening was, indeed, rather a product of moments when consciousness seemed half to slip away. Unfortunately such moments increased week by week, till it became common speech that 'something was wrong with all Nahum's folks'. When the early saxifrage came out it had another strange colour; not quite like that of the skunk-cabbage, but plainly related and equally unknown to anyone who saw it. Nahum took some blossoms to Arkham and shewed them to the editor of the *Gazette*, but that dignitary did no more than write a humorous article about them, in which the dark fears of rustics were held up to polite ridicule. It was a mistake of Nahum's to tell a stolid city man about the way the great, overgrown mourning-cloak butterflies behaved in connexion with these saxifrages.

April brought a kind of madness to the country folk, and began that disuse of the road past Nahum's which led to its ultimate abandonment. It was the vegetation. All the orchard trees blossomed forth in strange colours, and through the stony soil of the yard and adjacent pasturage there sprang up a bizarre growth which only a botanist could connect with the proper flora of the region. No sane wholesome colours were anywhere to be seen except in the green grass and leafage; but everywhere those hectic and prismatic variants of some diseased, underlying primary tone without a place among the known tints of earth. The Dutchman's breeches became a thing of sinister menace, and the bloodroots grew insolent in their chromatic perversion. Ammi and the Gardners thought that most of the colours had a sort of haunting familiarity, and decided that they reminded one of the brittle globule in the meteor. Nahum ploughed and sowed the ten-acre pasture and the upland lot, but did nothing with the land around the house. He knew it would be of no use, and hoped that the summer's strange growths would draw all the poison from the soil. He was prepared for almost anything now, and had grown used to the sense of something near him waiting to be heard. The shunning of his house by neighbours told on him, of course; but it told on his wife more. The boys were better off, being at school each day; but they could not help being frightened by the gossip. Thaddeus, an especially sensitive youth, suffered the most.

In May the insects came, and Nahum's place became a nightmare of buzzing and crawling. Most of the creatures seemed not quite usual in their aspects and motions, and their nocturnal habits contradicted all former experience. The Gardners took to watching at night – watching in all directions at random for something . . . they could not tell what. It was then that they all owned that Thaddeus had been right about the trees. Mrs Gardner was the next to see it from the window as she watched the swollen boughs of a maple against a moonlit sky. The boughs surely moved, and there was no wind. It must be the sap. Strangeness had come into everything growing now. Yet it was none of Nahum's family at all who made the next discovery. Familiarity had dulled them, and what they could not see was glimpsed by a timid windmill salesman from Bolton who drove by one night in ignorance of the country legends. What he told in Arkham was given a short paragraph in the *Gazette;* and it was there that all the farmers, Nahum included, saw it first. The night had been dark and the buggy-lamps faint, but around a farm in the valley which everyone knew from the account must be Nahum's the darkness had been less thick. A dim though distinct luminosity seemed to inhere in all the vegetation, grass, leaves, and blossoms alike, while at one moment a detached piece of the phosphorescence appeared to stir furtively in the yard near the barn.

The grass had so far seemed untouched, and the cows were freely pastured in the lot near the house, but toward the end of May the milk began to be bad. Then Nahum had the cows driven to the uplands, after which the trouble ceased. Not long after this the change in grass and leaves became apparent to the eye. All the verdure was going grey, and was developing a highly singular quality of brittleness. Ammi was now the only person who ever visited the place, and his visits were becoming fewer and fewer. When school closed the Gardners were virtually cut off from the world, and sometimes let Ammi do their errands in town. They were failing curiously both physically and mentally, and no one was surprised when the news of Mrs Gardner's madness stole around.

It happened in June, about the anniversary of the meteor's fall, and the poor woman screamed about things in the air which she could not describe. In her raving there was not a single specific noun, but only verbs and pronouns. Things moved and changed and fluttered, and ears tingled to impulses which were not wholly sounds. Something was taken away – she was being drained of something – something was fastening itself on her that ought not to be – someone must make it keep off – nothing was ever still in the night – the walls and windows shifted. Nahum did not send her to the county asylum, but let her wander about the house as long as she was harmless to herself and others. Even when her expression changed he did nothing. But when the boys grew afraid of her, and Thaddeus nearly fainted at the way she made faces at him, he decided to keep her locked in the attic. By July she had ceased to speak and crawled on all fours, and before that month was over Nahum got the mad notion that she was slightly luminous in the dark, as he now clearly saw was the case with the nearby vegetation.

It was a little before this that the horses had stampeded. Something had aroused them in the night, and their neighing and kicking in their stalls had been terrible. There seemed virtually nothing to do to calm them, and when Nahum opened the stable door they all bolted out like frightened woodland deer. It took a week to track all four, and when found they were seen to be quite useless and unmanageable. Something had snapped in their brains, and each one had to be shot for its own good. Nahum borrowed a horse from Ammi for his haying, but found it would not approach the barn. It shied, balked, and whinnied, and in the end he could do nothing but drive it into the yard while the men used their own strength to get the heavy wagon near enough the hayloft for convenient pitching. And all the while the vegetation was turning grey and brittle. Even the flowers whose hues had been so strange were greying now, and the fruit was coming out grey and dwarfed and tasteless. The asters and goldenrod bloomed grey and distorted, and the roses and zinneas and hollyhocks in the front yard were such blasphemous-looking things that Nahum's oldest boy Zenas cut them down. The strangely puffed insects died about that time, even the bees that had left their hives and taken to the woods.

By September all the vegetation was fast crumbling to a greyish powder, and Nahum feared that the trees would die before the poison was out of the soil. His wife now had spells of terrific screaming, and he and the boys were in a constant state of nervous tension. They shunned people now, and when school opened the boys did not go. But it was Ammi, on one of his rare visits, who first realised that the well water was no longer good. It had an evil taste that was not exactly foetid nor exactly salty, and Ammi advised his friend to dig another well on higher ground to use till the soil was good again. Nahum, however, ignored the warning, for he had by that time become calloused to strange and unpleasant things. He and the boys continued to use the tainted supply, drinking it as listlessly and mechanically as they ate their meagre and ill-cooked meals and did their thankless and monotonous chores through the aimless days. There was something of stolid resignation about them all, as if they walked half in another world between lines of nameless guards to a certain and familiar doom.

Thaddeus went mad in September after a visit to the well. He had gone with a pail and had come back empty-handed, shrieking and waving his arms, and sometimes lapsing into an inane titter or a whisper about 'the moving colours down there'. Two in one family was pretty bad, but Nahum was very brave about it. He let the boy run about for a week until he began stumbling and hurting himself, and then he shut him in an attic room across the hall from his mother's. The way they screamed at each other from behind their locked doors was very terrible, especially to little Merwin, who fancied they talked in some terrible language that was not of earth. Merwin was getting frightfully imaginative, and his restlessness was worse after the shutting away of the brother who had been his greatest playmate.

Almost at the same time the mortality among the livestock commenced. Poultry turned greyish and died very quickly, their meat being found dry and noisome upon cutting. Hogs grew inordinately fat, then suddenly began to undergo loathsome changes which no one could explain. Their meat was of course useless, and Nahum was at his wit's end. No rural veterinary would approach his place, and the city veterinary from Arkham was openly baffled. The swine began growing grey and brittle and falling to pieces before they died, and their eyes and muzzles developed singular alterations.

It was very inexplicable, for they had never been fed from the tainted vegetation. Then something struck the cows. Certain areas or sometimes the whole body would be uncannily shrivelled or compressed, and atrocious collapses or disintegrations were common. In the last stages – and death was always the result – there would be a greying and turning brittle like that which beset the hogs. There could be no question of poison, for all the cases occurred in a locked and undisturbed barn. No bites of prowling things could have brought the virus, for what live beast of earth can pass through solid obstacles? It must be only natural disease – yet what disease could wreak such results was beyond any mind's guessing. When the harvest came there was not an animal surviving on the place, for the stock and poultry were dead and the dogs had run away. These dogs, three in number, had all vanished one night and were never heard of again. The five cats had left some time before, but their going was scarcely noticed since there now seemed to be no mice, and only Mrs Gardner had made pets of the graceful felines.

On the nineteenth of October Nahum staggered into Ammi's house with hideous news. The death had come to poor Thaddeus in his attic room, and it had come in a way which could not be told. Nahum had dug a grave in the railed family plot behind the farm, and had put therein what he found. There could have been nothing from outside, for the small barred window and locked door were intact; but it was much as it had been in the barn. Ammi and his wife consoled the stricken man as best they could, but shuddered as they did so. Stark terror seemed to cling round the Gardners and all they touched, and the very presence of one in the house was a breath from regions unnamed and unnamable. Ammi accompanied Nahum home with the greatest reluctance, and did what he might to calm the hysterical sobbing of little Merwin. Zenas needed no calming. He had come of late to do nothing but stare into space and obey what his father told him; and Ammi thought that his fate was very merciful. Now and then Merwin's screams were answered faintly from the attic, and in response to an inquiring look Nahum said that his wife was getting very feeble. When night approached, Ammi managed to get away; for not even friendship could make him stay in that spot when the faint glow of the vegetation began and the trees may or may not have swayed without wind. It was really lucky for Ammi that he was not more imaginative. Even as things were, his mind was bent ever so slightly; but had he been able to connect and reflect upon all the portents around him he must inevitably have turned a total maniac. In the twilight he hastened home, the screams of the mad woman and the nervous child ringing horribly in his ears.

Three days later Nahum lurched into Ammi's kitchen in the early morning, and in the absence of his host stammered out a desperate tale once more, while Mrs Pierce listened in a clutching fright. It was little Merwin this time. He was gone. He had gone out late at night with a lantern and pail for water, and had never come back. He'd been going to pieces for days, and hardly knew what he was about. Screamed at everything. There had been a frantic shriek from the yard then, but before the father could get to the door, the boy was gone. There was no glow from the lantern he had taken, and of the child himself no trace. At the time Nahum thought the lantern and pail were gone too; but when dawn came, and the man had plodded back from his all-night search of the woods and fields, he had found some very curious things near the well. There was a crushed and apparently somewhat melted mass of iron which had certainly been the lantern; while a bent bail and twisted iron hoops beside it, both half-fused, seemed to hint at the remnants of the pail. That was all. Nahum was past imagining, Mrs Pierce was blank, and Ammi, when he had reached home and heard the tale, could give no guess. Merwin was gone, and there would be no use in telling the people around, who shunned all Gardners now. No use, either, in telling the city people at Arkham who laughed at everything. Thad was gone, and now Merwin was gone. Something was creeping and creeping and waiting to be seen and felt and heard. Nahum would go soon, and he wanted Ammi to look after his wife and Zenas if they survived him. It must all be a judgment of some sort, though he could not fancy what for, since he had always walked uprightly in the Lord's ways so far as he knew.

For over two weeks Ammi saw nothing of Nahum; and then, worried about what might have happened, he overcame his fears and paid the Gardner place a visit. There was no smoke from the great chimney, and for a moment the visitor was apprehensive of the worst. The aspect of the whole farm was shocking – greyish withered grass and leaves on the ground, vines falling in brittle wreckage from archaic walls and gables, and great bare trees clawing up at the grey November sky with a studied malevolence which Ammi could not but feel had come from some subtle change in the tilt of the branches. But Nahum was alive, after all. He was weak, and lying on a couch in the low-ceiled kitchen, but perfectly conscious and able to give simple orders to Zenas. The room was deadly cold; and as Ammi visibly shivered, the host shouted huskily to Zenas for more wood. Wood, indeed, was sorely needed; since the cavernous fireplace was unlit and empty, with a cloud of soot blowing about in the chill wind that came down the chimney. Presently Nahum asked him if the extra wood had made him any more comfortable, and then Ammi saw what had happened. The stoutest cord had broken at last, and the hapless farmer's mind was proof against more sorrow.

Questioning tactfully, Ammi could get no clear data at all about the missing Zenas. 'In the well – he lives in the well – ' was all that the clouded father would say. Then there flashed across the visitor's mind a sudden thought of the mad wife, and he changed his line of inquiry. 'Nabby? Why, here she is!' was the surprised response of poor Nahum, and Ammi soon saw that he must search for himself. Leaving the harmless babbler on the couch, he took the keys from their nail beside the door and climbed the creaking stairs to the attic. It was very close and noisome up there, and no sound could be heard from any direction. Of the four doors in sight, only one was locked, and on this he tried various keys on the ring he had taken. The third key proved the right one, and after some fumbling Ammi threw open the low white door.

It was quite dark inside, for the window was small and half-obscured by the crude wooden bars; and Ammi could see nothing at all on the wide-planked floor. The stench was beyond enduring, and before proceeding further he had to retreat to another room and return with his lungs filled with breathable air. When he did enter he saw something dark in the corner, and upon seeing it more clearly he screamed outright. While he screamed he thought a momentary cloud eclipsed the window, and a second later he felt himself brushed as if by some hateful current of vapour. Strange colours danced before his eyes; and had not a present horror numbed him he would have thought of the globule in the meteor that the geologist's hammer had shattered, and of the morbid vegetation that had sprouted in the spring. As it was he thought only of the blasphemous monstrosity which confronted him, and which all too clearly had shared the nameless fate of young Thaddeus and the livestock. But the terrible thing about this horror was that it very slowly and perceptibly moved as it continued to crumble.

Ammi would give me no added particulars to this scene, but the shape in the corner does not reappear in his tale as a moving object. There are things which cannot be mentioned, and what is done in common humanity is sometimes cruelly judged by the law. I gathered that no moving thing was left in that attic room, and that to leave anything capable of motion there would have been a deed so monstrous as to damn any accountable being to eternal torment. Anyone but a stolid farmer would have fainted or gone mad, but Ammi walked conscious through that low doorway and locked the accursed secret behind him. There would be Nahum to deal with now; he must be fed and tended, and removed to some place where he could be cared for.

Commencing his descent of the dark stairs, Ammi heard a thud below him. He even thought a scream had been suddenly choked off, and recalled nervously the clammy vapour which had brushed by him in that frightful room above. What presence had his cry and entry started up? Halted by some vague fear, he heard still further sounds below. Indubitably there was a sort of heavy dragging, and a most detestably sticky noise as of some fiendish and unclean species of suction. With an associative sense goaded to feverish heights, he thought unaccountably of what he had seen upstairs. Good God! What eldritch dream-world was this into which he had blundered? He dared move neither backward nor forward, but stood there trembling at the black curve of the boxed-in staircase. Every trifle of the scene burned itself into his brain. The sounds, the sense of dread expectancy, the darkness, the steepness of the narrow steps – and merciful heaven! . . . the faint but unmistakable luminosity of all the woodwork in sight; steps, sides, exposed laths, and beams alike!

Then there burst forth a frantic whinny from Ammi's horse outside, followed at once by a clatter which told of a frenzied runaway. In another moment horse and buggy had gone beyond earshot, leaving the frightened man on the dark stairs to guess what had sent them. But that was not all. There had been another sound out there. A sort of liquid splash – water – it must have been the well. He had left Hero untied near it, and a buggy-wheel must have brushed the coping and knocked in a stone. And still the pale phosphorescence glowed in that detestably ancient woodwork. God! how old the house was! Most of it built before 1670, and the gambrel roof not later than 1730.

A feeble scratching on the floor downstairs now sounded distinctly, and Ammi's grip tightened on a heavy stick he had picked up in the attic for some purpose. Slowly nerving himself, he finished his descent and walked boldly toward the kitchen. But he did not complete the walk, because what he sought was no longer there. It had come to meet him, and it was still alive after a fashion. Whether it had crawled or whether it had been dragged by any external force, Ammi could not say; but the death had been at it. Everything had happened in the last half-hour, but collapse, greying, and disintegration were already far advanced. There was a horrible brittleness, and dry fragments were scaling off. Ammi could not touch it, but looked horrifiedly into the distorted parody that had been a face. 'What was it, Nahum – what was it?' he whispered, and the cleft, bulging lips were just able to crackle out a final answer.

'Nothin' . . . nothin' . . . the colour . . . it burns . . . cold an' wet . . . but it burns . . . it lived in the well . . . I seen it . . . a kind o' smoke . . . jest like the flowers last spring . . . the well shone at night . . . Thad an' Mernie an' Zenas . . . everything alive . . . suckin' the life out of everything . . . in that stone . . . it must a' come in that stone . . . pizened the whole place . . . dun't know what it wants . . . that round thing them men from the college dug outen the stone . . . they smashed it . . . it was that same colour . . . jest the same, like the flowers an' plants . . . must a' ben more of 'em . . . seeds . . . seeds . . . they growed . . . I seen it the fust time this week . . . must a' got strong on Zenas . . . he was a big boy, full o' life . . . it beats down your mind an' then gits ye . . . burns ye up . . . in the well water . . . you was right about that . . . evil water . . . Zenas never come back from the well . . . can't git away . . . draws ye . . . ye know summ'at's comin', but 'tain't no use . . . I seen it time an' agin senct Zenas was took . . . whar's Nabby, Ammi? . . . my head's no good . . . dun't know how long senct I fed her . . . it'll git her ef we ain't keerful . . . jest a colour . . . her face is gettin' to hev that colour sometimes towards night . . . an' it burns an' sucks . . . it come from some place whar things ain't as they is here . . . one o' them professors said so . . . he was right . . . look out, Ammi, it'll do suthin' more . . . sucks the life out . . . '

But that was all. That which spoke could speak no more because it had completely caved in. Ammi laid a red checked tablecloth over what was left and reeled out the back door into the fields. He climbed the slope to the ten-acre pasture and stumbled home by the north road and the woods. He could not pass that well from which his horse had run away. He had looked at it through the window, and had seen that no stone was missing from the rim. Then the lurching buggy had not dislodged anything after all – the splash had been something else – something which went into the well after it had done with poor Nahum . . .

When Ammi reached his house the horse and buggy had arrived before him and thrown his wife into fits of anxiety. Reassuring her without explanations, he set out at once for Arkham and notified the authorities that the Gardner family was no more. He indulged in no details, but merely told of the deaths of Nahum and Nabby, that of Thaddeus being already known, and mentioned that the cause seemed to be the same strange ailment which had killed the livestock. He also stated that Merwin and Zenas had disappeared. There was considerable questioning at the police station, and in the end Ammi was compelled to take three officers to the Gardner farm, together with the coroner, the medical examiner, and the veterinary who had treated the diseased animals. He went much against his will, for the afternoon was advancing and he feared the fall of night over that accursed place, but it was some comfort to have so many people with him.

The six men drove out in a democrat-wagon, following Ammi's buggy, and arrived at the pest-ridden farmhouse about four o'clock. Used as the officers were to gruesome experiences, not one remained unmoved at what was found in the attic and under the red checked tablecloth on the floor below. The whole aspect of the farm with its grey desolation was terrible enough, but those two crumbling objects were beyond all bounds. No one could look long at them, and even the medical examiner admitted that there was very little to examine. Specimens could be analysed, of course, so he busied himself in obtaining them – and here it develops that a very puzzling aftermath occurred at the college laboratory where the two phials of dust were finally taken. Under the spectroscope both samples gave off an unknown spectrum, in which many of the baffling bands were precisely like those which the strange meteor had yielded in the previous year. The property of emitting this spectrum vanished in a month, the dust thereafter consisting mainly of alkaline phosphates and carbonates.

Ammi would not have told the men about the well if he had thought they meant to do anything then and there. It was getting toward sunset, and he was anxious to be away. But he could not help glancing nervously at the stony curb by the great sweep, and when a detective questioned him he admitted that Nahum had feared something down there – so much so that he had never even thought of searching it for Merwin or Zenas. After that nothing would do but that they empty and explore the well immediately, so Ammi had to wait trembling while pail after pail of rank water was hauled up and splashed on the soaking ground outside. The men sniffed in disgust at the fluid, and toward the last held their noses against the foetor they were uncovering. It was not so long a job as they had feared it would be, since the water was phenomenally low. There is no need to speak too exactly of what they found. Merwin and Zenas were both there, in part, though the vestiges were mainly skeletal. There were also a small deer and a large dog in about the same state, and a number of bones of smaller animals. The ooze and slime at the bottom seemed inexplicably porous and bubbling, and a man who descended on hand-holds with a long pole found that he could sink the wooden shaft to any depth in the mud of the floor without meeting any solid obstruction.

Twilight had now fallen, and lanterns were brought from the house. Then, when it was seen that nothing further could be gained from the well, everyone went indoors and conferred in the ancient sitting-room while the intermittent light of a spectral half-moon played wanly on the grey desolation outside. The men were frankly nonplussed by the entire case, and could find no convincing common element to link the strange vegetable conditions, the unknown disease of livestock and humans, and the unaccountable deaths of Merwin and Zenas in the tainted well. They had heard the common country talk, it is true; but could not believe that anything contrary to natural law had occurred. No doubt the meteor had poisoned the soil, but the illness of persons and animals who had eaten nothing grown in that soil was another matter. Was it the well water? Very possibly. It might be a good idea to analyse it. But what peculiar madness could have made both boys jump into the well? Their deeds were so similar – and the fragments shewed that they had both suffered from the grey brittle death. Why was everything so grey and brittle?

It was the coroner, seated near a window overlooking the yard, who first noticed the glow about the well. Night had fully set in, and all the abhorrent grounds seemed faintly luminous with more than the fitful moonbeams; but this new glow was something definite and distinct, and appeared to shoot up from the black pit like a softened ray from a searchlight, giving dull reflections in the little ground pools where the water had been emptied. It had a very queer colour, and as all the men clustered round the window Ammi gave a violent start. For this strange beam of ghastly miasma was to him of no unfamiliar hue. He had seen that colour before, and feared to think what it might mean. He had seen it in the nasty brittle globule in that aërolite two summers ago, had seen it in the crazy vegetation of the springtime, and had thought he had seen it for an instant that very morning against the small barred window of that terrible attic room where nameless things had happened. It had flashed there a second, and a clammy and hateful current of vapour had brushed past him – and then poor Nahum had been taken by something of that colour. He had said so at the last – said it was the globule and the plants. After that had come the runaway in the yard and the splash in the well – and now that well was belching forth to the night a pale insidious beam of the same daemoniac tint.

It does credit to the alertness of Ammi's mind that he puzzled even at that tense moment over a point which was essentially scientific. He could not but wonder at his gleaning of the same impression from a vapour glimpsed in the daytime, against a window opening on the morning sky, and from a nocturnal exhalation seen as a phosphorescent mist against the black and blasted landscape. It wasn't right – it was against Nature – and he thought of those terrible last words of his stricken friend, 'It come from some place whar things ain't as they is here . . . one o' them professors said so . . .'

All three horses outside, tied to a pair of shrivelled saplings by the road, were now neighing and pawing frantically. The wagon driver started for the door to do something, but Ammi laid a shaky hand on his shoulder. 'Dun't go out thar,' he whispered. 'They's more to this nor what we know. Nahum said somethin' lived in the well that sucks your life out. He said it must be some'at growed from a round ball like one we all seen in the meteor stone that fell a year ago June. Sucks an' burns, he said, an' is jest a cloud of colour like that light out thar now, that ye can hardly see an' can't tell what it is. Nahum thought it feeds on everything livin' an' gits stronger all the time. He said he seen it this last week. It must be somethin' from away off in the sky like the men from the college last year says the meteor stone was. The way it's made an' the way it works ain't like no way o' God's world. It's some'at from beyond.'

So the men paused indecisively as the light from the well grew stronger and the hitched horses pawed and whinnied in increasing frenzy. It was truly an awful moment, with terror in that ancient and accursed house itself, four monstrous sets of fragments – two from the house and two from the well – in the woodshed behind, and that shaft of unknown and unholy iridescence from the slimy depths in front. Ammi had restrained the driver on impulse, forgetting how uninjured he himself was after the clammy brushing of that coloured vapour in the attic room, but perhaps it is just as well that he acted as he did. No one will ever know what was abroad that night; and though the blasphemy from beyond had not so far hurt any human of unweakened mind, there is no telling what it might not have done at that last moment, and with its seemingly increased strength and the special signs of purpose it was soon to display beneath the half-clouded moonlit sky.

All at once one of the detectives at the window gave a short, sharp gasp. The others looked at him, and then quickly followed his own gaze upward to the point at which its idle straying had been suddenly arrested. There was no need for words. What had been disputed in country gossip was disputable no longer, and it is because of the thing which every man of that party agreed in whispering later on that the strange days are never talked about in Arkham. It is necessary to premise that there was no wind at that hour of the evening. One did arise not long afterward, but there was absolutely none then. Even the dry tips of the lingering hedge-mustard, grey and blighted, and the fringe on the roof of the standing democrat-wagon were unstirred.

And yet amid that tense, godless calm the high bare boughs of all the trees in the yard were moving. They were twitching morbidly and spasmodically, clawing in convulsive and epileptic madness at the moonlit clouds; scratching impotently in the noxious air as if jerked by some alien and bodiless line of linkage with subterrene horrors writhing and struggling below the black roots.

Not a man breathed for several seconds. Then a cloud of darker depth passed over the moon, and the silhouette of clutching branches faded out momentarily. At this there was a general cry; muffled with awe, but husky and almost identical from every throat. For the terror had not faded with the silhouette, and in a fearsome instant of deeper darkness the watchers saw wriggling at that treetop height a thousand tiny points of faint and unhallowed radiance, tipping each bough like the fire of St Elmo or the flames that came down on the apostles' heads at Pentecost. It was a monstrous constellation of unnatural light, like a glutted swarm of corpse-fed fireflies dancing hellish sarabands over an accursed marsh; and its colour was that same nameless intrusion which Ammi had come to recognise and dread. All the while the shaft of phosphorescence from the well was getting brighter and brighter, bringing to the minds of the huddled men a sense of doom and abnormality which far outraced any image their conscious minds could form. It was no longer *shining* out, it was *pouring* out; and as the shapeless stream of unplaceable colour left the well it seemed to flow directly into the sky.

The veterinary shivered, and walked to the front door to drop the heavy extra bar across it. Ammi shook no less, and had to tug and point for lack of a controllable voice when he wished to draw notice to the growing luminosity of the trees. The neighing and stamping of the horses had become utterly frightful, but not a soul of that group in the old house would have ventured forth for any earthly reward. With the moments the shining of the trees increased, while their restless branches seemed to strain more and more toward verticality. The wood of the well-sweep was shining now, and presently a policeman dumbly pointed to some wooden sheds and bee-hives near the stone wall on the west. They were commencing to shine, too, though the tethered vehicles of the visitors seemed so far unaffected. Then there was a wild commotion and clopping in the road, and as Ammi quenched the lamp for better seeing they realised that the span of frantic greys had broke their sapling and run off with the democrat-wagon.

The shock served to loosen several tongues, and embarrassed whispers were exchanged. 'It spreads on everything organic that's been around here,' muttered the medical examiner. No one replied, but the man who had been in the well gave a hint that his long pole must have stirred up something intangible. 'It was awful,' he added. 'There was no bottom at all. Just ooze and bubbles and the feeling of something lurking under there.' Ammi's horse still pawed and screamed deafeningly in the road outside, and nearly drowned its owner's faint quaver as he mumbled his formless reflections. 'It come from that stone . . . it growed down thar . . . it got everything livin' . . . it fed itself on 'em, mind and body . . . Thad an' Mernie, Zenas an' Nabby . . . Nahum was the last . . . they all drunk the water . . . it got strong on 'em . . . it come from beyond, whar things ain't like they be here . . . now it's goin' home . . . '

At this point, as the column of unknown colour flared suddenly stronger and began to weave itself into fantastic suggestions of shape which each spectator later described differently, there came from poor tethered Hero such a sound as no man before or since ever heard from a horse. Every person in that low-pitched sitting room stopped his ears, and Ammi turned away from the window in horror and nausea. Words could not convey it – when Ammi looked out again the hapless beast lay huddled inert on the moonlit ground between the splintered shafts of the buggy. That was the last of Hero till they buried him next day. But the present was no time to mourn, for almost at this instant a detective silently called attention to something terrible in the very room with them. In the absence of the lamplight it was clear that a faint phosphorescence had begun to pervade the entire apartment. It glowed on the broad-planked floor and the fragment of rag carpet, and shimmered over the sashes of the small-paned windows. It ran up and down the exposed corner-posts, coruscated about the shelf and mantel, and infected the very doors and furniture. Each minute saw it strengthen, and at last it was very plain that healthy living things must leave that house.

Ammi shewed them the back door and the path up through the fields to the ten-acre pasture. They walked and stumbled as in a dream, and did not dare look back till they were far away on the high ground. They were glad of the path, for they could not have gone the front way, by that well. It was bad enough passing the glowing barn and sheds, and those shining orchard trees with their gnarled, fiendish contours; but thank heaven the branches did their worst twisting high up. The moon went under some very black clouds as they crossed the rustic bridge over Chapman's Brook, and it was blind groping from there to the open meadows.

When they looked back toward the valley and the distant Gardner place at the bottom they saw a fearsome sight. All the farm was shining with the hideous unknown blend of colour; trees, buildings, and even such grass and herbage as had not been wholly changed to lethal grey brittleness. The boughs were all straining skyward, tipped with tongues of foul flame, and lambent tricklings of the same monstrous fire were creeping about the ridgepoles of the house, barn, and sheds. It was a scene from a vision of Fuseli, and over all the rest reigned that riot of luminous amorphousness, that alien and undimensioned rainbow of cryptic poison from the well – seething, feeling, lapping, reaching, scintillating, straining, and malignly bubbling in its cosmic and unrecognisable chromaticism.

Then without warning the hideous thing shot vertically up toward the sky like a rocket or meteor, leaving behind no trail and disappearing through a round and curiously regular hole in the clouds before any man could gasp or cry out. No watcher can ever forget that sight, and Ammi stared blankly at the stars of Cygnus, Deneb twinkling above the others, where the unknown colour had melted into the Milky Way. But his gaze was the next moment called swiftly to earth by the crackling in the valley. It was just that. Only a wooden ripping and crackling, and not an explosion, as so many others of the party vowed. Yet the outcome was the same, for in one feverish, kaleidoscopic instant there burst up from that doomed and accursed farm a gleamingly eruptive cataclysm of unnatural sparks and substance, blurring the glance of the few who saw it, and sending forth to the zenith a bombarding cloudburst of such coloured and fantastic fragments as our universe must needs disown. Through quickly reclosing vapours they followed the great morbidity that had vanished, and in another second they had vanished too. Behind and below was only a darkness to which the men dared not return, and all about was a mounting wind which seemed to sweep down in black, frore gusts from interstellar space. It shrieked and howled, and lashed the fields and distorted woods in a mad cosmic frenzy, till soon the trembling party realised it would be no use waiting for the moon to shew what was left down there at Nahum's.

Too awed even to hint theories, the seven shaking men trudged back toward Arkham by the north road. Ammi was worse than his fellows, and begged them to see him inside his own kitchen, instead of keeping straight on to town. He did not wish to cross the nighted, wind-whipped woods alone to his home on the main road. For he had had an added shock that the others were spared, and was crushed forever with a brooding fear he dared not even mention for many years to come. As the rest of the watchers on that tempestuous hill had stolidly set their faces toward the road, Ammi had looked back an instant at the shadowed valley of desolation so lately sheltering his ill-starred friend. And from that stricken, far-away spot he had seen something feebly rise, only to sink down again upon the place from which the great shapeless horror had shot into the sky. It was just a colour – but not any colour of our earth or heavens. And because Ammi recognised that colour, and knew that this last faint remnant must still lurk down there in the well, he has never been quite right since.

Ammi would never go near the place again. It is over half a century now since the horror happened, but he has never been there, and will be glad when the new reservoir blots it out. I shall be glad, too, for I do not like the way the sunlight changed colour around the mouth of that abandoned well I passed. I hope the water will always be very deep – but even so, I shall never drink it. I do not think I shall visit the Arkham country hereafter. Three of the men who had been with Ammi returned the next morning to see the ruins by daylight, but there were not any real ruins. Only the bricks of the chimney, the stones of the cellar, some mineral and metallic litter here and there, and the rim of that nefandous well. Save for Ammi's dead horse, which they towed away and buried, and the buggy which they shortly returned to him, everything that had ever been living had gone. Five eldritch acres of dusty grey desert remained, nor has anything ever grown there since. To this day it sprawls open to the sky like a great spot eaten by acid in the woods and fields, and the few who have ever dared glimpse it in spite of the rural tales have named it 'the blasted heath'.

The rural tales are queer. They might be even queerer if city men and college chemists could be interested enough to analyse the water from that disused well, or the grey dust that no wind seems ever to disperse. Botanists, too, ought to study the stunted flora on the borders of that spot, for they might shed light on the country notion that the blight is spreading – little by little, perhaps an inch a year. People say the colour of the neighbouring herbage is not quite right in the spring, and that wild things leave queer prints in the light winter snow. Snow never seems quite so heavy on the blasted heath as it is elsewhere. Horses – the few that are left in this motor age – grow skittish in the silent valley; and hunters cannot depend on their dogs too near the splotch of greyish dust.

They say the mental influences are very bad, too. Numbers went queer in the years after Nahum's taking, and always they lacked the power to get away. Then the stronger-minded folk all left the region, and only the foreigners tried to live in the crumbling old homesteads. They could not stay, though; and one sometimes wonders what insight beyond ours their wild, weird stores of whispered magic have given them. Their dreams at night, they protest, are very horrible in that grotesque country; and surely the very look of the dark realm is enough to stir a morbid fancy. No traveller has ever escaped a sense of strangeness in those deep ravines, and artists shiver as they paint thick woods whose mystery is as much of the spirit as of the eye. I myself am curious about the sensation I derived from my one lone walk before Ammi told me his tale. When twilight came I had vaguely wished some clouds would gather, for an odd timidity about the deep skyey voids above had crept into my soul.

Do not ask me for my opinion. I do not know – that is all. There was no one but Ammi to question; for Arkham people will not talk about the strange days, and all three professors who saw the aërolite and its coloured globule are dead. There were other globules – depend upon that. One must have fed itself and escaped, and probably there was another which was too late. No doubt it is still down the well – I know there was something wrong with the sunlight I saw above that miasmal brink. The rustics say the blight creeps an inch a year, so perhaps there is a kind of growth or nourishment even now. But whatever daemon hatchling is there, it must be tethered to something or else it would quickly spread. Is it fastened to the roots of those trees that claw the air? One of the current Arkham tales is about fat oaks that shine and move as they ought not to do at night.

What it is, only God knows. In terms of matter I suppose the thing Ammi described would be called a gas, but this gas obeyed laws that are not of our cosmos. This was no fruit of such worlds and suns as shine on the telescopes and photographic plates of our observatories. This was no breath from the skies whose motions and dimensions our astronomers measure or deem too vast to measure. It was just a colour out of space – a frightful messenger from unformed realms of infinity beyond all Nature as we know it; from realms whose mere existence stuns the brain and numbs us with the black extra-cosmic gulfs it throws open before our frenzied eyes.

I doubt very much if Ammi consciously lied to me, and I do not think his tale was all a freak of madness as the townfolk had fore-warned. Something terrible came to the hills and valleys on that meteor, and something terrible – though I know not in what pro-portion – still remains. I shall be glad to see the water come. Meanwhile I hope nothing will happen to Ammi. He saw so much of the thing – and its influence was so insidious. Why has he never been able to move away? How clearly he recalled those dying words of Nahum's – 'can't git away . . . draws ye . . . ye know summ'at's comin', but 'tain't no use . . . ' Ammi is such a good old man – when the reservoir gang gets to work I must write the chief engineer to keep a sharp watch on him. I would hate to think of him as the grey, twisted, brittle monstrosity which persists more and more in troubling my sleep.

The History of the Necronomicon

Original title *Al Azif* – *azif* being the word used by Arabs to designate that nocturnal sound (made by insects) suppos'd to be the howling of daemons.

Composed by Abdul Alhazred, a mad poet of Sanaá, in Yemen, who is said to have flourished during the period of the Ommiade caliphs, circa 700 A.D. He visited the ruins of Babylon and the subterranean secrets of Memphis and spent ten years alone in the great southern desert of Arabia – the Roba el Khaliyeh or 'Empty Space' of the ancients – and 'Dahna' or 'Crimson' desert of the modern Arabs, which is held to be inhabited by protective evil spirits and monsters of death. Of this desert many strange and unbelievable marvels are told by those who pretend to have penetrated it. In his last years Alhazred dwelt in Damascus, where the *Necronomicon* (*Al Azif*) was written, and of his final death or disappearance (738 A.D.) many terrible and conflicting things are told. He is said by Ebn Khallikan (12th cent. biographer) to have been seized by an invisible monster in broad daylight and devoured horribly before a large number of fright-frozen witnesses. Of his madness many things are told. He claimed to have seen fabulous Irem, or City of Pillars, and to have found beneath the ruins of a certain nameless desert town the shocking annals and secrets of a race older than mankind. He was only an indifferent Moslem, worshipping unknown entities whom he called Yog-Sothoth and Cthulhu.

In A.D. 950 the *Azif*, which had gained a considerable tho' surreptitious circulation amongst the philosophers of the age, was secretly translated into Greek by Theodorus Philetas of Constantinople under the title *Necronomicon*. For a century it impelled certain experimenters to terrible attempts, when it was suppressed and burnt by the patriarch Michael. After this it is only heard of furtively, but (1228) Olaus Wormius made a Latin translation later in the Middle Ages, and the

Latin text was printed twice – once in the fifteenth century in black-letter (evidently in Germany) and once in the seventeenth (prob. Spanish) – both editions being without identifying marks, and located as to time and place by internal typographical evidence only. The work both Latin and Greek was banned by Pope Gregory IX in 1232, shortly after its Latin translation, which called attention to it. The Arabic original was lost as early as Wormius' time, as indicated by his prefatory note; and no sight of the Greek copy – which was printed in Italy between 1500 and 1550 – has been reported since the burning of a certain Salem man's library in 1692. An English translation made by Dr Dee was never printed, and exists only in fragments recovered from the original manuscript. Of the Latin texts now existing one (15th cent.) is known to be in the British Museum under lock and key, while another (17th cent.) is in the Bibliothèque Nationale at Paris. A seventeenth-century edition is in the Widener Library at Harvard, and in the library of Miskatonic University at Arkham. Also in the library of the University of Buenos Ayres. Numerous other copies probably exist in secret, and a fifteenth-century one is persistently rumoured to form part of the collection of a celebrated American millionaire. A still vaguer rumour credits the preservation of a sixteenth-century Greek text in the Salem family of Pickman; but if it was so preserved, it vanished with the artist R. U. Pickman, who disappeared early in 1926. The book is rigidly suppressed by the authorities of most countries, and by all branches of organised ecclesiasticism. Reading leads to terrible consequences. It was from rumours of this book (of which relatively few of the general public know) that R. W. Chambers is said to have derived the idea of his early novel *The King in Yellow*.

Chronology

Al Azif written circa 730 A.D. at Damascus by Abdul Alhazred
Tr. to Greek 950 A.D. as *Necronomicon* by Theodorus Philetas
Burnt by Patriarch Michael 1050 (Greek text). Arabic text now lost
Olaus translates Gr. to Latin 1228
1232 Latin ed. (and Gr.) suppr. by Pope Gregory IX
14— Black-letter printed edition (Germany)
15— Gr. text printed in Italy
16— Spanish reprint of Latin text

Fungi from Yuggoth

1 THE BOOK

The place was dark and dusty and half-lost
In tangles of old alleys near the quays,
Reeking of strange things brought in from the seas,
And with queer curls of fog that west winds tossed.
Small lozenge panes, obscured by smoke and frost,
Just shewed the books, in piles like twisted trees,
Rotting from floor to roof – congeries
Of crumbling elder lore at little cost.

I entered, charmed, and from a cobwebbed heap
Took up the nearest tome and thumbed it through,
Trembling at curious words that seemed to keep
Some secret, monstrous if one only knew.
   Then, looking for some seller old in craft,
   I could find nothing but a voice that laughed.

2 PURSUIT

I held the book beneath my coat, at pains
To hide the thing from sight in such a place;
Hurrying through the ancient harbor lanes
With often-turning head and nervous pace.
Dull, furtive windows in old tottering brick
Peered at me oddly as I hastened by,
And thinking what they sheltered, I grew sick
For a redeeming glimpse of clean blue sky.

No one had seen me take the thing – but still
A blank laugh echoed in my whirling head,
And I could guess what nighted worlds of ill
Lurked in that volume I had coveted.
   The way grew strange – the walls alike and madding –
   And far behind me, unseen feet were padding.

3 THE KEY

I do not know what windings in the waste
Of those strange sea-lanes brought me home once more,
But on my porch I trembled, white with haste
To get inside and bolt the heavy door.
I had the book that told the hidden way
Across the void and through the space-hung screens
That hold the undimensioned worlds at bay,
And keep lost aeons to their own demesnes.

At last the key was mine to those vague visions
Of sunset spires and twilight woods that brood
Dim in the gulfs beyond this earth's precisions,
Lurking as memories of infinitude.
    The key was mine, but as I sat there mumbling,
    The attic window shook with a faint fumbling.

4 RECOGNITION

The day had come again, when as a child
I saw – just once – that hollow of old oaks,
Grey with a ground-mist that enfolds and chokes
The slinking shapes which madness has defiled.
It was the same – an herbage rank and wild
Clings round an altar whose carved sign invokes
That Nameless One to whom a thousand smokes
Rose, aeons gone, from unclean towers up-piled.

I saw the body spread on that dank stone,
And knew those things which feasted were not men;
I knew this strange, grey world was not my own,
But Yuggoth, past the starry voids – and then
    The body shrieked at me with a dead cry,
    And all too late I knew that it was I!

5 HOMECOMING

The daemon said that he would take me home
To the pale, shadowy land I half recalled
As a high place of stair and terrace, walled
With marble balustrades that sky-winds comb,
While miles below a maze of dome on dome
And tower on tower beside a sea lies sprawled.
Once more, he told me, I would stand enthralled
On those old heights, and hear the far-off foam.

All this he promised, and through sunset's gate
He swept me, past the lapping lakes of flame,
And red-gold thrones of gods without a name
Who shriek in fear at some impending fate.
   Then a black gulf with sea-sounds in the night:
   'Here was your home,' he mocked, 'when you had sight!'

6 THE LAMP

We found the lamp inside those hollow cliffs
Whose chiseled sign no priest in Thebes could read,
And from whose caverns frightened hieroglyphs
Warned every living creature of earth's breed.
No more was there – just that one brazen bowl
With traces of a curious oil within;
Fretted with some obscurely patterned scroll,
And symbols hinting vaguely of strange sin.

Little the fears of forty centuries meant
To us as we bore off our slender spoil,
And when we scanned it in our darkened tent
We struck a match to test the ancient oil.
   It blazed – great God! . . . But the vast shapes we saw
   In that mad flash have seared our lives with awe.

7 ZAMAN'S HILL

The great hill hung close over the old town,
A precipice against the main street's end;
Green, tall, and wooded, looking darkly down
Upon the steeple at the highway bend.
Two hundred years the whispers had been heard
About what happened on the man-shunned slope –
Tales of an oddly mangled deer or bird,
Or of lost boys whose kin had ceased to hope.

One day the mail-man found no village there,
Nor were its folk or houses seen again;
People came out from Aylesbury to stare –
Yet they all told the mail-man it was plain
   That he was mad for saying he had spied
   The great hill's gluttonous eyes, and jaws stretched wide.

8 THE PORT

Ten miles from Arkham I had struck the trail
That rides the cliff-edge over Boynton Beach,
And hoped that just at sunset I could reach
The crest that looks on Innsmouth in the vale.
Far out at sea was a retreating sail,
White as hard years of ancient winds could bleach,
But evil with some portent beyond speech,
So that I did not wave my hand or hail.

Sails out of lnnsmouth! echoing old renown
Of long-dead times. But now a too-swift night
Is closing in, and I have reached the height
Whence I so often scan the distant town.
    The spires and roofs are there – but look! the gloom
    Sinks on dark lanes, as lightless as the tomb!

9 THE COURTYARD

It was the city I had known before,
The ancient, leprous town where mongrel throngs
Chant to strange gods, and beat unhallowed gongs
In crypts beneath foul alleys near the shore.
The rotting, fish-eyed houses leered at me
From where they leaned, drunk and half-animate,
As edging through the filth I passed the gate
To the black courtyard where the man would be.

The dark walls closed me in, and loud I cursed
That ever I had come to such a den,
When suddenly a score of windows burst
Into wild light, and swarmed with dancing men:
    Mad, soundless revels of the dragging dead –
    And not a corpse had either hands or head!

10 THE PIGEON-FLYERS

They took me slumming, where gaunt walls of brick
Bulge outward with a viscous stored-up evil,
And twisted faces, thronging foul and thick,
Wink messages to alien god and devil.
A million fires were blazing in the streets,
And from flat roofs a furtive few would fly
Bedraggled birds into the yawning sky
While hidden drums droned on with measured beats.

I knew those fires were brewing monstrous things,
And that those birds of space had been *Outside* –
I guessed to what dark planet's crypts they plied,
And what they brought from Thog beneath their wings.
  The others laughed – till struck too mute to speak
  By what they glimpsed in one bird's evil beak.

11 THE WELL

Farmer Seth Atwood was past eighty when
He tried to sink that deep well by his door,
With only Eb to help him bore and bore.
We laughed, and hoped he'd soon be sane again.
And yet, instead, young Eb went crazy, too,
So that they shipped him to the county farm.
Seth bricked the well-mouth up as tight as glue –
Then hacked an artery in his gnarled left arm.

After the funeral we felt bound to get
Out to that well and rip the bricks away,
But all we saw were iron hand-holds set
Down a black hole deeper than we could say.
  And yet we put the bricks back – for we found
  The hole too deep for any line to sound.

12 THE HOWLER

They told me not to take the Briggs' Hill path
That used to be the highroad through to Zoar,
For Goody Watkins, hanged in seventeen-four,
Had left a certain monstrous aftermath.
Yet when I disobeyed, and had in view
The vine-hung cottage by the great rock slope,
I could not think of elms or hempen rope,
But wondered why the house still seemed so new.

Stopping a while to watch the fading day,
I heard faint howls, as from a room upstairs,
When through the ivied panes one sunset ray
Struck in, and caught the howler unawares.
  I glimpsed – and ran in frenzy from the place,
  And from a four-pawed thing with human face.

13 HESPERIA

The winter sunset, flaming beyond spires
And chimneys half-detached from this dull sphere,
Opens great gates to some forgotten year
Of elder splendours and divine desires.
Expectant wonders burn in those rich fires,
Adventure-fraught, and not untinged with fear;
A row of sphinxes where the way leads clear
Toward walls and turrets quivering to far lyres.

It is the land where beauty's meaning flowers,
Where every unplaced memory has a source,
Where the great river Time begins its course
Down the vast void in starlit streams of hours.
   Dreams bring us close – but ancient lore repeats
   That human tread has never soiled these streets.

14 STAR-WINDS

It is a certain hour of twilight glooms,
Mostly in autumn, when the star-wind pours
Down hilltop streets, deserted out-of-doors,
But shewing early lamplight from snug rooms.
The dead leaves rush in strange, fantastic twists,
And chimney-smoke whirls round with alien grace,
Heeding geometries of outer space,
While Fomalhaut peers in through southward mists.

This is the hour when moonstruck poets know
What fungi sprout in Yuggoth, and what scents
And tints of flowers fill Nithon's continents,
Such as in no poor earthly garden blow.
   Yet for each dream these winds to us convey,
   A dozen more of ours they sweep away!

15 ANTARKTOS

Deep in my dream the great bird whispered queerly
Of the black cone amid the polar waste;
Pushing above the ice-sheet lone and drearly,
By storm-crazed aeons battered and defaced.
Hither no living earth-shapes take their courses,
And only pale auroras and faint suns
Glow on that pitted rock, whose primal sources
Are guessed at dimly by the Elder Ones.

If men should glimpse it, they would merely wonder
What tricky mound of Nature's build they spied;
But the bird told of vaster parts, that under
The mile-deep ice-shroud crouch and brood and bide.
    God help the dreamer whose mad visions shew
    Those dead eyes set in crystal gulfs below!

16 THE WINDOW

The house was old, with tangled wings outthrown,
Of which no one could ever half keep track,
And in a small room somewhat near the back
Was an odd window sealed with ancient stone.
There, in a dream-plagued childhood, quite alone
I used to go, where night reigned vague and black,
Parting the cobwebs with a curious lack
Of fear, and with a wonder each time grown.

One later day I brought the masons there
To find what view my dim forbears had shunned,
But as they pierced the stone, a rush of air
Burst from the alien voids that yawned beyond.
    They fled – but I peered through and found unrolled
    All the wild worlds of which my dreams had told.

17 A MEMORY

There were great steppes, and rocky table-lands
Stretching half-limitless in starlit night,
With alien campfires shedding feeble light
On beasts with tinkling bells, in shaggy bands.
Far to the south the plain sloped low and wide
To a dark zigzag line of wall that lay
Like a huge python of some primal day
Which endless time had chilled and petrified.

I shivered oddly in the cold, thin air,
And wondered where I was and how I came,
When a cloaked form against a campfire's glare
Rose and approached, and called me by my name.
    Staring at that dead face beneath the hood,
    I ceased to hope – because I understood.

18 THE GARDENS OF YIN

Beyond that wall, whose ancient masonry
Reached almost to the sky in moss-thick towers,
There would be terraced gardens, rich with flowers,
And flutter of bird and butterfly and bee.
There would be walks, and bridges arching over
Warm lotos-pools reflecting temple eaves,
And cherry-trees with delicate boughs and leaves
Against a pink sky where the herons hover.

All would be there, for had not old dreams flung
Open the gate to that stone-lanterned maze
Where drowsy streams spin out their winding ways,
Trailed by green vines from bending branches hung?
    I hurried – but when the wall rose, grim and great,
    I found there was no longer any gate.

19 THE BELLS

Year after year I heard that faint, far ringing
Of deep-toned bells on the black midnight wind;
Peals from no steeple I could ever find,
But strange, as if across some great void winging.
I searched my dreams and memories for a clue,
And thought of all the chimes my visions carried;
Of quiet Innsmouth, where the white gulls tarried
Around an ancient spire that once I knew.

Always perplexed I heard those far notes falling,
Till one March night the bleak rain splashing cold
Beckoned me back through gateways of recalling
To elder towers where the mad clappers tolled.
    They tolled – but from the sunless tides that pour
    Through sunken valleys on the sea's dead floor.

20 NIGHT-GAUNTS

Out of what crypt they crawl, I cannot tell,
But every night I see the rubbery things,
Black, horned, and slender, with membraneous wings,
And tails that bear the bifid barb of hell.
They come in legions on the north wind's swell,
With obscene clutch that titillates and stings,
Snatching me off on monstrous voyagings
To grey worlds hidden deep in nightmare's well.

Over the jagged peaks of Thok they sweep,
Heedless of all the cries I try to make,
And down the nether pits to that foul lake
Where the puffed shoggoths splash in doubtful sleep.
   But oh! if only they would make some sound,
   Or wear a face where faces should be found!

21 NYARLATHOTEP

And at the last from inner Egypt came
The strange dark One to whom the fellahs bowed;
Silent and lean and cryptically proud,
And wrapped in fabrics red as sunset flame.
Throngs pressed around, frantic for his commands,
But leaving, could not tell what they had heard;
While through the nations spread the awestruck word
That wild beasts followed him and licked his hands.

Soon from the sea a noxious birth began;
Forgotten lands with weedy spires of gold;
The ground was cleft, and mad auroras rolled
Down on the quaking citadels of man.
   Then, crushing what he chanced to mould in play,
   The idiot Chaos blew Earth's dust away.

22 AZATHOTH

Out in the mindless void the daemon bore me,
Past the bright clusters of dimensioned space,
Till neither time nor matter stretched before me,
But only Chaos, without form or place.
Here the vast Lord of All in darkness muttered
Things he had dreamed but could not understand,
While near him shapeless bat-things flopped and fluttered
In idiot vortices that ray-streams fanned.

They danced insanely to the high, thin whining
Of a cracked flute clutched in a monstrous paw,
Whence flow the aimless waves whose chance combining
Gives each frail cosmos its eternal law.
  'I am His Messenger,' the daemon said,
   As in contempt he struck his Master's head.

23 MIRAGE

I do not know if ever it existed –
That lost world floating dimly on Time's stream –
And yet I see it often, violet-misted,
And shimmering at the back of some vague dream.
There were strange towers and curious lapping rivers,
Labyrinths of wonder, and low vaults of light,
And bough-crossed skies of flame, like that which quivers
Wistfully just before a winter's night.

Great moors led off to sedgy shores unpeopled,
Where vast birds wheeled, while on a windswept hill
There was a village, ancient and white-steepled,
With evening chimes for which I listen still.
　I do not know what land it is – or dare
　Ask when or why I was, or will be, there.

24 THE CANAL

Somewhere in dream there is an evil place
Where tall, deserted buildings crowd along
A deep, black, narrow channel, reeking strong
Of frightful things whence oily currents race.
Lanes with old walls half meeting overhead
Wind off to streets one may or may not know,
And feeble moonlight sheds a spectral glow
Over long rows of windows, dark and dead.

There are no footfalls, and the one soft sound
Is of the oily water as it glides
Under stone bridges, and along the sides
Of its deep flume, to some vague ocean bound.
　None lives to tell when that stream washed away
　Its dream-lost region from the world of clay.

25 ST TOAD'S

'Beware St Toad's cracked chimes!' I heard him scream
As I plunged into those mad lanes that wind
In labyrinths obscure and undefined
South of the river where old centuries dream.
He was a furtive figure, bent and ragged,
And in a flash had staggered out of sight,
So still I burrowed onward in the night
Toward where more roof-lines rose, malign and jagged.

No guide-book told of what was lurking here –
But now I heard another old man shriek:
'Beware St Toad's cracked chimes!' And growing weak,
I paused, when a third greybeard croaked in fear:
    'Beware St Toad's cracked chimes!' Aghast, I fled –
    Till suddenly that black spire loomed ahead.

26 THE FAMILIARS

John Whateley lived about a mile from town,
Up where the hills began to huddle thick;
We never thought his wits were very quick,
Seeing the way he let his farm run down.
He used to waste his time on some queer books
He'd found around the attic of his place,
Till funny lines got creased into his face,
And folks all said they didn't like his looks.

When he began those night-howls we declared
He'd better be locked up away from harm,
So three men from the Aylesbury town farm
Went for him – but came back alone and scared.
    They'd found him talking to two crouching things
    That at their step flew off on great black wings.

27 THE ELDER PHAROS

From Leng, where rocky peaks climb bleak and bare
Under cold stars obscure to human sight,
There shoots at dusk a single beam of light
Whose far blue rays make shepherds whine in prayer.
They say (though none has been there) that it comes
Out of a pharos in a tower of stone,
Where the last Elder One lives on alone,
Talking to Chaos with the beat of drums.

The Thing, they whisper, wears a silken mask
Of yellow, whose queer folds appear to hide
A face not of this earth, though none dares ask
Just what those features are, which bulge inside.
    Many, in man's first youth, sought out that glow,
    But what they found, no one will ever know.

28 EXPECTANCY

I cannot tell why some things hold for me
A sense of unplumbed marvels to befall,
Or of a rift in the horizon's wall
Opening to worlds where only gods can be.
There is a breathless, vague expectancy,
As of vast ancient pomps I half recall,
Or wild adventures, uncorporeal,
Ecstasy-fraught, and as a day-dream free.

It is in sunsets and strange city spires,
Old villages and woods and misty downs,
South winds, the sea, low hills, and lighted towns,
Old gardens, half-heard songs, and the moon's fires.
   But though its lure alone makes life worth living,
   None gains or guesses what it hints at giving.

29 NOSTALGIA

Once every year, in autumn's wistful glow,
The birds fly out over an ocean waste,
Calling and chattering in a joyous haste
To reach some land their inner memories know.
Great terraced gardens where bright blossoms blow,
And lines of mangoes luscious to the taste,
And temple-groves with branches interlaced
Over cool paths – all these their vague dreams shew.

They search the sea for marks of their old shore –
For the tall city, white and turreted –
But only empty waters stretch ahead,
So that at last they turn away once more.
   Yet sunken deep where alien polyps throng,
   The old towers miss their lost, remembered song.

30 BACKGROUND

I never can be tied to raw, new things,
For I first saw the light in an old town,
Where from my window huddled roofs sloped down
To a quaint harbour rich with visionings.
Streets with carved doorways where the sunset beams
Flooded old fanlights and small window-panes,
And Georgian steeples topped with gilded vanes –
These were the sights that shaped my childhood dreams.

Such treasures, left from times of cautious leaven,
Cannot but loose the hold of flimsier wraiths
That flit with shifting ways and muddled faiths
Across the changeless walls of earth and heaven.
    They cut the moment's thongs and leave me free
    To stand alone before eternity.

31 THE DWELLER

It had been old when Babylon was new;
None knows how long it slept beneath that mound,
Where in the end our questing shovels found
Its granite blocks and brought it back to view.
There were vast pavements and foundation-walls,
And crumbling slabs and statues, carved to shew
Fantastic beings of some long ago
Past anything the world of man recalls.

And then we saw those stone steps leading down
Through a choked gate of graven dolomite
To some black haven of eternal night
Where elder signs and primal secrets frown.
    We cleared a path – but raced in mad retreat
    When from below we heard those clumping feet.

32 ALIENATION

His solid flesh had never been away,
For each dawn found him in his usual place,
But every night his spirit loved to race
Through gulfs and worlds remote from common day.
He had seen Yaddith, yet retained his mind,
And come back safely from the Ghooric zone,
When one still night across curved space was thrown
That beckoning piping from the voids behind.

He waked that morning as an older man,
And nothing since has looked the same to him.
Objects around float nebulous and dim –
False, phantom trifles of some vaster plan.
    His folk and friends are now an alien throng
    To which he struggles vainly to belong.

33 HARBOUR WHISTLES

Over old roofs and past decaying spires
The harbour whistles chant all through the night;
Throats from strange ports, and beaches far and white,
And fabulous oceans, ranged in motley choirs.
Each to the other alien and unknown,
Yet all, by some obscurely focussed force
From brooding gulfs beyond the Zodiac's course,
Fused into one mysterious cosmic drone.

Through shadowy dreams they send a marching line
Of still more shadowy shapes and hints and views;
Echoes from outer voids, and subtle clues
To things which they themselves cannot define.
  And always in that chorus, faintly blent,
  We catch some notes no earth-ship ever sent.

34 RECAPTURE

The way led down a dark, half-wooded heath
Where moss-grey boulders humped above the mould,
And curious drops, disquieting and cold,
Sprayed up from unseen streams in gulfs beneath.
There was no wind, nor any trace of sound
In puzzling shrub, or alien-featured tree,
Nor any view before – till suddenly,
Straight in my path, I saw a monstrous mound.

Half to the sky those steep sides loomed upspread,
Rank-grassed, and cluttered by a crumbling flight
Of lava stairs that scaled the fear-topped height
In steps too vast for any human tread.
  I shrieked – and knew what primal star and year
  Had sucked me back from man's dream-transient sphere!

35 EVENING STAR

I saw it from that hidden, silent place
Where the old wood half shuts the meadow in.
It shone through all the sunset's glories – thin
At first, but with a slowly brightening face.
Night came, and that lone beacon, amber-hued,
Beat on my sight as never it did of old;
The evening star – but grown a thousandfold
More haunting in this hush and solitude.

It traced strange pictures on the quivering air –
Half-memories that had always filled my eyes –
Vast towers and gardens; curious seas and skies
Of some dim life – I never could tell where.
  But now I knew that through the cosmic dome
  Those rays were calling from my far, lost home.

36 CONTINUITY

There is in certain ancient things a trace
Of some dim essence – more than form or weight;
A tenuous aether, indeterminate,
Yet linked with all the laws of time and space.
A faint, veiled sign of continuities
That outward eyes can never quite descry;
Of locked dimensions harbouring years gone by,
And out of reach except for hidden keys.

It moves me most when slanting sunbeams glow
On old farm buildings set against a hill,
And paint with life the shapes which linger still
From centuries less a dream than this we know.
  In that strange light I feel I am not far
  From the fixt mass whose sides the ages are.

The Shadow Over Innsmouth

I

During the winter of 1927–28 officials of the Federal government made a strange and secret investigation of certain conditions in the ancient Massachusetts seaport of Innsmouth. The public first learned of it in February, when a vast series of raids and arrests occurred, followed by the deliberate burning and dynamiting – under suitable precautions – of an enormous number of crumbling, worm-eaten, and supposedly empty houses along the abandoned waterfront. Uninquiring souls let this occurrence pass as one of the major clashes in a spasmodic war on liquor.

Keener news-followers, however, wondered at the prodigious number of arrests, the abnormally large force of men used in making them, and the secrecy surrounding the disposal of the prisoners. No trials, or even definite charges, were reported; nor were any of the captives seen thereafter in the regular gaols of the nation. There were vague statements about disease and concentration camps, and later about dispersal in various naval and military prisons, but nothing positive ever developed. Innsmouth itself was left almost depopulated, and is even now only beginning to shew signs of a sluggishly revived existence.

Complaints from many liberal organisations were met with long confidential discussions, and representatives were taken on trips to certain camps and prisons. As a result, these societies became surprisingly passive and reticent. Newspaper men were harder to manage, but seemed largely to cooperate with the government in the end. Only one paper – a tabloid always discounted because of its wild policy – mentioned the deep-diving submarine that discharged torpedoes downward in the marine abyss just beyond Devil Reef. That item, gathered by chance in a haunt of sailors, seemed indeed rather far-fetched; since the low, black reef lies a full mile and a half out from Innsmouth Harbour.

People around the country and in the nearby towns muttered a great deal among themselves, but said very little to the outer world. They had talked about dying and half-deserted Innsmouth for nearly a century, and nothing new could be wilder or more hideous than what they had whispered and hinted years before. Many things had taught them secretiveness, and there was now no need to exert pressure on them. Besides, they really knew very little; for wide salt marshes, desolate and unpeopled, keep neighbours off from Innsmouth on the landward side.

But at last I am going to defy the ban on speech about this thing. Results, I am certain, are so thorough that no public harm save a shock of repulsion could ever accrue from a hinting of what was found by those horrified raiders at Innsmouth. Besides, what was found might possibly have more than one explanation. I do not know just how much of the whole tale has been told even to me, and I have many reasons for not wishing to probe deeper. For my contact with this affair has been closer than that of any other layman, and I have carried away impressions which are yet to drive me to drastic measures.

It was I who fled frantically out of Innsmouth in the early morning hours of July 16, 1927, and whose frightened appeals for government inquiry and action brought on the whole reported episode. I was willing enough to stay mute while the affair was fresh and uncertain; but now that it is an old story, with public interest and curiosity gone, I have an odd craving to whisper about those few frightful hours in that ill-rumoured and evilly shadowed seaport of death and blasphemous abnormality. The mere telling helps me to restore confidence in my own faculties; to reassure myself that I was not simply the first to succumb to a contagious nightmare hallucination. It helps me, too, in making up my mind regarding a certain terrible step which lies ahead of me.

I never heard of Innsmouth till the day before I saw it for the first and – so far – last time. I was celebrating my coming of age by a tour of New England – sightseeing, antiquarian, and genealogical – and had planned to go directly from ancient Newburyport to Arkham, whence my mother's family was derived. I had no car, but was travelling by train, trolley, and motor-coach, always seeking the cheapest possible route. In Newburyport they told me that the steam train was the thing to take to Arkham; and it was only at the station ticket-office, when I demurred at the high fare, that I learned about Innsmouth. The stout, shrewd-faced agent, whose speech shewed him to be no local man, seemed sympathetic toward my efforts at economy, and made a suggestion that none of my other informants had offered.

'You *could* take that old bus, I suppose,' he said with a certain hesitation, 'but it ain't thought much of hereabouts. It goes through Innsmouth – you may have heard about that – and so the people don't like it. Run by an Innsmouth fellow – Joe Sargent – but never gets any custom from here, or Arkham either, I guess. Wonder it keeps running at all. I s'pose it's cheap enough, but I never see more'n two or three people in it – nobody but those Innsmouth folks. Leaves the Square – front of Hammond's Drug Store – at 10 a.m. and 7 p.m. unless they've changed lately. Looks like a terrible rattletrap – I've never ben on it.'

That was the first I ever heard of shadowed Innsmouth. Any reference to a town not shewn on common maps or listed in recent guide-books would have interested me, and the agent's odd manner of allusion roused something like real curiosity. A town able to inspire such dislike in its neighbours, I thought, must be at least rather unusual, and worthy of a tourist's attention. If it came before Arkham I would stop off there – and so I asked the agent to tell me something about it. He was very deliberate, and spoke with an air of feeling slightly superior to what he said.

'Innsmouth? Well, it's a queer kind of a town down at the mouth of the Manuxet. Used to be almost a city – quite a port before the War of 1812 – but all gone to pieces in the last hundred years or so. No railroad now – B. & M. never went through, and the branch line from Rowley was given up years ago.

'More empty houses than there are people, I guess, and no business to speak of except fishing and lobstering. Everybody trades mostly here or in Arkham or Ipswich. Once they had quite a few mills, but nothing's left now except one gold refinery running on the leanest kind of part time.

'That refinery, though, used to be a big thing, and Old Man Marsh, who owns it, must be richer'n Croesus. Queer old duck, though, and sticks mighty close in his home. He's supposed to have developed some skin disease or deformity late in life that makes him keep out of sight. Grandson of Captain Obed Marsh, who founded the business. His mother seems to've ben some kind of foreigner – they say a South Sea islander – so everybody raised Cain when he married an Ipswich girl fifty years ago. They always do that about Innsmouth people, and folks here and hereabouts always try to cover up any Innsmouth blood they have in 'em. But Marsh's children and grandchildren look just like anyone else so far's I can see. I've had 'em pointed out to me here – though, come to think of it, the elder children don't seem to be around lately. Never saw the old man.

'And why is everybody so down on Innsmouth? Well, young fellow, you mustn't take too much stock in what people around here say. They're hard to get started, but once they do get started they never let up. They've ben telling things about Innsmouth – whispering 'em, mostly – for the last hundred years, I guess, and I gather they're more scared than anything else. Some of the stories would make you laugh – about old Captain Marsh driving bargains with the devil and bringing imps out of hell to live in Innsmouth, or about some kind of devil-worship and awful sacrifices in some place near the wharves that people stumbled on around 1845 or thereabouts – but I come from Panton, Vermont, and that kind of story don't go down with me.

'You ought to hear, though, what some of the old-timers tell about the black reef off the coast – Devil Reef, they call it. It's well above water a good part of the time, and never much below it, but at that you could hardly call it an island. The story is that there's a whole legion of devils seen sometimes on that reef – sprawled about, or darting in and out of some kind of caves near the top. It's a rugged, uneven thing, a good bit over a mile out, and toward the end of shipping days sailors used to make big detours just to avoid it.

'That is, sailors that didn't hail from Innsmouth. One of the things they had against old Captain Marsh was that he was supposed to land on it sometimes at night when the tide was right. Maybe he did, for I dare say the rock formation was interesting, and it's just barely possible he was looking for pirate loot and maybe finding it; but there was talk of his dealing with daemons there. Fact is, I guess on the whole it was really the Captain that gave the bad reputation to the reef.

'That was before the big epidemic of 1846, when over half the folks in Innsmouth was carried off. They never did quite figure out what the trouble was, but it was probably some foreign kind of disease brought from China or somewhere by the shipping. It surely was bad enough – there was riots over it, and all sorts of ghastly doings that I don't believe ever got outside of town – and it left the place in awful shape. Never came back – there can't be more'n 300 or 400 people living there now.

'But the real thing behind the way folks feel is simply race prejudice – and I don't say I'm blaming those that hold it. I hate those Innsmouth folks myself, and I wouldn't care to go to their town. I s'pose you know – though I can see you're a Westerner by your talk – what a lot our New England ships used to have to do with queer ports in Africa, Asia, the South Seas, and everywhere else, and what queer kinds of people they sometimes brought back with 'em. You've probably heard about the Salem man that came home with a Chinese wife, and maybe you know there's still a bunch of Fiji Islanders somewhere around Cape Cod.

'Well, there must be something like that back of the Innsmouth people. The place always was badly cut off from the rest of the country by marshes and creeks, and we can't be sure about the ins and outs of the matter; but it's pretty clear that old Captain Marsh must have brought home some odd specimens when he had all three of his ships in commission back in the twenties and thirties. There certainly is a strange kind of streak in the Innsmouth folks today – I don't know how to explain it, but it sort of makes you crawl. You'll notice a little in Sargent if you take his bus. Some of 'em have queer narrow heads with flat noses and bulgy, stary eyes that never seem to shut, and their skin ain't quite right. Rough and scabby, and the sides of their necks are all shrivelled or creased up. Get bald, too, very young. The older fellows look the worst – fact is, I don't believe I've ever seen a very old chap of that kind. Guess they must die of looking in the glass! Animals hate 'em – they used to have lots of horse trouble before autos came in.

'Nobody around here or in Arkham or Ipswich will have anything to do with 'em, and they act kind of offish themselves when they come to town or when anyone tries to fish on their grounds. Queer how fish are always thick off Innsmouth Harbour when there ain't any anywhere else around – but just try to fish there yourself and see how the folks chase you off! Those people used to come here on the railroad – walking and taking the train at Rowley after the branch was dropped – but now they use that bus.

'Yes, there's a hotel in Innsmouth – called the Gilman House – but I don't believe it can amount to much. I wouldn't advise you to try it. Better stay over here and take the ten o'clock bus tomorrow morning; then you can get an evening bus there for Arkham at eight o'clock. There was a factory inspector who stopped at the Gilman a couple of years ago, and he had a lot of unpleasant hints about the place. Seems they get a queer crowd there, for this fellow heard voices in other rooms – though most of 'em was empty – that gave him the shivers. It was foreign talk, he thought, but he said the bad thing about it was the kind of voice that sometimes spoke. It sounded so unnatural – slopping-like, he said – that he didn't dare undress and go to sleep. Just waited up and lit out the first thing in the morning. The talk went on most all night.

'This fellow – Casey, his name was – had a lot to say about how the Innsmouth folks watched him and seemed kind of on guard. He found the Marsh refinery a queer place – it's in an old mill on the lower falls of the Manuxet. What he said tallied up with what I'd heard. Books in bad shape, and no clear account of any kind of dealings. You know it's always ben a kind of mystery where the Marshes get the gold they refine. They've never seemed to do much buying in that line, but years ago they shipped out an enormous lot of ingots.

'Used to be talk of a queer foreign kind of jewellery that the sailors and refinery men sometimes sold on the sly, or that was seen once or twice on some of the Marsh womenfolks. People allowed maybe old Captain Obed traded for it in some heathen port, especially since he was always ordering stacks of glass beads and trinkets such as sea-faring men used to get for native trade. Others thought and still think he'd found an old pirate cache out on Devil Reef. But here's a funny thing. The old Captain's ben dead these sixty years, and there ain't ben a good-sized ship out of the place since the Civil War; but just the same the Marshes still keep on buying a few of those native trade things – mostly glass and rubber gewgaws, they tell me. Maybe the Innsmouth folks like 'em to look at themselves –

Gawd knows they've gotten to be about as bad as South Sea canni-bals and Guinea savages.

'That plague of '46 must have taken off the best blood in the place. Anyway, they're a doubtful lot now, and the Marshes and the other rich folks are as bad as any. As I told you, there probably ain't more'n 400 people in the whole town in spite of all the streets they say there are. I guess they're what they call "white trash" down South – lawless and sly, and full of secret doings. They get a lot of fish and lobsters and do exporting by truck. Queer how the fish swarm right there and nowhere else.

'Nobody can ever keep track of these people, and state school officials and census men have a devil of a time. You can bet that prying strangers ain't welcome around Innsmouth. I've heard personally of more'n one business or government man that's disappeared there, and there's loose talk of one who went crazy and is out at Danvers now. They must have fixed up some awful scare for that fellow.

'That's why I wouldn't go at night if I was you. I've never ben there and have no wish to go, but I guess a daytime trip couldn't hurt you – even though the people hereabouts will advise you not to make it. If you're just sightseeing, and looking for old-time stuff, Innsmouth ought to be quite a place for you.'

And so I spent part of that evening at the Newburyport Public Library looking up data about Innsmouth. When I had tried to question the natives in the shops, the lunch room, the garages, and the fire station, I had found them even harder to get started than the ticket-agent had predicted; and realised that I could not spare the time to overcome their first instinctive reticences. They had a kind of obscure suspiciousness, as if there were something amiss with anyone too much interested in Innsmouth. At the Y.M.C.A., where I was stopping, the clerk merely discouraged my going to such a dismal, decadent place; and the people at the library shewed much the same attitude. Clearly, in the eyes of the educated, Innsmouth was merely an exaggerated case of civic degeneration.

The Essex County histories on the library shelves had very little to say, except that the town was founded in 1643, noted for ship-building before the Revolution, a seat of great marine prosperity in the early nineteenth century, and later a minor factory centre using the Manuxet as power. The epidemic and riots of 1846 were very sparsely treated, as if they formed a discredit to the county.

References to decline were few, though the significance of the later record was unmistakable. After the Civil War all industrial life was confined to the Marsh Refining Company, and the marketing of gold ingots formed the only remaining bit of major commerce aside from the eternal fishing. That fishing paid less and less as the price of the commodity fell and large-scale corporations offered competition, but there was never a dearth of fish around Innsmouth Harbour. Foreigners seldom settled there, and there was some discreetly veiled evidence that a number of Poles and Portuguese who had tried it had been scattered in a peculiarly drastic fashion.

Most interesting of all was a glancing reference to the strange jewellery vaguely associated with Innsmouth. It had evidently impressed the whole countryside more than a little, for mention was made of specimens in the museum of Miskatonic University at Arkham, and in the display room of the Newburyport Historical Society. The fragmentary descriptions of these things were bald and prosaic, but they hinted to me an undercurrent of persistent strangeness. Something about them seemed so odd and provocative that I could not put them out of my mind, and despite the relative lateness of the hour I resolved to see the local sample – said to be a large, queerly proportioned thing evidently meant for a tiara – if it could possibly be arranged.

The librarian gave me a note of introduction to the curator of the Society, a Miss Anna Tilton, who lived nearby, and after a brief explanation that ancient gentlewoman was kind enough to pilot me into the closed building, since the hour was not outrageously late. The collection was a notable one indeed, but in my present mood I had eyes for nothing but the bizarre object which glistened in a corner cupboard under the electric lights.

It took no excessive sensitiveness to beauty to make me literally gasp at the strange, unearthly splendour of the alien, opulent phantasy that rested there on a purple velvet cushion. Even now I can hardly describe what I saw, though it was clearly enough a sort of tiara, as the description had said. It was tall in front, and with a very large and curiously irregular periphery, as if designed for a head of almost freakishly elliptical outline. The material seemed to be predominantly gold, though a weird lighter lustrousness hinted at some strange alloy with an equally beautiful and scarcely identifiable metal. Its condition was almost perfect, and one could have spent hours in studying the striking and puzzlingly untraditional designs – some simply geometrical, and some plainly marine – chased or moulded in high relief on its surface with a craftsmanship of incredible skill and grace.

The longer I looked, the more the thing fascinated me; and in this fascination there was a curiously disturbing element hardly to be classified or accounted for. At first I decided that it was the queer other-worldly quality of the art which made me uneasy. All other art objects I had ever seen either belonged to some known racial or national stream, or else were consciously modernistic defiances of every recognised stream. This tiara was neither. It clearly belonged to some settled technique of infinite maturity and perfection, yet that technique was utterly remote from any – Eastern or Western, ancient or modern – which I had ever heard of or seen exemplified. It was as if the workmanship were that of another planet.

However, I soon saw that my uneasiness had a second and perhaps equally potent source residing in the pictorial and mathematical suggestions of the strange designs. The patterns all hinted of remote secrets and unimaginable abysses in time and space, and the monotonously aquatic nature of the reliefs became almost sinister. Among these reliefs were fabulous monsters of abhorrent grotesqueness and malignity – half ichthyic and half batrachian in suggestion – which one could not dissociate from a certain haunting and uncomfortable sense of pseudo-memory, as if they called up some image from deep cells and tissues whose retentive functions are wholly primal and awesomely ancestral. At times I fancied that every contour of these blasphemous fish-frogs was overflowing with the ultimate quintessence of unknown and inhuman evil.

In odd contrast to the tiara's aspect was its brief and prosy history as related by Miss Tilton. It had been pawned for a ridiculous sum at a shop in State Street in 1873, by a drunken Innsmouth man shortly afterward killed in a brawl. The Society had acquired it directly from the pawnbroker, at once giving it a display worthy of its quality. It was labelled as of probable East-Indian or Indo-Chinese provenance, though the attribution was frankly tentative.

Miss Tilton, comparing all possible hypotheses regarding its origin and its presence in New England, was inclined to believe that it formed part of some exotic pirate hoard discovered by old Captain Obed Marsh. This view was surely not weakened by the insistent offers of purchase at a high price which the Marshes began to make as soon as they knew of its presence, and which they repeated to this day despite the Society's unvarying determination not to sell.

As the good lady shewed me out of the building she made it clear that the pirate theory of the Marsh fortune was a popular one among the intelligent people of the region. Her own attitude toward shadowed Innsmouth – which she had never seen – was one of disgust at a community slipping far down the cultural scale, and she assured me that the rumours of devil-worship were partly justified by a peculiar secret cult which had gained force there and engulfed all the orthodox churches.

It was called, she said, 'The Esoteric Order of Dagon', and was undoubtedly a debased, quasi-pagan thing imported from the East a century before, at a time when the Innsmouth fisheries seemed to be going barren. Its persistence among a simple people was quite natural in view of the sudden and permanent return of abundantly fine fishing, and it soon came to be the greatest influence on the town, replacing Freemasonry altogether and taking up headquarters in the old Masonic Hall on New Church Green.

All this, to the pious Miss Tilton, formed an excellent reason for shunning the ancient town of decay and desolation; but to me it was merely a fresh incentive. To my architectural and historical anticipations was now added an acute anthropological zeal, and I could scarcely sleep in my small room at the 'Y' as the night wore away.

2

Shortly before ten the next morning I stood with one small valise in front of Hammond's Drug Store in old Market Square waiting for the Innsmouth bus. As the hour for its arrival drew near I noticed a general drift of the loungers to other places up the street, or to the Ideal Lunch across the square. Evidently the ticket-agent had not exaggerated the dislike which local people bore toward Innsmouth and its denizens. In a few moments a small motor-coach of extreme decrepitude and dirty grey colour rattled down State Street, made a turn, and drew up at the curb beside me. I felt immediately that it was the right one; a guess which the half-illegible sign on the wind-shield – '*Arkham-Innsmouth-Newb'port*' – soon verified.

There were only three passengers – dark, unkempt men of sullen visage and somewhat youthful cast – and when the vehicle stopped they clumsily shambled out and began walking up State Street in a silent, almost furtive fashion. The driver also alighted, and I watched him as he went into the drug store to make some purchase. This, I reflected, must be the Joe Sargent mentioned by the ticket-agent; and even before I noticed any details there spread over me a wave of spontaneous aversion which could be neither checked nor explained. It suddenly struck me as very natural that the local people should not wish to ride on a bus owned and driven by this man, or to visit any oftener than possible the habitat of such a man and his kinsfolk.

When the driver came out of the store I looked at him more carefully and tried to determine the source of my evil impression. He was a thin, stoop-shouldered man not much under six feet tall, dressed in shabby blue civilian clothes and wearing a frayed grey golf cap. His age was perhaps thirty-five, but the odd, deep creases in the sides of his neck made him seem older when one did not study his dull, expressionless face. He had a narrow head, bulging, watery blue eyes that seemed never to wink, a flat nose, a receding forehead and chin, and singularly undeveloped ears. His long, thick lip and coarse-pored, greyish cheeks seemed almost beardless except for some sparse yellow hairs that straggled and curled in irregular patches; and in places the surface seemed queerly irregular, as if peeling from some cutaneous disease. His hands were large and heavily veined, and had a very unusual greyish-blue tinge. The fingers were strikingly short in proportion to the rest of the structure, and seemed to have a tendency to curl closely into the huge palm. As he walked toward the bus I observed his peculiarly shambling gait and saw that his feet were inordinately immense. The more I studied them the more I wondered how he could buy any shoes to fit them.

A certain greasiness about the fellow increased my dislike. He was evidently given to working or lounging around the fish docks, and carried with him much of their characteristic smell. Just what foreign blood was in him I could not even guess. His oddities certainly did not look Asiatic, Polynesian, Levantine, or negroid, yet I could see why the people found him alien. I myself would have thought of biological degeneration rather than alienage.

I was sorry when I saw that there would be no other passengers on the bus. Somehow I did not like the idea of riding alone with this driver. But as leaving time obviously approached I conquered my qualms and followed the man aboard, extending him a dollar bill and murmuring the single word 'Innsmouth'. He looked curiously at me for a second as he returned forty cents change without speaking. I took a seat far behind him, but on the same side of the bus, since I wished to watch the shore during the journey.

At length the decrepit vehicle started with a jerk, and rattled noisily past the old brick buildings of State Street amidst a cloud of vapour from the exhaust. Glancing at the people on the sidewalks, I thought I detected in them a curious wish to avoid looking at the bus – or at least a wish to avoid seeming to look at it. Then we turned to the left into High Street, where the going was smoother; flying by stately old mansions of the early republic and still older colonial farmhouses, passing the Lower Green and Parker River, and finally emerging into a long, monotonous stretch of open shore country.

The day was warm and sunny, but the landscape of sand, sedge-grass, and stunted shrubbery became more and more desolate as we proceeded. Out the window I could see the blue water and the sandy line of Plum Island, and we presently drew very near the beach as our narrow road veered off from the main highway to Rowley and Ipswich. There were no visible houses, and I could tell by the state of the road that traffic was very light hereabouts. The small, weather-worn telephone poles carried only two wires. Now and then we crossed crude wooden bridges over tidal creeks that wound far inland and promoted the general isolation of the region.

Once in a while I noticed dead stumps and crumbling foundation-walls above the drifting sand, and recalled the old tradition quoted in one of the histories I had read, that this was once a fertile and thickly settled countryside. The change, it was said, came simultaneously with the Innsmouth epidemic of 1846, and was thought by simple folk to have a dark connexion with hidden forces of evil. Actually, it was caused by the unwise cutting of woodlands near the shore, which robbed the soil of its best protection and opened the way for waves of wind-blown sand.

At last we lost sight of Plum Island and saw the vast expanse of the open Atlantic on our left. Our narrow course began to climb steeply, and I felt a singular sense of disquiet in looking at the lonely crest ahead where the rutted roadway met the sky. It was as if the bus were about to keep on in its ascent, leaving the sane earth altogether and merging with the unknown arcana of upper air and cryptical sky. The smell of the sea took on ominous implications, and the silent driver's bent, rigid back and narrow head became more and more hateful. As I looked at him I saw that the back of his head was almost as hairless as his face, having only a few straggling yellow strands upon a grey scabrous surface.

Then we reached the crest and beheld the outspread valley beyond, where the Manuxet joins the sea just north of the long line of cliffs that culminate in Kingsport Head and veer off toward Cape Ann. On the far, misty horizon I could just make out the dizzy profile of the Head, topped by the queer ancient house of which so many legends are told; but for the moment all my attention was captured by the nearer panorama just below me. I had, I realised, come face to face with rumour-shadowed Innsmouth.

It was a town of wide extent and dense construction, yet one with a portentous dearth of visible life. From the tangle of chimney-pots scarcely a wisp of smoke came, and the three tall steeples loomed stark and unpainted against the seaward horizon. One of them was crumbling down at the top, and in that and another there were only black gaping holes where clock-dials should have been. The vast huddle of sagging gambrel roofs and peaked gables conveyed with offensive clearness the idea of wormy decay, and as we approached along the now descending road I could see that many roofs had wholly caved in. There were some large square Georgian houses, too, with hipped roofs, cupolas, and railed 'widow's walks'. These were mostly well back from the water, and one or two seemed to be in moderately sound condition. Stretching inland from among them I saw the rusted, grass-grown line of the abandoned railway, with leaning telegraph-poles now devoid of wires, and the half-obscured lines of the old carriage roads to Rowley and Ipswich.

The decay was worst close to the waterfront, though in its very midst I could spy the white belfry of a fairly well-preserved brick structure which looked like a small factory. The harbour, long clogged with sand, was enclosed by an ancient stone breakwater, on which I could begin to discern the minute forms of a few seated fishermen, and at whose end were what looked like the foundations of a bygone lighthouse. A sandy tongue had formed inside this barrier, and upon it I saw a few decrepit cabins, moored dories, and scattered lobster-pots. The only deep water seemed to be where the river poured out past the belfried structure and turned southward to join the ocean at the breakwater's end.

Here and there the ruins of wharves jutted out from the shore to end in indeterminate rottenness, those farthest south seeming the most decayed. And far out at sea, despite a high tide, I glimpsed a long, black line scarcely rising above the water yet carrying a sugges-tion of odd latent malignancy. This, I knew, must be Devil Reef. As I looked, a subtle, curious sense of beckoning seemed superadded to the grim repulsion; and oddly enough, I found this overtone more disturbing than the primary impression.

We met no one on the road, but presently began to pass deserted farms in varying stages of ruin. Then I noticed a few inhabited houses with rags stuffed in the broken windows and shells and dead fish lying about the littered yards. Once or twice I saw listless-looking people working in barren gardens or digging clams on the fishy-smelling beach below, and groups of dirty, simian-visaged children playing around weed-grown doorsteps. Somehow these people seemed more disquieting than the dismal buildings, for almost every one had certain peculiarities of face and motions which I instinctively disliked with-out being able to define or comprehend them. For a second I thought this typical physique suggested some picture I had seen, perhaps in a book, under circumstances of particular horror or melancholy; but this pseudo-recollection passed very quickly.

As the bus reached a lower level I began to catch the steady note of a waterfall through the unnatural stillness. The leaning, unpainted houses grew thicker, lined both sides of the road, and displayed more urban tendencies than did those we were leaving behind. The pan-orama ahead had contracted to a street scene, and in spots I could see where a cobblestone pavement and stretches of brick sidewalk had formerly existed. All the houses were apparently deserted, and there were occasional gaps where tumbledown chimneys and cellar walls told of buildings that had collapsed. Pervading everything was the most nauseous fishy odour imaginable.

Soon cross streets and junctions began to appear; those on the left leading to shoreward realms of unpaved squalor and decay, while those on the right shewed vistas of departed grandeur. So far I had seen no people in the town, but there now came signs of a sparse habitation – curtained windows here and there, and an occasional battered motor-car at the curb. Pavement and sidewalks were increasingly well defined, and though most of the houses were quite old – wood and brick structures of the early nineteenth century – they were obviously kept fit for habitation. As an amateur antiquarian I almost lost my olfactory disgust and my feeling of menace and repulsion amidst this rich, unaltered survival from the past.

But I was not to reach my destination without one very strong impression of poignantly disagreeable quality. The bus had come to a sort of open concourse or radial point with churches on two sides and the bedraggled remains of a circular green in the centre, and I was looking at a large pillared hall on the right-hand junction ahead. The structure's once white paint was now grey and peeling, and the black and gold sign on the pediment was so faded that I could only with difficulty make out the words 'Esoteric Order of Dagon'. This, then, was the former Masonic Hall now given over to a degraded cult. As I strained to decipher this inscription my notice was distracted by the raucous tones of a cracked bell across the street, and I quickly turned to look out the window on my side of the coach.

The sound came from a squat-towered stone church of manifestly later date than most of the houses, built in a clumsy Gothic fashion and having a disproportionately high basement with shuttered windows. Though the hands of its clock were missing on the side I glimpsed, I knew that those hoarse strokes were telling the hour of eleven. Then suddenly all thoughts of time were blotted out by an onrushing image of sharp intensity and unaccountable horror which had seized me before I knew what it really was. The door of the church basement was open, revealing a rectangle of blackness inside. And as I looked, a certain object crossed or seemed to cross that dark rectangle, burning into my brain a momentary conception of nightmare which was all the more maddening because analysis could not shew a single nightmarish quality in it.

It was a living object – the first except the driver that I had seen since entering the compact part of the town – and had I been in a steadier mood I would have found nothing whatever of terror in it. Clearly, as I realised a moment later, it was the pastor; clad in some peculiar vestments doubtless introduced since the Order of Dagon had modified the ritual of the local churches. The thing which had probably caught my first subconscious glance and supplied the touch of bizarre horror was the tall tiara he wore; an almost exact duplicate of the one Miss Tilton had shewn me the previous evening. This, acting on my imagination, had supplied namelessly sinister qualities to the indeterminate face and robed, shambling form beneath it. There was not, I soon decided, any reason why I should have felt that shuddering touch of evil pseudo-memory. Was it not natural that a local mystery cult should adopt among its regimentals an unique type of head-dress made familiar to the community in some strange way – perhaps as treasure-trove?

A very thin sprinkling of repellent-looking youngish people now became visible on the sidewalks – lone individuals, and silent knots of two or three. The lower floors of the crumbling houses sometimes harboured small shops with dingy signs, and I noticed a parked truck or two as we rattled along. The sound of waterfalls became more and more distinct, and presently I saw a fairly deep river-gorge ahead, spanned by a wide, iron-railed highway bridge beyond which a large square opened out. As we clanked over the bridge I looked out on both sides and observed some factory buildings on the edge of the grassy bluff or part way down. The water far below was very abundant, and I could see two vigorous sets of falls upstream on my right and at least one downstream on my left. From this point the noise was quite deafening. Then we rolled into the large semicircular square across the river and drew up on the right-hand side in front of a tall, cupola-crowned building with remnants of yellow paint and with a half-effaced sign proclaiming it to be the Gilman House.

I was glad to get out of that bus, and at once proceeded to check my valise in the shabby hotel lobby. There was only one person in sight – an elderly man without what I had come to call the 'Innsmouth look' – and I decided not to ask him any of the questions which bothered me, remembering that odd things had been noticed in this hotel. Instead, I strolled out on the square, from which the bus had already gone, and studied the scene minutely and appraisingly.

One side of the cobble-stoned open space was the straight line of the river; the other was a semicircle of slant-roofed brick buildings of about the 1800 period, from which several streets radiated away to the southeast, south, and southwest. Lamps were depressingly few and small – all low-powered incandescents – and I was glad that my plans called for departure before dark, even though I knew the moon would be bright. The buildings were all in fair condition, and included perhaps a dozen shops in current operation; of which one was a grocery of the First National chain, others a dismal restaurant, a drug store, and a wholesale fish-dealer's office, and still another, at the eastern extremity of the square near the river, an office of the town's only industry – the Marsh Refining Company. There were perhaps ten people visible, and four or five automobiles and motor trucks stood scattered about. I did not need to be told that this was the civic centre of Innsmouth. Eastward I could catch blue glimpses of the harbour, against which rose the decaying remains of three once beautiful Georgian steeples. And toward the shore on the opposite bank of the river I saw the white belfry surmounting what I took to be the Marsh refinery.

For some reason or other I chose to make my first inquiries at the chain grocery, whose personnel was not likely to be native to Innsmouth. I found a solitary boy of about seventeen in charge, and was pleased to note the brightness and affability which promised cheerful information. He seemed exceptionally eager to talk, and I soon gathered that he did not like the place, its fishy smell, or its furtive people. A word with any outsider was a relief to him. He hailed from Arkham, boarded with a family who came from Ipswich, and went back home whenever he got a moment off. His family did not like him to work in Innsmouth, but the chain had transferred him there and he did not wish to give up his job.

There was, he said, no public library or chamber of commerce in Innsmouth, but I could probably find my way about. The street I had come down was Federal. West of that were the fine old residence streets – Broad, Washington, Lafayette, and Adams – and east of it were the shoreward slums. It was in these slums – along Main

Street – that I would find the old Georgian churches, but they were all long abandoned. It would be well not to make oneself too conspicuous in such neighbourhoods – especially north of the river – since the people were sullen and hostile. Some strangers had even disappeared.

Certain spots were almost forbidden territory, as he had learned at considerable cost. One must not, for example, linger much around the Marsh refinery, or around any of the still used churches, or around the pillared Order of Dagon Hall at New Church Green. Those churches were very odd – all violently disavowed by their respective denominations elsewhere, and apparently using the queerest kind of ceremonials and clerical vestments. Their creeds were heterodox and mysterious, involving hints of certain marvellous transformations leading to bodily immortality – of a sort – on this earth. The youth's own pastor – Dr Wallace of Asbury M. E. Church in Arkham – had gravely urged him not to join any church in Innsmouth.

As for the Innsmouth people – the youth hardly knew what to make of them. They were as furtive and seldom seen as animals that live in burrows, and one could hardly imagine how they passed the time apart from their desultory fishing. Perhaps – judging from the quantities of bootleg liquor they consumed – they lay for most of the daylight hours in an alcoholic stupor. They seemed sullenly banded together in some sort of fellowship and understanding – despising the world as if they had access to other and preferable spheres of entity. Their appearance – especially those staring, unwinking eyes which one never saw shut – was certainly shocking enough; and their voices were disgusting. It was awful to hear them chanting in their churches at night, and especially during their main festivals or revivals, which fell twice a year on April 30th and October 31st.

They were very fond of the water, and swam a great deal in both river and harbour. Swimming races out to Devil Reef were very common, and everyone in sight seemed well able to share in this arduous sport. When one came to think of it, it was generally only rather young people who were seen about in public, and of these the oldest were apt to be the most tainted-looking. When exceptions did occur, they were mostly persons with no trace of aberrancy, like the old clerk at the hotel. One wondered what became of the bulk of the older folk, and whether the 'Innsmouth look' were not a strange and insidious disease-phenomenon which increased its hold as years advanced.

Only a very rare affliction, of course, could bring about such vast and radical anatomical changes in a single individual after maturity – changes involving osseous factors as basic as the shape of the skull – but then, even this aspect was no more baffling and unheard-of than the visible features of the malady as a whole. It would be hard, the youth implied, to form any real conclusions regarding such a matter, since one never came to know the natives personally no matter how long one might live in Innsmouth.

The youth was certain that many specimens even worse than the worst visible ones were kept locked indoors in some places. People sometimes heard the queerest kind of sounds. The tottering water-front hovels north of the river were reputedly connected by hidden tunnels, being thus a veritable warren of unseen abnormalities. What kind of foreign blood – if any – these beings had, it was impossible to tell. They sometimes kept certain especially repulsive characters out of sight when government agents and others from the outside world came to town.

It would be of no use, my informant said, to ask the natives anything about the place. The only one who would talk was a very aged but normal-looking man who lived at the poorhouse on the north rim of the town and spent his time walking about or lounging around the fire station. This hoary character, Zadok Allen, was ninety-six years old and somewhat touched in the head, besides being the town drunkard. He was a strange, furtive creature who constantly looked over his shoulder as if afraid of something, and when sober could not be persuaded to talk at all with strangers. He was, however, unable to resist any offer of his favourite poison; and once drunk would furnish the most astonishing fragments of whispered reminiscence.

After all, though, little useful data could be gained from him, since his stories were all insane, incomplete hints of impossible marvels and horrors which could have no source save in his own disordered fancy. Nobody ever believed him, but the natives did not like him to drink and talk with strangers; and it was not always safe to be seen questioning him. It was probably from him that some of the wildest popular whispers and delusions were derived.

Several non-native residents had reported monstrous glimpses from time to time, but between old Zadok's tales and the malformed denizens it was no wonder such illusions were current. None of the non-natives ever stayed out late at night, there being a widespread impression that it was not wise to do so. Besides, the streets were loathsomely dark.

As for business – the abundance of fish was certainly almost uncanny, but the natives were taking less and less advantage of it. Moreover, prices were falling and competition was growing. Of course the town's real business was the refinery, whose commercial office was on the square only a few doors east of where we stood. Old Man Marsh was never seen, but sometimes went to the works in a closed, curtained car.

There were all sorts of rumours about how Marsh had come to look. He had once been a great dandy, and people said he still wore the frock-coated finery of the Edwardian age, curiously adapted to certain deformities. His sons had formerly conducted the office in the square, but latterly they had been keeping out of sight a good deal and leaving the brunt of affairs to the younger generation. The sons and their sisters had come to look very queer, especially the elder ones; and it was said that their health was failing.

One of the Marsh daughters was a repellent, reptilian-looking woman who wore an excess of weird jewellery clearly of the same exotic tradition as that to which the strange tiara belonged. My informant had noticed it many times, and had heard it spoken of as coming from some secret hoard, either of pirates or of daemons. The clergymen – or priests, or whatever they were called nowadays – also wore this kind of ornament as a head-dress; but one seldom caught glimpses of them. Other specimens the youth had not seen, though many were rumoured to exist around Innsmouth.

The Marshes, together with the other three gently bred families of the town – the Waites, the Gilmans, and the Eliots – were all very retiring. They lived in immense houses along Washington Street, and several were reputed to harbour in concealment certain living kinsfolk whose personal aspect forbade public view, and whose deaths had been reported and recorded.

Warning me that many of the street signs were down, the youth drew for my benefit a rough but ample and painstaking sketch map of the town's salient features. After a moment's study I felt sure that it would be of great help, and pocketed it with profuse thanks. Disliking the dinginess of the single restaurant I had seen, I bought a fair supply of cheese crackers and ginger wafers to serve as a lunch later on. My programme, I decided, would be to thread the principal streets, talk with any non-natives I might encounter, and catch the eight o'clock coach for Arkham. The town, I could see, formed a significant and exaggerated example of communal decay; but being no sociologist I would limit my serious observations to the field of architecture.

Thus I began my systematic though half-bewildered tour of Innsmouth's narrow, shadow-blighted ways. Crossing the bridge and turning toward the roar of the lower falls, I passed close to the Marsh refinery, which seemed oddly free from the noise of industry. This building stood on the steep river bluff near a bridge and an open confluence of streets which I took to be the earliest civic centre, displaced after the Revolution by the present Town Square.

Re-crossing the gorge on the Main Street bridge, I struck a region of utter desertion which somehow made me shudder. Collapsing huddles of gambrel roofs formed a jagged and fantastic skyline, above which rose the ghoulish, decapitated steeple of an ancient church. Some houses along Main Street were tenanted, but most were tightly boarded up. Down unpaved side streets I saw the black, gaping windows of deserted hovels, many of which leaned at perilous and incredible angles through the sinking of part of the foundations. Those windows stared so spectrally that it took courage to turn eastward toward the waterfront. Certainly, the terror of a deserted house swells in geometrical rather than arithmetical progression as houses multiply to form a city of stark desolation. The sight of such endless avenues of fishy-eyed vacancy and death, and the thought of such linked infinities of black, brooding compartments given over to cobwebs and memories and the conqueror worm, start up vestigial fears and aversions that not even the stoutest philosophy can disperse.

Fish Street was as deserted as Main, though it differed in having many brick and stone warehouses still in excellent shape. Water Street was almost its duplicate, save that there were great seaward gaps where wharves had been. Not a living thing did I see, except for the scattered fishermen on the distant breakwater, and not a sound did I hear save the lapping of the harbour tides and the roar of the falls in the Manuxet. The town was getting more and more on my nerves, and I looked behind me furtively as I picked my way back over the tottering Water Street bridge. The Fish Street bridge, according to the sketch, was in ruins.

North of the river there were traces of squalid life – active fish-packing houses in Water Street, smoking chimneys and patched roofs here and there, occasional sounds from indeterminate sources, and infrequent shambling forms in the dismal streets and unpaved lanes – but I seemed to find this even more oppressive than the southerly desertion. For one thing, the people were more hideous and abnormal than those near the centre of the town; so that I was several times evilly reminded of something utterly fantastic which I could not quite place. Undoubtedly the alien strain in the Innsmouth folk was stronger here than farther inland – unless, indeed, the 'Innsmouth look' were a disease rather than a blood strain, in which case this district might be held to harbour the more advanced cases.

One detail that annoyed me was the *distribution* of the few faint sounds I heard. They ought naturally to have come wholly from the visibly inhabited houses, yet in reality were often strongest inside the most rigidly boarded-up façades. There were creakings, scurryings, and hoarse doubtful noises; and I thought uncomfortably about the hidden tunnels suggested by the grocery boy. Suddenly I found myself wondering what the voices of those denizens would be like. I had heard no speech so far in this quarter, and was unaccountably anxious not to do so.

Pausing only long enough to look at two fine but ruinous old churches at Main and Church Streets, I hastened out of that vile waterfront slum. My next logical goal was New Church Green, but somehow or other I could not bear to repass the church in whose basement I had glimpsed the inexplicably frightening form of that strangely diademed priest or pastor. Besides, the grocery youth had told me that the churches, as well as the Order of Dagon Hall, were not advisable neighbourhoods for strangers.

Accordingly I kept north along Main to Martin, then turning in-land, crossing Federal Street safely north of the Green, and entering the decayed patrician neighbourhood of northern Broad, Washington, Lafayette, and Adams Streets. Though these stately old avenues were ill-surfaced and unkempt, their elm-shaded dignity had not entirely departed. Mansion after mansion claimed my gaze, most of them decrepit and boarded up amidst neglected grounds, but one or two in each street shewing signs of occupancy. In Washington Street there was a row of four or five in excellent repair and with finely tended lawns and gardens. The most sumptuous of these – with wide terraced parterres extending back the whole way to Lafayette Street – I took to be the home of Old Man Marsh, the afflicted refinery owner.

In all these streets no living thing was visible, and I wondered at the complete absence of cats and dogs from Innsmouth. Another thing which puzzled and disturbed me, even in some of the best-preserved mansions, was the tightly shuttered condition of many third-story and attic windows. Furtiveness and secretiveness seemed universal in this hushed city of alienage and death, and I could not escape the sensation of being watched from ambush on every hand by sly, staring eyes that never shut.

I shivered as the cracked stroke of three sounded from a belfry on my left. Too well did I recall the squat church from which those notes came. Following Washington Street toward the river, I now faced a new zone of former industry and commerce, noting the ruins of a factory ahead, and seeing others, with the traces of an old railway station and covered railway bridge beyond, up the gorge on my right.

The uncertain bridge now before me was posted with a warning sign, but I took the risk and crossed again to the south bank where traces of life reappeared. Furtive, shambling creatures stared cryptically in my direction, and more normal faces eyed me coldly and curiously. Innsmouth was rapidly becoming intolerable, and I turned down Paine Street toward the Square in the hope of getting some vehicle to take me to Arkham before the still-distant starting-time of that sinister bus.

It was then that I saw the tumbledown fire station on my left, and noticed the red-faced, bushy-bearded, watery-eyed old man in non-descript rags who sat on a bench in front of it talking with a pair of unkempt but not abnormal-looking firemen. This, of course, must be Zadok Allen, the half-crazed, liquorish nonagenarian whose tales of old Innsmouth and its shadow were so hideous and incredible.

3

It must have been some imp of the perverse – or some sardonic pull from dark, hidden sources – which made me change my plans as I did. I had long before resolved to limit my observations to architecture alone, and I was even then hurrying toward the Square in an effort to get quick transportation out of this festering city of death and decay; but the sight of old Zadok Allen set up new currents in my mind and made me slacken my pace uncertainly.

I had been assured that the old man could do nothing but hint at wild, disjointed, and incredible legends, and I had been warned that the natives made it unsafe to be seen talking to him; yet the thought of this aged witness to the town's decay, with memories going back to the early days of ships and factories, was a lure that no amount of reason could make me resist. After all, the strangest and maddest of myths are often merely symbols or allegories based upon truth – and old Zadok must have seen everything which went on around Innsmouth for the last ninety years. Curiosity flared up beyond sense and caution, and in my youthful egotism I fancied I might be able to sift a nucleus of real history from the confused, extravagant outpouring I would probably extract with the aid of raw whiskey.

I knew that I could not accost him then and there, for the firemen would surely notice and object. Instead, I reflected, I would prepare by getting some bootleg liquor at a place where the grocery boy had told me it was plentiful. Then I would loaf near the fire station in apparent casualness, and fall in with old Zadok after he had started on one of his frequent rambles. The youth said that he was very restless, seldom sitting around the station for more than an hour or two at a time.

A quart bottle of whiskey was easily, though not cheaply, obtained in the rear of a dingy variety-store just off the Square in Eliot Street. The dirty-looking fellow who waited on me had a touch of the staring 'Innsmouth look', but was quite civil in his way, being perhaps used to the custom of such convivial strangers – truckmen, gold-buyers, and the like – as were occasionally in town.

Reentering the Square I saw that luck was with me, for – shuffling out of Paine Street around the corner of the Gilman House – I glimpsed nothing less than the tall, lean, tattered form of old Zadok Allen himself. In accordance with my plan, I attracted his attention by brandishing my newly purchased bottle, and soon realised that he had begun to shuffle wistfully after me as I turned into Waite Street on my way to the most deserted region I could think of.

I was steering my course by the map the grocery boy had prepared, and was aiming for the wholly abandoned stretch of southern water-front which I had previously visited. The only people in sight there had been the fishermen on the distant breakwater; and by going a few squares south I could get beyond the range of these, finding a pair of seats on some abandoned wharf and being free to question old Zadok unobserved for an indefinite time. Before I reached Main Street I could hear a faint and wheezy 'Hey, Mister!' behind me, and I presently allowed the old man to catch up and take copious pulls from the quart bottle.

I began putting out feelers as we walked along to Water Street and turned southward amidst the omnipresent desolation and crazily tilted ruins, but found that the aged tongue did not loosen as quickly as I had expected. At length I saw a grass-grown opening toward the sea between crumbling brick walls, with the weedy length of an earth-and-masonry wharf projecting beyond. Piles of moss-covered stones near the water promised tolerable seats, and the scene was sheltered from all possible view by a ruined warehouse on the north. Here, I thought, was the ideal place for a long secret colloquy; so I guided my companion down the lane and picked out spots to sit in among the mossy stones. The air of death and desertion was ghoulish, and the smell of fish almost insufferable; but I was resolved to let nothing deter me.

About four hours remained for conversation if I were to catch the eight o'clock coach for Arkham, and I began to dole out more liquor to the ancient tippler, meanwhile eating my own frugal lunch. In my donations I was careful not to overshoot the mark, for I did not wish Zadok's vinous garrulousness to pass into a stupor. After an hour his furtive taciturnity shewed signs of disappearing, but much to my disappointment he still sidetracked my questions about Innsmouth and its shadow-haunted past. He would babble of current topics, revealing a wide acquaintance with newspapers and a great tendency to philosophise in a sententious village fashion.

Toward the end of the second hour I feared my quart of whiskey would not be enough to produce results, and was wondering whether I had better leave old Zadok and go back for more. Just then, however, chance made the opening which my questions had been unable to make; and the wheezing ancient's rambling took a turn that caused me to lean forward and listen alertly. My back was toward the fishy-smelling sea, but he was facing it, and something or other had caused his wandering gaze to light on the low, distant line of Devil Reef, then shewing plainly and almost fascinatingly above the waves. The sight seemed to displease him, for he began a series of weak curses which ended in a confidential whisper and a knowing leer. He bent toward me, took hold of my coat lapel, and hissed out some hints that could not be mistaken.

'Thar's whar it all begun – that cursed place of all wickedness whar the deep water starts. Gate o' hell – sheer drop daown to a bottom no saoundin'-line kin tech. Ol' Cap'n Obed done it – him that faound aout more'n was good fer him in the Saouth Sea islands.

'Everybody was in a bad way them days. Trade fallin' off, mills losin' business – even the new ones – an' the best of our menfolks kilt a-privateerin' in the War of 1812 or lost with the *Elizy* brig an' the *Ranger* scow – both of 'em Gilman venters. Obed Marsh he had three ships afloat – brigantine *Columby*, brig *Hetty*, an' barque *Sumatry Queen*. He was the only one as kep' on with the East-Injy an' Pacific trade, though Esdras Martin's barkentine *Malay Pride* made a venter as late as 'twenty-eight.

'Never was nobody like Cap'n Obed – old limb o' Satan! Heh, heh! I kin mind him a-tellin' abaout furren parts, an' callin' all the folks stupid fer goin' to Christian meetin' an' bearin' their burdens meek an' lowly. Says they'd orter git better gods like some o' the folks in the Injies – gods as ud bring 'em good fishin' in return for their sacrifices, an' ud reely answer folks's prayers.

'Matt Eliot, his fust mate, talked a lot, too, only he was agin' folks's doin' any heathen things. Told abaout an island east of Otaheité whar they was a lot o' stone ruins older'n anybody knew anything abaout, kind o' like them on Ponape, in the Carolines, but with carvin's of faces that looked like the big statues on Easter Island. They was a little volcanic island near thar, too, whar they was other ruins with diff'rent carvin's – ruins all wore away like they'd ben under the sea onct, an' with picters of awful monsters all over 'em.

'Wal, Sir, Matt he says the natives araound thar had all the fish they cud ketch, an' sported bracelets an' armlets an' head rigs made aout of a queer kind o' gold an' covered with picters o' monsters jest like the ones carved over the ruins on the little island – sorter fish-like frogs or frog-like fishes that was drawed in all kinds o' positions like they was human bein's. Nobody cud git aout o' them whar they got all the stuff, an' all the other natives wondered haow they managed to find fish in plenty even when the very next islands had lean pickin's. Matt he got to wonderin' too, an' so did Cap'n Obed. Obed he notices, besides, that lots of the han'some young folks ud drop aout o' sight fer good from year to year, an' that they wa'n't many old folks araound. Also, he thinks some of the folks looks durned queer even fer Kanakys.

'It took Obed to git the truth aout o' them heathen. I dun't know haow he done it, but he begun by tradin' fer the gold-like things they wore. Ast 'em whar they come from, an' ef they cud git more, an' finally wormed the story aout o' the old chief – Walakea, they called him. Nobody but Obed ud ever a believed the old yeller devil, but the Cap'n cud read folks like they was books. Heh, heh! Nobody never believes me naow when I tell 'em, an' I dun't s'pose you will, young feller – though come to look at ye, ye hev kind o' got them sharp-readin' eyes like Obed had.'

The old man's whisper grew fainter, and I found myself shuddering at the terrible and sincere portentousness of his intonation, even though I knew his tale could be nothing but drunken phantasy.

'Wal, Sir, Obed he larnt that they's things on this arth as most folks never heerd abaout – an' wouldn't believe ef they did hear. It seems these Kanakys was sacrificin' heaps o' their young men an' maidens to some kind o' god-things that lived under the sea, an' gittin' all kinds o' favour in return. They met the things on the little islet with the queer ruins, an' it seems them awful picters o' frog-fish monsters was supposed to be picters o' these things. Mebbe they was the kind o' critters as got all the mermaid stories an' sech started. They had all kinds o' cities on the sea-bottom, an' this island was heaved up from thar. Seems they was some of the things alive in the stone buildin's when the island come up sudden to the surface.

That's haow the Kanakys got wind they was daown thar. Made sign-talk as soon as they got over bein' skeert, an' pieced up a bargain afore long.

'Them things liked human sacrifices. Had had 'em ages afore, but lost track o' the upper world arter a time. What they done to the victims it ain't fer me to say, an' I guess Obed wa'n't none too sharp abaout askin'. But it was all right with the heathens, because they'd ben havin' a hard time an' was desp'rate abaout everything. They give a sarten number o' young folks to the sea-things twict every year – May-Eve an' Hallowe'en – reg'lar as cud be. Also give some o' the carved knick-knacks they made. What the things agreed to give in return was plenty o' fish – they druv 'em in from all over the sea – an' a few gold-like things naow an' then.

'Wal, as I says, the natives met the things on the little volcanic islet – goin' thar in canoes with the sacrifices et cet'ry, and bringin' back any of the gold-like jools as was comin' to 'em. At fust the things didn't never go onto the main island, but arter a time they come to want to. Seems they hankered arter mixin' with the folks, an' havin' j'int ceremonies on the big days – May-Eve an' Hallowe'en. Ye see, they was able to live both in an' aout o' water – what they call amphibians, I guess. The Kanakys told 'em as haow folks from the other islands might wanta wipe 'em aout ef they got wind o' their bein' thar, but they says they dun't keer much, because they cud wipe aout the hull brood o' humans ef they was willin' to bother – that is, any as didn't hev sarten signs sech as was used onct by the lost Old Ones, whoever they was. But not wantin' to bother, they'd lay low when anybody visited the island.

'When it come to matin' with them toad-lookin' fishes, the Kanakys kind o' balked, but finally they larnt something as put a new face on the matter. Seems that human folks has got a kind o' relation to sech water-beasts – that everything alive come aout o' the water onct, an' only needs a little change to go back agin. Them things told the Kanakys that ef they mixed bloods there'd be children as ud look human at fust, but later turn more'n more like the things, till finally they'd take to the water an' jine the main lot o' things daown thar. An' this is the important part, young feller – them as turned into fish things an' went into the water *wouldn't never die*. Them things never died excep' they was kilt violent.

'Wal, Sir, it seems by the time Obed knowed them islanders they was all full o' fish blood from them deep-water things. When they got old an' begun to shew it, they was kep' hid until they felt like takin' to the water an' quittin' the place. Some was more teched than others, an' some never did change quite enough to take to the water; but mostly they turned aout jest the way them things said. Them as was born more like the things changed arly, but them as was nearly human sometimes stayed on the island till they was past seventy, though they'd usually go daown under fer trial trips afore that. Folks as had took to the water gen'rally come back a good deal to visit, so's a man ud often be a-talkin' to his own five-times-great-grandfather, who'd left the dry land a couple o' hundred years or so afore.

'Everybody got aout o' the idee o' dyin' – excep' in canoe wars with the other islanders, or as sacrifices to the sea-gods daown below, or from snake-bite or plague or sharp gallopin' ailments or somethin' afore they cud take to the water – but simply looked forrad to a kind o' change that wa'n't a bit horrible arter a while. They thought what they'd got was well wuth all they'd had to give up – an' I guess Obed kind o' come to think the same hisself when he'd chewed over old Walakea's story a bit. Walakea, though, was one of the few as hadn't got none of the fish blood – bein' of a royal line that intermarried with royal lines on other islands.

'Walakea he shewed Obed a lot o' rites an' incantations as had to do with the sea-things, an' let him see some o' the folks in the village as had changed a lot from human shape. Somehaow or other, though, he never would let him see one of the reg'lar things from right aout o' the water. In the end he give him a funny kind o' thingumajig made aout o' lead or something, that he said ud bring up the fish things from any place in the water whar they might be a nest of 'em. The idee was to drop it daown with the right kind o' prayers an' sech. Walakea allaowed as the things was scattered all over the world, so's anybody that looked abaout cud find a nest an' bring 'em up ef they was wanted.

'Matt he didn't like this business at all, an' wanted Obed shud keep away from the island; but the Cap'n was sharp fer gain, an' faound he cud git them gold-like things so cheap it ud pay him to make a specialty of 'em. Things went on that way fer years, an' Obed got enough o' that gold-like stuff to make him start the refinery in

Waite's old run-daown fullin' mill. He didn't dass sell the pieces like they was, fer folks ud be all the time askin' questions. All the same his crews ud git a piece an' dispose of it naow and then, even though they was swore to keep quiet; an' he let his women-folks wear some o' the pieces as was more human-like than most.

'Wal, come abaout 'thutty-eight – when I was seven year' old – Obed he faound the island people all wiped aout between v'yages. Seems the other islanders had got wind o' what was goin' on, an' had took matters into their own hands. S'pose they musta had, arter all, them old magic signs as the sea-things says was the only things they was afeard of. No tellin' what any o' them Kanakys will chance to git a holt of when the sea-bottom throws up some island with ruins older'n the deluge. Pious cusses, these was – they didn't leave nothin' standin' on either the main island or the little volcanic islet excep' what parts of the ruins was too big to knock daown. In some places they was little stones strewed abaout – like charms – with somethin' on 'em like what ye call a swastika naowadays. Prob'ly them was the Old Ones' signs. Folks all wiped aout, no trace o' no gold-like things, an' none o' the nearby Kanakys ud breathe a word abaout the matter. Wouldn't even admit they'd ever ben any people on that island.

'That naturally hit Obed pretty hard, seein' as his normal trade was doin' very poor. It hit the whole of Innsmouth, too, because in seafarin' days what profited the master of a ship gen'lly profited the crew proportionate. Most o' the folks araound the taown took the hard times kind o' sheep-like an' resigned, but they was in bad shape because the fishin' was peterin' aout an' the mills wa'n't doin' none too well.

'Then's the time Obed he begun a-cursin' at the folks fer bein' dull sheep an' prayin' to a Christian heaven as didn't help 'em none. He told 'em he'd knowed of folks as prayed to gods that give somethin' ye reely need, an' says ef a good bunch o' men ud stand by him, he cud mebbe git a holt o' sarten paowers as ud bring plenty o' fish an' quite a bit o' gold. O' course them as sarved on the *Sumatry Queen* an' seed the island knowed what he meant, an' wa'n't none too anxious to git clost to sea-things like they'd heerd tell on, but them as didn't know what 'twas all abaout got kind o' swayed by what Obed had to say, an' begun to ast him what he cud do to set 'em on the way to the faith as ud bring 'em results.'

Here the old man faltered, mumbled, and lapsed into a moody and apprehensive silence, glancing nervously over his shoulder and then turning back to stare fascinatedly at the distant black reef. When I spoke to him he did not answer, so I knew I would have to let him finish the bottle. The insane yarn I was hearing interested me profoundly, for I fancied there was contained within it a sort of crude allegory based upon the strangenesses of Innsmouth and elaborated by an imagination at once creative and full of scraps of exotic legend. Not for a moment did I believe that the tale had any really substantial foundation; but none the less the account held a hint of genuine terror, if only because it brought in references to strange jewels clearly akin to the malign tiara I had seen at Newburyport. Perhaps the ornaments had, after all, come from some strange island; and possibly the wild stories were lies of the bygone Obed himself rather than of this antique toper.

I handed Zadok the bottle, and he drained it to the last drop. It was curious how he could stand so much whiskey, for not even a trace of thickness had come into his high, wheezy voice. He licked the nose of the bottle and slipped it into his pocket, then beginning to nod and whisper softly to himself. I bent close to catch any articulate words he might utter, and thought I saw a sardonic smile behind the stained, bushy whiskers. Yes – he was really forming words, and I could grasp a fair proportion of them.

'Poor Matt – Matt he allus was agin' it – tried to line up the folks on his side, an' had long talks with the preachers – no use – they run the Congregational parson aout o' taown, an' the Methodist feller quit – never did see Resolved Babcock, the Baptist parson, agin – Wrath o' Jehovy – I was a mighty little critter, but I heerd what I heerd an' seen what I seen – Dagon an' Ashtoreth – Belial an' Beëlzebub – Golden Caff an' the idols o' Canaan an' the Philistines – Babylonish abominations – *Mene, mene, tekel, upharsin* – '

He stopped again, and from the look in his watery blue eyes I feared he was close to a stupor after all. But when I gently shook his shoulder he turned on me with astonishing alertness and snapped out some more obscure phrases.

'Dun't believe me, hey? Heh, heh, heh – then jest tell me, young feller, why Cap'n Obed an' twenty odd other folks used to row aout to Devil Reef in the dead o' night an' chant things so laoud ye cud hear 'em all over taown when the wind was right? Tell me that, hey? An' tell me why Obed was allus droppin' heavy things daown into the deep water t'other side o' the reef whar the bottom shoots daown like a cliff lower'n ye kin saound? Tell me what he done with that funny-shaped lead thingumajig as Walakea give him? Hey, boy? An' what did they all haowl on May-Eve, an' agin the next Hallowe'en? An' why'd the new church parsons – fellers as used to be sailors – wear them queer robes an' cover theirselves with them gold-like things Obed brung? Hey?'

The watery blue eyes were almost savage and maniacal now, and the dirty white beard bristled electrically. Old Zadok probably saw me shrink back, for he had begun to cackle evilly.

'Heh, heh, heh, heh! Beginnin' to see, hey? Mebbe ye'd like to a ben me in them days, when I seed things at night aout to sea from the cupalo top o' my haouse. Oh, I kin tell ye, little pitchers hev big ears, an' I wa'n't missin' nothin' o' what was gossiped abaout Cap'n Obed an' the folks aout to the reef! Heh, heh, heh! Haow abaout the night I took my pa's ship's glass up to the cupalo an' seed the reef a-bristlin' thick with shapes that dove off quick soon's the moon riz? Obed an' the folks was in a dory, but them shapes dove off the far side into the deep water an' never come up . . . Haow'd ye like to be a little shaver alone up in a cupalo a-watchin' shapes *as wa'n't human shapes*? . . . Hey? . . . Heh, heh, heh, heh . . . '

The old man was getting hysterical, and I began to shiver with a nameless alarm. He laid a gnarled claw on my shoulder, and it seemed to me that its shaking was not altogether that of mirth.

'S'pose one night ye seed somethin' heavy heaved offen Obed's dory beyond the reef, an' then larned nex' day a young feller was missin' from home? hey? Did anybody ever see hide or hair o' Hiram Gilman agin? Did they? An' Nick Pierce, an' Luelly Waite, an' Adoniram Saouthwick, an' Henry Garrison? hey? Heh, heh, heh, heh . . . Shapes talkin' sign language with their hands . . . them as had reel hands . . .

'Wal, Sir, that was the time Obed begun to git on his feet agin. Folks see his three darters a-wearin' gold-like things as nobody'd never see on 'em afore, an' smoke started comin' aout o' the refin'ry chimbly. Other folks were prosp'rin', too – fish begun to swarm into the harbour fit to kill, an' heaven knows what sized cargoes we begun to ship aout to Newb'ryport, Arkham, an' Boston. 'Twas then Obed got the ol' branch railrud put through. Some Kingsport fishermen heerd abaout the ketch an' come up in sloops, but they was all lost. Nobody never see 'em agin. An' jest then our folks organised the Esoteric Order o' Dagon, an' bought Masonic Hall offen Calvary Commandery for it . . . heh, heh, heh! Matt Eliot was a Mason an' agin' the sellin', but he dropped aout o' sight jest then.

'Remember, I ain't sayin' Obed was set on hevin' things jest like they was on that Kanaky isle. I dun't think he aimed at fust to do no mixin', nor raise no younguns to take to the water an' turn into fishes with eternal life. He wanted them gold things, an' was willin' to pay heavy, an' I guess the *others* was satisfied fer a while . . .

'Come in 'forty-six the taown done some lookin' an' thinkin' fer itself. Too many folks missin' – too much wild preachin' at meetin' of a Sunday – too much talk abaout that reef. I guess I done a bit by tellin' Selectman Mowry what I see from the cupalo. They was a party one night as follered Obed's craowd aout to the reef, an' I heerd shots betwixt the dories. Nex' day Obed an' thutty-two others was in gaol, with everbody a-wonderin' jest what was afoot an' jest what charge agin' 'em cud be got to holt. God, ef anybody'd look'd ahead . . . a couple o' weeks later, when nothin' had ben throwed into the sea fer that long . . . '

Zadok was shewing signs of fright and exhaustion, and I let him keep silence for a while, though glancing apprehensively at my watch. The tide had turned and was coming in now, and the sound of the waves seemed to arouse him. I was glad of that tide, for at high water the fishy smell might not be so bad. Again I strained to catch his whispers.

'That awful night . . . I seed 'em . . . I was up in the cupalo . . . hordes of 'em . . . swarms of 'em . . . all over the reef an' swimmin' up the harbour into the Manuxet . . . God, what happened in the streets of Innsmouth that night . . . they rattled our door, but pa wouldn't open . . . then he clumb aout the kitchen winder with his musket to find Selectman Mowry an' see what he cud do . . . Maounds o' the dead an' the dyin' . . . shots an' screams . . . shaoutin' in Ol' Squar an' Taown Squar an' New Church Green . . . gaol throwed open . . . proclamation . . . treason . . . called it the plague when folks come in an' faound haff our people missin' . . . nobody left but them as ud jine in with Obed an' them things or else keep quiet . . . never heerd o' my pa no more . . . '

The old man was panting, and perspiring profusely. His grip on my shoulder tightened.

'Everything cleaned up in the mornin' – but they was *traces* . . . Obed he kinder takes charge an' says things is goin' to be changed . . . *others'll* worship with us at meetin'-time, an' sarten haouses hez got to entertain *guests* . . . *they* wanted to mix like they done with the Kanakys, an' he fer one didn't feel baound to stop 'em. Far gone, was Obed . . . jest like a crazy man on the subjeck. He says they brung us fish an' treasure, an' shud hev what they hankered arter . . .

'Nothin' was to be diff'runt on the aoutside, only we was to keep shy o' strangers ef we knowed what was good fer us. We all hed to take the Oath o' Dagon, an' later on they was secon' an' third Oaths that some on us took. Them as ud help special, ud git special rewards – gold an' sech – No use balkin', fer they was millions of 'em daown thar. They'd ruther not start risin' an' wipin' aout humankind, but ef they was gave away an' forced to, they cud do a lot toward jest that. We didn't hev them old charms to cut 'em off like folks in the Saouth Sea did, an' them Kanakys wudn't never give away their secrets.

'Yield up enough sacrifices an' savage knick-knacks an' harbourage in the taown when they wanted it, an' they'd let well enough alone. Wudn't bother no strangers as might bear tales aoutside – that is, withaout they got pryin'. All in the band of the faithful – Order o' Dagon – an' the children shud never die, but go back to the Mother Hydra an' Father Dagon what we all come from onct – *Iä! Iä! Cthulhu fhtagn! Ph'nglui mglw'nafh Cthulhu R'lyeh wgah-nagl fhtagn* – '

Old Zadok was fast lapsing into stark raving, and I held my breath. Poor old soul – to what pitiful depths of hallucination had his liquor, plus his hatred of the decay, alienage, and disease around him, brought that fertile, imaginative brain! He began to moan now, and tears were coursing down his channelled cheeks into the depths of his beard.

'God, what I seen senct I was fifteen year' old – *Mene, mene, tekel, upharsin!* – the folks as was missin', an' them as kilt theirselves – them as told things in Arkham or Ipswich or sech places was all called crazy, like you're a-callin' me right naow – but God, what I seen – They'd a kilt me long ago fer what I know, only I'd took the fust an' secon' Oaths o' Dagon offen Obed, so was pertected unlessen a jury of 'em proved I told things knowin' an' delib'rit . . . but I wudn't take the third Oath – I'd a died ruther'n take that –

'It got wuss araound Civil War time, *when children born senct 'forty-six begun to grow up* – some of 'em, that is. I was afeard – never did no pryin' arter that awful night, an' never see one of – *them* – clost to in all my life. That is, never no full-blooded one. I went to the war, an' ef I'd a had any guts or sense I'd a never come back, but settled away from here. But folks wrote me things wa'n't so bad. That, I s'pose, was because gov'munt draft men was in taown arter 'sixty-three. Arter the war it was jest as bad agin. People begun to fall off – mills an' shops shet daown – shippin' stopped an' the harbour choked up – railrud give up – but *they* . . . they never stopped swimmin' in an' aout o' the river from that cursed reef o' Satan – an' more an' more attic winders got a-boarded up, an' more an' more noises was heerd in haouses as wa'n't s'posed to hev nobody in 'em . . .

'Folks aoutside hev their stories abaout us – s'pose you've heerd a plenty on 'em, seein' what questions ye ast – stories abaout things they've seed naow an' then, an' abaout that queer joolry as still comes in from somewhars an' ain't quite all melted up – but nothin' never gits def'nite. Nobody'll believe nothin'. They call them gold-like things pirate loot, an' allaow the Innsmouth folks hez furren blood or is distempered or somethin'. Besides, them that lives here shoo off as many strangers as they kin, an' encourage the rest not to git very cur'ous, specially raound night time. Beasts balk at the critters – hosses wuss'n mules – but when they got autos that was all right.

'In 'forty-six Cap'n Obed took a second wife *that nobody in the taown never see* – some says he didn't want to, but was made to by them as he'd called in – had three children by her – two as disappeared young, but one gal as looked like anybody else an' was eddicated in Europe. Obed finally got her married off by a trick to an Arkham feller as didn't suspect nothin'. But nobody aoutside'll hev nothin' to do with Innsmouth folks naow. Barnabas Marsh that runs the refin'ry naow is Obed's grandson by his fust wife – son of Onesiphorus, his eldest son, *but his mother was another o' them as wa'n't never seed aoutdoors.*

'Right naow Barnabas is abaout changed. Can't shet his eyes no more, an' is all aout o' shape. They say he still wears clothes, but he'll take to the water soon. Mebbe he's tried it already – they do sometimes go daown fer little spells afore they go fer good. Ain't ben seed abaout in public fer nigh on ten year'. Dun't know haow his poor wife kin feel – she come from Ipswich, an' they nigh lynched Barnabas when he courted her fifty odd year' ago. Obed he died in 'seventy-eight, an' all the next gen'ration is gone naow – the fust wife's children dead, an' the rest . . . God knows . . .'

The sound of the incoming tide was now very insistent, and little by little it seemed to change the old man's mood from maudlin tearfulness to watchful fear. He would pause now and then to renew those nervous glances over his shoulder or out toward the reef, and despite the wild absurdity of his tale, I could not help beginning to share his vague apprehensiveness. Zadok now grew shriller, and seemed to be trying to whip up his courage with louder speech.

'Hey, yew, why dun't ye say somethin'? Haow'd ye like to be livin' in a taown like this, with everything a-rottin' an' a-dyin', an' boarded-up monsters crawlin' an' bleatin' an' barkin' an' hoppin' araoun' black cellars an' attics every way ye turn? Hey? Haow'd ye like to hear the haowlin' night arter night from the churches an' Order o' Dagon Hall, *an' know what's doin' part o' the haowlin'*? Haow'd ye like to hear what comes from that awful reef every May-Eve an' Hallowmass? Hey? Think the old man's crazy, eh? Wal, Sir, *let me tell ye that ain't the wust*!'

Zadok was really screaming now, and the mad frenzy of his voice disturbed me more than I care to own.

'Curse ye, dun't set thar a-starin' at me with them eyes – I tell Obed Marsh he's in hell, an' hez got to stay thar! Heh, heh . . . in hell, I says! Can't git me – I hain't done nothin' nor told nobody nothin' –

'Oh, you, young feller? Wal, even ef I hain't told nobody nothin' yet, I'm a-goin' to naow! You jest set still an' listen to me, boy – this is what I ain't never told nobody . . . I says I didn't do no pryin' arter that night – *but I faound things aout jest the same*!

'Yew want to know what the reel horror is, hey? Wal, it's this – it ain't what them fish devils *hez done, but what they're a-goin' to do*! They're a-bringin' things up aout o' whar they come from into the taown – ben doin' it fer years, an' slackenin' up lately. Them haouses north o' the river betwixt Water an' Main Streets is full of 'em – them devils *an' what they brung* – an' when they git ready . . . I say, *when they git ready* . . . ever hear tell of a *shoggoth*? . . .

'Hey, d'ye hear me? I tell ye *I know what them things be – I seen 'em one night when* . . . EH — AHHHH — AH! E'YAAHHHH . . .'

The hideous suddenness and inhuman frightfulness of the old man's shriek almost made me faint. His eyes, looking past me toward the malodorous sea, were positively starting from his head, while his face was a mask of fear worthy of Greek tragedy. His bony claw dug monstrously into my shoulder, and he made no motion as I turned my head to look at whatever he had glimpsed.

There was nothing that I could see. Only the incoming tide, with perhaps one set of ripples more local than the long-flung line of breakers. But now Zadok was shaking me, and I turned back to watch the melting of that fear-frozen face into a chaos of twitching eyelids and mumbling gums. Presently his voice came back – albeit as a trembling whisper.

'*Git aout o' here!* Git aout o' here! *They seen us* – git aout fer your life! Dun't wait fer nothin' – *they know naow* – Run fer it – quick – *aout o' this taown* –'

Another heavy wave dashed against the loosening masonry of the bygone wharf, and changed the mad ancient's whisper to another inhuman and blood-curdling scream.

'E – YAAHHHH! . . . YHAAAAAAA! . . .'

Before I could recover my scattered wits he had relaxed his clutch on my shoulder and dashed wildly inland toward the street, reeling northward around the ruined warehouse wall.

I glanced back at the sea, but there was nothing there. And when I reached Water Street and looked along it toward the north there was no remaining trace of Zadok Allen.

4

I can hardly describe the mood in which I was left by this harrowing episode – an episode at once mad and pitiful, grotesque and terrifying. The grocery boy had prepared me for it, yet the reality left me none the less bewildered and disturbed. Puerile though the story was, old Zadok's insane earnestness and horror had communicated to me a mounting unrest which joined with my earlier sense of loathing for the town and its blight of intangible shadow.

Later I might sift the tale and extract some nucleus of historic allegory; just now I wished to put it out of my head. The hour had grown perilously late – my watch said 7:15, and the Arkham bus left Town Square at eight – so I tried to give my thoughts as neutral and practical a cast as possible, meanwhile walking rapidly through the deserted streets of gaping roofs and leaning houses toward the hotel where I had checked my valise and would find my bus.

Though the golden light of late afternoon gave the ancient roofs and decrepit chimneys an air of mystic loveliness and peace, I could not help glancing over my shoulder now and then. I would surely be very glad to get out of malodorous and fear-shadowed Innsmouth, and wished there were some other vehicle than the bus driven by that sinister-looking fellow Sargent. Yet I did not hurry too precipitately, for there were architectural details worth viewing at every silent corner; and I could easily, I calculated, cover the necessary distance in a half-hour.

Studying the grocery youth's map and seeking a route I had not traversed before, I chose Marsh Street instead of State for my approach to Town Square. Near the corner of Fall Street I began to see scattered groups of furtive whisperers, and when I finally reached the Square I saw that almost all the loiterers were congregated around the door of the Gilman House. It seemed as if many bulging, watery, unwinking eyes looked oddly at me as I claimed my valise in the lobby, and I hoped that none of these unpleasant creatures would be my fellow-passengers on the coach.

The bus, rather early, rattled in with three passengers somewhat before eight, and an evil-looking fellow on the sidewalk muttered a few indistinguishable words to the driver. Sargent threw out a mail-bag and a roll of newspapers, and entered the hotel; while the passengers – the same men whom I had seen arriving in Newburyport that morning – shambled to the sidewalk and exchanged some faint guttural words with a loafer in a language I could have sworn was not English. I boarded the empty coach and took the same seat I had taken before, but was hardly settled before Sargent reappeared and began mumbling in a throaty voice of peculiar repulsiveness.

I was, it appeared, in very bad luck. There had been something wrong with the engine, despite the excellent time made from Newburyport, and the bus could not complete the journey to Arkham. No, it could not possibly be repaired that night, nor was there any other way of getting transportation out of Innsmouth, either to Arkham or elsewhere. Sargent was sorry, but I would have to stop over at the Gilman. Probably the clerk would make the price easy for me, but there was nothing else to do. Almost dazed by this sudden obstacle, and violently dreading the fall of night in this decaying and half-unlighted town, I left the bus and reentered the hotel lobby, where the sullen, queer-looking night clerk told me I could have Room 428 on next the top floor – large, but without running water – for a dollar.

Despite what I had heard of this hotel in Newburyport, I signed the register, paid my dollar, let the clerk take my valise, and followed that sour, solitary attendant up three creaking flights of stairs past dusty corridors which seemed wholly devoid of life. My room, a dismal rear one with two windows and bare, cheap furnishings, overlooked a dingy courtyard otherwise hemmed in by low, deserted brick blocks, and commanded a view of decrepit westward-stretching roofs with a marshy countryside beyond. At the end of the corridor was a bathroom – a discouraging relique with ancient marble bowl, tin tub, faint electric light, and musty wooden panelling around all the plumbing fixtures.

It being still daylight, I descended to the Square and looked around for a dinner of some sort, noticing as I did so the strange glances I received from the unwholesome loafers. Since the grocery was closed, I was forced to patronise the restaurant I had shunned before, a stooped, narrow-headed man with staring, unwinking eyes, and a flat-nosed wench with unbelievably thick, clumsy hands being in attendance. The service was of the counter type, and it relieved me to find that much was evidently served from cans and packages. A bowl of vegetable soup with crackers was enough for me, and I soon headed back for my cheerless room at the Gilman, getting an evening paper and a flyspecked magazine from the evil-visaged clerk at the rickety stand beside his desk.

As twilight deepened I turned on the one feeble electric bulb over the cheap, iron-framed bed, and tried as best I could to continue the reading I had begun. I felt it advisable to keep my mind wholesomely occupied, for it would not do to brood over the abnormalities of this ancient, blight-shadowed town while I was still within its borders. The insane yarn I had heard from the aged drunkard did not promise very pleasant dreams, and I felt I must keep the image of his wild, watery eyes as far as possible from my imagination.

Also, I must not dwell on what that factory inspector had told the Newburyport ticket-agent about the Gilman House and the voices of its nocturnal tenants – not on that, nor on the face beneath the tiara in the black church doorway; the face for whose horror my conscious mind could not account. It would perhaps have been easier to keep my thoughts from disturbing topics had the room not been so gruesomely musty. As it was, the lethal mustiness blended hideously with the town's general fishy odour and persistently focussed one's fancy on death and decay.

Another thing that disturbed me was the absence of a bolt on the door of my room. One had been there, as marks clearly shewed, but there were signs of recent removal. No doubt it had become out of order, like so many other things in this decrepit edifice. In my nervousness I looked around and discovered a bolt on the clothes-press which seemed to be of the same size, judging from the marks, as the one formerly on the door. To gain a partial relief from the general tension I busied myself by transferring this hardware to the vacant place with the aid of a handy three-in-one device including a screw-driver which I kept on my key-ring. The bolt fitted perfectly, and I was somewhat relieved when I knew that I could shoot it firmly upon retiring. Not that I had any real apprehension of its need, but that any symbol of security was welcome in an environment of this kind. There were adequate bolts on the two lateral doors to connecting rooms, and these I proceeded to fasten.

I did not undress, but decided to read till I was sleepy and then lie down with only my coat, collar, and shoes off. Taking a pocket flashlight from my valise, I placed it in my trousers, so that I could read my watch if I woke up later in the dark. Drowsiness, however, did not come; and when I stopped to analyse my thoughts I found to my disquiet that I was really unconsciously listening for something – listening for something which I dreaded but could not name. That inspector's story must have worked on my imagination more deeply than I had suspected. Again I tried to read, but found that I made no progress.

After a time I seemed to hear the stairs and corridors creak at intervals as if with footsteps, and wondered if the other rooms were beginning to fill up. There were no voices, however, and it struck me that there was something subtly furtive about the creaking. I did not like it, and debated whether I had better try to sleep at all. This town had some queer people, and there had undoubtedly been several disappearances. Was this one of those inns where travellers were slain for their money? Surely I had no look of excessive prosperity. Or were the townsfolk really so resentful about curious visitors? Had my obvious sightseeing, with its frequent map-consultations, aroused unfavourable notice? It occurred to me that I must be in a highly nervous state to let a few random creakings set me off speculating in this fashion – but I regretted none the less that I was unarmed.

At length, feeling a fatigue which had nothing of drowsiness in it, I bolted the newly outfitted hall door, turned off the light, and threw myself down on the hard, uneven bed – coat, collar, shoes, and all. In the darkness every faint noise of the night seemed magnified, and a flood of doubly unpleasant thoughts swept over me. I was sorry I had put out the light, yet was too tired to rise and turn it on again. Then, after a long, dreary interval, and prefaced by a fresh creaking of stairs and corridor, there came that soft, damnably unmistakable sound which seemed like a malign fulfilment of all my apprehensions. Without the least shadow of a doubt, the lock on my hall door was being tried – cautiously, furtively, tentatively – with a key.

My sensations upon recognising this sign of actual peril were perhaps less rather than more tumultuous because of my previous vague fears. I had been, albeit without definite reason, instinctively on my guard – and that was to my advantage in the new and real crisis, whatever it might turn out to be. Nevertheless the change in the menace from vague premonition to immediate reality was a profound shock, and fell upon me with the force of a genuine blow. It never once occurred to me that the fumbling might be a mere mistake. Malign purpose was all I could think of, and I kept deathly quiet, awaiting the would-be intruder's next move.

After a time the cautious rattling ceased, and I heard the room to the north entered with a pass-key. Then the lock of the connecting door to my room was softly tried. The bolt held, of course, and I heard the floor creak as the prowler left the room. After a moment there came another soft rattling, and I knew that the room to the south of me was being entered. Again a furtive trying of a bolted connecting door, and again a receding creaking. This time the creaking went along the hall and down the stairs, so I knew that the prowler had realised the bolted condition of my doors and was giving up his attempt for a greater or lesser time, as the future would shew.

The readiness with which I fell into a plan of action proves that I must have been subconsciously fearing some menace and considering possible avenues of escape for hours. From the first I felt that the unseen fumbler meant a danger not to be met or dealt with, but only to be fled from as precipitately as possible. The one thing to do was to get out of that hotel alive as quickly as I could, and through some channel other than the front stairs and lobby.

Rising softly and throwing my flashlight on the switch, I sought to light the bulb over my bed in order to choose and pocket some belongings for a swift, valiseless flight. Nothing, however, happened; and I saw that the power had been cut off. Clearly, some cryptic, evil movement was afoot on a large scale – just what, I could not say. As I stood pondering with my hand on the now useless switch I heard a muffled creaking on the floor below, and thought I could barely distinguish voices in conversation. A moment later I felt less sure that the deeper sounds were voices, since the apparent hoarse barkings and loose-syllabled croakings bore so little resemblance to recognised human speech. Then I thought with renewed force of what the factory inspector had heard in the night in this mouldering and pestilential building.

Having filled my pockets with the flashlight's aid, I put on my hat and tiptoed to the windows to consider chances of descent. Despite the state's safety regulations there was no fire escape on this side of the hotel, and I saw that my windows commanded only a sheer three-story drop to the cobbled courtyard. On the right and left, however, some ancient brick business blocks abutted on the hotel; their slant roofs coming up to a reasonable jumping distance from my fourth-story level. To reach either of these lines of buildings I would have to be in a room two doors from my own – in one case on the north and in the other case on the south – and my mind instantly set to work calculating what chances I had of making the transfer.

I could not, I decided, risk an emergence into the corridor, where my footsteps would surely be heard, and where the difficulties of entering the desired room would be insuperable. My progress, if it was to be made at all, would have to be through the less solidly built connecting doors of the rooms, the locks and bolts of which I would have to force violently, using my shoulder as a battering-ram whenever they were set against me. This, I thought, would be possible owing to the rickety nature of the house and its fixtures; but I realised I could not do it noiselessly. I would have to count on sheer speed, and the chance of getting to a window before any hostile forces became coordinated enough to open the right door toward me with a passkey. My own outer door I reinforced by pushing the bureau against it – little by little, in order to make a minimum of sound.

I perceived that my chances were very slender, and was fully prepared for any calamity. Even getting to another roof would not solve the problem, for there would then remain the task of reaching the ground and escaping from the town. One thing in my favour was the deserted and ruinous state of the abutting buildings, and the number of skylights gaping blackly open in each row.

Gathering from the grocery boy's map that the best route out of town was southward, I glanced first at the connecting door on the south side of the room. It was designed to open in my direction, hence I saw – after drawing the bolt and finding other fastenings in place – it was not a favourable one for forcing. Accordingly abandoning it as a route, I cautiously moved the bedstead against it to hamper any attack which might be made on it later from the next room. The door on the north was hung to open away from me, and this – though a test proved it to be locked or bolted from the other side – I knew must be my route. If I could gain the roofs of the buildings in Paine Street and descend successfully to the ground level, I might perhaps dart through the courtyard and the adjacent or opposite buildings to Washington or Bates – or else emerge in Paine and edge around southward into Washington. In any case, I would aim to strike Washington somehow and get quickly out of the Town Square region. My preference would be to avoid Paine, since the fire station there might be open all night.

As I thought of these things I looked out over the squalid sea of decaying roofs below me, now brightened by the beams of a moon not much past full. On the right the black gash of the river-gorge clove the panorama, abandoned factories and railway station clinging barnacle-like to its sides. Beyond it the rusted railway and the Rowley road led off through a flat, marshy terrain dotted with islets of higher and dryer scrub-grown land. On the left the creek-threaded country-side was nearer, the narrow road to Ipswich gleaming white in the moonlight. I could not see from my side of the hotel the southward route toward Arkham which I had determined to take.

I was irresolutely speculating on when I had better attack the northward door, and on how I could least audibly manage it, when I noticed that the vague noises underfoot had given place to a fresh and heavier creaking of the stairs. A wavering flicker of light shewed through my transom, and the boards of the corridor began to groan with a ponderous load. Muffled sounds of possible vocal origin approached, and at length a firm knock came at my outer door.

For a moment I simply held my breath and waited. Eternities seemed to elapse, and the nauseous fishy odour of my environment seemed to mount suddenly and spectacularly. Then the knocking was repeated – continuously, and with growing insistence. I knew that the time for action had come, and forthwith drew the bolt of the northward connecting door, bracing myself for the task of battering it open. The knocking waxed louder, and I hoped that its volume would cover the sound of my efforts. At last beginning my attempt, I lunged again and again at the thin panelling with my left shoulder, heedless of shock or pain. The door resisted even more than I had expected, but I did not give in. And all the while the clamour at the outer door increased.

Finally the connecting door gave, but with such a crash that I knew those outside must have heard. Instantly the outside knocking became a violent battering, while keys sounded ominously in the hall doors of the rooms on both sides of me. Rushing through the newly opened connexion, I succeeded in bolting the northerly hall door before the lock could be turned; but even as I did so I heard the hall door of the third room – the one from whose window I had hoped to reach the roof below – being tried with a pass-key.

For an instant I felt absolute despair, since my trapping in a chamber with no window egress seemed complete. A wave of almost abnormal horror swept over me, and invested with a terrible but unexplainable singularity the flashlight-glimpsed dust prints made by the intruder who had lately tried my door from this room. Then, with a dazed automatism which persisted despite hopelessness, I made for the next connecting door and performed the blind motion of pushing at it in an effort to get through and – granting that fastenings might be as providentially intact as in this second room – bolt the hall door beyond before the lock could be turned from outside.

Sheer fortunate chance gave me my reprieve – for the connecting door before me was not only unlocked but actually ajar. In a second I was through, and had my right knee and shoulder against a hall door which was visibly opening inward. My pressure took the opener off guard, for the thing shut as I pushed, so that I could slip the well-conditioned bolt as I had done with the other door. As I gained this respite I heard the battering at the two other doors abate, while a confused clatter came from the connecting door I had shielded with the bedstead. Evidently the bulk of my assailants had entered the southerly room and were massing in a lateral attack. But at the same moment a pass-key sounded in the next door to the north, and I knew that a nearer peril was at hand.

The northward connecting door was wide open, but there was no time to think about checking the already turning lock in the hall. All I could do was to shut and bolt the open connecting door, as well as its mate on the opposite side – pushing a bedstead against the one and a bureau against the other, and moving a washstand in front of the hall door. I must, I saw, trust to such makeshift barriers to shield me till I could get out the window and on the roof of the Paine Street block. But even in this acute moment my chief horror was something apart from the immediate weakness of my defences. I was shuddering because not one of my pursuers, despite some hideous pantings, gruntings, and subdued barkings at odd intervals, was uttering an unmuffled or intelligible vocal sound.

As I moved the furniture and rushed toward the windows I heard a frightful scurrying along the corridor toward the room north of me, and perceived that the southward battering had ceased. Plainly, most of my opponents were about to concentrate against the feeble connecting door which they knew must open directly on me. Outside, the moon played on the ridgepole of the block below, and I saw that the jump would be desperately hazardous because of the steep surface on which I must land.

Surveying the conditions, I chose the more southerly of the two windows as my avenue of escape; planning to land on the inner slope of the roof and make for the nearest skylight. Once inside one of the decrepit brick structures I would have to reckon with pursuit; but I hoped to descend and dodge in and out of yawning doorways along the shadowed courtyard, eventually getting to Washington Street and slipping out of town toward the south.

The clatter at the northerly connecting door was now terrific, and I saw that the weak panelling was beginning to splinter. Obviously, the besiegers had brought some ponderous object into play as a battering-ram. The bedstead, however, still held firm; so that I had at least a faint chance of making good my escape. As I opened the window I noticed that it was flanked by heavy velour draperies suspended from a pole by brass rings, and also that there was a large projecting catch for the shutters on the exterior. Seeing a possible means of avoiding the dangerous jump, I yanked at the hangings and brought them down, pole and all; then quickly hooking two of the rings in the shutter catch and flinging the drapery outside. The heavy folds reached fully to the abutting roof, and I saw that the rings and catch would be likely to bear my weight. So, climbing out of the window and down the improvised rope ladder, I left behind me forever the morbid and horror-infested fabric of the Gilman House.

I landed safely on the loose slates of the steep roof, and succeeded in gaining the gaping black skylight without a slip. Glancing up at the window I had left, I observed it was still dark, though far across the crumbling chimneys to the north I could see lights ominously blazing in the Order of Dagon Hall, the Baptist church, and the Congregational church which I recalled so shiveringly. There had seemed to be no one in the courtyard below, and I hoped there would be a chance to get away before the spreading of a general alarm. Flashing my pocket lamp into the skylight, I saw that there were no steps down. The distance was slight, however, so I clambered over the brink and dropped; striking a dusty floor littered with crumbling boxes and barrels.

The place was ghoulish-looking, but I was past minding such impressions and made at once for the staircase revealed by my flashlight – after a hasty glance at my watch, which shewed the hour to be 2 a.m. The steps creaked, but seemed tolerably sound; and I raced down past a barn-like second story to the ground floor. The desolation was complete, and only echoes answered my footfalls. At length I reached the lower hall, at one end of which I saw a faint luminous rectangle marking the ruined Paine Street doorway. Heading the other way, I found the back door also open; and darted out and down five stone steps to the grass-grown cobblestones of the courtyard.

The moonbeams did not reach down here, but I could just see my way about without using the flashlight. Some of the windows on the Gilman House side were faintly glowing, and I thought I heard confused sounds within. Walking softly over to the Washington Street side I perceived several open doorways, and chose the nearest as my route out. The hallway inside was black, and when I reached the opposite end I saw that the street door was wedged immovably shut. Resolved to try another building, I groped my way back toward the courtyard, but stopped short when close to the doorway.

For out of an opened door in the Gilman House a large crowd of doubtful shapes was pouring – lanterns bobbing in the darkness, and horrible croaking voices exchanging low cries in what was certainly not English. The figures moved uncertainly, and I realised to my relief that they did not know where I had gone; but for all that they sent a shiver of horror through my frame. Their features were indistinguishable, but their crouching, shambling gait was abominably repellent. And worst of all, I perceived that one figure was strangely robed, and unmistakably surmounted by a tall tiara of a design altogether too familiar. As the figures spread throughout the courtyard, I felt my fears increase. Suppose I could find no egress from this building on the street side? The fishy odour was detestable, and I wondered I could stand it without fainting. Again groping toward the street, I opened a door off the hall and came upon an empty room with closely shuttered but sashless windows. Fumbling in the rays of my flashlight, I found I could open the shutters; and in another moment had climbed outside and was carefully closing the aperture in its original manner.

I was now in Washington Street, and for the moment saw no living thing nor any light save that of the moon. From several directions in the distance, however, I could hear the sound of hoarse voices, of footsteps, and of a curious kind of pattering which did not sound quite like footsteps. Plainly I had no time to lose. The points of the compass were clear to me, and I was glad that all the street-lights were turned off, as is often the custom on strongly moonlit nights in unprosperous rural regions. Some of the sounds came from the south, yet I retained my design of escaping in that direction. There would, I knew, be plenty of deserted doorways to shelter me in case I met any person or group who looked like pursuers.

I walked rapidly, softly, and close to the ruined houses. While hatless and dishevelled after my arduous climb, I did not look especially noticeable; and stood a good chance of passing unheeded if forced to encounter any casual wayfarer. At Bates Street I drew into a yawning vestibule while two shambling figures crossed in front of me, but was soon on my way again and approaching the open space where Eliot Street obliquely crosses Washington at the intersection of South. Though I had never seen this space, it had looked dangerous to me on the grocery youth's map, since the moonlight would have free play there. There was no use trying to evade it, for any alternative course would involve detours of possibly disastrous visibility and delaying effect. The only thing to do was to cross it boldly and openly, imitating the typical shamble of the Innsmouth folk as best I could, and trusting that no one – or at least no pursuer of mine – would be there.

Just how fully the pursuit was organised – and indeed, just what its purpose might be – I could form no idea. There seemed to be unusual activity in the town, but I judged that the news of my escape from the Gilman had not yet spread. I would, of course, soon have to shift from Washington to some other southward street; for that party from the hotel would doubtless be after me. I must have left dust prints in that last old building, revealing how I had gained the street.

The open space was, as I had expected, strongly moonlit; and I saw the remains of a park-like, iron-railed green in its centre. Fortunately no one was about, though a curious sort of buzz or roar seemed to be increasing in the direction of Town Square. South Street was very wide, leading directly down a slight declivity to the waterfront and commanding a long view out at sea; and I hoped that no one would be glancing up it from afar as I crossed in the bright moonlight.

My progress was unimpeded, and no fresh sound arose to hint that I had been spied. Glancing about me, I involuntarily let my pace slacken for a second to take in the sight of the sea, gorgeous in the burning moonlight at the street's end. Far out beyond the breakwater was the dim, dark line of Devil Reef, and as I glimpsed it I could not help thinking of all the hideous legends I had heard in the last thirty-four hours – legends which portrayed this ragged rock as a veritable gateway to realms of unfathomed horror and inconceivable abnormality.

Then, without warning, I saw the intermittent flashes of light on the distant reef. They were definite and unmistakable, and awaked in my mind a blind horror beyond all rational proportion. My muscles tightened for panic flight, held in only by a certain unconscious caution and half-hypnotic fascination. And to make matters worse, there now flashed forth from the lofty cupola of the Gilman House, which loomed up to the northeast behind me, a series of analogous though differently spaced gleams which could be nothing less than an answering signal.

Controlling my muscles, and realising afresh how plainly visible I was, I resumed my brisker and feignedly shambling pace, though keeping my eyes on that hellish and ominous reef as long as the opening of South Street gave me a seaward view. What the whole proceeding meant, I could not imagine, unless it involved some strange rite connected with Devil Reef, or unless some party had landed from a ship on that sinister rock. I now bent to the left around the ruinous green, still gazing toward the ocean as it blazed in the spectral summer moonlight, and watching the cryptical flashing of those nameless, unexplainable beacons.

It was then that the most horrible impression of all was borne in upon me – the impression which destroyed my last vestige of self-control and set me running frantically southward past the yawning black doorways and fishily staring windows of that deserted nightmare street. For at a closer glance I saw that the moonlit waters between the reef and the shore were far from empty. They were alive with a teeming horde of shapes swimming inward toward the town; and even at my vast distance and in my single moment of perception I could tell that the bobbing heads and flailing arms were alien and aberrant in a way scarcely to be expressed or consciously formulated.

My frantic running ceased before I had covered a block, for at my left I began to hear something like the hue and cry of organised pursuit. There were footsteps and guttural sounds, and a rattling motor wheezed south along Federal Street. In a second all my plans were utterly changed – for if the southward highway were blocked ahead of me, I must clearly find another egress from Innsmouth. I paused and drew into a gaping doorway, reflecting how lucky I was to have left the moonlit open space before these pursuers came down the parallel street.

A second reflection was less comforting. Since the pursuit was down another street, it was plain that the party was not following me directly. It had not seen me, but was simply obeying a general plan of cutting off my escape. This, however, implied that all roads leading out of Innsmouth were similarly patrolled; for the denizens could not have known what route I intended to take. If this were so, I would have to make my retreat across country away from any road; but how could I do that in view of the marshy and creek-riddled nature of all the surrounding region? For a moment my brain reeled – both from sheer hopelessness and from a rapid increase in the omnipresent fishy odour.

Then I thought of the abandoned railway to Rowley, whose solid line of ballasted, weed-grown earth still stretched off to the north-west from the crumbling station on the edge of the river-gorge. There was just a chance that the townsfolk would not think of that, since its brier-choked desertion made it half-impassable, and the unlikeliest of all avenues for a fugitive to choose. I had seen it clearly from my hotel window, and knew about how it lay. Most of its earlier length was uncomfortably visible from the Rowley road, and from high places in the town itself; but one could perhaps crawl inconspicuously through the undergrowth. At any rate, it would form my only chance of deliverance, and there was nothing to do but try it.

Drawing inside the hall of my deserted shelter, I once more con-sulted the grocery boy's map with the aid of the flashlight. The immediate problem was how to reach the ancient railway; and I now saw that the safest course was ahead to Babson Street, then west to Lafayette – there edging around but not crossing an open space homologous to the one I had traversed – and subsequently back northward and westward in a zigzagging line through Lafayette, Bates, Adams, and Bank Streets – the latter skirting the river-gorge – to the abandoned and dilapidated station I had seen from my window. My reason for going ahead to Babson was that I wished neither to re-cross the earlier open space nor to begin my westward course along a cross street as broad as South.

Starting once more, I crossed the street to the right-hand side in order to edge around into Babson as inconspicuously as possible. Noises still continued in Federal Street, and as I glanced behind me I thought I saw a gleam of light near the building through which I had escaped. Anxious to leave Washington Street, I broke into a quiet dog-trot, trusting to luck not to encounter any observing eye. Next the corner of Babson Street I saw to my alarm that one of the houses was still inhabited, as attested by curtains at the window; but there were no lights within, and I passed it without disaster.

In Babson Street, which crossed Federal and might thus reveal me to the searchers, I clung as closely as possible to the sagging, uneven buildings; twice pausing in a doorway as the noises behind me momentarily increased. The open space ahead shone wide and desolate under the moon, but my route would not force me to cross it. During my second pause I began to detect a fresh distribution of the vague sounds; and upon looking cautiously out from cover beheld a motor-car darting across the open space, bound outward along Eliot Street, which there intersects both Babson and Lafayette.

As I watched – choked by a sudden rise in the fishy odour after a short abatement – I saw a band of uncouth, crouching shapes loping and shambling in the same direction; and knew that this must be the party guarding the Ipswich road, since that highway forms an extension of Eliot Street. Two of the figures I glimpsed were in voluminous robes, and one wore a peaked diadem which glistened whitely in the moonlight. The gait of this figure was so odd that it sent a chill through me – for it seemed to me the creature was almost *hopping*.

When the last of the band was out of sight I resumed my progress, darting around the corner into Lafayette Street, and crossing Eliot very hurriedly lest stragglers of the party be still advancing along that thoroughfare. I did hear some croaking and clattering sounds far off toward Town Square, but accomplished the passage without disaster. My greatest dread was in re-crossing broad and moonlit South Street – with its seaward view – and I had to nerve myself for the ordeal. Someone might easily be looking, and possible Eliot Street stragglers could not fail to glimpse me from either of two points. At the last moment I decided I had better slacken my trot and make the crossing as before in the shambling gait of an average Innsmouth native.

When the view of the water again opened out – this time on my right – I was half-determined not to look at it at all. I could not, however, resist, but cast a sidelong glance as I carefully and imitatively shambled toward the protecting shadows ahead. There was no ship visible, as I had half expected there would be. Instead, the first thing which caught my eye was a small rowboat pulling in toward the abandoned wharves and laden with some bulky, tarpaulin-covered object. Its rowers, though distantly and indistinctly seen, were of an especially repellent aspect. Several swimmers were still discernible; while on the far black reef I could see a faint, steady glow unlike the winking beacon visible before, and of a curious colour which I could not precisely identify. Above the slant roofs ahead and to the right there loomed the tall cupola of the Gilman House, but it was completely dark. The fishy odour, dispelled for a moment by some merciful breeze, now closed in again with maddening intensity.

I had not quite crossed the street when I heard a muttering band advancing along Washington from the north. As they reached the broad open space where I had had my first disquieting glimpse of the moonlit water I could see them plainly only a block away – and was horrified by the bestial abnormality of their faces and the dog-like sub-humanness of their crouching gait. One man moved in a positively simian way, with long arms frequently touching the ground; while another figure – robed and tiaraed – seemed to progress in an almost hopping fashion. I judged this party to be the one I had seen in the Gilman's courtyard – the one, therefore, most closely on my trail. As some of the figures turned to look in my direction I was transfixed with fright, yet managed to preserve the casual, shambling gait I had assumed. To this day I do not know whether they saw me or not. If they did, my stratagem must have deceived them, for they passed on across the moonlit space without varying their course – meanwhile croaking and jabbering in some hateful guttural patois I could not identify.

Once more in shadow, I resumed my former dog-trot past the leaning and decrepit houses that stared blankly into the night. Having crossed to the western sidewalk I rounded the nearest corner into Bates Street, where I kept close to the buildings on the southern side. I passed two houses shewing signs of habitation, one of which had faint lights in upper rooms, yet met with no obstacle. As I turned into Adams Street I felt measurably safer, but received a shock when a man reeled out of a black doorway directly in front of me. He proved, however, too hopelessly drunk to be a menace, so that I reached the dismal ruins of the Bank Street warehouses in safety.

No one was stirring in that dead street beside the river-gorge, and the roar of the waterfalls quite drowned my footsteps. It was a long dog-trot to the ruined station, and the great brick warehouse walls around me seemed somehow more terrifying than the fronts of private houses. At last I saw the ancient arcaded station – or what was left of it – and made directly for the tracks that started from its farther end.

The rails were rusty but mainly intact, and not more than half the ties had rotted away. Walking or running on such a surface was very difficult; but I did my best, and on the whole made very fair time. For some distance the line kept on along the gorge's brink, but at length I reached the long covered bridge where it crossed the chasm at a dizzy height. The condition of this bridge would determine my next step. If humanly possible, I would use it; if not, I would have to risk more street wandering and take the nearest intact highway bridge.

The vast, barn-like length of the old bridge gleamed spectrally in the moonlight, and I saw that the ties were safe for at least a few feet within. Entering, I began to use my flashlight, and was almost knocked down by the cloud of bats that flapped past me. About half way across there was a perilous gap in the ties which I feared for a moment would halt me; but in the end I risked a desperate jump which fortunately succeeded.

I was glad to see the moonlight again when I emerged from that macabre tunnel. The old tracks crossed River Street at grade, and at once veered off into a region increasingly rural and with less and less of Innsmouth's abhorrent fishy odour. Here the dense growth of weeds and briers hindered me and cruelly tore my clothes, but I was none the less glad that they were there to give me concealment in case of peril. I knew that much of my route must be visible from the Rowley road.

The marshy region began very shortly, with the single track on a low, grassy embankment where the weedy growth was somewhat thinner. Then came a sort of island of higher ground, where the line passed through a shallow open cut choked with bushes and brambles. I was very glad of this partial shelter, since at this point the Rowley road was uncomfortably near according to my window view. At the end of the cut it would cross the track and swerve off to a safer distance; but meanwhile I must be exceedingly careful. I was by this time thankfully certain that the railway itself was not patrolled.

Just before entering the cut I glanced behind me, but saw no pursuer. The ancient spires and roofs of decaying Innsmouth gleamed lovely and ethereal in the magic yellow moonlight, and I thought of how they must have looked in the old days before the shadow fell. Then, as my gaze circled inland from the town, something less tranquil arrested my notice and held me immobile for a second.

What I saw – or fancied I saw – was a disturbing suggestion of undulant motion far to the south; a suggestion which made me conclude that a very large horde must be pouring out of the city along the level Ipswich road. The distance was great, and I could distinguish nothing in detail; but I did not at all like the look of that moving column. It undulated too much, and glistened too brightly in the rays of the now westering moon. There was a suggestion of sound, too, though the wind was blowing the other way – a suggestion of bestial scraping and bellowing even worse than the muttering of the parties I had lately overheard.

All sorts of unpleasant conjectures crossed my mind. I thought of those very extreme Innsmouth types said to be hidden in crumbling, centuried warrens near the waterfront. I thought, too, of those nameless swimmers I had seen. Counting the parties so far glimpsed, as well as those presumably covering other roads, the number of my pursuers must be strangely large for a town as depopulated as Innsmouth.

Whence could come the dense personnel of such a column as I now beheld? Did those ancient, unplumbed warrens teem with a twisted, uncatalogued, and unsuspected life? Or had some unseen ship indeed landed a legion of unknown outsiders on that hellish reef? Who were they? Why were they there? And if such a column of them was scouring the Ipswich road, would the patrols on the other roads be likewise augmented?

I had entered the brush-grown cut and was struggling along at a very slow pace when that damnable fishy odour again waxed dominant. Had the wind suddenly changed eastward, so that it blew in from the sea and over the town? It must have, I concluded, since I now began to hear shocking guttural murmurs from that hitherto silent direction. There was another sound, too – a kind of wholesale, colossal flopping or pattering which somehow called up images of the most detestable sort. It made me think illogically of that unpleasantly undulating column on the far-off Ipswich road.

And then both stench and sounds grew stronger, so that I paused shivering and grateful for the cut's protection. It was here, I recalled, that the Rowley road drew so close to the old railway before crossing westward and diverging. Something was coming along that road, and I must lie low till its passage and vanishment in the distance. Thank heaven these creatures employed no dogs for tracking – though perhaps that would have been impossible amidst the omnipresent regional odour. Crouched in the bushes of that sandy cleft I felt reasonably safe, even though I knew the searchers would have to cross the track in front of me not much more than a hundred yards away. I would be able to see them, but they could not, except by a malign miracle, see me.

All at once I began dreading to look at them as they passed. I saw the close moonlit space where they would surge by, and had curious thoughts about the irredeemable pollution of that space. They would perhaps be the worst of all Innsmouth types – something one would not care to remember.

The stench waxed overpowering, and the noises swelled to a bestial babel of croaking, baying, and barking without the least suggestion of human speech. Were these indeed the voices of my pursuers? Did they have dogs after all? So far I had seen none of the lower animals in Innsmouth. That flopping or pattering was monstrous – I could not look upon the degenerate creatures responsible for it. I would keep my eyes shut till the sounds receded toward the west. The horde was very close now – the air foul with their hoarse snarlings, and the ground almost shaking with their alien-rhythmed footfalls. My breath nearly ceased to come, and I put every ounce of will power into the task of holding my eyelids down.

I am not even yet willing to say whether what followed was a hideous actuality or only a nightmare hallucination. The later action of the government, after my frantic appeals, would tend to confirm it as a monstrous truth; but could not an hallucination have been repeated under the quasi-hypnotic spell of that ancient, haunted, and shadowed town? Such places have strange properties, and the legacy of insane legend might well have acted on more than one human imagination amidst those dead, stench-cursed streets and huddles of rotting roofs and crumbling steeples. Is it not possible that the germ of an actual contagious madness lurks in the depths of that shadow over Innsmouth? Who can be sure of reality after hearing things like the tale of old Zadok Allen? The government men never found poor Zadok, and have no conjectures to make as to what became of him. Where does madness leave off and reality begin? Is it possible that even my latest fear is sheer delusion?

But I must try to tell what I thought I saw that night under the mocking yellow moon – saw surging and hopping down the Rowley road in plain sight in front of me as I crouched among the wild brambles of that desolate railway cut. Of course my resolution to keep my eyes shut had failed. It was foredoomed to failure – for who could crouch blindly while a legion of croaking, baying entities of unknown source flopped noisomely past, scarcely more than a hundred yards away?

I thought I was prepared for the worst, and I really ought to have been prepared considering what I had seen before. My other pursuers had been accursedly abnormal – so should I not have been ready to face a *strengthening* of the abnormal element; to look upon forms in which there was no mixture of the normal at all? I did not open my eyes until the raucous clamour came loudly from a point obviously straight ahead. Then I knew that a long section of them must be plainly in sight where the sides of the cut flattened out and the road crossed the track – and I could no longer keep myself from sampling whatever horror that leering yellow moon might have to shew.

It was the end, for whatever remains to me of life on the surface of this earth, of every vestige of mental peace and confidence in the integrity of Nature and of the human mind. Nothing that I could have imagined – nothing, even, that I could have gathered had I credited old Zadok's crazy tale in the most literal way – would be in any way comparable to the daemoniac, blasphemous reality that I saw – or believe I saw. I have tried to hint what it was in order to postpone the horror of writing it down baldly. Can it be possible that this planet has actually spawned such things; that human eyes have truly seen, as objective flesh, what man has hitherto known only in febrile phantasy and tenuous legend?

And yet I saw them in a limitless stream – flopping, hopping, croaking, bleating – surging inhumanly through the spectral moonlight in a grotesque, malignant saraband of fantastic nightmare. And some of them had tall tiaras of that nameless whitish-gold metal . . . and some were strangely robed . . . and one, who led the way, was clad in a ghoulishly humped black coat and striped trousers, and had a man's felt hat perched on the shapeless thing that answered for a head . . .

I think their predominant colour was a greyish-green, though they had white bellies. They were mostly shiny and slippery, but the ridges of their backs were scaly. Their forms vaguely suggested the anthropoid, while their heads were the heads of fish, with prodigious bulging eyes that never closed. At the sides of their necks were palpitating gills, and their long paws were webbed. They hopped irregularly, sometimes on two legs and sometimes on four. I was somehow glad that they had no more than four limbs. Their croaking, baying voices, clearly used for articulate speech, held all the dark shades of expression which their staring faces lacked.

But for all of their monstrousness they were not unfamiliar to me. I knew too well what they must be – for was not the memory of that evil tiara at Newburyport still fresh? They were the blasphemous fish-frogs of the nameless design – living and horrible – and as I saw them I knew also of what that humped, tiaraed priest in the black church basement had so fearsomely reminded me. Their number was past guessing. It seemed to me that there were limitless swarms of them – and certainly my momentary glimpse could have shewn only the least fraction. In another instant everything was blotted out by a merciful fit of fainting; the first I had ever had.

5

It was a gentle daylight rain that awaked me from my stupor in the brush-grown railway cut, and when I staggered out to the roadway ahead I saw no trace of any prints in the fresh mud. The fishy odour, too, was gone. Innsmouth's ruined roofs and toppling steeples loomed up greyly toward the southeast, but not a living creature did I spy in all the desolate salt marshes around. My watch was still going, and told me that the hour was past noon.

The reality of what I had been through was highly uncertain in my mind, but I felt that something hideous lay in the background. I must get away from evil-shadowed Innsmouth – and accordingly I began to test my cramped, wearied powers of locomotion. Despite weakness, hunger, horror, and bewilderment I found myself after a long time able to walk; so started slowly along the muddy road to Rowley. Before evening I was in the village, getting a meal and providing myself with presentable clothes. I caught the night train to Arkham, and the next day talked long and earnestly with government officials there; a process I later repeated in Boston. With the main result of these colloquies the public is now familiar – and I wish, for normality's sake, there were nothing more to tell. Perhaps it is madness that is overtaking me – yet perhaps a greater horror – or a greater marvel – is reaching out.

As may well be imagined, I gave up most of the foreplanned features of the rest of my tour – the scenic, architectural, and antiquarian diversions on which I had counted so heavily. Nor did I dare look for that piece of strange jewellery said to be in the Miskatonic University Museum. I did, however, improve my stay in Arkham by collecting some genealogical notes I had long wished to possess; very rough and hasty data, it is true, but capable of good use later on when I might have time to collate and codify them. The curator of the historical society there – Mr E. Lapham Peabody – was very courteous about assisting me, and expressed unusual interest when I told him I was a grandson of Eliza Orne of Arkham, who was born in 1867 and had married James Williamson of Ohio at the age of seventeen.

It seemed that a maternal uncle of mine had been there many years before on a quest much like my own; and that my grandmother's family was a topic of some local curiosity. There had, Mr Peabody said, been considerable discussion about the marriage of her father, Benjamin Orne, just after the Civil War, since the ancestry of the bride was peculiarly puzzling. That bride was understood to have been an orphaned Marsh of New Hampshire – a cousin of the Essex County Marshes – but her education had been in France and she knew very little of her family. A guardian had deposited funds in a Boston bank to maintain her and her French governess; but that guardian's name was unfamiliar to Arkham people, and in time he dropped out of sight, so that the governess assumed his role by court appointment. The Frenchwoman – now long dead – was very taciturn, and there were those who said she could have told more than she did.

But the most baffling thing was the inability of anyone to place the recorded parents of the young woman – Enoch and Lydia (Meserve) Marsh – among the known families of New Hampshire. Possibly, many suggested, she was the natural daughter of some Marsh of prominence – she certainly had the true Marsh eyes. Most of the puzzling was done after her early death, which took place at the birth of my grandmother – her only child. Having formed some disagreeable impressions connected with the name of Marsh, I did not welcome the news that it belonged on my own ancestral tree; nor was I pleased by Mr Peabody's suggestion that I had the true Marsh eyes myself. However, I was grateful for data which I knew would prove valuable; and took copious notes and lists of book references regarding the well-documented Orne family.

I went directly home to Toledo from Boston, and later spent a month at Maumee recuperating from my ordeal. In September I entered Oberlin for my final year, and from then till the next June was busy with studies and other wholesome activities – reminded of the bygone terror only by occasional official visits from government men in connexion with the campaign which my pleas and evidence had started. Around the middle of July – just a year after the Innsmouth experience – I spent a week with my late mother's family in Cleveland, checking some of my new genealogical data with the various notes, traditions, and bits of heirloom material in existence there, and seeing what kind of connected chart I could construct.

I did not exactly relish the task, for the atmosphere of the Williamson home had always depressed me. There was a strain of morbidity there, and my mother had never encouraged my visiting her parents as a child, although she always welcomed her father when he came to Toledo. My Arkham-born grandmother had seemed strange and almost terrifying to me, and I do not think I grieved when she disappeared. I was eight years old then, and it was said that she had wandered off in grief after the suicide of my uncle Douglas, her eldest son. He had shot himself after a trip to New England – the same trip, no doubt, which had caused him to be recalled at the Arkham Historical Society.

This uncle had resembled her, and I had never liked him either. Something about the staring, unwinking expression of both of them had given me a vague, unaccountable uneasiness. My mother and uncle Walter had not looked like that. They were like their father, though poor little cousin Lawrence – Walter's son – had been an almost perfect duplicate of his grandmother before his condition took him to the permanent seclusion of a sanitarium at Canton. I had not seen him in four years, but my uncle once implied that his state, both mental and physical, was very bad. This worry had probably been a major cause of his mother's death two years before.

My grandfather and his widowed son Walter now comprised the Cleveland household, but the memory of older times hung thickly over it. I still disliked the place, and tried to get my researches done as quickly as possible. Williamson records and traditions were supplied in abundance by my grandfather, though for Orne material I had to depend on my uncle Walter, who put at my disposal the contents of all his files, including notes, letters, cuttings, heirlooms, photographs, and miniatures.

It was in going over the letters and pictures on the Orne side that I began to acquire a kind of terror of my own ancestry. As I have said, my grandmother and uncle Douglas had always disturbed me. Now, years after their passing, I gazed at their pictured faces with a measurably heightened feeling of repulsion and alienation. I could not at first understand the change, but gradually a horrible sort of *comparison* began to obtrude itself on my unconscious mind despite the steady refusal of my consciousness to admit even the least suspicion of it. It was clear that the typical expression of these faces now suggested something it had not suggested before – something which would bring stark panic if too openly thought of.

But the worst shock came when my uncle shewed me the Orne jewellery in a downtown safe-deposit vault. Some of the items were delicate and inspiring enough, but there was one box of strange old pieces descended from my mysterious great-grandmother which my uncle was almost reluctant to produce. They were, he said, of very grotesque and almost repulsive design, and had never to his knowledge been publicly worn, though my grandmother used to enjoy looking at them. Vague legends of bad luck clustered around them, and my great-grandmother's French governess had said they ought not to be worn in New England, though it would be quite safe to wear them in Europe.

As my uncle began slowly and grudgingly to unwrap the things he urged me not to be shocked by the strangeness and frequent hideousness of the designs. Artists and archaeologists who had seen them pronounced the workmanship superlatively and exotically ex-quisite, though no one seemed able to define their exact material or assign them to any specific art tradition. There were two armlets, a tiara, and a kind of pectoral; the latter having in high relief certain figures of almost unbearable extravagance.

During this description I had kept a tight rein on my emotions, but my face must have betrayed my mounting fears. My uncle looked concerned, and paused in his unwrapping to study my countenance. I motioned to him to continue, which he did with renewed signs of reluctance. He seemed to expect some demonstration when the first piece – the tiara – became visible, but I doubt if he expected quite what actually happened. I did not expect it, either, for I thought I was thoroughly forewarned regarding what the jewellery would turn out to be. What I did was to faint silently away, just as I had done in that brier-choked railway cut a year before.

From that day on my life has been a nightmare of brooding and apprehension, nor do I know how much is hideous truth and how much madness. My great-grandmother had been a Marsh of unknown source whose husband lived in Arkham – and did not old Zadok say that the daughter of Obed Marsh by a monstrous mother was married to an Arkham man through a trick? What was it the ancient toper had muttered about the likeness of my eyes to Captain Obed's? In Arkham, too, the curator had told me I had the true Marsh eyes. Was Obed Marsh my own great-great-grandfather? Who – or *what* – then, was my great-great-grandmother? But perhaps this was all madness. Those whitish-gold ornaments might easily have been bought from some Innsmouth sailor by the father of my great-grandmother, whoever he was. And that look in the staring-eyed faces of my grand-mother and self-slain uncle might be sheer fancy on my part – sheer fancy, bolstered up by the Innsmouth shadow which had so darkly coloured my imagination. But why had my uncle killed himself after an ancestral quest in New England?

For more than two years I fought off these reflections with partial success. My father secured me a place in an insurance office, and I buried myself in routine as deeply as possible. In the winter of 1930–31, however, the dreams began. They were very sparse and insidious at first, but increased in frequency and vividness as the weeks went by. Great watery spaces opened out before me, and I seemed to wander through titanic sunken porticos and labyrinths of weedy Cyclopean walls with grotesque fishes as my companions. Then the *other shapes* began to appear, filling me with nameless horror the moment I awoke. But during the dreams they did not horrify me at all – I was one with them, wearing their unhuman trappings, treading their aqueous ways, and praying monstrously at their evil sea-bottom temples.

There was much more than I could remember, but even what I did remember each morning would be enough to stamp me as a madman or a genius if ever I dared write it down. Some frightful influence, I felt, was seeking gradually to drag me out of the sane world of wholesome life into unnamable abysses of blackness and alienage; and the process told heavily on me. My health and appearance grew steadily worse, till finally I was forced to give up my position and adopt the static, secluded life of an invalid. Some odd nervous affliction had me in its grip, and I found myself at times almost unable to shut my eyes.

It was then that I began to study the mirror with mounting alarm. The slow ravages of disease are not pleasant to watch, but in my case there was something subtler and more puzzling in the background. My father seemed to notice it, too, for he began looking at me curiously and almost affrightedly. What was taking place in me? Could it be that I was coming to resemble my grandmother and uncle Douglas?

One night I had a frightful dream in which I met my grandmother under the sea. She lived in a phosphorescent palace of many terraces, with gardens of strange leprous corals and grotesque brachiate efflorescences, and welcomed me with a warmth that may have been sardonic. She had changed – as those who take to the water change – and told me she had never died. Instead, she had gone to a spot her dead son had learned about, and had leaped to a realm whose wonders – destined for him as well – he had spurned with a smoking pistol. This was to be my realm, too – I could not escape it. I would never die, but would live with those who had lived since before man ever walked the earth.

I met also that which had been her grandmother. For eighty thousand years Pth'thya-l'yi had lived in Y'ha-nthlei, and thither she had gone back after Obed Marsh was dead. Y'ha-nthlei was not destroyed when the upper-earth men shot death into the sea. It was hurt, but not destroyed. The Deep Ones could never be destroyed, even though the palaeogean magic of the forgotten Old Ones might sometimes check them. For the present they would rest; but some day, if they remembered, they would rise again for the tribute Great Cthulhu craved. It would be a city greater than Innsmouth next time. They had planned to spread, and had brought up that which would help them, but now they must wait once more. For bringing the upper-earth men's death I must do a penance, but that would not be heavy. This was the dream in which I saw a *shoggoth* for the first time, and the sight set me awake in a frenzy of screaming. That morning the mirror definitely told me I had acquired *the Innsmouth look*.

So far I have not shot myself as my uncle Douglas did. I bought an automatic and almost took the step, but certain dreams deterred me. The tense extremes of horror are lessening, and I feel queerly drawn toward the unknown sea-deeps instead of fearing them. I hear and do strange things in sleep, and awake with a kind of exaltation instead of terror. I do not believe I need to wait for the full change as most have waited. If I did, my father would probably shut me up in a sanitarium as my poor little cousin is shut up. Stupendous and unheard-of splendours await me below, and I shall seek them soon. *Iä-R'lyeh! Cthulhu fhtagn! Iä! Iä!* No, I shall not shoot myself – I cannot be made to shoot myself!

I shall plan my cousin's escape from that Canton madhouse, and together we shall go to marvel-shadowed Innsmouth. We shall swim out to that brooding reef in the sea and dive down through black abysses to Cyclopean and many-columned Y'ha-nthlei, and in that lair of the Deep Ones we shall dwell amidst wonder and glory for ever.

The Dreams in the Witch House

Whether the dreams brought on the fever or the fever brought on the dreams Walter Gilman did not know. Behind everything crouched the brooding, festering horror of the ancient town, and of the mouldy, unhallowed garret gable where he wrote and studied and wrestled with figures and formulae when he was not tossing on the meagre iron bed. His ears were growing sensitive to a preternatural and intolerable degree, and he had long ago stopped the cheap mantel clock whose ticking had come to seem like a thunder of artillery. At night the subtle stirring of the black city outside, the sinister scurrying of rats in the wormy partitions, and the creaking of hidden timbers in the centuried house, were enough to give him a sense of strident pandemonium. The darkness always teemed with unexplained sound – and yet he sometimes shook with fear lest the noises he heard should subside and allow him to hear certain other, fainter, noises which he suspected were lurking behind them.

He was in the changeless, legend-haunted city of Arkham, with its clustering gambrel roofs that sway and sag over attics where witches hid from the King's men in the dark, olden days of the Province. Nor was any spot in that city more steeped in macabre memory than the gable room which harboured him – for it was this house and this room which had likewise harboured old Keziah Mason, whose flight from Salem Gaol at the last no one was ever able to explain. That was in 1692 – the gaoler had gone mad and babbled of a small, white-fanged furry thing which scuttled out of Keziah's cell, and not even Cotton Mather could explain the curves and angles smeared on the grey stone walls with some red, sticky fluid.

Possibly Gilman ought not to have studied so hard. Non-Euclidean calculus and quantum physics are enough to stretch any brain; and when one mixes them with folklore, and tries to trace a strange background of multi-dimensional reality behind the ghoulish hints of the Gothic tales and the wild whispers of the chimney-corner, one can hardly expect to be wholly free from mental tension. Gilman came from Haverhill, but it was only after he had entered college in Arkham that he began to connect his mathematics with the fantastic legends of elder magic. Something in the air of the hoary town worked obscurely on his imagination. The professors at Miskatonic had urged him to slacken up, and had voluntarily cut down his course at several points. Moreover, they had stopped him from consulting the dubious old books on forbidden secrets that were kept under lock and key in a vault at the university library. But all these precautions came late in the day, so that Gilman had some terrible hints from the dreaded *Necronomicon* of Abdul Alhazred, the fragmentary *Book of Eibon,* and the suppressed *Unaussprechlichen Kulten* of von Junzt to correlate with his abstract formulae on the properties of space and the linkage of dimensions known and unknown.

He knew his room was in the old Witch House – that, indeed, was why he had taken it. There was much in the Essex County records about Keziah Mason's trial, and what she had admitted under pressure to the Court of Oyer and Terminer had fascinated Gilman beyond all reason. She had told Judge Hathorne of lines and curves that could be made to point out directions leading through the walls of space to other spaces beyond, and had implied that such lines and curves were frequently used at certain midnight meetings in the dark valley of the white stone beyond Meadow Hill and on the unpeopled island in the river. She had spoken also of the Black Man, of her oath, and of her new secret name of Nahab. Then she had drawn those devices on the walls of her cell and vanished.

Gilman believed strange things about Keziah, and had felt a queer thrill on learning that her dwelling was still standing after more than 235 years. When he heard the hushed Arkham whispers about Keziah's persistent presence in the old house and the narrow streets, about the irregular human tooth-marks left on certain sleepers in that and other houses, about the childish cries heard near May-Eve, and Hallowmass, about the stench often noted in the old house's attic just after those dreaded seasons, and about the small, furry, sharp-toothed thing which haunted the mouldering structure and the town and nuzzled people curiously in the black hours before dawn, he resolved to live in the place at any cost. A room was easy to secure, for the house was unpopular, hard to rent, and long given over to cheap lodgings. Gilman could not have told what he expected to find there, but he knew he wanted to be in the building where some circumstance had more or less suddenly given a mediocre old woman of the seventeenth century an insight into mathematical depths perhaps beyond the utmost modern delvings of Planck, Heisenberg, Einstein, and de Sitter.

He studied the timber and plaster walls for traces of cryptic designs at every accessible spot where the paper had peeled, and within a week managed to get the eastern attic room where Keziah was held to have practiced her spells. It had been vacant from the first – for no one had ever been willing to stay there long – but the Polish landlord had grown wary about renting it. Yet nothing whatever happened to Gilman till about the time of the fever. No ghostly Keziah flitted through the sombre halls and chambers, no small furry thing crept into his dismal eyrie to nuzzle him, and no record of the witch's incantations rewarded his constant search. Sometimes he would take walks through shadowy tangles of unpaved musty-smelling lanes where eldritch brown houses of unknown age leaned and tottered and leered mockingly through narrow, small-paned windows. Here he knew strange things had happened once, and there was a faint suggestion behind the surface that everything of that monstrous past might not – at least in the darkest, narrowest, and most intricately crooked alleys – have utterly perished. He also rowed out twice to the ill-regarded island in the river, and made a sketch of the singular angles described by the moss-grown rows of grey standing stones whose origin was so obscure and immemorial.

Gilman's room was of good size but queerly irregular shape, the north wall slanting perceptibly inward from the outer to the inner end, while the low ceiling slanted gently downward in the same direction. Aside from an obvious rat-hole and the signs of other stopped-up ones, there was no access – nor any appearance of a former avenue of access – to the space which must have existed between the slanting wall and the straight outer wall on the house's north side, though a view from the exterior shewed where a window had been boarded up at a very remote date. The loft above the ceiling – which must have had a slanting floor – was likewise inaccessible. When Gilman climbed up a ladder to the cobwebbed level loft above the rest of the attic he found vestiges of a bygone aperture tightly and heavily covered with ancient planking and secured by the stout wooden pegs common in colonial carpentry. No amount of persuasion, however, could induce the stolid landlord to let him investigate either of these two closed spaces.

As time wore along, his absorption in the irregular wall and ceiling of his room increased; for he began to read into the odd angles a mathematical significance which seemed to offer vague clues regarding their purpose. Old Keziah, he reflected, might have had excellent reasons for living in a room with peculiar angles; for was it not through certain angles that she claimed to have gone outside the boundaries of the world of space we know? His interest gradually veered away from the unplumbed voids beyond the slanting surfaces, since it now appeared that the purpose of those surfaces concerned the side he was already on.

The touch of brain-fever and the dreams began early in February. For some time, apparently, the curious angles of Gilman's room had been having a strange, almost hypnotic effect on him; and as the bleak winter advanced he had found himself staring more and more intently at the corner where the down-slanting ceiling met the inward-slanting wall. About this period his inability to concentrate on his formal studies worried him considerably, his apprehensions about the mid-year examinations being very acute. But the exaggerated sense of hearing was scarcely less annoying. Life had become an insistent and almost unendurable cacophony, and there was that constant, terrifying impression of *other* sounds – perhaps from regions beyond life – trembling on the very brink of audibility. So far as concrete noises went, the rats in the ancient partitions were the worst. Sometimes their scratching seemed not only furtive but deliberate. When it came from beyond the slanting north wall it was mixed with a sort of dry rattling – and when it came from the century-closed loft above the slanting ceiling Gilman always braced himself as if expecting some horror which only bided its time before descending to engulf him utterly.

The dreams were wholly beyond the pale of sanity, and Gilman felt that they must be a result, jointly, of his studies in mathematics and in folklore. He had been thinking too much about the vague regions which his formulae told him must lie beyond the three dimensions we know, and about the possibility that old Keziah Mason – guided by some influence past all conjecture – had actually found the gate to those regions. The yellowed county records containing her testimony and that of her accusers were so damnably suggestive of things beyond human experience – and the descriptions of the darting little furry object which served as her familiar were so painfully realistic despite their incredible details.

That object – no larger than a good-sized rat and quaintly called by the townspeople 'Brown Jenkin' – seemed to have been the fruit of a remarkable case of sympathetic herd-delusion, for in 1692 no less than eleven persons had testified to glimpsing it. There were recent rumours, too, with a baffling and disconcerting amount of agreement. Witnesses said it had long hair and the shape of a rat, but that its sharp-toothed, bearded face was evilly human while its paws were like tiny human hands. It took messages betwixt old Keziah and the devil, and was nursed on the witch's blood – which it sucked like a vampire. Its voice was a kind of loathsome titter, and it could speak all languages. Of all the bizarre monstrosities in Gilman's dreams, nothing filled him with greater panic and nausea than this blasphemous and diminutive hybrid, whose image flitted across his vision in a form a thousandfold more hateful than anything his waking mind had deduced from the ancient records and the modern whispers.

Gilman's dreams consisted largely in plunges through limitless abysses of inexplicably coloured twilight and bafflingly disordered sound; abysses whose material and gravitational properties, and whose relation to his own entity, he could not even begin to explain. He did not walk or climb, fly or swim, crawl or wriggle; yet always experienced a mode of motion partly voluntary and partly involuntary. Of his own condition he could not well judge, for sight of his arms, legs, and torso seemed always cut off by some odd disarrangement of perspective; but he felt that his physical organisation and faculties were somehow marvellously transmuted and obliquely projected – though not without a certain grotesque relationship to his normal proportions and properties.

The abysses were by no means vacant, being crowded with indescribably angled masses of alien-hued substance, some of which appeared to be organic while others seemed inorganic. A few of the organic objects tended to awake vague memories in the back of his mind, though he could form no conscious idea of what they mockingly resembled or suggested. In the later dreams he began to distinguish separate categories into which the organic objects appeared to be divided, and which seemed to involve in each case a radically different species of conduct-pattern and basic motivation. Of these categories one seemed to him to include objects slightly less illogical and irrelevant in their motions than the members of the other categories.

All the objects – organic and inorganic alike – were totally beyond description or even comprehension. Gilman sometimes compared the inorganic masses to prisms, labyrinths, clusters of cubes and planes, and Cyclopean buildings; and the organic things struck him variously as groups of bubbles, octopi, centipedes, living Hindoo idols, and intricate Arabesques roused into a kind of ophidian anim-ation. Everything he saw was unspeakably menacing and horrible; and whenever one of the organic entities appeared by its motions to be noticing him, he felt a stark, hideous fright which generally jolted him awake. Of how the organic entities moved, he could tell no more than of how he moved himself. In time he observed a further mystery – the tendency of certain entities to appear suddenly out of empty space, or to disappear totally with equal suddenness. The shrieking, roaring confusion of sound which permeated the abysses was past all analysis as to pitch, timbre, or rhythm, but seemed to be synchronous with vague visual changes in all the indefinite objects, organic and inorganic alike. Gilman had a constant sense of dread that it might rise to some unbearable degree of intensity during one or another of its obscure, relentlessly inevitable fluctuations.

But it was not in these vortices of complete alienage that he saw Brown Jenkin. That shocking little horror was reserved for certain lighter, sharper dreams which assailed him just before he dropped into the fullest depths of sleep. He would be lying in the dark fighting to keep awake when a faint lambent glow would seem to shimmer around the centuried room, shewing in a violet mist the convergence of angled planes which had seized his brain so insidiously. The horror would appear to pop out of the rat-hole in the corner and patter toward him over the sagging, wide-planked floor with evil expectancy in its tiny, bearded human face – but mercifully, this dream always melted away before the object got close enough to nuzzle him. It had hellishly long, sharp, canine teeth. Gilman tried to stop up the rat-hole every day, but each night the real tenants of the partitions would gnaw away the obstruction, whatever it might be. Once he had the landlord nail tin over it, but the next night the rats gnawed a fresh hole – in making which they pushed or dragged out into the room a curious little fragment of bone.

Gilman did not report his fever to the doctor, for he knew he could not pass the examinations if ordered to the college infirmary when every moment was needed for cramming. As it was, he failed in Calculus D and Advanced General Psychology, though not without hope of making up lost ground before the end of the term. It was in March when the fresh element entered his lighter preliminary dreaming, and the nightmare shape of Brown Jenkin began to be companioned by the nebulous blur which grew more and more to resemble a bent old woman. This addition disturbed him more than he could account for, but finally he decided that it was like an ancient crone whom he had twice actually encountered in the dark tangle of lanes near the abandoned wharves. On those occasions the evil, sardonic, and seemingly unmotivated stare of the beldame had set him almost shivering – especially the first time, when an overgrown rat darting across the shadowed mouth of a neighbouring alley had made him think irrationally of Brown Jenkin. Now, he reflected, those nervous fears were being mirrored in his disordered dreams.

That the influence of the old house was unwholesome, he could not deny; but traces of his early morbid interest still held him there. He argued that the fever alone was responsible for his nightly phantasies, and that when the touch abated he would be free from the monstrous visions. Those visions, however, were of abhorrent vividness and convincingness, and whenever he awaked he retained a vague sense of having undergone much more than he remembered. He was hideously sure that in unrecalled dreams he had talked with both Brown Jenkin and the old woman, and that they had been urging him to go somewhere with them and to meet a third being of greater potency.

Toward the end of March he began to pick up in his mathematics, though other studies bothered him increasingly. He was getting an intuitive knack for solving Riemannian equations, and astonished

Professor Upham by his comprehension of fourth-dimensional and other problems which had floored all the rest of the class. One afternoon there was a discussion of possible freakish curvatures in space, and of theoretical points of approach or even contact between our part of the cosmos and various other regions as distant as the farthest stars or the trans-galactic gulfs themselves – or even as fabulously remote as the tentatively conceivable cosmic units beyond the whole Einsteinian space-time continuum. Gilman's handling of this theme filled everyone with admiration, even though some of his hypothetical illustrations caused an increase in the always plentiful gossip about his nervous and solitary eccentricity. What made the students shake their heads was his sober theory that a man might – given mathematical knowledge admittedly beyond all likelihood of human acquirement – step deliberately from the earth to any other celestial body which might lie at one of an infinity of specific points in the cosmic pattern.

Such a step, he said, would require only two stages; first, a passage out of the three-dimensional sphere we know, and second, a passage back to the three-dimensional sphere at another point, perhaps one of infinite remoteness. That this could be accomplished without loss of life was in many cases conceivable. Any being from any part of three-dimensional space could probably survive in the fourth dimension; and its survival of the second stage would depend upon what alien part of three-dimensional space it might select for its re-entry. Denizens of some planets might be able to live on certain others – even planets belonging to other galaxies, or to similar-dimensional phases of other space-time continua – though of course there must be vast numbers of mutually uninhabitable even though mathematically juxtaposed bodies or zones of space.

It was also possible that the inhabitants of a given dimensional realm could survive entry to many unknown and incomprehensible realms of additional or indefinitely multiplied dimensions – be they within or outside the given space-time continuum – and that the converse would be likewise true. This was a matter for speculation, though one could be fairly certain that the type of mutation involved in a passage from any given dimensional plane to the next higher plane would not be destructive of biological integrity as we under-stand it. Gilman could not be very clear about his reasons for this last assumption, but his haziness here was more than overbalanced by his clearness on other complex points. Professor Upham especially liked his demonstration of the kinship of higher mathematics to certain phases of magical lore transmitted down the ages from an ineffable antiquity – human or pre-human – whose knowledge of the cosmos and its laws was greater than ours.

Around the first of April Gilman worried considerably because his slow fever did not abate. He was also troubled by what some of his fellow-lodgers said about his sleep-walking. It seemed that he was often absent from his bed, and that the creaking of his floor at certain hours of the night was remarked by the man in the room below. This fellow also spoke of hearing the tread of shod feet in the night; but Gilman was sure he must have been mistaken in this, since shoes as well as other apparel were always precisely in place in the morning. One could develop all sorts of aural delusions in this morbid old house – for did not Gilman himself, even in daylight, now feel certain that noises other than rat-scratchings came from the black voids beyond the slanting wall and above the slanting ceiling? His pathologically sensitive ears began to listen for faint footfalls in the immemorially sealed loft overhead, and sometimes the illusion of such things was agonisingly realistic.

However, he knew that he had actually become a somnambulist; for twice at night his room had been found vacant, though with all his clothing in place. Of this he had been assured by Frank Elwood, the one fellow-student whose poverty forced him to room in this squalid and unpopular house. Elwood had been studying in the small hours and had come up for help on a differential equation, only to find Gilman absent. It had been rather presumptuous of him to open the unlocked door after knocking had failed to rouse a response, but he had needed the help very badly and thought that his host would not mind a gentle prodding awake. On neither occasion, though, had Gilman been there – and when told of the matter he wondered where he could have been wandering, barefoot and with only his night-clothes on. He resolved to investigate the matter if reports of his sleep-walking continued, and thought of sprinkling flour on the floor of the corridor to see where his footsteps might lead. The door was the only conceivable egress, for there was no possible foothold outside the narrow window.

As April advanced Gilman's fever-sharpened ears were disturbed by the whining prayers of a superstitious loom-fixer named Joe Mazurewicz, who had a room on the ground floor. Mazurewicz had told long, rambling stories about the ghost of old Keziah and the furry, sharp-fanged, nuzzling thing, and had said he was so badly haunted at times that only his silver crucifix – given him for the purpose by Father Iwanicki of St Stanislaus' Church – could bring him relief. Now he was praying because the Witches' Sabbath was drawing near. May-Eve was Walpurgis-Night, when hell's blackest evil roamed the earth and all the slaves of Satan gathered for nameless rites and deeds. It was always a very bad time in Arkham, even though the fine folks up in Miskatonic Avenue and High and Saltonstall Streets pretended to know nothing about it. There would be bad doings – and a child or two would probably be missing. Joe knew about such things, for his grandmother in the old country had heard tales from her grandmother. It was wise to pray and count one's beads at this season. For three months Keziah and Brown Jenkin had not been near Joe's room, nor near Paul Choynski's room, nor anywhere else – and it meant no good when they held off like that. They must be up to something.

Gilman dropped in at a doctor's office on the 16th of the month, and was surprised to find his temperature was not as high as he had feared. The physician questioned him sharply, and advised him to see a nerve specialist. On reflection, he was glad he had not consulted the still more inquisitive college doctor. Old Waldron, who had curtailed his activities before, would have made him take a rest – an impossible thing now that he was so close to great results in his equations. He was certainly near the boundary between the known universe and the fourth dimension, and who could say how much farther he might go?

But even as these thoughts came to him he wondered at the source of his strange confidence. Did all of this perilous sense of imminence come from the formulae on the sheets he covered day by day? The soft, stealthy, imaginary footsteps in the sealed loft above were unnerving. And now, too, there was a growing feeling that somebody was constantly persuading him to do something terrible which he could not do. How about the somnambulism? Where did he go sometimes in the night? And what was that faint suggestion of sound which once in a while seemed to trickle through the maddening confusion of identifiable sounds even in broad daylight and full wakefulness? Its rhythm did not correspond to anything on earth, unless perhaps to the cadence of one or two unmentionable Sabbat-chants, and sometimes he feared it corresponded to certain attributes of the vague shrieking or roaring in those wholly alien abysses of dream.

The dreams were meanwhile getting to be atrocious. In the lighter preliminary phase the evil old woman was now of fiendish distinctness, and Gilman knew she was the one who had frightened him in the slums. Her bent back, long nose, and shrivelled chin were unmistakable, and her shapeless brown garments were like those he remembered. The expression on her face was one of hideous malevolence and exultation, and when he awaked he could recall a croaking voice that persuaded and threatened. He must meet the Black Man, and go with them all to the throne of Azathoth at the centre of ultimate Chaos. That was what she said. He must sign in his own blood the book of Azathoth and take a new secret name now that his independent delvings had gone so far. What kept him from going with her and Brown Jenkin and the other to the throne of Chaos where the thin flutes pipe mindlessly was the fact that he had seen the name 'Azathoth' in the *Necronomicon*, and knew it stood for a primal evil too horrible for description.

The old woman always appeared out of thin air near the corner where the downward slant met the inward slant. She seemed to crystallise at a point closer to the ceiling than to the floor, and every night she was a little nearer and more distinct before the dream shifted. Brown Jenkin, too, was always a little nearer at the last, and its yellowish-white fangs glistened shockingly in that unearthly violet phosphorescence. Its shrill loathsome tittering stuck more and more in Gilman's head, and he could remember in the morning how it had pronounced the words 'Azathoth' and 'Nyarlathotep'.

In the deeper dreams everything was likewise more distinct, and Gilman felt that the twilight abysses around him were those of the fourth dimension. Those organic entities whose motions seemed least flagrantly irrelevant and unmotivated were probably projections of life-forms from our own planet, including human beings. What the others were in their own dimensional sphere or spheres he dared not try to think. Two of the less irrelevantly moving things – a rather large congeries of iridescent, prolately spheroidal bubbles and a very much smaller polyhedron of unknown colours and rapidly shifting surface angles – seemed to take notice of him and follow him about or float ahead as he changed position among the titan prisms, labyrinths, cube-and-plane clusters, and quasi-buildings; and all the while the vague shrieking and roaring waxed louder and louder, as if approaching some monstrous climax of utterly unendurable intensity.

During the night of April 19–20 the new development occurred. Gilman was half-involuntarily moving about in the twilight abysses with the bubble-mass and the small polyhedron floating ahead, when he noticed the peculiarly regular angles formed by the edges of some gigantic neighbouring prism-clusters. In another second he was out of the abyss and standing tremulously on a rocky hillside bathed in intense, diffused green light. He was barefooted and in his night-clothes, and when he tried to walk discovered that he could scarcely lift his feet. A swirling vapour hid everything but the immediate sloping terrain from sight, and he shrank from the thought of the sounds that might surge out of that vapour.

Then he saw the two shapes laboriously crawling toward him – the old woman and the little furry thing. The crone strained up to her knees and managed to cross her arms in a singular fashion, while Brown Jenkin pointed in a certain direction with a horribly anthropoid fore paw which it raised with evident difficulty. Spurred by an impulse he did not originate, Gilman dragged himself forward along a course determined by the angle of the old woman's arms and the direction of the small monstrosity's paw, and before he had shuffled three steps he was back in the twilight abysses. Geometrical shapes seethed around him, and he fell dizzily and interminably. At last he woke in his bed in the crazily angled garret of the eldritch old house.

He was good for nothing that morning, and stayed away from all his classes. Some unknown attraction was pulling his eyes in a seemingly irrelevant direction, for he could not help staring at a certain vacant spot on the floor. As the day advanced the focus of his unseeing eyes changed position, and by noon he had conquered the impulse to stare at vacancy. About two o'clock he went out for lunch, and as he threaded the narrow lanes of the city he found himself turning always to the southeast. Only an effort halted him at a cafeteria in Church Street, and after the meal he felt the unknown pull still more strongly.

He would have to consult a nerve specialist after all – perhaps there was a connexion with his somnambulism – but meanwhile he might at least try to break the morbid spell himself. Undoubtedly he could still manage to walk away from the pull; so with great resolution he headed against it and dragged himself deliberately north along Garrison Street. By the time he had reached the bridge over the Miskatonic he was in a cold perspiration, and he clutched at the iron railing as he gazed upstream at the ill-regarded island whose regular lines of ancient standing stones brooded sullenly in the afternoon sunlight.

Then he gave a start. For there was a clearly visible living figure on that desolate island, and a second glance told him it was certainly the strange old woman whose sinister aspect had worked itself so disastrously into his dreams. The tall grass near her was moving, too, as if some other living thing were crawling close to the ground. When the old woman began to turn toward him he fled precipitately off the bridge and into the shelter of the town's labyrinthine waterfront alleys. Distant though the island was, he felt that a monstrous and invincible evil could flow from the sardonic stare of that bent, ancient figure in brown.

The southeastward pull still held, and only with tremendous resolution could Gilman drag himself into the old house and up the rickety stairs. For hours he sat silent and aimless, with his eyes shifting gradually westward. About six o'clock his sharpened ears caught the whining prayers of Joe Mazurewicz two floors below, and in desperation he seized his hat and walked out into the sunset-golden streets, letting the now directly southward pull carry him where it might. An hour later darkness found him in the open fields beyond Hangman's Brook, with the glimmering spring stars shining ahead. The urge to walk was gradually changing to an urge to leap mystically into space, and suddenly he realised just where the source of the pull lay.

It was in the sky. A definite point among the stars had a claim on him and was calling him. Apparently it was a point somewhere between Hydra and Argo Navis, and he knew that he had been urged toward it ever since he had awaked soon after dawn. In the morning it had been underfoot; afternoon found it rising in the southeast, and now it was roughly south but wheeling toward the west. What was the meaning of this new thing? Was he going mad? How long would it last? Again mustering his resolution, Gilman turned and dragged himself back to the sinister old house.

Mazurewicz was waiting for him at the door, and seemed both anxious and reluctant to whisper some fresh bit of superstition. It was about the witch light. Joe had been out celebrating the night before – it was Patriots' Day in Massachusetts – and had come home after midnight. Looking up at the house from outside, he had thought at first that Gilman's window was dark; but then he had seen the faint violet glow within. He wanted to warn the gentleman about that glow, for everybody in Arkham knew it was Keziah's witch light which played near Brown Jenkin and the ghost of the old crone herself. He had not mentioned this before, but now he must tell about it because it meant that Keziah and her long-toothed familiar were haunting the young gentleman. Sometimes he and Paul Choynski and Landlord Dombrowski thought they saw that light seeping out of cracks in the sealed loft above the young gentleman's room, but they had all agreed not to talk about that. However, it would be better for the gentleman to take another room and get a crucifix from some good priest like Father Iwanicki.

As the man rambled on Gilman felt a nameless panic clutch at his throat. He knew that Joe must have been half drunk when he came home the night before, yet this mention of a violet light in the garret window was of frightful import. It was a lambent glow of this sort which always played about the old woman and the small furry thing in those lighter, sharper dreams which prefaced his plunge into unknown abysses, and the thought that a wakeful second person could see the dream-luminance was utterly beyond sane harbourage. Yet where had the fellow got such an odd notion? Had he himself talked as well as walked around the house in his sleep? No, Joe said, he had not – but he must check up on this. Perhaps Frank Elwood could tell him something, though he hated to ask.

Fever – wild dreams – somnambulism – illusions of sounds – a pull toward a point in the sky – and now a suspicion of insane sleep-talking! He must stop studying, see a nerve specialist, and take himself in hand. When he climbed to the second story he paused at Elwood's door but saw that the other youth was out. Reluctantly he continued up to his garret room and sat down in the dark. His gaze was still pulled to the southwest, but he also found himself listening intently for some sound in the closed loft above, and half imagining that an evil violet light seeped down through an infinitesimal crack in the low, slanting ceiling.

That night as Gilman slept the violet light broke upon him with heightened intensity, and the old witch and small furry thing – getting closer than ever before – mocked him with inhuman squeals and devilish gestures. He was glad to sink into the vaguely roaring twilight abysses, though the pursuit of that iridescent bubble-congeries and that kaleidoscopic little polyhedron was menacing and irritating. Then came the shift as vast converging planes of a slippery-looking substance loomed above and below him – a shift which ended in a flash of delirium and a blaze of unknown, alien light in which yellow, carmine, and indigo were madly and inextricably blended.

He was half lying on a high, fantastically balustraded terrace above a boundless jungle of outlandish, incredible peaks, balanced planes, domes, minarets, horizontal discs poised on pinnacles, and numberless forms of still greater wildness – some of stone and some of metal – which glittered gorgeously in the mixed, almost blistering glare from a polychromatic sky. Looking upward he saw three stupendous discs of flame, each of a different hue, and at a different height above an infinitely distant curving horizon of low mountains. Behind him tiers of higher terraces towered aloft as far as he could see. The city below stretched away to the limits of vision, and he hoped that no sound would well up from it.

The pavement from which he easily raised himself was of a veined, polished stone beyond his power to identify, and the tiles were cut in bizarre-angled shapes which struck him as less asymmetrical than based on some unearthly symmetry whose laws he could not comprehend. The balustrade was chest-high, delicate, and fantastically wrought, while along the rail were ranged at short intervals little figures of grotesque design and exquisite workmanship. They, like the whole balustrade, seemed to be made of some sort of shining metal whose colour could not be guessed in this chaos of mixed effulgences; and their nature utterly defied conjecture. They represented some ridged, barrel-shaped object with thin horizontal arms radiating spoke-like from a central ring, and with vertical knobs or bulbs projecting from the head and base of the barrel. Each of these knobs was the hub of a system of five long, flat, triangularly tapering arms arranged around it like the arms of a starfish – nearly horizontal, but curving slightly away from the central barrel. The base of the bottom knob was fused to the long railing with so delicate a point of contact that several figures had been broken off and were missing. The figures were about four and a half inches in height, while the spiky arms gave them a maximum diameter of about two and a half inches.

When Gilman stood up the tiles felt hot to his bare feet. He was wholly alone, and his first act was to walk to the balustrade and look dizzily down at the endless, Cyclopean city almost two thousand feet below. As he listened he thought a rhythmic confusion of faint musical pipings covering a wide tonal range welled up from the narrow streets beneath, and he wished he might discern the denizens of the place. The sight turned him giddy after a while, so that he would have fallen to the pavement had he not clutched instinctively at the lustrous balustrade. His right hand fell on one of the projecting figures, the touch seeming to steady him slightly. It was too much, however, for the exotic delicacy of the metal-work, and the spiky figure snapped off under his grasp. Still half-dazed, he continued to clutch it as his other hand seized a vacant space on the smooth railing.

But now his oversensitive ears caught something behind him, and he looked back across the level terrace. Approaching him softly though without apparent furtiveness were five figures, two of which were the sinister old woman and the fanged, furry little animal. The other three were what sent him unconscious – for they were living entities about eight feet high, shaped precisely like the spiky images on the balustrade, and propelling themselves by a spider-like wriggling of their lower set of starfish-arms.

Gilman awakened in his bed, drenched by a cold perspiration and with a smarting sensation in his face, hands, and feet. Springing to the floor, he washed and dressed in frantic haste, as if it were necessary for him to get out of the house as quickly as possible. He did not know where he wished to go, but felt that once more he would have to sacrifice his classes. The odd pull toward that spot in the sky between Hydra and Argo had abated, but another of even greater strength had taken its place. Now he felt that he must go north – infinitely north. He dreaded to cross the bridge that gave a view of the desolate island in the Miskatonic, so went over the Peabody Avenue bridge. Very often he stumbled, for his eyes and ears were chained to an extremely lofty point in the blank blue sky.

After about an hour he got himself under better control, and saw that he was far from the city. All around him stretched the bleak emptiness of salt marshes, while the narrow road ahead led to Innsmouth – that ancient, half-deserted town which Arkham people were so curiously unwilling to visit. Though the northward pull had not diminished, he resisted it as he had resisted the other pull, and finally found that he could almost balance the one against the other. Plodding back to town and getting some coffee at a soda fountain, he dragged himself into the public library and browsed aimlessly among the lighter magazines. Once he met some friends who remarked how oddly sunburned he looked, but he did not tell them of his walk. At three o'clock he took some lunch at a restaurant, noting meanwhile that the pull had either lessened or divided itself. After that he killed the time at a cheap cinema show, seeing the inane performance over and over again without paying any attention to it.

About nine at night he drifted homeward and stumbled into the ancient house. Joe Mazurewicz was whining unintelligible prayers, and Gilman hastened up to his own garret chamber without pausing to see if Elwood was in. It was when he turned on the feeble electric light that the shock came. At once he saw there was something on the table which did not belong there, and a second look left no room for doubt. Lying on its side – for it could not stand up alone – was the exotic spiky figure which in his monstrous dream he had broken off the fantastic balustrade. No detail was missing. The ridged, barrel-shaped centre, the thin, radiating arms, the knobs at each end, and the flat, slightly outward-curving starfish-arms spreading from those knobs – all were there. In the electric light the colour seemed to be a kind of iridescent grey veined with green, and Gilman could see amidst his horror and bewilderment that one of the knobs ended in a jagged break corresponding to its former point of attachment to the dream-railing.

Only his tendency toward a dazed stupor prevented him from screaming aloud. This fusion of dream and reality was too much to bear. Still dazed, he clutched at the spiky thing and staggered down-stairs to Landlord Dombrowski's quarters. The whining prayers of the superstitious loom-fixer were still sounding through the mouldy halls, but Gilman did not mind them now. The landlord was in, and greeted him pleasantly. No, he had not seen that thing before and did not know anything about it. But his wife had said she found a funny tin thing in one of the beds when she fixed the rooms at noon, and maybe that was it. Dombrowski called her, and she waddled in. Yes, that was the thing. She had found it in the young gentleman's bed – on the side next the wall. It had looked very queer to her, but of course the young gentleman had lots of queer things in his room – books and curios and pictures and markings on paper. She certainly knew nothing about it.

So Gilman climbed upstairs again in a mental turmoil, convinced that he was either still dreaming or that his somnambulism had run to incredible extremes and led him to depredations in unknown places. Where had he got this outré thing? He did not recall seeing it in any museum in Arkham. It must have been somewhere, though; and the sight of it as he snatched it in his sleep must have caused the odd dream-picture of the balustraded terrace. Next day he would make some very guarded inquiries – and perhaps see the nerve specialist.

Meanwhile he would try to keep track of his somnambulism. As he went upstairs and across the garret hall he sprinkled about some flour which he had borrowed – with a frank admission as to its purpose – from the landlord. He had stopped at Elwood's door on the way, but had found all dark within. Entering his room, he placed the spiky thing on the table, and lay down in complete mental and physical exhaustion without pausing to undress. From the closed loft above the slanting ceiling he thought he heard a faint scratching and padding, but he was too disorganised even to mind it. That cryptical pull from the north was getting very strong again, though it seemed now to come from a lower place in the sky.

In the dazzling violet light of dream the old woman and the fanged, furry thing came again and with a greater distinctness than on any former occasion. This time they actually reached him, and he felt the crone's withered claws clutching at him. He was pulled out of bed and into empty space, and for a moment he heard a rhythmic roaring and saw the twilight amorphousness of the vague abysses seething around him. But that moment was very brief, for presently he was in a crude, windowless little space with rough beams and planks rising to a peak just above his head, and with a curious slanting floor underfoot. Propped level on that floor were low cases full of books of every degree of antiquity and disintegration, and in the centre were a table and bench, both apparently fastened in place. Small objects of unknown shape and nature were ranged on the tops of the cases, and in the flaming violet light Gilman thought he saw a counterpart of the spiky image which had puzzled him so horribly. On the left the floor fell abruptly away, leaving a black triangular gulf out of which, after a second's dry rattling, there presently climbed the hateful little furry thing with the yellow fangs and bearded human face.

The evilly grinning beldame still clutched him, and beyond the table stood a figure he had never seen before – a tall, lean man of dead black colouration but without the slightest sign of negroid features; wholly devoid of either hair or beard, and wearing as his only garment a shapeless robe of some heavy black fabric. His feet were indistinguishable because of the table and bench, but he must have been shod, since there was a clicking whenever he changed position. The man did not speak, and bore no trace of expression on his small, regular features. He merely pointed to a book of prodigious size which lay open on the table, while the beldame thrust a huge grey quill into Gilman's right hand. Over everything was a pall of intensely maddening fear, and the climax was reached when the furry thing ran up the dreamer's clothing to his shoulders and then down his left arm, finally biting him sharply in the wrist just below his cuff. As the blood spurted from this wound Gilman lapsed into a faint.

He awaked on the morning of the 22nd with a pain in his left wrist, and saw that his cuff was brown with dried blood. His recollections were very confused, but the scene with the black man in the unknown space stood out vividly. The rats must have bitten him as he slept, giving rise to the climax of that frightful dream. Opening the door, he saw that the flour on the corridor floor was undisturbed except for the huge prints of the loutish fellow who roomed at the other end of the garret. So he had not been sleep-walking this time. But something would have to be done about those rats. He would speak to the landlord about them. Again he tried to stop up the hole at the base of the slanting wall, wedging in a candlestick which seemed of about the right size. His ears were ringing horribly, as if with the residual echoes of some horrible noise heard in dreams.

As he bathed and changed clothes he tried to recall what he had dreamed after the scene in the violet-litten space, but nothing definite would crystallise in his mind. That scene itself must have corresponded to the sealed loft overhead, which had begun to attack his imagination so violently, but later impressions were faint and hazy. There were suggestions of the vague, twilight abysses, and of still vaster, blacker abysses beyond them – abysses in which all fixed suggestions of form were absent. He had been taken there by the bubble-congeries and the little polyhedron which always dogged him; but they, like himself, had changed to wisps of milky, barely luminous mist in this farther void of ultimate blackness. Something else had gone on ahead – a larger wisp which now and then condensed into nameless approximations of form – and he thought that their progress had not been in a straight line, but rather along the alien curves and spirals of some ethereal vortex which obeyed laws unknown to the physics and mathematics of any conceivable cosmos. Eventually there had been a hint of vast, leaping shadows, of a monstrous, half-acoustic pulsing, and of the thin, monotonous piping of an unseen flute – but that was all. Gilman decided he had picked up that last conception from what he had read in the *Necronomicon* about the mindless entity Azathoth, which rules all time and space from a curiously environed black throne at the centre of Chaos.

When the blood was washed away the wrist wound proved very slight, and Gilman puzzled over the location of the two tiny punctures. It occurred to him that there was no blood on the bedspread where he had lain – which was very curious in view of the amount on his skin and cuff. Had he been sleep-walking within his room, and had the rat bitten him as he sat in some chair or paused in some less rational position? He looked in every corner for brownish drops or stains, but did not find any. He had better, he thought, sprinkle flour within the room as well as outside the door – though after all no further proof of his sleep-walking was needed. He knew he did walk – and the thing to do now was to stop it. He must ask Frank Elwood for help. This morning the strange pulls from space seemed lessened, though they were replaced by another sensation even more inexplicable. It was a vague, insistent impulse to fly away from his present situation, but held not a hint of the specific direction in which he wished to fly. As he picked up the strange spiky image on the table he thought the older northward pull grew a trifle stronger; but even so, it was wholly overruled by the newer and more bewildering urge.

He took the spiky image down to Elwood's room, steeling himself against the whines of the loom-fixer which welled up from the ground floor. Elwood was in, thank heaven, and appeared to be stirring about. There was time for a little conversation before leaving for breakfast and college, so Gilman hurriedly poured forth an account of his recent dreams and fears. His host was very sympathetic, and agreed that something ought to be done. He was shocked by his guest's drawn, haggard aspect, and noticed the queer, abnormal-looking sunburn which others had remarked during the past week. There was not much, though, that he could say. He had not seen Gilman on any sleep-walking expedition, and had no idea what the curious image could be. He had, though, heard the French-Canadian who lodged just under Gilman talking to Mazurewicz one evening. They were telling each other how badly they dreaded the coming of Walpurgis-Night, now only a few days off; and were exchanging pitying comments about the poor, doomed young gentleman. Des-rochers, the fellow under Gilman's room, had spoken of nocturnal footsteps both shod and unshod, and of the violet light he saw one night when he had stolen fearfully up to peer through Gilman's keyhole. He had not dared to peer, he told Mazurewicz, after he had glimpsed that light through the cracks around the door. There had been soft talking, too – and as he began to describe it his voice had sunk to an inaudible whisper.

Elwood could not imagine what had set these superstitious creatures gossiping, but supposed their imaginations had been roused by Gilman's late hours and somnolent walking and talking on the one hand, and by the nearness of traditionally feared May-Eve on the other hand. That Gilman talked in his sleep was plain, and it was obviously from Desrochers' keyhole-listenings that the delusive notion of the violet dream-light had got abroad. These simple people were quick to imagine they had seen any odd thing they had heard about. As for a plan of action – Gilman had better move down to Elwood's room and avoid sleeping alone. Elwood would, if awake, rouse him whenever he began to talk or rise in his sleep. Very soon, too, he must see the specialist. Meanwhile they would take the spiky image around to the various museums and to certain professors, seeking identification and stating that it had been found in a public rubbish-can. Also, Dombrowski must attend to the poisoning of those rats in the walls.

Braced up by Elwood's companionship, Gilman attended classes that day. Strange urges still tugged at him, but he could sidetrack them with considerable success. During a free period he shewed the queer image to several professors, all of whom were intensely interested, though none of them could shed any light upon its nature or origin. That night he slept on a couch which Elwood had had the landlord bring to the second-story room, and for the first time in weeks was wholly free from disquieting dreams. But the feverishness still hung on, and the whines of the loom-fixer were an unnerving influence.

During the next few days Gilman enjoyed an almost perfect immunity from morbid manifestations. He had, Elwood said, shewed no tendency to talk or rise in his sleep; and meanwhile the landlord was putting rat-poison everywhere. The only disturbing element was the talk among the superstitious foreigners, whose imaginations had become highly excited. Mazurewicz was always trying to make him get a crucifix, and finally forced one upon him which he said had been blessed by the good Father Iwanicki. Desrochers, too, had something to say – in fact, he insisted that cautious steps had sounded in the now vacant room above him on the first and second nights of Gilman's absence from it. Paul Choynski thought he heard sounds in the halls and on the stairs at night, and claimed that his door had been softly tried, while Mrs Dombrowski vowed she had seen Brown Jenkin for the first time since All-Hallows. But such naive reports could mean very little, and Gilman let the cheap metal crucifix hang idly from a knob on his host's dresser.

For three days Gilman and Elwood canvassed the local museums in an effort to identify the strange spiky image, but always without success. In every quarter, however, interest was intense; for the utter alienage of the thing was a tremendous challenge to scientific curiosity. One of the small radiating arms was broken off and subjected to chemical analysis, and the result is still talked about in college circles. Professor Ellery found platinum, iron, and tellurium in the strange alloy; but mixed with these were at least three other apparent elements of high atomic weight which chemistry was absolutely powerless to classify. Not only did they fail to correspond with any known element, but they did not even fit the vacant places reserved for probable elements in the periodic system. The mystery remains unsolved to this day, though the image is on exhibition at the museum of Miskatonic University.

On the morning of April 27 a fresh rat-hole appeared in the room where Gilman was a guest, but Dombrowski tinned it up during the day. The poison was not having much effect, for scratchings and scurryings in the walls were virtually undiminished. Elwood was out late that night, and Gilman waited up for him. He did not wish to go to sleep in a room alone – especially since he thought he had glimpsed in the evening twilight the repellent old woman whose image had become so horribly transferred to his dreams. He wondered who she was, and what had been near her rattling the tin can in a rubbish-heap at the mouth of a squalid courtyard. The crone had seemed to notice him and leer evilly at him – though perhaps this was merely his imagination.

The next day both youths felt very tired, and knew they would sleep like logs when night came. In the evening they drowsily discussed the mathematical studies which had so completely and perhaps harmfully engrossed Gilman, and speculated about the linkage with ancient magic and folklore which seemed so darkly probable. They spoke of old Keziah Mason, and Elwood agreed that Gilman had good scientific grounds for thinking she might have stumbled on strange and significant information. The hidden cults to which these witches belonged often guarded and handed down surprising secrets from elder, forgotten aeons; and it was by no means impossible that Keziah had actually mastered the art of passing through dimensional gates. Tradition emphasises the uselessness of material barriers in halting a witch's motions; and who can say what underlies the old tales of broomstick rides through the night?

Whether a modern student could ever gain similar powers from mathematical research alone, was still to be seen. Success, Gilman added, might lead to dangerous and unthinkable situations; for who could foretell the conditions pervading an adjacent but normally inaccessible dimension? On the other hand, the picturesque possibilities were enormous. Time could not exist in certain belts of space, and by entering and remaining in such a belt one might preserve one's life and age indefinitely, never suffering organic metabolism or deterioration except for slight amounts incurred during visits to one's own or similar planes. One might, for example, pass into a timeless dimension and emerge at some remote period of the earth's history as young as before.

Whether anybody had ever managed to do this, one could hardly conjecture with any degree of authority. Old legends are hazy and ambiguous, and in historic times all attempts at crossing forbidden gaps seem complicated by strange and terrible alliances with beings and messengers from outside. There was the immemorial figure of the deputy or messenger of hidden and terrible powers – the 'Black Man' of the witch-cult, and the 'Nyarlathotep' of the *Necronomicon*. There was, too, the baffling problem of the lesser messengers or intermediaries – the quasi-animals and queer hybrids which legend depicts as witches' familiars. As Gilman and Elwood retired, too sleepy to argue further, they heard Joe Mazurewicz reel into the house half-drunk, and shuddered at the desperate wildness of his whining prayers.

That night Gilman saw the violet light again. In his dream he had heard a scratching and gnawing in the partitions, and thought that someone fumbled clumsily at the latch. Then he saw the old woman and the small furry thing advancing toward him over the carpeted floor. The beldame's face was alight with inhuman exultation, and the little yellow-toothed morbidity tittered mockingly as it pointed at the heavily sleeping form of Elwood on the other couch across the room. A paralysis of fear stifled all attempts to cry out. As once before, the hideous crone seized Gilman by the shoulders, yanking him out of bed and into empty space. Again the infinitude of the shrieking twilight abysses flashed past him, but in another second he thought he was in a dark, muddy, unknown alley of foetid odours, with the rotting walls of ancient houses towering up on every hand.

Ahead was the robed black man he had seen in the peaked space in the other dream, while from a lesser distance the old woman was beckoning and grimacing imperiously. Brown Jenkin was rubbing itself with a kind of affectionate playfulness around the ankles of the black man, which the deep mud largely concealed. There was a dark open doorway on the right, to which the black man silently pointed. Into this the grimacing crone started, dragging Gilman after her by his pajama sleeve. There were evil-smelling staircases which creaked ominously, and on which the old woman seemed to radiate a faint violet light; and finally a door leading off a landing. The crone fumbled with the latch and pushed the door open, motioning to Gilman to wait and disappearing inside the black aperture.

The youth's oversensitive ears caught a hideous strangled cry, and presently the beldame came out of the room bearing a small, senseless form which she thrust at the dreamer as if ordering him to carry it. The sight of this form, and the expression on its face, broke the spell. Still too dazed to cry out, he plunged recklessly down the noisome staircase and into the mud outside, halting only when seized and choked by the waiting black man. As consciousness departed he heard the faint, shrill tittering of the fanged, rat-like abnormality.

On the morning of the 29th Gilman awaked into a maelstrom of horror. The instant he opened his eyes he knew something was terribly wrong, for he was back in his old garret room with the slanting wall and ceiling, sprawled on the now unmade bed. His throat was aching inexplicably, and as he struggled to a sitting posture he saw with growing fright that his feet and pajama-bottoms were brown with caked mud. For the moment his recollections were hopelessly hazy, but he knew at least that he must have been sleep-walking. Elwood had been lost too deeply in slumber to hear and stop him. On the floor were confused muddy prints, but oddly enough they did not extend all the way to the door. The more Gilman looked at them, the more peculiar they seemed; for in addition to those he could recognise as his there were some smaller, almost round markings – such as the legs of a large chair or table might make, except that most of them tended to be divided into halves. There were also some curious muddy rat-tracks leading out of a fresh hole and back into it again. Utter bewilderment and the fear of madness racked Gilman as he staggered to the door and saw that there were no muddy prints outside. The more he remembered of his hideous dream the more terrified he felt, and it added to his desperation to hear Joe Mazurewicz chanting mournfully two floors below.

Descending to Elwood's room he roused his still-sleeping host and began telling of how he had found himself, but Elwood could form no idea of what might really have happened. Where Gilman could have been, how he got back to his room without making tracks in the hall, and how the muddy, furniture-like prints came to be mixed with his in the garret chamber, were wholly beyond conjecture. Then there were those dark, livid marks on his throat, as if he had tried to strangle himself. He put his hands up to them, but found that they did not even approximately fit. While they were talking Desrochers dropped in to say that he had heard a terrific clattering overhead in the dark small hours. No, there had been no one on the stairs after midnight – though just before midnight he had heard faint footfalls in the garret, and cautiously descending steps he did not like. It was, he added, a very bad time of year for Arkham. The young gentleman had better be sure to wear the crucifix Joe Mazurewicz had given him. Even the daytime was not safe, for after dawn there had been strange sounds in the house – especially a thin, childish wail hastily choked off.

Gilman mechanically attended classes that morning, but was wholly unable to fix his mind on his studies. A mood of hideous apprehension and expectancy had seized him, and he seemed to be awaiting the fall of some annihilating blow. At noon he lunched at the University Spa, picking up a paper from the next seat as he waited for dessert. But he never ate that dessert; for an item on the paper's first page left him limp, wild-eyed, and able only to pay his check and stagger back to Elwood's room.

There had been a strange kidnapping the night before in Orne's Gangway, and the two-year-old child of a clod-like laundry worker named Anastasia Wolejko had completely vanished from sight. The mother, it appeared, had feared the event for some time; but the reasons she assigned for her fear were so grotesque that no one took them seriously. She had, she said, seen Brown Jenkin about the place now and then ever since early in March, and knew from its grimaces and titterings that little Ladislas must be marked for sacrifice at the awful Sabbat on Walpurgis-Night. She had asked her neighbour Mary Czanek to sleep in the room and try to protect the child, but Mary had not dared. She could not tell the police, for they never believed such things. Children had been taken that way every year ever since she could remember. And her friend Pete Stowacki would not help because he wanted the child out of the way anyhow.

But what threw Gilman into a cold perspiration was the report of a pair of revellers who had been walking past the mouth of the gangway just after midnight. They admitted they had been drunk, but both vowed they had seen a crazily dressed trio furtively entering the dark passageway. There had, they said, been a huge robed negro, a little old woman in rags, and a young white man in his night-clothes. The old woman had been dragging the youth, while around the feet of the negro a tame rat was rubbing and weaving in the brown mud.

Gilman sat in a daze all the afternoon, and Elwood – who had meanwhile seen the papers and formed terrible conjectures from them – found him thus when he came home. This time neither could doubt but that something hideously serious was closing in around them. Between the phantasms of nightmare and the realities of the objective world a monstrous and unthinkable relationship was crystallising, and only stupendous vigilance could avert still more direful developments. Gilman must see a specialist sooner or later, but not just now, when all the papers were full of this kidnapping business.

Just what had really happened was maddeningly obscure, and for a moment both Gilman and Elwood exchanged whispered theories of the wildest kind. Had Gilman unconsciously succeeded better than he knew in his studies of space and its dimensions? Had he actually slipped outside our sphere to points unguessed and unimaginable?

Where – if anywhere – had he been on those nights of daemoniac alienage? The roaring twilight abysses – the green hillside – the blistering terrace – the pulls from the stars – the ultimate black vortex – the black man – the muddy alley and the stairs – the old witch and the fanged, furry horror – the bubble-congeries and the little polyhedron – the strange sunburn – the wrist wound – the unexplained image – the muddy feet – the throat-marks – the tales and fears of the superstitious foreigners – what did all this mean? To what extent could the laws of sanity apply to such a case?

There was no sleep for either of them that night, but next day they both cut classes and drowsed. This was April 30th, and with the dusk would come the hellish Sabbat-time which all the foreigners and the superstitious old folk feared. Mazurewicz came home at six o'clock and said people at the mill were whispering that the Walpurgis-revels would be held in the dark ravine beyond Meadow Hill where the old white stone stands in a place queerly void of all plant-life. Some of them had even told the police and advised them to look there for the missing Wolejko child, but they did not believe anything would be done. Joe insisted that the poor young gentleman wear his nickel-chained crucifix, and Gilman put it on and dropped it inside his shirt to humour the fellow.

Late at night the two youths sat drowsing in their chairs, lulled by the rhythmical praying of the loom-fixer on the floor below. Gilman listened as he nodded, his preternaturally sharpened hearing seeming to strain for some subtle, dreaded murmur beyond the noises in the ancient house. Unwholesome recollections of things in the *Necronomicon* and the Black Book welled up, and he found himself swaying to infandous rhythms said to pertain to the blackest ceremonies of the Sabbat and to have an origin outside the time and space we comprehend.

Presently he realised what he was listening for – the hellish chant of the celebrants in the distant black valley. How did he know so much about what they expected? How did he know the time when Nahab and her acolyte were due to bear the brimming bowl which would follow the black cock and the black goat? He saw that Elwood had dropped asleep, and tried to call out and waken him. Something, however, closed his throat. He was not his own master. Had he signed the black man's book after all?

Then his fevered, abnormal hearing caught the distant, windborne notes. Over miles of hill and field and alley they came, but he recognised them none the less. The fires must be lit, and the dancers must be starting in. How could he keep himself from going? What was it that had enmeshed him? Mathematics – folklore – the house – old Keziah – Brown Jenkin . . . and now he saw that there was a fresh rat-hole in the wall near his couch. Above the distant chanting and the nearer praying of Joe Mazurewicz came another sound – a stealthy, determined scratching in the partitions. He hoped the electric lights would not go out. Then he saw the fanged, bearded little face in the rat-hole – the accursed little face which he at last realised bore such a shocking, mocking resemblance to old Keziah's – and heard the faint fumbling at the door.

The screaming twilight abysses flashed before him, and he felt himself helpless in the formless grasp of the iridescent bubble-congeries. Ahead raced the small, kaleidoscopic polyhedron, and all through the churning void there was a heightening and acceleration of the vague tonal pattern which seemed to foreshadow some unutterable and unendurable climax. He seemed to know what was coming – the monstrous burst of Walpurgis-rhythm in whose cosmic timbre would be concentrated all the primal, ultimate space-time seethings which lie behind the massed spheres of matter and sometimes break forth in measured reverberations that penetrate faintly to every layer of entity and give hideous significance throughout the worlds to certain dreaded periods.

But all this vanished in a second. He was again in the cramped, violet-litten peaked space with the slanting floor, the low cases of ancient books, the bench and table, the queer objects, and the triangular gulf at one side. On the table lay a small white figure – an infant boy, unclothed and unconscious – while on the other side stood the monstrous, leering old woman with a gleaming, grotesque-hafted knife in her right hand, and a queerly proportioned pale metal bowl covered with curiously chased designs and having delicate lateral handles in her left. She was intoning some croaking ritual in a language which Gilman could not understand, but which seemed like something guardedly quoted in the *Necronomicon*.

As the scene grew clear he saw the ancient crone bend forward and extend the empty bowl across the table – and unable to control his own motions, he reached far forward and took it in both hands, noticing as he did so its comparative lightness. At the same moment the disgusting form of Brown Jenkin scrambled up over the brink of the triangular black gulf on his left. The crone now motioned him to hold the bowl in a certain position while she raised the huge, grotesque knife above the small white victim as high as her right hand could reach. The fanged, furry thing began tittering a continuation of the unknown ritual, while the witch croaked loathsome responses. Gilman felt a gnawing, poignant abhorrence shoot through his mental and emotional paralysis, and the light metal bowl shook in his grasp. A second later the downward motion of the knife broke the spell completely, and he dropped the bowl with a resounding bell-like clangour while his hands darted out frantically to stop the monstrous deed.

In an instant he had edged up the slanting floor around the end of the table and wrenched the knife from the old woman's claws, sending it clattering over the brink of the narrow triangular gulf. In another instant, however, matters were reversed; for those murderous claws had locked themselves tightly around his own throat, while the wrinkled face was twisted with insane fury. He felt the chain of the cheap crucifix grinding into his neck, and in his peril wondered how the sight of the object itself would affect the evil creature. Her strength was altogether superhuman, but as she continued her choking he reached feebly in his shirt and drew out the metal symbol, snapping the chain and pulling it free.

At sight of the device the witch seemed struck with panic, and her grip relaxed long enough to give Gilman a chance to break it entirely. He pulled the steel-like claws from his neck, and would have dragged the beldame over the edge of the gulf had not the claws received a fresh access of strength and closed in again. This time he resolved to reply in kind, and his own hands reached out for the creature's throat. Before she saw what he was doing he had the chain of the crucifix twisted about her neck, and a moment later he had tightened it enough to cut off her breath. During her last struggle he felt something bite at his ankle, and saw that Brown Jenkin had come to her aid. With one savage kick he sent the morbidity over the edge of the gulf and heard it whimper on some level far below.

Whether he had killed the ancient crone he did not know, but he let her rest on the floor where she had fallen. Then, as he turned away, he saw on the table a sight which nearly snapped the last thread of his reason. Brown Jenkin, tough of sinew and with four tiny hands of daemoniac dexterity, had been busy while the witch was throttling him, and his efforts had been in vain. What he had prevented the knife from doing to the victim's chest, the yellow fangs of the furry blasphemy had done to a wrist – and the bowl so lately on the floor stood full beside the small lifeless body.

In his dream-delirium Gilman heard the hellish, alien-rhythmed chant of the Sabbat coming from an infinite distance, and knew the black man must be there. Confused memories mixed themselves with his mathematics, and he believed his subconscious mind held the *angles* which he needed to guide him back to the normal world – alone and unaided for the first time. He felt sure he was in the immemorially sealed loft above his own room, but whether he could ever escape through the slanting floor or the long-stopped egress he doubted greatly. Besides, would not an escape from a dream-loft bring him merely into a dream-house – an abnormal projection of the actual place he sought? He was wholly bewildered as to the relation betwixt dream and reality in all his experiences.

The passage through the vague abysses would be frightful, for the Walpurgis-rhythm would be vibrating, and at last he would have to hear that hitherto veiled cosmic pulsing which he so mortally dreaded. Even now he could detect a low, monstrous shaking whose tempo he suspected all too well. At Sabbat-time it always mounted and reached through to the worlds to summon the initiate to name-less rites. Half the chants of the Sabbat were patterned on this faintly overheard pulsing which no earthly ear could endure in its unveiled spatial fulness. Gilman wondered, too, whether he could trust his instinct to take him back to the right part of space. How could he be sure he would not land on that green-litten hillside of a far planet, on the tessellated terrace above the city of tentacled monsters somewhere beyond the galaxy, or in the spiral black vor-tices of that ultimate void of Chaos wherein reigns the mindless daemon-sultan Azathoth?

Just before he made the plunge the violet light went out and left him in utter blackness. The witch – old Keziah – Nahab – that must have meant her death. And mixed with the distant chant of the Sabbat and the whimpers of Brown Jenkin in the gulf below he thought he heard another and wilder whine from unknown depths. Joe Mazurewicz – the prayers against the Crawling Chaos now turning to an inexplicably triumphant shriek – worlds of sardonic actuality impinging on vortices of febrile dream – Iä! Shub-Niggurath! The Goat with a Thousand Young . . .

They found Gilman on the floor of his queerly angled old garret room long before dawn, for the terrible cry had brought Desrochers and Choynski and Dombrowski and Mazurewicz at once, and had even wakened the soundly sleeping Elwood in his chair. He was alive, and with open, staring eyes, but seemed largely unconscious. On his throat were the marks of murderous hands, and on his left ankle was a distressing rat-bite. His clothing was badly rumpled, and Joe's crucifix was missing. Elwood trembled, afraid even to speculate on what new form his friend's sleep-walking had taken. Mazurewicz seemed half-dazed because of a 'sign' he said he had had in response to his prayers, and he crossed himself frantically when the squealing and whimpering of a rat sounded from beyond the slanting partition.

When the dreamer was settled on his couch in Elwood's room they sent for Dr Malkowski – a local practitioner who would repeat no tales where they might prove embarrassing – and he gave Gilman two hypodermic injections which caused him to relax in something like natural drowsiness. During the day the patient regained consciousness at times and whispered his newest dream disjointedly to Elwood. It was a painful process, and at its very start brought out a fresh and disconcerting fact.

Gilman – whose ears had so lately possessed an abnormal sensitiveness – was now stone deaf. Dr Malkowski, summoned again in haste, told Elwood that both ear-drums were ruptured, as if by the impact of some stupendous sound intense beyond all human conception or endurance. How such a sound could have been heard in the last few hours without arousing all the Miskatonic Valley was more than the honest physician could say.

Elwood wrote his part of the colloquy on paper, so that a fairly easy communication was maintained. Neither knew what to make of the whole chaotic business, and decided it would be better if they thought as little as possible about it. Both, though, agreed that they must leave this ancient and accursed house as soon as it could be arranged. Evening papers spoke of a police raid on some curious revellers in a ravine beyond Meadow Hill just before dawn, and mentioned that the white stone there was an object of age-long superstitious regard. Nobody had been caught, but among the scattering fugitives had been glimpsed a huge negro. In another column it was stated that no trace of the missing child Ladislas Wolejko had been found.

The crowning horror came that very night. Elwood will never forget it, and was forced to stay out of college the rest of the term because of the resulting nervous breakdown. He had thought he heard rats in the partitions all the evening, but paid little attention to them. Then, long after both he and Gilman had retired, the atrocious shrieking began. Elwood jumped up, turned on the lights, and rushed over to his guest's couch. The occupant was emitting sounds of veritably inhuman nature, as if racked by some torment beyond description. He was writhing under the bedclothes, and a great red stain was beginning to appear on the blankets.

Elwood scarcely dared to touch him, but gradually the screaming and writhing subsided. By this time Dombrowski, Choynski, Desrochers, Mazurewicz, and the top-floor lodger were all crowding into the doorway, and the landlord had sent his wife back to telephone for Dr Malkowski. Everybody shrieked when a large rat-like form suddenly jumped out from beneath the ensanguined bedclothes and scuttled across the floor to a fresh, open hole close by. When the doctor arrived and began to pull down those frightful covers Walter Gilman was dead.

It would be barbarous to do more than suggest what had killed Gilman. There had been virtually a tunnel through his body – something had eaten his heart out. Dombrowski, frantic at the failure of his constant rat-poisoning efforts, cast aside all thought of his lease and within a week had moved with all his older lodgers to a dingy but less ancient house in Walnut Street. The worst thing for a while was keeping Joe Mazurewicz quiet; for the brooding loom-fixer would never stay sober, and was constantly whining and muttering about spectral and terrible things.

It seems that on that last hideous night Joe had stooped to look at the crimson rat-tracks which led from Gilman's couch to the nearby hole. On the carpet they were very indistinct, but a piece of open flooring intervened between the carpet's edge and the baseboard. There Mazurewicz had found something monstrous – or thought he had, for no one else could quite agree with him despite the undeniable queerness of the prints. The tracks on the flooring were certainly vastly unlike the average prints of a rat, but even Choynski and Desrochers would not admit that they were like the prints of four tiny human hands.

The house was never rented again. As soon as Dombrowski left it the pall of its final desolation began to descend, for people shunned it both on account of its old reputation and because of the new foetid odour. Perhaps the ex-landlord's rat-poison had worked after all, for not long after his departure the place became a neighbourhood nuisance. Health officials traced the smell to the closed spaces above and beside the eastern garret room, and agreed that the number of dead rats must be enormous. They decided, however, that it was not worth their while to hew open and disinfect the long-sealed spaces; for the foetor would soon be over, and the locality was not one which encouraged fastidious standards. Indeed, there were always vague local tales of unexplained stenches upstairs in the Witch House just after May-Eve and Hallowmass. The neighbours grumblingly acquiesced in the inertia – but the foetor none the less formed an additional count against the place. Toward the last the house was condemned as an habitation by the building inspector.

Gilman's dreams and their attendant circumstances have never been explained. Elwood, whose thoughts on the entire episode are sometimes almost maddening, came back to college the next autumn and graduated in the following June. He found the spectral gossip of the town much diminished, and it is indeed a fact that – notwithstanding certain reports of a ghostly tittering in the deserted house which lasted almost as long as that edifice itself – no fresh appearances either of old Keziah or of Brown Jenkin have been muttered of since Gilman's death. It is rather fortunate that Elwood was not in Arkham in that later year when certain events abruptly renewed the local whispers about elder horrors. Of course he heard about the matter afterward and suffered untold torments of black and bewildered speculation; but even that was not as bad as actual nearness and several possible sights would have been.

In March, 1931, a gale wrecked the roof and great chimney of the vacant Witch House, so that a chaos of crumbling bricks, blackened, moss-grown shingles, and rotting planks and timbers crashed down into the loft and broke through the floor beneath. The whole attic story was choked with debris from above, but no one took the trouble to touch the mess before the inevitable razing of the decrepit structure. That ultimate step came in the following December, and it was when Gilman's old room was cleared out by reluctant, apprehensive workmen that the gossip began.

Among the rubbish which had crashed through the ancient slanting ceiling were several things which made the workmen pause and call in the police. Later the police in turn called in the coroner and several professors from the university. There were bones – badly crushed and splintered, but clearly recognisable as human – whose manifestly modern date conflicted puzzlingly with the remote period at which their only possible lurking-place, the low, slant-floored loft overhead, had supposedly been sealed from all human access. The coroner's physician decided that some belonged to a small child, while certain others – found mixed with shreds of rotten brownish cloth – belonged to a rather undersized, bent female of advanced years. Careful sifting of debris also disclosed many tiny bones of rats caught in the collapse, as well as older rat-bones gnawed by small fangs in a fashion now and then highly productive of controversy and reflection.

Other objects found included the mingled fragments of many books and papers, together with a yellowish dust left from the total disintegration of still older books and papers. All, without exception, appeared to deal with black magic in its most advanced and horrible forms; and the evidently recent date of certain items is still a mystery as unsolved as that of the modern human bones. An even greater mystery is the absolute homogeneity of the crabbed, archaic writing found on a wide range of papers whose conditions and watermarks suggest age differences of at least 150 to 200 years. To some, though, the greatest mystery of all is the variety of utterly inexplicable objects – objects whose shapes, materials, types of workmanship, and purposes baffle all conjecture – found scattered amidst the wreckage in evidently diverse states of injury. One of these things – which excited several Miskatonic professors profoundly – is a badly damaged monstrosity plainly resembling the strange image which Gilman gave to the college museum, save that it is larger, wrought of some peculiar bluish stone instead of metal, and possessed of a singularly angled pedestal with undecipherable hieroglyphics.

Archaeologists and anthropologists are still trying to explain the bizarre designs chased on a crushed bowl of light metal whose inner side bore ominous brownish stains when found. Foreigners and credulous grandmothers are equally garrulous about the modern nickel crucifix with broken chain mixed in the rubbish and shiveringly identified by Joe Mazurewicz as that which he had given poor Gilman many years before. Some believe this crucifix was dragged up to the sealed loft by rats, while others think it must have been on the floor in some corner of Gilman's old room all the time. Still others, including Joe himself, have theories too wild and fantastic for sober credence.

When the slanting wall of Gilman's room was torn out, the once sealed triangular space between that partition and the house's north wall was found to contain much less structural debris, even in proportion to its size, than the room itself, though it had a ghastly layer of older materials which paralysed the wreckers with horror. In brief, the floor was a veritable ossuary of the bones of small children – some fairly modern, but others extending back in infinite gradations to a period so remote that crumbling was almost complete. On this deep bony layer rested a knife of great size, obvious antiquity, and grotesque, ornate, and exotic design – above which the debris was piled.

In the midst of this debris, wedged between a fallen plank and a cluster of cemented bricks from the ruined chimney, was an object destined to cause more bafflement, veiled fright, and openly superstitious talk in Arkham than anything else discovered in the haunted and accursed building. This object was the partly crushed skeleton of a huge, diseased rat, whose abnormalities of form are still a topic of debate and source of singular reticence among the members of Miskatonic's department of comparative anatomy. Very little concerning this skeleton has leaked out, but the workmen who found it whisper in shocked tones about the long, brownish hairs with which it was associated.

The bones of the tiny paws, it is rumoured, imply prehensile characteristics more typical of a diminutive monkey than of a rat; while the small skull with its savage yellow fangs is of the utmost anomalousness, appearing from certain angles like a miniature, monstrously degraded parody of a human skull. The workmen crossed themselves in fright when they came upon this blasphemy, but later burned candles of gratitude in St Stanislaus' Church because of the shrill, ghostly tittering they felt they would never hear again.

The Thing on the Doorstep

I

It is true that I have sent six bullets through the head of my best friend, and yet I hope to shew by this statement that I am not his murderer. At first I shall be called a madman – madder than the man I shot in his cell at the Arkham Sanitarium. Later some of my readers will weigh each statement, correlate it with the known facts, and ask themselves how I could have believed otherwise than as I did after facing the evidence of that horror – that thing on the doorstep.

Until then I also saw nothing but madness in the wild tales I have acted on. Even now I ask myself whether I was misled – or whether I am not mad after all. I do not know – but others have strange things to tell of Edward and Asenath Derby, and even the stolid police are at their wits' ends to account for that last terrible visit. They have tried weakly to concoct a theory of a ghastly jest or warning by discharged servants, yet they know in their hearts that the truth is something infinitely more terrible and incredible.

So I say that I have not murdered Edward Derby. Rather have I avenged him, and in so doing purged the earth of a horror whose survival might have loosed untold terrors on all mankind. There are black zones of shadow close to our daily paths, and now and then some evil soul breaks a passage through. When that happens, the man who knows must strike before reckoning the consequences.

I have known Edward Pickman Derby all his life. Eight years my junior, he was so precocious that we had much in common from the time he was eight and I sixteen. He was the most phenomenal child scholar I have ever known, and at seven was writing verse of a sombre, fantastic, almost morbid cast which astonished the tutors surrounding him. Perhaps his private education and coddled seclusion had something to do with his premature flowering. An only child, he had organic weaknesses which startled his doting parents and caused them to keep him closely chained to their side. He was never allowed out without his nurse, and seldom had a chance to play unconstrainedly with other children. All this doubtless fostered a strange, secretive inner life in the boy, with imagination as his one avenue of freedom.

At any rate, his juvenile learning was prodigious and bizarre; and his facile writings such as to captivate me despite my greater age. About that time I had leanings toward art of a somewhat grotesque cast, and I found in this younger child a rare kindred spirit. What lay behind our joint love of shadows and marvels was, no doubt, the ancient, mouldering, and subtly fearsome town in which we lived – witch-cursed, legend-haunted Arkham, whose huddled, sagging gambrel roofs and crumbling Georgian balustrades brood out the centuries beside the darkly muttering Miskatonic.

As time went by I turned to architecture and gave up my design of illustrating a book of Edward's daemoniac poems, yet our comrade-ship suffered no lessening. Young Derby's odd genius developed remarkably, and in his eighteenth year his collected nightmare-lyrics made a real sensation when issued under the title *Azathoth and Other Horrors*. He was a close correspondent of the notorious Baudelairean poet Justin Geoffrey, who wrote *The People of the Monolith* and died screaming in a madhouse in 1926 after a visit to a sinister, ill-regarded village in Hungary.

In self-reliance and practical affairs, however, Derby was greatly retarded because of his coddled existence. His health had improved, but his habits of childish dependence were fostered by overcareful parents; so that he never travelled alone, made independent decisions, or assumed responsibilities. It was early seen that he would not be equal to a struggle in the business or professional arena, but the family fortune was so ample that this formed no tragedy. As he grew to years of manhood he retained a deceptive aspect of boyishness. Blond and blue-eyed, he had the fresh complexion of a child; and his attempts to raise a moustache were discernible only with difficulty. His voice was soft and light, and his pampered, unexercised life gave him a juvenile chubbiness rather than the paunchiness of premature middle age. He was of good height, and his handsome face would have made him a notable gallant had not his shyness held him to seclusion and bookishness.

Derby's parents took him abroad every summer, and he was quick to seize on the surface aspects of European thought and expression. His Poe-like talents turned more and more toward the decadent, and other artistic sensitivenesses and yearnings were half-aroused in him. We had great discussions in those days. I had been through Harvard, had studied in a Boston architect's office, had married, and had finally returned to Arkham to practice my profession – settling in the family homestead in Saltonstall Street since my father had moved to Florida for his health. Edward used to call almost every evening, till I came to regard him as one of the household. He had a characteristic way of ringing the doorbell or sounding the knocker that grew to be a veritable code signal, so that after dinner I always listened for the familiar three brisk strokes followed by two more after a pause. Less frequently I would visit at his house and note with envy the obscure volumes in his constantly growing library.

Derby went through Miskatonic University in Arkham, since his parents would not let him board away from them. He entered at sixteen and completed his course in three years, majoring in English and French literature and receiving high marks in everything but mathematics and the sciences. He mingled very little with the other students, though looking enviously at the 'daring' or 'Bohemian' set – whose superficially 'smart' language and meaninglessly ironic pose he aped, and whose dubious conduct he wished he dared adopt.

What he did do was to become an almost fanatical devotee of subterranean magical lore, for which Miskatonic's library was and is famous. Always a dweller on the surface of phantasy and strangeness, he now delved deep into the actual runes and riddles left by a fabulous past for the guidance or puzzlement of posterity. He read things like the frightful *Book of Eibon*, the *Unaussprechlichen Kulten* of von Junzt, and the forbidden *Necronomicon* of the mad Arab Abdul Alhazred, though he did not tell his parents he had seen them. Edward was twenty when my son and only child was born, and seemed pleased when I named the newcomer Edward Derby Upton, after him.

By the time he was twenty-five Edward Derby was a prodigiously learned man and a fairly well-known poet and *fantaisiste*, though his lack of contacts and responsibilities had slowed down his literary growth by making his products derivative and overbookish. I was perhaps his closest friend – finding him an inexhaustible mine of vital theoretical topics, while he relied on me for advice in whatever matters he did not wish to refer to his parents. He remained single – more through shyness, inertia, and parental protectiveness than through inclination – and moved in society only to the slightest and most perfunctory extent. When the war came both health and ingrained timidity kept him at home. I went to Plattsburg for a commission, but never got overseas.

So the years wore on. Edward's mother died when he was thirty-four, and for months he was incapacitated by some odd psychological malady. His father took him to Europe, however, and he managed to pull out of his trouble without visible effects. Afterward he seemed to feel a sort of grotesque exhilaration, as if of partial escape from some unseen bondage. He began to mingle in the more 'advanced' college set despite his middle age, and was present at some extremely wild doings – on one occasion paying heavy blackmail (which he borrowed of me) to keep his presence at a certain affair from his father's notice. Some of the whispered rumours about the wild Miskatonic set were extremely singular. There was even talk of black magic and of happenings utterly beyond credibility.

2

Edward was thirty-eight when he met Asenath Waite. She was, I judge, about twenty-three at the time, and was taking a special course in mediaeval metaphysics at Miskatonic. The daughter of a friend of mine had met her before – in the Hall School at Kingsport – and had been inclined to shun her because of her odd reputation. She was dark, smallish, and very good-looking except for overprotuberant eyes; but something in her expression alienated extremely sensitive people. It was, however, largely her origin and conversation which caused average folk to avoid her. She was one of the Innsmouth Waites, and dark legends have clustered for generations about crumbling, half-deserted Innsmouth and its people. There are tales of horrible bargains about the year 1850, and of a strange element 'not quite human' in the ancient families of the run-down fishing port – tales such as only old-time Yankees can devise and repeat with proper awesomeness.

Asenath's case was aggravated by the fact that she was Ephraim Waite's daughter – the child of his old age by an unknown wife who always went veiled. Ephraim lived in a half-decayed mansion in Washington Street, Innsmouth, and those who had seen the place (Arkham folk avoid going to Innsmouth whenever they can) declared that the attic windows were always boarded, and that strange sounds sometimes floated from within as evening drew on. The old man was known to have been a prodigious magical student in his day, and legend averred that he could raise or quell storms at sea according to his whim. I had seen him once or twice in my youth as he came to Arkham to consult forbidden tomes at the college library, and had hated his wolfish, saturnine face with its tangle of iron-grey beard. He had died insane – under rather queer circumstances – just before his daughter (by his will made a nominal ward of the principal) entered the Hall School, but she had been his morbidly avid pupil and looked fiendishly like him at times.

The friend whose daughter had gone to school with Asenath Waite repeated many curious things when the news of Edward's acquaintance with her began to spread about. Asenath, it seemed, had posed as a kind of magician at school, and had really seemed able to accomplish some highly baffling marvels. She professed to be able to raise thunderstorms, though her seeming success was generally laid to some uncanny knack at prediction. All animals markedly disliked her, and she could make any dog howl by certain motions of her right hand. There were times when she displayed snatches of knowledge and language very singular – and very shocking – for a young girl; when she would frighten her schoolmates with leers and winks of an inexplicable kind, and would seem to extract an obscene and zestful irony from her present situation.

Most unusual, though, were the well-attested cases of her influence over other persons. She was, beyond question, a genuine hypnotist. By gazing peculiarly at a fellow-student she would often give the latter a distinct feeling of *exchanged personality* – as if the subject were placed momentarily in the magician's body and able to stare half across the room at her real body, whose eyes blazed and protruded with an alien expression. Asenath often made wild claims about the nature of consciousness and about its independence of the physical frame – or at least from the life-processes of the physical frame. Her crowning rage, however, was that she was not a man, since she believed a male brain had certain unique and far-reaching cosmic powers. Given a man's brain, she declared, she could not only equal but surpass her father in mastery of unknown forces.

Edward met Asenath at a gathering of 'intelligentsia' held in one of the students' rooms, and could talk of nothing else when he came to see me the next day. He had found her full of the interests and erudition which engrossed him most, and was in addition wildly taken with her appearance. I had never seen the young woman, and recalled casual references only faintly, but I knew who she was. It seemed rather regrettable that Derby should become so upheaved about her; but I said nothing to discourage him, since infatuation thrives on opposition. He was not, he said, mentioning her to his father.

In the next few weeks I heard of very little but Asenath from young Derby. Others now remarked Edward's autumnal gallantry, though they agreed that he did not look even nearly his actual age, or seem at all inappropriate as an escort for his bizarre divinity. He was only a trifle paunchy despite his indolence and self-indulgence, and his face was absolutely without lines. Asenath, on the other hand, had the premature crow's feet which come from the exercise of an intense will.

About this time Edward brought the girl to call on me, and I at once saw that his interest was by no means one-sided. She eyed him continually with an almost predatory air, and I perceived that their intimacy was beyond untangling. Soon afterward I had a visit from old Mr Derby, whom I had always admired and respected. He had heard the tales of his son's new friendship, and had wormed the whole truth out of 'the boy'. Edward meant to marry Asenath, and had even been looking at houses in the suburbs. Knowing my usually great influence with his son, the father wondered if I could help to break the ill-advised affair off; but I regretfully expressed my doubts. This time it was not a question of Edward's weak will but of the woman's strong will. The perennial child had transferred his dependence from the parental image to a new and stronger image, and nothing could be done about it.

The wedding was performed a month later – by a justice of the peace, according to the bride's request. Mr Derby, at my advice, offered no opposition; and he, my wife, my son, and I attended the brief ceremony – the other guests being wild young people from the college. Asenath had bought the old Crowninshield place in the country at the end of High Street, and they proposed to settle there after a short trip to Innsmouth, whence three servants and some books and household goods were to be brought. It was probably not so much consideration for Edward and his father as a personal wish to be near the college, its library, and its crowd of 'sophisticates', that made Asenath settle in Arkham instead of returning permanently home.

When Edward called on me after the honeymoon I thought he looked slightly changed. Asenath had made him get rid of the undeveloped moustache, but there was more than that. He looked soberer and more thoughtful, his habitual pout of childish rebelliousness being exchanged for a look almost of genuine sadness. I was puzzled to decide whether I liked or disliked the change. Certainly, he seemed for the moment more normally adult than ever before. Perhaps the marriage was a good thing – might not the *change* of dependence form a start toward actual *neutralisation*, leading ultimately to responsible independence? He came alone, for Asenath was very busy. She had brought a vast store of books and apparatus from Innsmouth (Derby shuddered as he spoke the name), and was finishing the restoration of the Crowninshield house and grounds.

Her home in – that town – was a rather disquieting place, but certain objects in it had taught him some surprising things. He was progressing fast in esoteric lore now that he had Asenath's guidance. Some of the experiments she proposed were very daring and radical – he did not feel at liberty to describe them – but he had confidence in her powers and intentions. The three servants were very queer – an incredibly aged couple who had been with old Ephraim and referred occasionally to him and to Asenath's dead mother in a cryptic way, and a swarthy young wench who had marked anomalies of feature and seemed to exude a perpetual odour of fish.

3

For the next two years I saw less and less of Derby. A fortnight would sometimes slip by without the familiar three-and-two strokes at the front door; and when he did call – or when, as happened with increasing infrequency, I called on him – he was very little disposed to converse on vital topics. He had become secretive about those occult studies which he used to describe and discuss so minutely, and preferred not to talk of his wife. She had aged tremendously since her marriage, till now – oddly enough – she seemed the elder of the two. Her face held the most concentratedly determined expression I had ever seen, and her whole aspect seemed to gain a vague, unplaceable repulsiveness. My wife and son noticed it as much as I, and we all ceased gradually to call on her – for which, Edward admitted in one of his boyishly tactless moments, she was unmitigatedly grateful. Occasionally the Derbys would go on long trips – ostensibly to Europe, though Edward sometimes hinted at obscurer destinations.

It was after the first year that people began talking about the change in Edward Derby. It was very casual talk, for the change was purely psychological; but it brought up some interesting points. Now and then, it seemed, Edward was observed to wear an expression and to do things wholly incompatible with his usual flabby nature. For example – although in the old days he could not drive a car, he was now seen occasionally to dash into or out of the old Crowninshield driveway with Asenath's powerful Packard, handling it like a master, and meeting traffic entanglements with a skill and determination utterly alien to his accustomed nature. In such cases he seemed always to be just back from some trip or just starting on one – what sort of trip, no one could guess, although he mostly favoured the Innsmouth road.

Oddly, the metamorphosis did not seem altogether pleasing. People said he looked too much like his wife, or like old Ephraim Waite himself, in these moments – or perhaps these moments seemed unnatural because they were so rare. Sometimes, hours after starting out in this way, he would return listlessly sprawled on the rear seat of the car while an obviously hired chauffeur or mechanic drove. Also, his preponderant aspect on the streets during his decreasing round of social contacts (including, I may say, his calls on me) was the old-time indecisive one – its irresponsible childishness even more marked than in the past. While Asenath's face aged, Edward's – aside from those exceptional occasions – actually relaxed into a kind of exaggerated immaturity, save when a trace of the new sadness or understanding would flash across it. It was really very puzzling. Meanwhile the Derbys almost dropped out of the gay college circle – not through their own disgust, we heard, but because something about their present studies shocked even the most callous of the other decadents.

It was in the third year of the marriage that Edward began to hint openly to me of a certain fear and dissatisfaction. He would let fall remarks about things 'going too far', and would talk darkly about the need of 'saving his identity'. At first I ignored such references, but in time I began to question him guardedly, remembering what my friend's daughter had said about Asenath's hypnotic influence over the other girls at school – the cases where students had thought they were in her body looking across the room at themselves. This questioning seemed to make him at once alarmed and grateful, and once he mumbled something about having a serious talk with me later.

About this time old Mr Derby died, for which I was afterward very thankful. Edward was badly upset, though by no means disorganised. He had seen astonishingly little of his parent since his marriage, for Asenath had concentrated in herself all his vital sense of family linkage. Some called him callous in his loss – especially since those jaunty and confident moods in the car began to increase. He now wished to move back into the old Derby mansion, but Asenath insisted on staying in the Crowninshield house, to which she had become well adjusted.

Not long afterward my wife heard a curious thing from a friend – one of the few who had not dropped the Derbys. She had been out to the end of High Street to call on the couple, and had seen a car shoot briskly out of the drive with Edward's oddly confident and almost sneering face above the wheel. Ringing the bell, she had been told by the repulsive wench that Asenath was also out, but had chanced to look up at the house in leaving. There, at one of Edward's library windows, she had glimpsed a hastily withdrawn face – a face whose expression of pain, defeat, and wistful hopelessness was poignant beyond description. It was – incredibly enough in view of its usual domineering cast – Asenath's; yet the caller had vowed that in that instant the sad, muddled eyes of poor Edward were gazing out from it.

Edward's calls now grew a trifle more frequent, and his hints occasionally became concrete. What he said was not to be believed, even in centuried and legend-haunted Arkham; but he threw out his dark lore with a sincerity and convincingness which made one fear for his sanity. He talked about terrible meetings in lonely places, of

Cyclopean ruins in the heart of the Maine woods beneath which vast staircases led down to abysses of nighted secrets, of complex angles that led through invisible walls to other regions of space and time, and of hideous exchanges of personality that permitted explorations in remote and forbidden places, on other worlds, and in different space-time continua.

He would now and then back up certain crazy hints by exhibiting objects which utterly nonplussed me – elusively coloured and bafflingly textured objects like nothing ever heard of on earth, whose insane curves and surfaces answered no conceivable purpose and followed no conceivable geometry. These things, he said, came 'from outside'; and his wife knew how to get them. Sometimes – but always in frightened and ambiguous whispers – he would suggest things about old Ephraim Waite, whom he had seen occasionally at the college library in the old days. These adumbrations were never specific, but seemed to revolve around some especially horrible doubt as to whether the old wizard were really dead – in a spiritual as well as corporeal sense.

At times Derby would halt abruptly in his revelations, and I wondered whether Asenath could possibly have divined his speech at a distance and cut him off through some unknown sort of telepathic mesmerism – some power of the kind she had displayed at school. Certainly, she suspected that he told me things, for as the weeks passed she tried to stop his visits with words and glances of a most inexplicable potency. Only with difficulty could he get to see me, for although he would pretend to be going somewhere else, some invisible force would generally clog his motions or make him forget his destination for the time being. His visits usually came when Asenath was away – 'away in her own body', as he once oddly put it. She always found out later – the servants watched his goings and comings – but evidently she thought it inexpedient to do anything drastic.

4

Derby had been married more than three years on that August day when I got the telegram from Maine. I had not seen him for two months, but had heard he was away 'on business'. Asenath was supposed to be with him, though watchful gossips declared there was someone upstairs in the house behind the doubly curtained windows. They had watched the purchases made by the servants. And now the town marshal of Chesuncook had wired of the draggled madman who stumbled out of the woods with delirious ravings and screamed to me for protection. It was Edward – and he had been just able to recall his own name and my name and address.

Chesuncook is close to the wildest, deepest, and least explored forest belt in Maine, and it took a whole day of feverish jolting through fantastic and forbidding scenery to get there in a car. I found Derby in a cell at the town farm, vacillating between frenzy and apathy. He knew me at once, and began pouring out a meaningless, half-incoherent torrent of words in my direction.

'Dan – for God's sake! The pit of the shoggoths! Down the six thousand steps . . . the abomination of abominations . . . I never would let her take me, and then I found myself there . . . Iä! Shub-Niggurath! . . . The shape rose up from the altar, and there were 500 that howled . . . The Hooded Thing bleated "Kamog! Kamog!" – that was old Ephraim's secret name in the coven . . . I was there, where she promised she wouldn't take me . . . A minute before I was locked in the library, and then I was there where she had gone with my body – in the place of utter blasphemy, the unholy pit where the black realm begins and the watcher guards the gate . . . I saw a shoggoth – it changed shape . . . I can't stand it . . . I won't stand it . . . I'll kill her if she ever sends me there again . . . I'll kill that entity . . . her, him, it . . . I'll kill it! I'll kill it with my own hands!'

It took me an hour to quiet him, but he subsided at last. The next day I got him decent clothes in the village, and set out with him for Arkham. His fury of hysteria was spent, and he was inclined to be silent, though he began muttering darkly to himself when the car passed through Augusta – as if the sight of a city aroused unpleasant memories. It was clear that he did not wish to go home; and considering the fantastic delusions he seemed to have about his wife – delusions undoubtedly springing from some actual hypnotic ordeal to which he had been subjected – I thought it would be better if he did not. I would, I resolved, put him up myself for a time, no matter what unpleasantness it would make with Asenath. Later I would help him get a divorce, for most assuredly there were mental factors which made this marriage suicidal for him. When we struck open country again Derby's muttering faded away, and I let him nod and drowse on the seat beside me as I drove.

During our sunset dash through Portland the muttering commenced again, more distinctly than before, and as I listened I caught a stream of utterly insane drivel about Asenath. The extent to which she had preyed on Edward's nerves was plain, for he had woven a whole set of hallucinations around her. His present predicament, he mumbled furtively, was only one of a long series. She was getting hold of him, and he knew that some day she would never let go. Even now she probably let him go only when she had to, because she couldn't hold on long at a time. She constantly took his body and went to nameless places for nameless rites, leaving him in her body and locking him upstairs – but sometimes she couldn't hold on, and he would find himself suddenly in his own body again in some far-off, horrible, and perhaps unknown place. Sometimes she'd get hold of him again and sometimes she couldn't. Often he was left stranded somewhere as I had found him . . . time and again he had to find his way home from frightful distances, getting somebody to drive the car after he found it.

The worst thing was that she was holding on to him longer and longer at a time. She wanted to be a man – to be fully human – that was why she got hold of him. She had sensed the mixture of fine-wrought brain and weak will in him. Some day she would crowd him out and disappear with his body – disappear to become a great magician like her father and leave him marooned in that female shell that wasn't even quite human. Yes, he knew about the Innsmouth blood now. There had been traffick with things from the sea – it was horrible . . . And old Ephraim – he had known the secret, and when he grew old did a hideous thing to keep alive . . . he wanted to live forever . . . Asenath would succeed – one successful demonstration had taken place already.

As Derby muttered on I turned to look at him closely, verifying the impression of change which an earlier scrutiny had given me. Paradoxically, he seemed in better shape than usual – harder, more normally developed, and without the trace of sickly flabbiness caused by his indolent habits. It was as if he had been really active and properly exercised for the first time in his coddled life, and I judged that Asenath's force must have pushed him into unwonted channels of motion and alertness. But just now his mind was in a pitiable state, for he was mumbling wild extravagances about his wife, about black magic, about old Ephraim, and about some revelation which would convince even me. He repeated names which I recognised from bygone browsings in forbidden volumes, and at times made me shudder with a certain thread of mythological consistency – of convincing coherence – which ran through his maundering. Again and again he would pause, as if to gather courage for some final and terrible disclosure.

'Dan, Dan, don't you remember him – the wild eyes and the unkempt beard that never turned white? He glared at me once, and I never forgot it. Now *she* glares that way. *And I know why*! He found it in the *Necronomicon* – the formula. I don't dare tell you the page yet, but when I do you can read and understand. Then you will know what has engulfed me. On, on, on, on – body to body to body – he means never to die. The life-glow – he knows how to break the link . . . it can flicker on a while even when the body is dead. I'll give you hints, and maybe you'll guess. Listen, Dan – do you know why my wife always takes such pains with that silly backhand writing? Have you ever seen a manuscript of old Ephraim's? Do you want to know why I shivered when I saw some hasty notes Asenath had jotted down?

'Asenath . . . *is there such a person*? Why did they half think there was poison in old Ephraim's stomach? Why do the Gilmans whisper about the way he shrieked – like a frightened child – when he went mad and Asenath locked him up in the padded attic room where – the other – had been? *Was it old Ephraim's soul that was locked in? Who locked in whom*? Why had he been looking for months for someone with a fine mind and a weak will? Why did he curse that his daughter wasn't a son? Tell me, Daniel Upton – *what devilish exchange was perpetrated in the house of horror where that blasphemous monster had his trusting, weak-willed, half-human child at his mercy*? Didn't he make it permanent – as she'll do in the end with me? Tell me why that thing that calls itself Asenath writes differently when off guard, *so that you can't tell its script from* . . . '

Then the thing happened. Derby's voice was rising to a thin treble scream as he raved, when suddenly it was shut off with an almost mechanical click. I thought of those other occasions at my home when his confidences had abruptly ceased – when I had half fancied that some obscure telepathic wave of Asenath's mental force was intervening to keep him silent. This, though, was something altogether different – and, I felt, infinitely more horrible. The face beside me was twisted almost unrecognisably for a moment, while through the whole body there passed a shivering motion – as if all the bones, organs, muscles, nerves, and glands were readjusting themselves to a radically different posture, set of stresses, and general personality.

Just where the supreme horror lay, I could not for my life tell; yet there swept over me such a swamping wave of sickness and repulsion – such a freezing, petrifying sense of utter alienage and abnormality – that my grasp of the wheel grew feeble and uncertain. The figure beside me seemed less like a lifelong friend than like some monstrous intrusion from outer space – some damnable, utterly accursed focus of unknown and malign cosmic forces.

I had faltered only a moment, but before another moment was over my companion had seized the wheel and forced me to change places with him. The dusk was now very thick, and the lights of Portland far behind, so I could not see much of his face. The blaze of his eyes, though, was phenomenal; and I knew that he must now be in that queerly energised state – so unlike his usual self – which so many people had noticed. It seemed odd and incredible that listless Edward Derby – he who could never assert himself, and who had never learned to drive – should be ordering me about and taking the wheel of my own car, yet that was precisely what had happened. He did not speak for some time, and in my inexplicable horror I was glad he did not.

In the lights of Biddeford and Saco I saw his firmly set mouth, and shivered at the blaze of his eyes. The people were right – he did look damnably like his wife and like old Ephraim when in these moods. I did not wonder that the moods were disliked – there was certainly something unnatural and diabolic in them, and I felt the sinister element all the more because of the wild ravings I had been hearing. This man, for all my lifelong knowledge of Edward Pickman Derby, was a stranger – an intrusion of some sort from the black abyss.

He did not speak until we were on a dark stretch of road, and when he did his voice seemed utterly unfamiliar. It was deeper, firmer, and more decisive than I had ever known it to be, while its accent and pronunciation were altogether changed – though vaguely, remotely, and rather disturbingly recalling something I could not quite place. There was, I thought, a trace of very profound and very genuine irony in the timbre – not the flashy, meaninglessly jaunty pseudo-irony of the callow 'sophisticate', which Derby had habitually affected, but something grim, basic, pervasive, and potentially evil. I marvelled at the self-possession so soon following the spell of panic-struck muttering.

'I hope you'll forget my attack back there, Upton,' he was saying. 'You know what my nerves are, and I guess you can excuse such things. I'm enormously grateful, of course, for this lift home.

'And you must forget, too, any crazy things I may have been saying about my wife – and about things in general. That's what comes from overstudy in a field like mine. My philosophy is full of bizarre concepts, and when the mind gets worn out it cooks up all sorts of imaginary concrete applications. I shall take a rest from now on – you probably won't see me for some time, and you needn't blame Asenath for it.

'This trip was a bit queer, but it's really very simple. There are certain Indian relics in the north woods – standing stones, and all that – which mean a good deal in folklore, and Asenath and I are following that stuff up. It was a hard search, so I seem to have gone off my head. I must send somebody for the car when I get home. A month's relaxation will put me back on my feet.'

I do not recall just what my own part of the conversation was, for the baffling alienage of my seatmate filled all my consciousness. With every moment my feeling of elusive cosmic horror increased, till at length I was in a virtual delirium of longing for the end of the drive. Derby did not offer to relinquish the wheel, and I was glad of the speed with which Portsmouth and Newburyport flashed by.

At the junction where the main highway runs inland and avoids Innsmouth I was half afraid my driver would take the bleak shore road that goes through that damnable place. He did not, however, but darted rapidly past Rowley and Ipswich toward our destination. We reached Arkham before midnight, and found the lights still on at the old Crowninshield house. Derby left the car with a hasty repetition of his thanks, and I drove home alone with a curious feeling of relief. It had been a terrible drive – all the more terrible because I could not quite tell why – and I did not regret Derby's forecast of a long absence from my company.

5

The next two months were full of rumours. People spoke of seeing Derby more and more in his new energised state, and Asenath was scarcely ever in to her few callers. I had only one visit from Edward, when he called briefly in Asenath's car – duly reclaimed from wherever he had left it in Maine – to get some books he had lent me. He was in his new state, and paused only long enough for some evasively polite remarks. It was plain that he had nothing to discuss with me when in this condition – and I noticed that he did not even trouble to give the old three-and-two signal when ringing the doorbell. As on that evening in the car, I felt a faint, infinitely deep horror which I could not explain; so that his swift departure was a prodigious relief.

In mid-September Derby was away for a week, and some of the decadent college set talked knowingly of the matter – hinting at a meeting with a notorious cult-leader, lately expelled from England, who had established headquarters in New York. For my part I could not get that strange ride from Maine out of my head. The transformation I had witnessed had affected me profoundly, and I caught myself again and again trying to account for the thing – and for the extreme horror it had inspired in me.

But the oddest rumours were those about the sobbing in the old Crowninshield house. The voice seemed to be a woman's, and some of the younger people thought it sounded like Asenath's. It was heard only at rare intervals, and would sometimes be choked off as if by force. There was talk of an investigation, but this was dispelled one day when Asenath appeared in the streets and chatted in a sprightly way with a large number of acquaintances – apologising for her recent absences and speaking incidentally about the nervous breakdown and hysteria of a guest from Boston. The guest was never seen, but Asenath's appearance left nothing to be said. And then someone complicated matters by whispering that the sobs had once or twice been in a man's voice.

One evening in mid-October I heard the familiar three-and-two ring at the front door. Answering it myself, I found Edward on the steps, and saw in a moment that his personality was the old one which I had not encountered since the day of his ravings on that terrible ride from Chesuncook. His face was twitching with a mixture of odd emotions in which fear and triumph seemed to share dominion, and he looked furtively over his shoulder as I closed the door behind him.

Following me clumsily to the study, he asked for some whiskey to steady his nerves. I forbore to question him, but waited till he felt like beginning whatever he wanted to say. At length he ventured some information in a choking voice.

'Asenath has gone, Dan. We had a long talk last night while the servants were out, and I made her promise to stop preying on me. Of course I had certain – certain occult defences I never told you about. She had to give in, but got frightfully angry. Just packed up and started for New York – walked right out to catch the 8:20 in to Boston. I suppose people will talk, but I can't help that. You needn't mention that there was any trouble – just say she's gone on a long research trip.

'She's probably going to stay with one of her horrible groups of devotees. I hope she'll go west and get a divorce – anyhow, I've made her promise to keep away and let me alone. It was horrible, Dan – she was stealing my body – crowding me out – making a prisoner of me. I laid low and pretended to let her do it, but I had to be on the watch. I could plan if I was careful, for she can't read my mind literally, or in detail. All she could read of my planning was a sort of general mood of rebellion – and she always thought I was helpless. Never thought I could get the best of her . . . but I had a spell or two that worked.'

Derby looked over his shoulder and took some more whiskey.

'I paid off those damned servants this morning when they got back. They were ugly about it, and asked questions, but they went. They're her kind – Innsmouth people – and were hand and glove with her. I hope they'll let me alone – I didn't like the way they laughed when they walked away. I must get as many of Dad's old servants again as I can. I'll move back home now.

'I suppose you think I'm crazy, Dan – but Arkham history ought to hint at things that back up what I've told you – and what I'm going to tell you. You've seen one of the changes, too – in your car after I told you about Asenath that day coming home from Maine. That was when she got me – drove me out of my body. The last thing of the ride I remember was when I was all worked up trying to tell you *what that she-devil is.* Then she got me, and in a flash I was back at the house – in the library where those damned servants had me locked up – and in that cursed fiend's body . . . that isn't even human . . . You know, it was she you must have ridden home with . . . that preying wolf in my body . . . You ought to have known the difference!'

I shuddered as Derby paused. Surely, I *had* known the difference – yet could I accept an explanation as insane as this? But my distracted caller was growing even wilder.

'I had to save myself – I had to, Dan! She'd have got me for good at Hallowmass – they hold a Sabbat up there beyond Chesuncook, and the sacrifice would have clinched things. She'd have got me for good . . . she'd have been I, and I'd have been she . . . forever . . . too late . . . My body'd have been hers for good . . . She'd have been a man, and fully human, just as she wanted to be . . . I suppose she'd have put me out of the way – killed her own ex-body with me in it, damn her, *just as she did before* – just as she, he, or it did before . . . '

Edward's face was now atrociously distorted, and he bent it uncomfortably close to mine as his voice fell to a whisper.

'You must know what I hinted in the car – *that she isn't Asenath at all, but really old Ephraim himself.* I suspected it a year and a half ago, but I know it now. Her handwriting shews it when she's off guard – sometimes she jots down a note in writing that's just like her father's manuscripts, stroke for stroke – and sometimes she says things that nobody but an old man like Ephraim could say. He changed forms with her when he felt death coming – she was the only one he could find with the right kind of brain and a weak enough will – he got her body permanently, just as she almost got mine, and then poisoned the old body he'd put her into. Haven't you seen old Ephraim's soul glaring out of that she-devil's eyes dozens of times . . . and out of mine when she had control of my body?'

The whisperer was panting, and paused for breath. I said nothing, and when he resumed his voice was nearer normal. This, I reflected, was a case for the asylum, but I would not be the one to send him there.

Perhaps time and freedom from Asenath would do its work. I could see that he would never wish to dabble in morbid occultism again.

'I'll tell you more later – I must have a long rest now. I'll tell you something of the forbidden horrors she led me into – something of the age-old horrors that even now are festering in out-of-the-way corners with a few monstrous priests to keep them alive. Some people know things about the universe that nobody ought to know, and can do things that nobody ought to be able to do. I've been in it up to my neck, but that's the end. Today I'd burn that damned *Necronomicon* and all the rest if I were librarian at Miskatonic.

'But she can't get me now. I must get out of that accursed house as soon as I can, and settle down at home. You'll help me, I know, if I need help. Those devilish servants, you know . . . and if people should get too inquisitive about Asenath. You see, I can't give them her address . . . Then there are certain groups of searchers – certain cults, you know – that might misunderstand our breaking up . . . some of them have damnably curious ideas and methods. I know you'll stand by me if anything happens – even if I have to tell you a lot that will shock you . . . '

I had Edward stay and sleep in one of the guest-chambers that night, and in the morning he seemed calmer. We discussed certain possible arrangements for his moving back into the Derby mansion, and I hoped he would lose no time in making the change. He did not call the next evening, but I saw him frequently during the ensuing weeks. We talked as little as possible about strange and unpleasant things, but discussed the renovation of the old Derby house, and the travels which Edward promised to take with my son and me the following summer.

Of Asenath we said almost nothing, for I saw that the subject was a peculiarly disturbing one. Gossip, of course, was rife; but that was no novelty in connexion with the strange ménage at the old Crowninshield house. One thing I did not like was what Derby's banker let fall in an overexpansive mood at the Miskatonic Club – about the cheques Edward was sending regularly to a Moses and Abigail Sargent and a Eunice Babson in Innsmouth. That looked as if those evil-faced servants were extorting some kind of tribute from him – yet he had not mentioned the matter to me.

I wished that the summer – and my son's Harvard vacation – would come, so that we could get Edward to Europe. He was not, I soon saw, mending as rapidly as I had hoped he would; for there was something a bit hysterical in his occasional exhilaration, while his moods of fright and depression were altogether too frequent. The old Derby house was ready by December, yet Edward constantly put off moving. Though he hated and seemed to fear the Crown-inshield place, he was at the same time queerly enslaved by it. He could not seem to begin dismantling things, and invented every kind of excuse to postpone action. When I pointed this out to him he appeared unaccountably frightened. His father's old butler – who was there with other reacquired family servants – told me one day that Edward's occasional prowlings about the house, and especially down the cellar, looked odd and unwholesome to him. I wondered if Asenath had been writing disturbing letters, but the butler said there was no mail which could have come from her.

6

It was about Christmas that Derby broke down one evening while calling on me. I was steering the conversation toward next summer's travels when he suddenly shrieked and leaped up from his chair with a look of shocking, uncontrollable fright – a cosmic panic and loathing such as only the nether gulfs of nightmare could bring to any sane mind.

'My brain! My brain! God, Dan – it's tugging – from beyond – knocking – clawing – that she-devil – even now – Ephraim – Kamog! Kamog! – The pit of the shoggoths – Iä! Shub-Niggurath! The Goat with a Thousand Young! . . .

'The flame – the flame . . . beyond body, beyond life . . . in the earth . . . oh, God! . . . '

I pulled him back to his chair and poured some wine down his throat as his frenzy sank to a dull apathy. He did not resist, but kept his lips moving as if talking to himself. Presently I realised that he was trying to talk to me, and bent my ear to his mouth to catch the feeble words.

' . . . again, again . . . she's trying . . . I might have known . . . nothing can stop that force; not distance, nor magic, nor death . . . it comes and comes, mostly in the night . . . I can't leave . . . it's horrible . . . oh, God, Dan, *if you only knew as I do just how horrible it is* . . . '

When he had slumped down into a stupor I propped him with pillows and let normal sleep overtake him. I did not call a doctor, for I knew what would be said of his sanity, and wished to give nature a chance if I possibly could. He waked at midnight, and I put him to bed upstairs, but he was gone by morning. He had let himself quietly out of the house – and his butler, when called on the wire, said he was at home pacing restlessly about the library.

Edward went to pieces rapidly after that. He did not call again, but I went daily to see him. He would always be sitting in his library, staring at nothing and having an air of abnormal *listening*. Sometimes he talked rationally, but always on trivial topics. Any mention of his trouble, of future plans, or of Asenath would send him into a frenzy. His butler said he had frightful seizures at night, during which he might eventually do himself harm.

I had a long talk with his doctor, banker, and lawyer, and finally took the physician with two specialist colleagues to visit him. The spasms that resulted from the first questions were violent and pitiable – and that evening a closed car took his poor struggling body to the Arkham Sanitarium. I was made his guardian and called on him twice weekly – almost weeping to hear his wild shrieks, awesome whispers, and dreadful, droning repetitions of such phrases as 'I had to do it – I had to do it . . . it'll get me . . . it'll get me . . . down there . . . down there in the dark . . . Mother, mother! Dan! Save me . . . save me . . . '

How much hope of recovery there was, no one could say; but I tried my best to be optimistic. Edward must have a home if he emerged, so I transferred his servants to the Derby mansion, which would surely be his sane choice. What to do about the Crowninshield place with its complex arrangements and collections of utterly inexplicable objects I could not decide, so left it momentarily untouched – telling the Derby housemaid to go over and dust the chief rooms once a week, and ordering the furnace man to have a fire on those days.

The final nightmare came before Candlemas – heralded, in cruel irony, by a false gleam of hope. One morning late in January the sanitarium telephoned to report that Edward's reason had suddenly come back. His continuous memory, they said, was badly impaired; but sanity itself was certain. Of course he must remain some time for observation, but there could be little doubt of the outcome. All going well, he would surely be free in a week.

I hastened over in a flood of delight, but stood bewildered when a nurse took me to Edward's room. The patient rose to greet me, extending his hand with a polite smile; but I saw in an instant that he bore the strangely energised personality which had seemed so foreign to his own nature – the competent personality I had found so vaguely horrible, and which Edward himself had once vowed was the intruding soul of his wife. There was the same blazing vision – so like Asenath's and old Ephraim's – and the same firm mouth; and when he spoke I could sense the same grim, pervasive irony in his voice – the deep irony so redolent of potential evil. This was the person who had driven my car through the night five months before – the person I had not seen since that brief call when he had forgotten the old-time doorbell signal and stirred such nebulous fears in me – and now he filled me with the same dim feeling of blasphemous alienage and ineffable cosmic hideousness.

He spoke affably of arrangements for release – and there was nothing for me to do but assent, despite some remarkable gaps in his recent memories. Yet I felt that something was terribly, inexplicably wrong and abnormal. There were horrors in this thing that I could not reach. This was a sane person – but was it indeed the Edward Derby I had known? If not, who or what was it – *and where was Edward*? Ought it to be free or confined . . . or ought it to be extirpated from the face of the earth? There was a hint of the abysmally sardonic in everything the creature said – the Asenath-like eyes lent a special and baffling mockery to certain words about the 'early liberty earned by an *especially close confinement*'. I must have behaved very awkwardly, and was glad to beat a retreat.

All that day and the next I racked my brain over the problem. What had happened? What sort of mind looked out through those alien eyes in Edward's face? I could think of nothing but this dimly terrible enigma, and gave up all efforts to perform my usual work. The second morning the hospital called up to say that the recovered patient was unchanged, and by evening I was close to a nervous collapse – a state I admit, though others will vow it coloured my subsequent vision. I have nothing to say on this point except that no madness of mine could account for *all* the evidence.

7

It was in the night – after that second evening – that stark, utter horror burst over me and weighted my spirit with a black, clutching panic from which it can never shake free. It began with a telephone call just before midnight. I was the only one up, and sleepily took down the receiver in the library. No one seemed to be on the wire, and I was about to hang up and go to bed when my ear caught a very faint suspicion of sound at the other end. Was someone trying under great difficulties to talk? As I listened I thought I heard a sort of half-liquid bubbling noise – '*glub . . . glub . . . glub*' – which had an odd suggestion of inarticulate, unintelligible word and syllable divisions. I called, 'Who is it?' But the only answer was '*glub-glub . . . glub-glub.*' I could only assume that the noise was mechanical; but fancying that it might be a case of a broken instrument able to receive but not to send, I added, 'I can't hear you. Better hang up and try Information.' Immediately I heard the receiver go on the hook at the other end.

This, I say, was just before midnight. When that call was traced afterward it was found to come from the old Crowninshield house, though it was fully half a week from the housemaid's day to be there. I shall only hint what was found at that house – the upheaval in a remote cellar storeroom, the tracks, the dirt, the hastily rifled wardrobe, the baffling marks on the telephone, the clumsily used stationery, and the detestable stench lingering over everything. The police, poor fools, have their smug little theories, and are still searching for those sinister discharged servants – who have dropped out of sight amidst the present furore. They speak of a ghoulish revenge for things that were done, and say I was included because I was Edward's best friend and adviser.

Idiots! – do they fancy those brutish clowns could have forged that handwriting? Do they fancy they could have brought what later came? Are they blind to the changes in that body that was Edward's? As for me, *I now believe all that Edward Derby ever told me.* There are horrors beyond life's edge that we do not suspect, and once in a while man's evil prying calls them just within our range. Ephraim – Asenath – that devil called them in, and they engulfed Edward as they are engulfing me.

Can I be sure that I am safe? Those powers survive the life of the physical form. The next day – in the afternoon, when I pulled out of my prostration and was able to walk and talk coherently – I went to the madhouse and shot him dead for Edward's and the world's sake, but can I be sure till he is cremated? They are keeping the body for some silly autopsies by different doctors – but I say he must be cremated. *He must be cremated – he who was not Edward Derby when I shot him.* I shall go mad if he is not, for I may be the next. But my will is not weak – and I shall not let it be undermined by the terrors I know are seething around it. One life – Ephraim, Asenath, and Edward – who now? I *will not* be driven out of my body . . . I *will not* change souls with that bullet-ridden lich in the madhouse!

But let me try to tell coherently of that final horror. I will not speak of what the police persistently ignored – the tales of that dwarfed, grotesque, malodorous thing met by at least three wayfarers in High Street just before two o'clock, and the nature of the single footprints in certain places. I will say only that just about two the doorbell and knocker waked me – doorbell and knocker both, plied alternately and uncertainly in a kind of weak desperation, *and each trying to keep to Edward's old signal of three-and-two strokes.*

Roused from sound sleep, my mind leaped into a turmoil. Derby at the door – and remembering the old code! That new personality had not remembered it . . . was Edward suddenly back in his rightful state? Why was he here in such evident stress and haste? Had he been released ahead of time, or had he escaped? Perhaps, I thought as I flung on a robe and bounded downstairs, his return to his own self had brought raving and violence, revoking his discharge and driving him to a desperate dash for freedom. Whatever had happened, he was good old Edward again, and I would help him!

When I opened the door into the elm-arched blackness a gust of insufferably foetid wind almost flung me prostrate. I choked in nausea, and for a second scarcely saw the dwarfed, humped figure on the steps. The summons had been Edward's, but who was this foul, stunted parody? Where had Edward had time to go? His ring had sounded only a second before the door opened.

The caller had on one of Edward's overcoats – its bottom almost touching the ground, and its sleeves rolled back yet still covering the hands. On the head was a slouch hat pulled low, while a black silk muffler concealed the face. As I stepped unsteadily forward, the figure made a semi-liquid sound like that I had heard over the telephone – '*glub . . . glub . . .* ' – and thrust at me a large, closely written paper impaled on the end of a long pencil. Still reeling from the morbid and unaccountable foetor, I seized this paper and tried to read it in the light from the doorway.

Beyond question, it was in Edward's script. But why had he written when he was close enough to ring – and why was the script so awkward, coarse, and shaky? I could make out nothing in the dim half light, so edged back into the hall, the dwarf figure clumping mechanically after but pausing on the inner door's threshold. The odour of this singular messenger was really appalling, and I hoped (not in vain, thank God!) that my wife would not wake and confront it.

Then, as I read the paper, I felt my knees give under me and my vision go black. I was lying on the floor when I came to, that accursed sheet still clutched in my fear-rigid hand. This is what it said.

DAN – go to the sanitarium and kill it. Exterminate it. It isn't Edward Derby any more. She got me – it's Asenath – *and she has been dead three months and a half*. I lied when I said she had gone away. I killed her. I had to. It was sudden, but we were alone and I was in my right body. I saw a candlestick and smashed her head in. She would have got me for good at Hallowmass.

I buried her in the farther cellar storeroom under some old boxes and cleaned up all the traces. The servants suspected next morning, but they have such secrets that they dare not tell the police. I sent them off, but God knows what they – and others of the cult – will do.

I thought for a while I was all right, and then I felt the tugging at my brain. I knew what it was – I ought to have remembered. A soul like hers – or Ephraim's – is half detached, and keeps right on after death as long as the body lasts. She was getting me – making me change bodies with her – *seizing my body and putting me in that corpse of hers buried in the cellar*.

I knew what was coming – that's why I snapped and had to go to the asylum. Then it came – I found myself choked in the dark – in Asenath's rotting carcass down there in the cellar under the boxes where I put it. And I knew she must be in my body at the sanitarium – *permanently*, for it was after Hallowmass, and the sacrifice would work even without her being there – sane, and ready for release as a menace to the world. I was desperate, *and in spite of everything I clawed my way out.*

I'm too far gone to talk – I couldn't manage to telephone – but I can still write. I'll get fixed up somehow and bring you this last word and warning. *Kill that fiend* if you value the peace and comfort of the world. *See that it is cremated.* If you don't, it will live on and on, body to body forever, and I can't tell you what it will do. Keep clear of black magic, Dan, it's the devil's business. Goodbye – you've been a great friend. Tell the police whatever they'll believe – and I'm damnably sorry to drag all this on you. I'll be at peace before long – this thing won't hold together much more. Hope you can read this. *And kill that thing – kill it.*

Yours – E<small>D</small>

It was only afterward that I read the last half of this paper, for I had fainted at the end of the third paragraph. I fainted again when I saw and smelled what cluttered up the threshold where the warm air had struck it. The messenger would not move or have consciousness any more.

The butler, tougher-fibred than I, did not faint at what met him in the hall in the morning. Instead, he telephoned the police. When they came I had been taken upstairs to bed, but the – other mass – lay where it had collapsed in the night. The men put handkerchiefs to their noses.

What they finally found inside Edward's oddly assorted clothes was mostly liquescent horror. There were bones, too – and a crushed-in skull. Some dental work positively identified the skull as Asenath's.

The Shadow out of Time

I

After twenty-two years of nightmare and terror, saved only by a desperate conviction of the mythical source of certain impressions, I am unwilling to vouch for the truth of that which I think I found in Western Australia on the night of July 17–18, 1935. There is reason to hope that my experience was wholly or partly an hallucination – for which, indeed, abundant causes existed. And yet, its realism was so hideous that I sometimes find hope impossible. If the thing did happen, then man must be prepared to accept notions of the cosmos, and of his own place in the seething vortex of time, whose merest mention is paralysing. He must, too, be placed on guard against a specific lurking peril which, though it will never engulf the whole race, may impose monstrous and unguessable horrors upon certain venturesome members of it. It is for this latter reason that I urge, with all the force of my being, a final abandonment of all attempts at unearthing those fragments of unknown, primordial masonry which my expedition set out to investigate.

Assuming that I was sane and awake, my experience on that night was such as has befallen no man before. It was, moreover, a frightful confirmation of all I had sought to dismiss as myth and dream. Mercifully there is no proof, for in my fright I lost the awesome object which would – if real and brought out of that noxious abyss – have formed irrefutable evidence. When I came upon the horror I was alone – and I have up to now told no one about it. I could not stop the others from digging in its direction, but chance and the shifting sand have so far saved them from finding it. Now I must formulate some definitive statement – not only for the sake of my own mental balance, but to warn such others as may read it seriously.

These pages – much in whose earlier parts will be familiar to close readers of the general and scientific press – are written in the cabin of the ship that is bringing me home. I shall give them to my son, Prof. Wingate Peaslee of Miskatonic University – the only member of my family who stuck to me after my queer amnesia of long ago, and the man best informed on the inner facts of my case. Of all living persons, he is least likely to ridicule what I shall tell of that fateful night. I did not enlighten him orally before sailing, because I think he had better have the revelation in written form. Reading and re-reading at leisure will leave with him a more convincing picture than my confused tongue could hope to convey. He can do as he thinks best with this account – shewing it, with suitable comment, to any quarters where it will be likely to accomplish good. It is for the sake of such readers as are unfamiliar with the earlier phases of my case that I am prefacing the revelation itself with a fairly ample summary of its background.

My name is Nathaniel Wingate Peaslee, and those who recall the newspaper tales of a generation back – or the letters and articles in psychological journals six or seven years ago – will know who and what I am. The press was filled with the details of my strange amnesia in 1908–13, and much was made of the traditions of horror, madness, and witchcraft which lurk behind the ancient Massachusetts town then and now forming my place of residence. Yet I would have it known that there is nothing whatever of the mad or sinister in my heredity and early life. This is a highly important fact in view of the shadow which fell so suddenly upon me from *outside* sources. It may be that centuries of dark brooding had given to crumbling, whisper-haunted Arkham a peculiar vulnerability as regards such shadows – though even this seems doubtful in the light of those other cases which I later came to study. But the chief point is that my own ancestry and background are altogether normal. What came, came from *somewhere else* – where, I even now hesitate to assert in plain words.

I am the son of Jonathan and Hannah (Wingate) Peaslee, both of wholesome old Haverhill stock. I was born and reared in Haverhill – at the old homestead in Boardman Street near Golden Hill – and did not go to Arkham till I entered Miskatonic University at the age of eighteen. That was in 1889. After my graduation I studied economics at Harvard, and came back to Miskatonic as Instructor of Political Economy in 1895. For thirteen years more my life ran smoothly and happily. I married Alice Keezar of Haverhill in 1896, and my three children, Robert K., Wingate, and Hannah, were born in 1898, 1900, and 1903, respectively. In 1898 I became an associate professor, and in 1902 a full professor. At no time had I the least interest in either occultism or abnormal psychology.

It was on Thursday, May 14, 1908, that the queer amnesia came. The thing was quite sudden, though later I realised that certain brief, glimmering visions of several hours previous – chaotic visions which disturbed me greatly because they were so unprecedented – must have formed premonitory symptoms. My head was aching, and I had a singular feeling – altogether new to me – that someone else was trying to get possession of my thoughts.

The collapse occurred about 10:20 a.m., while I was conducting a class in Political Economy VI – history and present tendencies of economics – for juniors and a few sophomores. I began to see strange shapes before my eyes, and to feel that I was in a grotesque room other than the classroom. My thoughts and speech wandered from my subject, and the students saw that something was gravely amiss. Then I slumped down, unconscious in my chair, in a stupor from which no one could arouse me. Nor did my rightful faculties again look out upon the daylight of our normal world for five years, four months, and thirteen days.

It is, of course, from others that I have learned what followed. I shewed no sign of consciousness for sixteen and a half hours, though removed to my home at 27 Crane Street and given the best of medical attention. At 3 a.m. May 15 my eyes opened and I began to speak, but before long the doctors and my family were thoroughly frightened by the trend of my expression and language. It was clear that I had no remembrance of my identity or of my past, though for some reason I seemed anxious to conceal this lack of knowledge. My eyes gazed strangely at the persons around me, and the flexions of my facial muscles were altogether unfamiliar.

Even my speech seemed awkward and foreign. I used my vocal organs clumsily and gropingly, and my diction had a curiously stilted quality, as if I had laboriously learned the English language from books. The pronunciation was barbarously alien, whilst the idiom seemed to include both scraps of curious archaism and expressions of a wholly incomprehensible cast. Of the latter one in particular was very potently – even terrifiedly – recalled by the youngest of the physicians twenty years afterward. For at that late period such a phrase began to have an actual currency – first in England and then in the United States – and though of much complexity and indisputable newness, it reproduced in every least particular the mystifying words of the strange Arkham patient of 1908.

Physical strength returned at once, although I required an odd amount of re-education in the use of my hands, legs, and bodily apparatus in general. Because of this and other handicaps inherent in the mnemonic lapse, I was for some time kept under strict medical care. When I saw that my attempts to conceal the lapse had failed, I admitted it openly, and became eager for information of all sorts. Indeed, it seemed to the doctors that I had lost interest in my proper personality as soon as I found the case of amnesia accepted as a natural thing. They noticed that my chief efforts were to master certain points in history, science, art, language, and folklore – some of them tremendously abstruse, and some childishly simple – which remained, very oddly in many cases, outside my consciousness.

At the same time they noticed that I had an inexplicable command of many almost unknown sorts of knowledge – a command which I seemed to wish to hide rather than display. I would inadvertently refer, with casual assurance, to specific events in dim ages outside the range of accepted history – passing off such references as a jest when I saw the surprise they created. And I had a way of speaking of the future which two or three times caused actual fright. These uncanny flashes soon ceased to appear, though some observers laid their vanishment more to a certain furtive caution on my part than to any waning of the strange knowledge behind them. Indeed, I seemed anomalously avid to absorb the speech, customs, and perspectives of the age around me, as if I were a studious traveller from a far, foreign land.

As soon as permitted, I haunted the college library at all hours, and shortly began to arrange for those odd travels, and special courses at American and European universities, which evoked so much comment during the next few years. I did not at any time suffer from a lack of learned contacts, for my case had a mild celebrity among the psychologists of the period. I was lectured upon as a typical example of secondary personality – even though I seemed to puzzle the lecturers now and then with some bizarre symptom or some queer trace of carefully veiled mockery.

Of real friendliness, however, I encountered little. Something in my aspect and speech seemed to excite vague fears and aversions in everyone I met, as if I were a being infinitely removed from all that is normal and healthful. This idea of a black, hidden horror connected with incalculable gulfs of some sort of *distance* was oddly widespread and persistent. My own family formed no exception. From the moment of my strange waking my wife had regarded me with extreme horror and loathing, vowing that I was some utter alien usurping the body of her husband. In 1910 she obtained a legal divorce, nor would she ever consent to see me even after my return to normalcy in 1913. These feelings were shared by my elder son and my small daughter, neither of whom I have ever seen since.

Only my second son Wingate seemed able to conquer the terror and repulsion which my change aroused. He indeed felt that I was a stranger, but though only eight years old held fast to a faith that my proper self would return. When it did return he sought me out, and the courts gave me his custody. In succeeding years he helped me with the studies to which I was driven, and today at thirty-five he is a professor of psychology at Miskatonic. But I do not wonder at the horror I caused – for certainly, the mind, voice, and facial expression of the being that awaked on May 15, 1908 were not those of Nathaniel Wingate Peaslee.

I will not attempt to tell much of my life from 1908 to 1913, since readers may glean all the outward essentials – as I largely had to do – from files of old newspapers and scientific journals. I was given charge of my funds, and spent them slowly and on the whole wisely, in travel and in study at various centres of learning. My travels, however, were singular in the extreme, involving long visits to remote and desolate places. In 1909 I spent a month in the Himalayas, and in 1911 aroused much attention through a camel trip into the unknown deserts of Arabia. What happened on those journeys I have never been able to learn. During the summer of 1912 I chartered a ship and sailed in the Arctic north of Spitzbergen, afterward shewing signs of disappointment. Later in that

year I spent weeks alone beyond the limits of previous or subsequent exploration in the vast limestone cavern systems of western
Virginia – black labyrinths so complex that no retracing of my steps
could even be considered.

My sojourns at the universities were marked by abnormally rapid
assimilation, as if the secondary personality had an intelligence enormously superior to my own. I have found, also, that my rate of reading
and solitary study was phenomenal. I could master every detail of a
book merely by glancing over it as fast as I could turn the leaves; while
my skill at interpreting complex figures in an instant was veritably
awesome. At times there appeared almost ugly reports of my power to
influence the thoughts and acts of others, though I seemed to have
taken care to minimise displays of this faculty.

Other ugly reports concerned my intimacy with leaders of occultist
groups, and scholars suspected of connexion with nameless bands of
abhorrent elder-world hierophants. These rumours, though never
proved at the time, were doubtless stimulated by the known tenor of
some of my reading – for the consultation of rare books at libraries
cannot be effected secretly. There is tangible proof – in the form
of marginal notes – that I went minutely through such things as
the Comte d'Erlette's *Cultes des Goules*, Ludvig Prinn's *De Vermis
Mysteriis*, the *Unaussprechlichen Kulten* of von Junzt, the surviving fragments of the puzzling *Book of Eibon*, and the dreaded *Necronomicon* of
the mad Arab Abdul Alhazred. Then, too, it is undeniable that a fresh
and evil wave of underground cult activity set in about the time of my
odd mutation.

In the summer of 1913 I began to display signs of ennui and
flagging interest, and to hint to various associates that a change
might soon be expected in me. I spoke of returning memories of my
earlier life – though most auditors judged me insincere, since all the
recollections I gave were casual, and such as might have been learned
from my old private papers. About the middle of August I returned
to Arkham and reopened my long-closed house in Crane Street.
Here I installed a mechanism of the most curious aspect, constructed
piecemeal by different makers of scientific apparatus in Europe and
America, and guarded carefully from the sight of anyone intelligent
enough to analyse it. Those who did see it – a workman, a servant,
and the new housekeeper – say that it was a queer mixture of rods,

wheels, and mirrors, though only about two feet tall, one foot wide, and one foot thick. The central mirror was circular and convex. All this is borne out by such makers of parts as can be located.

On the evening of Friday, Sept. 26, I dismissed the housekeeper and the maid till noon of the next day. Lights burned in the house till late, and a lean, dark, curiously foreign-looking man called in an automobile. It was about 1 a.m. that the lights were last seen. At 2:15 a.m. a policeman observed the place in darkness, but with the stranger's motor still at the curb. By four o'clock the motor was certainly gone. It was at six that a hesitant, foreign voice on the telephone asked Dr Wilson to call at my house and bring me out of a peculiar faint. This call – a long-distance one – was later traced to a public booth in the North Station in Boston, but no sign of the lean foreigner was ever unearthed.

When the doctor reached my house he found me unconscious in the sitting-room – in an easy-chair with a table drawn up before it. On the polished table-top were scratches shewing where some heavy object had rested. The queer machine was gone, nor was anything afterward heard of it. Undoubtedly the dark, lean foreigner had taken it away. In the library grate were abundant ashes evidently left from the burning of every remaining scrap of paper on which I had written since the advent of the amnesia. Dr Wilson found my breathing very peculiar, but after an hypodermic injection it became more regular.

At 11:15 a.m., Sept. 27, I stirred vigorously, and my hitherto mask-like face began to shew signs of expression. Dr Wilson remarked that the expression was not that of my secondary personality, but seemed much like that of my normal self. About 11:30 I muttered some very curious syllables – syllables which seemed unrelated to any human speech. I appeared, too, to struggle against something. Then, just after noon – the housekeeper and the maid having meanwhile returned – I began to mutter in English.

' . . . of the orthodox economists of that period, Jevons typifies the prevailing trend toward scientific correlation. His attempt to link the commercial cycle of prosperity and depression with the physical cycle of the solar spots forms perhaps the apex of . . . '

Nathaniel Wingate Peaslee had come back – a spirit in whose time-scale it was still that Thursday morning in 1908, with the economics class gazing up at the battered desk on the platform.

2

My reabsorption into normal life was a painful and difficult process. The loss of over five years creates more complications than can be imagined, and in my case there were countless matters to be adjusted. What I heard of my actions since 1908 astonished and disturbed me, but I tried to view the matter as philosophically as I could. At last regaining custody of my second son Wingate, I settled down with him in the Crane Street house and endeavoured to resume teaching – my old professorship having been kindly offered me by the college.

I began work with the February, 1914, term, and kept at it just a year. By that time I realised how badly my experience had shaken me. Though perfectly sane – I hoped – and with no flaw in my original personality, I had not the nervous energy of the old days. Vague dreams and queer ideas continually haunted me, and when the outbreak of the world war turned my mind to history I found myself thinking of periods and events in the oddest possible fashion. My conception of *time* – my ability to distinguish between con-secutiveness and simultaneousness – seemed subtly disordered; so that I formed chimerical notions about living in one age and casting one's mind all over eternity for knowledge of past and future ages.

The war gave me strange impressions of *remembering* some of its far-off *consequences* – as if I knew how it was coming out and could look *back* upon it in the light of future information. All such quasi-memories were attended with much pain, and with a feeling that some artificial psychological barrier was set against them. When I diffidently hinted to others about my impressions I met with varied responses. Some persons looked uncomfortably at me, but men in the mathematics department spoke of new developments in those theories of relativity – then discussed only in learned circles – which were later to become so famous. Dr Albert Einstein, they said, was rapidly reducing *time* to the status of a mere dimension.

But the dreams and disturbed feelings gained on me, so that I had to drop my regular work in 1915. Certain of the impressions were taking an annoying shape – giving me the persistent notion that my amnesia had formed some unholy sort of *exchange*; that the secondary personality had indeed been an intruding force from unknown regions, and that my own personality had suffered displacement. Thus I was driven to vague and frightful speculations concerning the whereabouts of my true self during the years that another had held my body. The curious knowledge and strange conduct of my body's late tenant troubled me more and more as I learned further details from persons, papers, and magazines. Queernesses that had baffled others seemed to harmonise terribly with some background of black knowledge which festered in the chasms of my subconscious. I began to search feverishly for every scrap of information bearing on the studies and travels of *that other one* during the dark years.

Not all of my troubles were as semi-abstract as this. There were the dreams – and these seemed to grow in vividness and concreteness. Knowing how most would regard them, I seldom mentioned them to anyone but my son or certain trusted psychologists, but eventually I commenced a scientific study of other cases in order to see how typical or non-typical such visions might be among amnesia victims. My results, aided by psychologists, historians, anthropologists, and mental specialists of wide experience, and by a study that included all records of split personalities from the days of daemoniac-possession legends to the medically realistic present, at first bothered me more than they consoled me.

I soon found that my dreams had indeed no counterpart in the overwhelming bulk of true amnesia cases. There remained, however, a tiny residue of accounts which for years baffled and shocked me with their parallelism to my own experience. Some of them were bits of ancient folklore; others were case-histories in the annals of medicine; one or two were anecdotes obscurely buried in standard histories. It thus appeared that, while my special kind of affliction was prodigiously rare, instances of it had occurred at long intervals ever since the beginning of man's annals. Some centuries might contain one, two, or three cases; others none – or at least none whose record survived.

The essence was always the same – a person of keen thoughtfulness seized with a strange secondary life and leading for a greater or lesser period an utterly alien existence typified at first by vocal and bodily awkwardness, and later by a wholesale acquisition of scientific, historic, artistic, and anthropological knowledge; an acquisition carried on with feverish zest and with a wholly abnormal absorptive power. Then a sudden return of the rightful consciousness, intermittently plagued ever after with vague unplaceable dreams suggesting fragments of some hideous memory elaborately blotted out. And the close resemblance of those nightmares to my own – even in some of the smallest particulars – left no doubt in my mind of their significantly typical nature. One or two of the cases had an added ring of faint, blasphemous familiarity, as if I had heard of them before through some cosmic channel too morbid and frightful to contemplate. In three instances there was specific mention of such an unknown machine as had been in my house before the second change.

Another thing that cloudily worried me during my investigation was the somewhat greater frequency of cases where a brief, elusive glimpse of the typical nightmares was afforded to persons not visited with well-defined amnesia. These persons were largely of mediocre mind or less – some so primitive that they could scarcely be thought of as vehicles for abnormal scholarship and preternatural mental acquisitions. For a second they would be fired with alien force – then a backward lapse and a thin, swift-fading memory of un-human horrors.

There had been at least three such cases during the past half century – one only fifteen years before. Had something been *groping blindly through time* from some unsuspected abyss in Nature? Were these faint cases monstrous, sinister *experiments* of a kind and authorship utterly beyond sane belief? Such were a few of the formless speculations of my weaker hours – fancies abetted by myths which my studies uncovered. For I could not doubt but that certain persistent legends of immemorial antiquity, apparently unknown to the victims and physicians connected with recent amnesia cases, formed a striking and awesome elaboration of memory lapses such as mine.

Of the nature of the dreams and impressions which were growing so clamorous I still almost fear to speak. They seemed to savour of madness, and at times I believed I was indeed going mad. Was there a special type of delusion afflicting those who had suffered lapses of memory? Conceivably, the efforts of the subconscious mind to fill up a perplexing blank with pseudo-memories might give rise to strange imaginative vagaries. This, indeed (though an alternative folklore theory finally seemed to me more plausible), was the belief of many of the alienists who helped me in my search for parallel cases, and who shared my puzzlement at the exact resemblances sometimes discovered. They did not call the condition true insanity, but classed it rather among neurotic disorders. My course in trying to track it down and analyse it, instead of vainly seeking to dismiss or forget it, they heartily endorsed as correct according to the best psychological principles. I especially valued the advice of such physicians as had studied me during my possession by the other personality.

My first disturbances were not visual at all, but concerned the more abstract matters which I have mentioned. There was, too, a feeling of profound and inexplicable horror concerning *myself*. I developed a queer fear of seeing my own form, as if my eyes would find it something utterly alien and inconceivably abhorrent. When I did glance down and behold the familiar human shape in quiet grey or blue clothing I always felt a curious relief, though in order to gain this relief I had to conquer an infinite dread. I shunned mirrors as much as possible, and was always shaved at the barber's.

It was a long time before I correlated any of these disappointed feelings with the fleeting visual impressions which began to develop. The first such correlation had to do with the odd sensation of an external, artificial restraint on my memory. I felt that the snatches of sight I experienced had a profound and terrible meaning, and a frightful connexion with myself, but that some purposeful influence held me from grasping that meaning and that connexion. Then came that queerness about the element of *time*, and with it desperate efforts to place the fragmentary dream-glimpses in the chronological and spatial pattern.

The glimpses themselves were at first merely strange rather than horrible. I would seem to be in an enormous vaulted chamber whose lofty stone groinings were well-nigh lost in the shadows overhead. In whatever time or place the scene might be, the principle of the arch was known as fully and used as extensively as by the Romans. There were colossal round windows and high arched doors, and pedestals or tables each as tall as the height of an ordinary room. Vast shelves of dark wood lined the walls, holding what seemed to be volumes of immense size with strange hieroglyphs on their backs. The exposed stonework held curious carvings, always in curvilinear mathematical designs, and there were chiselled inscriptions in the same characters that the huge books bore. The dark granite masonry was of a monstrous megalithic type, with lines of convex-topped blocks fitting the concave-bottomed courses which rested upon them. There were no chairs, but the tops of the vast pedestals were littered with books, papers, and what seemed to be writing materials – oddly figured jars of a purplish metal, and rods with stained tips. Tall as the pedestals were, I seemed at times able to view them from above. On some of them were great globes of luminous crystal serving as lamps, and inexplicable machines formed of vitreous tubes and metal rods. The windows were glazed, and latticed with stout-looking bars. Though I dared not approach and peer out them, I could see from where I was the waving tops of singular fern-like growths. The floor was of massive octagonal flagstones, while rugs and hangings were entirely lacking.

Later I had visions of sweeping through Cyclopean corridors of stone, and up and down gigantic inclined planes of the same monstrous masonry. There were no stairs anywhere, nor was any passage-way less than thirty feet wide. Some of the structures through which I floated must have towered into the sky for thousands of feet. There were multiple levels of black vaults below, and never-opened trap-doors, sealed down with metal bands and holding dim suggestions of some special peril. I seemed to be a prisoner, and horror hung broodingly over everything I saw. I felt that the mocking curvilinear hieroglyphs on the walls would blast my soul with their message were I not guarded by a merciful ignorance.

Still later my dreams included vistas from the great round windows, and from the titanic flat roof, with its curious gardens, wide barren area, and high, scalloped parapet of stone, to which the top-most of the inclined planes led. There were almost endless leagues of giant buildings, each in its garden, and ranged along paved roads fully two hundred feet wide. They differed greatly in aspect, but few were less than five hundred feet square or a thousand feet high. Many seemed so limitless that they must have had a frontage of several thousand feet, while some shot up to mountainous altitudes in the grey, steamy heavens. They seemed to be mainly of stone or concrete, and most of them embodied the oddly curvilinear type of masonry noticeable in the building that held me. Roofs were flat and garden-covered, and tended to have scalloped parapets. Sometimes there were terraces and higher levels, and wide cleared spaces amidst the gardens. The great roads held hints of motion, but in the earlier visions I could not resolve this impression into details.

In certain places I beheld enormous dark cylindrical towers which climbed far above any of the other structures. These appeared to be of a totally unique nature, and shewed signs of prodigious age and dilapidation. They were built of a bizarre type of square-cut basalt masonry, and tapered slightly toward their rounded tops. Nowhere in any of them could the least traces of windows or other apertures save huge doors be found. I noticed also some lower buildings – all crumbling with the weathering of aeons – which resembled these dark cylindrical towers in basic architecture. Around all these aberrant piles of square-cut masonry there hovered an inexplicable aura of menace and concentrated fear, like that bred by the sealed trap-doors.

The omnipresent gardens were almost terrifying in their strangeness, with bizarre and unfamiliar forms of vegetation nodding over broad paths lined with curiously carven monoliths. Abnormally vast fern-like growths predominated; some green, and some of a ghastly, fungoid pallor. Among them rose great spectral things resembling calamites, whose bamboo-like trunks towered to fabulous heights. Then there were tufted forms like fabulous cycads, and grotesque dark-green shrubs and trees of coniferous aspect. Flowers were small, colourless, and unrecognisable, blooming in geometrical beds and at large among the greenery. In a few of the terrace and roof-top gardens were larger and more vivid blossoms of almost offensive contours and seeming to suggest artificial breeding. Fungi of inconceivable size, outlines, and colours speckled the scene in patterns bespeaking some unknown but well-established horticultural tradition. In the larger gardens on the ground there seemed to be some attempt to preserve the irregularities of Nature, but on the roofs there was more selectiveness, and more evidences of the topiary art.

The skies were almost always moist and cloudy, and sometimes I would seem to witness tremendous rains. Once in a while, though, there would be glimpses of the sun – which looked abnormally large – and of the moon, whose markings held a touch of difference from the normal that I could never quite fathom. When – very rarely – the night sky was clear to any extent, I beheld constellations which were nearly beyond recognition. Known outlines were sometimes approximated, but seldom duplicated; and from the position of the few groups I could recognise, I felt I must be in the earth's southern hemisphere, near the Tropic of Capricorn. The far horizon was always steamy and indistinct, but I could see that great jungles of unknown tree-ferns, calamites, lepidodendra, and sigillaria lay outside the city, their fantastic frondage waving mockingly in the shifting vapours. Now and then there would be suggestions of motion in the sky, but these my early visions never resolved.

By the autumn of 1914 I began to have infrequent dreams of strange floatings over the city and through the regions around it. I saw interminable roads through forests of fearsome growths with mottled, fluted, and banded trunks, and past other cities as strange as the one which persistently haunted me. I saw monstrous constructions of black or iridescent stone in glades and clearings where perpetual twilight reigned, and traversed long causeways over swamps so dark that I could tell but little of their moist, towering vegetation. Once I saw an area of countless miles strown with age-blasted basaltic ruins whose architecture had been like that of the few windowless, round-topped towers in the haunting city. And once I saw the sea – a boundless steamy expanse beyond the colossal stone piers of an enormous town of domes and arches. Great shapeless suggestions of shadow moved over it, and here and there its surface was vexed with anomalous spoutings.

3

As I have said, it was not immediately that these wild visions began to hold their terrifying quality. Certainly, many persons have dreamed intrinsically stranger things – things compounded of unrelated scraps of daily life, pictures, and reading, and arranged in fantastically novel forms by the unchecked caprices of sleep. For some time I accepted the visions as natural, even though I had never before been an extravagant dreamer. Many of the vague anomalies, I argued, must have come from trivial sources too numerous to track down; while others seemed to reflect a common text-book knowledge of the plants and other conditions of the primitive world of a hundred and fifty million years ago – the world of the Permian or Triassic age. In the course of some months, however, the element of terror did figure with accumulating force. This was when the dreams began so unfailingly to have the aspect of *memories*, and when my mind began to link them with my growing abstract disturbances – the feeling of mnemonic restraint, the curious impressions regarding *time*, the sense of a loathsome exchange with my secondary personality of 1908–13, and, considerably later, the inexplicable loathing of my own person.

As certain definite details began to enter the dreams, their horror increased a thousandfold – until by October, 1915, I felt I must do something. It was then that I began an intensive study of other cases of amnesia and visions, feeling that I might thereby objectivise my trouble and shake clear of its emotional grip. However, as before mentioned, the result was at first almost exactly opposite. It disturbed me vastly to find that my dreams had been so closely duplicated; especially since some of the accounts were too early to admit of any geological knowledge – and therefore of any idea of primitive landscapes – on the subjects' part. What is more, many of these accounts supplied very horrible details and explanations in connexion with the visions of great buildings and jungle gardens – and other things. The actual sights and vague impressions were bad enough, but what was hinted or asserted by some of the other dreamers savoured of madness and blasphemy. Worst of all, my own pseudo-memory was aroused to wilder dreams and hints of coming revelations. And yet most doctors deemed my course, on the whole, an advisable one.

I studied psychology systematically, and under the prevailing stimulus my son Wingate did the same – his studies leading eventually to his present professorship. In 1917 and 1918 I took special courses at Miskatonic. Meanwhile my examination of medical, historical, and anthropological records became indefatigable, involving travels to distant libraries, and finally including even a reading of the hideous books of forbidden elder lore in which my secondary personality had been so disturbingly interested. Some of the latter were the actual copies I had consulted in my altered state, and I was greatly disturbed by certain marginal notations and ostensible *corrections* of the hideous text in a script and idiom which somehow seemed oddly un-human.

These markings were mostly in the respective languages of the various books, all of which the writer seemed to know with equal though obviously academic facility. One note appended to von Junzt's *Unaussprechlichen Kulten*, however, was alarmingly otherwise. It consisted of certain curvilinear hieroglyphs in the same ink as that of the German corrections, but following no recognised human pattern. And these hieroglyphs were closely and unmistakably akin to the characters constantly met with in my dreams – characters whose meaning I would sometimes momentarily fancy I knew or was just on the brink of recalling. To complete my black confusion, my librarians assured me that, in view of previous examinations and records of consultation of the volumes in question, all of these notations must have been made by myself in my secondary state. This despite the fact that I was and still am ignorant of three of the languages involved.

Piecing together the scattered records, ancient and modern, anthropological and medical, I found a fairly consistent mixture of myth and hallucination whose scope and wildness left me utterly dazed. Only one thing consoled me – the fact that the myths were of such early existence. What lost knowledge could have brought pictures of the Palaeozoic or Mesozoic landscape into these primitive fables, I could not even guess, but the pictures had been there. Thus, a basis existed for the formation of a fixed type of delusion. Cases of amnesia no doubt created the general myth-pattern – but afterward the fanciful accretions of the myths must have reacted on amnesia sufferers and coloured their pseudo-memories. I myself had read and heard all the early tales during my memory lapse – my quest had amply proved that. Was it not natural, then, for my subsequent dreams and emotional impressions to become coloured and moulded by what my memory subtly held over from my secondary state? A few of the myths had significant connexions with other cloudy legends of the pre-human world, especially those Hindoo tales involving stupefying gulfs of time and forming part of the lore of modern theosophists.

Primal myth and modern delusion joined in their assumption that mankind is only one – perhaps the least – of the highly evolved and dominant races of this planet's long and largely unknown career. Things of inconceivable shape, they implied, had reared towers to the sky and delved into every secret of Nature before the first amphibian forbear of man had crawled out of the hot sea three hundred million years ago. Some had come down from the stars; a few were as old as the cosmos itself; others had arisen swiftly from terrene germs as far behind the first germs of our life-cycle as those germs are behind ourselves. Spans of thousands of millions of years, and linkages with other galaxies and universes, were freely spoken of. Indeed, there was no such thing as time in its humanly accepted sense.

But most of the tales and impressions concerned a relatively late race, of a queer and intricate shape resembling no life-form known to science, which had lived till only fifty million years before the advent of man. This, they indicated, was the greatest race of all, because it alone had conquered the secret of time. It had learned all things that ever were known *or ever would be known* on the earth, through the power of its keener minds to project themselves into the past and future, even through gulfs of millions of years, and study the lore of every age. From the accomplishments of this race arose all legends of *prophets*, including those in human mythology.

In its vast libraries were volumes of texts and pictures holding the whole of earth's annals – histories and descriptions of every species that had ever been or that ever would be, with full records of their arts, their achievements, their languages, and their psychologies. With this aeon-embracing knowledge, the Great Race chose from every era and life-form such thoughts, arts, and processes as might suit its own nature and situation. Knowledge of the past, secured through a kind of mind-casting outside the recognised senses, was harder to glean than knowledge of the future.

In the latter case the course was easier and more material. With suitable mechanical aid a mind would project itself forward in time, feeling its dim, extra-sensory way till it approached the desired period. Then, after preliminary trials, it would seize on the best discoverable representative of the highest of that period's life-forms, entering the organism's brain and setting up therein its own vibrations while the displaced mind would strike back to the period of the displacer, remaining in the latter's body till a reverse process was set up. The projected mind, in the body of the organism of the future, would then pose as a member of the race whose outward form it wore, learning as quickly as possible all that could be learned of the chosen age and its massed information and techniques.

Meanwhile the displaced mind, thrown back to the displacer's age and body, would be carefully guarded. It would be kept from harming the body it occupied, and would be drained of all its knowledge by trained questioners. Often it could be questioned in its own language, when previous quests into the future had brought back records of that language. If the mind came from a body whose language the Great Race could not physically reproduce, clever machines would be made, on which the alien speech could be played as on a musical instrument. The Great Race's members were immense rugose cones ten feet high, and with head and other organs attached to foot-thick, distensible limbs spreading from the apexes. They spoke by the clicking or scraping of huge paws or claws attached to the end of two of their four limbs, and walked by the expansion and contraction of a viscous layer attached to their vast ten-foot bases.

When the captive mind's amazement and resentment had worn off, and when (assuming that it came from a body vastly different from the Great Race's) it had lost its horror at its unfamiliar temporary form, it was permitted to study its new environment and experience a wonder and wisdom approximating that of its displacer. With suitable precautions, and in exchange for suitable services, it was allowed to rove all over the habitable world in titan airships or on the huge boat-like atomic-engined vehicles which traversed the great roads, and to delve freely into the libraries containing the records of the planet's past and future. This reconciled many captive minds to their lot, since none were other than keen, and to such minds the unveiling of hidden mysteries of earth – closed chapters of inconceivable pasts and dizzying vortices of future time which include the years ahead of their own natural ages – forms always, despite the abysmal horrors often unveiled, the supreme experience of life.

Now and then certain captives were permitted to meet other captive minds seized from the future – to exchange thoughts with consciousnesses living a hundred or a thousand or a million years before or after their own ages. And all were urged to write copiously in their own languages of themselves and their respective periods; such documents to be filed in the great central archives.

It may be added that there was one sad special type of captive whose privileges were far greater than those of the majority. These were the dying *permanent* exiles, whose bodies in the future had been seized by keen-minded members of the Great Race who, faced with death, sought to escape mental extinction. Such melancholy exiles were not as common as might be expected, since the longevity of the Great Race lessened its love of life – especially among those superior minds capable of projection. From cases of the permanent projection of elder minds arose many of those lasting changes of personality noticed in later history – including mankind's.

As for the ordinary cases of exploration – when the displacing mind had learned what it wished in the future, it would build an apparatus like that which had started its flight and reverse the process of projection. Once more it would be in its own body in its own age, while the lately captive mind would return to that body of the future to which it properly belonged. Only when one or the other of the bodies had died during the exchange was this restoration impossible. In such cases, of course, the exploring mind had – like those of the death-escapers – to live out an alien-bodied life in the future; or else the captive mind – like the dying permanent exiles – had to end its days in the form and past age of the Great Race.

This fate was least horrible when the captive mind was also of the Great Race – a not infrequent occurrence, since in all its periods that race was intensely concerned with its own future. The number of dying permanent exiles of the Great Race was very slight – largely because of the tremendous penalties attached to displacements of future Great Race minds by the moribund. Through projection, arrangements were made to inflict these penalties on the offending minds in their new future bodies – and sometimes forced re-exchanges were effected. Complex cases of the displacement of exploring or already captive minds by minds in various regions of the past had been known and carefully rectified. In every age since the discovery of mind-projection, a minute but well-recognised element of the population consisted of Great Race minds from past ages, sojourning for a longer or shorter while.

When a captive mind of alien origin was returned to its own body in the future, it was purged by an intricate mechanical hypnosis of all it had learned in the Great Race's age – this because of certain troublesome consequences inherent in the general carrying forward of knowledge in large quantities. The few existing instances of clear transmission had caused, and would cause at known future times, great disasters. And it was largely in consequence of two cases of the kind (said the old myths) that mankind had learned what it had concerning the Great Race. Of all things surviving *physically and directly* from that aeon-distant world, there remained only certain ruins of great stones in far places and under the sea, and parts of the text of the frightful *Pnakotic Manuscripts*.

Thus the returning mind reached its own age with only the faintest and most fragmentary visions of what it had undergone since its seizure. All memories that could be eradicated were eradicated, so that in most cases only a dream-shadowed blank stretched back to the time of the first exchange. Some minds recalled more than others, and the chance joining of memories had at rare times brought hints of the forbidden past to future ages. There probably never was a time when groups or cults did not secretly cherish certain of these hints. In the *Necronomicon* the presence of such a cult among human beings was suggested – a cult that sometimes gave aid to minds voyaging down the aeons from the days of the Great Race.

And meanwhile the Great Race itself waxed well-nigh omniscient, and turned to the task of setting up exchanges with the minds of other planets, and of exploring their pasts and futures. It sought likewise to fathom the past years and origin of that black, aeon-dead orb in far space whence its own mental heritage had come – for the mind of the Great Race was older than its bodily form. The beings of a dying elder world, wise with the ultimate secrets, had looked ahead for a new world and species wherein they might have long life; and had sent their minds en masse into that future race best adapted to house them – the cone-shaped things that peopled our earth a billion years ago. Thus the Great Race came to be, while the myriad minds sent backward were left to die in the horror of strange shapes. Later the race would again face death, yet would live through another forward migration of its best minds into the bodies of others who had a longer physical span ahead of them.

Such was the background of intertwined legend and hallucination. When, around 1920, I had my researches in coherent shape, I felt a slight lessening of the tension which their earlier stages had increased. After all, and in spite of the fancies prompted by blind emotions, were not most of my phenomena readily explainable? Any chance might have turned my mind to dark studies during the amnesia – and then I read the forbidden legends and met the members of ancient and ill-regarded cults. That, plainly, supplied the material for the dreams and disturbed feelings which came after the return of memory. As for the marginal notes in dream hieroglyphs and languages unknown to me, but laid at my door by librarians – I might easily have picked up a smattering of the tongues during my secondary state, while the hieroglyphs were doubtless coined by my fancy from descriptions in old legends, and *afterward* woven into my dreams. I tried to verify certain points through conversation with known cult-leaders, but never succeeded in establishing the right connexions.

At times the parallelism of so many cases in so many distant ages continued to worry me as it had at first, but on the other hand I reflected that the excitant folklore was undoubtedly more universal in the past than in the present. Probably all the other victims whose cases were like mine had had a long and familiar knowledge of the tales I had learned only when in my secondary state. When these victims had lost their memory, they had associated themselves with the creatures of their household myths – the fabulous invaders supposed to displace men's minds – and had thus embarked upon quests for knowledge which they thought they could take back to a fancied, non-human past. Then when their memory returned, they reversed the associative process and thought of themselves as the former captive minds instead of as the displacers. Hence the dreams and pseudo-memories following the conventional myth-pattern.

Despite the seeming cumbrousness of these explanations, they came finally to supersede all others in my mind – largely because of the greater weakness of any rival theory. And a substantial number of eminent psychologists and anthropologists gradually agreed with me. The more I reflected, the more convincing did my reasoning seem, till in the end I had a really effective bulwark against the visions and impressions which still assailed me. Suppose I did see strange things at night? These were only what I had heard and read of. Suppose I did have odd loathings and perspectives and pseudo-memories? These, too, were only echoes of myths absorbed in my secondary state. Nothing that I might dream, nothing that I might feel, could be of any actual significance.

Fortified by this philosophy, I greatly improved in nervous equi-librium, even though the visions (rather than the abstract impressions) steadily became more frequent and more disturbingly detailed. In 1922 I felt able to undertake regular work again, and put my newly gained knowledge to practical use by accepting an instructorship in psychology at the university. My old chair of political economy had long been adequately filled – besides which, methods of teaching economics had changed greatly since my heyday. My son was at this time just entering on the post-graduate studies leading to his present professorship, and we worked together a great deal.

4

I continued, however, to keep a careful record of the *outré* dreams which crowded upon me so thickly and vividly. Such a record, I argued, was of genuine value as a psychological document. The glimpses still seemed damnably like *memories*, though I fought off this impression with a goodly measure of success. In writing, I treated the phantasmata as things seen; but at all other times I brushed them aside like any gossamer illusions of the night. I had never mentioned such matters in common conversation; though reports of them, filtering out as such things will, had aroused sundry rumours regarding my mental health. It is amusing to reflect that these rumours were confined wholly to laymen, without a single champion among physicians or psychologists.

Of my visions after 1914 I will here mention only a few, since fuller accounts and records are at the disposal of the serious stud-ent. It is evident that with time the curious inhibitions somewhat waned, for the scope of my visions vastly increased. They have never, though, become other than disjointed fragments seemingly without clear motivation. Within the dreams I seemed gradually to acquire a greater and greater freedom of wandering. I floated through many strange buildings of stone, going from one to the other along mammoth underground passages which seemed to form the common avenues of transit. Sometimes I encountered those gigantic sealed trap-doors in the lowest level, around which such an aura of fear and forbiddenness clung. I saw tremendous tessellated pools, and rooms of curious and inexplicable utensils of myriad sorts. Then there were colossal caverns of intricate machinery whose outlines and purpose were wholly strange to me, and whose *sound* manifested itself only after many years of dreaming. I may here remark that sight and sound are the only senses I have ever exercised in the visionary world.

The real horror began in May, 1915, when I first saw the *living things*. This was before my studies had taught me what, in view of the myths and case histories, to expect. As mental barriers wore down, I beheld great masses of thin vapour in various parts of the building and in the streets below. These steadily grew more solid and distinct, till at last I could trace their monstrous outlines with uncomfortable ease. They seemed to be enormous iridescent cones, about ten feet high and ten feet wide at the base, and made up of some ridgy, scaly, semi-elastic matter. From their apexes projected four flexible, cylindrical members, each a foot thick, and of a ridgy substance like that of the cones themselves. These members were sometimes contracted almost to nothing, and sometimes extended to any distance up to about ten feet. Terminating two of them were enormous claws or nippers. At the end of a third were four red, trumpet-like appendages. The fourth terminated in an irregular yellowish globe some two feet in diameter and having three great dark eyes ranged along its central circumference. Surmounting this head were four slender grey stalks bearing flower-like appendages, whilst from its nether side dangled eight greenish antennae or tentacles. The great base of the central cone was fringed with a rubbery, grey substance which moved the whole entity through expansion and contraction.

Their actions, though harmless, horrified me even more than their appearance – for it is not wholesome to watch monstrous objects doing what one has known only human beings to do. These objects moved intelligently around the great rooms, getting books from the shelves and taking them to the great tables, or vice versa, and sometimes writing diligently with a peculiar rod gripped in the greenish head-tentacles. The huge nippers were used in carrying books and in conversation – speech consisting of a kind of clicking and scraping. The objects had no clothing, but wore satchels or knapsacks suspended from the top of the conical trunk. They commonly carried their head and its supporting member at the level of the cone top, although it was frequently raised or lowered. The other three great members tended to rest downward on the sides of the cone, contracted to about five feet each, when not in use. From their rate of reading, writing, and operating their machines (those on the tables seemed somehow connected with thought) I concluded that their intelligence was enormously greater than man's.

Afterward I saw them everywhere; swarming in all the great chambers and corridors, tending monstrous machines in vaulted crypts, and racing along the vast roads in gigantic boat-shaped cars. I ceased to be afraid of them, for they seemed to form supremely natural parts of their environment. Individual differences amongst them began to be manifest, and a few appeared to be under some kind of restraint. These latter, though shewing no physical variation, had a diversity of gestures and habits which marked them off not only from the majority, but very largely from one another. They wrote a great deal in what seemed to my cloudy vision a vast variety of characters – never the typical curvilinear hieroglyphs of the majority. A few, I fancied, used our own familiar alphabet. Most of them worked much more slowly than the general mass of the entities.

All this time *my own part* in the dreams seemed to be that of a disembodied consciousness with a range of vision wider than the normal; floating freely about, yet confined to the ordinary avenues and speeds of travel. Not until August, 1915, did any suggestions of bodily existence begin to harass me. I say *harass*, because the first phase was a purely abstract though infinitely terrible association of my previously noted body-loathing with the scenes of my visions. For a while my chief concern during dreams was to avoid looking down at myself, and I recall how grateful I was for the total absence of large mirrors in the strange rooms. I was mightily troubled by the fact that I always saw the great tables – whose height could not be under ten feet – from a level not below that of their surfaces.

And then the morbid temptation to look down at myself became greater and greater, till one night I could not resist it. At first my downward glance revealed nothing whatever. A moment later I perceived that this was because my head lay at the end of a flexible neck of enormous length. Retracting this neck and gazing down very sharply, I saw the scaly, rugose, iridescent bulk of a vast cone ten feet tall and ten feet wide at the base. That was when I waked half of Arkham with my screaming as I plunged madly up from the abyss of sleep.

Only after weeks of hideous repetition did I grow half-reconciled to these visions of myself in monstrous form. In the dreams I now moved bodily among the other unknown entities, reading terrible books from the endless shelves and writing for hours at the great tables with a stylus managed by the green tentacles that hung down from my head. Snatches of what I read and wrote would linger in my memory. There were horrible annals of other worlds and other universes, and of stirrings of formless life outside of all universes. There were records of strange orders of beings which had peopled the world in forgotten pasts, and frightful chronicles of grotesque-bodied intelligences which would people it millions of years after the death of the last human being. And I learned of chapters in human history whose existence no scholar of today has ever suspected. Most of these writings were in the language of the hieroglyphs, which I studied in a queer way with the aid of droning machines, and which was evidently an agglutinative speech with root systems utterly un-like any found in human languages. Other volumes were in other unknown tongues learned in the same queer way. A very few were in languages I knew. Extremely clever pictures, both inserted in the records and forming separate collections, aided me immensely. And all the time I seemed to be setting down a history of my own age in English. On waking, I could recall only minute and meaningless scraps of the unknown tongues which my dream-self had mastered, though whole phrases of the history stayed with me.

I learned – even before my waking self had studied the parallel cases or the old myths from which the dreams doubtless sprang –

that the entities around me were of the world's greatest race, which had conquered time and had sent exploring minds into every age. I knew, too, that I had been snatched from my age while *another* used my body in that age, and that a few of the other strange forms housed similarly captured minds. I seemed to talk, in some odd language of claw-clickings, with exiled intellects from every corner of the solar system.

There was a mind from the planet we know as Venus, which would live incalculable epochs to come, and one from an outer moon of Jupiter six million years in the past. Of earthly minds there were some from the winged, star-headed, half-vegetable race of palaeogean Antarctica; one from the reptile people of fabled Valusia; three from the furry pre-human Hyperborean worshippers of Tsathoggua; one from the wholly abominable Tcho-Tchos; two from the arachnid denizens of earth's last age; five from the hardy coleopterous species immediately following mankind, to which the Great Race was some day to transfer its keenest minds en masse in the face of horrible peril; and several from different branches of humanity.

I talked with the mind of Yiang-Li, a philosopher from the cruel empire of Tsan-Chan, which is to come in A.D. 5000; with that of a general of the great-headed brown people who held South Africa in B.C. 50,000; with that of a twelfth-century Florentine monk named Bartolomeo Corsi; with that of a king of Lomar who had ruled that terrible polar land 100,000 years before the squat, yellow Inutos came from the west to engulf it; with that of Nug-Soth, a magician of the dark conquerors of A.D. 16,000; with that of a Roman named Titus Sempronius Blaesus, who had been a quaestor in Sulla's time; with that of Khephnes, an Egyptian of the 14th Dynasty who told me the hideous secret of Nyarlathotep; with that of a priest of Atlantis' middle kingdom; with that of a Suffolk gentleman of Cromwell's day, James Woodville; with that of a court astronomer of pre-Inca Peru; with that of the Australian physicist Nevil Kingston-Brown, who will die in A.D. 2518; with that of an archimage of vanished Yhe in the Pacific; with that of Theodotides, a Graeco-Bactrian official of B.C. 200; with that of an aged Frenchman of Louis XIII's time named Pierre-Louis Mont-magny; with that of Crom-Ya, a Cimmerian chieftain of B.C. 15,000;

and with so many others that my brain cannot hold the shocking secrets and dizzying marvels I learned from them.

I awaked each morning in a fever, sometimes frantically trying to verify or discredit such information as fell within the range of modern human knowledge. Traditional facts took on new and doubtful aspects, and I marvelled at the dream-fancy which could invent such surprising addenda to history and science. I shivered at the mysteries the past may conceal, and trembled at the menaces the future may bring forth. What was hinted in the speech of post-human entities of the fate of mankind produced such an effect on me that I will not set it down here. After man there would be the mighty beetle civilisation, the bodies of whose members the cream of the Great Race would seize when the monstrous doom overtook the elder world. Later, as the earth's span closed, the transferred minds would again migrate through time and space – to another stopping-place in the bodies of the bulbous vegetable entities of Mercury. But there would be races after them, clinging pathetically to the cold planet and burrowing to its horror-filled core, before the utter end.

Meanwhile, in my dreams, I wrote endlessly in that history of my own age which I was preparing – half voluntarily and half through promises of increased library and travel opportunities – for the Great Race's central archives. The archives were in a colossal subterranean structure near the city's centre, which I came to know well through frequent labours and consultations. Meant to last as long as the race, and to withstand the fiercest of earth's convulsions, this titan repository surpassed all other buildings in the massive, mountain-like firmness of its construction.

The records, written or printed on great sheets of a curiously tenacious cellulose fabric, were bound into books that opened from the top, and were kept in individual cases of a strange, extremely light rustless metal of greyish hue, decorated with mathematical designs and bearing the title in the Great Race's curvilinear hiero-glyphs. These cases were stored in tiers of rectangular vaults – like closed, locked shelves – wrought of the same rustless metal and fastened by knobs with intricate turnings. My own history was assigned a specific place in the vaults of the lowest or vertebrate level – the section devoted to the culture of mankind and of the furry and reptilian races immediately preceding it in terrestrial dominance.

But none of the dreams ever gave me a full picture of daily life. All were the merest misty, disconnected fragments, and it is certain that these fragments were not unfolded in their rightful sequence. I have, for example, a very imperfect idea of my own living arrangements in the dream-world, though I seem to have possessed a great stone room of my own. My restrictions as a prisoner gradually disappeared, so that some of the visions included vivid travels over the mighty jungle roads, sojourns in strange cities, and explorations of some of the vast dark windowless ruins from which the Great Race shrank in curious fear. There were also long sea-voyages in enormous, many-decked boats of incredible swiftness, and trips over wild regions in closed, projectile-like airships lifted and moved by electrical repulsion. Beyond the wide, warm ocean were other cities of the Great Race, and on one far continent I saw the crude villages of the black-snouted, winged creatures who would evolve as a dominant stock after the Great Race had sent its foremost minds into the future to escape the creeping horror. Flatness and exuberant green life were always the keynote of the scene. Hills were low and sparse, and usually displayed signs of volcanic forces.

Of the animals I saw, I could write volumes. All were wild; for the Great Race's mechanised culture had long since done away with domestic beasts, while food was wholly vegetable or synthetic. Clumsy reptiles of great bulk floundered in steaming morasses, fluttered in the heavy air, or spouted in the seas and lakes; and among these I fancied I could vaguely recognise lesser, archaic prototypes of many forms – dinosaurs, pterodactyls, ichthyosaurs, labyrinthodonts, rhamphorhynci, plesiosaurs, and the like – made familiar through palaeontology. Of birds or mammals there were none that I could discern.

The ground and swamps were constantly alive with snakes, lizards, and crocodiles, while insects buzzed incessantly amidst the lush vegetation. And far out at sea unspied and unknown monsters spouted mountainous columns of foam into the vaporous sky. Once I was taken under the ocean in a gigantic submarine vessel with searchlights, and glimpsed some living horrors of awesome magnitude. I saw also the ruins of incredible sunken cities, and the wealth of crinoid, brachiopod, coral, and ichthyic life which everywhere abounded.

Of the physiology, psychology, folkways, and detailed history of the Great Race my visions preserved but little information, and many of the scattered points I here set down were gleaned from my study of old legends and other cases rather than from my own dreaming. For in time, of course, my reading and research caught up with and passed the dreams in many phases; so that certain dream-fragments were explained in advance, and formed verifications of what I had learned. This consolingly established my belief that similar reading and research, accomplished by my secondary self, had formed the source of the whole terrible fabric of pseudo-memories.

The period of my dreams, apparently, was one somewhat less than 150,000,000 years ago, when the Palaeozoic age was giving place to the Mesozoic. The bodies occupied by the Great Race represented no surviving – or even scientifically known – line of terrestrial evolution, but were of a peculiar, closely homogeneous, and highly specialised organic type inclining as much to the vegetable as to the animal state. Cell-action was of an unique sort almost precluding fatigue, and wholly eliminating the need of sleep. Nourishment, assimilated through the red trumpet-like appendages on one of the great flexible limbs, was always semi-fluid and in many aspects wholly unlike the food of existing animals. The beings had but two of the senses which we recognise – sight and hearing, the latter accomplished through the flower-like appendages on the grey stalks above their heads – but of other and incomprehensible senses (not, however, well utilisable by alien captive minds inhabiting their bodies) they possessed many. Their three eyes were so situated as to give them a range of vision wider than the normal. Their blood was a sort of deep-greenish ichor of great thickness. They had no sex, but reproduced through seeds or spores which clustered on their bases and could be developed only under water. Great, shallow tanks were used for the growth of their young – which were, however, reared only in small numbers on account of the longevity of individuals, four or five thousand years being the common life span.

Markedly defective individuals were quietly disposed of as soon as their defects were noticed. Disease and the approach of death were, in the absence of a sense of touch or of physical pain, recognised by purely visual symptoms. The dead were incinerated with dignified ceremonies. Once in a while, as before mentioned, a keen mind would escape death by forward projection in time; but such cases were not numerous. When one did occur, the exiled mind from the future was treated with the utmost kindness till the dissolution of its unfamiliar tenement.

The Great Race seemed to form a single loosely knit nation or league, with major institutions in common, though there were four definite divisions. The political and economic system of each unit was a sort of fascistic socialism, with major resources rationally distributed, and power delegated to a small governing board elected by the votes of all able to pass certain educational and psychological tests. Family organisation was not overstressed, though ties among persons of common descent were recognised, and the young were generally reared by their parents.

Resemblances to human attitudes and institutions were, of course, most marked in those fields where on the one hand highly abstract elements were concerned, or where on the other hand there was a dominance of the basic, unspecialised urges common to all organic life. A few added likenesses came through conscious adoption as the Great Race probed the future and copied what it liked. Industry, highly mechanised, demanded but little time from each citizen; and the abundant leisure was filled with intellectual and aesthetic activities of various sorts. The sciences were carried to an unbelievable height of development, and art was a vital part of life, though at the period of my dreams it had passed its crest and meridian. Technology was enormously stimulated through the constant struggle to survive, and to keep in existence the physical fabric of great cities, imposed by the prodigious geologic upheavals of those primal days.

Crime was surprisingly scanty, and was dealt with through highly efficient policing. Punishments ranged from privilege-deprivation and imprisonment to death or major emotion-wrenching, and were never administered without a careful study of the criminal's motivations. Warfare, largely civil for the last few millennia though sometimes waged against reptilian and octopodic invaders, or against the winged, star-headed Old Ones who centred in the Antarctic, was infrequent though infinitely devastating. An enormous army, using camera-like weapons which produced tremendous electrical effects, was kept on hand for purposes seldom mentioned, but obviously connected with the ceaseless fear of the dark, windowless elder ruins and of the great sealed trap-doors in the lowest sub-terrene levels.

This fear of the basalt ruins and trap-doors was largely a matter of unspoken suggestion – or, at most, of furtive quasi-whispers. Everything specific which bore on it was significantly absent from such books as were on the common shelves. It was the one subject lying altogether under a taboo among the Great Race, and seemed to be connected alike with horrible bygone struggles, and with that future peril which would some day force the race to send its keener minds ahead en masse in time. Imperfect and fragmentary as were the other things presented by dreams and legends, this matter was still more bafflingly shrouded. The vague old myths avoided it – or perhaps all allusions had for some reason been excised. And in the dreams of myself and others, the hints were peculiarly few. Members of the Great Race never intentionally referred to the matter, and what could be gleaned came only from some of the more sharply observant captive minds.

According to these scraps of information, the basis of the fear was a horrible elder race of half-polypous, utterly alien entities which had come through space from immeasurably distant universes and had dominated the earth and three other solar planets about six hundred million years ago. They were only partly material – as we understand matter – and their type of consciousness and media of perception differed wholly from those of terrestrial organisms. For example, their senses did not include that of sight, their mental world being a strange, non-visual pattern of impressions. They were, however, sufficiently material to use implements of normal matter when in cosmic areas containing it; and they required housing – albeit of a peculiar kind. Though their *senses* could penetrate all material barriers, their *substance* could not; and certain forms of electrical energy could wholly destroy them. They had the power of aerial motion despite the absence of wings or any other visible means of levitation. Their minds were of such texture that no exchange with them could be effected by the Great Race.

When these things had come to the earth they had built mighty basalt cities of windowless towers, and had preyed horribly upon the beings they found. Thus it was when the minds of the Great Race sped across the void from that obscure trans-galactic world known in the disturbing and debatable Eltdown Shards as Yith. The newcomers, with the instruments they created, had found it easy to subdue the predatory entities and drive them down to those caverns of inner earth which they had already joined to their abodes and begun to inhabit. Then they had sealed the entrances and left them to their fate, afterward occupying most of their great cities and preserving certain important buildings for reasons connected more with superstition than with indifference, boldness, or scient-ific and historical zeal.

But as the aeons passed, there came vague, evil signs that the Elder Things were growing strong and numerous in the inner world. There were sporadic irruptions of a particularly hideous character in certain small and remote cities of the Great Race, and in some of the deserted elder cities which the Great Race had not peopled – places where the paths to the gulfs below had not been properly sealed or guarded. After that greater precautions were taken, and many of the paths were closed for ever – though a few were left with sealed trap-doors for strategic use in fighting the Elder Things if ever they broke forth in unexpected places; fresh rifts caused by that selfsame geologic change which had choked some of the paths and had slowly lessened the number of outer-world structures and ruins surviving from the conquered entities.

The irruptions of the Elder Things must have been shocking beyond all description, since they had permanently coloured the psychology of the Great Race. Such was the fixed mood of horror that the very *aspect* of the creatures was left unmentioned – at no time was I able to gain a clear hint of what they looked like. There were veiled suggestions of a monstrous *plasticity*, and of temporary *lapses of visibility*, while other fragmentary whispers referred to their control and military use of *great winds*. Singular *whistling* noises, and colossal footprints made up of five circular toe-marks, seemed also to be associated with them.

It was evident that the coming doom so desperately feared by the Great Race – the doom that was one day to send millions of keen

minds across the chasm of time to strange bodies in the safer future –
had to do with a final successful irruption of the Elder Beings.
Mental projections down the ages had clearly foretold such a horror,
and the Great Race had resolved that none who could escape should
face it. That the foray would be a matter of vengeance, rather than
an attempt to reoccupy the outer world, they knew from the planet's
later history – for their projections shewed the coming and going
of subsequent races untroubled by the monstrous entities. Perhaps these entities had come to prefer earth's inner abysses to the
variable, storm-ravaged surface, since light meant nothing to them.
Perhaps, too, they were slowly weakening with the aeons. Indeed, it
was known that they would be quite dead in the time of the post-
human beetle race which the fleeing minds would tenant. Meanwhile the Great Race maintained its cautious vigilance, with potent
weapons ceaselessly ready despite the horrified banishing of the
subject from common speech and visible records. And always the
shadow of nameless fear hung about the sealed trap-doors and the
dark, windowless elder towers.

5

That is the world of which my dreams brought me dim, scattered
echoes every night. I cannot hope to give any true idea of the horror
and dread contained in such echoes, for it was upon a wholly
intangible quality – the sharp sense of *pseudo-memory* – that such
feelings mainly depended. As I have said, my studies gradually gave
me a defence against these feelings, in the form of rational psychological explanations; and this saving influence was augmented by
the subtle touch of accustomedness which comes with the passage
of time. Yet in spite of everything the vague, creeping terror would
return momentarily now and then. It did not, however, engulf
me as it had before, and after 1922 I lived a very normal life of work
and recreation.

In the course of years I began to feel that my experience –
together with the kindred cases and the related folklore – ought to
be definitely summarised and published for the benefit of serious
students; hence I prepared a series of articles briefly covering the
whole ground and illustrated with crude sketches of some of the

shapes, scenes, decorative motifs, and hieroglyphs remembered from the dreams. These appeared at various times during 1928 and 1929 in the *Journal of the American Psychological Society*, but did not attract much attention. Meanwhile I continued to record my dreams with the minutest care, even though the growing stack of reports attained troublesomely vast proportions.

On July 10, 1934, there was forwarded to me by the Psychological Society the letter which opened the culminating and most horrible phase of the whole mad ordeal. It was postmarked Pilbarra, Western Australia, and bore the signature of one whom I found, upon inquiry, to be a mining engineer of considerable prominence. Enclosed were some very curious snapshots. I will reproduce the text in its entirety, and no reader can fail to understand how tremendous an effect it and the photographs had upon me.

I was, for a time, almost stunned and incredulous; for although I had often thought that some basis of fact must underlie certain phases of the legends which had coloured my dreams, I was none the less unprepared for anything like a tangible survival from a lost world remote beyond all imagination. Most devastating of all were the photographs – for here, in cold, incontrovertible realism, there stood out against a background of sand certain worn-down, water-ridged, storm-weathered blocks of stone whose slightly convex tops and slightly concave bottoms told their own story. And when I studied them with a magnifying glass I could see all too plainly, amidst the batterings and pittings, the traces of those vast curvilinear designs and occasional hieroglyphs whose significance had become so hideous to me. But here is the letter, which speaks for itself.

Prof. N. W. Peaslee
c/o Am. Psychological Society
30, E. 41st Street
N.Y. City, U.S.A.

49, Dampier Street
Pilbarra, W. Australia
18 May, 1934

My dear Sir

A recent conversation with Dr E. M. Boyle of Perth, and some papers with your articles which he has just sent me, make it advisable for me to tell you about certain things I have seen in the Great Sandy Desert east of our gold field here. It would seem, in view of the peculiar legends about old cities with huge stonework and strange designs and hieroglyphs which you describe, that I have come upon something very important.

The black fellows have always been full of talk about 'great stones with marks on them', and seem to have a terrible fear of such things. They connect them in some way with their common racial legends about Buddai, the gigantic old man who lies asleep for ages underground with his head on his arm, and who will some day awake and eat up the world. There are some very old and half-forgotten tales of enormous underground huts of great stones, where passages lead down and down, and where horrible things have happened. The black fellows claim that once some warriors, fleeing in battle, went down into one and never came back, but that frightful winds began to blow from the place soon after they went down. However, there usually isn't much in what these natives say.

But what I have to tell is more than this. Two years ago, when I was prospecting about 500 miles east in the desert, I came on a lot of queer pieces of dressed stone perhaps 3 x 2 x 2 feet in size, and weathered and pitted to the very limit. At first I couldn't find any of the marks the black fellows told about, but when I looked close enough I could make out some deeply carved lines in spite of the weathering. They were peculiar curves, just like what the blacks had tried to describe. I imagine there must have been 30 or 40 blocks, some nearly buried in the sand, and all within a circle perhaps a quarter of a mile's diameter.

When I saw some, I looked around closely for more, and made a careful reckoning of the place with my instruments. I also took pictures of 10 or 12 of the most typical blocks, and will enclose the prints for you to see. I turned my information and pictures over to the government at Perth, but they have done nothing with them. Then I met Dr Boyle, who had read your articles in the *Journal of the American Psychological Society*, and in time happened to mention the stones. He was enormously interested, and became quite excited when I shewed him my snapshots, saying that the stones and markings were just like those of the masonry you had dreamed about and seen described in legends. He meant to write you, but was delayed. Meanwhile he sent me most of the magazines with your articles, and I saw at once from your drawings and descriptions that my stones are certainly the kind you mean. You can appreciate this from the enclosed prints. Later on you will hear directly from Dr Boyle.

Now I can understand how important all this will be to you. Without question we are faced with the remains of an unknown civilisation older than any dreamed of before, and forming a basis for your legends. As a mining engineer, I have some knowledge of geology, and can tell you that these blocks are so ancient they frighten me. They are mostly sandstone and granite, though one is almost certainly made of a queer sort of *cement* or *concrete*. They bear evidence of water action, as if this part of the world had been submerged and come up again after long ages – all since these blocks were made and used. It is a matter of hundreds of thousands of years – or heaven knows how much more. I don't like to think about it.

In view of your previous diligent work in tracking down the legends and everything connected with them, I cannot doubt but that you will want to lead an expedition to the desert and make some archaeological excavations. Both Dr Boyle and I are prepared to cooperate in such work if you – or organisations known to you – can furnish the funds. I can get together a dozen miners for the heavy digging – the blacks would be of no use, for I've found that they have an almost maniacal fear of this particular spot. Boyle and I are saying nothing to others, for you very obviously ought to have precedence in any discoveries or credit.

The place can be reached from Pilbarra in about 4 days by motor tractor – which we'd need for our apparatus. It is some-what west and south of Warburton's path of 1873, and 100 miles southeast of Joanna Spring. We could float things up the De Grey River instead of starting from Pilbarra – but all that can be talked over later. Roughly, the stones lie at a point about 22° 3' 14" South Latitude, 125° 0' 39" East Longitude. The climate is tropical, and the desert conditions are trying. Any expedition had better be made in winter – June or July or August. I shall welcome further correspondence upon this subject, and am keenly eager to assist in any plan you may devise. After studying your articles I am deeply impressed with the profound significance of the whole matter. Dr Boyle will write later. When rapid communication is needed, a cable to Perth can be relayed by wireless.

Hoping profoundly for an early message,

Believe me,

Most faithfully yours,

ROBERT B. F. MACKENZIE

Of the immediate aftermath of this letter, much can be learned from the press. My good fortune in securing the backing of Miskatonic University was great, and both Mr Mackenzie and Dr Boyle proved invaluable in arranging matters at the Australian end. We were not too specific with the public about our objects, since the whole matter would have lent itself unpleasantly to sensational and jocose treatment by the cheaper newspapers. As a result, printed reports were sparing; but enough appeared to tell of our quest for reported Australian ruins and to chronicle our various preparatory steps.

Professors William Dyer of the college's geology department (leader of the Miskatonic Antarctic Expedition of 1930–31), Ferdinand C. Ashley of the department of ancient history, and Tyler M. Freeborn of the department of anthropology – together with my son Wingate – accompanied me. My correspondent Mackenzie came to Arkham early in 1935 and assisted in our final preparations. He proved to be a tremendously competent and affable man of about fifty, admirably well-read, and deeply familiar with all the conditions of Australian travel. He had tractors waiting at Pilbarra, and we chartered a tramp steamer of sufficiently light draught to get up the river to that point. We were prepared to excavate in the most careful and scientific fashion, sifting every particle of sand, and disturbing nothing which might seem to be in or near its original situation.

Sailing from Boston aboard the wheezy *Lexington* on March 28, 1935, we had a leisurely trip across the Atlantic and Mediterranean, through the Suez Canal, down the Red Sea, and across the Indian Ocean to our goal. I need not tell how the sight of the low, sandy West Australian coast depressed me, and how I detested the crude mining town and dreary gold fields where the tractors were given their last loads. Dr Boyle, who met us, proved to be elderly, pleasant, and intelligent – and his knowledge of psychology led him into many long discussions with my son and me.

Discomfort and expectancy were oddly mingled in most of us when at length our party of eighteen rattled forth over the arid leagues of sand and rock. On Friday, May 31, we forded a branch of the De Grey and entered the realm of utter desolation. A certain positive terror grew on me as we advanced to this actual site of the elder world behind the legends – a terror of course abetted by the fact that my disturbing dreams and pseudo-memories still beset me with unabated force.

It was on Monday, June 3, that we saw the first of the half-buried blocks. I cannot describe the emotions with which I actually touched – in objective reality – a fragment of Cyclopean masonry in every respect like the blocks in the walls of my dream-buildings. There was a distinct trace of carving – and my hands trembled as I recognised part of a curvilinear decorative scheme made hellish to me through years of tormenting nightmare and baffling research.

A month of digging brought a total of some 1250 blocks in varying stages of wear and disintegration. Most of these were carven megaliths with curved tops and bottoms. A minority were smaller, flatter, plain-surfaced, and square or octagonally cut – like those of the floors and pavements in my dreams – while a few were singularly massive and curved or slanted in such a manner as to suggest use in vaulting or groining, or as parts of arches or round window casings. The deeper – and the farther north and east – we dug, the more blocks we found, though we still failed to discover any trace of arrangement among them. Professor Dyer was appalled at the measureless age of the fragments, and Freeborn found traces of symbols which fitted darkly into certain Papuan and Polynesian legends of infinite antiquity. The condition and scattering of the blocks told mutely of vertiginous cycles of time and geologic upheavals of cosmic savagery.

We had an aeroplane with us, and my son Wingate would often go up to different heights and scan the sand-and-rock waste for signs of dim, large-scale outlines – either differences of level or trails of scattered blocks. His results were virtually negative; for whenever he would one day think he had glimpsed some significant trend, he would on his next trip find the impression replaced by another equally insubstantial – a result of the shifting, wind-blown sand. One or two of these ephemeral suggestions, though, affected me queerly and disagreeably. They seemed, after a fashion, to dovetail horribly with something which I had dreamed or read, but which I could no longer remember. There was a terrible *pseudo-familiarity* about them – which somehow made me look furtively and apprehensively over the abominable, sterile terrain toward the north and northeast.

Around the first week in July I developed an unaccountable set of mixed emotions about that general northeasterly region. There was horror, and there was curiosity – but more than that, there was a persistent and perplexing illusion of *memory*. I tried all sorts of psychological expedients to get these notions out of my head, but met with no success. Sleeplessness also gained upon me, but I almost welcomed this because of the resultant shortening of my dream-periods. I acquired the habit of taking long, lone walks in the desert late at night – usually to the north or northeast, whither the sum of my strange new impulses seemed subtly to pull me.

Sometimes, on these walks, I would stumble over nearly buried fragments of the ancient masonry. Though there were fewer visible blocks here than where we had started, I felt sure that there must be a vast abundance beneath the surface. The ground was less level than at our camp, and the prevailing high winds now and then piled the sand into fantastic temporary hillocks – exposing some traces of the elder stones while it covered other traces. I was queerly anxious to have the excavations extend to this territory, yet at the same time dreaded what might be revealed. Obviously, I was getting into a rather bad state – all the worse because I could not account for it.

An indication of my poor nervous health can be gained from my response to an odd discovery which I made on one of my nocturnal rambles. It was on the evening of July 11th, when a gibbous moon flooded the mysterious hillocks with a curious pallor. Wandering somewhat beyond my usual limits, I came upon a great stone which seemed to differ markedly from any we had yet encountered. It was almost wholly covered, but I stooped and cleared away the sand with my hands, later studying the object carefully and supplementing the moonlight with my electric torch. Unlike the other very large rocks, this one was perfectly square-cut, with no convex or concave surface. It seemed, too, to be of a dark basaltic substance wholly dissimilar to the granite and sandstone and occasional concrete of the now familiar fragments.

Suddenly I rose, turned, and ran for the camp at top speed. It was a wholly unconscious and irrational flight, and only when I was close to my tent did I fully realise why I had run. Then it came to me. The queer dark stone was something which I had dreamed and read about, and which was linked with the uttermost horrors of the aeon-old legendry. It was one of the blocks of that basaltic elder masonry which the fabled Great Race held in such fear – the tall, windowless ruins left by those brooding, half-material, alien Things that festered in earth's nether abysses and against whose wind-like, invisible forces the trap-doors were sealed and the sleepless sentinels posted.

I remained awake all that night, but by dawn realised how silly I had been to let the shadow of a myth upset me. Instead of being frightened, I should have had a discoverer's enthusiasm. The next forenoon I told the others about my find, and Dyer, Freeborn, Boyle, my son, and I set out to view the anomalous block. Failure, however, confronted us. I had formed no clear idea of the stone's location, and a late wind had wholly altered the hillocks of shifting sand.

6

I come now to the crucial and most difficult part of my narrative – all the more difficult because I cannot be quite certain of its reality. At times I feel uncomfortably sure that I was not dreaming or deluded; and it is this feeling – in view of the stupendous implications which the objective truth of my experience would raise – which impels me to make this record. My son – a trained psychologist with the fullest and most sympathetic knowledge of my whole case – shall be the primary judge of what I have to tell.

First let me outline the externals of the matter, as those at the camp know them. On the night of July 17–18, after a windy day, I retired early but could not sleep. Rising shortly before eleven, and

afflicted as usual with that strange feeling regarding the northeast-
ward terrain, I set out on one of my typical nocturnal walks, seeing
and greeting only one person – an Australian miner named Tupper –
as I left our precincts. The moon, slightly past full, shone from a
clear sky and drenched the ancient sands with a white, leprous radiance which seemed to me somehow infinitely evil. There was no
longer any wind, nor did any return for nearly five hours, as amply
attested by Tupper and others who did not sleep through the night.
The Australian last saw me walking rapidly across the pallid, secret-
guarding hillocks toward the northeast.

About 3:30 a.m. a violent wind blew up, waking everyone in camp
and felling three of the tents. The sky was unclouded, and the
desert still blazed with that leprous moonlight. As the party saw to
the tents my absence was noted, but in view of my previous walks
this circumstance gave no one alarm. And yet as many as three
men – all Australians – seemed to feel something sinister in the
air. Mackenzie explained to Prof. Freeborn that this was a fear
picked up from black fellow folklore – the natives having woven a
curious fabric of malignant myth about the high winds which at
long intervals sweep across the sands under a clear sky. Such winds,
it is whispered, blow out of the great stone huts under the ground
where terrible things have happened – and are never felt except
near places where the big marked stones are scattered. Close to four
the gale subsided as suddenly as it had begun, leaving the sand hills
in new and unfamiliar shapes.

It was just past five, with the bloated, fungoid moon sinking in
the west, when I staggered into camp – hatless, tattered, features
scratched and ensanguined, and without my electric torch. Most of
the men had returned to bed, but Prof. Dyer was smoking a pipe in
front of his tent. Seeing my winded and almost frenzied state, he
called Dr Boyle, and the two of them got me on my cot and made me
comfortable. My son, roused by the stir, soon joined them, and they
all tried to force me to lie still and attempt sleep.

But there was no sleep for me. My psychological state was very
extraordinary – different from anything I had previously suffered.
After a time I insisted upon talking – nervously and elaborately
explaining my condition. I told them I had become fatigued, and
had lain down in the sand for a nap. There had, I said, been dreams

even more frightful than usual – and when I was awaked by the sudden high wind my overwrought nerves had snapped. I had fled in panic, frequently falling over half-buried stones and thus gaining my tattered and bedraggled aspect. I must have slept long – hence the hours of my absence.

Of anything strange either seen or experienced I hinted absolutely nothing – exercising the greatest self-control in that respect. But I spoke of a change of mind regarding the whole work of the expedition, and earnestly urged a halt in all digging toward the northeast. My reasoning was patently weak – for I mentioned a dearth of blocks, a wish not to offend the superstitious miners, a possible shortage of funds from the college, and other things either untrue or irrelevant. Naturally, no one paid the least attention to my new wishes – not even my son, whose concern for my health was very obvious.

The next day I was up and around the camp, but took no part in the excavations. Seeing that I could not stop the work, I decided to return home as soon as possible for the sake of my nerves, and made my son promise to fly me in the plane to Perth – a thousand miles to the southwest – as soon as he had surveyed the region I wished let alone. If, I reflected, the thing I had seen was still visible, I might decide to attempt a specific warning even at the cost of ridicule. It was just conceivable that the miners who knew the local folklore might back me up. Humouring me, my son made the survey that very afternoon, flying over all the terrain my walk could possibly have covered. Yet nothing of what I had found remained in sight. It was the case of the anomalous basalt block all over again – the shifting sand had wiped out every trace. For an instant I half regretted having lost a certain awesome object in my stark fright – but now I know that the loss was merciful. I can still believe my whole experience an illusion – especially if, as I devoutly hope, that hellish abyss is never found.

Wingate took me to Perth July 20, though declining to abandon the expedition and return home. He stayed with me until the 25th, when the steamer for Liverpool sailed. Now, in the cabin of the *Empress*, I am pondering long and frantically on the entire matter, and have decided that my son at least must be informed. It shall rest with him whether to diffuse the matter more widely. In order to meet any eventuality I have prepared this summary of my background – as already known in a scattered way to others – and will now tell as briefly as possible what seemed to happen during my absence from the camp that hideous night.

Nerves on edge, and whipped into a kind of perverse eagerness by that inexplicable, dread-mingled, pseudo-mnemonic urge toward the northeast, I plodded on beneath the evil, burning moon. Here and there I saw, half-shrouded by the sand, those primal Cyclopean blocks left from nameless and forgotten aeons. The incalculable age and brooding horror of this monstrous waste began to oppress me as never before, and I could not keep from thinking of my maddening dreams, of the frightful legends which lay behind them, and of the present fears of natives and miners concerning the desert and its carven stones.

And yet I plodded on as if to some eldritch rendezvous – more and more assailed by bewildering fancies, compulsions, and pseudo-memories. I thought of some of the possible contours of the lines of stones as seen by my son from the air, and wondered why they seemed at once so ominous and so familiar. Something was fumbling and rattling at the latch of my recollection, while another unknown force sought to keep the portal barred.

The night was windless, and the pallid sand curved upward and downward like frozen waves of the sea. I had no goal, but somehow ploughed along as if with fate-bound assurance. My dreams welled up into the waking world, so that each sand-embedded megalith seemed part of endless rooms and corridors of pre-human masonry, carved and hieroglyphed with symbols that I knew too well from years of custom as a captive mind of the Great Race. At moments I fancied I saw those omniscient conical horrors moving about at their accustomed tasks, and I feared to look down lest I find myself one with them in aspect. Yet all the while I saw the sand-covered blocks as well as the rooms and corridors; the evil, burning moon as well as the lamps of luminous crystal; the endless desert as well as the waving ferns and cycads beyond the windows. I was awake and dreaming at the same time.

I do not know how long or how far – or indeed, in just what direction – I had walked when I first spied the heap of blocks bared by the day's wind. It was the largest group in one place that I had

so far seen, and so sharply did it impress me that the visions of
fabulous aeons faded suddenly away. Again there were only the
desert and the evil moon and the shards of an unguessed past. I
drew close and paused, and cast the added light of my electric torch
over the tumbled pile. A hillock had blown away, leaving a low,
irregularly round mass of megaliths and smaller fragments some
forty feet across and from two to eight feet high.

From the very outset I realised that there was some utterly unprecedented quality about these stones. Not only was the mere
number of them quite without parallel, but something in the sand-
worn traces of design arrested me as I scanned them under the
mingled beams of the moon and my torch. Not that any one differed essentially from the earlier specimens we had found. It was
something subtler than that. The impression did not come when
I looked at one block alone, but only when I ran my eye over several almost simultaneously. Then, at last, the truth dawned upon
me. The curvilinear patterns on many of these blocks were *closely
related* – parts of one vast decorative conception. For the first time
in this aeon-shaken waste I had come upon a mass of masonry in its
old position – tumbled and fragmentary, it is true, but none the less
existing in a very definite sense.

Mounting at a low place, I clambered laboriously over the heap,
here and there clearing away the sand with my fingers, and constantly striving to interpret varieties of size, shape, and style, and
relationships of design. After a while I could vaguely guess at the
nature of the bygone structure, and at the designs which had once
stretched over the vast surfaces of the primal masonry. The perfect
identity of the whole with some of my dream-glimpses appalled and
unnerved me. This was once a Cyclopean corridor thirty feet tall,
paved with octagonal blocks and solidly vaulted overhead. There
would have been rooms opening off on the right, and at the farther
end one of those strange inclined planes would have wound down
to still lower depths.

I started violently as these conceptions occurred to me, for there
was more in them than the blocks themselves had supplied. How
did I know that this level should have been far underground? How
did I know that the plane leading upward should have been behind
me? How did I know that the long subterrene passage to the Square

of Pillars ought to lie on the left one level above me? How did I know that the room of machines, and the rightward-leading tunnel to the central archives, ought to lie two levels below? How did I know that there would be one of those horrible, metal-banded trapdoors at the very bottom, four levels down? Bewildered by this intrusion from the dream-world, I found myself shaking and bathed in a cold perspiration.

Then, as a last, intolerable touch, I felt that faint, insidious stream of cool air trickling upward from a depressed place near the centre of the huge heap. Instantly, as once before, my visions faded, and I saw again only the evil moonlight, the brooding desert, and the spreading tumulus of palaeogean masonry. Something real and tangible, yet fraught with infinite suggestions of nighted mystery, now confronted me. For that stream of air could argue but one thing – a hidden gulf of great size beneath the disordered blocks on the surface.

My first thought was of the sinister black fellow legends of vast underground huts among the megaliths where horrors happen and great winds are born. Then thoughts of my own dreams came back, and I felt dim pseudo-memories tugging at my mind. What manner of place lay below me? What primal, inconceivable source of age-old myth-cycles and haunting nightmares might I be on the brink of uncovering? It was only for a moment that I hesitated, for more than curiosity and scientific zeal was driving me on and working against my growing fear.

I seemed to move almost automatically, as if in the clutch of some compelling fate. Pocketing my torch, and struggling with a strength that I had not thought I possessed, I wrenched aside first one titan fragment of stone and then another, till there welled up a strong draught whose dampness contrasted oddly with the desert's dry air. A black rift began to yawn, and at length – when I had pushed away every fragment small enough to budge – the leprous moonlight blazed on an aperture of ample width to admit me.

I drew out my torch and cast a brilliant beam into the opening. Below me was a chaos of tumbled masonry, sloping roughly down toward the north at an angle of about forty-five degrees, and evidently the result of some bygone collapse from above. Between its surface and the ground level was a gulf of impenetrable blackness at whose upper edge were signs of gigantic, stress-heaved vaulting. At this point, it appeared, the desert's sands lay directly upon a floor of some titan structure of earth's youth – how preserved through aeons of geologic convulsion I could not then and cannot now even attempt to guess.

In retrospect, the barest idea of a sudden, lone descent into such a doubtful abyss – and at a time when one's whereabouts were unknown to any living soul – seems like the utter apex of insanity. Perhaps it was – yet that night I embarked without hesitancy upon such a descent. Again there was manifest that lure and driving of fatality which had all along seemed to direct my course. With torch flashing intermittently to save the battery, I commenced a mad scramble down the sinister, Cyclopean incline below the opening – sometimes facing forward as I found good hand and foot holds, and at other times turning to face the heap of megaliths as I clung and fumbled more precariously. In two directions beside me, distant walls of carven, crumbling masonry loomed dimly under the direct beams of my torch. Ahead, however, was only unbroken blackness.

I kept no track of time during my downward scramble. So seething with baffling hints and images was my mind, that all objective matters seemed withdrawn into incalculable distances. Physical sensation was dead, and even fear remained as a wraith-like, inactive gargoyle leering impotently at me. Eventually I reached a level floor strown with fallen blocks, shapeless fragments of stone, and sand and detritus of every kind. On either side – perhaps thirty feet apart – rose massive walls culminating in huge groinings. That they were carved I could just discern, but the nature of the carvings was beyond my perception. What held me the most was the vaulting overhead. The beam from my torch could not reach the roof, but the lower parts of the monstrous arches stood out distinctly. And so perfect was their identity with what I had seen in countless dreams of the elder world, that I trembled actively for the first time.

Behind and high above, a faint luminous blur told of the distant moonlit world outside. Some vague shred of caution warned me that I should not let it out of my sight, lest I have no guide for my return. I now advanced toward the wall on my left, where the traces of carving were plainest. The littered floor was nearly as hard to traverse as the downward heap had been, but I managed to pick my difficult way. At one place I heaved aside some blocks and kicked away the detritus to see what the pavement was like, and shuddered at the utter, fateful familiarity of the great octagonal stones whose buckled surface still held roughly together.

Reaching a convenient distance from the wall, I cast the torchlight slowly and carefully over its worn remnants of carving. Some bygone influx of water seemed to have acted on the sandstone surface, while there were curious incrustations which I could not explain. In places the masonry was very loose and distorted, and I wondered how many aeons more this primal, hidden edifice could keep its remaining traces of form amidst earth's heavings.

But it was the carvings themselves that excited me most. Despite their time-crumbled state, they were relatively easy to trace at close range; and the complete, intimate familiarity of every detail almost stunned my imagination. That the major attributes of this hoary masonry should be familiar, was not beyond normal credibility. Powerfully impressing the weavers of certain myths, they had become embodied in a stream of cryptic lore which, somehow coming to my notice during the amnesic period, had evoked vivid images in my subconscious mind. But how could I explain the exact and minute fashion in which each line and spiral of these strange designs tallied with what I had dreamt for more than a score of years? What obscure, forgotten iconography could have reproduced each subtle shading and nuance which so persistently, exactly, and unvaryingly besieged my sleeping vision night after night?

For this was no chance or remote resemblance. Definitely and absolutely, the millennially ancient, aeon-hidden corridor in which I stood was the original of something I knew in sleep as intimately as I knew my own house in Crane Street, Arkham. True, my dreams shewed the place in its undecayed prime; but the identity was no less real on that account. I was wholly and horribly oriented. The particular structure I was in was known to me. Known, too, was its place in that terrible elder city of dreams. That I could visit unerringly any point in that structure or in that city which had escaped the changes and devastations of uncounted ages, I realised with hideous and instinctive certainty. What in God's name could all this mean? How had I come to know what I knew? And what awful reality could lie behind those antique tales of the beings who had dwelt in this labyrinth of primordial stone?

Words can convey only fractionally the welter of dread and bewilderment which ate at my spirit. I knew this place. I knew what lay before me, and what had lain overhead before the myriad towering stories had fallen to dust and debris and the desert. No need now, I thought with a shudder, to keep that faint blur of moonlight in view. I was torn betwixt a longing to flee and a feverish mixture of burning curiosity and driving fatality. What had happened to this monstrous megalopolis of eld in the millions of years since the time of my dreams? Of the subterrene mazes which had underlain the city and linked all its titan towers, how much had still survived the writhings of earth's crust?

Had I come upon a whole buried world of unholy archaism? Could I still find the house of the writing-master, and the tower where S'gg'ha, a captive mind from the star-headed vegetable carnivores of Antarctica, had chiselled certain pictures on the blank spaces of the walls? Would the passage at the second level down, to the hall of the alien minds, be still unchoked and traversable? In that hall the captive mind of an incredible entity – a half-plastic denizen of the hollow interior of an unknown trans-Plutonian planet eighteen million years in the future – had kept a certain thing which it had modelled from clay.

I shut my eyes and put my hand to my head in a vain, pitiful effort to drive these insane dream-fragments from my consciousness. Then, for the first time, I felt acutely the coolness, motion, and dampness of the surrounding air. Shuddering, I realised that a vast chain of aeon-dead black gulfs must indeed be yawning somewhere beyond and below me. I thought of the frightful chambers and corridors and inclines as I recalled them from my dreams. Would the way to the central archives still be open? Again that driving fatality tugged insistently at my brain as I recalled the awesome records that once lay cased in those rectangular vaults of rustless metal.

There, said the dreams and legends, had reposed the whole history, past and future, of the cosmic space-time continuum – written by captive minds from every orb and every age in the solar system. Madness, of course – but had I not now stumbled into a nighted world as mad as I? I thought of the locked metal shelves, and of the curious knob-twistings needed to open each one. My own came vividly into my consciousness. How often had I gone through that intricate routine of varied turns and pressures in the terrestrial vertebrate section on the lowest level! Every detail was fresh and familiar. If there were such a vault as I had dreamed of, I could open it in a moment. It was then that madness took me utterly. An instant later, and I was leaping and stumbling over the rocky debris toward the well-remembered incline to the depths below.

7

From that point forward my impressions are scarcely to be relied on – indeed, I still possess a final, desperate hope that they all form parts of some daemoniac dream – or illusion born of delirium. A fever raged in my brain, and everything came to me through a kind of haze – sometimes only intermittently. The rays of my torch shot feebly into the engulfing blackness, bringing phantasmal flashes of hideously familiar walls and carvings, all blighted with the decay of ages. In one place a tremendous mass of vaulting had fallen, so that I had to clamber over a mighty mound of stones reaching almost to the ragged, grotesquely stalactited roof. It was all the ultimate apex of nightmare, made worse by the blasphemous tug of pseudo-memory. One thing only was unfamiliar, and that was my own size in relation to the monstrous masonry. I felt oppressed by a sense of unwonted smallness, as if the sight of these towering walls from a mere human body was something wholly new and abnormal. Again and again I looked nervously down at myself, vaguely disturbed by the human form I possessed.

Onward through the blackness of the abyss I leaped, plunged, and staggered – often falling and bruising myself, and once nearly shattering my torch. Every stone and corner of that daemoniac gulf was known to me, and at many points I stopped to cast beams of light through choked and crumbling yet familiar archways. Some rooms had totally collapsed; others were bare or debris-filled. In a few I saw masses of metal – some fairly intact, some broken, and some crushed or battered – which I recognised as the colossal pedestals or tables of my dreams. What they could in truth have been, I dared not guess.

I found the downward incline and began its descent – though after a time halted by a gaping, ragged chasm whose narrowest point could not be much less than four feet across. Here the stonework had fallen through, revealing incalculable inky depths beneath. I knew there were two more cellar levels in this titan edifice, and trembled with fresh panic as I recalled the metal-clamped trap-door on the lowest one. There could be no guards now – for what had lurked beneath had long since done its hideous work and sunk into its long decline. By the time of the post-human beetle race it would be quite dead. And yet, as I thought of the native legends, I trembled anew.

It cost me a terrible effort to vault that yawning chasm, since the littered floor prevented a running start – but madness drove me on. I chose a place close to the left-hand wall – where the rift was least wide and the landing-spot reasonably clear of dangerous debris – and after one frantic moment reached the other side in safety. At last gaining the lower level, I stumbled on past the archway of the room of machines, within which were fantastic ruins of metal half-buried beneath fallen vaulting. Everything was where I knew it would be, and I climbed confidently over the heaps which barred the entrance of a vast transverse corridor. This, I realised, would take me under the city to the central archives.

Endless ages seemed to unroll as I stumbled, leaped, and crawled along that debris-cluttered corridor. Now and then I could make out carvings on the age-stained walls – some familiar, others seemingly added since the period of my dreams. Since this was a subterrene house-connecting highway, there were no archways save when the route led through the lower levels of various buildings. At some of these intersections I turned aside long enough to look down well-remembered corridors and into well-remembered rooms. Twice only did I find any radical changes from what I had dreamed of – and in one of these cases I could trace the sealed-up outlines of the archway I remembered.

I shook violently, and felt a curious surge of retarding weakness, as I steered a hurried and reluctant course through the crypt of one of those great windowless ruined towers whose alien basalt masonry bespoke a whispered and horrible origin. This primal vault was round and fully two hundred feet across, with nothing carved upon the dark-hued stonework. The floor was here free from anything save dust and sand, and I could see the apertures leading upward and downward. There were no stairs or inclines – indeed, my dreams had pictured those elder towers as wholly untouched by the fabulous Great Race. Those who had built them had not needed stairs or inclines. In the dreams, the downward aperture had been tightly sealed and nervously guarded. Now it lay open – black and yawning, and giving forth a current of cool, damp air. Of what limitless caverns of eternal night might brood below, I would not permit myself to think.

Later, clawing my way along a badly heaped section of the corridor, I reached a place where the roof had wholly caved in. The debris rose like a mountain, and I climbed up over it, passing through a vast empty space where my torchlight could reveal neither walls nor vaulting. This, I reflected, must be the cellar of the house of the metal-purveyors, fronting on the third square not far from the archives. What had happened to it I could not conjecture.

I found the corridor again beyond the mountain of detritus and stones, but after a short distance encountered a wholly choked place where the fallen vaulting almost touched the perilously sagging ceiling. How I managed to wrench and tear aside enough blocks to afford a passage, and how I dared disturb the tightly packed fragments when the least shift of equilibrium might have brought down all the tons of superincumbent masonry to crush me to nothingness, I do not know. It was sheer madness that impelled and guided me – if, indeed, my whole underground adventure was not – as I hope – a hellish delusion or phase of dreaming. But I did make – or dream that I made – a passage that I could squirm through. As I wriggled over the mound of debris – my torch, switched continuously on, thrust deeply within my mouth – I felt myself torn by the fantastic stalactites of the jagged floor above me.

I was now close to the great underground archival structure which seemed to form my goal. Sliding and clambering down the farther side of the barrier, and picking my way along the remaining stretch of corridor with hand-held, intermittently flashing torch, I came at last to a low, circular crypt with arches – still in a marvellous state of preservation – opening off on every side. The walls, or such parts of them as lay within reach of my torchlight, were densely hiero-glyphed and chiselled with typical curvilinear symbols – some added since the period of my dreams.

This, I realised, was my fated destination, and I turned at once through a familiar archway on my left. That I could find a clear passage up and down the incline to all the surviving levels, I had oddly little doubt. This vast, earth-protected pile, housing the annals of all the solar system, had been built with supernal skill and strength to last as long as that system itself. Blocks of stupendous size, poised with mathematical genius and bound with cements of incredible toughness, had combined to form a mass as firm as the planet's rocky core. Here, after ages more prodigious than I could sanely grasp, its buried bulk stood in all its essential contours; the vast, dust-drifted floors scarce sprinkled with the litter elsewhere so dominant.

The relatively easy walking from this point onward went curiously to my head. All the frantic eagerness hitherto frustrated by obstacles now took itself out in a kind of febrile speed, and I literally raced along the low-roofed, monstrously well-remembered aisles beyond the archway. I was past being astonished by the familiarity of what I saw. On every hand the great hieroglyphed metal shelf-doors loomed monstrously; some yet in place, others sprung open, and still others bent and buckled under bygone geological stresses not quite strong enough to shatter the titan masonry. Here and there a dust-covered heap below a gaping empty shelf seemed to indicate where cases had been shaken down by earth-tremors. On occasional pillars were great symbols or letters proclaiming classes and sub-classes of volumes.

Once I paused before an open vault where I saw some of the accustomed metal cases still in position amidst the omnipresent gritty dust. Reaching up, I dislodged one of the thinner specimens with some difficulty, and rested it on the floor for inspection. It was titled in the prevailing curvilinear hieroglyphs, though something in the arrangement of the characters seemed subtly unusual. The odd mechanism of the hooked fastener was perfectly well known to me, and I snapped up the still rustless and workable lid and drew out the book within. The latter, as expected, was some twenty by fifteen inches in area, and two inches thick; the thin metal covers opening at the top. Its tough cellulose pages seemed unaffected by the myriad cycles of time they had lived through, and I studied the queerly pigmented, brush-drawn letters of the text – symbols utterly unlike either the usual curved hieroglyphs or any alphabet known to human scholarship – with a haunting, half-aroused memory. It came to me that this was the language used by a captive mind I had known slightly in my dreams – a mind from a large asteroid on which had survived much of the archaic life and lore of the primal planet whereof it formed a fragment. At the same time I recalled that this level of the archives was devoted to volumes dealing with the non-terrestrial planets.

As I ceased poring over this incredible document I saw that the light of my torch was beginning to fail, hence quickly inserted the extra battery I always had with me. Then, armed with the stronger radiance, I resumed my feverish racing through unending tangles of aisles and corridors – recognising now and then some familiar shelf, and vaguely annoyed by the acoustic conditions which made my footfalls echo incongruously in these catacombs of aeon-long death and silence. The very prints of my shoes behind me in the millennially untrodden dust made me shudder. Never before, if my mad dreams held anything of truth, had human feet pressed upon those immemorial pavements. Of the particular goal of my insane racing, my conscious mind held no hint. There was, however, some force of evil potency pulling at my dazed will and buried recollections, so that I vaguely felt I was not running at random.

I came to a downward incline and followed it to profounder depths. Floors flashed by me as I raced, but I did not pause to explore them. In my whirling brain there had begun to beat a certain rhythm which set my right hand twitching in unison. I wanted to unlock something, and felt that I knew all the intricate twists and pressures needed to do it. It would be like a modern safe with a combination lock. Dream or not, I had once known and still knew. How any dream – or scrap of unconsciously absorbed legend – could have taught me a detail so minute, so intricate, and so complex, I did not attempt to explain to myself. I was beyond all coherent thought. For was not this whole experience – this shocking familiarity with a set of unknown ruins, and this monstrously exact identity of everything before me with what only dreams and scraps of myth could have suggested – a horror beyond all reason? Probably it was my basic conviction then – as it is now during my saner moments – that I was not awake at all, and that the entire buried city was a fragment of febrile hallucination.

Eventually I reached the lowest level and struck off to the right of the incline. For some shadowy reason I tried to soften my steps, even though I lost speed thereby. There was a space I was afraid to cross on this last, deeply buried floor, and as I drew near it I recalled what thing in that space I feared. It was merely one of the metal-barred and closely guarded trap-doors. There would be no guards now, and on that account I trembled and tiptoed as I had done in passing through that black basalt vault where a similar trap-door had yawned. I felt a current of cool, damp air, as I had felt there, and wished that my course led in another direction. Why I had to take the particular course I was taking, I did not know.

When I came to the space I saw that the trap-door yawned widely open. Ahead the shelves began again, and I glimpsed on the floor before one of them a heap very thinly covered with dust, where a number of cases had recently fallen. At the same moment a fresh wave of panic clutched me, though for some time I could not discover why. Heaps of fallen cases were not uncommon, for all through the aeons this lightless labyrinth had been racked by the heavings of earth and had echoed at intervals to the deafening clatter of toppling objects. It was only when I was nearly across the space that I realised why I shook so violently.

Not the heap, but something about the dust of the level floor was troubling me. In the light of my torch it seemed as if that dust were not as even as it ought to be – there were places where it looked thinner, as if it had been disturbed not many months before. I could not be sure, for even the apparently thinner places were dusty enough; yet a certain suspicion of regularity in the fancied unevenness was highly disquieting. When I brought the torchlight close to one of the queer places I did not like what I saw – for the illusion of regularity became very great. It was as if there were regular lines of composite impressions – impressions that went in threes, each slightly over a foot square, and consisting of five nearly circular three-inch prints, one in advance of the other four.

These possible lines of foot-square impressions appeared to lead in two directions, as if something had gone somewhere and returned. They were of course very faint, and may have been illusions or accidents; but there was an element of dim, fumbling terror about the way I thought they ran. For at one end of them was the heap of cases which must have clattered down not long before, while at the other end was the ominous trap-door with the cool, damp wind, yawning unguarded down to abysses past imagination.

8

That my strange sense of compulsion was deep and overwhelming is shewn by its conquest of my fear. No rational motive could have drawn me on after that hideous suspicion of prints and the creeping dream-memories it excited. Yet my right hand, even as it shook with fright, still twitched rhythmically in its eagerness to turn a lock it hoped to find. Before I knew it I was past the heap of lately fallen cases and running on tiptoe through aisles of utterly un-broken dust toward a point which I seemed to know morbidly, horribly well. My mind was asking itself questions whose origin and relevancy I was only beginning to guess. Would the shelf be reachable by a human body? Could my human hand master all the aeon-remembered motions of the lock? Would the lock be undamaged and workable? And what would I do – what dare I do – with what (as I now commenced to realise) I both hoped and feared to find? Would it prove the awesome, brain-shattering truth of something past normal conception, or shew only that I was dreaming?

The next I knew I had ceased my tiptoe racing and was standing still, staring at a row of maddeningly familiar hieroglyphed shelves. They were in a state of almost perfect preservation, and only three of the doors in this vicinity had sprung open. My feelings toward these shelves cannot be described – so utter and insistent was the sense of old acquaintance. I was looking high up, at a row near the top and wholly out of my reach, and wondering how I could climb to best advantage. An open door four rows from the bottom would help, and the locks of the closed doors formed possible holds for hands and feet. I would grip the torch between my teeth as I had in other places where both hands were needed. Above all, I must make no noise. How to get down what I wished to remove would be difficult, but I could probably hook its movable fastener in my coat collar and carry it like a knapsack. Again I wondered whether the lock would be undamaged. That I could repeat each familiar motion I had not the least doubt. But I hoped the thing would not scrape or creak – and that my hand could work it properly.

Even as I thought these things I had taken the torch in my mouth and begun to climb. The projecting locks were poor supports; but as I had expected, the opened shelf helped greatly. I used both the difficultly swinging door and the edge of the aperture itself in my ascent, and managed to avoid any loud creaking. Balanced on the upper edge of the door, and leaning far to my right, I could just reach the lock I sought. My fingers, half-numb from climbing, were very clumsy at first; but I soon saw that they were anatomically adequate. And the memory-rhythm was strong in them. Out of unknown gulfs of time the intricate secret motions had somehow reached my brain correctly in every detail – for after less than five minutes of trying there came a click whose familiarity was all the more startling because I had not consciously anticipated it. In another instant the metal door was slowly swinging open with only the faintest grating sound.

Dazedly I looked over the row of greyish case-ends thus exposed, and felt a tremendous surge of some wholly inexplicable emotion. Just within reach of my right hand was a case whose curving hiero-glyphs made me shake with a pang infinitely more complex than one of mere fright. Still shaking, I managed to dislodge it amidst a shower of gritty flakes, and ease it over toward myself without any violent noise. Like the other case I had handled, it was slightly more than twenty by fifteen inches in size, with curved mathematical designs in low relief. In thickness it just exceeded three inches. Crudely wedging it between myself and the surface I was climbing, I fumbled with the fastener and finally got the hook free. Lifting the cover, I shifted the heavy object to my back, and let the hook catch hold of my collar. Hands now free, I awkwardly clambered down to the dusty floor, and prepared to inspect my prize.

Kneeling in the gritty dust, I swung the case around and rested it in front of me. My hands shook, and I dreaded to draw out the book within almost as much as I longed – and felt compelled – to do so. It had very gradually become clear to me what I ought to find, and this realisation nearly paralysed my faculties. If the thing were there – and if I were not dreaming – the implications would be quite beyond the power of the human spirit to bear. What tormented me most was my momentary inability to feel that my surroundings were a dream. The sense of reality was hideous – and again becomes so as I recall the scene.

At length I tremblingly pulled the book from its container and stared fascinatedly at the well-known hieroglyphs on the cover. It seemed to be in prime condition, and the curvilinear letters of the title held me in almost as hypnotised a state as if I could read them. Indeed, I cannot swear that I did not actually read them in some transient and terrible access of abnormal memory. I do not know how long it was before I dared to lift that thin metal cover. I temporised and made excuses to myself. I took the torch from my mouth and shut it off to save the battery. Then, in the dark, I screwed up my courage – finally lifting the cover without turning on the light. Last of all I did indeed flash the torch upon the exposed page – steeling myself in advance to suppress any sound no matter what I should find.

I looked for an instant, then almost collapsed. Clenching my teeth, however, I kept silence. I sank wholly to the floor and put a hand to my forehead amidst the engulfing blackness. What I dreaded and expected was there. Either I was dreaming, or time and space had become a mockery. I must be dreaming – but I would test the horror by carrying this thing back and shewing it to my son if it were indeed a reality. My head swam frightfully, even though there were no visible objects in the unbroken gloom to swirl around me. Ideas and images of the starkest terror – excited by vistas which my glimpse had opened up – began to throng in upon me and cloud my senses.

I thought of those possible prints in the dust, and trembled at the sound of my own breathing as I did so. Once again I flashed on the light and looked at the page as a serpent's victim may look at his destroyer's eyes and fangs. Then, with clumsy fingers in the dark, I closed the book, put it in its container, and snapped the lid and the curious hooked fastener. This was what I must carry back to the outer world if it truly existed – if the whole abyss truly existed – if I, and the world itself, truly existed.

Just when I tottered to my feet and commenced my return I cannot be certain. It comes to me oddly – as a measure of my sense of separation from the normal world – that I did not even once look at my watch during those hideous hours underground. Torch in hand, and with the ominous case under one arm, I eventually found myself tiptoeing in a kind of silent panic past the draught-giving abyss and those lurking suggestions of prints. I lessened my precautions as I climbed up the endless inclines, but could not shake off a shadow of apprehension which I had not felt on the downward journey.

I dreaded having to re-pass through that black basalt crypt that was older than the city itself, where cold draughts welled up from unguarded depths. I thought of that which the Great Race had feared, and of what might still be lurking – be it ever so weak and dying – down there. I thought of those possible five-circle prints and of what my dreams had told me of such prints – and of strange winds and whistling noises associated with them. And I thought of the tales of the modern blacks, wherein the horror of great winds and nameless subterrene ruins was dwelt upon.

I knew from a carven wall symbol the right floor to enter, and came at last – after passing that other book I had examined – to the great circular space with the branching archways. On my right, and at once recognisable, was the arch through which I had arrived. This I now entered, conscious that the rest of my course would be harder because of the tumbled state of the masonry outside the archive building. My new metal-cased burden weighed upon me, and I found it harder and harder to be quiet as I stumbled among debris and fragments of every sort.

Then I came to the ceiling-high mound of debris through which I had wrenched a scanty passage. My dread at wriggling through again was infinite; for my first passage had made some noise, and I now – after seeing those possible prints – dreaded sound above all things. The case, too, doubled the problem of traversing the narrow crevice. But I clambered up the barrier as best I could, and pushed the case through the aperture ahead of me. Then, torch in mouth, I scrambled through myself – my back torn as before by stalactites. As I tried to grasp the case again, it fell some distance ahead of me down the slope of the debris, making a disturbing clatter and arousing echoes which sent me into a cold perspiration. I lunged for it at once, and regained it without further noise – but a moment afterward the slipping of blocks under my feet raised a sudden and unprecedented din.

The din was my undoing. For, falsely or not, I thought I heard it answered in a terrible way from spaces far behind me. I thought I heard a shrill, whistling sound, like nothing else on earth, and beyond any adequate verbal description. It may have been only my imagination. If so, what followed has a grim irony – since, save for the panic of this thing, the second thing might never have happened.

As it was, my frenzy was absolute and unrelieved. Taking my torch in my hand and clutching feebly at the case, I leaped and bounded wildly ahead with no idea in my brain beyond a mad desire to race out of these nightmare ruins to the waking world of desert and moonlight which lay so far above. I hardly knew it when I reached the mountain of debris which towered into the vast blackness beyond the caved-in roof, and bruised and cut myself repeatedly in scrambling up its steep slope of jagged blocks and fragments. Then came the great disaster. Just as I blindly crossed the summit, unprepared for the sudden dip ahead, my feet slipped utterly and I found myself involved in a mangling avalanche of sliding masonry whose cannon-loud uproar split the black cavern air in a deafening series of earth-shaking reverberations.

I have no recollection of emerging from this chaos, but a momentary fragment of consciousness shews me as plunging and tripping and scrambling along the corridor amidst the clangour – case and torch still with me. Then, just as I approached that primal basalt crypt I had so dreaded, utter madness came. For as the echoes of the avalanche died down, there became audible a repetition of that frightful, alien whistling I thought I had heard before. This time there was no doubt about it – and what was worse, it came from a point not behind but *ahead of me*.

Probably I shrieked aloud then. I have a dim picture of myself as flying through the hellish basalt vault of the Elder Things, and hearing that damnable alien sound piping up from the open, unguarded door of limitless nether blacknesses. There was a wind, too – not merely a cool, damp draught, but a violent, purposeful blast belching savagely and frigidly from that abominable gulf whence the obscene whistling came.

There are memories of leaping and lurching over obstacles of every sort, with that torrent of wind and shrieking sound growing moment by moment, and seeming to curl and twist purposefully around me as it struck out wickedly from the spaces behind and beneath. Though in my rear, that wind had the odd effect of hindering instead of aiding my progress; as if it acted like a noose or lasso thrown around me. Heedless of the noise I made, I clattered over a great barrier of blocks and was again in the structure that led to the surface. I recall glimpsing the archway to the room of machines and almost crying out as I saw the incline leading down to where one of those blasphemous trap-doors must be yawning two levels below. But instead of crying out I muttered over and over to myself that this was all a dream from which I must soon awake. Perhaps I was in camp – perhaps I was at home in Arkham. As these hopes bolstered up my sanity I began to mount the incline to the higher level.

I knew, of course, that I had the four-foot cleft to re-cross, yet was too racked by other fears to realise the full horror until I came almost upon it. On my descent, the leap across had been easy – but could I clear the gap as readily when going uphill, and hampered by fright, exhaustion, the weight of the metal case, and the anomalous back-ward tug of that daemon wind? I thought of these things at the last moment, and thought also of the nameless entities which might be lurking in the black abysses below the chasm.

My wavering torch was growing feeble, but I could tell by some obscure memory when I neared the cleft. The chill blasts of wind and the nauseous whistling shrieks behind me were for the moment like a merciful opiate, dulling my imagination to the horror of the yawning gulf ahead. And then I became aware of the added blasts and whistling *in front of me* – tides of abomination surging up through the cleft itself from depths unimagined and unimaginable.

Now, indeed, the essence of pure nightmare was upon me. Sanity departed – and ignoring everything except the animal impulse of flight, I merely struggled and plunged upward over the incline's debris as if no gulf had existed. Then I saw the chasm's edge, leaped frenziedly with every ounce of strength I possessed, and was instantly engulfed in a pandaemoniac vortex of loathsome sound and utter, materially tangible blackness.

This is the end of my experience, so far as I can recall. Any further impressions belong wholly to the domain of phantasmagoric delirium. Dream, madness, and memory merged wildly together in a series of fantastic, fragmentary delusions which can have no relation to anything real. There was a hideous fall through incalculable leagues of viscous, sentient darkness, and a babel of noises utterly alien to all that we know of the earth and its organic life. Dormant, rudimentary senses seemed to start into vitality within me, telling of pits and voids peopled by floating horrors and leading to sunless crags and oceans and teeming cities of windowless basalt towers upon which no light ever shone.

Secrets of the primal planet and its immemorial aeons flashed through my brain without the aid of sight or sound, and there were known to me things which not even the wildest of my former dreams had ever suggested. And all the while cold fingers of damp vapour clutched and picked at me, and that eldritch, damnable whistling shrieked fiendishly above all the alternations of babel and silence in the whirlpools of darkness around.

Afterward there were visions of the Cyclopean city of my dreams – not in ruins, but just as I had dreamed of it. I was in my conical, non-human body again, and mingled with crowds of the Great Race and the captive minds who carried books up and down the lofty corridors and vast inclines. Then, superimposed upon these pictures, were frightful momentary flashes of a non-visual consciousness involving desperate struggles, a writhing free from clutching tentacles of whistling wind, an insane, bat-like flight through half-solid air, a feverish burrowing through the cyclone-whipped dark, and a wild stumbling and scrambling over fallen masonry.

Once there was a curious, intrusive flash of half-sight – a faint, diffuse suspicion of bluish radiance far overhead. Then there came a dream of wind-pursued climbing and crawling – of wriggling into a blaze of sardonic moonlight through a jumble of debris which slid and collapsed after me amidst a morbid hurricane. It was the evil, monotonous beating of that maddening moonlight which at last told me of the return of what I had once known as the objective, waking world.

I was clawing prone through the sands of the Australian desert, and around me shrieked such a tumult of wind as I had never before known on our planet's surface. My clothing was in rags, and my whole body was a mass of bruises and scratches. Full consciousness returned very slowly, and at no time could I tell just where true memory left off and delirious dream began. There had seemed to be a mound of titan blocks, an abyss beneath it, a monstrous revelation from the past, and a nightmare horror at the end – but how much of this was real? My flashlight was gone, and likewise any metal case I may have discovered. Had there been such a case – or any abyss – or any mound? Raising my head, I looked behind me, and saw only the sterile, undulant sands of the waste.

The daemon wind died down, and the bloated, fungoid moon sank reddeningly in the west. I lurched to my feet and began to stagger southwestward toward the camp. What in truth had happened to me? Had I merely collapsed in the desert and dragged a dream-racked body over miles of sand and buried blocks? If not, how could I bear to live any longer? For in this new doubt all my faith in the myth-born unreality of my visions dissolved once more into the hellish older doubting. If that abyss was real, then the Great Race was real – and its blasphemous reachings and seizures in the cosmos-wide vortex of time were no myths or nightmares, but a terrible, soul-shattering actuality.

Had I, in full hideous fact, been drawn back to a pre-human world of a hundred and fifty million years ago in those dark, baffling days of the amnesia? Had my present body been the vehicle of a fright-ful alien consciousness from palaeogean gulfs of time? Had I, as the captive mind of those shambling horrors, indeed known that accursed city of stone in its primordial heyday, and wriggled down those familiar corridors in the loathsome shape of my captor? Were those tormenting dreams of more than twenty years the offspring of stark, monstrous *memories*? Had I once veritably talked with minds from reachless corners of time and space, learned the universe's secrets past and to come, and written the annals of my own world for the metal cases of those titan archives? And were those others – those shocking Elder Things of the mad winds and daemon pipings – in truth a lingering, lurking menace, waiting and slowly weakening in black abysses while varied shapes of life drag out their multi-millennial courses on the planet's age-racked surface?

I do not know. If that abyss and what it held were real, there is no hope. Then, all too truly, there lies upon this world of man a mocking and incredible shadow out of time. But mercifully, there is no proof that these things are other than fresh phases of my myth-born dreams. I did not bring back the metal case that would have been a proof, and so far those subterrene corridors have not been found. If the laws of the universe are kind, they will never be found. But I must tell my son what I saw or thought I saw, and let him use his judgment as a psychologist in gauging the reality of my experience, and communicating this account to others.

I have said that the awful truth behind my tortured years of dreaming hinges absolutely upon the actuality of what I thought I saw in those Cyclopean buried ruins. It has been hard for me literally to set down the crucial revelation, though no reader can have failed to guess it. Of course it lay in that book within the metal case – the case which I pried out of its forgotten lair amidst the undisturbed dust of a million centuries. No eye had seen, no hand had touched that book since the advent of man to this planet. And yet, when I flashed my torch upon it in that frightful megalithic abyss, I saw that the queerly pigmented letters on the brittle, aeon-browned cellulose pages were not indeed any nameless hieroglyphs of earth's youth. They were, instead, the letters of our familiar alphabet, spelling out the words of the English language in my own handwriting.

Supernatural Horror in Literature

Introduction

The oldest and strongest emotion of mankind is fear, and the oldest and strongest kind of fear is fear of the unknown. These facts few psychologists will dispute, and their admitted truth must establish for all time the genuineness and dignity of the weirdly horrible tale as a literary form. Against it are discharged all the shafts of a materialistic sophistication which clings to frequently felt emotions and external events, and of a naively insipid idealism which deprecates the aesthetic motive and calls for a didactic literature to uplift the reader toward a suitable degree of smirking optimism. But in spite of all this opposition the weird tale has survived, developed, and attained remarkable heights of perfection; founded as it is on a profound and elementary principle whose appeal, if not always universal, must necessarily be poignant and permanent to minds of the requisite sensitiveness.

The appeal of the spectrally macabre is generally narrow because it demands from the reader a certain degree of imagination and a capacity for detachment from every-day life. Relatively few are free enough from the spell of the daily routine to respond to rappings from outside, and tales of ordinary feelings and events, or of common sentimental distortions of such feelings and events, will always take first place in the taste of the majority; rightly, perhaps, since of course these ordinary matters make up the greater part of human experience. But the sensitive are always with us, and sometimes a curious streak of fancy invades an obscure corner of the very hardest head; so that no amount of rationalisation, reform, or Freudian analysis can quite annul the thrill of the chimney-corner whisper or the lonely wood. There is here involved a psychological pattern or tradition as real and as deeply grounded in mental experience as any other pattern or tradition of mankind; coeval with the religious feeling and closely related to many aspects of it, and too much a part of our inmost biological heritage to lose keen potency over a very important, though not numerically great, minority of our species.

Man's first instincts and emotions formed his response to the environment in which he found himself. Definite feelings based on pleasure and pain grew up around the phenomena whose causes and effects he understood, whilst around those which he did not understand – and the universe teemed with them in the early days – were naturally woven such personifications, marvellous interpretations, and sensations of awe and fear as would be hit upon by a race having few and simple ideas and limited experience. The unknown, being likewise the unpredictable, became for our primitive forefathers a terrible and omnipotent source of boons and calamities visited upon mankind for cryptic and wholly extra-terrestrial reasons, and thus clearly belonging to spheres of existence whereof we know nothing and wherein we have no part. The phenomenon of dreaming likewise helped to build up the notion of an unreal or spiritual world; and in general, all the conditions of savage dawn-life so strongly conduced toward a feeling of the supernatural, that we need not wonder at the thoroughness with which man's very hereditary essence has become saturated with religion and superstition. That saturation must, as a matter of plain scientific fact, be regarded as virtually permanent so far as the subconscious mind and inner instincts are concerned; for though the area of the unknown has been steadily contracting for thousands of years, an infinite reservoir of mystery still engulfs most of the outer cosmos, whilst a vast residuum of powerful inherited associations clings around all the objects and processes that were once mysterious, however well they may now be explained. And more than this, there is an actual physiological fixation of the old instincts in our nervous tissue, which would make them obscurely operative even were the conscious mind to be purged of all sources of wonder.

Because we remember pain and the menace of death more vividly than pleasure, and because our feelings toward the beneficent aspects of the unknown have from the first been captured and formalised by conventional religious rituals, it has fallen to the lot of the darker and more maleficent side of cosmic mystery to figure chiefly in our popular supernatural folklore. This tendency, too, is naturally enhanced by the fact that uncertainty and danger are always closely allied, thus making any kind of an unknown world a world of peril and evil possibilities. When to this sense of fear and evil the inevitable fascination of wonder and curiosity is superadded, there is born a composite body of keen emotion and imaginative provocation whose vitality must of necessity endure as long as the human race itself. Children will always be afraid of the dark, and men with minds sensitive to hereditary impulse will always tremble at the thought of the hidden and fathomless worlds of strange life which may pulsate in the gulfs beyond the stars, or press hideously upon our own globe in unholy dimensions which only the dead and the moonstruck can glimpse.

With this foundation, no one need wonder at the existence of a literature of cosmic fear. It has always existed, and always will exist; and no better evidence of its tenacious vigour can be cited than the impulse which now and then drives writers of totally opposite leanings to try their hands at it in isolated tales, as if to discharge from their minds certain phantasmal shapes which would otherwise haunt them. Thus Dickens wrote several eerie narratives; Browning, the hideous poem 'Childe Roland'; Henry James, *The Turn of the Screw*; Dr Holmes, the subtle novel *Elsie Venner*; F. Marion Crawford, 'The Upper Berth' and a number of other examples; Mrs Charlotte Perkins Gilman, social worker, 'The Yellow Wall Paper'; whilst the humourist W. W. Jacobs produced that able melodramatic bit called 'The Monkey's Paw'.

This type of fear-literature must not be confounded with a type externally similar but psychologically widely different; the literature of mere physical fear and the mundanely gruesome. Such writing, to be sure, has its place, as has the conventional or even whimsical or humorous ghost story where formalism or the author's knowing wink removes the true sense of the morbidly unnatural; but these things are not the literature of cosmic fear in its purest sense. The true weird tale has something more than secret murder, bloody bones, or a sheeted form clanking chains according to rule. A certain atmosphere of breathless and unexplainable dread of outer, unknown forces must be present; and there must be a hint, expressed with a seriousness and portentousness becoming its subject, of that most terrible conception of the human brain – a malign and particular suspension or defeat of those fixed laws of Nature which are our only safeguard against the assaults of chaos and the daemons of unplumbed space.

Naturally we cannot expect all weird tales to conform absolutely to any theoretical model. Creative minds are uneven, and the best of fabrics have their dull spots. Moreover, much of the choicest weird work is unconscious, appearing in memorable fragments scattered through material whose massed effect may be of a very different cast. Atmosphere is the all-important thing, for the final criterion of authenticity is not the dovetailing of a plot but the creation of a given sensation. We may say, as a general thing, that a weird story whose intent is to teach or produce a social effect, or one in which the horrors are finally explained away by natural means, is not a genuine tale of cosmic fear; but it remains a fact that such narratives often possess, in isolated sections, atmospheric touches which fulfil every condition of true supernatural horror-literature. Therefore we must judge a weird tale not by the author's intent, or by the mere mechanics of the plot, but by the emotional level which it attains at its least mundane point. If the proper sensations are excited, such a 'high spot' must be admitted on its own merits as weird literature, no matter how prosaically it is later dragged down. The one test of the really weird is simply this – whether or not there be excited in the reader a profound sense of dread, and of contact with unknown spheres and powers; a subtle attitude of awed listening, as if for the beating of black wings or the scratching of outside shapes and entities on the known universe's utmost rim. And of course, the more completely and unifiedly a story conveys this atmosphere, the better it is as a work of art in the given medium.

The Dawn of the Horror-Tale

As may naturally be expected of a form so closely connected with primal emotion, the horror-tale is as old as human thought and speech themselves.

Cosmic terror appears as an ingredient of the earliest folklore of all races, and is crystallised in the most archaic ballads, chronicles, and sacred writings. It was, indeed, a prominent feature of the elaborate ceremonial magic, with its rituals for the evocation of daemons and spectres, which flourished from prehistoric times, and which reached its highest development in Egypt and the Semitic nations. Fragments like the *Book of Enoch* and the *Claviculae* of Solomon well illustrate the power of the weird over the ancient Eastern mind, and upon such things were based enduring systems and traditions whose echoes extend obscurely even to the present time. Touches of this transcendental fear are seen in classic literature, and there is evidence of its still greater emphasis in a ballad literature which paralleled the classic stream but vanished for lack of a written medium. The Middle Ages, steeped in fanciful darkness, gave it an enormous impulse toward expression; and East and West alike were busy preserving and amplifying the dark heritage, both of random folklore and of academically formulated magic and cabbalism, which had descended to them. Witch, werewolf, vampire, and ghoul brooded ominously on the lips of bard and grandam, and needed but little encouragement to take the final step across the boundary that divides the chanted tale or song from the formal literary composition. In the Orient, the weird tale tended to assume a gorgeous colouring and sprightliness which almost transmuted it into sheer phantasy. In the West, where the mystical Teuton had come down from his black Boreal forests and the Celt remembered strange sacrifices in Druidic groves, it assumed a terrible intensity and convincing seriousness of atmosphere which doubled the force of its half-told, half-hinted horrors.

Much of the power of Western horror-lore was undoubtedly due to the hidden but often suspected presence of a hideous cult of nocturnal worshippers whose strange customs – descended from pre-Aryan and pre-agricultural times when a squat race of Mongoloids roved over Europe with their flocks and herds – were rooted in the most revolting fertility-rites of immemorial antiquity. This secret religion, stealthily handed down amongst peasants for thousands of years despite the outward reign of the Druidic, Graeco-Roman, and Christian faiths in the regions involved, was marked by wild 'Witches' Sabbaths' in lonely woods and atop distant hills on Walpurgis-Night and Hallowe'en, the traditional breeding-seasons of the goats and sheep and cattle; and became the source of vast riches of sorcery-legend, besides provoking extensive witchcraft-prosecutions of which the Salem affair forms the chief American example. Akin to it in essence, and perhaps connected with it in fact, was the frightful secret system of inverted theology or Satan-worship which produced such horrors as the famous 'Black Mass'; whilst operating toward the same end we may note the activities of those whose aims were somewhat more scientific or philosophical – the astrologers, cabbalists, and alchemists of the Albertus Magnus or Raymond Lully type, with whom such rude ages invariably abound. The prevalence and depth of the mediaeval horror-spirit in Europe, intensified by the dark despair which waves of pestilence brought, may be fairly gauged by the grotesque carvings slyly introduced into much of the finest later Gothic ecclesiastical work of the time; the daemoniac gargoyles of Notre Dame and Mont St Michel being among the most famous specimens. And throughout the period, it must be remembered, there existed amongst educated and uneducated alike a most unquestioning faith in every form of the supernatural; from the gentlest of Christian doctrines to the most monstrous morbidities of witchcraft and black magic. It was from no empty background that the Renaissance magicians and alchemists – Nostradamus, Trithemius, Dr John Dee, Robert Fludd, and the like – were born.

In this fertile soil were nourished types and characters of sombre myth and legend which persist in weird literature to this day, more or less disguised or altered by modern technique. Many of them were taken from the earliest oral sources, and form part of mankind's permanent heritage. The shade which appears and demands the burial of its bones, the daemon lover who comes to bear away his still living bride, the death-fiend or psychopomp riding the night-wind, the man-wolf, the sealed chamber, the deathless sorcerer – all these may be found in that curious body of mediaeval lore which the late Mr Baring-Gould so effectively assembled in book form. Wherever the mystic Northern blood was strongest, the atmosphere of the popular tales became most intense; for in the Latin races there is a touch of basic rationality which denies to even their strangest superstitions many of the overtones of glamour so characteristic of our own forest-born and ice-fostered whisperings.

Just as all fiction first found extensive embodiment in poetry, so is it in poetry that we first encounter the permanent entry of the weird into standard literature. Most of the ancient instances, curiously enough, are in prose; as the werewolf incident in Petronius, the gruesome passages in Apuleius, the brief but celebrated letter of Pliny the Younger to Sura, and the odd compilation *On Wonderful Events* by the Emperor Hadrian's Greek freedman, Phlegon. It is in Phlegon that we first find that hideous tale of the corpse-bride, 'Philinnion and Machates', later related by Proclus and in modern times forming the inspiration of Goethe's 'Bride of Corinth' and Washington Irving's 'German Student'. But by the time the old Northern myths take literary form, and in that later time when the weird appears as a steady element in the literature of the day, we find it mostly in metrical dress; as indeed we find the greater part of the strictly imaginative writing of the Middle Ages and Renaissance. The Scandinavian Eddas and Sagas thunder with cosmic horror, and shake with the stark fear of Ymir and his shapeless spawn; whilst our own Anglo-Saxon *Beowulf* and the later Continental Nibelung tales are full of eldritch weirdness. Dante is a pioneer in the classic capture of macabre atmosphere, and in Spenser's stately stanzas will be seen more than a few touches of fantastic terror in landscape, incident, and character. Prose literature gives us Malory's *Morte d'Arthur*, in which are presented many ghastly situations taken from early ballad sources – the theft of the sword and silk from the corpse in Chapel Perilous by Sir Launcelot, the ghost of Sir Gawaine, and the tomb-fiend seen by Sir Galahad – whilst other and cruder specimens were doubtless set forth in the cheap and sensational 'chapbooks' vulgarly hawked about and devoured by the ignorant. In Elizabethan drama, with its *Dr Faustus*, the witches in *Macbeth*, the ghost in *Hamlet*, and the horrible gruesomeness of Webster, we may easily discern the strong hold of the daemoniac on the public mind; a hold intensified by the very real fear of living witchcraft, whose terrors, first wildest on the Continent, begin to echo loudly in English ears as the witch-hunting crusades of James the First gain headway. To the lurking mystical prose of the ages is added a long line of treatises on witchcraft and daemonology which aid in exciting the imagination of the reading world.

Through the seventeenth and into the eighteenth century we behold a growing mass of fugitive legendry and balladry of darksome cast; still, however, held down beneath the surface of polite and accepted literature. Chapbooks of horror and weirdness multiplied, and we glimpse the eager interest of the people through fragments like Defoe's 'Apparition of Mrs Veal', a homely tale of a dead woman's spectral visit to a distant friend, written to advertise covertly a badly selling theological disquisition on death. The upper orders of society were now losing faith in the supernatural, and indulging in a period of classic rationalism. Then, beginning with the translations of Eastern tales in Queen Anne's reign and taking definite form toward the middle of the century, comes the revival of romantic feeling – the era of new joy in Nature, and in the radiance of past times, strange scenes, bold deeds, and incredible marvels. We feel it first in the poets, whose utterances take on new qualities of wonder, strangeness, and shuddering. And finally, after the timid appearance of a few weird scenes in the novels of the day – such as Smollett's *Adventures of Ferdinand, Count Fathom* – the released instinct precipitates itself in the birth of a new school of writing; the 'Gothic' school of horrible and fantastic prose fiction, long and short, whose literary posterity is destined to become so numerous, and in many cases so resplendent in artistic merit. It is, when one reflects upon it, genuinely remarkable that weird narration as a fixed and academically recognised literary form should have been so late of final birth. The impulse and atmosphere are as old as man, but the typical weird tale of standard literature is a child of the eighteenth century.

The Early Gothic Novel

The shadow-haunted landscapes of 'Ossian', the chaotic visions of William Blake, the grotesque witch-dances in Burns's 'Tam O'Shanter', the sinister daemonism of Coleridge's *Christabel* and *Ancient Mariner*, the ghostly charm of James Hogg's 'Kilmeny', and the more restrained approaches to cosmic horror in *Lamia* and many of Keats's other poems, are typical British illustrations of the advent of the weird to formal literature. Our Teutonic cousins of the Continent were equally receptive to the rising flood, and Bürger's 'Wild Huntsman' and the even more famous daemon-bridegroom ballad of 'Lenore' – both imitated in English by Scott, whose respect for the supernatural was always great – are only a taste of the eerie wealth which German song had commenced to provide. Thomas Moore adapted from such sources the legend of the ghoulish statue-bride (later used by Prosper Mérimée in 'The

Venus of Ille', and traceable back to great antiquity) which echoes so shiveringly in his ballad of 'The Ring'; whilst Goethe's deathless masterpiece *Faust*, crossing from mere balladry into the classic, cosmic tragedy of the ages, may be held as the ultimate height to which this German poetic impulse arose.

But it remained for a very sprightly and worldly Englishman – none other than Horace Walpole himself – to give the growing impulse definite shape and become the actual founder of the literary horror-story as a permanent form. Fond of mediaeval romance and mystery as a dilettante's diversion, and with a quaintly imitated Gothic castle as his abode at Strawberry Hill, Walpole in 1764 published *The Castle of Otranto*, a tale of the supernatural which, though thoroughly unconvincing and mediocre in itself, was destined to exert an almost unparalleled influence on the literature of the weird. First venturing it only as a translation by one 'William Marshal, Gent.' from the Italian of a mythical 'Onuphrio Muralto', the author later acknowledged his connexion with the book and took pleasure in its wide and instantaneous popularity – a popularity which extended to many editions, early dramatisation, and wholesale imitation both in England and in Germany.

The story – tedious, artificial, and melodramatic – is further impaired by a brisk and prosaic style whose urbane sprightliness nowhere permits the creation of a truly weird atmosphere. It tells of Manfred, an unscrupulous and usurping prince determined to found a line, who after the mysterious sudden death of his only son Conrad on the latter's bridal morn, attempts to put away his wife Hippolita and wed the lady destined for the unfortunate youth – the lad, by the way, having been crushed by the preternatural fall of a gigantic helmet in the castle courtyard. Isabella, the widowed bride, flees from this design, and encounters in subterranean crypts beneath the castle a noble young preserver, Theodore, who seems to be a peasant yet strangely resembles the old lord Alfonso who ruled the domain before Manfred's time. Shortly thereafter supernatural phenomena assail the castle in divers ways; fragments of gigantic armour being discovered here and there, a portrait walking out of its frame, a thunderclap destroying the edifice, and a colossal armoured spectre of Alfonso rising out of the ruins to ascend through parting clouds to the bosom of St Nicholas. Theodore, having

wooed Manfred's daughter Matilda and lost her through death –
for she is slain by her father by mistake – is discovered to be the
son of Alfonso and rightful heir to the estate. He concludes the tale
by wedding Isabella and preparing to live happily ever after, whilst
Manfred – whose usurpation was the cause of his son's supernatural
death and his own supernatural harassings – retires to a monastery
for penitence, his saddened wife seeking asylum in a neighbouring
convent.

Such is the tale; flat, stilted, and altogether devoid of the true
cosmic horror which makes weird literature. Yet such was the thirst
of the age for those touches of strangeness and spectral antiquity
which it reflects, that it was seriously received by the soundest
readers and raised in spite of its intrinsic ineptness to a pedestal of
lofty importance in literary history. What it did above all else was to
create a novel type of scene, puppet-characters, and incidents; which,
handled to better advantage by writers more naturally adapted to
weird creation, stimulated the growth of an imitative Gothic school
which in turn inspired the real weavers of cosmic terror – the line of
actual artists beginning with Poe. This novel dramatic paraphernalia
consisted first of all of the Gothic castle, with its awesome antiquity,
vast distances and ramblings, deserted or ruined wings, damp corridors, unwholesome hidden catacombs, and galaxy of ghosts and
appalling legends, as a nucleus of suspense and daemoniac fright. In
addition, it included the tyrannical and malevolent nobleman as
villain; the saintly, long-persecuted, and generally insipid heroine
who undergoes the major terrors and serves as a point of view and
focus for the reader's sympathies; the valorous and immaculate hero,
always of high birth but often in humble disguise; the convention of
high-sounding foreign names, mostly Italian, for the characters; and
the infinite array of stage properties which includes strange lights,
damp trap-doors, extinguished lamps, mouldy hidden manuscripts,
creaking hinges, shaking arras, and the like. All this paraphernalia
reappears with amusing sameness, yet sometimes with tremendous
effect, throughout the history of the Gothic novel; and is by no
means extinct even today, though subtler technique now forces it to
assume a less naive and obvious form. An harmonious milieu for a
new school had been found, and the writing world was not slow to
grasp the opportunity.

German romance at once responded to the Walpole influence, and soon became a byword for the weird and ghastly. In England one of the first imitators was the celebrated Mrs Barbauld, then Miss Aikin, who in 1773 published an unfinished fragment called 'Sir Bertrand', in which the strings of genuine terror were truly touched with no clumsy hand. A nobleman on a dark and lonely moor, attracted by a tolling bell and distant light, enters a strange and ancient turreted castle whose doors open and close and whose bluish will-o'-the-wisps lead up mysterious staircases toward dead hands and animated black statues. A coffin with a dead lady, whom Sir Bertrand kisses, is finally reached; and upon the kiss the scene dissolves to give place to a splendid apartment where the lady, restored to life, holds a banquet in honour of her rescuer. Walpole admired this tale, though he accorded less respect to an even more prominent offspring of his *Otranto – The Old English Baron*, by Clara Reeve, published in 1777. Truly enough, this tale lacks the real vibration to the note of outer darkness and mystery which distinguishes Mrs Barbauld's fragment; and though less crude than Walpole's novel, and more artistically economical of horror in its possession of only one spectral figure, it is nevertheless too definitely insipid for greatness. Here again we have the virtuous heir to the castle disguised as a peasant and restored to his heritage through the ghost of his father; and here again we have a case of wide popularity leading to many editions, dramatisation, and ultimate translation into French. Miss Reeve wrote another weird novel, unfortunately unpublished and lost.

The Gothic novel was now settled as a literary form, and instances multiply bewilderingly as the eighteenth century draws toward its close. *The Recess*, written in 1785 by Mrs Sophia Lee, has the historic element, revolving round the twin daughters of Mary, Queen of Scots; and though devoid of the supernatural, employs the Walpole scenery and mechanism with great dexterity. Five years later, and all existing lamps are paled by the rising of a fresh luminary of wholly superior order – Mrs Ann Radcliffe (1764–1823), whose famous novels made terror and suspense a fashion, and who set new and higher standards in the domain of macabre and fear-inspiring atmosphere despite a provoking custom of destroying her own phantoms at the last through laboured mechanical explanations. To the familiar Gothic trappings of her predecessors Mrs Radcliffe added a genuine sense of the unearthly in scene and incident which closely approached genius; every touch of setting and action contributing artistically to the impression of illimitable frightfulness which she wished to convey. A few sinister details like a track of blood on castle stairs, a groan from a distant vault, or a weird song in a nocturnal forest can with her conjure up the most powerful images of imminent horror, surpassing by far the extravagant and toilsome elaborations of others. Nor are these images in themselves any the less potent because they are explained away before the end of the novel. Mrs Radcliffe's visual imagination was very strong, and appears as much in her delightful landscape touches – always in broad, glamorously pictorial outline, and never in close detail – as in her weird phantasies. Her prime weaknesses, aside from the habit of prosaic disillusionment, are a tendency toward erroneous geography and history and a fatal predilection for bestrewing her novels with insipid little poems, attributed to one or another of the characters.

Mrs Radcliffe wrote six novels; *The Castles of Athlin and Dunbayne* (1789), *A Sicilian Romance* (1790), *The Romance of the Forest* (1791), *The Mysteries of Udolpho* (1794), *The Italian* (1797), and *Gaston de Blondeville*, composed in 1802 but first published posthumously in 1826. Of these *Udolpho* is by far the most famous, and may be taken as a type of the early Gothic tale at its best. It is the chronicle of Emily, a young Frenchwoman transplanted to an ancient and portentous castle in the Apennines through the death of her parents and the marriage of her aunt to the lord of the castle – the scheming nobleman Montoni. Mysterious sounds, opened doors, frightful legends, and a nameless horror in a niche behind a black veil all operate in quick succession to unnerve the heroine and her faithful attendant Annette; but finally, after the death of her aunt, she escapes with the aid of a fellow-prisoner whom she has discovered. On the way home she stops at a château filled with fresh horrors – the abandoned wing where the departed châtelaine dwelt, and the bed of death with the black pall – but is finally restored to security and happiness with her lover Valancourt, after the clearing-up of a secret which seemed for a time to involve her birth in mystery. Clearly, this is only the familiar material re-worked; but it is so well re-worked that *Udolpho* will always be a classic. Mrs Radcliffe's characters are puppets, but they are less markedly so than those of her forerunners. And in atmospheric creation she stands preeminent among those of her time.

Of Mrs Radcliffe's countless imitators, the American novelist Charles Brockden Brown stands the closest in spirit and method. Like her, he injured his creations by natural explanations; but also like her, he had an uncanny atmospheric power which gives his horrors a frightful vitality as long as they remain unexplained. He differed from her in contemptuously discarding the external Gothic paraphernalia and properties and choosing modern American scenes for his mysteries; but this repudiation did not extend to the Gothic spirit and type of incident. Brown's novels involve some memorably frightful scenes, and excel even Mrs Radcliffe's in describing the operations of the perturbed mind. *Edgar Huntly* starts with a sleep-walker digging a grave, but is later impaired by touches of Godwinian didacticism. *Ormond* involves a member of a sinister secret brotherhood. That and *Arthur Mervyn* both describe the plague of yellow fever, which the author had witnessed in Philadelphia and New York. But Brown's most famous book is *Wieland; or, The Transformation* (1798), in which a Pennsylvania German, engulfed by a wave of religious fanaticism, hears voices and slays his wife and children as a sacrifice. His sister Clara, who tells the story, narrowly escapes. The scene, laid at the woodland estate of Mittingen on the Schuylkill's remote reaches, is drawn with extreme vividness; and the terrors of Clara, beset by spectral tones, gathering fears, and the sound of strange footsteps in the lonely house, are all shaped with truly artistic force. In the end a lame ventriloquial explanation is offered, but the atmosphere is genuine while it lasts. Carwin, the malign ventriloquist, is a typical villain of the Manfred or Montoni type.

The Apex of Gothic Romance

Horror in literature attains a new malignity in the work of Matthew Gregory Lewis (1775–1818), whose novel *The Monk* (1796) achieved marvellous popularity and earned him the nickname of 'Monk' Lewis. This young author, educated in Germany and saturated with a body of wild Teuton lore unknown to Mrs Radcliffe, turned to terror in forms more violent than his gentle predecessor had ever dared to think of, and produced as a result a masterpiece of active nightmare whose general Gothic cast is spiced with added stores of ghoulishness. The story is one of a Spanish monk, Ambrosio, who from a state of overproud virtue is tempted to the very nadir of evil by a fiend in the guise of the maiden Matilda; and who is finally, when awaiting death at the Inquisition's hands, induced to purchase escape at the price of his soul from the Devil, because he deems both body and soul already lost. Forthwith the mocking Fiend snatches him to a lonely place, tells him he has sold his soul in vain since both pardon and a chance for salvation were approaching at the moment of his hideous bargain, and completes the sardonic betrayal by rebuking him for his unnatural crimes, and casting his body down a precipice whilst his soul is borne off for ever to perdition. The novel contains some appalling descriptions such as the incantation in the vaults beneath the convent cemetery, the burning of the convent, and the final end of the wretched abbot. In the sub-plot where the Marquis de las Cisternas meets the spectre of his erring ancestress, The Bleeding Nun, there are many enormously potent strokes; notably the visit of the animated corpse to the Marquis's bedside, and the cabbalistic ritual whereby the Wandering Jew helps him to fathom and banish his dead tormentor. Nevertheless *The Monk* drags sadly when read as a whole. It is too long and too diffuse, and much of its potency is marred by flippancy and by an awkwardly excessive reaction against those canons of decorum which Lewis at first despised as prudish. One great thing may be said of the author; that he never ruined his ghostly visions with a natural explanation. He succeeded in breaking up the Radcliffian tradition and expanding the field of the Gothic novel. Lewis wrote much more than *The Monk*. His drama, *The Castle Spectre*, was produced in 1798, and he later found time to pen other fictions in ballad form – *Tales of Terror* (1799), *Tales of Wonder* (1801), and a succession of translations from the German.

Gothic romances, both English and German, now appeared in multitudinous and mediocre profusion. Most of them were merely ridiculous in the light of mature taste, and Miss Austen's famous satire *Northanger Abbey* was by no means an unmerited rebuke to a school which had sunk far toward absurdity. This particular school was petering out, but before its final subordination there arose its last and greatest figure in the person of Charles Robert Maturin (1782–1824), an obscure and eccentric Irish clergyman. Out of an ample body of miscellaneous writing which includes one confused Radcliffian imitation called *Fatal Revenge; or, The Family of Montorio* (1807), Maturin at length evolved the vivid horror-masterpiece of *Melmoth the Wanderer* (1820), in which the Gothic tale climbed to altitudes of sheer spiritual fright which it had never known before.

Melmoth is the tale of an Irish gentleman who, in the seventeenth century, obtained a preternaturally extended life from the Devil at the price of his soul. If he can persuade another to take the bargain off his hands, and assume his existing state, he can be saved; but this he can never manage to effect, no matter how assiduously he haunts those whom despair has made reckless and frantic. The framework of the story is very clumsy, involving tedious length, digressive episodes, narratives within narratives, and laboured dovetailing and coincidences; but at various points in the endless rambling there is felt a pulse of power undiscoverable in any previous work of this kind – a kinship to the essential truth of human nature, an understanding of the profoundest sources of actual cosmic fear, and a white heat of sympathetic passion on the writer's part which makes the book a true document of aesthetic self-expression rather than a mere clever compound of artifice. No unbiased reader can doubt that with *Melmoth* an enormous stride in the evolution of the horror-tale is represented. Fear is taken out of the realm of the conventional and exalted into a hideous cloud over mankind's very destiny. Maturin's shudders, the work of one capable of shuddering himself, are of the sort that convince. Mrs Radcliffe and Lewis are fair game for the parodist, but it would be difficult to find a false note in the feverishly intensified action and high atmospheric tension of the Irishman, whose less sophisticated emotions and strain of Celtic mysticism gave him the finest possible natural equipment for his task. Without a doubt Maturin is a man of authentic genius, and he was so recognised by Balzac, who grouped Melmoth with Molière's Don Juan, Goethe's Faust, and Byron's Manfred as the supreme allegorical figures of modern European literature, and wrote a whimsical piece called 'Melmoth Reconciled', in which the Wanderer succeeds in passing his infernal bargain on to a Parisian bank defaulter, who in turn hands it along a chain of victims until a

revelling gambler dies with it in his possession, and by his damnation ends the curse. Scott, Rossetti, Thackeray, and Baudelaire
are the other titans who gave Maturin their unqualified admiration,
and there is much significance in the fact that Oscar Wilde, after his
disgrace and exile, chose for his last days in Paris the assumed name
of 'Sebastian Melmoth'.

Melmoth contains scenes which even now have not lost their
power to evoke dread. It begins with a deathbed – an old miser is
dying of sheer fright because of something he has seen, coupled
with a manuscript he has read and a family portrait which hangs in an
obscure closet of his centuried home in County Wicklow. He sends
to Trinity College, Dublin, for his nephew John; and the latter upon
arriving notes many uncanny things. The eyes of the portrait in the
closet glow horribly, and twice a figure strangely resembling the
portrait appears momentarily at the door. Dread hangs over that
house of the Melmoths, one of whose ancestors, 'J. Melmoth, 1646',
the portrait represents. The dying miser declares that this man –
at a date slightly before 1800 – is alive. Finally the miser dies,
and the nephew is told in the will to destroy both the portrait
and a manuscript to be found in a certain drawer. Reading the
manuscript, which was written late in the seventeenth century by
an Englishman named Stanton, young John learns of a terrible
incident in Spain in 1677, when the writer met a horrible fellow-
countryman and was told of how he had stared to death a priest
who tried to denounce him as one filled with fearsome evil. Later,
after meeting the man again in London, Stanton is cast into a
madhouse and visited by the stranger, whose approach is heralded
by spectral music and whose eyes have a more than mortal glare.
Melmoth the Wanderer – for such is the malign visitor – offers
the captive freedom if he will take over his bargain with the Devil;
but like all others whom Melmoth has approached, Stanton is
proof against temptation. Melmoth's description of the horrors
of a life in a madhouse, used to tempt Stanton, is one of the most
potent passages of the book. Stanton is at length liberated, and
spends the rest of his life tracking down Melmoth, whose family
and ancestral abode he discovers. With the family he leaves the
manuscript, which by young John's time is sadly ruinous and fragmentary. John destroys both portrait and manuscript, but in sleep

is visited by his horrible ancestor, who leaves a black and blue mark on his wrist.

Young John soon afterward receives as a visitor a shipwrecked Spaniard, Alonzo de Monçada, who has escaped from compulsory monasticism and from the perils of the Inquisition. He has suffered horribly – and the descriptions of his experiences under torment and in the vaults through which he once essays escape are classic – but had the strength to resist Melmoth the Wanderer when approached at his darkest hour in prison. At the house of a Jew who sheltered him after his escape he discovers a wealth of manuscript relating other exploits of Melmoth including his wooing of an Indian island maiden, Immalee, who later comes to her birthright in Spain and is known as Donna Isidora; and his horrible marriage to her by the corpse of a dead anchorite at midnight in the ruined chapel of a shunned and abhorred monastery. Monçada's narrative to young John takes up the bulk of Maturin's four-volume book; this disproportion being considered one of the chief technical faults of the composition.

At last the colloquies of John and Monçada are interrupted by the entrance of Melmoth the Wanderer himself, his piercing eyes now fading, and decrepitude swiftly overtaking him. The term of his bargain has approached its end, and he has come home after a century and a half to meet his fate. Warning all others from the room, no matter what sounds they may hear in the night, he awaits the end alone. Young John and Monçada hear frightful ululations, but do not intrude till silence comes toward morning. They then find the room empty. Clayey footprints lead out a rear door to a cliff overlooking the sea, and near the edge of the precipice is a track indicating the forcible dragging of some heavy body. The Wanderer's scarf is found on a crag some distance below the brink, but nothing further is ever seen or heard of him.

Such is the story, and none can fail to notice the difference between this modulated, suggestive, and artistically moulded horror and – to use the words of Professor George Saintsbury – 'the artful but rather jejune rationalism of Mrs Radcliffe, and the too often puerile extravagance, the bad taste, and the sometimes slipshod style of Lewis'. Maturin's style in itself deserves particular praise, for its forcible directness and vitality lift it altogether above the pompous artificialities of which his predecessors are guilty. Professor Edith Birkhead, in her history of the Gothic novel, justly observes that with all his faults Maturin was the greatest as well as the last of the Goths. *Melmoth* was widely read and eventually dramatised, but its late date in the evolution of the Gothic tale deprived it of the tumultuous popularity of *Udolpho* and *The Monk*.

The Aftermath of Gothic Fiction

Meanwhile other hands had not been idle, so that above the dreary plethora of trash like Marquis von Grosse's *Horrid Mysteries* (1796), Mrs Roche's *Children of the Abbey* (1796), Miss Dacre's *Zofloya; or, The Moor* (1806), and the poet Shelley's schoolboy effusions *Zastrozzi* (1810) and *St Irvyne* (1811) (both imitations of *Zofloya*) there arose many memorable weird works both in English and German. Classic in merit, and markedly different from its fellows because of its foundation in the Oriental tale rather than the Walpolesque Gothic novel, is the celebrated *History of the Caliph Vathek* by the wealthy dilettante William Beckford, first written in the French language but published in an English translation before the appearance of the original. Eastern tales, introduced to European literature early in the eighteenth century through Galland's French translation of the inexhaustibly opulent *Arabian Nights*, had become a reigning fashion, being used both for allegory and for amusement. The sly humour which only the Eastern mind knows how to mix with weirdness had captivated a sophisticated generation, till Bagdad and Damascus names became as freely strown through popular literature as dashing Italian and Spanish ones were soon to be. Beckford, well read in Eastern romance, caught the atmosphere with unusual receptivity; and in his fantastic volume reflected very potently the haughty luxury, sly disillusion, bland cruelty, urbane treachery, and shadowy spectral horror of the Saracen spirit. His seasoning of the ridiculous seldom mars the force of his sinister theme, and the tale marches onward with a phantasmagoric pomp in which the laughter is that of skeletons feasting under Arabesque domes. *Vathek* is a tale of the grandson of the Caliph Haroun, who, tormented by that ambition for super-terrestrial power, pleasure, and learning which animates the average Gothic villain or Byronic hero (essentially cognate types), is lured by an evil genius to seek the subterranean throne of the mighty and fabulous pre-Adamite sultans in the fiery halls of Eblis, the Mahometan Devil. The descriptions of Vathek's palaces and diversions, of his scheming sorceress-mother Carathis and her witch-tower with the fifty one-eyed negresses, of his pilgrimage to the haunted ruins of Istakhar (Persepolis) and of the impish bride Nouronihar whom he treacherously acquired on the way, of Istakhar's primordial towers and terraces in the burning moonlight of the waste, and of the terrible Cyclopean halls of Eblis, where, lured by glittering promises, each victim is compelled to wander in anguish for ever, his right hand upon his blazingly ignited and eternally burning heart, are triumphs of weird colouring which raise the book to a permanent place in English letters. No less notable are the three *Episodes of Vathek*, intended for insertion in the tale as narratives of Vathek's fellow-victims in Eblis' infernal halls, which remained unpublished throughout the author's life-time and were discovered as recently as 1909 by the scholar Lewis Melville whilst collecting material for his *Life and Letters of William Beckford*. Beckford, however, lacks the essential mysticism which marks the acutest form of the weird; so that his tales have a certain knowing Latin hardness and clearness preclusive of sheer panic fright.

But Beckford remained alone in his devotion to the Orient. Other writers, closer to the Gothic tradition and to European life in general, were content to follow more faithfully in the lead of Walpole. Among the countless producers of terror-literature in these times may be mentioned the Utopian economic theorist William Godwin, who followed his famous but non-supernatural *Caleb Williams* (1794) with the intendedly weird *St Leon* (1799), in which the theme of the elixir of life, as developed by the imaginary secret order of 'Rosicrucians', is handled with ingeniousness if not with atmospheric convincing-ness. This element of Rosicrucianism, fostered by a wave of popular magical interest exemplified in the vogue of the charlatan Cagliostro and the publication of Francis Barrett's *The Magus* (1801), a curious and compendious treatise on occult principles and ceremonies, of which a reprint was made as lately as 1896, figures in Bulwer-Lytton and in many late Gothic novels, especially that remote and enfeebled posterity which straggled far down into the nineteenth century and was represented by George W. M. Reynolds' *Faust and the Demon* and *Wagner, the Wehr-wolf. Caleb Williams*, though non-supernatural, has many authentic touches of terror. It is the tale of a servant persecuted by a master whom he has found guilty of murder, and displays an invention and skill which have kept it alive in a fashion to this day. It was dramatised as *The Iron Chest*, and in that form was almost equally celebrated. Godwin, however, was too much the conscious teacher and prosaic man of thought to create a genuine weird masterpiece.

His daughter, the wife of Shelley, was much more successful; and her inimitable *Frankenstein; or, The Modern Prometheus* (1818) is one of the horror-classics of all time. Composed in competition with her husband, Lord Byron, and Dr John William Polidori in an effort to prove supremacy in horror-making, Mrs Shelley's *Frankenstein* was the only one of the rival narratives to be brought to an elaborate completion; and criticism has failed to prove that the best parts are due to Shelley rather than to her. The novel, somewhat tinged but scarcely marred by moral didacticism, tells of the artificial human being moulded from charnel fragments by Victor Frank-enstein, a young Swiss medical student. Created by its designer 'in the mad pride of intellectuality', the monster possesses full intell-igence but owns a hideously loathsome form. It is rejected by mankind, becomes embittered, and at length begins the successive murder of all whom young Frankenstein loves best, friends and family. It demands that Frankenstein create a wife for it; and when the student finally refuses in horror lest the world be populated with such monsters, it departs with a hideous threat 'to be with him on his wedding night'. Upon that night the bride is strangled, and from that time on Frankenstein hunts down the monster, even into the wastes of the Arctic. In the end, whilst seeking shelter on the ship of the man who tells the story, Frankenstein himself is killed by the shocking object of his search and creation of his presumptuous pride. Some of the scenes in *Frankenstein* are unforgettable, as when the newly animated monster enters its creator's room, parts the curtains of his bed, and gazes at him in the yellow moonlight with watery eyes – 'if eyes they may be called'. Mrs Shelley wrote other novels, including the fairly notable *Last Man*; but never duplicated the success of her first effort. It has the true touch of cosmic fear, no matter how much the movement may lag in places. Dr Polidori developed his competing idea as a long short story, 'The Vampyre'; in which we behold a suave villain of the true Gothic or Byronic type, and encounter some excellent passages of stark fright, including a terrible nocturnal experience in a shunned Grecian wood.

In this same period Sir Walter Scott frequently concerned himself with the weird, weaving it into many of his novels and poems, and sometimes producing such independent bits of narration as 'The Tapestried Chamber' or 'Wandering Willie's Tale' in *Redgauntlet*, in the latter of which the force of the spectral and the diabolic is enhanced by a grotesque homeliness of speech and atmosphere. In 1830 Scott published his *Letters on Demonology and Witchcraft*, which still forms one of our best compendia of European witch-lore. Washington Irving is another famous figure not unconnected with the weird; for though most of his ghosts are too whimsical and humorous to form genuinely spectral literature, a distinct inclination in this direction is to be noted in many of his productions. 'The German Student' in *Tales of a Traveller* (1824) is a slyly concise and effective presentation of the old legend of the dead bride, whilst woven into the comic tissue of 'The Money-Diggers' in the same volume is more than one hint of piratical apparitions in the realms which Captain Kidd once roamed. Thomas Moore also joined the ranks of the macabre artists in the poem *Alciphron*, which he later elaborated into the prose novel of *The Epicurean* (1827). Though merely relating the adventures of a young Athenian duped by the artifice of cunning Egyptian priests, Moore manages to infuse much genuine horror into his account of subterranean frights and wonders beneath the primordial temples of Memphis. De Quincey more than once revels in grotesque and arabesque terrors, though with a desultoriness and learned pomp which deny him the rank of specialist.

This era likewise saw the rise of William Harrison Ainsworth, whose romantic novels teem with the eerie and the gruesome. Capt. Marryat, besides writing such short tales as 'The Werewolf', made a memorable contribution in *The Phantom Ship* (1839), founded on the legend of the Flying Dutchman, whose spectral and accursed vessel sails for ever near the Cape of Good Hope. Dickens now rises with occasional weird bits like 'The Signalman', a tale of ghostly warning conforming to a very common pattern and touched with a verisimilitude which allies it as much with the coming psychological school as with the dying Gothic school. At this time a wave of interest in spiritualistic charlatanry, mediumism, Hindoo theosophy, and such matters, much like that of the present day, was flourishing; so that the number of weird tales with a 'psychic' or pseudo-scientific basis became very considerable. For a number of these the prolific and popular Lord Edward Bulwer-Lytton was responsible; and despite the large doses of turgid rhetoric and empty romanticism in his products, his success in the weaving of a certain kind of bizarre charm cannot be denied.

'The House and the Brain', which hints of Rosicrucianism and at a malign and deathless figure perhaps suggested by Louis XV's mysterious courtier St Germain, yet survives as one of the best short haunted-house tales ever written. The novel *Zanoni* (1842) contains similar elements more elaborately handled, and introduces a vast unknown sphere of being pressing on our own world and guarded by a horrible 'Dweller of the Threshold' who haunts those who try to enter and fail. Here we have a benign brotherhood kept alive from age to age till finally reduced to a single member, and as a hero an ancient Chaldaean sorcerer surviving in the pristine bloom of youth to perish on the guillotine of the French Revolution. Though full of the conventional spirit of romance, marred by a ponderous network of symbolic and didactic meanings, and left unconvincing through lack of perfect atmospheric realisation of the situations hinging on the spectral world, *Zanoni* is really an excellent performance as a romantic novel, and can be read with genuine interest today by the not too sophisticated reader. It is amusing to note that in describing an attempted initiation into the ancient brotherhood the author cannot escape using the stock Gothic castle of Walpolian lineage.

In *A Strange Story* (1862) Bulwer-Lytton shews a marked improvement in the creation of weird images and moods. The novel, despite enormous length, a highly artificial plot bolstered up by opportune coincidences, and an atmosphere of homiletic pseudo-science designed to please the matter-of-fact and purposeful Victorian reader, is exceedingly effective as a narrative, evoking instantaneous and unflagging interest, and furnishing many potent – if somewhat melodramatic – tableaux and climaxes. Again we have the mysterious user of life's elixir in the person of the soulless magician Margrave, whose dark exploits stand out with dramatic vividness against the modern background of a quiet English town and of the Australian bush; and again we have shadowy intimations of a vast spectral world of the unknown in the very air about us – this time handled with much greater power and vitality than in *Zanoni*. One of the two great incantation passages, where the hero is driven by a luminous evil spirit to rise at night in his sleep, take a strange Egyptian wand, and evoke nameless presences in the haunted and mausoleum-facing pavilion of a famous Renaissance alchemist, truly stands among the major terror scenes of literature. Just enough is suggested, and just little enough is told. Unknown words are twice dictated to the sleep-walker, and as he repeats them the ground trembles, and all the dogs of the countryside begin to bay at half-seen amorphous shadows that stalk athwart the moonlight. When a third set of unknown words is prompted, the sleep-walker's spirit suddenly rebels at uttering them, as if the soul could recognise ultimate abysmal horrors concealed from the mind; and at last an apparition of an absent sweetheart and good angel breaks the malign spell. This fragment well illustrates how far Lord Lytton was capable of progressing beyond his usual pomp and stock romance toward that crystalline essence of artistic fear which belongs to the domain of poetry. In describing certain details of incantations, Lytton was greatly indebted to his amusingly serious occult studies, in the course of which he came in touch with that odd French scholar and cabbalist Alphonse-Louis Constant ('Eliphas Lévi'), who claimed to possess the secrets of ancient magic, and to have evoked the spectre of the old Grecian wizard Apollonius of Tyana, who lived in Nero's time.

The romantic, semi-Gothic, quasi-moral tradition here represented was carried far down the nineteenth century by such authors as Joseph Sheridan LeFanu, Thomas Preskett Prest with his famous *Varney, the Vampyre* (1847), Wilkie Collins, the late Sir H. Rider Haggard (whose *She* is really remarkably good), Sir A. Conan Doyle, H. G. Wells, and Robert Louis Stevenson – the latter of whom, despite an atrocious tendency toward jaunty mannerisms, created permanent classics in 'Markheim', 'The Body-Snatcher', and *Dr Jekyll and Mr Hyde*. Indeed, we may say that this school still survives; for to it clearly belong such of our contemporary horror-tales as specialise in events rather than atmospheric details, address the intellect rather than the impressionistic imagination, cultivate a luminous glamour rather than a malign tensity or psychological verisimilitude, and take a definite stand in sympathy with mankind and its welfare. It has its undeniable strength, and because of its 'human element' commands a wider audience than does the sheer artistic nightmare. If not quite so potent as the latter, it is because a diluted product can never achieve the intensity of a concentrated essence.

Quite alone both as a novel and as a piece of terror-literature stands the famous *Wuthering Heights* (1847) by Emily Brontë, with its mad vista of bleak, windswept Yorkshire moors and the violent, distorted lives they foster. Though primarily a tale of life, and of human passions in agony and conflict, its epically cosmic setting affords room for horror of the most spiritual sort. Heathcliff, the modified Byronic villain-hero, is a strange dark waif found in the streets as a small child and speaking only a strange gibberish till adopted by the family he ultimately ruins. That he is in truth a diabolic spirit rather than a human being is more than once suggested, and the unreal is further approached in the experience of the visitor who encounters a plaintive child-ghost at a bough-brushed upper window. Between Heathcliff and Catherine Earnshaw is a tie deeper and more terrible than human love. After her death he twice disturbs her grave, and is haunted by an impalpable presence which can be nothing less than her spirit. The spirit enters his life more and more, and at last he becomes confident of some imminent mystical reunion. He says he feels a strange change approaching, and ceases to take nourishment. At night he either walks abroad or opens the casement by his bed. When he dies the casement is still swinging open to the pouring rain, and a queer smile pervades the stiffened face. They bury him in a grave beside the mound he has haunted for eighteen years, and small shepherd boys say that he yet walks with his Catherine in the churchyard and on the moor when it rains. Their faces, too, are sometimes seen on rainy nights behind that upper casement at Wuthering Heights. Miss Brontë's eerie terror is no mere Gothic echo, but a tense expression of man's shuddering reaction to the unknown. In this respect, *Wuthering Heights* becomes the symbol of a literary transition, and marks the growth of a new and sounder school.

Spectral Literature on the Continent

On the Continent literary horror fared well. The celebrated short tales and novels of Ernst Theodor Wilhelm Hoffmann (1776–1822) are a byword for mellowness of background and maturity of form, though they incline to levity and extravagance, and lack the exalted moments of stark, breathless terror which a less sophisticated writer might have achieved. Generally they convey the grotesque rather than the terrible. Most artistic of all the Continental weird tales is the German classic *Undine* (1811), by Friedrich Heinrich Karl, Baron de la Motte Fouqué. In this story of a water-spirit who married a mortal and gained a human soul there is a delicate fineness of craftsmanship which makes it notable in any department of literature, and an easy naturalness which places it close to the genuine folk-myth. It is, in fact, derived from a tale told by the Renaissance physician and alchemist Paracelsus in his *Treatise on Elemental Sprites.*

Undine, daughter of a powerful water-prince, was exchanged by her father as a small child for a fisherman's daughter, in order that she might acquire a soul by wedding a human being. Meeting the noble youth Huldbrand at the cottage of her foster-father by the sea at the edge of a haunted wood, she soon marries him, and accompanies him to his ancestral castle of Ringstetten. Huldbrand, however, eventually wearies of his wife's supernatural affiliations, and especially of the appearances of her uncle, the malicious woodland waterfall-spirit Kühleborn; a weariness increased by his growing affection for Bertalda, who turns out to be the fisherman's child for whom Undine was exchanged. At length, on a voyage down the Danube, he is provoked by some innocent act of his devoted wife to utter the angry words which consign her back to her supernatural element; from which she can, by the laws of her species, return only once – to kill him, whether she will or no, if ever he prove unfaithful to her memory. Later, when Huldbrand is about to be married to Bertalda, Undine returns for her sad duty, and bears his life away in tears. When he is buried among his fathers in the village churchyard a veiled, snow-white female figure appears among the mourners, but after the prayer is seen no more. In her place is seen a little silver spring, which murmurs its way almost completely around the new grave, and empties into a neighbouring lake. The villagers shew it to this day, and say that Undine and her Huldbrand are thus united in death. Many passages and atmospheric touches in this tale reveal Fouqué as an accomplished artist in the field of the macabre; especially the descriptions of the haunted wood with its gigantic snow-white man and various unnamed terrors, which occur early in the narrative.

Not so well known as *Undine*, but remarkable for its convincing realism and freedom from Gothic stock devices, is *The Amber Witch* of Wilhelm Meinhold, another product of the German fantastic genius of the earlier nineteenth century. This tale, which is laid in the time of the Thirty Years' War, purports to be a clergyman's manuscript found in an old church at Coserow, and centres round the writer's daughter, Maria Schweidler, who is wrongly accused of witchcraft. She has found a deposit of amber which she keeps secret for various reasons, and the unexplained wealth obtained from this lends colour to the accusation; an accusation instigated by the malice of the wolf-hunting nobleman Wittich Appelmann, who has vainly pursued her with ignoble designs. The deeds of a real witch, who afterward comes to a horrible supernatural end in prison, are glibly imputed to the hapless Maria; and after a typical witchcraft trial with forced confessions under torture she is about to be burned at the stake when saved just in time by her lover, a noble youth from a neighbouring district. Meinhold's great strength is in his air of casual and realistic verisimilitude, which intensifies our suspense and sense of the unseen by half persuading us that the menacing events must somehow be either the truth or very close to the truth. Indeed, so thorough is this realism that a popular magazine once published the main points of *The Amber Witch* as an actual occurrence of the seventeenth century!

[In the present generation German horror-fiction is most notably represented by Hanns Heinz Ewers, who brings to bear on his dark conceptions an effective knowledge of modern psychology. Novels like *The Sorcerer's Apprentice* and *Alraune*, and short stories like 'The Spider', contain distinctive qualities which raise them to a classic level.]

But France as well as Germany has been active in the realm of weirdness. Victor Hugo, in such tales as *Hans of Iceland*, and Balzac, in *The Wild Ass's Skin*, *Séraphîta*, and *Louis Lambert*, both employ supernaturalism to a greater or less extent, though generally only as a means to some more human end, and without the sincere and daemonic intensity which characterises the born artist in shadows. It is in Théophile Gautier that we first seem to find an authentic French sense of the unreal world, and here there appears a spectral mastery which, though not continuously used, is recognisable at once as something alike genuine and profound. Short tales like 'Avatar', 'The Foot of the Mummy', and 'Clarimonde' display glimpses of forbidden visits that allure, tantalise, and sometimes horrify; whilst the Egyptian visions evoked in 'One of Cleopatra's Nights' are of the keenest and most expressive potency. Gautier captured the inmost soul of aeon-weighted Egypt, with its cryptic life and Cyclopean architecture, and uttered once and for all the eternal horror of its nether world of catacombs, where to the end of time millions of stiff, spiced corpses will stare up in the blackness with glassy eyes, awaiting some awesome and unrelatable summons. Gustave Flaubert ably continued the tradition of Gautier in orgies of poetic phantasy like *The Temptation of St Anthony*, and but for a strong realistic bias might have been an arch-weaver of tapestried terrors. Later on we see the stream divide, producing strange poets and *fantaisistes* of the Symbolist and Decadent schools whose dark interests really centre more in abnormalities of human thought and instinct than in the actual supernatural, and subtle story-tellers whose thrills are quite directly derived from the night-black wells of cosmic unreality. Of the former class of 'artists in sin' the illustrious poet Baudelaire, influenced vastly by Poe, is the supreme type; whilst the psychological novelist Joris-Karl Huysmans, a true child of the eighteen-nineties, is at once the summation and finale. The latter and purely narrative class is continued by Prosper Mérimée, whose 'Venus of Ille' presents in terse and convincing prose the same ancient statue-bride theme which Thomas Moore cast in ballad form in 'The Ring'.

The horror-tales of the powerful and cynical Guy de Maupassant, written as his final madness gradually overtook him, present individualities of their own; being rather the morbid outpourings of a realistic mind in a pathological state than the healthy imaginative products of a vision naturally disposed toward phantasy and sensitive to the normal illusions of the unseen. Nevertheless they are of the keenest interest and poignancy, suggesting with marvellous force the imminence of nameless terrors, and the relentless dogging of an ill-starred individual by hideous and menacing representatives of the outer blackness. Of these stories 'The Horla' is generally regarded as the masterpiece. Relating the advent to France of an invisible being who lives on water and milk, sways the minds of others, and seems to be the vanguard of a horde of extra-terrestrial organisms arrived on earth to subjugate and overwhelm mankind, this tense narrative is perhaps without a peer in its particular department, notwithstanding its indebtedness to a tale by the American Fitz-James O'Brien for details in describing the actual presence of the unseen monster. Other potently dark creations of de Maupassant are 'Who Knows?', 'The Spectre', 'He?', 'The Diary of a Madman', 'The White Wolf', 'On the River', and the grisly verses entitled 'Horror'.

The collaborators Erckmann-Chatrian enriched French literature with many spectral fancies like *The Man-Wolf*, in which a transmitted curse works toward its end in a traditional Gothic-castle setting. Their power of creating a shuddering midnight atmosphere was tremendous despite a tendency toward natural explanations and scientific wonders; and few short tales contain greater horror than 'The Invisible Eye', where a malignant old hag weaves nocturnal hypnotic spells which induce the successive occupants of a certain inn chamber to hang themselves on a cross-beam. 'The Owl's Ear' and 'The Waters of Death' are full of engulfing darkness and mystery, the latter embodying the familiar overgrown-spider theme so frequently employed by weird fictionists. Villiers de l'Isle-Adam likewise followed the macabre school; his 'Torture by Hope', the tale of a stake-condemned prisoner permitted to escape in order to feel the pangs of recapture, being held by some to constitute the most harrowing short story in literature. This type, however, is less a part of the weird tradition than a class peculiar to itself – the so-called *conte cruel*, in which the wrenching of the emotions is accomplished through dramatic tantalisations, frustrations, and gruesome physical horrors. Almost wholly devoted to this form is the living writer Maurice Level, whose very brief episodes have lent themselves so readily to theatrical adaptation in the 'thrillers' of the Grand Guignol. As a matter of fact, the French genius is more naturally suited to this dark realism than to the suggestion of the unseen, since the latter process requires, for its best and most sympathetic development on a large scale, the inherent mysticism of the Northern mind.

A very flourishing, though till recently quite hidden, branch of weird literature is that of the Jews, kept alive and nourished in obscurity by the sombre heritage of early Eastern magic, apocalyptic literature, and cabbalism. The Semitic mind, like the Celtic and Teutonic, seems to possess marked mystical inclinations; and the wealth of underground horror-lore surviving in ghettoes and synagogues must be much more considerable than is generally imagined. Cabbalism itself, so prominent during the Middle Ages, is a system of philosophy explaining the universe as emanations of the Deity, and involving the existence of strange spiritual realms and beings apart from the visible world, of which dark glimpses may be obtained through certain secret incantations. Its ritual is bound up with mystical interpretations of the Old Testament, and attributes an esoteric significance to each letter of the Hebrew alphabet – a circumstance which has imparted to Hebrew letters a sort of spectral glamour and potency in the popular literature of magic. Jewish folklore has preserved much of the terror and mystery of the past, and when more thoroughly studied is likely to exert considerable influence on weird fiction. The best examples of its literary use so far are the German novel *The Golem*, by Gustav Meyrink, and the drama *The Dybbuk*, by the Jewish writer using the pseudonym 'Ansky'. [The former, with its haunting shadowy suggestions of marvels and horrors just beyond reach, is laid in Prague, and describes with singular mastery that city's ancient ghetto with its spectral, peaked gables. The name is derived from a fabulous artificial giant supposed to be made and animated by mediaeval rabbis according to a certain cryptic formula.] *The Dybbuk*, translated and produced in America in 1925 [and more recently produced as an opera], describes with singular power the possession of a living body by the evil soul of a dead man. Both golems and dybbuks are fixed types, and serve as frequent ingredients of later Jewish tradition.

Edgar Allan Poe

In the eighteen-thirties occurred a literary dawn directly affecting not only the history of the weird tale, but that of short fiction as a whole, and indirectly moulding the trends and fortunes of a great European aesthetic school. It is our good fortune as Americans to be able to claim that dawn as our own, for it came in the person of our illustrious and unfortunate fellow-countryman Edgar Allan Poe. Poe's fame has been subject to curious undulations, and it is now a fashion amongst the 'advanced intelligentsia' to minimise his importance both as an artist and as an influence; but it would be hard for any mature and reflective critic to deny the tremendous value of his work and the pervasive potency of his mind as an opener of artistic vistas. True, his type of outlook may have been anticipated; but it was he who first realised its possibilities and gave it supreme form and systematic expression. True also, that subsequent writers may have produced greater single tales than his; but again we must comprehend that it was only he who taught them by example and precept the art which they, having the way cleared for them and given an explicit guide, were perhaps able to carry to greater lengths. Whatever his limitations, Poe did that which no one else ever did or could have done; and to him we owe the modern horror-story in its final and perfected state.

Before Poe the bulk of weird writers had worked largely in the dark; without an understanding of the psychological basis of the horror appeal, and hampered by more or less of conformity to certain empty literary conventions such as the happy ending, virtue rewarded, and in general a hollow moral didacticism, acceptance of popular standards and values, and striving of the author to obtrude his own emotions into the story and take sides with the partisans of the majority's artificial ideas. Poe, on the other hand, perceived the essential impersonality of the real artist, and knew that the function of creative fiction is merely to express and interpret events and sensations as they are, regardless of how they tend or what they prove – good or evil, attractive or repulsive, stimulating or depressing – with the author always acting as a vivid and detached chronicler rather than as a teacher, sympathiser, or vendor of opinion. He saw clearly that all phases of life and thought are equally eligible as subject-matter for the artist, and being inclined by temperament to strangeness and gloom, decided to be the interpreter of those powerful feelings, and frequent happenings which attend pain rather than pleasure, decay rather than growth, terror rather than tranquillity, and which are fundamentally either adverse or indifferent to the tastes and traditional outward sentiments of mankind, and to the health, sanity, and normal expansive welfare of the species.

Poe's spectres thus acquired a convincing malignity possessed by none of their predecessors, and established a new standard of realism in the annals of literary horror. The impersonal and artistic intent, moreover, was aided by a scientific attitude not often found before, whereby Poe studied the human mind rather than the usages of Gothic fiction, and worked with an analytical knowledge of terror's true sources which doubled the force of his narratives and emancipated him from all the absurdities inherent in merely conventional shudder-coining. This example having been set, later authors were naturally forced to conform to it in order to compete at all; so that in this way a definite change began to affect the main stream of macabre writing. Poe, too, set a fashion in consummate craftsmanship; and although today some of his own work seems slightly melodramatic and unsophisticated, we can constantly trace his influence in such things as the maintenance of a single mood and achievement of a single impression in a tale, and the rigorous paring down of incidents to such as have a direct bearing on the plot and will figure prominently in the climax. Truly may it be said that Poe invented the short story in its present form. His elevation of disease, perversity, and decay to the level of artistically expressible themes was likewise infinitely far-reaching in effect; for avidly seized, sponsored, and intensified by his eminent French admirer Charles Pierre Baudelaire, it became the nucleus of the principal aesthetic movements in France, thus making Poe in a sense the father of the Decadents and the Symbolists.

Poet and critic by nature and supreme attainment, logician and philosopher by taste and mannerism, Poe was by no means immune from defects and affectations. His pretence to profound and obscure scholarship, his blundering ventures in stilted and laboured pseudo-humour, and his often vitriolic outbursts of critical prejudice must all be recognised and forgiven. Beyond and above them, and dwarfing them to insignificance, was a master's vision of the terror that stalks about and within us, and the worm that writhes and slavers in the hideously close abyss. Penetrating to every festering horror in the gaily painted mockery called existence, and in the solemn masquerade called human thought and feelings, that vision had power to project itself in blackly magical crystallisations and transmutations, till there bloomed in the sterile America of the 'thirties and 'forties such a moon-nourished garden of gorgeous poison fungi as not even the nether slope of Saturn might boast. Verses and tales alike sustain the burthen of cosmic panic. The raven whose noisome beak pierces the heart, the ghouls that toll iron bells in pestilential steeples, the vault of Ulalume in the black October night, the shocking spires and domes under the sea, the 'wild, weird clime that lieth, sublime, out of Space – out of Time' – all these things and more leer at us amidst maniacal rattlings in the seething nightmare of the poetry. And in the prose there yawn open for us the very jaws of the pit – inconceivable abnormalities slyly hinted into a horrible half-knowledge by words whose innocence we scarcely doubt till the cracked tension of the speaker's hollow voice bids us fear their nameless implications; daemoniac patterns and presences slumbering noxiously till waked for one phobic instant into a shrieking revelation that cackles itself to sudden madness or explodes in memorable and cataclysmic echoes. A Witches' Sabbath of horror flinging off decorous robes is flashed before us – a sight the more monstrous because of the scientific skill with which every particular is marshalled and brought into an easy apparent relation to the known gruesomeness of material life.

Poe's tales, of course, fall into several classes; some of which contain a purer essence of spiritual horror than others. The tales of logic and ratiocination, forerunners of the modern detective story, are not to be included at all in weird literature, whilst certain others, probably influenced considerably by Hoffmann, possess an extravagance which relegates them to the borderline of the grotesque. Still a third group deal with abnormal psychology and monomania in such a way as to express terror but not weirdness. A substantial residuum, however, represent the literature of supernatural horror in its acutest form; and give their author a permanent and unassailable place as deity and fountain-head of all modern diabolic fiction. Who can forget the terrible swollen ship poised on the billow-chasm's edge in 'MS. Found in a Bottle' –

the dark intimations of her unhallowed age and monstrous growth, her sinister crew of unseeing greybeards, and her frightful southward rush under full sail through the ice of the Antarctic night, sucked onward by some resistless devil-current toward a vortex of eldritch enlightenment which must end in destruction? Then there is the unutterable 'M. Valdemar', kept together by hypnotism for seven months after his death, and uttering frantic sounds but a moment before the breaking of the spell leaves him 'a nearly liquid mass of loathsome – of detestable – putrescence'. In the *Narrative of A. Gordon Pym* the voyagers reach first a strange south polar land of murderous savages where nothing is white and where vast rocky ravines have the form of titanic Egyptian letters spelling terrible primal arcana of earth; and thereafter a still more mysterious realm where everything is white, and where shrouded giants and snowy-plumed birds guard a cryptic cataract of mist which empties from immeasurable celestial heights into a torrid milky sea. 'Metzengerstein' horrifies with its malign hints of a monstrous metempsychosis – the mad nobleman who burns the stable of his hereditary foe; the colossal unknown horse that issues from the blazing building after the owner has perished therein; the vanishing bit of ancient tapestry where was shewn the giant horse of the victim's ancestor in the Crusades; the madman's wild and constant riding on the great horse, and his fear and hatred of the steed; the meaningless prophecies that brood obscurely over the warring houses; and finally, the burning of the madman's palace and the death therein of the owner, borne helpless into the flames and up the vast staircases astride the beast he has ridden so strangely. Afterward the rising smoke of the ruins takes the form of a gigantic horse. 'The Man of the Crowd', telling of one who roams day and night to mingle with streams of people as if afraid to be alone, has quieter effects, but implies nothing less of cosmic fear. Poe's mind was never far from terror and decay, and we see in every tale, poem, and philosophical dialogue a tense eagerness to fathom unplumbed wells of night, to pierce the veil of death, and to reign in fancy as lord of the frightful mysteries of time and space.

Certain of Poe's tales possess an almost absolute perfection of artistic form which makes them veritable beacon-lights in the province of the short story. Poe could, when he wished, give to his prose a richly poetic cast, employing that archaic and Orientalised style with jewelled phrase, quasi-Biblical repetition, and recurrent burthen so successfully used by later writers like Oscar Wilde and Lord Dunsany; and in the cases where he has done this we have an effect of lyrical phantasy almost narcotic in essence – an opium pageant of dream in the language of dream, with every unnatural colour and grotesque image bodied forth in a symphony of corresponding sound. 'The Masque of the Red Death', 'Silence – A Fable', and 'Shadow – A Parable' are assuredly poems in every sense of the word save the metrical one, and owe as much of their power to aural cadence as to visual imagery. But it is in two of the less openly poetic tales, 'Ligeia' and 'The Fall of the House of Usher' – especially the latter – that one finds those very summits of artistry whereby Poe takes his place at the head of fictional miniaturists. Simple and straightforward in plot, both of these tales owe their supreme magic to the cunning development which appears in the selection and collocation of every least incident. 'Ligeia' tells of a first wife of lofty and mysterious origin, who after death returns through a preternatural force of will to take possession of the body of a second wife, imposing even her physical appearance on the temporarily reanimated corpse of her victim at the last moment. Despite a suspicion of prolixity and top-heaviness, the narrative reaches its terrific climax with relentless power. 'Usher', whose superiority in detail and proportion is very marked, hints shudderingly of obscure life in inorganic things, and displays an abnormally linked trinity of entities at the end of a long and isolated family history – a brother, his twin sister, and their incredibly ancient house all sharing a single soul and meeting one common dissolution at the same moment.

These bizarre conceptions, so awkward in unskilful hands, become under Poe's spell living and convincing terrors to haunt our nights; and all because the author understood so perfectly the very mechanics and physiology of fear and strangeness – the essential details to emphasise, the precise incongruities and conceits to select as preliminaries or concomitants to horror, the exact incidents and allusions to throw out innocently in advance as symbols or prefigurings of each major step toward the hideous dénouement to come, the nice adjustments of cumulative force and the unerring accuracy in linkage of parts which make for faultless unity throughout and thunderous effectiveness at the climactic moment, the delicate nuances of scenic and landscape value to select in establishing and sustaining the desired mood and vitalising the desired illusion – principles of this kind, and dozens of obscurer ones too elusive to be described or even fully comprehended by any ordinary commentator. Melodrama and unsophistication there may be – we are told of one fastidious Frenchman who could not bear to read Poe except in Baudelaire's urbane and Gallically modulated translation – but all traces of such things are wholly overshadowed by a potent and inborn sense of the spectral, the morbid, and the horrible which gushed forth from every cell of the artist's creative mentality and stamped his macabre work with the ineffaceable mark of supreme genius. Poe's weird tales are *alive* in a manner that few others can ever hope to be.

Like most *fantaisistes*, Poe excels in incidents and broad narrative effects rather than in character drawing. His typical protagonist is generally a dark, handsome, proud, melancholy, intellectual, highly sensitive, capricious, introspective, isolated, and sometimes slightly mad gentleman of ancient family and opulent circumstances; usually deeply learned in strange lore, and darkly ambitious of penetrating to forbidden secrets of the universe. Aside from a high-sounding name, this character obviously derives little from the early Gothic novel; for he is clearly neither the wooden hero nor the diabolical villain of Radcliffian or Ludovician romance. Indirectly, however, he does possess a sort of genealogical connexion, since his gloomy, ambitious, and anti-social qualities savour strongly of the typical Byronic hero, who in turn is definitely an offspring of the Gothic Manfreds, Montonis, and Ambrosios. More particular qualities appear to be derived from the psychology of Poe himself, who certainly possessed much of the depression, sensitiveness, mad aspiration, loneliness, and extravagant freakishness which he attributes to his haughty and solitary victims of Fate.

The Weird Tradition in America

The public for whom Poe wrote, though grossly unappreciative of his art, was by no means unaccustomed to the horrors with which he dealt. America, besides inheriting the usual dark folklore of Europe, had an additional fund of weird associations to draw upon; so that spectral legends had already been recognised as fruitful subject-matter for literature. Charles Brockden Brown had achieved phenomenal fame with his Radcliffian romances, and Washington Irving's lighter treatment of eerie themes had quickly become classic. This additional fund proceeded, as Paul Elmer More has pointed out, from the keen spiritual and theological interests of the first colonists, plus the strange and forbidding nature of the scene into which they were plunged. The vast and gloomy virgin forests in whose perpetual twilight all terrors might well lurk; the hordes of coppery Indians whose strange, saturnine visages and violent customs hinted strongly at traces of infernal origin; the free rein given under the influence of Puritan theocracy to all manner of notions respecting man's relation to the stern and vengeful God of the Calvinists, and to the sulphureous Adversary of that God, about whom so much was thundered in the pulpits each Sunday; and the morbid introspection developed by an isolated backwoods life devoid of normal amusements and of the recreational mood, harassed by commands for theological self-examination, keyed to unnatural emotional repression, and forming above all a mere grim struggle for survival – all these things conspired to produce an environment in which the black whisperings of sinister grandams were heard far beyond the chimney corner, and in which tales of witchcraft and unbelievable secret monstrosities lingered long after the dread days of the Salem nightmare.

Poe represents the newer, more disillusioned, and more technically finished of the weird schools that rose out of this propitious milieu. Another school – the tradition of moral values, gentle restraint, and mild, leisurely phantasy tinged more or less with the whimsical – was represented by another famous, misunderstood, and lonely figure in American letters – the shy and sensitive Nathaniel Hawthorne, scion of antique Salem and great-grandson of one of the bloodiest of the old witchcraft judges. In Hawthorne we have none of the violence, the daring, the high colouring, the intense dramatic sense, the cosmic malignity, and the undivided and impersonal artistry of Poe. Here, instead, is a gentle soul cramped by the Puritanism of early New England; shadowed and wistful, and grieved at an unmoral universe which everywhere transcends the conventional patterns thought by our forefathers to represent divine and immutable law. Evil, a very real force to Hawthorne, appears on every hand as a lurking and conquering adversary; and the visible world becomes in his fancy a theatre of infinite tragedy and woe, with unseen half-existent influences hovering over it and through it, battling for supremacy and moulding the destinies of the hapless mortals who form its vain and self-deluded population. The heritage of American weirdness was his to a most intense degree, and he saw a dismal throng of vague spectres behind the common phenomena of life; but he was not disinterested enough to value impressions, sensations, and beauties of narration for their own sake. He must needs weave his phantasy into some quietly melancholy fabric of didactic or allegorical cast, in which his meekly resigned cynicism may display with naive moral appraisal the perfidy of a human race which he cannot cease to cherish and mourn despite his insight into its hypocrisy. Supernatural horror, then, is never a primary object with Hawthorne, though its impulses were so deeply woven into his personality that he cannot help suggesting it with the force of genius when he calls upon the unreal world to illustrate the pensive sermon he wishes to preach.

Hawthorne's intimations of the weird, always gentle, elusive, and restrained, may be traced throughout his work. The mood that produced them found one delightful vent in the Teutonised retelling of classic myths for children contained in *A Wonder Book* and *Tanglewood Tales*, and at other times exercised itself in casting a certain strangeness and intangible witchery or malevolence over events not meant to be actually supernatural; as in the macabre posthumous novel *Dr Grimshawe's Secret*, which invests with a peculiar sort of repulsion a house existing to this day in Salem, and abutting on the ancient Charter Street Burying Ground. In *The Marble Faun*, whose design was sketched out in an Italian villa reputed to be haunted, a tremendous background of genuine phantasy and mystery palpitates just beyond the common reader's sight; and glimpses of fabulous blood in mortal veins are hinted at during the course of a romance which cannot help being interesting despite the persistent incubus of moral allegory, anti-Popery propaganda, and a Puritan prudery which has caused the late D. H. Lawrence to express a longing to treat the author in a highly undignified manner. *Septimius Felton*, a posthumous novel whose idea was to have been elaborated and incorporated into the unfinished *Dolliver Romance*, touches on the Elixir of Life in a more or less capable fashion;

whilst the notes for a never-written tale to be called 'The Ancestral Footstep' shew what Hawthorne would have done with an intensive treatment of an old English superstition – that of an ancient and accursed line whose members left footprints of blood as they walked – which appears incidentally in both *Septimius Felton* and *Dr Grimshawe's Secret*.

Many of Hawthorne's shorter tales exhibit weirdness, either of atmosphere or of incident, to a remarkable degree. 'Edward Randolph's Portrait', in *Legends of the Province House*, has its diabolic moments. 'The Minister's Black Veil' (founded on an actual incident) and 'The Ambitious Guest' imply much more than they state, whilst 'Ethan Brand' – a fragment of a longer work never completed – rises to genuine heights of cosmic fear with its vignette of the wild hill country and the blazing, desolate lime-kilns, and its delineation of the Byronic 'unpardonable sinner', whose troubled life ends with a peal of fearful laughter in the night as he seeks rest amidst the flames of the furnace. Some of Hawthorne's notes tell of weird tales he would have written had he lived longer – an especially vivid plot being that concerning a baffling stranger who appeared now and then in public assemblies, and who was at last followed and found to come and go from a very ancient grave.

But foremost as a finished, artistic unit among all our author's weird material is the famous and exquisitely wrought novel, *The House of the Seven Gables*, in which the relentless working out of an ancestral curse is developed with astonishing power against the sinister background of a very ancient Salem house – one of those peaked Gothic affairs which formed the first regular building-up of our New England coast towns, but which gave way after the seventeenth century to the more familiar gambrel-roofed or classic Georgian types now known as 'Colonial'. Of these old gabled Gothic houses scarcely a dozen are to be seen today in their original condition throughout the United States, but one well known to Hawthorne still stands in Turner Street, Salem, and is pointed out with doubtful authority as the scene and inspiration of the romance. Such an edifice, with its spectral peaks, its clustered chimneys, its overhanging second story, its grotesque corner-brackets, and its diamond-paned lattice windows, is indeed an object well calculated to evoke sombre reflections, typifying as it does the dark Puritan age of concealed horror and witch-whispers which preceded the beauty, rationality, and spaciousness of the eighteenth century. Hawthorne saw many in his youth, and knew the black tales connected with some of them. He heard, too, many rumours of a curse upon his own line as the result of his great-grandfather's severity as a witchcraft judge in 1692.

From this setting came the immortal tale – New England's greatest contribution to weird literature – and we can feel in an instant the authenticity of the atmosphere presented to us. Stealthy horror and disease lurk within the weather-blackened, moss-crusted, and elm-shadowed walls of the archaic dwelling so vividly displayed, and we grasp the brooding malignity of the place when we read that its builder – old Colonel Pyncheon – snatched the land with peculiar ruthlessness from its original settler, Matthew Maule, whom he condemned to the gallows as a wizard in the year of the panic. Maule died cursing old Pyncheon – 'God will give him blood to drink' – and the waters of the old well on the seized land turned bitter. Maule's carpenter son consented to build the great gabled house for his father's triumphant enemy, but the old Colonel died strangely on the day of its dedication. Then followed generations of odd vicissitudes, with queer whispers about the dark powers of the Maules, and peculiar and sometimes terrible ends befalling the Pyncheons.

The overshadowing malevolence of the ancient house – almost as alive as Poe's House of Usher, though in a subtler way – pervades the tale as a recurrent motif pervades an operatic tragedy; and when the main story is reached, we behold the modern Pyncheons in a pitiable state of decay. Poor old Hepzibah, the eccentric reduced gentlewoman; child-like, unfortunate Clifford, just released from undeserved imprisonment; sly and treacherous Judge Pyncheon, who is the old Colonel all over again – all these figures are tremendous symbols, and are well matched by the stunted vegetation and anaemic fowls in the garden. It was almost a pity to supply a fairly happy ending, with a union of sprightly Phoebe, cousin and last scion of the Pyncheons, to the prepossessing young man who turns out to be the last of the Maules. This union, presumably, ends the curse. Hawthorne avoids all violence of diction or movement, and keeps his implications of terror well in the background; but occasional glimpses amply serve to sustain the mood and redeem the work from pure allegorical aridity. Incidents like the bewitching of Alice Pyncheon in the early eighteenth century, and the spectral music of her harpsichord which precedes a death in the family – the latter a variant of an immemorial type of Aryan myth – link the action directly with the supernatural; whilst the dead nocturnal vigil of old Judge Pyncheon in the ancient parlour, with his frightfully ticking watch, is stark horror of the most poignant and genuine sort. The way in which the Judge's death is first adumbrated by the motions and sniffing of a strange cat outside the window, long before the fact is suspected either by the reader or by any of the characters, is a stroke of genius which Poe could not have surpassed. Later the strange cat watches intently outside that same window in the night and on the next day, for – something. It is clearly the psychopomp of primeval myth, fitted and adapted with infinite deftness to its latter-day setting.

But Hawthorne left no well-defined literary posterity. His mood and attitude belonged to the age which closed with him, and it is the spirit of Poe – who so clearly and realistically understood the natural basis of the horror-appeal and the correct mechanics of its achievement – which survived and blossomed. Among the earliest of Poe's disciples may be reckoned the brilliant young Irishman Fitz-James O'Brien (1828–1862), who became naturalised as an American and perished honourably in the Civil War. It is he who gave us 'What Was It?', the first well-shaped short story of a tangible but invisible being, and the prototype of de Maupassant's 'Horla'; he also who created the inimitable 'Diamond Lens', in which a young microscopist falls in love with a maiden of an infinitesimal world which he has discovered in a drop of water. O'Brien's early death undoubtedly deprived us of some masterful tales of strangeness and terror, though his genius was not, properly speaking, of the same titan quality which characterised Poe and Hawthorne.

Closer to real greatness was the eccentric and saturnine journalist Ambrose Bierce, born in 1842; who likewise entered the Civil War, but survived to write some immortal tales and to disappear in 1913 in as great a cloud of mystery as any he ever evoked from his nightmare fancy. Bierce was a satirist and pamphleteer of note, but the bulk of his artistic reputation must rest upon his grim and savage short stories; a large number of which deal with the Civil War and form the most vivid and realistic expression which that conflict has yet received in fiction. Virtually all of Bierce's tales are tales of horror; and whilst many of them treat only of the physical and psychological horrors within Nature, a substantial proportion admit the malignly supernatural and form a leading element in America's fund of weird literature. Mr Samuel Loveman, a living poet and critic who was personally acquainted with Bierce, thus sums up the genius of the great shadow-maker in the preface to some of his letters.

> In Bierce, the evocation of horror becomes for the first time, not so much the prescription or perversion of Poe and Maupassant, but an atmosphere definite and uncannily precise. Words, so simple that one would be prone to ascribe them to the limit-ations of a literary hack, take on an unholy horror, a new and unguessed transformation. In Poe one finds it a *tour de force*, in Maupassant a nervous engagement of the flagellated climax. To Bierce, simply and sincerely, diabolism held in its tormented depth, a legitimate and reliant means to the end. Yet a tacit confirmation with Nature is in every instance insisted upon.
>
> In 'The Death of Halpin Frayser', flowers, verdure, and the boughs and leaves of trees are magnificently placed as an oppos-ing foil to unnatural malignity. Not the accustomed golden world, but a world pervaded with the mystery of blue and the breathless recalcitrance of dreams, is Bierce's. Yet, curiously, inhumanity is not altogether absent.

The 'inhumanity' mentioned by Mr Loveman finds vent in a rare strain of sardonic comedy and graveyard humour, and a kind of delight in images of cruelty and tantalising disappointment. The former quality is well illustrated by some of the subtitles in the darker narratives; such as 'One does not always eat what is on the table', describing a body laid out for a coroner's inquest, and 'A man though naked may be in rags', referring to a frightfully mangled corpse.

Bierce's work is in general somewhat uneven. Many of the stories are obviously mechanical, and marred by a jaunty and common-placely artificial style derived from journalistic models; but the grim malevolence stalking through all of them is unmistakable, and several stand out as permanent mountain-peaks of American weird writing.

'The Death of Halpin Frayser', called by Frederic Taber Cooper the most fiendishly ghastly tale in the literature of the Anglo-Saxon race, tells of a body skulking by night without a soul in a weird and horribly ensanguined wood, and of a man beset by ancestral memories who met death at the claws of that which had been his fervently loved mother. 'The Damned Thing', frequently copied in popular anthologies, chronicles the hideous devastations of an invisible entity that waddles and flounders on the hills and in the wheatfields by night and day. 'The Suitable Surroundings' evokes with singular subtlety yet apparent simplicity a piercing sense of the terror which may reside in the written word. In the story the weird author Colston says to his friend Marsh, 'You are brave enough to read me in a street-car, but – in a deserted house – alone – in the forest – at night! Bah! I have a manuscript in my pocket that would kill you!' Marsh reads the manuscript in 'the suitable surroundings' – and it does kill him. 'The Middle Toe of the Right Foot' is clumsily developed, but has a powerful climax. A man named Manton has horribly killed his two children and his wife, the latter of whom lacked the middle toe of the right foot. Ten years later he returns much altered to the neighbourhood; and, being secretly recognised, is provoked into a bowie-knife duel in the dark, to be held in the now abandoned house where his crime was committed. When the moment of the duel arrives a trick is played upon him, and he is left without an antagonist, shut in a night-black ground-floor room of the reputedly haunted edifice, with the thick dust of a decade on every hand. No knife is drawn against him, for only a thorough scare is intended; but on the next day he is found crouched in a corner with distorted face, dead of sheer fright at something he has seen. The only clue visible to the discoverers is one having terrible implications: 'In the dust of years that lay thick upon the floor – leading from the door by which they had entered, straight across the room to within a yard of Manton's crouching corpse – were three parallel lines of footprints – light but definite impressions of bare feet, the outer ones those of small children, the inner a woman's. From the point at which they ended they did not return; they pointed all one way.' And, of course, the woman's prints shewed a lack of the middle toe of the right foot. 'The Spook House', told with a severely homely air of journalistic verisimilitude, conveys terrible hints of shocking mystery. In 1858 an entire family of seven persons disappears suddenly and unaccountably from a plantation house in eastern Kentucky, leaving all its possessions untouched – furniture, clothing, food supplies, horses, cattle, and slaves. About a year later two men of high standing are forced by a storm to take shelter in the deserted dwelling, and in so doing stumble into a strange subterranean room lit by an unaccountable greenish light and having an iron door which cannot be opened from within. In this room lie the decayed corpses of all the missing family; and as one of the discoverers rushes forward to embrace a body he seems to recognise, the other is so overpowered by a strange foetor that he accidentally shuts his companion in the vault and loses consciousness. Recovering his senses six weeks later, the survivor is unable to find the hidden room; and the house is burned during the Civil War. The imprisoned discoverer is never seen or heard of again.

Bierce seldom realises the atmospheric possibilities of his themes as vividly as Poe; and much of his work contains a certain touch of naiveté, prosaic angularity, or early-American provincialism which contrasts somewhat with the efforts of later horror-masters. Nevertheless the genuineness and artistry of his dark intimations are always unmistakable, so that his greatness is in no danger of eclipse. As arranged in his definitively collected works, Bierce's weird tales occur mainly in two volumes, *Can Such Things Be?* and *In the Midst of Life*. The former, indeed, is almost wholly given over to the supernatural.

Much of the best in American horror-literature has come from pens not mainly devoted to that medium. Oliver Wendell Holmes's historic *Elsie Venner* suggests with admirable restraint an unnatural ophidian element in a young woman pre-natally influenced, and sustains the atmosphere with finely discriminating landscape touches. In *The Turn of the Screw* Henry James triumphs over his inevitable pomposity and prolixity sufficiently well to create a truly potent air of sinister menace, depicting the hideous influence of two dead and evil servants, Peter Quint and the governess Miss Jessel, over a small boy and girl who had been under their care. James is perhaps too diffuse, too unctuously urbane, and too much addicted to subtleties of speech to realise fully all the wild and devastating horror in his situations; but for all that there is a rare and mounting tide of fright, culminating in the death of the little boy, which gives the novelette a permanent place in its special class.

F. Marion Crawford produced several weird tales of varying quality, now collected in a volume entitled *Wandering Ghosts*. 'For the Blood Is the Life' touches powerfully on a case of moon-cursed vampirism near an ancient tower on the rocks of the lonely South Italian sea-coast. 'The Dead Smile' treats of family horrors in an old house and an ancestral vault in Ireland, and introduces the banshee with considerable force. 'The Upper Berth', however, is Crawford's weird masterpiece, and is one of the most tremendous horror-stories in all literature. In this tale of a suicide-haunted stateroom such things as the spectral salt-water dampness, the strangely open porthole, and the nightmare struggle with the nameless object are handled with incomparable dexterity.

Very genuine, though not without the typical mannered extra-vagance of the eighteen-nineties, is the strain of horror in the early work of Robert W. Chambers, since renowned for products of a very different quality. *The King in Yellow*, a series of vaguely connected short stories having as a background a monstrous and suppressed book whose perusal brings fright, madness, and spectral tragedy, really achieves notable heights of cosmic fear in spite of uneven interest and a somewhat trivial and affected cultivation of the Gallic studio atmosphere made popular by Du Maurier's *Trilby*. The most powerful of its tales, perhaps, is 'The Yellow Sign', in which is introduced a silent and terrible churchyard watchman with a face like a puffy grave-worm's. A boy, describing a tussle he has had with this creature, shivers and sickens as he relates a certain detail. 'Well, sir, it's Gawd's truth that when I 'it 'im 'e grabbed me wrists, sir, and when I twisted 'is soft, mushy fist one of 'is fingers come off in me 'and.' An artist, who after seeing him has shared with another a strange dream of a nocturnal hearse, is shocked by the voice with which the watchman accosts him. The fellow emits a muttering sound that fills the head like thick oily smoke from a fat-rendering vat or an odour of noisome decay. What he mumbles is merely this: 'Have you found the Yellow Sign?'

A weirdly hieroglyphed onyx talisman, picked up in the street by the sharer of his dream, is shortly given the artist; and after stumbling queerly upon the hellish and forbidden book of horrors the two learn, among other hideous things which no sane mortal should know, that this talisman is indeed the nameless Yellow Sign handed down from the accursed cult of Hastur – from primordial Carcosa, whereof the volume treats, and some nightmare memory of which seems to lurk latent and ominous at the back of all men's minds. Soon they hear the rumbling of the black-plumed hearse driven by the flabby and corpse-faced watchman. He enters the night-shrouded house in quest of the Yellow Sign, all bolts and bars rotting at his touch. And when the people rush in, drawn by a scream that no human throat could utter, they find three forms on the floor – two dead and one dying. One of the dead shapes is far gone in decay. It is the churchyard watchman, and the doctor exclaims, 'That man must have been dead for months.' It is worth observing that the author derives most of the names and allusions connected with his eldritch land of primal memory from the tales of Ambrose Bierce. Other early works of Mr Chambers displaying the outré and macabre element are *The Maker of Moons* and *In Search of the Unknown*. One cannot help regretting that he did not further develop a vein in which he could so easily have become a recognised master.

Horror material of authentic force may be found in the work of the New England realist Mary E. Wilkins, whose volume of short tales, *The Wind in the Rose-Bush*, contains a number of noteworthy achievements. In 'The Shadows on the Wall' we are shewn with consummate skill the response of a staid New England household to uncanny tragedy; and the sourceless shadow of the poisoned brother well prepares us for the climactic moment when the shadow of the secret murderer, who has killed himself in a neighbouring city, suddenly appears beside it. Charlotte Perkins Gilman, in 'The Yellow Wall Paper', rises to a classic level in subtly delineating the madness which crawls over a woman dwelling in the hideously papered room where a madwoman was once confined.

[In 'The Dead Valley' the eminent architect and mediaevalist Ralph Adams Cram achieves a memorably potent degree of vague regional horror through subtleties of atmosphere and description.]

Still further carrying on our spectral tradition is the gifted and versatile humourist Irvin S. Cobb, whose work both early and recent contains some finely weird specimens. 'Fishhead', an early achievement, is banefully effective in its portrayal of unnatural affinities between a hybrid idiot and the strange fish of an isolated lake, which at the last avenge their biped kinsman's murder. Later work of Mr Cobb introduces an element of possible science, as in the tale of hereditary memory where a modern man with a negroid strain utters words in African jungle speech when run down by a train under visual and aural circumstances recalling the maiming of his black ancestor by a rhinoceros a century before.

[Extremely high in artistic stature is the novel *The Dark Chamber* (1927), by the late Leonard Cline. This is the tale of a man who – with the characteristic ambition of the Gothic or Byronic hero-villain – seeks to defy Nature and recapture every moment of his past life through the abnormal stimulation of memory. To this end he employs endless notes, records, mnemonic objects, and pictures – and finally odours, music, and exotic drugs. At last his ambition goes beyond his personal life and reaches toward the black abysses of *hereditary* memory – even back to pre-human days amidst the steaming swamps of the Carboniferous age, and to still more unimaginable deeps of primal time and entity. He calls for madder music and takes stronger drugs, and finally his great dog grows oddly afraid of him. A noxious animal stench encompasses him, and he grows vacant-faced and sub-human. In the end he takes to the woods, howling at night beneath windows. He is finally found in a thicket, mangled to death. Beside him is the mangled corpse of his dog. They have killed each other. The atmosphere of this novel is malevolently potent, much attention being paid to the central figure's sinister home and household.

A less subtle and well-balanced but nevertheless highly effective creation is Herbert S. Gorman's novel, *The Place Called Dagon*, which relates the dark history of a western Massachusetts backwater where the descendants of refugees from the Salem witchcraft still keep alive the morbid and degenerate horrors of the Black Sabbat.

Sinister House, by Leland Hall, has touches of magnificent atmosphere but is marred by a somewhat mediocre romanticism.

Very notable in their way are some of the weird conceptions of the novelist and short-story writer Edward Lucas White, most of whose themes arise from actual dreams. 'The Song of the Sirens' has a very pervasive strangeness, while such things as 'Lukundoo' and 'The Snout' rouse darker apprehensions. Mr White imparts a very peculiar quality to his tales – an oblique sort of glamour which has its own distinctive type of convincingness.]

Of younger Americans, none strikes the note of cosmic terror so well as the California poet, artist, and fictionist Clark Ashton Smith, whose bizarre writings, drawings, paintings, and stories are the delight of a sensitive few. Mr Smith has for his background a universe of remote and paralysing fright – jungles of poisonous and iridescent blossoms on the moons of Saturn, evil and grotesque temples in Atlantis, Lemuria, and forgotten elder worlds, and dank morasses of spotted death-fungi in spectral countries beyond earth's rim. His longest and most ambitious poem, *The Hashish-Eater*, is in pentameter blank verse; and opens up chaotic and incredible vistas of kaleidoscopic nightmare in the spaces between the stars. In sheer daemonic strangeness and fertility of conception, Mr Smith is perhaps unexcelled by any other writer dead or living. Who else has seen such gorgeous, luxuriant, and feverishly distorted visions of infinite spheres and multiple dimensions and lived to tell the tale? [His short stories deal powerfully with other galaxies, worlds, and dimensions, as well as with strange regions and aeons on the earth. He tells of primal Hyperborea and its black amorphous god Tsathoggua; of the lost continent Zothique, and of the fabulous, vampire-curst land of Averoigne in mediaeval France. Some of Mr Smith's best work can be found in the brochure entitled *The Double Shadow and Other Fantasies* (1933).]

The Weird Tradition in the British Isles

Recent British literature, besides including the three or four greatest *fantaisistes* of the present age, has been gratifyingly fertile in the element of the weird. Rudyard Kipling has often approached it; and has, despite the omnipresent mannerisms, handled it with indubitable mastery in such tales as 'The Phantom 'Rickshaw', 'The Finest Story in the World', 'The Recrudescence of Imray', and 'The Mark of the Beast'. This latter is of particular poignancy; the pictures of the naked leper-priest who mewed like an otter, of the spots which appeared on the chest of the man that priest cursed, of the growing carnivorousness of the victim and of the fear which horses began to display toward him, and of the eventually half-accomplished transformation of that victim into a leopard, being things which no reader is ever likely to forget. The final defeat of the malignant sorcery does not impair the force of the tale or the validity of its mystery.

Lafcadio Hearn, strange, wandering, and exotic, departs still farther from the realm of the real; and with the supreme artistry of a sensitive poet weaves phantasies impossible to an author of the solid roast-beef type. His *Fantastics*, written in America, contains some of the most impressive ghoulishness in all literature; whilst his *Kwaidan*, written in Japan, crystallises with matchless skill and delicacy the eerie lore and whispered legends of that richly colourful nation. Still more of Hearn's weird wizardry of language is shewn in some of his translations from the French, especially from Gautier and Flaubert. His version of the latter's *Temptation of St Anthony* is a classic of fevered and riotous imagery clad in the magic of singing words.

Oscar Wilde may likewise be given a place amongst weird writers, both for certain of his exquisite fairy tales, and for his vivid *Picture of Dorian Gray*, in which a marvellous portrait for years assumes the duty of ageing and coarsening instead of its original, who meanwhile plunges into every excess of vice and crime without the outward loss of youth, beauty, and freshness. There is a sudden and potent climax when Dorian Gray, at last become a murderer, seeks to destroy the painting whose changes testify to his moral degeneracy. He stabs it with a knife, and a hideous cry and crash are heard; but when the servants enter they find it in all its pristine loveliness. 'Lying on the floor was a dead man, in evening dress, with a knife in his heart. He was withered, wrinkled, and loathsome of visage. It was not till they had examined the rings that they recognised who it was.'

Matthew Phipps Shiel, author of many weird, grotesque, and adventurous novels and tales, occasionally attains a high level of horrific magic. 'Xélucha' is a noxiously hideous fragment, but is excelled by Mr Shiel's undoubted masterpiece, 'The House of Sounds', floridly written in the 'yellow 'nineties', and re-cast with more artistic restraint in the early twentieth century. This story, in final form, deserves a place among the foremost things of its kind. It tells of a creeping horror and menace trickling down the centuries on a sub-arctic island off the coast of Norway; where, amidst the sweep of daemon winds and the ceaseless din of hellish waves and cataracts, a vengeful dead man built a brazen tower of terror. It is vaguely like, yet infinitely unlike, Poe's 'Fall of the House of Usher'. [In the novel *The Purple Cloud* Mr Shiel describes with tremendous power a curse which came out of the arctic to destroy mankind, and which for a time appears to have left but a single inhabitant on our planet. The sensations of this lone survivor as he realises his position, and roams through the corpse-littered and treasure-strown cities of the world as their absolute master, are delivered with a skill and artistry falling little short of actual majesty. Unfortunately the second half of the book, with its conventionally romantic element, involves a distinct 'letdown'.]

Better known than Shiel is the ingenious Bram Stoker, who created many starkly horrific conceptions in a series of novels whose poor technique sadly impairs their net effect. *The Lair of the White Worm*, dealing with a gigantic primitive entity that lurks in a vault beneath an ancient castle, utterly ruins a magnificent idea by a development almost infantile. *The Jewel of Seven Stars*, touching on a strange Egyptian resurrection, is less crudely written. But best of all is the famous *Dracula*, which has become almost the standard modern exploitation of the frightful vampire myth. Count Dracula, a vampire, dwells in a horrible castle in the Carpathians, but finally migrates to England with the design of populating the country with fellow vampires. How an Englishman fares within Dracula's stronghold of terrors, and how the dead fiend's plot for domination is at last defeated, are elements which unite to form a tale now justly assigned a permanent place in English letters. *Dracula* evoked many similar novels of supernatural horror, among which the best are perhaps *The Beetle*, by Richard Marsh, *Brood of the Witch-Queen*, by 'Sax Rohmer' (Arthur Sarsfield Ward), and *The Door of the Unreal*, by Gerald Biss. The latter handles quite dexterously the standard werewolf superstition. Much subtler and more artistic, and told with singular skill through the juxtaposed narratives of the several characters, is the novel *Cold Harbour*, by Francis Brett Young, in which an ancient house of strange malignancy is powerfully delineated. The mocking and well-nigh omnipotent fiend Humphrey Furnival holds echoes of the Manfred-Montoni type of early Gothic 'villain', but is redeemed from triteness by many clever individualities. Only the slight diffuseness of explanation at the close, and the somewhat too free use of divination as a plot factor, keep this tale from approaching absolute perfection.

[In the novel *Witch Wood* John Buchan depicts with tremendous force a survival of the evil Sabbat in a lonely district of Scotland. The description of the black forest with the evil stone, and of the terrible cosmic adumbrations when the horror is finally extirpated, will repay one for wading through the very gradual action and plethora of Scottish dialect. Some of Mr Buchan's short stories are also extremely vivid in their spectral intimations; 'The Green Wilde-beest', a tale of African witchcraft, 'The Wind in the Portico', with its awakening of dead Britanno-Roman horrors, and 'Skule Skerry', with its touches of sub-arctic fright, being especially remarkable.]

Clemence Housman, in the brief novelette 'The Were-wolf', attains a high degree of gruesome tension and achieves to some extent the atmosphere of authentic folklore. [In *The Elixir of Life* Arthur Ransome attains some darkly excellent effects despite a general naiveté of plot, while H. B. Drake's *The Shadowy Thing* summons up strange and terrible vistas. George Macdonald's *Lilith* has a compelling *bizarrerie* all its own; the first and simpler of the two versions being perhaps the more effective.]

Deserving of distinguished notice as a forceful craftsman to whom an unseen mystic world is ever a close and vital reality is the poet Walter de la Mare, whose haunting verse and exquisite prose alike bear consistent traces of a strange vision reaching deeply into veiled spheres of beauty and terrible and forbidden dimensions of being. In the novel *The Return* we see the soul of a dead man reach out of its grave of two centuries and fasten itself upon the flesh of the living, so that even the face of the victim becomes that which had long ago returned to dust. Of the shorter tales, of which several volumes exist, many are unforgettable for their command of fear's and sorcery's darkest ramifications; notably 'Seaton's Aunt', in which there lowers a noxious background of malignant vampirism; 'The Tree', which tells of a frightful vegetable growth in the yard of a starving artist; 'Out of the Deep', wherein we are given leave to imagine what thing answered the summons of a dying wastrel in a dark lonely house when he pulled a long-feared bell-cord in the attic chamber of his dread-haunted boyhood; ['A Recluse', which hints at what sent a chance guest flying from a house in the night;] 'Mr Kempe', which shews us a mad clerical hermit in quest of the human soul, dwelling in a frightful sea-cliff region beside an archaic abandoned chapel; and 'All-Hallows', a glimpse of daemoniac forces besieging a lonely mediaeval church and miraculously restoring the rotting masonry. De la Mare does not make fear the sole or even the dominant element of most of his tales, being apparently more interested in the subtleties of character involved. Occasionally he sinks to sheer whimsical phantasy of the Barrie order. Still, he is among the very few to whom unreality is a vivid, living presence; and as such he is able to put into his occasional fear-studies a keen potency which only a rare master can achieve. His poem 'The Listeners' restores the Gothic shudder to modern verse.

The weird short story has fared well of late, an important contributor being the versatile E. F. Benson, whose 'The Man Who Went Too Far' breathes whisperingly of a house at the edge of a dark wood, and of Pan's hoof-mark on the breast of a dead man. Mr Benson's volume, *Visible and Invisible*, contains several stories of singular power; notably 'Negotium Perambulans', whose unfolding reveals an abnormal monster from an ancient ecclesiastical panel which performs an act of miraculous vengeance in a lonely village on the Cornish coast, and 'The Horror-Horn', through which lopes a terrible half-human survival dwelling on unvisited Alpine peaks. ['The Face', in another collection, is lethally potent in its relentless aura of doom. H. R. Wakefield, in his collections *They Return at Evening* and *Others Who Return*, manages now and then to achieve great heights of horror despite a vitiating air of sophistication. The most notable stories are 'The Red Lodge' with its slimy aqueous evil, 'He Cometh and He Passeth By', 'And He Shall Sing . . . ', 'The Cairn', 'Look Up There!', 'Blind Man's Buff', and that bit of lurking millennial horror, 'The Seventeenth Hole at Duncaster'. Mention has been made of the weird work of H. G. Wells and A. Conan Doyle. The former, in 'The Ghost of Fear', reaches a very high level; while all the items in *Thirty Strange Stories* have strong fantastic implications. Doyle now and then struck a powerfully spectral note, as in 'The Captain of the *Pole-Star*', a tale of arctic ghostliness, and 'Lot No. 249', wherein the reanimated mummy theme is used with more than ordinary skill. Hugh Walpole, of the same family as the founder of Gothic fiction, has sometimes approached the bizarre with much success, his short story 'Mrs Lunt' carrying a very poignant shudder.] John Metcalfe, in the collection published as *The Smoking Leg*, attains now and then a rare pitch of potency, the tale entitled 'The Bad Lands' containing graduations of horror that strongly savour of genius. More whimsical and inclined toward the amiable and innocuous phantasy of Sir J. M. Barrie are the short tales of E. M. Forster, grouped under the title of *The Celestial Omnibus*. Of these only one, dealing with a glimpse of Pan and his aura of fright, may be said to hold the true element of cosmic horror. [Mrs H. D. Everett, though adhering to very old and conventional models, occasionally reaches singular heights of spiritual terror in her collection of short stories. L. P. Hartley is notable for his incisive and extremely ghastly tale, 'A Visitor from Down Under'.] May Sinclair's *Uncanny Stories* contain more of traditional occultism than of that creative treatment of fear which marks mastery in this field, and are inclined to lay more stress on human emotions and psychological delving than upon the stark phenomena of a cosmos utterly unreal. It may be well to remark here that occult believers are probably less effective than materialists in delineating the spectral and the fantastic, since to them the phantom world is so commonplace a reality that they tend to refer to it with less awe, remoteness, and impressiveness than do those who see in it an absolute and stupendous violation of the natural order.

[Of rather uneven stylistic quality, but vast occasional power in its suggestion of lurking worlds and beings behind the ordinary surface of life, is the work of William Hope Hodgson, known today far less than it deserves to be. Despite a tendency toward conventionally sentimental conceptions of the universe, and of man's relation to it and to his fellows, Mr Hodgson is perhaps second only to Algernon Blackwood in his serious treatment of unreality. Few can equal him in adumbrating the nearness of nameless forces and monstrous besieging entities through casual hints and insignificant details, or in conveying feelings of the spectral and the abnormal in connexion with regions or buildings.

In *The Boats of the 'Glen Carrig'* (1907) we are shewn a variety of malign marvels and accursed unknown lands as encountered by the survivors of a sunken ship. The brooding menace in the earlier parts of the book is impossible to surpass, though a letdown in the direction of ordinary romance and adventure occurs toward the end. An inaccurate and pseudo-romantic attempt to reproduce eighteenth-century prose detracts from the general effect, but the really profound nautical erudition everywhere displayed is a compensating factor.

The House on the Borderland (1908) – perhaps the greatest of all Mr Hodgson's works – tells of a lonely and evilly regarded house in Ireland which forms a focus for hideous other-world forces and sustains a siege by blasphemous hybrid anomalies from a hidden abyss below. The wanderings of the narrator's spirit through limitless light-years of cosmic space and kalpas of eternity, and its witnessing of the solar system's final destruction, constitute something almost unique in standard literature. And everywhere there is manifest the author's power to suggest vague, ambushed horrors in natural scenery. But for a few touches of commonplace sentimentality this book would be a classic of the first water.

The Ghost Pirates (1909), regarded by Mr Hodgson as rounding out a trilogy with the two previously mentioned works, is a powerful account of a doomed and haunted ship on its last voyage, and of the terrible sea-devils (of quasi-human aspect, and perhaps the spirits of bygone buccaneers) that besiege it and finally drag it down to an unknown fate. With its command of maritime knowledge, and its clever selection of hints and incidents suggestive of latent horrors in Nature, this book at times reaches enviable peaks of power.

The Night Land (1912) is a long-extended (583 pp.) tale of the earth's infinitely remote future – billions of billions of years ahead, after the death of the sun. It is told in a rather clumsy fashion, as the dreams of a man in the seventeenth century, whose mind merges with its own future incarnation; and is seriously marred by painful verboseness, repetitiousness, artificial and nauseously sticky romantic sentimentality, and an attempt at archaic language even more grotesque and absurd than that in '*Glen Carrig*'.

Allowing for all its faults, it is yet one of the most potent pieces of macabre imagination ever written. The picture of a night-black, dead planet, with the remains of the human race concentrated in a stupendously vast metal pyramid and besieged by monstrous, hybrid, and altogether unknown forces of the darkness, is something that no reader can ever forget. Shapes and entities of an altogether non-human and inconceivable sort – the prowlers of the black, man-forsaken, and unexplored world outside the pyramid – are *suggested* and *partly* described with ineffable potency; while the night-bound landscape with its chasms and slopes and dying volcanism takes on an almost sentient terror beneath the author's touch.

Midway in the book the central figure ventures outside the pyramid on a quest through death-haunted realms untrod by man for millions of years – and in his slow, minutely described, day-by-day progress over unthinkable leagues of immemorial blackness there is a sense of cosmic alienage, breathless mystery, and terrified expectancy unrivalled in the whole range of literature. The last quarter of the book drags woefully, but fails to spoil the tremendous power of the whole.

Mr Hodgson's later volume, *Carnacki, the Ghost-Finder*, consists of several longish short stories published many years before in magazines. In quality it falls conspicuously below the level of the other books. We here find a more or less conventional stock figure of the 'infallible detective' type – the progeny of M. Dupin and Sherlock Holmes, and the close kin of Algernon Blackwood's John Silence – moving through scenes and events badly marred by an atmosphere of professional 'occultism'. A few of the episodes, however, are of undeniable power, and afford glimpses of the peculiar genius characteristic of the author.]

Naturally it is impossible in a brief sketch to trace out all the classic modern uses of the terror element. The ingredient must of necessity enter into all work both prose and verse treating broadly of life; and we are therefore not surprised to find a share in such writers as the poet Browning, whose 'Childe Roland to the Dark Tower Came' is instinct with hideous menace, or the novelist Joseph Conrad, who often wrote of the dark secrets within the sea, and of the daemoniac driving power of Fate as influencing the lives of lonely and maniacally resolute men. Its trail is one of infinite ramifications; but we must here confine ourselves to its appearance in a relatively unmixed state, where it determines and dominates the work of art containing it.

Somewhat separate from the main British stream is that current of weirdness in Irish literature which came to the fore in the Celtic Renaissance of the later nineteenth and early twentieth centuries.

Ghost and fairy lore have always been of great prominence in Ireland, and for over an hundred years have been recorded by a line of such faithful transcribers and translators as William Carleton, T. Crofton Croker, Lady Wilde – mother of Oscar Wilde – Douglas Hyde, and W. B. Yeats. Brought to notice by the modern movement, this body of myth has been carefully collected and studied; and its salient features reproduced in the work of later figures like Yeats, J. M. Synge, 'A. E.', Lady Gregory, Padraic Colum, James Stephens, and their colleagues.

Whilst on the whole more whimsically fantastic than terrible, such folklore and its consciously artistic counterparts contain much that falls truly within the domain of cosmic horror. Tales of burials in sunken churches beneath haunted lakes, accounts of death-heralding banshees and sinister changelings, ballads of spectres and 'the unholy creatures of the raths' – all these have their poignant and definite shivers, and mark a strong and distinctive element in weird literature. Despite homely grotesqueness and absolute naiveté, there is genuine nightmare in the class of narrative represented by the yarn of Teig O'Kane, who in punishment for his wild life was ridden all night by a hideous corpse that demanded burial and drove him from churchyard to churchyard as the dead rose up loathsomely in each one and refused to accommodate the newcomer with a berth. Yeats, undoubtedly the greatest figure of the Irish revival if not the greatest of all living poets, has accomplished notable things both in original work and in the codification of old legends.

The Modern Masters

The best horror-tales of today, profiting by the long evolution of the type, possess a naturalness, convincingness, artistic smoothness, and skilful intensity of appeal quite beyond comparison with anything in the Gothic work of a century or more ago. Technique, craftsmanship, experience, and psychological knowledge have advanced tremendously with the passing years, so that much of the older work seems naive and artificial; redeemed, when redeemed at all, only by a genius which conquers heavy limitations. The tone of jaunty and inflated romance, full of false motivation and investing every conceivable event with a counterfeit significance and carelessly inclusive glamour,

is now confined to lighter and more whimsical phases of supernatural writing. Serious weird stories are either made realistically
intense by close consistency and perfect fidelity to Nature except in
the one supernatural direction which the author allows himself,
or else cast altogether in the realm of phantasy, with atmosphere
cunningly adapted to the visualisation of a delicately exotic world of
unreality beyond space and time, in which almost anything may
happen if it but happen in true accord with certain types of imagination and illusion normal to the sensitive human brain. This, at
least, is the dominant tendency, though of course many great contemporary writers slip occasionally into some of the flashy postures
of immature romanticism, or into bits of the equally empty and
absurd jargon of pseudo-scientific 'occultism', now at one of its
periodic high tides.

Of living creators of cosmic fear raised to its most artistic pitch, few
if any can hope to equal the versatile Arthur Machen, author of some
dozen tales long and short, in which the elements of hidden horror
and brooding fright attain an almost incomparable substance and
realistic acuteness. Mr Machen, a general man of letters and master
of an exquisitely lyrical and expressive prose style, has perhaps put
more conscious effort into his picaresque *Chronicle of Clemendy*, his
refreshing essays, his vivid autobiographical volumes, his fresh and
spirited translations, and above all his memorable epic of the sensitive aesthetic mind, *The Hill of Dreams*, in which the youthful hero
responds to the magic of that ancient Welsh environment which is
the author's own, and lives a dream-life in the Roman city of Isca
Silurum, now shrunk to the relic-strown village of Caerleon-on-
Usk. But the fact remains that his powerful horror-material of the
'nineties and earlier nineteen-hundreds stands alone in its class, and
marks a distinct epoch in the history of this literary form.

Mr Machen, with an impressionable Celtic heritage linked to keen
youthful memories of the wild domed hills, archaic forests, and
cryptical Roman ruins of the Gwent countryside, has developed an
imaginative life of rare beauty, intensity, and historic background.
He has absorbed the mediaeval mystery of dark woods and ancient
customs, and is a champion of the Middle Ages in all things –
including the Catholic faith. He has yielded, likewise, to the spell of

the Britanno-Roman life which once surged over his native region, and finds strange magic in the fortified camps, tessellated pavements, fragments of statues, and kindred things which tell of the day when classicism reigned and Latin was the language of the country. A young American poet, Frank Belknap Long, Jun., has well summarised this dreamer's rich endowments and wizardry of expression in the sonnet 'On Reading Arthur Machen':

> There is a glory in the autumn wood;
> The ancient lanes of England wind and climb
> Past wizard oaks and gorse and tangled thyme
> To where a fort of mighty empire stood:
> There is a glamour in the autumn sky;
> The reddened clouds are writhing in the glow
> Of some great fire, and there are glints below
> Of tawny yellow where the embers die.
>
> I wait, for he will show me, clear and cold,
> High-rais'd in splendour, sharp against the North,
> The Roman eagles, and thro' mists of gold
> The marching legions as they issue forth:
>   I wait, for I would share with him again
>   The ancient wisdom, and the ancient pain.

Of Mr Machen's horror-tales the most famous is perhaps 'The Great God Pan' (1894), which tells of a singular and terrible experiment and its consequences. A young woman, through surgery of the brain-cells, is made to see the vast and monstrous deity of Nature, and becomes an idiot in consequence, dying less than a year later. Years afterward a strange, ominous, and foreign-looking child named Helen Vaughan is placed to board with a family in rural Wales, and haunts the woods in unaccountable fashion. A little boy is thrown out of his mind at sight of someone or something he spies with her, and a young girl comes to a terrible end in similar fashion. All this mystery is strangely interwoven with the Roman rural deities of the place, as sculptured in antique fragments. After another lapse of years, a woman of strangely exotic beauty appears in society, drives her husband to horror and death, causes an artist to paint unthinkable paintings of Witches' Sabbaths, creates an epidemic of suicide among the men of her acquaintance, and is finally discovered to be a frequenter of the lowest dens of vice in London, where even the most callous degenerates are shocked at her enormities. Through the clever comparing of notes on the part of those who have had word of her at various stages of her career, this woman is discovered to be the girl Helen Vaughan, who is the child – by no mortal father – of the young woman on whom the brain experiment was made. She is a daughter of hideous Pan himself, and at the last is put to death amidst horrible transmutations of form involving changes of sex and a descent to the most primal manifestations of the life-principle.

But the charm of the tale is in the telling. No one could begin to describe the cumulative suspense and ultimate horror with which every paragraph abounds without following fully the precise order in which Mr Machen unfolds his gradual hints and revelations. Melodrama is undeniably present, and coincidence is stretched to a length which appears absurd upon analysis; but in the malign witchery of the tale as a whole these trifles are forgotten, and the sensitive reader reaches the end with only an appreciative shudder and a tendency to repeat the words of one of the characters: 'It is too incredible, too monstrous; such things can never be in this quiet world . . . Why, man, if such a case were possible, our earth would be a nightmare.'

Less famous and less complex in plot than 'The Great God Pan', but definitely finer in atmosphere and general artistic value, is the curious and dimly disquieting chronicle called 'The White People', whose central portion purports to be the diary or notes of a little girl whose nurse has introduced her to some of the forbidden magic and soul-blasting traditions of the noxious witch-cult – the cult whose whispered lore was handed down long lines of peasantry throughout Western Europe, and whose members sometimes stole forth at night, one by one, to meet in black woods and lonely places for the revolting orgies of the Witches' Sabbath. Mr Machen's narrative, a triumph of skilful selectiveness and restraint, accumulates enormous power as it flows on in a stream of innocent childish prattle; introducing allusions to strange 'nymphs', 'Dôls', 'voolas', 'White, Green, and Scarlet Ceremonies', 'Aklo letters', 'Chian language', 'Mao games', and the like. The rites learned by the nurse from her witch grandmother are taught to the child by the time she is three years old, and her artless accounts of the dangerous secret revelations possess a lurking terror generously mixed with pathos. Evil charms well known to anthropologists are described with juvenile naiveté, and finally there comes a winter afternoon journey into the old Welsh hills, performed under an imaginative spell which lends to the wild scenery an added weird-ness, strangeness, and suggestion of grotesque sentience. The details of this journey are given with marvellous vividness, and form to the keen critic a masterpiece of fantastic writing, with almost unlimited power in the intimation of potent hideousness and cosmic aberr-ation. At length the child – whose age is then thirteen – comes upon a cryptic and banefully beautiful thing in the midst of a dark and inaccessible wood. She flees in awe, but is permanently altered and repeatedly revisits the wood. In the end horror overtakes her in a manner deftly prefigured by an anecdote in the prologue, but she poisons herself in time. Like the mother of Helen Vaughan in The Great God Pan, she has seen that frightful deity. She is dis-covered dead in the dark wood beside the cryptic thing she found; and that thing – a whitely luminous statue of Roman workmanship about which dire mediaeval rumours had clustered – is affrightedly hammered into dust by the searchers.

In the episodic novel *The Three Impostors*, a work whose merit as a whole is somewhat marred by an imitation of the jaunty Stevenson manner, occur certain tales which perhaps represent the high-water mark of Machen's skill as a terror-weaver. Here we find in its most artistic form a favourite weird conception of the author's; the notion that beneath the mounds and rocks of the wild Welsh hills dwell subterraneously that squat primitive race whose vestiges gave rise to our common folk legends of fairies, elves, and the 'little people', and whose acts are even now responsible for certain unexplained disappearances, and occasional substitutions of strange dark 'changelings' for normal infants. This theme receives its finest treatment in the episode entitled 'The Novel of the Black Seal'; where a professor, having discovered a singular identity between certain characters scrawled on Welsh limestone rocks and those existing in a prehistoric black seal from Babylon, sets out on a course of discovery which leads him to unknown and terrible things. A queer passage in the ancient geographer Solinus, a series of mysterious disappearances in the lonely reaches of Wales, a strange idiot son born to a rural mother after a fright in which her inmost faculties were shaken; all these things suggest to the professor a hideous connexion and a condition revolting to any friend and respecter of the human race. He hires the idiot boy, who jabbers strangely at times in a repulsive hissing voice, and is subject to odd epileptic seizures. Once, after such a seizure in the professor's study by night, disquieting odours and evidences of unnatural presences are found; and soon after that the professor leaves a bulky document and goes into the weird hills with feverish expectancy and strange terror in his heart. He never returns, but beside a fantastic stone in the wild country are found his watch, money, and ring, done up with catgut in a parchment bearing the same terrible characters as those on the black Babylonish seal and the rock in the Welsh mountains.

The bulky document explains enough to bring up the most hideous vistas. Professor Gregg, from the massed evidence presented by the Welsh disappearances, the rock inscription, the accounts of ancient geographers, and the black seal, has decided that a frightful race of dark primal beings of immemorial antiquity and wide former diffusion still dwells beneath the hills of unfrequented Wales. Further research has unriddled the message of the black seal, and proved that the idiot boy, a son of some father more terrible than mankind, is the heir of monstrous memories and possibilities. That strange night in the study the professor invoked 'the awful transmutation of the hills' by the aid of the black seal, and aroused in the hybrid idiot the horrors of his shocking paternity. He 'saw his body swell and become distended as a bladder, while the face blackened . . . ' And then the supreme effects of the invocation appeared, and Professor Gregg knew the stark frenzy of cosmic panic in its darkest form. He knew the abysmal gulfs of abnormality that he had opened, and went forth into the wild hills prepared and resigned. He would meet the unthinkable 'Little People' – and his document ends with a rational observation: 'If I unhappily do not return from my journey, there is no need to conjure up here a picture of the awfulness of my fate.'

Also in *The Three Impostors* is the 'Novel of the White Powder', which approaches the absolute culmination of loathsome fright.

Francis Leicester, a young law student nervously worn out by seclusion and overwork, has a prescription filled by an old apothecary none too careful about the state of his drugs. The substance, it later turns out, is an unusual salt which time and varying temperature have accidentally changed to something very strange and terrible; nothing less, in short, than the mediaeval *Vinum Sabbati*, whose consumption at the horrible orgies of the Witches' Sabbath gave rise to shocking transformations and – if injudiciously used – to unutterable consequences. Innocently enough, the youth regularly imbibes the powder in a glass of water after meals, and at first seems substantially benefited. Gradually, however, his improved spirits take the form of dissipation; he is absent from home a great deal, and appears to have undergone a repellent psychological change. One day an odd livid spot appears on his right hand, and he afterward returns to his seclusion, finally keeping himself shut within his room and admitting none of the household. The doctor calls for an interview, and departs in a palsy of horror, saying that he can do no more in that house. Two weeks later the patient's sister, walking outside, sees a monstrous thing at the sickroom window; and servants report that food left at the locked door is no longer touched. Summons at the door bring only a sound of shuffling and a demand in a thick gurgling voice to be let alone. At last an awful happening is reported by a shuddering housemaid. The ceiling of the room below Leicester's is stained with a hideous black fluid, and a pool of viscid abomination has dripped to the bed beneath. Dr Haberden, now persuaded to return to the house, breaks down the young man's door and strikes again and again with an iron bar at the blasphemous semi-living thing he finds there. It is 'a dark and putrid mass, seething with corruption and hideous rottenness, neither liquid nor solid, but melting and changing'. Burning points like eyes shine out of its midst, and before it is despatched it tries to lift what might have been an arm. Soon afterward the physician, unable to endure the memory of what he has beheld, dies at sea while bound for a new life in America.

Mr Machen returns to the daemoniac 'Little People' in 'The Red Hand' and 'The Shining Pyramid'; and in *The Terror*, a wartime story, he treats with very potent mystery the effect of man's modern repudiation of spirituality on the beasts of the world, which are thus led to question his supremacy and to unite for his extermination. Of utmost delicacy, and passing from mere horror into true mysticism, is *The Great Return*, a story of the Graal, also a product of the war period. Too well known to need description here is the tale of 'The Bowmen'; which, taken for authentic narration, gave rise to the widespread legend of the 'Angels of Mons' – ghosts of the old English archers of Crécy and Agincourt who fought in 1914 beside the hard-pressed ranks of England's glorious 'Old Contemptibles'.

Less intense than Mr Machen in delineating the extremes of stark fear, yet infinitely more closely wedded to the idea of an unreal world constantly pressing upon ours, is the inspired and prolific Algernon Blackwood, amidst whose voluminous and uneven work may be found some of the finest spectral literature of this or any age. Of the quality of Mr Blackwood's genius there can be no dispute; for no one has even approached the skill, seriousness, and minute fidelity with which he records the overtones of strangeness in ordinary things and experiences, or the preternatural insight with which he builds up detail by detail the complete sensations and perceptions leading from reality into supernormal life or vision. Without notable command of the poetic witchery of mere words, he is the one absolute and unquestioned master of weird atmosphere; and can evoke what amounts almost to a story from a simple fragment of humourless psychological description. Above all others he understands how fully some sensitive minds dwell forever on the borderland of dream, and how relatively slight is the distinction betwixt those images formed from actual objects and those excited by the play of the imagination.

Mr Blackwood's lesser work is marred by several defects such as ethical didacticism, occasional insipid whimsicality, the flatness of benignant supernaturalism, and a too free use of the trade jargon of modern 'occultism'. A fault of his more serious efforts is that diffuseness and long-windedness which results from an excessively elaborate attempt, under the handicap of a somewhat bald and journalistic style devoid of intrinsic magic, colour, and vitality, to visualise precise sensations and nuances of uncanny suggestion. But in spite of all this, the major products of Mr Blackwood attain a genuinely classic level, and evoke as does nothing else in literature an awed and convinced sense of the immanence of strange spiritual spheres or entities.

The well-nigh endless array of Mr Blackwood's fiction includes both novels and shorter tales, the latter sometimes independent and sometimes arrayed in series. Foremost of all must be reckoned 'The Willows', in which the nameless presences on a desolate Danube island are horribly felt and recognised by a pair of idle voyagers. Here art and restraint in narrative reach their very highest development, and an impression of lasting poignancy is produced without a single strained passage or a single false note. Another amazingly potent though less artistically finished tale is 'The Wendigo', where we are confronted by horrible evidences of a vast forest daemon about which North Woods lumbermen whisper at evening. The manner in which certain footprints tell certain unbelievable things is really a marked triumph in craftsmanship. In 'An Episode in a Lodging House' we behold frightful presences summoned out of black space by a sorcerer, and 'The Listener' tells of the awful psychic residuum creeping about an old house where a leper died. In the volume titled *Incredible Adventures* occur some of the finest tales which the author has yet produced, leading the fancy to wild rites on nocturnal hills, to secret and terrible aspects lurking behind stolid scenes, and to unimaginable vaults of mystery below the sands and pyramids of Egypt; all with a serious finesse and delicacy that convince where a cruder or lighter treatment would merely amuse. Some of these accounts are hardly stories at all, but rather studies in elusive impressions and half-remembered snatches of dream. Plot is everywhere negligible, and atmosphere reigns untrammelled.

John Silence – Physician Extraordinary is a book of five related tales, through which a single character runs his triumphant course. Marred only by traces of the popular and conventional detective-story atmosphere – for Dr Silence is one of those benevolent geniuses who employ their remarkable powers to aid worthy fellow-men in difficulty – these narratives contain some of the author's best work, and produce an illusion at once emphatic and lasting. The opening tale, 'A Psychical Invasion', relates what befell a sensitive author in a house once the scene of dark deeds, and how a legion of fiends was exorcised. 'Ancient Sorceries', perhaps the finest tale in the book, gives an almost hypnotically vivid account of an old French town where once the unholy Sabbath was kept by all the people in the form of cats. In 'The Nemesis of Fire' a hideous elemental is evoked by new-spilt blood, whilst 'Secret Worship' tells of a German school where Satanism held sway, and where long afterward an evil aura remained. 'The Camp of the Dog' is a werewolf tale, but is weakened by moralisation and professional 'occultism'.

Too subtle, perhaps, for definite classification as horror-tales, yet possibly more truly artistic in an absolute sense, are such delicate phantasies as *Jimbo* or *The Centaur*. Mr Blackwood achieves in these novels a close and palpitant approach to the inmost substance of dream, and works enormous havock with the conventional barriers between reality and imagination.

Unexcelled in the sorcery of crystalline singing prose, and supreme in the creation of a gorgeous and languorous world of iridescently exotic vision, is Edward John Moreton Drax Plunkett, Eighteenth Baron Dunsany, whose tales and short plays form an almost unique element in our literature. Inventor of a new mythology and weaver of surprising folklore, Lord Dunsany stands dedicated to a strange world of fantastic beauty, and pledged to eternal warfare against the coarseness and ugliness of diurnal reality. His point of view is the most truly cosmic of any held in the literature of any period. As sensitive as Poe to dramatic values and the significance of isolated words and details, and far better equipped rhetorically through a simple lyric style based on the prose of the King James Bible, this author draws with tremendous effectiveness on nearly every body of myth and legend within the circle of European culture, producing a composite or eclectic cycle of phantasy in which Eastern colour, Hellenic form, Teutonic sombreness, and Celtic wistfulness are so superbly blended that each sustains and supplements the rest without sacrifice of perfect congruity and homogeneity. In most cases Dunsany's lands are fabulous – 'beyond the East', or 'at the edge of the world'. His system of original personal and place names, with roots drawn from classical, Oriental, and other sources, is a marvel of versatile inventiveness and poetic discrimination; as one may see from such specimens as 'Argimenes', 'Bethmoora', 'Poltarnees', 'Camorak', 'Illuriel', or 'Sardathrion'.

Beauty rather than terror is the keynote of Dunsany's work. He loves the vivid green of jade and of copper domes, and the delicate flush of sunset on the ivory minarets of impossible dream-cities. Humour and irony, too, are often present to impart a gentle cynicism and modify what might otherwise possess a naive intensity. Nevertheless, as is inevitable in a master of triumphant unreality, there are occasional touches of cosmic fright which come well within the authentic tradition. Dunsany loves to hint slyly and adroitly of monstrous things and incredible dooms, as one hints in a fairy tale. In *The Book of Wonder* we read of Hlo-hlo, the gigantic spider-idol which does not always stay at home; of what the Sphinx feared in the forest; of Slith, the thief who jumps over the edge of the world after seeing a certain light lit and knowing *who* lit it; of the anthropophagous Gibbelins, who inhabit an evil tower and guard a treasure; of the Gnoles, who live in the forest and from whom it is not well to steal; of the City of Never, and the eyes that watch in the Under Pits; and of kindred things of darkness. *A Dreamer's Tales* tells of the mystery that sent forth all men from Bethmoora in the desert; of the vast gate of Perdóndaris, that was carved from a *single piece* of ivory; and of the voyage of poor old Bill, whose captain cursed the crew and paid calls on nasty-looking isles new-risen from the sea, with low thatched cottages having evil, obscure windows.

Many of Dunsany's short plays are replete with spectral fear. In *The Gods of the Mountain* seven beggars impersonate the seven green idols on a distant hill, and enjoy ease and honour in a city of worshippers until they hear that *the real idols are missing from their wonted seats*. A very ungainly sight in the dusk is reported to them – 'rock should not walk in the evening' – and at last, as they sit awaiting the arrival of a troop of dancers, they note that the approaching footsteps are heavier than those of good dancers ought to be. Then things ensue, and in the end the presumptuous blasphemers are turned to green jade statues by the very walking statues whose sanctity they outraged. But mere plot is the very least merit of this marvellously effective play. The incidents and developments are those of a supreme master, so that the whole forms one of the most important contributions of the present age not only to drama, but to literature in general. *A Night at an Inn* tells of four thieves who have stolen the emerald eye of Klesh, a monstrous Hindoo god. They lure to their room and succeed in slaying the three priestly avengers who are on their track, but in the night Klesh comes gropingly for his eye; and having gained it and departed, calls each of the despoilers out into the darkness for an unnamed punishment. In *The Laughter of the Gods* there is a doomed city at the jungle's edge, and a ghostly lutanist heard only by those about to die (cf. Alice's spectral harpsichord in Hawthorne's *House of the Seven Gables*); whilst *The Queen's Enemies* retells the anecdote of Herodotus in which a vengeful princess invites her foes to a subterranean banquet and lets in the Nile to drown them.

But no amount of mere description can convey more than a fraction of Lord Dunsany's pervasive charm. His prismatic cities and unheard-of rites are touched with a sureness which only mastery can engender, and we thrill with a sense of actual participation in his secret mysteries. To the truly imaginative he is a talisman and a key unlocking rich storehouses of dream and fragmentary memory, so that we may think of him not only as a poet, but as one who makes each reader a poet as well.

At the opposite pole of genius from Lord Dunsany, and gifted with an almost diabolic power of calling horror by gentle steps from the midst of prosaic daily life, is the scholarly Montague Rhodes James, Provost of Eton College, antiquary of note, and recognised authority on mediaeval manuscripts and cathedral history. Dr James, long fond of telling spectral tales at Christmastide, has become by slow degrees a literary weird fictionist of the very first rank, and has developed a distinctive style and method likely to serve as models for an enduring line of disciples.

The art of Dr James is by no means haphazard, and in the preface to one of his collections he has formulated three very sound rules for macabre composition. A ghost story, he believes, should have a familiar setting in the modern period, in order to approach closely the reader's sphere of experience. Its spectral phenomena, moreover, should be malevolent rather than beneficent, since *fear* is the emotion primarily to be excited. And finally, the technical patois of 'occultism' or pseudo-science ought carefully to be avoided, lest the charm of casual verisimilitude be smothered in unconvincing pedantry.

Dr James, practicing what he preaches, approaches his themes in a light and often conversational way. Creating the illusion of every-day events, he introduces his abnormal phenomena cautiously and gradually, relieved at every turn by touches of homely and prosaic detail, and sometimes spiced with a snatch or two of anti-quarian scholarship. Conscious of the close relation between present weirdness and accumulated tradition, he generally provides remote historical antecedents for his incidents, thus being able to utilise very aptly his exhaustive knowledge of the past, and his ready and convincing command of archaic diction and colouring. A favour-ite scene for a James tale is some centuried cathedral, which the author can describe with all the familiar minuteness of a specialist in that field.

Sly humorous vignettes and bits of life-like genre portraiture and characterisation are often to be found in Dr James's narratives, and serve in his skilled hands to augment the general effect rather than to spoil it, as the same qualities would tend to do with a lesser crafts-man. In inventing a new type of ghost, he has departed considerably from the conventional Gothic tradition; for where the older stock ghosts were pale and stately, and apprehended chiefly through the sense of sight, the average James ghost is lean, dwarfish, and hairy – a sluggish, hellish night-abomination midway betwixt beast and man – and usually *touched* before it is *seen*. Sometimes the spectre is of still more eccentric composition; a roll of flannel with spidery eyes, or an invisible entity which moulds itself in bedding and shews *a face of crumpled linen*. Dr James has, it is clear, an intelligent and scientific knowledge of human nerves and feelings, and knows just how to apportion statement, imagery, and subtle suggestions in order to secure the best results with his readers. He is an artist in incident and arrangement rather than in atmosphere, and reaches the emotions more often through the intellect than directly. This method, of course, with its occasional absences of sharp climax, has its draw-backs as well as its advantages; and many will miss the thorough atmospheric tension which writers like Machen are careful to build up with words and scenes. But only a few of the tales are open to the charge of tameness. Generally the laconic unfolding of abnormal events in adroit order is amply sufficient to produce the desired effect of cumulative horror.

The short stories of Dr James are contained in four small collections, entitled respectively *Ghost-Stories of an Antiquary*, *More Ghost Stories of an Antiquary*, *A Thin Ghost and Others*, and *A Warning to the Curious*. There is also a delightful juvenile phantasy, *The Five Jars*, which has its spectral adumbrations. Amidst this wealth of material it is hard to select a favourite or especially typical tale, though each reader will no doubt have such preferences as his temperament may determine.

'Count Magnus' is assuredly one of the best, forming as it does a veritable Golconda of suspense and suggestion. Mr Wraxall is an English traveller of the middle nineteenth century, sojourning in Sweden to secure material for a book. Becoming interested in the ancient family of De la Gardie, near the village of Råbäck, he studies its records, and finds particular fascination in the builder of the existing manor-house, one Count Magnus, of whom strange and terrible things are whispered. The Count, who flourished early in the seventeenth century, was a stern landlord, and famous for his severity toward poachers and delinquent tenants. His cruel punishments were bywords, and there were dark rumours of influences which even survived his interment in the great mausoleum he built near the church – as in the case of the two peasants who hunted on his preserves one night a century after his death. There were hideous screams in the woods, and near the tomb of Count Magnus an unnatural laugh and the clang of a great door. Next morning the priest found the two men; one a maniac, and the other dead, with the flesh of his face sucked from the bones.

Mr Wraxall hears all these tales, and stumbles on more guarded references to a *Black Pilgrimage* once taken by the Count; a pilgrimage to Chorazin in Palestine, one of the cities denounced by Our Lord in the Scriptures, and in which old priests say that Antichrist is to be born. No one dares to hint just what that Black Pilgrimage was, or what strange being or thing the Count brought back as a companion. Meanwhile Mr Wraxall is increasingly anxious to explore the mausoleum of Count Magnus, and finally secures permission to do so, in the company of a deacon. He finds several monuments and three copper sarcophagi, one of which is the Count's. Round the edge of this latter are several bands of engraved scenes, including a singular and hideous delineation of a pursuit – the pursuit of a frantic man through a forest by a squat muffled figure with a devil-fish's tentacle, directed by a tall cloaked man on a neighbouring hillock. The sarcophagus has three massive steel padlocks, one of which is lying open on the floor, reminding the traveller of a metallic clash he heard the day before when passing the mausoleum and wishing idly that he might see Count Magnus.

His fascination augmented, and the key being accessible, Mr Wraxall pays the mausoleum a second and solitary visit and finds another padlock unfastened. The next day, his last in Råbäck, he again goes alone to bid the long-dead Count farewell. Once more queerly impelled to utter a whimsical wish for a meeting with the buried nobleman, he now sees to his disquiet that only one of the padlocks remains on the great sarcophagus. Even as he looks, that last lock drops noisily to the floor, and there comes a sound as of creaking hinges. Then the monstrous lid appears very slowly to rise, and Mr Wraxall flees in panic fear without refastening the door of the mausoleum.

During his return to England the traveller feels a curious uneasiness about his fellow-passengers on the canal-boat which he employs for the earlier stages. Cloaked figures make him nervous, and he has a sense of being watched and followed. Of twenty-eight persons whom he counts, only twenty-six appear at meals; and the missing two are always a tall cloaked man and a shorter muffled figure. Completing his water travel at Harwich, Mr Wraxall takes frankly to flight in a closed carriage, but sees two cloaked figures at a crossroad. Finally he lodges at a small house in a village and spends the time making frantic notes. On the second morning he is found dead, and during the inquest seven jurors faint at sight of the body. The house where he stayed is never again inhabited, and upon its demolition half a century later his manuscript is discovered in a forgotten cupboard.

In 'The Treasure of Abbot Thomas' a British antiquary unriddles a cipher on some Renaissance painted windows, and thereby discovers a centuried hoard of gold in a niche half way down a well in the courtyard of a German abbey. But the crafty depositor had set a guardian over that treasure, and something in the black well twines its arms around the searcher's neck in such a manner that the quest is abandoned, and a clergyman sent for. Each night after that the discoverer feels a stealthy presence and detects a horrible odour of mould outside the door of his hotel room, till finally the clergyman makes a daylight replacement of the stone at the mouth of the treasure-vault in the well – out of which something had come in the dark to avenge the disturbing of old Abbot Thomas's gold. As he completes his work the cleric observes a curious toad-like carving on the ancient well-head, with the Latin motto '*Depositum custodi* – keep that which is committed to thee.'

Other notable James tales are 'The Stalls of Barchester Cathedral', in which a grotesque carving comes curiously to life to avenge the secret and subtle murder of an old Dean by his ambitious successor; 'Oh, Whistle, and I'll Come to You, My Lad', which tells of the horror summoned by a strange metal whistle found in a mediaeval church ruin; and 'An Episode of Cathedral History', where the dismantling of a pulpit uncovers an archaic tomb whose lurking daemon spreads panic and pestilence. Dr James, for all his light touch, evokes fright and hideousness in their most shocking forms, and will certainly stand as one of the few really creative masters in his darksome province.

For those who relish speculation regarding the future, the tale of supernatural horror provides an interesting field. Combated by a mounting wave of plodding realism, cynical flippancy, and sophisticated disillusionment, it is yet encouraged by a parallel tide of growing mysticism, as developed both through the fatigued reaction of 'occultists' and religious fundamentalists against materialistic discovery and through the stimulation of wonder and fancy by such enlarged vistas and broken barriers as modern science has given us with its intra-atomic chemistry, advancing astrophysics, doctrines of relativity, and probings into biology and human thought. At the present moment the favouring forces would appear to have somewhat of an advantage, since there is unquestionably more cordiality shewn toward weird writings than when, thirty years ago, the best of Arthur Machen's work fell on the stony ground of the smart and cocksure 'nineties. Ambrose Bierce, almost unknown in his own time, has now reached something like general recognition.

Startling mutations, however, are not to be looked for in either direction. In any case an approximate balance of tendencies will continue to exist; and while we may justly expect a further subtilisation of technique, we have no reason to think that the general position of the spectral in literature will be altered. It is a narrow though essential branch of human expression, and will chiefly appeal as always to a limited audience with keen special sensibilities. Whatever universal masterpiece of tomorrow may be wrought from phantasm or terror will owe its acceptance rather to a supreme workmanship than to a sympathetic theme. Yet who shall declare the dark theme a positive handicap? Radiant with beauty, the Cup of the Ptolemies was carven of onyx.